HONOUR
AND
OBEY

Also by Malcolm Macdonald:

The Silver Highways
On a Far Wild Shore
Tessa D'Arblay
For They Shall Inherit
Goldeneye
Abigail
Sons of Fortune
The Rich Are with You Always
The World from Rough Stones

HONOUR
AND
OBEY

Malcolm Macdonald

St. Martin's Press
New York

Library of Congress Cataloging-in-Publication Data

Ross-Macdonald. Malcolm.
      Honour and obey / by Malcolm Macdonald.
         p.   cm.
   ISBN 0-312-01773-1
   I. Title.
PR6068.0827H6 1988
823'.914—dc19   87-38240
                                                   CIP

First published in Great Britain by Hodder & Stoughton Limited under the title *The Sky with Diamonds*.

First U.S. Edition

10 9 8 7 6 5 4 3 2 1

To Wendy
and for
Edna, Cecil and Derek

CONTENTS

PART ONE

OFF THE GROUND

CHAPTER ONE

A SOMERVILLE-BODIED Rolls-Royce was to be seen waiting at the door of number 32 Connaught Square, every weekday morning, at precisely ten o'clock. It was waiting for Mrs Julia Somerville herself, of course. A quarter of an hour later, when she arrived at the offices of the SPRP, dear old Captain Harcourt would lift an eyebrow and say, "A new Rolls-Royce, I see!"

And she would glance casually over her shoulder and reply, "Oh, is it?"

There was never a smile, for that would have spoiled their little start-of-the-day pleasantry.

This unending supply of new Rolls-Royces owed itself to George Somerville's proud boast that none of his firm's coach-built motors ever left the works without undergoing the personal Somerville test. What that meant, in fact, was that Julia either drove the car or was driven in it for a day or two – after which time it would not *dare* develop another fault. This practice had begun in the early years of their marriage, back in 1912, when George had bought his first rolling chassis, a Silver Ghost, and built what the newspapers of the day had called "the world's most luxurious motor phæton" for the Maharajah of Mysore. By chance Julia had noticed a slight mismatch in the West-of-England cloth upholstery, just as the vehicle was about to be shipped. George, in his gallant way, said his little girlie had saved the firm, and ever since then she had been Somerville's final arbiter of quality. Even some of the armoured cars they had built during the Great War had been brought to Connaught Square for her scrutiny.

The workmen at Somerville's did not think of her as "little girlie"; to them she was "the Boss." George ("the Guv'nor") had never told her that, and she was unlikely to hear it directly since she never visited the works – indeed, she was only vaguely aware of their direction. They were a few miles to the northwest of Connaught Square, somewhere beyond Paddington. Willesden? Kensal Green?

Wormwood Scrubs? Somewhere like that – one of those fringes of London one need never visit in the ordinary way.

So every morning at ten, the latest Somerville awaited the Boss's yea or nay. It might be anything from a sporty little open tourer to yet another "luxurious motor phæton"; to each she gave the same critical care. Julia enjoyed this mixture of routine and novelty – each day at ten, a little surprise. On the morning of this particular day the car was the regular Somerville body for the new Phantom chassis, but with the addition of half-silvered passenger windows; it had been ordered by a grand old lady of the theatre who nowadays preferred press photographers to take close-ups of their own flashbulbs rather than of her sadly ageing features.

On this morning, however, Julia's routine was disrupted. She had put on her hat and gloves (which, even now, she could never do without hearing the voice of her old governess, Miss Creen: "Never put on your gloves, my dear, in sight of the servants!") and was coming down to the hall when Mrs Crooke, the housekeeper, intercepted her.

Mrs Crooke waited until Julia reached the foot of the stair and then said, "The agency has sent a young woman for the place of nursery maid, madam. I wondered if you would care to see her for yourself this time?"

There was something a little odd in the request. The position was a minor one. Normally Miss Valentine, the governess, would see the girl. Still, after the dreadful things the last girl had done, perhaps it would be as well to vet this one herself? No, no, no. Miss Valentine would be mortally offended. Julia glanced at her watch and gave a tut of vexation.

She came to a decision. "I think Miss Valentine had better interview this . . . what's her name?"

Mrs Crooke gave a tight little smile. "Miss Imogen Davis." She watched closely for her mistress's response.

"Unusual name," Julia commented. "I have a cousin Imogen. Somewhere."

Mrs Crooke nodded. "I seem to remember as much, madam. Quite unsuitable for a servant. I'll suggest she chooses another. Jane or Kate or something more fitting."

But Julia shook her head; then, smiling to soften what might otherwise seem a rebuke, she remarked, "I don't think a mistress can give a girl a name any longer. Not these days."

"More's the pity."

Julia eyed her shrewdly. "Why do you especially think I should see this one? Is it after what happened with the last?"

Mrs Crooke gave an awkward shrug. "There's something about her . . . I don't know. She's not of the servant *class*. Yet she comes with the highest references. I just don't know."

12

Dear Mrs Crooke – the best housekeeper anyone could hope for, but such a snob! "I think Miss Valentine may conduct the interview," she said. "And if she approves, well, I shall no doubt see Miss *Imogen* Davis in the usual way."

Mrs Crooke gave a disappointed tilt of her head. "As you prefer, madam."

Julia added, "Convey my wish for Miss Valentine to be utterly frank about . . . well, we all know what she is to be utterly frank about!"

Mrs Crooke's ears flushed red as she agreed that indeed they did.

Moments later Julia had already dismissed the matter from her mind. Overnight rain lay in puddles on the two shallow front steps. Had they already been turned or would the undersides be good for another century of wear? She made a note to call in the stonemason.

Strong, the chauffeur, tucked away his chamois leather as soon as he heard the doorlatch; now he was holding open the car door for her.

"Good morning, Strong. What a blustery night."

"It promises better today, madam."

Strong was her weather expert. Before the war he had been Somerville's chief upholsterer, but gas had half-ruined his lungs and he could not go back to air laden with leather dust and all the alcohols they used.

Today was a Tuesday so, without needing to be told, he drove her directly to the head office of the SPRP at the far end of Bayswater. Every Tuesday, Wednesday, and Thursday she worked there until just before two, when she would return home for a light luncheon. Mondays and Fridays were usually her days for shopping, galleries, museums, and so on. The afternoons were for bridge, or being At Home, or going to matinées.

People said to her, "How you fit it all in I'll never know!"

What they were talking about, of course, was not the busy social whirl but the SPRP itself – the Society for . . . well, before we name it, let us first see how it came about.

It was Julia's own idea, prompted by something that happened toward the end of the war. From 1916 onward, Allbury, her family's ancestral home in Hertfordshire, had been run as a convalescent home for soldiers. Julia, though her son Robert was then three, and baby Lydia only one, had gone down there every Friday to Monday to relieve the regular nurses. On one occasion, toward the end of the summer of 1918, she had taken a convalescent, a Gunner Ashbury, to his home in Dalston in the East End of London for the christening of the fourth and latest little Ashbury. Afterwards, over the teacups, there had been a heated discussion about the difficulties of feeding a growing family on a dwindling purse. At one point Theresa Ashbury had canvassed Julia's opinion. Caught between husband and wife, she had given what seemed a diplomatic answer: The budget was certainly not lavish yet an adequate and wholesome diet should still be quite possible.

A disgruntled Theresa had muttered that it was all very well for some people to talk but she'd like to see them actually try it.

And Julia had astonished everyone, including herself, by saying, "Very well, and so I shall."

So, a few months later, the war being then over, Julia had rented a house three doors down the terrace from the Ashburys and had fed them and herself every meal for two weeks – at a saving of several shillings. It had not been difficult. It was simply that no one had ever shown Theresa Ashbury such elementary tricks as managing a stockpot, using butcher's bones and cheap end-of-the-day vegetables. If she wanted soup, she opened a tin.

It had astonished Julia, who, though brought up to expect the services of a cook, a housekeeper, and a dozen servants beside, had nonetheless been taught all those skills by her mother – on the grounds that, if you couldn't do it properly yourself, the servants would walk circles around you. Whether that were true or no, her early training had come in useful at the time of Theresa's challenge. The pennypinching produced those winning shillings.

Most other grand ladies of Bayswater, even if they had dared take up such a challenge, would have left it at that and dined out for weeks on their victory. Most other women in Dalston would have shrugged their shoulders, repeated that it was all very well for *some* . . . and reached for another tin of soup the moment Lady Bountiful had gone. But, just as Julia was not like most other women in Bayswater, so Theresa was not like most other women in Dalston. Over the two weeks of that challenge they were in each other's company a great deal of the time, and Julia was the first to admit that she had learned much more from Theresa than she had taught in return.

Between them they decided that if working people were ever to rise above their poverty, it could not be by higher wages alone. If the men brought home more money, much of the increase would be squandered – not wilfully but through simple ignorance of good housekeeping and domestic economy. In the last days of the challenge, when it was plain that Julia had "won," and neither of them cared a button for victory or defeat, Theresa had one final fling at an excuse. "It was easier for you," she said, "not having a load of screaming kids clinging round your skirts all the time."

The comment amused Julia. Many times during the days of the challenge she had envied Theresa and the other mothers their close and almost permanent relations with their children. Over the years since then she often thought of her own two – Robert, now away at school, independent already, and Lydia, still snug in the nursery and schoolroom. They wanted for nothing, yet both had given their love and their best childhood years to paid strangers. Still – that was the way of her world. Nothing could be done about it.

Such, at least, were the acceptable thoughts and recollections associated with those weeks in Dalston; but there was a deeper layer, dark and frightening . . . memories from which her mind would still recoil in a kind of terror.

Early on in the challenge, around the third or fourth day, the novelty of her situation had suddenly evaporated. The thought then gripped her: *What if this were all real?* In comfortable Bayswater, married to George with his thriving business, living in her big town house, cushioned by servants, it was impossible to imagine herself reduced to such poverty. But there in Dalston, lost in those acres of grimy brick, walking those mean streets where desperation seemed to hang on the very air, the impossible began to assume a nightmarish reality.

Money, a comfortable obsession until then, became a jealous god, demanding all her time, consuming every stray hint of pleasure. She went to sleep gnawing at it and awoke devoured by it.

And then, while the terror was still formless within her (because not capable of reasonable formulation), Theresa voiced the thought that gave it shape: "It's when you can't think beyond tonight's supper, innit? That's when you're trapped. Every day it's like a new prison cell where the window's too high. You can't see out, so you can't plan no escape. But having a few extra coins to rattle, so's you don't have to think only about supper and that, well, it's like standing on a chair so's you *can* look out the window, innit. Know what I mean? I wish I could talk like you, only there must be a word for it."

And it suddenly dawned on Julia that there was, indeed, a word for it – this ability – no, this *freedom* – to look beyond one's immediate despair. And that word, much to her surprise, was "responsibility." The way out of her own astonishing terror was a path that led, almost in one bound, to the founding of the SPRP.

"Responsibility" was such a comforting word. She had been raised on reassuring sermons about the *ir*responsibility of the working classes, as if they had made a deliberate moral choice to behave like that and therefore had only themselves to blame for their wretchedness.

"They will have these large families . . ."

"The amount they spend on weddings and funerals! They cast themselves upon the Jews for life."

"And the drink and the gambling! Just go down any back street. No, no, my dear – their poverty is quite voluntary, I assure you."

Julia had absorbed such opinions almost from the day she could talk. But the two weeks of the "Ashbury Challenge" had changed her perceptions for ever.

After that she had become quite a regular visitor at the Ashburys, witnessing their rise in the world as some token of personal deliverance. She watched Theresa learning to look out of her prison window and felt the vision as her own. With the extra money came the move to "a better street." It was, in fact, only around the corner but the streets of working-class Dalston were graded to a sixpence. The Gunner, as everyone called him, took a vegetable allotment beside the railway line, which he cultivated each evening, thus staying out of the pubs. Soon there was a further weekly sixpence to spare, and so the family made yet another move, this time to a house with a parlour and a piano.

"Pray, do enter, Fairy Godmother!" Theresa had said with shy daring as she let Julia into this latest household.

But it suddenly struck Julia that the words could not have been further from the truth. No magician had waved a magic wand over the Ashburys. No pumpkins had been turned into coaches. What they had done thousands of others might also do, if not millions. Already, indeed, one or two of Theresa's neighbours had taken pattern from her and were on the same highway. That was another thing about Theresa: She was a born teacher.

And so, in the summer of 1919, six eventful years ago, the SPRP, the Society for the Promotion of Responsible Parenthood, had been born. Julia was its creator, fund raiser, and administrator; Theresa its adjutant. She no longer lived in Dalston but in the warden's apartments of the rather grandly titled "City College," which was actually housed in the former Frog Lane Brewery, overlooking the City Road Basin of the Regent's Canal in Islington. There the society ran weekend "starter" courses for housewives from all over the East End.

Theresa had developed a shrewd instinct for sorting out their likely successes from their near-certain failures. Women in the first category were followed up and the more promising among them were selected for longer, five-day courses at the society's "Country College" – a former maltings at Ware, associated with the old brewery. The town of Ware is only a few miles from Allbury, which explains how Julia came to hear of the company's difficulties before most other people and was thus able to snap up both premises for a fraction of their price in an unforced sale.

Whenever people asked Julia, "How d'you manage to fit it all in?" she thought at once of Theresa, of whom the question could truly be asked. The woman seemed absolutely tireless. She not only ran the courses at the City College, she also trudged the streets to recruit the "students" and to follow up the hopefuls. And on at least one day each week she travelled down to Ware to guide the work of the Country College, too.

"It's easy," she would say. "As long as *you* keep raising the money, Mrs Somerville, *I* can cheerfully spend it." And then she'd give a roguish smile. "That was never my difficulty – spending the old spondulicks."

They were a perfectly matched pair. Julia's talent, as she had quickly discovered, lay in the business of organization, in raising and managing money. Theresa, on the other hand, could manage people, could teach, and, above all, knew how to ration the hours of the day so that everybody, from the least promising student to her own youngest child, got their fair share of her time. Indeed, so small was the overlap between their two spheres that a daily chat on the phone and a brief meeting once a month was all the consultation they needed. Whenever Julia's work took her inside other charities and she saw the time that was wasted in committees and in the supervision of routine tasks that needed none – then she knew how she managed to "fit it all in."

The SPRP's "head office" (as it was called in anticipation of the branch offices that would one day open in other cities up and down the country) was in a private house in Pembridge Square. When Strong drew up before it on this particular day there was nothing out of the ordinary. She handed him her usual list of minor defects – a "blip" in the french polish, which she had ringed with a yellow wax pencil; an unidentified squeak, probably beyond the hearing of most men, in the rear offside coachwork; and some uneven stitching in the driver's seat, which Strong himself had pointed out to her; then she left him to return the car to the works. He would bring it back at two, and she would then search for more blemishes . . . and so on until she could find none.

Dear old Captain Harcourt opened the door for her and said, "A new Rolls-Royce, I see."

She glanced casually over her shoulder and replied, "Oh, is it?"

And then they went to her office, where they ran through a list of fund-raising events that were to take place within the next few weeks. Julia was no public speaker. In fact, as she often said, she was rotten at doing any of the things that either raised the society's money or spent it. Her one great talent lay in organizing those geniuses who could do either or both.

After that they went through the ledgers. Then Julia telephoned Warne & Co., the society's stockbrokers, and discussed their investments, a conversation that almost always ended with her complaint that charities had to keep their funds in such safe investments, especially when equities were roaring away so famously.

Then Mrs Lacy, her secretary, brought her a cup of rosehip tea and a marie biscuit and they talked about Tallulah Bankhead in Noël Coward's "Fallen Angels" and agreed that the critics who had called it "vulgar, obscene, degenerate . . ." should visit the City College and have their eyes opened.

Then Julia dictated thank-you letters to donors, large and small. This was so routine she could not prevent her mind from wandering. What would it be like to be a great West End actress? Parties and night clubs and early-morning drives out into the country, where astonished yokels would fall off their bicycles at the sight of your fancy dress . . . would it be as wonderful as everybody imagined? Funny to think that those sorts of carryings-on were . . . well, *carrying on* not half a mile away from Connaught Square. All you needed to do was walk across the open space by Marble Arch and there it was, Mayfair, all around you. Yet in the almost-fourteen years she had lived there she had not once made that journey.

One day she would, of course – just as one day she would see the Pyramids and visit America and fly and learn to play the piano really properly and go walking in the Lake District . . . But just lately it had begun to dawn on her (or at least to hover at the outer rim of her consciousness) that some of these dreams would never come true.

Her younger sister, Dolly, would be the one to ask about high life in the West End. Wild little Dolly. It had always been her ambition to become a great West End actress – no, not always, but ever since the war. Perhaps that dream would never come true, either. Julia felt a familiar wave of sadness pass through her. She ought to try with Dolly, one more time.

They were an awful family for letting things slide. Since their parents had died, the pull of their diverse ambitions had carried them apart. No one *meant* it to happen; but they'd done little to stop it, either. Except with Dolly. She really had tried with Dolly.

Agnes was another matter. There she was, out in Kenya, reduced to a dutiful letter at Christmas and dutiful notes on birthdays. Still, when she was so far away, what else could one do?

And then there was Max. *What* could one say about Max? Prickly, lovable, incompetent . . . mad? Anyone would imagine that, what with all her trips to Ware, she'd often pop over to see her only surviving brother; but the truth was she couldn't bear to see the old place running itself down under his "care." He'd have made a wonderful landowner, Max – two hundred years ago.

No, since their parents had died they had all rather gone their separate ways. One really ought to Do Something about it. She gave an involuntary sigh.

"Is anything the matter, Mrs Somerville?" Mrs Lacy's face was filled with concern.

"Not in the least. My mind was wandering, I'm afraid. How many are left?"

"Three."

While she dictated the final letters Julia confined her musings safely to "Passion Island," which lay concealed in its brown paper wrappers in her handbag, awaiting her next private moment – for Julia could never quite own up to her addiction to romantic novels.

Would beautiful, spoiled, coquettish Joan Allison, already the cause of two suicides, go to San Francisco to stay with the Vandeerings, "one of the oldest and richest families in America," and there get the comeuppance she so richly deserved? Julia smiled to herself; of course she would. She'd fall hopelessly in love with the handsome young heartthrob who (quite unwittingly) would torment her, just as she had (not quite so unwittingly) tormented poor . . . whatsizname, the debonair society portrait painter who had then killed himself.

The telephone rang – the direct line into her office. Even as she leaned forward to lift the earpiece from its cradle, Julia had a premonition that something dreadful was about to happen.

CHAPTER TWO

STRONG WAS BACK even before Mrs Lacy rescued the earpiece from Julia's nerveless hand. "Whatever is the matter, Mrs Somerville?" she asked.

"I have to go home." The voice did not sound remotely like her own. "Something has happened to Mr Somerville."

No doubt Mrs Lacy made some reply but the words did not register. Nor – for the first time in her life – did Julia notice what sort of car Strong had brought for her. It was a model she had never seen before; that was all she noticed about it. But hadn't he been going to bring back the Phantom . . . lord, what did it matter now!

He opened the rear door for her.

"No, no," she told him. "I'll sit beside you. I want you to tell me what has happened. I'm afraid I didn't take in much of what Mr Opie was saying."

"I didn't see it myself, madam," he said as soon as they set off. "But I was there before the doctor moved him . . ."

"Yes, I had a word with the doctor, too. They both said he's unconscious. Tell me – they weren't just being . . . he's not dead, is he?"

The world seemed unreal. She had passed these houses every day for years, practically. Why were they so unfamiliar?

"You may set your mind at rest on that, madam. The Guv'nor was breathing regular and he had a good colour and all. It didn't look that bad a wound to me, not on the surface. I expect you'll find it's just concussion."

"I'm sorry – go on. You were telling me what happened."

"It seems he was hit by a falling chain. There was an overhead pulley-block, see? And the side plate must have worked loose so the chain sort of jumped off of the drive wheel."

She closed her eyes and gripped the edges of her seat. The description was too graphic; she could hear the rattle of the chain as it fell . . . smell the oil . . .

"I wouldn't say as it fell from all that high, neither," Strong added. "Twelve foot, maybe. I've seen men hit harder by worse – and off down the pub for a pint next day."

She reached across and gave his arm a grateful squeeze, but did not risk speaking. Judging by Dr Jordan's tone of voice, even down the phone, it was nothing so simple as that.

"You never asked what car this is," Strong prompted, determined to be jovial.

She let him talk. A human voice reading telephone numbers would be better than the silent screams that filled her mind.

"This is W.O.'s new Bentley. The Big Six. Well, she's six-and-a-half, really. Remember? They was testing the Four in France and they met the new Royce and had a race on the spot? And that was when W.O. decided to go for the Big Six." There was a pause before he added, "Beautiful, beautiful. Royce'll have to put their skates on now and all."

He was still praising the car as they pulled into Connaught Square. When he held open the door for her he said, "The Guv'nor's going to be all right, madam. I felt it the moment I saw him."

Too filled with dread to speak, she smiled her gratitude and turned toward her front door. Even at this extremity she could not forget that she was in public. She mounted the two steps calmly and did not fish for the keys until she arrived. Indoors she would be in public, too. The servants would be looking at her, seeking their cue. Later they would say, "Mrs Somerville was magnificent!" – meaning that she showed not a trace of emotion. No matter that inside herself she was on the verge of hysteria, that she wanted to rend her clothes, tear out her hair, fall to her knees and beg God not to do this to her . . .

Instead, she drew a deep breath and, preparing to be magnificent, lifted the key to the lock.

But someone must have been looking out for her arrival; the door opened before her hand was halfway there. "Oh, madam, what a terrible thing!" Mrs Crooke declared, watching her mistress keenly.

"Is Dr Jordan with him?"

"He's using the telephone. He wants to call in Sir John Woolaway."

"Of course. Anybody. The best . . ." She was already halfway up the stairs. But Mrs Crooke called after her, "They're in the morning room, madam."

It was such a shock to see George lying on the carpet – on his side, as if he were only pretending to sleep. He was still in his works overalls. She stood by the doorway and stared at him, then at Dr Jordan, who put his hand over the mouthpiece and said, "Best place." Then, quickly returning to the instrument, "Yes! I'm holding on here." Again the hand over the mouthpiece. "Sir John Woolaway."

"So I gather." She spoke at last. "What does he say?"

"No. They're still trying to find him. He *is* there. We know that much."

She knelt beside George.

"Please don't touch him," the doctor asked with respectful urgency.

Her hands hung limp at her sides. Now she was close to her husband she could see what damage the chain had done. There was dried blood on the back of his head and the bruising on his neck looked deep and angry. But his breathing was regular. She risked touching his hand; the skin was cold.

Sir John had obviously been located. As soon as he heard the circumstances of the accident and learned of George's condition, he promised he'd come without delay, and he'd send an ambulance, too.

"Your husband will go directly into University College Hospital," Jordan told her as he replaced the phone. He spoke as if that already made the outlook twice as hopeful. "Sir John is the best man in the world at this kind of thing, you know."

But his smile faded when Julia asked, "What exactly is 'this kind of thing'?"

"Well, we mustn't go jumping to conclusions," he said vaguely.

"I must go to my daughter," she told him. "I hope she hasn't seen . . ." she inclined her head toward George.

"No."

"Good. I'll post a maid at the door, just in case. And then I'll pack a bag. I'll stay at UCH with him."

"Oh but look . . ." he began, and then thought better of it.

Young Lydia was terrified. Yet, even at the tender age of ten, she had already absorbed that impulse of her class toward reserve and coolness. She ran to her mother, threw her pale little arms around her, hugged her tight – and uttered not a word.

Miss Valentine gestured toward the door and raised her eyebrows.

Julia nodded. The woman tiptoed away.

A maid, a stranger, dropped a curtsy and prepared to follow the governess out, also in silence.

Julia detained her briefly, saying, "You are Miss . . . I'm sorry. I've forgotten."

"Davis, madam. The new nursery . . ."

"Yes, of course. Imogen Davis. Of course. Well, Miss Davis, please go and stand outside the morning room door." Her eyes gestured down at Lydia, still clinging silently, eyes tight shut.

The maid, whose eyebrows had lifted a sardonic half-inch at being called *Miss* Davis, gave a nod and a wan little smile that was almost conspiratorial. It was not quite a servant's gesture, though the difference was subtle. Yet, watching her go, Julia, in whom it was quite instinctive to judge new servants, even in such awful circumstances as these, took an instant liking to her. Somehow she radiated confidence and reliability.

The minute they were alone, *en famille,* the rules changed. Lydia broke down and howled. Julia half-joined in, racking her body with almost silent sobs until, after a minute or so, she caught the distant clangour of the ambulance bell, still several streets away.

"Daddy isn't going to die, is he, Mummy?" Lydia asked.

"Of course not, dearest. I saw far worse injuries during the war, in soldiers who recovered completely." She gave another hug to prepare her to let go. "And Daddy has the best doctor in the world for . . . this sort of thing."

"What sort of thing?"

"Injuries to the head. D'you hear that ambulance? That's coming here, I expect. I must go and meet it." She released the child. "Listen, I'll probably go and stay with Daddy in hospital for a day or two. You will be terribly brave and good, won't you."

Lydia promised with a nod, then, dabbing her eyes with her pinny and fanning her face – preparing to revert to public rules – asked, "May Violet still come to tea tomorrow?"

"Of course, dear." She gave an encouraging smile. "We must go on as normally as possible. When Daddy gets better he'd hate to hear that we just moped around and made asses of ourselves."

She was still forcing the mood as she shut the door behind her; but the moment she was alone on the stair all her forebodings returned. As she went down the last flight, Dr Jordan emerged from the morning room, closing the door behind him. Imogen Davis stepped a little to one side.

"Sir John will have a word with you when he's completed his examination," he murmured. "D'you mind?"

She shook her head. "I must make a phone call."

Indeed, she ought to make a dozen calls but this was the one that could not wait.

"Max?" she said when he had at last been brought to the phone. "Listen, my dear – something rather awful has happened to George – an accident at the works. Yes, something fell on his head. He's still unconscious. No, I'm speaking from home. Sir John Woolaway is examining him now and it's pretty certain he's going into hospital – UCH in Gower Street – you know where it is? No, there's no point in that just yet. I'll let you know when he's conscious again and is allowed visitors. I'll be with him, of course. But the reason I'm ringing, Max, is could you pop over to Water End and let Robert know? I'd call his housemaster only you can manage to break the news so much better, dear. It's serious but not drastic, tell him – not life-and-death. It'd be so much better coming from you. Thank you, darling, you're such a brick. I knew you would and that's such a weight off my mind."

She drew a deep breath before she went on: "Listen, could I ask you to do one more tiny thing? At least, I hope it's tiny. Could you possibly find out where Dolly is and . . . no, I know you haven't, dear. I haven't either. I've tried, believe me. We get together, we meet for tea or something, and she's perfectly charming and full of contrition, and yes, it's been marvellous and we must see each other again soon . . . and then not a peep out of her, not a note – not a blind thing. Well, one can only do so much . . . Yes, all right, it'll be hard for you. I know that. But look at it from my . . . I mean, if I ring her with this news, well, it'll look like some kind of blackmail, won't it. Can't you see? Oh God, I can hear *noises* from the doctors. I must go now. I'll just leave it to you, Max. Do whatever you think fit, and I'll ring you again tomorrow – or sooner if there's any news. Tell Robert he may ring the hospital before prayers tonight. Bye!"

Dr Jordan had returned to the morning room. Julia waited outside. She had forgotten the new maid until the girl stepped forward and said, "I know I'm only new here, madam, but please call on me as if I'd been here years. I'll pull my weight whatever way I can."

It was unnerving. Her manner was as respectful as one could wish but her accent and tone were so perfectly middle class, she might have been an old school friend talking. Julia only just conquered an impulse to burst into tears. She blinked at the girl and smiled her thanks. "Tell me about yourself. I had to go out this morning."

"I know." Imogen's tone was affectionate. By some instinct she seemed to realize that her mistress did not want the usual servant's *curriculum vitae;* just the comfort of another human voice. "I know all about the SPRP, Mrs Somerville. I don't suppose you remember a *Mrs* Davis who came to one of your very first weekend courses in Islington? Mrs Consuelo Davis."

Julia's eyes brightened. "But of course! How could I forget! So you are her daughter?"

It all fell into place. Mrs Consuelo Davis had been married to a stock jobber in the City. They'd lost everything in some crash. He took to drink and fell in front of a bus. His poor wife hadn't the first idea of running a house without servants – until someone suggested the SPRP. Oh yes, Julia had cause and more to remember the name of Consuelo Davis; the woman had trodden so hard on her nightmares. But if a bonny, well-fed young thing like Miss Davis were the result, Julia could feel both relief and pride.

"And how is your mother these days?" she asked.

"She is very well, thank you," Imogen replied with an odd sort of coolness. Then, biting her lip at her own lapse, she added, "madam."

Julia knew when to leave well alone. "Do convey my regards to her," she said.

Miss Davis nodded. "She always spoke highly of you, Mrs Somerville – and Mrs Ashbury, of course. I could hardly believe my good fortune when the agency said there was a place here."

"So there you are – you may be new to this house, Miss Davis, but you're already no stranger." Julia glanced impatiently at the unyielding door. To her astonishment she heard Imogen reply, "Almost one of the family."

She spun in surprise to face the maid, expecting her to stammer out some apology for overstepping that indefinable barrier between friendliness and friendship. But Imogen was not in the least abashed. Indeed, she nodded vigorously as she added, "It's a very big family by now, Mrs Somerville. Indeed, there must be hundreds of women out there who'd drop everything to help you at such a dreadful time. Surely you know that?"

Again Julia felt that sudden lump in her throat and the almost intolerable pressure of tears behind her eyelids – but this time there was something more: the teeniest little suspicion that Imogen had stage-managed this emotional climax, as, indeed, she may have stage-managed the previous one, too.

It was that suspicion, rather than a renewed dose of her boundless self-discipline, which now prevented the tears from flowing. In any case, Sir John Woolaway himself opened the door at that moment and gravely beckoned her. Moments later she had completely forgotten the existence of Miss Imogen Davis.

Julia knew that, above all, she had to be told the truth; she also knew that neither of these grave gentlemen would give it her if they felt there was any risk of an unpleasant scene. So she faced them with a crisp, no-nonsense manner that could not have been further from her inward state. "Thank you for coming so quickly, Sir John," she said.

"It's as well I did, Mrs Somerville – and well I brought that ambulance, too. I'm afraid your husband will have to go into hospital for a day or so."

"I realize you will not want to commit yourself to any distant prognosis, Sir John, but, as you may know, we have quite a large engineering business that cannot wait until every *t* is crossed and every *i* has its dot. So anything you can tell me, even so early as this, will be helpful."

He sized her up before he risked saying, "I think, Mrs Somerville, that our patient will be away from his desk for some considerable time."

CHAPTER THREE

ON THE FIFTH day George opened his eyes properly and looked around. Before that there had been many false dawns – eyelids that flickered open to reveal nothing but ghoulish white crescents, whimperings such as dogs make when they hunt in dream packs. But this was a genuine awakening. It lasted no more than a quarter of a minute, and it was not repeated again that day, but there was no doubting the intelligence that had stared out from behind those eyelids, baffled and frightened as it was.

After that a new mood pervaded his sickroom, though to call it hope would be going too far. Indeed, Julia increasingly found herself wondering what "hope" might mean in such circumstances. Sir John looked in twice every day and sometimes of an evening, too. He always asked the nurses if they had noticed any sign of voluntary movement. The spinal reflexes were normal but George made not the slightest movement of his own accord. Even worse, he remained totally incontinent.

The signs that his coma was coming to an end made it vital for her to know exactly what was wrong with him and how soon they could expect a complete recovery. It was all very well to say he'd "be away from his desk for some considerable time," but George would want it in days and hours; and if she couldn't tell him, he'd suspect she was holding something back. She knew George; and Sir John did not.

So, after the great man had absorbed the news of his patient's slight recovery, she asked if she might speak with him outside.

"We may speak freely here," he assured her.

She nodded toward George.

"He can't hear us." He smiled as at a superstition.

But she knew better. George was lying there listening to everything. Indeed, acting on that belief, she had almost worn out her vocal cords these past days, reading him everything she could lay her hands on, from his favourite G.A. Henty adventures to the *Transactions of the Society of Automotive Engineers*. Now she went out to the anteroom, leaving Woolaway no choice but to follow. There she wasted no time. "If my husband is about to regain consciousness, Sir John, then I can promise you – the first thing he will wish to know is when he may return to the workshops."

The physician frowned.

"They are his life," she explained. "And they depend absolutely on him, too."

Sir John let a silence grow before he said, "Sit down, please, Mrs Somerville. What I have to tell you will, I'm afraid, be hard to bear."

She stared at him, open-mouthed.

"Please?" he insisted.

She obeyed. Already panic was rising within her. She wanted to reach across the ever-widening space between them and clamp his lips between her fingers.

"Yet," he went on, "having watched you these past days, having seen how well you cope, I have no doubt but that you *will* bear it."

He paused. She clasped her hands and gave him a tight little nod.

"I'm sorry to have to warn you that your husband may never recover all his faculties."

"But his eyes," she protested. "If you had seen . . ."

His raised finger silenced her. "His mental faculties may be unimpaired. We shall know the answer to that very soon – the next few weeks, in fact. But I'm afraid I can hold out no hope that he will ever walk or use his arms again."

Suddenly it was as if she and Sir John had ceased to occupy the same kind of space; he had become like some creature in an aquarium, talking at her down a long, invisible tube.

"You mean to say he's . . ."

There was a word, a special word for it.

Woolaway nodded. "Paralyzed. From the neck down."

She raised her hand to her mouth, bit her forefinger, but felt nothing. "His whole body?" she whispered.

"He will go on breathing, of course – as we see now. And his heart will continue to beat. All the muscles that do not respond to conscious control from his brain will go on functioning normally. Virtually normally."

Her mind, unwilling to face the enormity of this news, seized on that small qualification. "Virtually?"

His eyes fell. "I mean, he will remain incontinent."

A large, warm tear rolled down either cheek; she lowered her eyelids, sending more cascading after them. George . . . paralyzed! George – so vigorous and strong, so active, so proud of the skills in his fingers. It would destroy him. There wasn't a single job in the entire works that he couldn't do better than the craftsmen who worked at it every day of their lives – how often had he boasted that? He'd never be able to live with such a blow.

The tears ceased to flow. Her anguish had somehow gone too deep for such easy relief. Surprised, she discovered she was no longer sitting down but standing at the window, looking down into University Street.

People were walking around, going about their everyday business – quite unconscious of the fact that two fellow humans, not a dozen yards away, had just had their lives shattered.

Two women meeting, each surprised at finding the other there . . . laughing! How could they? A man, passing by, turning to admire their legs.

George without sex! How would he bear it? She remembered a time, a remote, distant time near the end of their honeymoon, when that overwhelming passion had seized her and she suddenly understood his frenzy. It had not happened often since; George found it indelicate in her. But his own pleasure was always enormous. What would he do now? And what of the third child she had promised him, as soon as the SPRP was on it feet? Life was as good as over – for both of them.

An arm went around her shoulder. She looked up in surprise, thinking it might be Sir John. But he had left the room; her comforter was one of the nurses, a sister, large and maternal. Julia took her arm and hugged it briefly. Then she blinked, drew a deep breath, and murmured, "All right now." She let the arm go.

The woman said, "You won't believe it, Mrs Somerville, but for many people this kind of tragedy proves in time to be the start of an amazingly rewarding life."

Her heart fell. Yes, she would have to grow used to comforters. Play the game. "I'm sure you're right, sister. But it's very hard to see it at the moment."

"I know. I'll bring you a cup of tea, shall I?"

Julia smiled and nodded.

It was all good practice for when George regained consciousness, for when she had to look him in the eye.

On Sir John's second visit, later that day, she exhausted the last remnant of hope. She asked him – again out of George's earshot – if he had ever known of a late recovery.

His eyes went large with sympathy. "I'm afraid not, Mrs Somerville."

"Not of any faculty? Not even in the slightest degree?"

There was a strange, awkward hesitation before he replied, "It would be quite wrong for me to raise the smallest hope, my dear. But when such a tragedy strikes a man – and this is the nearest tragedy to death itself – we have to search for the brighter elements in the picture. And far and away the brightest in your husband's case, if you will permit me to say so, is that he has *you* for a wife."

She accepted the compliment with a tight little smile and pressed on with, "If there is no hope that he will recover his faculties, then I'm quite sure his next question would be how long he might reasonably expect to live."

He bridled at that. Oh, it was much too early to start talking in those terms . . . wait till he regains consciousness . . . so much depends on his will to live . . . and so forth. She guessed that behind his cheery bluster lay an even more dire prognosis than any she had yet dared contemplate.

Over the next few days George's brief spells of consciousness grew in both duration and frequency. At last they endured long enough to allow him to take proper nourishment; the clumsy apparatus for passive feeding could be dismantled.

To everyone's consternation, though, he seemed unable to speak. He opened his mouth and made desperate efforts, but nothing emerged except the odd little gurgling noise, random utterances whose resemblance to words was as coincidental as the *ma-ma-ma* with which babies recruit their parents' delight; and, as with a baby, Julia hung on his every syllable, saying, "Yes, dear, this is Julia, I'm here. What is it? What are you trying to say? *I? You? Oh?* What is it, darling?"

All he could do was repeat his guttural cries until, exhausted, he fell back asleep.

Lydia was desperate to see her father but, naturally, she would not hear of it. She returned briefly to Connaught Square each day and painted as rosy a picture as possible – though she realized she would also have to prepare her for the shock of his homecoming, whenever that might be.

Every night of their lives she had heard her children say their prayers before tucking them in. Now, before the "sand in the left eye, sand in the right eye" and the "mind the bugs don't bite" rituals, she reminded Lydia how brave and strong their father had always been. "And when he comes home he's going to show us that same bravery and strength in a different way," she said. "If you and Robert could just see how he's fighting to get better, you'd both be so proud of him. This awful accident would have killed most men – but not your father. If anyone can triumph over it, he's the man."

The girl cried, of course, and Julia had to fight hard not to give in and join her; but she could also feel a kind of warmth in the child, something that in other circumstances would be called gladness – that her father was proving himself so fine a man.

Julia would stay at Lydia's bedside until she was fast asleep, and then she would touch her gently and yield at last to tears. No one saw her. No one would have suspected it.

The house ran smoothly in her absence; Captain Harcourt assured her all was well at Pembridge Square; and Mr Opie reported no difficulty at the works, either.

"I never felt less necessary," she commented to Max, who was the first visitor allowed.

"It's a case of the colonel's glass eye," he replied cryptically.

She had long ago ceased asking him to explain his more gnomic utterances; they were almost invariably gruesome, even when they were not frankly indecent.

"Did you find Dolly?" she asked.

He nodded curtly. "Appalled. Says she'll phone you."

"She's not in London, then?"

"Leamington Spa." He shook his head sadly. "The things they have to put up with, eh? What a bloody awful trade!" Then he went into the sickroom, where he bellowed, "Who goes there!" at George and pinched his cheeks.

People were rushing forward to pull him away when George opened his eyes and *smiled!*

"You're a bloody fool, Somerville," Max continued, still at the top of his voice. "You'll be out of this year's Le Mans for sure now. I suppose you know that?"

The noises from George's throat were the closest thing to laughter.

Max roared a few more nuggets of manly comfort before he said, "Well, old scout – mustn't outstay my welcome on my first day, what?" And he left.

Sir John arrived just as he was departing. "Bottle of Scotch wouldn't hurt," he growled at the distinguished physician. "I'll bring some tomorrow."

Julia hugged him tight. "You're wiser than all of us, Max."

He more than kept his word, for he brought not only the Scotch but also young Robert with him on the following day. "Intimations of mortality never harmed a chap," was his explanation.

They met first in the anteroom. Julia, willing now to try anything to restore George's power of speech, held out her arms to her son; but he stuck his hands awkwardly into his pockets and remarked, "Hello, Mater. Pretty rotten, what?"

She could see a sort of terror in his eyes – a frightened, bewildered little boy determined to be a man. She longed for some way of reaching him, of sharing the comfort she had been able to give so easily to young Lydia.

"Pretty rotten," she echoed. She remembered Dolly's description of the lad; "a robust little thug." That had been years ago but Robert had, if anything, grown to fit the description even better. "How've you been keeping?" she asked.

He shrugged. "School is school, don't you know." Then he brightened. "We beat Bedford Lower School yesterday. Thrashed them into the mud. I didn't disgrace us at the assault-at-arms, either."

"He won every bout," Max explained, as proud as if Robert were his own son. "Come on, young fellow!" And without a by-your-leave, he led the way into the sickroom. At the door he paused and, with a dramatic flourish of his hand, declaimed, "Behold – the wreckage of a man!" As he spoke he prodded a suddenly reluctant nephew toward the bed.

"Hello, Pater," Robert mumbled, taking up his father's hand. Its utter lifelessness shocked him and he dropped it as if the touch had scalded him.

"You're a positive wreck!" Max was booming down at George. In leaning over he was pushing the boy uncomfortably close, too. "Take more than a couple of spanners to put you right, old scout," he went on. "It's going to be a long haul. Are you sure you feel up to it?"

What's the alternative? Julia wondered.

As if in answer Max barked, "You wouldn't prefer the old service revolver to be left on the bedside table, what?" He thrust his hand in his pocket and, for one dreadful moment, everyone thought he was about to produce the weapon. But the bright metallic glint came from the silver stopper of an old leather hipflask; Julia recognized it as one that had been in the family for generations.

George laughed. This time there was no mistaking the sound. Not only that – he also said, "Max!" – somewhat slurred and hesitant, but the syllable was all there.

Max chuckled. "Caught you out, what? Take my tip. This is your man!" And he set the flask down ceremoniously upon the bedside table. "The whole *Titanic* in a pint. A luxury cruise to oblivion."

"Max," George repeated, then, shifting his focus, "Ro'ert . . . Romert."

Every muscle in Robert's body was now as tense as his father's were slack. "Beastly bad luck, Pater," he murmured. "Will you get better?"

"Ooo . . . ooo . . ."

"Soon?" Julia interpreted.

"Ya!" His mood was a blend of relief at being understood and anger that it should be necessary.

He had two small sips of whisky out of the silver cap, Max tipped the rest down his own throat and relished it loudly enough for the pair of them.

From that day on Max was a regular visitor, though he never

brought Robert again. His bluff humour was exactly what George required, as Julia soon realized. And no one else could supply it. No one else but Max could say, "Listen, Somerville, old sport – if ever you want the quick exit" – he made a pistol of his fist and shot himself behind the ear – and then the "barrel" was transformed into an emphatically pointing finger as it tapped his breast – "I'm your man."

No one else could say such things *and* make George laugh.

And George himself, once he'd got his tongue around a few words, improved at an astonishing pace. Before the week was out, only the occasional slurring or a furious hunt for a word would remind them of the disaster that might have been. In a curious way, the fact that he was not dumbstruck brought a mood of relief and near-happiness that none could have expected so soon.

Julia sat with him each evening. They talked of everything but his paralysis; she thought it best to let him raise the matter first.

By then they were preparing to move him back to Connaught Square.

"He'll need day and night nursing from now on," Sir John warned Julia. "Don't run away with the notion you can manage any of it yourself. It's a job for professionals."

But George had ideas of his own. The very first morning out of hospital, even before he saw Lydia, he made Julia telephone the works and arrange for Mr Opie to come over.

It was an amazing interview. George, who had no memory at all of the accident, had, it seemed, forgotten nothing of the work in hand. Had they sorted out the difficulty over that last batch of steel sheet? Was the new lot of chrome plating any better than before? And had that new American chappie turned up yet – what was his name?

"Eliot Baring IV!" Opie said. "He came last week."

"And?"

"Difficult to make him out, Guv'nor. Well built. You'd think he was a marine or a prize fighter. But very quiet, too – you'd never take him for an American until he opens his mouth. Knows his onions, though. You remember the way the wind used to howl around Sir Jock Drummond's Hispano-Suiza? He cured that in two days – driving around the Brooklands circuit at sixty, poking pencils and little strips of metal out the window. You never saw such a caper. But he found the answer for us. Simple, too."

"He's going to be worth his keep, then?"

"I'd say so, Guv'nor. You remember that annoying little problem with the new Phantom – the raindrops chasing round and round in circles in the quarter-light? That's what he's working on today. I'll bet he's got it licked by this evening."

Julia left them alone with the nurse and went to re-establish contact with the rest of her household. An hour later she met Opie, about to return to the works.

"What an amazing man, Mrs Somerville," he exclaimed. "Look at this." And he held out for her inspection a sheaf of paper covered with freehand sketches. Being engineering drawings they resembled the sort of work George used to do all the time – so much so that for one wild moment she thought he had magically recovered the faculty during the past hour.

It was impossible, of course, and yet here was Opie saying, "And look at this bit – and this" – pointing out two rather more childish-looking scribbles – "Mr Somerville did those himself."

"With his hands? His own hands?"

"No. You have to put the pencil between his teeth. Isn't it marvellous?" He saw her staring at the other drawings. "I did those. He told me what he wanted and I sketched it."

"His teeth?" she said – the idea just beginning to dawn on her.

"Yes, that's what this is for." He pointed to an unintelligible bit of engineering scribble at the heart of one of the drawings. "It's a miniature engineer's drafting board, where he can make drawings with his teeth. He had it all worked out, down to the last nut and bolt."

"But what is it? I can't make head nor tail of it."

"Why, it's an invalid carriage, see? Two driven wheels . . . differential . . . electric batteries. And these are the controls – all worked by mouth, using compressed air and rubber tubes, just like in a player piano. Amazing!"

Still she did not understand. "But he'll never get a licence to drive it on the public highway, surely?"

For a moment his bewilderment matched hers; then he threw back his head and laughed. "Why, bless us, Mrs Somerville, this isn't a road vehicle. It's something to carry him round the works. He's coming back to us – the Guv'nor, back on his own patch! It's going to be like old times again!"

CHAPTER FOUR

IT WAS WELL past midnight. They had no right to be making such a racket – laughing and slamming their car doors, rousing the whole neighbourhood. Without even drawing back her curtains Julia knew where it was all coming from. There was only one house that kept such hours: Alexander Deeping's, the central mansion on the far side of the square. "Dear Lexy" was London's most fashionable playwright – though "Darling Noël" was soon to dispute the title.

The noise was worse in winter, when there were no leaves on the trees; but even now, with the foliage at its thickest, it was still pretty intolerable. She had once tried getting up a petition among the other residents but they were all so besotted at having Dear Lexy for a neighbour that she got nowhere. Fortunately, George had always been a heavy sleeper. He hadn't been home two weeks and already he slept through most of his two-hourly turnings and changes.

She rose carefully and went to close the window, though she hated sleeping in a warm, airless room. As she slipped behind the heavy curtains the noise seemed to double. A girl laughed, that insistent, braying laugh of the dedicated young flapper determinedly *having fun*. Something about it reminded her of Dolly. Perhaps it was Dolly. These mindless, late-night carryings-on would be just her thing.

Julia peered across the square, though it was too dark and too far for her to recognize faces. Still, one never knew. Dolly had a characteristic walk, a characteristic way of flinging up her arms – come to think of it, Dolly had a characteristic way of doing everything.

Not a word from her, of course. She was no longer in Leamington Spa. That was all Mrs Lacy had been able to discover. Julia sighed. Why had she and her sister drifted apart? For absolutely no reason, as far as she could see. They certainly hadn't quarrelled. Naturally, the six years between their ages had prevented any very close friendship during childhood, but they had, nonetheless, enjoyed a lot of fun together. The war changed everything, especially with the death of their brother Billy. He and Dolly had been so close; "my bro" she always called him, proudly accepting his school slang and making it a particular endearment. When Billy was killed on the Somme, after the push toward Bapaume petered out, everything changed. Dolly chose to bury her grief in a wayward, dissolute life; all her seriousness seemed then to pass to Julia, leaving them with little in common.

Julia continued to peer among the trees, hoping that the laugh had been Dolly's, hoping for a sight of her. A vast, sleek Daimler drew up; of all the mobile things in sight, it was the only one that knew how to keep quiet. There was the ritual upper-class door-slam before it swept onward to reveal a little vignette of gaiety that caught Julia in a vulnerable moment.

Neither the man nor the woman was known to her, yet circumstances – the lateness of the hour, the enchantment of the dark and distance, the ambience of Connaught Square with its fine old houses and stately gardens, the woman's flowing silk gown, the man's evening dress, white scarf, and topper – these beguiling circumstances painted the pair of them vividly in her mind's eye: *He* was the most handsome man in London, mature and debonair; *she* had that rare, exquisite sort of beauty which laid an unquestioning world at her feet. As they mounted the steps to join the gay party, he put his arm about her and – this was the mental snapshot that lingered in Julia's vision long after they had gone – the woman laid her head on his shoulder, looked up into his eyes, and laughed.

That fine, silvery peal bewitched the very air. It was both innocent and knowing, virginal and sophisticated. It filled Julia with a sudden, wild longing to throw on a gown and dance across the square to join them. The two beautiful people swept into Alexander Deeping's house, leaving the night heady with the promises of romance. Already the racket from that place no longer seemed so strident. The saxophones were mellow; the drumbeat enticing. Julia pressed her nose against the pane until it hurt.

George made a few small noises. She parted the curtains and came back into the room, leaving the window open. The softly illuminated clock showed the hour to be almost two; at any moment now Nurse Sanders would come in to turn him and change his swaddling. As Julia crossed to her bed she heard railway wagons being shunted in the goods yards beyond Paddington, over half a mile away. The city night was full of noises; why let oneself be upset by so small an element in that vast tapestry?

Before she could step out of her slippers the nurse came in. The nightlight, held below her face, exaggerated its surprise. "Did they wake you, too?" she whispered, jerking her head toward the window. "Selfish beasts!"

Julia nodded; she went to the far side of George's bed and began folding down his covers in time with the nurse, who went on, "It's a great life for some!"

"I was thinking the same," Julia whispered back. "Luckily this fellow would sleep out the crack of doom." She rolled her husband toward the nurse and left the room while the more intimate operations were completed. When she returned the nurse had already retired to the dressing room; like everything else at Number 32, "dressing" had taken on a new meaning.

She lay in her own bed, beside his, listening to the noise of the party, idly daring herself to get up, dress . . . walk across the square. How did one gatecrash such affairs? Lady Ellesmere's ball had more gatecrashers than guests. It was all empty speculation, anyway; she'd never do such a thing.

George probably hadn't been asleep. He just couldn't bear her to be present at that most intimate revelation of his helplessness. Poor man, he'd be missing all that sort of thing. Not that he gave any sign of it.

Not that he would give any sign of it, either.

Were those urges in the head or down there?

If they were down there, then he wouldn't be missing anything. But if they were in the head? He'd just have to take his own medicine . . . all that *lie still, don't move, don't make a sound* . . . don't breathe, almost.

Laughter from across the square again. It was time for fun all over the world.

She turned on her reading light and took her long-neglected book from the bedside cabinet. She hadn't read a thing, or nothing she actually wanted to read, since before the accident.

This was called "Passion Island," by Juanita Savage. It seemed vaguely familiar: Joan Allison, beautiful, spoiled, flirtatious . . . debonair society portrait painter commits suicide in her garden . . . can't live without her . . . Such tosh! She settled herself for a long, delicious read. Then she came across her bookmark, a torn-off strip of SPRP notepaper, and she realized she had been reading this book on the day of George's accident. Ah yes – now she remembered the story. She skipped a whole section of it. But she read the next two chapters in mounting bewilderment – until she realized that the plot she'd had in mind belonged to the beginning of quite a different tale by some other author. Oddly enough, the discovery disappointed her, for, as soon as the characters fell into line with the actual plot of *this* book, their behaviour became entirely predictable and rather dull; there had been something refreshing in their earlier apparent waywardness.

She abandoned the book then and settled once more to sleep.

But a new routine is soon established. George had two good nurses, all round the clock; he had his wireless set, the best in the whole

Marconi range; he had his back numbers of all those engineering journals, which Miss Davis and the day nurse took it in turns to read to him; and Mr Opie called every morning with progress reports from the works – not least about job number 817, his all-purpose electrified wheelchair. Lydia spent an hour with him every afternoon after lessons, playing ludo; and he had a frequent visitor in Max . . . so what need had she to mope around the house, filling time, feeling guilty? She returned to as much of her old life as had survived, working at the SPRP, shopping, entertaining . . . everything as normal as possible.

Young Lydia turned out a real surprise. George had never really wanted a daughter, never understood her, could never be at ease with her. Hence Julia's promise to try for another son as soon as the SPRP was established. Robert, captain of junior boxing and second-row-forward in the First XV, was more his sort of chap – which was why the boy's behaviour was so hurtful. For Robert had declined to come home on his last exeat from school; instead, he'd gone to stay with his Uncle Max at Allbury. True, there was nothing especially remarkable in that; he'd spent several previous exeats there. But common decency suggested that the first one since his father's accident should be spent at home.

Lydia, by contrast, spent every snatched minute at her father's side. She made up stories and read them out in her earnest little treble – all about aeroplanes and speedboats and racing cars – things in which she had never before shown the slightest interest; and she did drawings of the huge, sleek cars that once again began to wait outside the house each morning at ten. One day she came into the bedroom absolutely bursting with excitement. She had discovered a new way of drawing cars – "Look, Daddy, look! You can actually see all four wheels at the same time!"

"Of course, I praised her to the skies," George told Julia later. "But between you and me, it looked as if the thing had been flattened by a steamroller."

"Why d'you say 'of course'?" she asked.

He shrugged and looked away. Even now he could not quite bring himself to confess that Lydia's concern and, even more, her total and unquestioning acceptance of the paralysis, had profoundly moved him – for, in a negative way, that would have been like confessing to how deep a wound Robert's rejection of it had caused.

Young Miss Davis had also proved a treasure. Indeed, the only unsuitable thing about her was her name, Imogen. In this modern, topsy-turvy world, where servants had become the true tyrants of the household and had to be given two afternoons off each week to bribe them to stay at all, she was a shining exception. She never seemed to take so much as a minute off. Every "free" afternoon she was with the master, helping to push him out in the park if the day were fine, or sitting by the open window reading to him, if it were not.

It seemed odd that George, who was so keen to get back to his modified drawing board, was not in the least interested in reading for himself. He said he'd find it uncomfortable to have someone sitting beside him, bored to death, just waiting for him to tell them when to turn the page. While there was some truth in that, it could not be denied that Miss Davis had a pretty little face as well as a beautiful, well-modulated speaking voice.

All in all, then, by the time autumn had transformed Hyde Park into its annual gold and russet wonderland, life at number 32, Connaught Square had resumed a remarkably even keel again, especially when one considered the nature of the tragedy that had overtaken it.

CHAPTER FIVE

"THE END OF THE HOUSE OF ALARD" struck Julia as one of the most chilling stories she had ever read. The idea that a great and powerful family, lords of the manor, masters of the whole countryside, could be reduced to poverty and forced to sell off their assets, bit by bit, filled her with terror. Or, rather, it reawakened all those terrors that had seized her during the days of Theresa Ashbury's challenge. As humiliation was heaped upon humiliation, she found she could not keep back her tears. It was all so real – the sort of tragedy that could descend upon any family. She used to steal back to the nursery, long after Lydia was asleep, and fret over her – tuck her in, straighten her pillows, tidy away stray locks of hair – until the child stirred and became uneasy. Why she did these things she could not say. But it brought her a kind of comfort, as if these trivial actions were unspoken promises to both her children.

"Why d'you read that rubbish, girlie?" George asked. "It only gives you the weeps."

Actually, his gruffness was mostly pretend, these days – a mask for his delight that his electric carriage was completed and that he was able to get round the works again. That place was his true home, not the grand house in Connaught Square.

Somerville's was a third-generation family business. The grandfather, James Somerville, had begun life as a blacksmith and had ended it as carriage maker to the nobility. The father, John, had continued and expanded the works; among other things the firm in his time had fitted out suites of railway coaches for almost every crowned head in Europe. Between them James and John had spanned the solid, prosperous reign of Queen Victoria. Toward the end of his life John had been one of the first to build coachwork for motor cars.

George, who had gone into the business at the age of twenty-five, in 1910, had expanded still further, into fitting out private yachts and those vast, floating palaces called luxury ocean liners. His real interest, however, lay in engineering. Before his time Somerville's coachwork had always been added to an existing chassis; often they built the chassis themselves, in the works, but always under licence and to the regular design. George had changed that approach; even when he took a standard Rolls-Royce chassis, he modified the suspension, moved the engine mountings, changed her centre of gravity – all to make his bodywork function better. People were beginning to say, "If you want to know what the next marque of Rolls will be like – look at the latest Somerville."

One thing he hated about all present-day cars was the way the radiator had to sit slap bang over the front axle, otherwise the car would roll wildly at every turn in the road. Everyone else seemed to think it a marvellous feature, God-given, immutable. The way the front wheels jutted forward, they said, made the car look like a panther about to spring. But George had a vision of a car body in which the radiator jutted forward, while the axle sat beneath the engine. Folk swore it couldn't be done, but he had designers who knew otherwise, toiling away in little secret huts dotted here and there about the works. Any day now a new and truly revolutionary Somerville-bodied Rolls-Royce would take the world by storm.

That had really been why he was so desperate to get back to the works – and why he *lived* there but merely refreshed himself at home.

Julia had been surprised at the readiness with which both Sir John and Dr Jordan had agreed to his return to work. It made her uneasy. With her usual bluntness she asked Jordan: "Are you only saying that because he hasn't long to live anyway and so might as well spend his days where he's happiest?"

"On the contrary, Mrs Somerville," came Jordan's practised reply. "Let me put it this way. Sir John has stressed to you the vital importance of personal hygiene in the management of your husband's incontinence. Most people in his condition who die do so as a result of kidney infection, not of the actual paralysis – because, you see, we have no magic bullet to kill the microbes once they enter the body. We have to get at them before they enter. But it is also true that people who are happy and fulfilled are much less prone to infection than those who are bored and miserable. So, although the management of his hygiene will be slightly more difficult . . ."

"A lot more difficult, surely?"

"Not necessarily. If he has a good nurse with him, one who'll stand no nonsense, I'd back him for a longer life at the works than if he were cooped up at home all day, hearing everything at second hand."

It all sounded reassuring, except on one point: Jordan would not be drawn into saying how long George might be expected to live, given these apparently ideal circumstances. "I've known some die within months," he said vaguely, "while others have soldiered on for years and years. It all depends on the temperament, you see. And luck. And constitution."

She was not reassured. Perhaps the dire situation that was then unfolding in her present bedtime reading, "The End of the House of Alard," influenced her; perhaps it was the morbid effect of the death of Queen Alexandra, which filled the paper for days at around that time; or it could have been Jordan's very eagerness to calm her fears – at all events, she felt impelled to visit the Westminster Library, where she spent an hour or so consulting some very weighty medical tomes.

To her utter dismay she learned that few people in George's condition survived beyond three years.

Three years! She felt sick. She had to read the section several times to make sure she hadn't misunderstood the jargon. But it was suddenly plain to her that she had been living in a fool's paradise.

Next morning, at the SPRP, she suddenly broke off what they were doing and asked Captain Harcourt if she might burden him with a problem that had nothing to do with the society.

"If it concerns you, Mrs Somerville," he replied, "then it has everything to do with the society."

Wonderful old Captain Harcourt! There was something most endearing about a man who, having retired from active service almost twenty years ago, still insisted on his rank. If he'd been a captain in the Guards, one might understand it; but he had been in the Commissariat – what was now the Army Service Corps – not exactly the regiment a gentleman would choose to flaunt. Was he truly as proud of it as he seemed? Or was he poking sly fun at all those snobbish ex-Guards captains who clung onto their rank while working as motor-car salesmen and moving-picture-theatre managers? One could never tell; he was such an opaque sort of fellow.

But Julia adored him; if she could have picked a father, he'd have been first, second, and third choice, all in one.

"Normally it's the sort of thing one would discuss with one's family," she began. "But Agnes is out in Kenya, and is the world's worst correspondent, anyway. Ask her for the old family recipe for honey cakes and she'll send you one for beeswax polish. And Dolly – you know how I've tried there. And as for Max . . . well, you know Max."

"I do indeed."

"He'd only tell me I was barking up a mare's nest or some such nonsense."

"This sounds serious." He closed the ledger and pushed all his papers to one side.

And then she told him.

He listened without interruption, nodding sympathetically whenever she paused. "Medical books!" he remarked in disgust when she had finished. "I remember I had to read a lot once, first aid and things, during the Boer War. And dash it if I didn't feel every symptom between page one and page five hundred. I know it's a different kettle of fish with you, but my point is, you see – medical books bring out the worst in a body. Or in a mind." He gazed at her reassuringly and then, rubbing the tips of his fingers together, continued. "Still, that's not really your worry, is it."

"No. I suppose my real worry is that even if Mr Somerville's death is a remote possibility, it's still much less remote than it was before the accident. And Robert is only twelve. One couldn't even think of his taking control of the business for another ten years, if that. I suppose at the back of my mind I've always had the thought that George would last at least until . . ."

"You have a good manager in Opie. He seems to have coped well these past few months?"

"Oh, he can bridge a few months' gap, possibly even a year. But a manager isn't an owner. They're two different animals. They don't look at the world in the same way at all."

A little smile began to play at the corner of his mouth. "Yes?" he prompted.

"Well . . ." She was disappointed that he seemed to have missed the obvious drift of her thought. "I have to face the possibility of a much longer gap. Five years? Six? Seven?"

"Yes?" he repeated.

She realized she'd have to spell it out almost as to a child. "Take me, for instance. I have the best possible housekeeper in Mrs Crooke. But she'd be lost without me. I'm the one who determines what sort of household it is, and then she runs it after my direction. You're a military man, Captain Harcourt, surely you understand – the chain of command, delegation, et cetera?"

He grinned and nodded affably but still, and to her mounting frustration, volunteered nothing. She tried another approach. "Here at the society it's different. You and Mrs Lacy could manage it all between you – and Mrs Ashbury, of course. You wouldn't even notice my absence . . ."

He laughed. "If you suppose that, Mrs Somerville, then you have no idea of your unique contribution to our work."

"But you've proved it, these last few months . . ."

"Oh, we can 'bridge a gap' – like Mr Opie. I can't deny that. But nothing more. Tell me now" – he leaned forward over her desk, rubbing his hands briskly – "this proprietor who is so different from a manager, what are his qualities? In other words, who are we looking for?"

What were George's qualities, she wondered? "I suppose he'd have to be able to do every job in the factory as well as his own men."

The Captain's eyebrows shot up in surprise.

"Mr Somerville can," she explained.

"But is that essential in all proprietors? Take your own . . ."

"The men respect him for it. And fear his judgement."

"No doubt. But take your own case – can you do every household task? Could you cook an eight-course dinner for forty? Can you starch lace and crimp it properly? Do an invisible mend?" He hastened on without waiting for a reply. "But let's leave that aside for a moment. Tell me what other qualities we're looking for."

"Well . . . he'd have to know about managing money, of course."

The Captain nodded confidently. "We know all about *that.*" He waved vaguely at the ledger and the filing cabinets.

"We?" she asked, mystified.

"I mean, *you.* If it came to interviewing someone, you'd know exactly what questions to ask him. He couldn't think he was dealing with some ignorant woman (forgive me) and just flannel his way through. You'd spot it a mile off. What else?"

"Good at managing people, I suppose." Something was eluding her. She knew there was some indefinable quality far more important than anything on this rather humdrum list.

"Of course. Anything else? What about vision?"

That was it! "Yes. He'd have to have an eye for the future. You've put your finger on it, Captain Harcourt. He'd have to know, by some kind of magic, what way things are going – how the industry will look five or ten years from now. *That's* the difference between a manager and a proprietor. If the proprietor can't sense the future and steer his firm to meet it, they'll all go down the drain, no matter how superb the day-to-day management might be." She gave it further thought. "In fact," she concluded, "if it came to a straight choice, one would have to pick a poor administrator with good vision of the future against a superb administrator with none."

The Captain relaxed again and, leaning back in his chair, observed, "And in all the Somerville tribe are you telling me there isn't one solitary person who fits the bill?"

"Both Mr Somerville's brothers were killed in the war – as you know."

He waited; his attitude suggested he was expecting a quite different answer. Then, with that characteristic little smile of his, as if he
saw a joke that the rest of the world would never grasp, he remarked, "Well, Mrs Somerville, we must hope you never have to
interview prospective candidates for your husband's proprietorial
chair. But against that sad day, it might not be a bad idea for you to
start visiting the works more frequently . . . familiarizing yourself
with its present operations?"

"Oh!" She dismissed the idea with a laugh. "I shouldn't be able to
make head nor tail of it."

"You know that for certain?"

"My husband has often told me so. I don't think women's minds
are made for understanding sprockets and gears and things. Anyway
– you say I should go there more frequently. Shall I tell you something? I have never been there at all! Indeed, I'm not exactly sure
where the Somerville Motor Works are. There now!"

He raised both hands, as if showing their emptiness. "I'm sorry,
Mrs Somerville. I seem to have been of no help at all."

"But you have," she insisted.

"I don't see how."

"Well . . . you've defined things for me. You've put firm lines
around all my vague shadows. You're always so good at that. And,
in a funny sort of way, I feel as if I *have* somehow reached a decision.
Don't ask me what. I just have a feeling that some doubt has been
settled."

She noticed that Strong was waiting outside. She glanced at the
clock and exclaimed, "Lord, I must fly! We'll finish the ledger
tomorrow."

At the door she paused and turned to face him. "That question you
asked – could I do all those household tasks – cook for forty, and so
on. You didn't let me answer."

He shrugged apologetically.

It checked her briefly for she hadn't intended a reprimand, but
then her own momentum carried her on. "My answer is, I don't
know – but I'd have a jolly good try."

"Good answer!" He stabbed a finger at her in a most uncharacteristic way. "Try to remember it."

On her way out she poked her head into Mrs Lacy's office. "I'm
just a teeny bit worried about Captain Harcourt," she confessed.
"Keep an eye on him, will you?"

"In what way, Mrs Somerville?" the woman asked in surprise.

"He seems a bit . . . well, he's not a drinking man, so it can't be
that. Lightheaded, I suppose I'd call it. Yes – just a little lightheaded."

Actually, she thought as she walked out to the waiting car, she herself was feeling a little lightheaded, too.

"The Guv'nor is still at the works, I suppose?" she asked the chauffeur.

"He'll be there a good hour yet, madam."

"A good hour," she echoed thoughtfully. "Let's go and collect him. Give him a surprise, eh?"

CHAPTER SIX

FORGE LANE TOOK its name from the original Somerville premises. By 1925 they had expanded into a vast U-shaped collection of buildings of various ages, occupying the entire northern side of the road and straggling on around its dead end to fill most of the southern side, too; but in Grandfather James's days, back in the 1830s, the forge had stood on the corner with the Scrubs road, which was then a country lane miles outside London. Indeed, only since the Great War had the ever-spreading tide of brick and stucco engulfed the nearby villages of Kensal Green and Harlesden Green, making them part of the great metropolis.

It was a most depressing part, too, as Julia now discovered. The four-mile drive from Pembridge Gardens took her from the early-Victorian grandeur of Bayswater, northward through the late-Victorian pretensions of North Kensington, then westward along the Harrow Road, among the bijou drabness of postwar suburbia – the very southernmost fringe of that "Metroland" so glowingly depicted in the posters of the Metropolitan Railway. Somehow their artists and photographers were always elsewhere on a day like this, bleak and chill, with waves of drizzle borne in upon a cutting easterly wind. As the car went up Ladbroke Grove and took the bridge over the canal, Strong pointed out one of the chimneys of the Somerville works, almost a mile away to the west.

The intervening space was occupied by two cemeteries, All Souls and St Mary's. George's family grave was down there in All Souls. How odd, she thought, that they had visited it so many times over the years and never once had he pointed out the works; the chimney was surely visible from down there, too. She felt a twinge of panic and almost told Strong to turn about.

It wasn't just the depressing surroundings, there was also the matter of explaining to George this sudden whim to acquaint herself with the works after thirteen years of contented ignorance. If the chauffeur hadn't at that moment called out, "Not far now, madam," she might easily have turned about for home.

They came upon the canal again at journey's end, for it marked the southern boundary of the works on that side of Forge Lane. The other boundaries were formed by the West London Railway line and the Great Western Railway line to its huge depot at Willesden, half a mile farther out of town – and, of course, by Scrubs Lane itself.

A tramcar accelerated past them as they turned into Forge Lane, its trolley pole spitting hot, defiant sparks into the winter rain. Julia thought she had never seen a landscape so drab. Even the half-mile stretch of parkland known as Wormwood Scrubs, which lies beyond the canal, did little to relieve the scene, for at its farther edge rose the gaunt walls of the huge penitentiary of the same name – and beside it loomed the no-less-forbidding pile of the Hammersmith Workhouse.

Back in Connaught Square, in George's study, hung an old photograph of the original blacksmith's forge, taken the day before it was demolished to make room for the expanding works. Grandfather James, already a successful proprietor, had been coaxed back into his old smock and apron for the occasion and stood there, grinning self-consciously before the open doorway, around which some ivy, grubbed up from the graveyard over the road, had been artistically draped. A couple of great shire horses had been given the afternoon off to help complete the illusion – which was so successful that for Julia this simulated rural idyll had coloured her mental picture of "the works" and left her completely unprepared for the shock of this industrial higgledy-piggledy.

How could George be so eager to journey here each day, she wondered? On the contrary, the impulse that had made his father buy the house in Connaught Square had never been more understandable.

Strong was peering from building to building; if she hadn't known otherwise, she'd have imagined he was a stranger here, too – and equally shocked at the sight of it all.

"Which are the offices?" she asked.

"That's the thing, madam. There isn't just the one set of offices. Those are what we call the stores offices. Those are the forge offices . . . the finishing offices . . ."

"What strange names. I've heard of finishing schools . . ."

"Oh, it's nothing to do with the offices, it's just that they're next to the finishing shops. As a matter of fact, most of the accounts people work in there."

"Most? Why not all?"

"Well, accounts for prewar customers are still over in the old place, backing onto the Rolls-Royce Service Station in Hythe Road."

"And what name do *they* go by?" she asked, half ironically.

"The Rolls-Royce offices – only it's nothing to do with Royce's."

She gave up. "And where did you used to work, Strong?"

He shot her an appreciative glance and she guessed that no one had openly remembered his former status in a long time. He pointed out the building with a touch of pride.

She remarked, "You must regret it at times. It's very good of you to go on working for the firm."

"Loyalty's a two-way street, madam," he replied awkwardly. "And you and the Guv'nor have kept it open both ways for me. I'll tell you a time when I don't regret it – and that's when we drive up Oxford Street and see that band of blind and crippled ex-soldiers, begging their bread in this land fit for heroes."

Julia could not help wondering whether the freedom of the streets, even on a day like this, would not be preferable to the clamorous, sooty, oil-reeking purgatory of Somerville's. "I suppose, now I'm here, I'd better get out," she sighed. "In which of the four offices is the Guv'nor likely to be?"

"Oh, there's more'n four." Strong's laughter was mostly from relief at being back on everyday ground.

"I don't wish to hear it."

"There's a man'll do us," he said, waving to attract the attention of a young fellow who was staring out at nothing in particular from the window of the finishing office. "He'll know where the Guv'nor is."

She had a vague impression of a young, handsome-looking fellow. Tall, too, unless the floor in there was raised. "Who is he?" she asked.

Strong was trying to attract his attention with a piece of comic pantomime – pointing to the sky, opening and closing an imaginary umbrella, and wringing out an equally imaginary wet cloth. The man saw him suddenly, grasped the point, and, after a rather stiff wave, vanished from the window.

Strong answered her question then. "He's our new engineer. The Yankee fellow, Eliot Baring the fourth."

"He sounds like royalty."

Strong chuckled. "He's taken a lot of what he calls joshing about that. 'Your majesty,' they call him. Or 'Oy, Baring – come forth!'"

The man himself came forth at that moment. Julia's eyes went wide. She had never seen anyone more handsome. He was the very image of the he-man – not the big, beefy type, but the tall, lean, sinewy kind. In the idiom of his favourite reading – to which he was every bit as addicted as Julia was to her romances – he had muscles like whipcord; his eyes were pale green flecked with gold, like desert

45

after rain; and he looked about as amenable as a wild mustang.

But appearances deceive. In fact, as she soon learned, he was shy to a degree, sensitive, unassuming . . . a most private person.

He was, however, as strong as he looked, and there was something in Julia that could not help responding to strong, physical-looking men. The cowhand, the marine, the Canadian Mountie – especially of the wiry, rangy kind – that type drew her like a magnet. It was a purely physical attraction; she just liked being near them. They radiated something – a sense of danger, an otherness . . . something she could never share; they held her with a fascination she could not then handle.

Later in life she learned to discount it – as part of that sad process called maturing. But back then, when she first met Eliot Baring and felt the power of it sweep over her in all its raw energy, she had no means of dealing with it. Which is not to imply that she went to pieces. Women of her class and breeding never do that. Outwardly she remained as calm and collected as ever – so that Baring had no idea what effect he was having upon her.

"Mrs Somerville?" he asked rather brusquely.

"Yes. And you are Mr Baring, I understand?"

"I couldn't find a presentable umbrella back there." He spoke almost as if it had been her fault.

"Oh – I'm so sorry. Ah – have you any idea where my husband might be?"

"I'll go find him," he snapped, turning on his heel – and taking the umbrella with him.

"No, no." She laughed and did a couple of skips to join him beneath its shelter. "I really just want to look around the works. The last thing I wish is to disturb him, if he's busy. Perhaps you'd be kind enough?"

"Oh . . ." He looked about, vaguely.

"Perhaps you're busy, too?"

"No. I'd come to a dead end. Where d'you want to begin?"

"I don't know. I've never been here before."

He was so astonished that he forgot his shyness for a moment. "Honest?" he asked.

She nodded. "So show me everything."

He took her straight to the nearest bit of shelter, which happened to be the finishing shop, where the distinctive metallic stripe was painted upon each car and every surface was given its final, incredible polish. It was all done by hand. The atmosphere was not factory-like at all; if anything, it reminded her of occasional glimpses into those rooms labelled "Staff Only" at the British Museum, where craftsmen worked in the same absorbed silence.

"The logical thing would be to start at the beginning," he observed, "where the chassis come in, and then to follow the work through each progressive stage."

"Let's do that," she agreed.

She saw one of the workmen nudge another and say, "The Boss."

"Unfortunately," Eliot was saying, "the works isn't laid out like that. We'd spend a lot of time out there running back and forth in the rain."

It was so exciting to be near him that she missed everything he said about the wonderful new pyroxylin finishes, except that they couldn't be sprayed on a damp day like this.

Then they made a dash across a little cobblestoned yard into another, much larger building; this one was filled with noisy machines and men hammering, filing, sawing, and doing other technical things to bits of metal.

"What's that smell?" she asked.

"Cutting oil. It stops the machine tools from overheating."

"It's not unpleasant."

He led her to a quieter area. "This workshop, by the way, has nothing to do with the coachbuilding – or only incidentally. We appear to have become jobbing engineers to most of North London."

The idea seemed to exasperate him.

"Why do they call you the Boss?" she asked.

For the first time he laughed. "Don't you know?"

"Because you're American?"

"No, ma'am. I'm not the Boss. That's you. I thought you knew."

"Oh yes?" She smiled. "What d'you call it? *Joshing* the newcomer?"

"I assure you."

"But I've never been here before. Those men couldn't possibly have recognized me."

"But they could, too." He gave a one-sided grin that sent her wild. "The Guv'nor has a big portrait of you on his desk. That's how I knew who you were. They call you the Boss because of those lists of defects you send back on each car. You never knew?"

"How absurd," she commented – feeling absurdly flattered, nonetheless. "What's next? All this clattering and banging means nothing to me."

"Next is where the chassis come in – mostly by rail."

There was another dash across another backyard, this time with more mud than cobblestones underfoot. "The reception shop, as it's called, was built here because, in the old days, when we did a lot of railway coachwork, the line happened to end here. That's how decisions get made hereabouts!"

"Where would you have put it?" she asked.

"Oh . . ." His eyes raked the ceiling. Then he shook his head, closing off the subject. He pointed to the nearest chassis. "That's a special. For Henry Seagrave's next attempt on the world land-speed record."

"Ah, yes." She remembered talk of it. "My husband's very keen it should remain British."

"Oh, I know it." He spoke as if there'd already been an argument about that. "And there's a regular Phantom chassis that's about to become very *un*regular. Behind it, a Hispano-Suiza we did ten years back, in the middle of the war."

"I remember it." She was delighted for some small point of contact with this vast, alien place.

She liked the way he said "we," even about things that had happened long before he joined the firm. She looked at the Hispano-Suiza. "What happened to her?"

"She's been returned for a complete rebuild. So we've stripped her down and put her here, ready to start the random walk."

"What sort of walk?"

He glanced sidelong at her, suddenly unsure of himself.

"Random?" she prompted.

He framed himself to explain. "Every chassis we unload here, Mrs Somerville, has to travel more than a quarter of a mile before it arrives at the finishing shop – which, as you saw, is practically next door to this place, where it all begins."

"I had no idea it was so large."

"That's not it, ma'am. If the workshops were laid out in their proper sequence, the total journey would be less than forty yards."

There was a weariness behind the assertion, as if he had made it so often it had been reduced to a ritual. But he also glanced at her, as if hoping she might take his part.

"It all looks very bustling and efficient," she remarked. "Despite the awkward layout."

He stared at her in a kind of contempt; she almost melted. "What's in there?" she asked, pointing to another hut.

"It wouldn't mean a thing to you."

"Why not let me be the judge of that?"

"It's nothing to do with the firm – I mean, not with coachbuilding."

"More jobbing engineering?"

"No, something else. I think your husband should be the one to explain about that. I'm not involved."

"Good Lord! How many businesses are being carried on here, then?"

He rounded on her. His annoyance erupted in an ironic smile. "Good question, ma'am."

For the rest of their tour (and "Random Walk" would be a better address for Somerville's than "Forge Lane," she decided) he stuck to the facts – everything from panel beating to something called "sacrificial protection." He was a good teacher and she learned more than she had expected to.

In between she pumped him for information about himself, his parents, his upbringing, his present lodgings, his ambitions. No one who has seen a well-trained upper-middle-class English lady in action will be surprised that she discovered almost everything there was to know about Eliot Baring IV. His shyness did not yield, but she batted on as if it were not there between them.

His family were bankers, distantly related to the Barings of London, who had gone spectacularly bust in the middle of the last century. His parents had loathed the idea of his taking up engineering but had sensibly compromised: If he would take a business degree first, and was then still set on the oily-fingered life, they'd drop their objections. Which was what he had done. He had a degree in business from some university called "Ivy League." He was twenty-six and single, and he rented the middle floor of an apartment house in Sussex Gardens, Paddington, two miles away. He walked to and from work along the canal bank; the canal people had gotten to know him quite well and he often rode with them.

"And what brought you to England?" she asked.

"Oh . . . reasons."

She thought he meant an unhappy love affair and dropped it.

"Somerville's is a hard place to leave," he added, suddenly.

"My husband would agree with you there."

"Often I don't get home till almost midnight."

"Good heavens! Do we work you so hard?"

"Oh no. I thought your husband . . . well, I guess you don't talk much business."

She shook her head.

"Well" – he was in an agony of shyness again – "part of my salary, so to speak, is, er, kind of, in, er, kind. I mean, I get to use the workshops and facilities. My own work. Hobby, he calls it."

"Is it a hobby? I'd love to see this . . . whatever it is. Is it here now?"

"Oh, hell!" he said. If he'd been a few years younger he'd have looked for a stone to kick. "I'll show you if you like."

It was almost a challenge. Without waiting for her acceptance he led the way past several buildings to something like a large garden shed down by the canal. The railway arches soared above it, cutting out most of the dull, winter light. It was unheated, too. The temperature seemed even colder inside than out.

"You work until late at night – *here?*" she asked.

"Home from home."

She looked around in the gathering gloom and saw that he was right. The place did, indeed, have a homelike atmosphere. A moment of deep nostalgia seized her as forgotten rooms in her life came suddenly to mind, bringing in their train the dreams they once embodied. "Oh yes! I used to long for a place just like this."

With that one unguarded statement she finally penetrated his shyness and forged a bond between them that surprised him as deeply as it pleased her. "You?" he asked.

She nodded and closed her eyes. "I was going to be an artist, starving in a garret, no – not starving, but not noticing that I'd forgotten to eat, and not even noticing the cold. Isn't that right?" She opened her eyes and stared at him.

He was attracted to her, too. She could sense it now. The power of it thrilled her; the sensation of playing with fire.

"Right." He spoke in boyish ruefulness, smiling with reluctance. Even more awkwardly he asked, "Do you regret it?"

She shook her head. "I did paint for a while, after my marriage. Indeed, my husband encouraged it – wisely as it happens, for the impulse soon burned itself out. Just a passing fad. But enough of all that. What is it keeps you here so late? No passing fad, I'm sure."

He went to the back of the room and returned holding what looked like a piece of sculpture, a crucifix. His pale, gold-green eyes almost glowed in the twilight. She felt as if he were bringing her a special gift.

"I can't even guess," she murmured, taking it carefully.

He switched on the light and she found she was holding a model aeroplane.

A hobby after all! She felt let down. But her pleasure sounded genuine as she said, "Oh, you must meet my son Robert. He had an absolute craze for these all last year."

His laugh was tolerant, beyond insult. "Did they look like this?" Gently he took the model back and held it at various flying angles.

Robert used to do the same, she remembered. But she saw the point of the question. This model plane was like none other she had seen. Nor was it like any of the real-life aeroplanes one saw cut in half in the *Illustrated London News*. Those planes were all canvas sails and wire and struts, or whatever one called them. Props? No, that was the bit that went around at the front.

"No," she agreed. "It's all sleek and smooth and . . ."

"Aerodynamic is the word," he told her. "The full-scale version of this baby will carry two dozen passengers – and their baggage – and some mail – in luxury – London to Paris – in ninety minutes. Two hours against a strong wind."

Her mouth dropped.

"I know." He laughed. "You thought I just built models."

After that she showered him with questions – had he started building the real thing? Why not? Where would he look for money, then? Wasn't Somerville's interested? What did George say? And so on.

He was not as forthcoming as his earlier enthusiasm had led her to expect. But when it came to the likely competitors he spoke more freely. Time was short. The ban against the German airplane industry was about to be lifted. Junker, Dornier, Messerschmidt, and Fokke would all repatriate the industries they had set up temporarily in Italy, Denmark, et cetera. They were already ahead of the world, despite their disadvantages; once they were back home there'd be no holding them. He had come to England because of the imperial connection. America's likely air routes were three or four thousand miles at the most but England's spanned half-way around the world. At least, that was how it had looked from the States.

"But not now you're here?" she prompted.

He shook his head. "I despair sometimes, ma'am, I truly do. Every other nation in the world supports its airplane industry – but not this one. It's that old red-flag-in-front-of-the-auto spirit all over again. It's etched deep in the English soul."

She could not remember when she had last felt so excited by an idea – never, probably. Every moment she was with him, there in that grimy little shed, watching him move, hearing him explain about the industry, seeing him handle his own model, she felt him grow in stature. If George wasn't backing Eliot Baring, then George was wrong.

It was a judgement she would never have dreamed of making before that day.

"We'd better go find your husband," he observed, replacing the model in its cradle.

"Has it a name?" she asked.

He shook his head. "I'm kinda superstitious. When she flies, then we'll name her. Until then she's just Baring One."

On their way back to the centre of the works, where he thought they might find George in one of those mystery sheds, they passed a giant waste bin filled with things that looked perfectly serviceable to her: a table lamp, a filing cabinet (broken but not beyond repair), masses of paper, blank on one side (on which the children would just love to scribble), a folding desk . . . it went on and on. The yard was covered, so the rain had damaged nothing.

"What waste!" she sighed. "Just because my husband can't get around as he used to – they must have hoped he wouldn't catch sight of this."

"Oh, I think most of it is his doing, Mrs Somerville. He's ordered a great turnout of his old office. This is stuff he can't – er – use any more. I don't think he wanted to pass it on."

"Well, perhaps that is understandable. Even so, the children would love to have some of this paper for scribbling on . . ."

"Company secrets, maybe?" he suggested.

"Which any rag-and-bone man – or whoever collects this stuff –

can now read! No, I'm going to take at least some of this home with me."

Lying just beneath the handful she selected was a large manilla envelope. The corner of it tore away as she lifted her haul – revealing what looked like quite a pretty little water colour. She laid the waste paper aside and pulled the painting out for a better look.

What she saw was . . . impossible. She prolonged the tear in the envelope and discovered . . . well, it was even more impossible. Two water colours. Two very particular water colours.

"Is something wrong, Mrs Somerville?"

She had actually forgotten he was there.

"They're rather pretty, aren't they," she remarked.

"They don't bother me," he said.

One of those topsy-turvy American compliments, she assumed.

"I think I'll take them, too," she added.

"I'm sure your husband's in that building." He pointed to a hut in the middle distance. "I can see his nurse."

"It doesn't matter now," she observed icily. "I've just realized I have to hurry home. If you see him, tell him I didn't wish to disturb him." She held out her hand. "And I want to thank you, Mr Baring, for making my first visit so interesting – but above all for showing me the Baring One. I don't suppose you believe in a woman's intuition?"

He was neatly caught between honesty and politeness.

She laughed. "No. Nor do I. Not really. Even so, I'm convinced you will one day make your fortune with that machine."

He could not accept it. He thrust his hands deep in his pockets, sniffed, gave an awkward shrug, and waited for her to be gone, taking the burden of her confidence with her.

The moment she was back in her car she put him from her mind. All the way home she fumed at George, at his dishonesty, at the way he patronized her.

The water colours were hers – views of Hyde Park painted the year after her marriage. She'd done only one to start with; George had taken it to his office and hung it over his desk. Then about two months later he had come home full of excitement because a customer, a noted collector of paintings, had admired it and asked if it was for sale. After a lot of dithering she had agreed to let him sell it – flattered, of course, that a noted connoisseur should see anything of merit in her work; the proceeds had gone to the Red Cross. The collector had commissioned a matching painting on the same terms – by which time the novelty and flattery had worn thin. That was, in fact, how she discovered that her artistic ambitions were (as she had told Baring) just a passing fad.

Now it was plain that the whole business of the "noted connoisseur" was a lie. George had simply patronized her; his true estimate of her skill had been stated when he discarded them into that rubbish bin. She felt cheated, sick, furious.

It would not have occurred to her to connect this quite uncharacteristic over-reaction with George's denial of himself to her – nor with her meeting with Eliot Baring and the attraction that now existed between them.

CHAPTER SEVEN

GEORGE CAME HOME in a fury, too. What the devil was she playing at, turning up unannounced at the works like that? She had no business there. And then to go traipsing all over it with young Baring (and no doubt getting an earful of his incessant whining about efficiency). And finally vanishing without a word – not even having the courtesy to let him know she was there? What did she mean by it?

Tell him, she dared herself.

But one look at his crippled body, at the hands which, mentally, were no doubt doubled into fists, helping to punch home his anger, but which in fact lay limp where gravity had spilled them – and she knew she could tell him nothing. Always at her mind's ear that insidious voice whispered that he had so little time left – how could she pollute it with her anger, her feelings, her needs?

A profound gloom filled her. She saw that in every difference between them, great or small, there would henceforth be a third advocate: his vegetable body. Between it and that voice of conscience in her ear, she would always lose.

He stormed at her a few minutes more and then, taking her silence for concession, grew somewhat more conciliatory. "It's no place for you, girlie. Nasty, smelly, dangerous. Only fit for us brutes of men, eh?"

"I suppose so." She shrugged.

"Of course it is." He softened further. "Bit of a shock, what?"

She was surprised.

"Well, I can see you've had a bit of a shock Tell me – what d'you think of young Baring?"

His anger never ran deep; he always looked for the exit fairly quickly. She accepted the one he was now offering. "More to the point, George, what do *you* think of him?"

"*Over*-Baring, I call him!" He laughed immoderately. "Good, what?"

"It hits the mark. He's very critical of the way the work is organized. On the other hand . . ."

George, who had been about to interrupt, changed his mind. "No, go on?"

"I was going to say, on the other hand, he's as proud as can be of Somerville's and of the work we do. I mean, he *is* loyal."

"That's it, girlie, you've got it! Damn good fellow underneath it all. Couldn't stomach him at first. But all that rudeness, you know, it's just for show. Behind it he's quite shy. You should have let me know you were coming. I could have warned you about him."

"Well, funnily enough, George" – she sat beside him and wiped a strand of hair off his forehead. He was losing it quite fast these days. Another five years and . . . She bit her lip when she realized what another five years might actually bring.

He saw it and misunderstood. "The fellow wasn't rude to *you,* was he? By God, if so . . ."

"No, darling." She forced a laugh. "I was only going to say that even without your warning I did actually manage to fathom the boy out for myself. It took me the best part of a minute but I did it."

"Ah." He gave a contrite smile. "I should have known. Your territory more than mine. Took me a week."

She rose and crossed the room, pretending to tidy this and that. "You had quite a turnout in your old office?" she prompted lightly, but behind that seeming indifference she was watching him like a cat.

"Useless stuff," he remarked without a trace of unease. "Tell you what, girlie. At the risk of sounding blasphemous, this new situation of mine is not without its advantages. In the old days I could be distracted from my work a dozen times an hour – picking up a hammer, pushing some clumsy oaf aside at his lathe – showing them how it should be done."

"Distracted? But I thought that was your work?"

"So did I." He grinned broadly. "So did I – oh yes! But it ain't, you know. My real work is all up here." He rolled his eyes briefly inside his head. "Oh, the new ideas I'm getting all the time!"

"For cars?"

"For everything!"

"Is that what's going on in all your secret huts?"

He frowned in bewilderment.

She laughed. "Young Baring is very loyal to you. He refused to take me anywhere near them – or tell me what they were for."

The frown deepened.

"You know – all those huts where . . . well, I don't know what was going on. He wouldn't even let me look through the windows."

"Silly ass! It's no secret at all. Well, not inside the firm. And certainly not from you. Not that you'd be interested, mind."

"Oh, but I would. Especially now that I know what it all looks like."

He grinned to himself. "Pandora was a woman! Well, let me see . . ." He paused before he announced, dramatically: "In one of them we're developing an articulated high-pressure hydraulic joint!"

He looked at her teasingly. "What, no fanfare of trumpets? Shall I go on?"

She shrugged crossly. "If you told me what it *does* on a car, I might be wiser."

"Not on a car, girlie. On a submarine. Or in an oil refinery. I'm talking about pressures of several thousand pounds per square inch. And articulated, too."

"Government work!" she declared excitedly. "Of course – that's why it's secret."

He clearly had not expected so obvious and sensible a comment from her. He frowned. "Not exactly. It isn't for anybody, or not yet. But when we've perfected it – who knows?"

"Why are we doing it, then, George?"

"Why do people climb mountains? I'm working on it because I read a paper in which someone alleged it would not be possible for at least another ten years." He gave a rueful laugh. "At times I think they may have been right."

"And you're working on other ideas, too? Similar ideas?"

"Oh lots." His tone expected congratulation.

"And they're all like this hydraulic joint – things that seem impossible?"

Her close questioning annoyed him. "In everything you say, girlie, you're only proving how unfitted a woman's mind is to discuss such topics." His smile grew steely and thin. "Stick to your trade, eh. It's what you're best at."

"Aha!" She pretended she was joking. "But what is my trade? Once I thought I was best of all at pretty little water colours."

"And so you were," he said easily. "And the Red Cross has ten pounds to prove it. I was always sorry you gave that up. I say, what's for dinner?"

That night she lay long awake, thinking back over young Baring's criticisms, remembering Strong's description of the way the offices were scattered all over the place, wandering in imagination among the motley of workshops, seeing again in her mind's eye those gangs of craftsmen pushing half-assembled cars from one shed to another wondering, wondering . . .

Next morning at the SPRP she had a most extraordinary visitor; his introductory letter, which had come some days previously, did nothing to prepare her for the man himself. She was used to ladies who, wishing to make substantial donations – fifty pounds or more, say – preferred to call at the society's offices and talk with her personally about its work before parting with their money. Sometimes they brought their husbands, who thought it clever to ask to "see the books." It always amused Julia to watch their condescension transform itself first into surprise and then something like respect. They usually said they'd no idea it was so big.

She would pretend to misunderstand. "The problem? Oh yes, it's big, all right."

Often they left a little poorer than they had intended.

Callers of this kind were usually solid, upper middle class people like herself. They communicated as much by their accents, gestures, silences, as by actual words. Even the war profiteers among them had generally acquired a smattering of such refinements.

But Mr Sidney Gold was something different.

His card, which had gilded edges, read: *Sidney Gold, Esq., Belvoir Hall, Lordship Lane, Dulwich, London S.E.* His attire, which Julia glimpsed as he stepped from his new Rolls-Royce and sauntered up the garden path, told quite a different story. (So did his car, actually. The shape of the door handles told her at once that the coachwork was by James Young of Bromley, but it took a second astonished glance to confirm that, where other cars would have had chrome or nickel plating, this one had gold.) If she'd been asked to place him by his appearance, it could only have been in a cartoon in *Punch,* where he would have been cast as a prosperous butcher out for a day at the races – or perhaps a bookmaker at the racecourse itself. He was wearing the loudest check plus-fours she had ever seen, and, like his brown bowler hat, they were at least a size too small. So were his gloves, which made his hands and fingers seem inflated. Even his stick was undersized, for it caused him to list to port as he leaned upon it, waiting for his knock to be answered.

As the door opened he caught sight of Julia, spying on him from her window, not ten feet away; she had wrongly assumed that the almost-closed venetian blinds shielded her from view. He tipped his hat and grinned at her. Dear God, he even had a gold tooth – a canine!

But he was, as his letter had said, intending to make a donation in the region of *fifty* pounds.

Mrs Lacy showed him in, brimming with amusement behind his back.

He was grinning, too. He held up a finger, suspending the formality of introductions, and walked directly to her window, where he closed the two venetian blinds that did not face the front door. "So!" he exclaimed, giving Julia a cheerful, affirmative nod. "That's for next time."

"Thank you, Mr Gold." Her welcome was guarded as she introduced herself and asked him to be seated.

"Good." He spoke as if she had passed a test. He opened the blinds again before he sat down, timing his movement precisely with hers. "I use mirrors in my office."

Not for self-inspection, she thought. "Your letter was very welcome."

"Yeah. I thought it might be." He had the commonest sort of South London accent and made no effort to disguise it. Rightly so, too, she realized, for his brash joviality, his preposterous dress, and his speech were all of a whole.

"Do smoke, if you wish," she told him.

"Ta," he replied. "Do you indulge?" His banana fingers, ringed with gold and amethysts, proffered a solid gold cigarette case. "Virginia this side – Turkish that."

She chose Turkish, a Balkan Sobranie. "I don't often. Once or twice a week, perhaps."

"Like my doctor," he commented with a note of irony that ended in a wheezy chuckle. He snapped the case shut and held his lighter toward her. The first spark kindled the flame. His hands smelled of . . . oil of cloves? Something vaguely oriental.

"You don't smoke?" she asked, relishing the dry, honeyed flavour of the tobacco.

He gave a confidential grin and pulled out a much larger case, full of half coronas; it, too, was of solid gold. While he went through the rituals of rolling the selected cigar near his ear, clipping and piercing its end, sucking it until it gleamed, warming it in the flame of his lighter, and finally puffing it to life, he addressed a number of remarks to his own hands: "Yeah, I first heard of your work through me sister-in-law's people. Fox, their name is. Live in Deptford – or in *Debt* and can't *afford,* I always say." Another throaty chuckle. "Your lot done their best for them, but there's no helping some, is there."

You haven't a single charitable corpuscle in your body, she thought. *Why are you going to part with this money?* "We can't succeed with everyone," she said.

"'Course you can't, Mrs Somerville." Sharp eyes stared at her suddenly through clouds of aromatic smoke. "'Course you can't." The eyes were cold and shrewd. Inside this jovial fellow lurked an altogether different man.

"We have succeeded with many," she added.

"Yes. That's why I come here, innit." He did not make it a question.

"Is it." Nor did she.

His eyes flickered around the room. She suspected that the interview was not going quite the way he had planned it; he wanted something from her that she was not yielding.

"No sense beating about the bush," he said, dipping into an inside pocket.

She realized he was going for his chequebook, but she wished to know a lot more about him before they reached that stage. "You'll surely want to cast an eye over our books?" she suggested.

The hand paused at his breast, the fingertips dithered behind the lapels in a glister of gold and amethyst. "Good idea," he said, only half-hiding his surprise. He obviously did not move in circles where "the books" were offered with such freedom (or, if they were, then they were not, so to speak, *the* books).

Would the figures mean anything to him? She watched him keenly. From the way his eyes moved up and down the columns, back and forth, comparing this figure with that, seeking the large items . . . she knew he was missing nothing.

"Good," he said crisply, closing the volume with a snap. "The investments seem on the cautious side, if I may venture so bold a comment?"

"That's the law on charities, Mr Gold. We have to select from a cautious list."

"Ah." It was obviously news to him. The hand again began to edge toward the inner pocket.

"I see you have a James Young body on your motor," she remarked affably. "What's your opinion of them?"

"They was handy," he replied in an oddly defensive tone. "Bromley's not that far from Dulwich."

"I honestly wasn't asking why you didn't go to Somerville's, you know. James Young are among the very best of firms."

He stared at her in surprise. "You mean you're *that* Somerville! Well, of course, I ought to of known."

"Ought you to?" What lay behind this charade, she wondered? Of course he knew she was *that* Somerville, else why be so defensive about choosing James Young? "Are you perhaps connected with our trade?"

He nodded ruefully. "At the very opposite end from yours, I hasten to say. But still and all . . ." He beamed expectantly at her.

"You have the advantage of me, I'm afraid. I know next to nothing about my husband's business."

The news appeared to please him. "Then allow me." He produced another card – a trade one this time – from his waistcoat pocket. "Private cards, right. Trade cards, left," he explained, tapping the two sets of pockets.

"So in your case the right hand *has* to know what the left is doing!" He laughed much too much.

The card informed her that he was the proprietor of Gold's Com-

58

mercial Bodies – charabancs, pantechnicons, delivery vans, automobile stores . . . "everything from 'earses to 'orse boxes," as he summed it up for her.

"A family business like ours?" she asked.

"It was." He gave a wry smile. "Used to be Fox's of Camberwell." He laughed. "And I suppose you ain't never heard of them, neither."

She passed him back the card.

"Keep it," he urged ambiguously. "You never know."

"Never know what?"

His hand made an awkward circle in the air and he repeated, "You just never know."

The scintillating fingers darted behind his lapel at last and he produced not a chequebook but a wallet. It was stuffed with fivers to the point where the stitching was strained. "Nice," he murmured, basking in her surprise.

Methodically he counted out ten fivers and then, pausing and looking at her, added another three. He hammered down the pile of notes with his fist, the fist of a bareknuckle fighter, she thought.

"Thank you, Mr Gold." She carried the notes to the safe. "It will be banked this lunchtime."

As she wrote him out his receipt she asked, "May I publish your name in our next list of donors?"

"No," he said quickly. "Don't do that."

"Of course not, if you don't wish it."

For a moment they stared at each other with nothing further to say.

What impelled Julia to speak as she did next is a mystery. Without pausing for thought she asked, "And why did you really come to see me today?"

He stared back with a frightening, almost reptilian calm, until she began to feel she had made a dreadful blunder. Then he gave a little grin and replied, "You just stay north of the river, Mrs Somerville. You'd run circles around us poor provincials down there." He drew a deep breath, squaring himself to some momentous decision. "You're quite right. I did have another purpose in coming here to see you."

"And still do, I think?"

He nodded. "I think the whole trade was shocked at what happened to your husband, Mrs Somerville. He's one of the most respected people there is. Ask anyone. George Somerville's one of the best. So I came here today, like, to scout out the ground. I've not spoken with others in the trade but I'm sure I may speak *for* them. If there was any question of help needed – if the work fell behind and it was a question of half a dozen skilled men wanted – or a shortage of stock or anything like that – well, I know we'd rally round . . ."

59

Julia didn't believe a word of it. Her first intuition, that he hadn't an ounce of charity about him, still ruled her. But she thanked him warmly and told him that her husband would be touched at his kindness, though, mercifully, no actual assistance was needed.

He was glad to hear it. "You can't believe your ears, can you!" he commented in disgust.

"Why, what have you heard?"

"Oh, nothing . . . well, maybe I'd better tell you. Else I look a right mug coming here like this. There's a whisper going around that your bankers is getting edgy. That's all."

Julia laughed at the very thought. Somerville's had banked with Wallis & Thorn since the year dot.

The response seemed to reassure him, for he joined in her laughter and added, "But then, I should know – my life! Those same whispers have seen me bankrupt more times than I've had hot dinners already."

As she led him to the door she felt it important for him to understand just how good things were at Somerville's. She explained that her husband had never been more mentally alert. "He has so many new ideas on the boil," she added.

He paused and then replied, in all seriousness, "I wouldn't go telling too many people that, if I was you, Mrs Somerville."

"Why ever not?"

"New ideas." He shook his head dubiously. "They're like sand in the Sahara in our trade. Lift the bonnet of any car and what do you find? A couple of Mad Inventors popping out like jack-in-a-boxes. No, we all know George Somerville. He's much too solid to go having new ideas all over the place."

She thanked him again and accompanied him to the front door. In the corner of her eye she saw Max waiting for her in Mrs Lacy's little office.

He came bounding out as soon as the front door was closed. "Who was the gold-plated Jew?" he asked.

CHAPTER EIGHT

MAX WAS THE *original* sort of English gentleman, the type that Dr
Arnold and the public schools set out to murder. They so nearly
succeeded that occasional survivors like Max are dubbed "eccentric,"
while the word "gentleman" has come to signify someone like
young Robert – a hearty, beefy, mindless conformist.

Your original English gentleman could build an empire but was
too wayward to run it properly, which is why, throughout the
Victorian era, he was steadily and ruthlessly transformed into his
latter-day namesake. By the time of the Great War there were no
empires left to build, and even the running of them had become the
White Man's Burden. In every sense of the word, Max's sort of
gentleman had nowhere left to run; so he stayed at home and became
an "eccentric," a figure of fun whose qualities had once been the very
jewel of the nation.

According to popular wisdom, one had to be mad to survive all
four years of that war – in the trenches, anyway. Max did. In attack
after attack he walked a charmed path through gunfire that felled his
men behind him like cornstalks at harvest. The only bullets that
scathed him came from the rear – one at the Somme and one at
Passchendaele in the final weeks of the war. By then people no
longer talked of that business of the severed German head, but it was
not exactly forgotten, either. In peace or war it was Max's peculiar
fate to be sniped at by his own.

As he and Julia watched Sidney Gold's gold-plated monstrosity
pull away from the kerb, he murmured, "Did you not prick him?
Did he not bleed?"

If you were in difficulties, Max could be bluff and to the point – as
he had been with George in hospital. But if the trouble was on his
side, he became oblique and obscure. Julia knew how to read him,
though. His turning up here, unannounced, was in itself a sign that
all was not well; now his reference to Jews and Shylock's question
was as good as confirmation: He was in trouble over money.

"How is the old place?" she asked.

"Marvellous," he assured her. "Never better. What did that fellow want?"

"He seemed pleasant enough."

"Made a big donation, I suppose?"

"He's interested in our work."

"They're all out for Number One, you know."

"Cast the first stone, then! To what do we owe this honour, Max?"

He shrugged awkwardly. "Happened to be in London." He turned from the window and ran his eye along a shelf of books, all dealing with charities, or the law, or accountancy. "Pity the Russian war's over," he said. "A great time we had of it."

"It was a squalid and forlorn excursion," she remarked, knowing she'd do better to hold her tongue.

But for once he did not argue. "We weren't actually trying to defeat the Reds," he observed. "That's what people don't understand. All we wanted to do was keep open a corridor to allow the Whites to escape butchery. God, they were some of the finest humans who ever breathed. Did I tell you of the Grand Ball they held at . . . I forget the hotel. In Vienna, anyway."

He had, but she shook her head. This was no idle reminiscence; somewhere in it would be clues.

So he told her again of the hundred White Russians who sat down to champagne and caviare and ten courses of Vienna's finest cuisine – the prince who drove a taxi, the archduke who ran a café, the pretty young grand duchess who was a striptease artiste, the dowager countess who donned gypsy rags and told fortunes. They were all there, as charming, as gay, as feckless as if the years since 1912 had simply been wiped from history. They toasted the murdered tsar and drank to impossible futures. They sang their plaintive Russian songs and wept like the children they were – brilliant, handsome, *divine* children. Everyone joined in – all the other diners – Venetians, Germans, Italians, even the English. They sang and wept with them. And when at last they played the tsarist anthem the entire dining room rose to its feet – "except the two little Jews who were waiting to play their expected part."

Last time Max had told this story they had been "two little Armenian jewellers."

"And when it was over," he concluded, "when the bill was presented, the first to move was the pretty little striptease duchess. She rose and walked over to the 'Court jewellers,' as everybody called them. And then, taking off her Fabergé pendant, she laid it carelessly before them. My God, I never saw anything more magnificent than that little woman! Not once did she even glance their way as they debated the price between themselves. They didn't tell her their decision, they simply counted out the money on a small silver tray.

And she – oh, such style! – she just scooped it up and gave it to the
head waiter, every last Schilling. She was only paying for herself, yet
it was probably enough for the entire meal for everyone. And then
she glided out like an empress." He sighed. "If one has to go down –
isn't that the way to do it, eh?"

"Is it, Max?" She stared him out. "Is that why you're in London?"

Casually he leafed through a copy of *Country Life* that lay across
the corner of her desk. "You don't know a good banker, I suppose?"
he asked.

She told George nothing of Max's troubles; what could George do
about it anyway? Max would sell off another farm, mortgage
another town property, and so limp on toward the next crisis. While
farm prices held up, he'd survive somehow.

But Sidney Gold's parting hint that all might not be well with
Somerville's – a hint that had blatantly fished for her response –
could not so easily be shrugged off.

"D'you know this man?" she asked her husband that evening as
they sat together after dinner. She fished out his card, intending to
hold it for him to read. But as soon as he saw the gilded edge he
laughed. "I should say so!" Then he frowned. "Has the blighter had
the nerve to call here?"

She asked what sort of man he was.

"A greater rogue never walked the earth. Is this SPRP business?
Don't tell me he's made a donation!"

"That's something I couldn't discuss anyway."

"Well, just be warned, girlie. Sidney Gold wouldn't part with a
brass farthing unless he saw a chance to get threepence back on it. Mr
Tenfold they call him. His father had a market stall somewhere south
of the river, and . . ."

"In Deptford?" she asked.

"Could be. South of the river's all one to me. Did he mention it?"

"He spoke of family connections there."

"Anyway, his sister married extremely well – Fox's of . . ."

"The commercial coachbuilders – Fox's of Camberwell? Oh, now
it all begins to fit."

His eyebrows shot up in surprise. "He *has* been talking! Yes. Fox's
of Camberwell. Did he tell you he stole the firm from his brother-in-
law? Keeps him on a three-pound pension. A very nasty piece of
work, our Sidney. Someone will murder him one of these days. Did
he talk about Somerville's at all? Did he connect you with . . ."

"Only to express conventional sympathy, you know."

"Ah."

She watched him carefully. There was a tension in him that had
not been there earlier. She risked adding, "He even offered to help
out in any way he could. But we don't need help, do we, darling?"

"Not from the likes of Sidney Gold, thank you." George laughed heartily enough – and yet, somehow, it was not as reassuring as it ought to have been.

When you are only a wife, and one who, until a few days earlier, did not even know precisely where your husband's business was located, how do you take its financial temperature?

Julia cudgelled her brains for days, seeking an answer. Could she perhaps call on their bankers, Wallis & Thorn, pretending to be an emissary for Max? "Please don't breathe a word of this to either of the menfolk just yet – only I wonder whether something can't be done for my brother? Could Somerville's arrange a guarantee – without his knowing, of course?"

It sounded plausible enough, surely? And their response would reveal something – a raised eyebrow or a pitying smile; it would be enough to show that Sidney Gold's smoke had a real fire at its heart.

No, they'd smell a rat. It would sound better if the request came through another bank. "Can you speak for this account?" All nice and impersonal. She thought at once of Crownfield's, the bankers to the SPRP. Their local agent, a Mr Crimmond, had always been most cordial.

In fact, when she at last seized the bull by the horns and called on him, he was so cordial she had to fight an urge to start behaving like a Daisy heroine, throwing herself on the gallant gentleman's mercy and fluttering appropriately grateful eyelashes at him once he had solved all her problems. Even in the days of her innocence – as she later called them – she was protected by instincts that lay far deeper than anything her lamentable education and shallow reading had given her for guidance.

Crimmond accepted her story without question and promised to use the bank's good offices to discover whether such guarantees might be arranged; he quite understood the need for total discretion at this early stage.

She was on the point of leaving when a further thought struck her. "Since I'm here," she added, "I may as well unburden myself of a slight misgiving – another matter for your complete discretion, Mr Crimmond."

"Whatever is in my power, Mrs Somerville."

"You may remember a week or ten days ago I paid in some eighty pounds in cash? Well, strictly between ourselves, most of that was a donation from a certain Sidney Gold." She fished out the trade card and handed it to him. "I may be wrong, but I just had a feeling, as he left, I just got the feeling that he hadn't finished his business with the society. Don't ask me in what way. But I'd like to know a little more about him."

"Ah – a woman's intuition!" he said.

within fifty paces. At first he was not absolutely sure. His

m slackened but he did not stop. A shunting engine gave a

mpatient hoots from somewhere beyond Somerville's. She

ning away from him, and stared briefly in its direction,

re to turn full circle before she stooped once more at the

e.

there was no doubt he had recognized her. He came to a halt

ated with himself whether or not to call out. In the end, to

oyance, he decided to press on and say nothing. In following

th her eyes she overbalanced and had to put out a hand to stay

getting mud and gravel all over her glove.

unplanned incident did the trick. She looked at the dirt in

t, then at the canal – actually, straight at him – so that he had

oice but to pretend suddenly to notice her.

h, hello!" she cried back cheerfully. "Fancy meeting you. I say,

a beastly mess." She displayed her glove.

plucked a neatly folded handkerchief from his breast pocket,

d at the green and greasy canal, thought better of it, and soaked

loth in a rain-filled jam jar on one of the intervening graves. He

ed her the wet kerchief. "D'you mind?" she asked, holding out

soiled glove, which she was still wearing. "Seeing that your

ds are already wet."

he touch of him was thrilling; she became acutely aware how

g it had been since any man had stirred her like that – or done

ything to satisfy such stirrings.

"Have you flown that model yet?" she asked, pleased at how calm

r voice sounded.

"Ready and waiting," he replied.

"For what? A day like this?"

He was looking at the grave. "Oh, I see. I had no idea." He darted

er a glance and added, "Long may it remain so. Exactly so."

"Amen," she said. "This flight – will it be public? I should love to

be there."

He pulled a rueful face. "It'll be all too public, I fear. I was on my

way to ask the Guv'nor now – do we have some private place where

I could fly her? Or maybe he knows somewhere, some country

park?"

"Ask me. I know just the place."

He licked his lips. "Oh?"

She glanced toward the gate. "It so happens that I'm motoring

down to the country for the day, in connection with my little

charity. It's at Ware, about twenty miles north of here. And, by an

equally fortunate chance, my brother's place, my old family home,

in fact, is just outside Ware. I could drop you off there and go about

my business while you conduct your tests – though I'd love to stay

and watch, if I may?"

It was the sort of remark that no
might.

He promised to do what he could. S
morning's work.

And then, having done all the safe and
risky one as well: She sought out Eliot Ba
who had so much as hinted that all was n

he came
momentu
series of
rose, tu
taking c
gravesic

Now
and de
her an
him v
herse

T
disg
no

w

l
t

CHAPTER NIN

SINCE BARING HAD so obligingly told her he walk
each day, that is where she chose to waylay him. C
was buried in All Souls cemetery, whose southern
canal, and George's father lay beside him, so sh
plausible reason in the world for being there, even
hour.

She found the graves in immaculate condition, as
should have been, for Tredwell, the night watchman
tended them every week. In short, there was nothing t
discreet vigil as she arranged and rearranged the flov
bought ten minutes earlier in the Harrow Road.

It was a fine morning, poised between autumn and win
silvery sun lost what little warmth it had in its struggle w
of misty smoke which hangs perpetually over London be
gale and the next. It was a day for driving down to the co
revel in the pure air and the last, fading gold of the season
would look splendid today.

Before long she caught sight of him, the very picture of
and energy among those whose ways were tuned to the
rhythms of the water. Even at that distance the vision of his ta
muscular frame rekindled all her earlier feelings.

The family plot was near enough to the canal bank to allow
discover her. Bending low over the grave, pretending to pluc
few weeds and smooth over the marble chippings, she peep
her right shoulder, waiting for the moment of recognition.

There was no faulting his eyesight. He knew who she was

The shock in his eyes told her he was aware of dangers in this arrangement – dangers from the point of view of *his* emotions (for she was sure he knew nothing of hers). Before he could say anything she added, "It's the usual sort of country house, you know. There's a walled deer park on the south side. Your only witnesses would be a colony of rooks."

"And the deer."

"Their ghosts, perhaps. And I could watch from an upstairs window, and if it fails, I could pretend I hadn't seen anything."

He laughed confidently. "It won't fail. But there are degrees of success."

The one topic on which she could always get him over his shyness was flying, she noticed.

"How long before you can be ready?" she asked.

"Oh . . . well . . ." He saw where she had rushed him and, seeking a little more time, gestured vaguely westward and asked if she were going on to the works.

"No," she replied crisply. "This is my" – she was about to say "annual" but changed her mind – "my monthly visit to the family plot. My vehicle's at the gate." It was not precisely a lie; there was a taxi rank there. "I'm going home to change into my country things. So – shall I collect you at the works at, say, half past ten?"

He conceded with a bend of the head. He licked his lips again. She wanted to touch them, touch his tongue, hold herself tight to him. "You're more than kind," he was saying. "Both of you. I shall have to ask the Guv'nor as a matter of courtesy."

His tone rose a little on the sentence. She realized he was testing her for signs of alarm at the thought.

"Half ten, then," she said easily.

But he was a belt-and-braces man. "Will you come to the main entrance or will I wait for you in Scrubs Lane?"

"I'll look for you exactly where you saw me the other day. If you want to speed things up, see if there's an open tourer ready for me to test. And if so, have it waiting, filled, and ticking over."

By half past ten the sun, being higher in the sky, had burned off some of that London pall. It was going to be a brilliant day, Julia thought happily. She found George in one of the research huts, with Nurse Ivory in attendance. Nurse Ivory was new and extremely efficient, though, at the moment, Julia observed, she was looking a bit glum. She made a mental note to inquire further on her return home that evening. George was obviously being difficult. "Why does Baring have to go down to Allbury at all?" he asked. "Isn't there the whole of Wormwood Scrubs just down the road?"

"He wants somewhere private."

"There'd be no one at Brookwood today. Why Allbury?"

"Perhaps I was wrong to suggest it."

"Yes, talking of which, when *did* you suggest it? You mentioned nothing when we spoke of him the other . . ."

"I'll call it off if you wish, George"

He saw how curmudgeonly it would make him appear. "No, no," he grumbled. "What's done is done. But don't let him lead you astray, eh, girlie? I know him. He'll want to stand in the back of the car holding his precious machine up while you break the speed limit for him. Just tell him no."

She laughed and bent to kiss him, but he turned his face away and told her not to fuss. Then he informed Nurse Ivory that she should have been a sailor. The way she was wheeling him around made him seasick.

"Someone forgot to put the batteries on charge," the nurse explained to Julia with weary resignation.

All the way back to the car Julia seethed with annoyance, chiefly that George's condition allowed him to get away with so much plain rudeness. If Nurse Ivory left in a huff – and who could blame her – she would be the third in almost as many weeks. And if the word spread, they'd stop applying altogether.

But the minute she saw the car, and young Baring standing beside it, she forgot George entirely.

It was, as she had requested, an open tourer – a beautiful sleeve-valve Daimler whose radiator was shoulder-tall and whose engine compartment seemed to stretch about a quarter of a mile down the road. The back seat was crammed with gear for his various tests. "Hope you don't mind?" he asked anxiously.

"It's all very exciting."

The largest item was the chest that held the Baring One itself in its knocked-down form; almost as large was what looked like a tripod for a two-ton camera, one foot of which was bolted to half a hundredweight of lead. Then came lesser boxes all stencilled with his name, plus coils of wire, hanks of fine chain, cable reels, bags filled with loose tools, and several flasks labelled "ether" or "light oil."

"A little different to your son's model airplanes," he remarked offhandedly.

She nodded. "Yes, I can see why that comment must have stung."

He pursed his lips in vexation.

"Will you drive?" she offered, but to her relief he shook his head and held open the driver's door for her. The very sight of this enormous, sleek machine filled her with pleasure, and the prospect of getting behind the wheel was even more thrilling.

"Of course," she said, as if making excuses for him, "you all drive on the wrong side of the road in America, don't you – the same as in France. It must be very off-putting for you here."

His crossness dissolved as he smiled at the idea. "No, I've gotten used to that, but I'd like to do some tests on the way."

"Breaking the speed limit?"

"I'm afraid so."

"I see! Well, swing the handle, there's a good fellow."

"You'll find she's already ticking over," he promised as he climbed in on the passenger side.

She gave the accelerator a skeptical prod. There was still not the faintest trace of vibration but she just managed to catch the rise and fall of the exhaust note above the clamour from the works. "But that's amazing," she cried.

"The finest engine ever built in my opinion."

She engaged bottom with one faint, well-oiled snick of the cogs. When she let in the clutch the bonnet gave a barely perceptible lift and the vast machine glided forward, still in that same eerie silence.

"The mightiest whisper in the world," he added.

"Is that their advertising motto?"

"It should be."

Using the sun for a compass she followed her nose, keeping the signs for Harrow to her left and taking anything that pointed northeastward, to Golders Green or Finchley or any of the other villages on the Great North Road.

"Hey, you can drive," he exclaimed.

"Did you think I only ever use a chauffeur? When we go down to the country I always drive – I mean even before my husband's accident, too."

"I don't mean just steering properly and not crashing the gears, I mean really driving. Is this the first time you've handled the double-six?"

"I'm afraid so." She revelled in his admiration. George took her driving so much for granted that he never noticed.

"Well, there you are."

As they approached Golders Green he told her, "If you make a left here, you'll pass one of the most exciting sights in London."

"You mean turn left," she corrected him. The signpost said Hendon. She understood then and followed his suggestion, swinging northward up the hill.

"We came here to the Aerial Pageant last year," she informed him. "I mean in 1924. We saw a whole squadron of Sopwith something. Not Camels."

"Snipe."

"That's the one. They did some mock bombing. It was very realistic and extremely frightening."

They purred on through the village and up to the hill crest. "Twelve miles an hour and still in top," she boasted.

"Pretty good. There it is!" His hand discovered the aerodrome a mile away to the northeast, a large expanse of green among the more broken landscape of farms and smallholdings.

"I remember it now. But we came by a different road."

"Yes, this way is new. I get the feeling they're building Hendon into something more than just an aerodrome, you know – now they've settled that disgraceful business – their treatment of Claude Grahame-White."

"I expect you come out here quite often?"

"Hey – pull over a mo," he said excitedly.

"Pullover?"

"Stop."

She halted swiftly. "Four-wheel brakes, too," she commented.

But he was staring at the airfield, where a large, three-engined aeroplane was taxiing downwind across the field. "Now what is she doing here?" he asked himself aloud.

"Is there something wrong?"

"If there was, they fixed it. She sounds okay. That's a de Havilland Sixty-six, by the way. Imperial Airways. They're ten a penny at Croydon but I never saw one here. De Havilland's own airfield is just a mile or so south of us here."

"It is . . . a beauty?" Julia ventured.

"A beauty!" He rounded scornfully on her. "You think that is beautiful?"

"Isn't it?"

His eyes raked the heavens. "Listen – if you exhumed some old naval architect from back in the days of Lord Nelson, and you told him all about these heavier-than-air machines, why he might just about come up with a design like that." He pulled a face. "It is *hawrible!*"

She laughed at his solemn intensity. "You know about these things."

"So do you," he assured her.

Her eyebrows rose.

"You do, too," he insisted. "I can tell from the way you drive. You have an instinct for engineering fitness. That's the great thing about engineering – if a thing is right, it *looks* right. You can surely tell whether a thing looks fit for its purpose or not. I mean, just look at that Sixty-six. Really look at it!"

The machine had finished taxiing and had turned, ready for take-off. It moved forward before the doubled roar of its engines carried to them. Julia had his comparison with old sailing ships to help her but, as it set off, lumbering over the grass, accelerating furiously like some underpowered little Austin Seven, she saw precisely what he meant. She couldn't have pointed to any particular flaw in it, nor (despite her preview of the Baring One) could she have told you what a *proper* aircraft ought to look like, yet she knew that poor old Sixty-six was as archaic as gas lighting and hansom cabs.

His talk of her engineering instinct was pure flattery, of course. But, she thought, perhaps she did have the tiniest beginnings of a critical faculty in that direction – and even that discovery was no small pleasure.

When the "clipper of the air" at last rose from the turf, the analogy with a sailing ship of old was even stronger.

"And that's when she's empty," Baring commented. "Imagine her with a full payload of fourteen."

She turned to him suddenly. "You're the only person I know who's ever treated me as if I might just not be a complete fool where engines and technical things are concerned. D'you know that?"

The direct assault embarrassed him but she did not relent. "Actually, I quite like being treated as an equal. Teach me. Tell me what an aeroplane ought to look like."

He laughed. "It's funny you should ask that, ma'am." And he reached for the box that held the Baring One. "Since we're halted I might as well set her up now."

He took several brass fittings from the box and attached them to the gigantic tripod, which he then stood upright with one extended leg on the floor of the car, the leg that was bolted to the massive lead weight; the two shorter legs he splayed across the back seat. It required a couple of minutes to assemble the Baring One. As it took shape Julia began to see it with fresh eyes – newly cleansed, so to speak, by their encounter with the DH 66. Even though she had seen the model before, it now seemed quite different. All at once she could imagine the full-scale version taking off from that same airfield. She could see it leaping forward at twice the speed, overtaking those cumbersome air clippers. And when it rose it would be like the tip of a razor-sharp scythe, utterly unlike the stately launchings of the old ladies of Imperial Airways. Already she felt impatient for the day.

Baring bolted the assembled model to the small platform at the top of the tripod. "How's your memory?" he asked. "If I call out strings of numbers – never mind what they mean – would you be able to remember them?"

"I'll try. But I'd prefer to know what they mean . . ."

Her keenness to take part seemed to please him. "I'm going to put the wing at different angles – it's adjustable, see? And then I'll measure how much lift we get for each angle at different speeds. Those are the figures I'll be calling out. Can you take her up to sixty?"

"Sixty!" she cried out. "The speed limit's only twenty, you realize. Ten in the villages."

"Don't I know it! Your laws are absurd. This beauty will do sixty without even trying – which is what I need. Velocity doesn't scale linearly, you see."

"Oh well I'm so glad you told me that. It makes all the difference."
She grinned at him. "Of course I'll do sixty. I just wanted you to
know what sacrifices I'm prepared to make for you."

She kept an eye on the speedometer and called out the reading at
every five-mph increment. He called the measurements back to her.
She felt exhilarated. She had once touched ninety going round
Brooklands on a practice day but had never gone over fifty on the
open road. Everyone ignored the 20-mph limit, of course, but mag-
istrates were not lenient on road hogs who did sixty.

The measurements on that first run were easy – zero all the way.

"Isn't that bad?" she asked when they slowed again.

"Nope. The wing angle, or the attack angle as it's called, was zero,
too. It means the flow is smooth over both surfaces."

"Smooth?" she queried. "Is that the proper word?"

"Okay." He laughed. "Laminar. The flow is laminar."

"That's better. 'Smooth' sounds like baby talk."

He leaned forward to see if she were serious. "Hey," he said. "You
really like to join in!"

"Yes," she agreed. "It's a matter of being part of it or just always a
spectator."

"Right! Can we go again? This time the attack angle is ten degrees."

"Ten degrees, cap'n!" She let out the clutch for another smooth
acceleration to three times the legal limit.

This time the numbers crept up: "Two, two point seven, three
point five, five point eight, eleven dead, seventeen . . . thirty-two
. . . fifty – and hold her there, for God's sake!"

His excitement communicated. She could sense these measurements were better than his most optimistic dreams. "It can't be," he
kept saying. "What were those figures again?"

She reeled them back while he wrote them down in a little pocket
book; it had a lockable clasp, she noticed. "Forty?" he queried. "Are
you sure that was only forty mph?"

"We'll do it again if you like."

"No. I'll believe you. It's just *this* I can't quite swallow." He
tapped the page with the backs of his fingers. "Let's try it again with
half that attack angle. Five degrees it is."

This time, though, they were forced to slow down before she even
reached the forty mark. "Chipping Barnet," she explained, pointing
to the village ahead. "There's a notorious speed trap here." She called
back the incomplete sequence of figures to him. He compared them
with the earlier set and said, "Okay, that's consistent enough for
anyone. Let's not risk your license any more."

"There's another fast stretch near Hatfield – or we can turn off here
and go cross-country to Ware, but it's slow."

"Let's go cross-country."

At thirty-five mph, top speed, it seemed like a crawl.

"What do those figures tell you?" she asked.

He gave a sardonic laugh. "That my engine is probably over-powered for the model. These lift figures are beyond my wildest . . . I mean, if they scale up to full size machine . . . 'Course, that's a big if."

She thought again of that full-scale machine taking off – and tried to relate it to these pranks along the lanes of Hertfordshire.

"What are you grinning at?" he asked, though he was grinning just as broadly himself.

"All this. I mean, it's so Heath-Robinson."

"What's that – Heath-Robinson?"

"He draws those funny cartoon machines – all string and wire and borrowed bits of this and that."

"Ah – yeah – we have a cartoonist like that. Rube Goldberg. Heath-Robinson, eh?" He scratched an ear, looked at his test rig, and added, "Yep, I guess so."

"Suppose you were one of the first passengers now, and someone told you that *this* was how she was first tested – in the back of a car breaking the speed limit along some country lane. Would you fly in her?"

"Would you?" he countered.

"Yes," she replied without hesitation. "Something tells me – actually, it must be that instinct you're so sure I possess – anyway, something tells me that this plane will not only get built, will not only fly – it's going to take the Blue Riband of the air."

"Oh, Mrs Somerville," he cried. "I wish you really were the boss!"

Suddenly he realized what he had said – or the other implications of what he had said. Though she kept her eyes on the road she could actually *feel* him turning scarlet behind her.

"I m-m-mean . . ." he began at once to stammer.

"I know what you mean," she told him.

Suddenly it struck her that the moment was absolutely right – the moment and the man. There would be no need to fish or prevaricate or go all about the houses. She could tell him the whole thing, straight and unvarnished.

She brought the car to an easy halt and turned to face him. "Listen, Eliot – I may call you Eliot?"

He nodded, swallowing his surprise.

"And you, of course, must call me Julia. I've been worried to death lately, Eliot, and I haven't known who to turn to. But now I feel sure you're the right person. In fact, I believe you're the only one who can possibly help me. May I be utterly frank with you? And will you be completely candid with me in return?"

He groped for the first word he remembered her saying and

echoed it. "Worried?"

Then he remembered, vaguely, the rest of what she had said. "About me?"

"No," she answered. "About Somerville's."

She knew she'd scored a bull's-eye when he lowered his gaze and said, "Unh-oh!"

CHAPTER TEN

MAX WATCHED his sister watching Baring test the machine. They were standing at the old nursery window, which gave the best view of the deer park.

"Are you and this fellow having an *affaire?*" he asked conversationally.

Julia kept her eyes on the scene below. "Don't be absurd. What ever put such an idea into your head?"

"There's an air of conspiracy between the pair of you."

"Oh that."

When she volunteered nothing further he said, "So there is something."

"Let's just watch this. I'll tell you later."

Baring had set up the tripod in the centre of an open space of rabbit-cropped turf, just inside the gateway to the park; its legs, now of equal length, were spiked into the ground and the huge leaden weight hung from the centre, supplemented by an even heavier wet-cell accumulator from the car. The top plate now held a sort of control panel, a neatly engineered contrivance of levers and switches, to which was attached a long "umbilical cord," as Baring called it, connecting the controls to the flying machine itself. At the centre was a miniature joystick, just as in a real cockpit.

The preparations seemed to take an eternity. Time and again the two watchers were sure the great moment had arrived, but there always seemed to be one more inspection to make. Baring checked and double-checked and checked again, ticking off lists in that lockable notebook of his. Finally, when they were almost ready to throw up the window and scream out their frustration, he walked with measured pace to the car and fetched one of the cans of ether. Filling the fuel reservoir in the body of the machine took a further age but at last it was done. Then there was only the slow plod back to the car to replace the ether can – and back to the tripod for one last check that the controls were in their neutral position. He paid the umbilicus through his hands on the final walk to the aircraft, inspecting every inch for at least the third time.

"He's doing it deliberately," Max said. His breath clouded the pane.

The sight of it stirred an ancient memory for Julia. "D'you remember my governess, Miss Creen?"

"Oh, I forgot to tell you. I saw her death notice in the *Telegraph* – the week of George's accident."

"Oh dear. I wish I'd known. I would've written."

"Talking of which, I don't suppose Dolly ever got in touch?"

Julia shook her head. "The moment I have an afternoon to spare, Max . . ." She felt angry at her own weakness, for Dolly's carelessness had hurt. "No, dammit. Let her mend this fence!"

"Anyway, what about Miss Creen?"

"I've just remembered something she once did. She hung me upside down for an hour in this room, by my heels. Just because I couldn't remember the kings and queens of England. It's astonishing, isn't it – the things one accepts as absolutely normal and natural when one's that age. I'm sure the parents would have had a fit if they'd known. But all I worried about was that someone would come in and see my knickers." She shook her head in amazement.

"The point is, d'you know the kings and queens of England now?"

"No."

Baring started the motor by swinging the prop. Nothing happened. He walked deliberately to the tripod and moved the lever a fraction of an inch. Then back for another swing. Again nothing happened.

This was repeated several more times, together with other small adjustments to the cable entry points and to a manual choke on the engine itself.

Both watchers had their noses pressed to the glass by now. Just as they were about to smash the pane in their frustration, Baring actually ran to the tripod, put the lever back to where it had been in the first place, and ran back to the plane again.

"Thank God even he can get impatient," Max commented.

At last it fired – two or three loud pops roared out in that quiet rural backwater and sent a great flock of rooks up from their perches, where they blundered around the sky in panic-stricken clamour.

The motor died, but the next swing started it again and this time it held. Gingerly he set the machine down, checked the umbilicus for tension, and ran inward to the tripod. There he set his hand to the throttle lever and increased the revs . . . and decreased them . . . and increased them – until he was accustomed to the degree of lash in the linkages.

Next he did a laborious check of the flap controls, which brought all their impatience back to the boil. But at last he began a slow and sustained increase in the revs.

"There!" Julia cried out as it began to taxi slowly forward.

But Baring immediately dropped it back to tickover and, taking out a wax pencil, made a mark upon the quadrant, beside the throttle lever. He brought it back to the mark, checked once more that the plane moved, and yet again throttled her back. He went on in this way until she had stop-start taxied through almost a full circle.

"He'll run out of fuel before he even starts," Max grumbled.

"First he has to check that the flow is laminar," she explained casually.

"Ah." Max peered more eagerly, in case he missed the moment.

Baring increased the revs until she began taxiing once more, but this time he went on increasing them – until the machine was fairly skimming along the ground. He moved another control and the tail lifted clear of the grass. This action, too, he repeated several times until he had the feel of it. Only then did he increase the revs still further.

"Now, surely!" Julia cried, twitching with unsuppressible excitement.

Max turned and looked at her in amazement.

The machine, gathering speed along its perfectly circular path, began to bounce alarmingly, even though the bumps were too small to be seen. One of those bounces finally propelled it into the air, where, after a couple of uncertain lurches, it climbed smoothly until it was about twenty feet above the ground. There at last it began to look like the real thing.

"Oh, I should have brought the camera up here," Julia cried out in vexation.

She could actually see it lying on the back seat of the car, next to one of the ether cans. A box Brownie with a patent leather strap.

On a sudden impulse the turned from the window and ran below, taking the stairs three at a time. She almost bowled over an astonished housemaid who was struggling to replace a broken pane in the front door. In the same headlong rush, anxious not to miss one moment of the trials, she grabbed up the camera and ran to the gateway of the deer park.

Baring had finished whatever tests he had intended making in level flight and was now causing the machine to climb and swoop along an aerial hogsback. Julia made a rapid survey of the scene. There was one obvious place to snap the plane in flight, where it would be silhouetted against a patch of sky between two large trees and with

Baring himself in profile.

She pulled back the sticking plaster that covered the little ruby-coloured porthole where the number of the exposure could be read. Number 4 was showing. Did whoever used it last remember to wind it on? Best be safe. She twisted the knob at the side. What an age it took! There was a hand in the porthole, with a pointing finger – did that come before the star? And would there be dots? It was years since she'd done this. The number 5 came so unexpectedly that she almost overran.

She firmed the sticking plaster back over the hole and cocked the shutter.

How tiny the scene looked in the viewfinder. She followed the switchback flight through two circuits but Eliot's control was so accurate that each time the plane came to the gap between the trees it was in one of the troughs, not visible against the sky.

She wanted to call out but did not dare distract him. Then he saw her. "Okay?" he shouted, noticing the camera.

"No," she yelled and gestured *higher!* – pointing to the gap where she wanted to frame it.

He took her meaning and brought the machine out of its climbs and dives, keeping it in high and level flight above the tree-line most of the circuit.

She snapped one of the whole scene and then, choosing her moment, ran in to get him in profile, close up, and with the machine in shot, too.

"Now see if you can land her," she challenged, running out beyond the circuit again. She wanted a shot with the plane all speed-blurred against the grass in the foreground and Eliot standing rock-like, dead-centre.

He brought the plane in smoothly for the landing, keeping it about three feet off the ground until she had her shot. He handled it skilfully by now so that, in the moments before touchdown, the simulation was perfect. The machine came toward Julia head-on and turned through its captive arc just inches above the grass. She, blind to everything but the plane itself, lost all sense of scale and saw it magically transformed into the real thing. It was a hundred yards away instead of only ten. For a moment there was even a suggestion of a pilot at the controls, and passengers peering nervously out through the windows down the side. Only when it touched down, and came to rest, and the motor died – all within a few feet – was the spell broken. But in that one brief illusion she knew she had seen the future.

There was a moment of total stillness and then Eliot moved, approaching the plane as if it were a shrine.

"That is *it*," he said, barely above a whisper.

Once again she lost touch with reality, though now it was Eliot himself who became the only solid element in her landscape. He was godlike at that moment. Her longing for him took her with a sudden, visceral force that seemed almost irresistible; but she gave herself the same answer she had given Max: *Don't be absurd.* Self-control, denial of emotion – the very meat and drink of an upper-class childhood – they were part of the Allbury air.

"That is it!" Eliot repeated much more loudly.

"Everything you hoped for?" she asked. The words seemed absurdly thin.

"And then some. Now I know what Kittyhawk was like. This is the poker player's royal flush . . . Tiny Tim's Christmas . . ."

"Let me take one more of you, holding the plane with exactly that smile on your face."

He held the plane but not the smile.

"What's next?" she asked, hoping to distract him into assuming it unconsciously again. "Between now and when she flies in earnest?"

"Oh, the boring bits."

She lingered, waiting for the smile to return. He was in any case so beautiful to look at she could have stayed an hour.

"Hurry up there," he told her.

The smile flashed back again but it was still with reluctance that she sprang the shutter and wound on. "What are the boring bits?"

"Unh, scaling up . . . working out stresses . . . testing different alloys . . . and, of course, money. Maybe I should do a quarter-scale version, something just about flyable, so I can raise money on it."

"I can't help you with any of those things," she answered sadly.

"Not even with the money?" He nodded toward the house. "What about your brother? This looks a fine place."

She laughed at the very idea. "What about your parents?"

"Oh no!" He was adamant on that. "The whole point is to show them, not involve them. Don't you know any bankers?"

She realized he was quite serious. "As a matter of fact, I do."

"Other than Somerville's bank?"

She nodded thoughtfully.

He did not press the point. "Would there be some kind of work-shop hereabouts?" he asked, peering toward the gateway. "I want to make a little adjustment to the engine while she's still warm."

They heard footsteps approaching across the gravel. It was Max. Julia relayed the question.

"There's a place round the back of the house where Fritz fiddles ineffectually with the lawn mower."

"I know. I'll show you," she said.

But Max took her arm. "He'll find it easily enough. It's the first double-door you come to. Used to be the coach house."

Baring hefted the model under his arm and, grabbing up the hank of control cable, set off to find the workshop.

"D'you think I'm not to be trusted?" she asked her brother grumpily.

He dismissed the accusation. "No. Quite the contrary. I believe an *affaire* would do you the world of good. But you promised to tell me about this conspiracy – or whatever it is – between you."

"Oh yes." The excitement had driven the business from her mind. Now it all came back in one depressing rush. "I think Somerville's may be heading for trouble."

His raised eyebrow made her react. "Don't jump to the conclusion Baring's being disloyal. Nor that he's been speaking behind . . . I mean, I truly had to drag it out of him. But he's as worried as anybody – even more so, perhaps, because he hasn't grown up with all the muddle and inefficiency."

"And what's wrong with Somerville's – in *his* opinion?" Max gave the word a sarcastic emphasis.

"It seems that George has changed greatly since the accident. I don't mean in all the obvious ways. Funnily enough, now that I come to think of it, George himself said as much to me only the other day. He told me he's no longer distracted by being able to do things himself. Instead he has lots more time for planning – developing new ideas . . ."

"Isn't that a good thing? It's such a grand day – shall we walk round through the coppice?"

They set off across the deer park. Julia relished the soft turf, the sun, the bright, cold air, the triumph of the maiden flight. Since Baring had spoken to her of his worries about the firm, a sense of impending crisis had hung over the day. Could she make Max see it?

"Have you mentioned it to George himself?" he asked.

"I tried."

Max chuckled. "And got a flea in your ear, I'll bet."

"I'm not interested in the business – I mean . . . not in meddling with it. But naturally I worry. It's the children I think of."

"Aren't these new ideas of George's . . ."

"I feel trapped, Max. Can't you understand? There are rumours about the firm's soundness – empty, no doubt, but still . . . And George is having the time of his life . . . and we're all dependent on him. You've never known that kind of dependence – that's the trouble. And who's thinking of the children?"

Max shrugged and stuck to his own line, repeating the question he had started: "Aren't these new ideas of George's any good then?"

"They might be if they concerned Somerville's regular business, but they just seem to be . . . well, just George responding to this and that wild engineering challenge. There's no immediate commercial prospect for any of it. One that he told me about is some new kind of valve that might be used in submarines or oil refineries. And there's another idea for protecting buried metal from rust. And another for

painting underwater by electricity. And something to scrape barna-
cles off ships' hulls at full speed . . ."

"But these all sound very useful."

"To someone – yes, I'm sure they are. But hardly to Somerville's,
Max. It's as if there's a sort of desperation in George nowadays. I
don't know. Perhaps these were ideas he always meant to work on
someday, but now . . ."

"Does he feel he may not have long to live?"

Julia could not bring herself to agree out loud; but her silence said
it for her.

Max spoke quietly. "Then I think your Mr Baring should keep his
thoughts to himself. I had an adjutant just like him. Would have won
the war with a single regiment if only the bullet that did for him had
got me instead. Take my advice, Ju, they're men of straw, that kind.
Have your *affaire* with him by all means but keep ahold of the reins."

"But what if it's true, Max? I've only lately started taking a direct
interest in the firm, so I know very little. Yet even that little fits
Baring's version in every detail."

"You think he's not clever enough to know that?"

"Max!" she exploded in scorn.

"Listen, little one." His tone suggested boundless patience. "If you
are going to start interesting yourself in business, you'd better also
start expecting the worst of everyone. Every man's hand is against
you. You turn your back and there's cold steel between your shoulder blades. Everyone inside the firm, from your partner down, will
cheat, steal, and leave you in the lurch. The only man you can rely on
is your sworn enemy. You know where you are with him."

"Oh, Max, how bleak!"

"Baring thinks George'll be dead soon. With you under his thumb
he could bleed Somerville's white to build his . . ."

"He's not like that. You don't understand. He's just not calculat-
ing like that."

"It makes no difference, my dear. You're probably right about
him, but as far as business is concerned, you'd better start behaving
as if he were. No other course is safe. All very depressing, I know.
But if you can't take it, why not stay at home like a good little wife
and leave all the worrying to George. Then you can go on believing
that all shy, handsome young men are wonderful and saintly and in
every way just tickety-boo."

"Oh, ha ha! You think I should just stay out of the business
anyway."

"Not at all. Your place in the firm is just as important as George's
– but it's at his side, relieving him of all domestic worries, buttering
him up. My God, you've been doing it superbly all these years – why
start questioning it now?"

Why did I never question it then? she thought. After a glum silence

she went on, "Anyway, if there is anything between Baring and me
. . . I mean anything at all . . . I mean it's only *so* big. And I'm the
one who's made all the running so far."

"Good." His clipped tone indicated he'd said all he wanted to say
on that topic. "As long as you keep it so. Power is for using."

A grassy lane led out of the coppice into a field, where an
unkempt horse stared at them over a sea of rotten hay stooks. Max
spoke again. "Take him to the Falcon at Perry Green for lunch, by
the way. I can't lay on a thing here."

She realized they had walked a considerable way without meeting
a soul. Where was everyone? Hedges that needed laying after the
summer's growth were as ragged as rooks' nests; ditches that should
by now be clean were still rank with weeds. "How many have you
working here now?" she asked.

"A dog and a stick."

The truth began to dawn on her. "That maid who was mending
the front door – is she now the only indoor servant you have?"

"Apart from Fritz. People don't need servants," he added vaguely.
"If the war taught us anything, it taught us that."

"Look – about lunch, all I want is some bread and cheese, and a
glass of beer. I'm sure Baring's the same."

"They do that sort of thing very well at the Falcon, I'm told."

She sighed. "Oh, Max, why didn't you *say?* When you saw me the
other day, you should have said. I thought you wanted a mortgage in
the usual way of business. I had no idea things were so . . ."

"Prices are back to those of grandpa's day – and they were bad
enough then, with men at only twelve shillings a week. One's jolly
lucky to get them for thirty now. And they all want days off. How
can we compete with the Empire? Hottentots work for nothing. And
America. Everyone protects their farmers except us."

She let him ramble on while she considered his problem. If he
couldn't farm the land, nor even staff the house, there wasn't much
point in his staying on here. But . . . Lord! *Sell* Allbury? It was
unthinkable. This land had been granted to Sir Roger Neville by
Henry VIII. The Nevilles were famous as England's greatest "untit-
led aristocrats." Without Allbury they'd just be . . . well, plain
commoners.

Lease it, then? The place was too far off the main road to become a
roadhouse. A hotel? The conversion would cost a fortune. So would
a school.

"Who's managing the estate accounts these days?" she asked.

He lashed out at a withered stalk of dock, scattering its seeds for
yards. "Hobbs was. Says the game's not worth the candle any
more."

"So nobody's doing them. I don't suppose you touch them?"

"I keep meaning to. I've laid in gallons of red ink."

"Would you like me to help?"

He looked surprised.

"I have picked up one or two wrinkles, you know, where accountancy's concerned. I'll come down one day next week."

He gave a knowing smile. "Alone?"

She laughed. "You are so determined, Max. Also, just a little old-fashioned, don't you think?"

They were approaching the back of the stables, where Baring could be heard tap-tap-tapping with a light hammer.

"Old-fashioned?" Max asked.

"Yes. This insistence that all married women must have *affaires* is very Edwardian, you know. Dear Mama, immediately after my confinement with Lydia, told me, 'Now you've given George two undoubted offspring, he can hardly complain if you let his friends add the tail-enders. Have your fling!' She thought it positively obscene that I loved George and didn't really want any other man."

"And now?"

"She had *affaires* with half the county. I'm sure Dolly wasn't by Papa."

Max repeated his question. "What about now – with George out of action, so to speak?"

She made no reply.

"Difficult topic," Max said.

"It's not a . . . I mean, there's nothing about it in the books I read – of course. Do you know anything about it, Max? Can we be quite certain it does put a man 'out of action,' as you call it? Has George said anything to you? I don't know. Do men talk about such things?"

Max passed a hand across his brow. "I thought *I* asked the awkward one. I'm like you – I honestly don't know. Seen plenty of chaps dead from the waist down, of course. But then, one doesn't simply walk up to a bloke's bedside – 'Hello Corporal Snooks, sorry about your paralysis, but do tell me – are you still getting your oats?' What's put the idea into your head? D'you suspect . . . anything?"

"Suspect is too strong. I just get a feeling sometimes – the way he looks at me. And then, when I asked Woolaway if George would be absolutely, totally paralyzed – of course, I didn't mean *that* but I think Woolaway thought I did. Anyway, he looked at me very oddly. I can't remember his exact words, but there was a sort of . . . awkwardness there."

Max had sense enough not to interrupt.

After further thought she went on, "You see, suppose he is . . . suppose he can? Should I . . . I mean it's as if he almost wishes I'd . . ." She sighed at the impossibility of conveying it all in the few necessary words. "Oh, forget it. Forget I spoke. It's probably all imagination. We'll find some way of coping."

Max let the silence settle before he went on. "How would George take it if . . . you know – if you did have this *affaire?*"

She closed her eyes and shivered. "Don't, Max! I just can't think about it. It's like . . . it's building up and up. It's oppressive."

"Ah," he replied.

When Julia, now rather regretting her frankness, added nothing further, he prompted, "So George isn't the only one who's changing."

With even greater reluctance she responded, "I don't know about George any more. Has he changed? Or am I seeing things more clearly? I'd hate to think – even to myself – that I'm cooling off because of *that,* you know. I'm sure it isn't that. But I'm beginning to feel I've been the most awful . . . blind . . . I just don't know. I've only lately realized it's possible for a man to be 'a splendid fellow and all that,' and yet be . . . well, not a terribly pleasant person."

Now it was Max who remained silent.

"You don't defend him?" she asked, more boldly. "I was reluctant to say anything because you and he have always been so . . . such hearty friends."

"I know what you mean," he agreed ambiguously.

"About my not wanting to talk? Or about George?" Without waiting for his reply she went on: "You see, when I said that about his desperation to do lots of things all at once – I mean, it applies to everything. It's as if he doesn't have the time to be pleasant any more. Not even pleasant, you know?"

Her brother gave her arm a reassuring squeeze.

Now she had broached the topic, and met no protest at it, there was no more holding back. "And yet I have a feeling that, perhaps, he's been like this for some time, only I haven't noticed. You know how one settles into a pattern and stops noticing things. Sometimes I even think he was *always* like that – and I was just too romantic to realize it. I'm not a very seeing person, am I."

Max folded his arms and stared toward the skyline. "How long do the quacks say he'll last?"

"Max!"

"Don't tell me it hadn't crossed your mind, too."

She nodded gloomily. "Perhaps I'm not the pleasantest person either. It's just this bloody . . . I mean, everything's frozen. If George were hale and hearty now – and I started having these ideas about him – I'd be seriously thinking of a divorce. But with things as they are . . ."

He turned the handle on the wicket door that opened into the stable yard. "All in all," he said, "it might be best not to start an *affaire* with this Baring chap."

PART TWO

UP AND AWAY

CHAPTER ELEVEN

HAT CHRISTMAS OF 1925 the world fell in for Julia. It began with the wireless. There was an arrangement whereby, if you had a treat for your children, you could send a note to the British Broadcasting Company and the jolly aunts and uncles who compèred the children's programmes would announce, for example, "If Lydia Somerville and her brother Robert will just go and look in the elephant's-foot umbrella stand in the hall, they'll have such a jolly surprise!" That, at least, was the announcement expected at half past five on Boxing Day afternoon. The jolly surprise was a number of tickets for "Peter Pan and Wendy" that very evening.

In those days, switching on a wireless was as complicated as starting a large domestic generating set. First you sat down and plugged in the headphones. Then you switched on valve number one, a large glass bulb shaped like a Russian church and crammed with futuristic bits of metal. After a while its filament glowed bright red. Then you switched on the second valve . . . and so on, until you faced a whole bank of glowing red filaments. Then there were dials with labels like *Grid Leak, Grid Bias +/−, Hum Adjustment Potentiometer, Aerial Tuning, HF Tuning, Coil Turret* . . . only after endless adjustments, back and forth among these mysterious controls could you place your hand to the mighty switch labelled *Speaker* – whereupon a vast papier-mâché trumpet would make everything rattle with words and music (or, more often, with "atmospherics" and "interference").

On that particular Boxing Day, try as she might, Julia could not "bring in" 2LO, the BBC's station. She could get Hilversum and Kalundborg, hundreds of miles off, but 2LO, whose transmitter was less than half a mile away on the roof of Selfridge's department store, remained obstinately silent.

"You've got it switched to Long," Robert growled with that special scorn which twelve-year-olds reserve for their mothers – indeed, for incompetent womanhood in general.

He eased her aside and took over; but, despite the switch to the correct wave band, he had no better success.

"I'll go and find Miss Davis," Julia told them. "She usually adjusts it for your father."

Imogen came at once. Four or five deft twiddles of the various knobs and the room resounded to the voice of the hearty uncle. But he was saying: "And those are all our greetings and messages for today, children."

The disappointment of at least two of those children was intense. If they had been a few years younger, it would have erupted in tears. Julia telephoned the studio at Savoy Hill, but the person she spoke to was regretfully adamant that the message could not be repeated.

Nothing daunted, Julia asked Imogen to keep an eye on Mr Somerville while she took the youngsters out to find a taxi. They stopped one just around the corner at Marble Arch and, a mere ten minutes later, a surprised "aunt" and "uncle," who had just come off the air, were searching their scripts for the message that had been delivered but not received. The two children, now in a high state of excitement, bundled back into the taxi and shouted "Faster" and "Don't spare the horses" all the way home. Not even the latest wonder of London, the new gyratory traffic system in Trafalgar Square, could deflect their enthusiasm.

They almost destroyed the elephant's foot in their search but the tickets were the crowning of the day, especially as the performance was actually within the next few hours and not some dreary infinitude away – like tomorrow.

"You can have high tea in the breakfast room," Julia said. "I'll go and tell Miss Davis."

At the time she noticed nothing untoward, though it did seem a little odd that Miss Davis should be standing so irresolutely in the middle of George's room, neither going to nor coming from anywhere in particular.

Much later that evening, when she and the children returned from the theatre, she made them go on tiptoe in case their father was asleep. As they crept upstairs Robert whispered, "Tick-tock-tick-tock . . ."

His sister rewarded him with whispered *oohs* and silent screams as she scampered ahead in disciplined quiet. At the landing Julia left them, saying, "I'll send Miss Davis to you with some hot milk."

All the locks and hinges in that engineer's household had lately undergone their annual lubrication, so she was into the dressing room before the sounds of her approach would have reached the bedroom.

There was no dramatic discovery. In a way, she decided later, it would have been better if there had been. The scene that met her eyes was ambiguous to the point of pain. Once again young Imogen stood irresolute in the centre of the room. She was fully clothed, or apparently so, but her face was flushed and her breathing rapid. George, despite his paralysis, was more of a revelation; there was a glazed look in his eye that once she had known so well. During that first year of their marriage she had seen it at least twice every day.

"Girlie!" he cried out with guilt-laden affability.

It was all she could do to reply, "Oh good. I just wanted to let you know we're back." To Imogen she added, "I'll give the children some hot milk."

"Oh, but I can do that, madam," the woman answered hastily.

"No, no – you stay and settle the master."

Master and mistress, she thought bitterly as she closed the door on the pair of them.

Why was she giving them this time to compose themselves, concoct a story? Because, at heart, she no longer cared? She flinched from the possibility and all it implied.

With each step her pain turned to rage. By the time she reached the stairhead she realized she was far too angry to face the children. Every red corpuscle in her urged her to go storming back and confront that hackney bitch with her suspicions . . . turn her out into the streets. Her heart was thumping itself all over her chest and her skin burned with a warrior fury.

But even then, even at the height of her rage, a more careful instinct was exploring the situation and making waves of caution. It would do no good to bring it out into the open like that. George had the whip hand here. He must know she would never leave him, not in his condition. That was his trump.

The Davis creature would obviously have to go. But a peremptory demand – "Either she leaves or I do!" – might, in those circumstances, easily backfire, especially if he were besotted with her.

No, she thought, *if I go back to the bedroom now and face them with his treachery, it'll be an angry, screaming, heedless couple – plus a harlot with a cool head and an agile mind.* When the moment came, as come it certainly would, Julia wanted to be the cool one.

She went down to the kitchen and heated the children's bedtime milk. And that was another twist of the same knife. For, later, as she watched them drink it, their eyes still alight with memories of the pantomime, she felt the big, solid, protective fabric of the house enclosing them all, and she knew that even if every other constraint melted away, for their sake alone she could not lift a finger nor drop the smallest hint to make George's behaviour public. If he had as little time left as seemed likely, how could she bequeath them any memorial of him but the finest?

That night she lay in her bed, a prisoner of his paralysis, too. What could she do?

She tested herself for some small spark of feeling, some remnant of a love she was once so sure would never fade. But there was nothing. She thought back to the time of their honeymoon in Paris. No, not their honeymoon – *his*. Toward the end of it, when the fear and bewilderment were behind her, George, for all his haste and clumsiness, had begun to awaken her responses. That was when she had learned he could not tolerate it. He had simply stopped "thrashing," as he called it, and lay there, frozen, as if counting down his anger – waiting for her *not* to move, *not* to gasp, *not* to do all the things that seemed to arise so naturally from within her.

And then, after a long silence, he had said, "My respect for you, girlie, is the most precious thing I have."

Nevertheless, "The Lad," as he called it, had needed "a good, sound thrash" several times a day. Oh, how they had raced back to their hotel – from the Louvre, from the Eiffel Tower, from Sacré Coeur . . . even now the very names conjured up those mad dashes by taxi, back to that delicious little room in Montmartre. She could see again "the sweet disorder of her dress" – the clothes spilled all over the floor. How grown-up she had suddenly felt, how wonderfully feminine, how fulfilled.

And even a year later, when Robert was on the way, The Lad still needed his "punishment" twice a day, every morning before getting up, every night before sleep. But by then she had trained herself not to move a single muscle.

She wondered she did not now feel more angry – that George must have trained his little whore to do all the things he had forbidden in his wife. Then she realized why. It was because she could not bring herself to envy the creature in the slightest degree, nor grudge her the briefest moment with him. The anger she felt was cold and deep, but it had nothing to do with them; it ran in an altogether different vein. She was angry at the waste of the years, at the stillbirth of so much pleasure – and at her own acceptance of it. Yes, she was angry with herself. And it was that, more than anything, which now separated her from George.

She stirred and settled in a new position.

"Girlie?" George whispered out of the dark behind her.

She made no response.

"You're the only one I love," he added. "My respect for you . . . well, don't you see – I just couldn't live with myself if I didn't keep that intact inside me."

The following morning Mr Sidney Gold once again called at the SPRP offices – and a very different Mr Sidney Gold, too. Gone was the ingratiating bonhomie, the would-be benefactor; in their place sat a carnivore.

"I like to keep my ear close to the ground, Mrs Somerville," he boasted. "Well, in this business you have to. It's the law of the jungle out there. And I'll tell you what the jungle drums are saying. Somerville's is finished. Down the drain. Wallis & Thorn will be calling in the loan next week. Then they'll put in the receiver – and you know what that means!"

"Not entirely, Mr Gold." She was quite calm. The man had been so abrupt with his news that her body was still working up its response. And after all, the poker face was now part of her daily make-up.

"No one's going to buy it as a going concern, because that's the one thing it's not. Not with the receiver in. He'll strip out the assets and sell them off piecemeal. You'll end up with pocket money."

He waited for her response. Her outward calm must have puzzled him.

"It's most kind of you to warn me," she said, "but, forgive me – I don't quite see *your* interest?"

"Believe me, Mrs Somerville," – his hand began a forlorn search for his heart – "it hurts me to be the bringer of such news. But . . ." He hesitated; seeing her still-calm face unnerved him. A wary chill invaded his eyes. He had prepared himself for anguish, perhaps even tears. From that point on his script was all benevolence and cheer. But now, like an actor who dries in mid-scene, he realized he was in sudden danger of revealing his pygmy self. "I'll tell no lie. I've always wanted a place north of the river. And I've always wanted to extend my business into the high-class end of the trade. I've got volume but no class. Somerville's has got class but no volume, or not a tenth of what you could have. I mean to say, it's the most respected name in engineering in England, after Rolls-Royce. And what are you doing? Next to nothing."

Julia's face remained a mask.

"You don't even pay your way," he added. "That's why you got all them bank loans. For these last years, Mrs Somerville, your hats and frocks, and servants and theatre tickets . . . they've all been bought by good old Uncle Wallis and jolly Uncle Thorn. They wasn't pound notes you was spending, they was pawn tickets. The whole firm has been popped down at Uncle's, and now Uncle's saying redeem it or else!" He chuckled. He liked his new script even though – or perhaps because – it was so spur-of-the-moment. "Funny, innit. There you was with your SPRP, lording it over all them common women, telling them how to manage the old geld – and there's your own darling husband at it worse than anyone!"

Julia was now so furious that she had to thrust her hands below her desk, not just to hide their trembling but to restrain herself from striking him. She could not so easily quell the tremor in her face.

He saw it – and misunderstood. She read his error in the smile he only half suppressed and it struck her it might be more convenient to foster his illusions than dispel them. So she allowed her lip to tremble, permitted her shaking hands to emerge from hiding and make little readjustments to her papers.

"I had no idea." Her tone was as neutral as she could manage.

"Of course not." He packed away his lower-class triumphalism and returned to his original pose as concerned carnivore. The speed with which he could make such changes amazed her only slightly less than his arrogant assumption that the new act was so superb it would immediately obliterate all memory of the old. "It's not a woman's place, is it. I mean, women are there to pick up the pieces. Make do and mend. But you, Mrs Somerville, you're, like, special – not only because of what happened to your husband but also because of" – he extended his hands to include everything around them – "all this. That's why I came to you sooner than go straight to your old man himself."

She drew breath to interrupt but the script was now remorseless.

"I mean, you want to come out of the crash with your beautiful home and kiddies secure and money in the bank. And I want . . . well, I already told you what I want. But what I didn't say was that I'm willing to pay over the odds for it. *Well* over. Providing, that is, we can make a good, quick job of it. The jackals and vultures will gather in no time, see? It's up to us, you and me together, to leave nothing around for scavengers like that."

He paused at last, waiting for some response from her.

"Thank heavens you came to me," she told him. "If things are as bad as you say, then we shall need good friends like you. Tell me what you think I should do?"

CHAPTER TWELVE

DEAR LEXY WAS proud of his reputation as England's most outspoken playwright. "There Is No News Today" had put the blundering generals of the Great War in their places – and almost landed him in prison. "Waste Blood Merchant" had done the same for war profiteers, though at much less risk to his own liberty. But by 1925 he was beginning to worry that Darling Noël was taking over his mantle. There had been "The Vortex" a couple of years earlier, all about dope fiends and the Older Woman. (It had caused poor old Sir Gerald du Maurier to explode: "The public are asking for filth . . . The younger generation are knocking at the door of the dustbin.") And 1925 itself had seen Tallulah Bankhead's sensational debut in "Fallen Angels," which was all about drink. ("Vulgar, obscene, degenerate . . ." The headlines had packed the house.) Poor Lexy was feeling distinctly upstaged.

He was astute enough to see what was happening. His sort of scandal-mongering was of the public, official kind – all about bungling generals and profiteers. Noël Coward's, by contrast, was private and personal – drink, drugs, and sex. It was more in tune with the times, which still could not face the terrible issues of the war. But damn the man! He'd cornered the market, leaving Lexy looking decidedly overblown and bombastic. It was plain to him that he'd have to move smartly in his young rival's direction; yet his public would still expect something of the old grandeur, the larger social significance, to survive.

For most of that year he racked his brains to hit upon the right theme. For bread and butter he tossed the public a couple of reviews – "Hopping Mad" was a sellout and even the less successful "The Purple Hat," a skit on the Michael Arlen best seller, did well enough to keep whole packs of wolves from the door. But the world expected more of him than that.

So far Darling Noël had not dealt with Money, so that was the obvious place to start. Old money versus new money? Aristocracy and the New Rich? No, that was just a different angle on war profiteers. Anyway, the theme itself had been done to death by Pinero and Galsworthy.

Money and corruption? The power of money . . . the abuse of power . . . getting people into your clutches? No, that was as old as Dickens, if not older. What, then, was *new* about money?

The Jews? Aha! Everyone was talking about the Jews. Thirty years ago they were penniless refugees from eastern Europe, all rather quaint and picturesque. Now they'd risen from being jobbing tailors and street-market traders to big proprietors worth thousands. They'd started out with everyone's sympathy but now society was turning against them. His play would show the Jews' side of the story, of course. Slap the public in the face – that was Noël's trick. Lots of wit, too. No difficulty there. Jews had bags of the stuff.

He had just decided upon this theme when he read an article in *John Bull* that made him decide to throw it all in the waste-paper basket and start again. This time his theme was Money and Sex. He had naturally considered such promising territory earlier but, being unable to get beyond White Slavery or the Kept Woman, had abandoned it. This magazine article, however, hinted at subtleties that had until then eluded him.

It began, like so many social pieces of that time, by reference to the fact that an entire generation of young men, born around the turn of the century, had been removed from the "social pot." Usually this sort of observation was a prelude to sermons against jazz, the Charleston, or Mayfair parties and Bright Young Things. But here was a more thoughtful piece.

Its writer was Wallace Baker, who was then quite unknown. But for its appearance in print, he might never have met Alexander Deeping. In which case – who knows? – he might also never have been drawn into Julia's circle. However, as he was by then seeing quite a bit of her sister Dolly, who, in turn, was soon to be found among Deeping's set, the whole chain of events could have been brought about by some completely different agency.

Anyway, this is how it *did* happen.

Thoughtful though that *John Bull* article might have been, it was also, undeniably, a piece of pure *whatiffery*.

Whatiffery is to the journalist what oases are to Bedouins. Consider a poor member of that fraternity who has spent several weeks researching some item and a further two weeks writing it up. His editor loves it . . . thinks it will make a wonderful lead for next summer's issue (this being December). His butcher, tailor, bookmaker, wine merchant . . . all share his pleasure, except for that bit about next summer. The air grows heavy with the stink of descending bailiffs; it is time for a piece of pure whatiffery – an article he can write (and usually does) on the backs of unpaid bills while his elbows never leave the bar counter. Whatiffery needs no research at all.

He starts with any item in that day's papers – CITY STOCKBROKER WINS DANCE TROPHY . . . "WHAT IS MAH-JONGG?" JUDGE ASKS – and he works it up into a sort of "Whither the City?" or "Whither Justice?" piece. If the papers yield nothing, he can pretend he overheard a remark in a café or on a bus. An imaginary brace of typists can always be relied on for good quotes – something like, "Oh, I much prefer *older* men . . ." or "No, I wouldn't call *that* sort of petty pilfering dishonest, not these days" – and so on.

For a couple of years, on and off, Wallace Baker and his creditors had been living off a series of whatiffery pieces on the "missing generation" theme. He had used it first to explain short skirts – surplus women desperate to attract the diminished stock of men. "Then how do you explain the almost complete disappearance of the female bosom?" a reader had countered. That led to a further article arguing that women were becoming more boylike, with their Eton-cropped hair, no waists, no bosoms, simply in order to *replace* the missing generation. Whatiffery is clearly not over-fastidious about facts and can point itself in any promising direction.

The idea that women might seek to replace men in outward form led to the further whatif that the replacement might extend to more fundamental economic and social levels, too. One must always personalize these things, so Baker pictured a woman running a family business whose intended managers lay among the Flanders poppies. It is a thriving concern but it needs to expand. To whom does she turn? To her banker, of course.

To quote from the article itself: "Picture that poor man, accustomed to dealing with a hearty fellow male, engaging in no-nonsense talk of turnover and margin, and settling the affair over a manly luncheon of sausages and beer, or eighteen holes at the links, when suddenly he finds himself face-to-face with a young and attractive widow in desperate need of a favour. Are not the temptations obvious? This touching scene, pregnant with moral dangers, must be enacted a hundred times a day up and down the land . . ." And so on. Paid by the word, obviously.

The piece was headed "Business Affaires." Deeping read it and called on the scribbler without delay. Older readers may remember that he later used the same title for his play, so there is little mystery as to what happened at that interview.

"I was wondering whether you might be prepared to share your research with me?" the playwright asked. "For a fee, of course."

Baker, unhampered by the fact that there *was* no research, mumbled about confidentiality . . . solemn promises of absolute anonymity to his informants in return for *devastating* frankness . . . files packed with material far too "luscious" to print . . . and so on. But give him a couple of days to transcribe a fair copy, changing all names and disguising nonessential but revealing details . . .

Dear Lexy, slavering at the mouth by now, could hardly wait to press ten steaming fivers into the incredulous journalist's hands. Fifty quid! The article itself had been lucky to earn fifteen.

Over the next two days Baker virtually wrote Deeping's play for him. Lexy thanked him profusely when he read the result and scampered home in high glee. His parting words were, "You have given me every scene, dear boy, every scene and every curtain. All I need do is confirm one or two points of procedure with my banker friend and we can start rehearsals next week!" He then pressed another fifty upon the fellow. Not even his dearest friend would have called Lexy mean.

"My banker friend" was none other than Douglas Crownfield, whose Notting Hill branch held the accounts of the SPRP. The promised visit was paid to the head office in Cavendish Square on the morning of New Year's Day, 1926. But to Lexy's chagrin, the banker, who had also read the *John Bull* article, merely laughed at the absurdity of its thesis.

"What?" he asked. "Do you suppose that an appealing flutter of the eyelashes could unlock the vaults that defy oxyacetylene and gelignite?"

Deeping decided at once to ignore him. The story was far too good to allow mere facts to stand in its way. (And in any case, before the morning was out, he was to arrive at what seemed a far more convincing explanation for Crownfield's scorn.)

The father of coincidence is hindsight; in the actual van of time, *all* events are orphans. By that unsired chance, Julia Somerville first visited Crownfield that same New Year's morning. Indeed, she arrived as Deeping was leaving.

At this point it ought to be explained that Wallace Baker, while inventing his "research" for Deeping, had realized it would look pretty fishy if all his supposed informants were women whose men had gone in the war. So to one of them, the one with the most luscious confession, he had ascribed "a husband lying in a coma following an accident at his family engineering business." Perhaps there *is* a God who works in mysterious ways, or perhaps Baker had read of George's accident, which was certainly reported in all the papers at the time, and his subconscious served it up when wanted.

At all events, this mythical woman's confession now nestled securely in Alexander Deeping's briefcase.

Lexy did not recognize Julia all at once but he had a vague idea they had met somewhere, and quite recently, too. That, in itself, was not at all remarkable; there were hundreds of such people on the fringes of his life. He did what he always did in such circumstances – chatted amiably until the half-known face or voice yielded some further clue.

"Hell-*oh!*" he cried. "Spiffing to see you! And tell me, how are you keeping?"

Julia knew him at once, as, indeed, would any other inhabitant of Connaught Square. And, being often in the same boat herself – and employing the same oar to row it – she twigged his dilemma. Feeling more than somewhat apprehensive about her interview with Crownfield, she decided to tease. "Why, Mr Deeping! How kind of you to inquire. I'm as well as can be expected, you know." (Sigh!)

Deeping's heart sank. Something unpleasant had plainly befallen this young woman – this rather attractive and apparently healthy young woman – and not only did she know him, she assumed he knew all about her tragedy or whatever it was. He tried every trick he knew to pry one small hint of it from her but she wriggled clear each time.

Poor Tommy Beecham once found himself in the same predicament when he met the Princess Royal in Hyde Park and just couldn't place her; all he could remember was that her brother was some kind of bigwig. So in desperation he finally asked, "And your dear brother, ma'am – what's he up to these days, eh?"

"Oh," she replied with a gay smile, "still King, you know."

Deeping, too, found he had no choice but to try an equally

dangerous frontal question: "And your man" – he even assumed a slight Irish accent to show that his usage was jocular – "how fares it with him?"

Julia, realizing the joke had reached its natural end, decided to let him down gently. He was, she realized, a much nicer fellow than his rather brittle public persona suggested – more handsome and charming, too. She lowered her eyes and answered, "My husband, you mean?"

He could not disguise his relief that here at last was one solid fact on which to build. He nodded sympathetically and waited.

"He still goes to the works each day, as you know. You probably see him being helped into his car every morning. But the doctors say he will never recover the power of his limbs."

Deeping, ever quick on his feet, suddenly realized who she was and why her face had been so familiar. He still couldn't think of her name but she was the Rolls-Royce lady who lived across the square. Her husband had had that appalling accident at his . . . *engineering works* . . . oh my God!

No wonder she had been so evasive!

The hair on his neck bristled. Substitute "total paralysis" for "coma" (didn't that journalist chappie say he'd altered such inessential details?) and . . . by harry, he was at that very moment carrying a doctored version of this poor woman's confession!

And who was her banker? Ha ha – none other than lofty, unseduceable Douglas Crownfield! Now it was clear why his denials had been so vehement and sarcastic. Suddenly Deeping *knew* he was on to a good thing.

The one thought that never crossed his mind was that now he realized that the tarnished heroine of his play was, in real life (as he supposed), a neighbour – and the equally tarnished hero was one of his close friends – he would have to replace them with some other case from the Wallace Baker files. On the contrary, he was now desperate to know her, and her husband, better. A single-minded man, Dear Lexy.

He realized now that he and this Mrs Somerville had never formally met – merely nodded at each other in the way that city neighbours do. He switched on his considerable charm; oh, but he had so often meant to call on them. They seemed to lead such interesting lives . . . all those beautiful cars belonging to such famous people – what a lot of tales they must have to tell . . . and those two lovely, vivacious children, always so well turned out and so courteous . . . In fact, he had actually written them a formal invitation . . . the maid had been on the point of carrying it across the square, on the very day that cruel accident had happened. But now that the ice was broken . . . and so forth.

He left her with an invitation to join him – and to bring George, naturally – in his box, the following week, for a gala performance of "The Purple Hat."

Indeed, he left her with more than that, for Julia, seeing the iron was hot, struck it a well-practised blow and extracted a cheque for twenty guineas for the SPRP. Deeping was happy enough to pay up. The play "Business Affaires" would earn him many times that in a single night.

Lord, he thought as he watched her being shown into Crownfield's office, what he would not give to become a fly on the wall in there during the next half hour!

CHAPTER THIRTEEN

CROWNFIELD WAS BORN Kronenfeld back in the 1870s; the whole family had become Crownfield during the Great War, when there was all that hysteria about German names. The Royal Family changed from Saxe-Coburg to Windsor; the Battenbergs became Mountbattens; indeed, for a time, such translations were so prevalent that fashionable London considered adopting German names *en masse* in order to be able to follow where royalty and its kinsmen had led.

Be that as it may, Douglas Crownfield was third-generation English, and as English as they come. After Eton and Oxford he had worked at Rothschild's before joining the family's own bank. Since his father's retirement in 1922 he had been the bank's senior working partner and, in name at least, its head.

Julia took an immediate liking to him. Tall, distinguished, patriarchal, he was the sort of man who had looked the patriarch at twenty – suits by Hooper, shirts by Izzard, shoes by Cobb – you know the type. Now, almost thirty years on, age had merely confirmed the status, deepening the voice and the lines of laughter around the eyes. But tragedy had also left its mark; the death of a young son in the war, sparing his amiable but dim-witted brother and a sister just turned eighteen, had lent an abiding melancholy to those same eyes – and it qualified that laughter, too.

She wondered whether to mention her business with Crimmond, who was, after all, this man's employee; but she decided it would be best, on the whole, to stick to her original plan and not muddy the water by any mention of the SPRP. She explained she had come on behalf of two men, neither of whom felt in a position to approach his own banker just at present.

"But they have asked you to come to me?" he surmised.

She hesitated. "I could not claim that."

"I see. Well, do tell me, anyway."

He listened in silence while she outlined, anonymously, first Max's problem then Baring's. As her narrative unfolded he began giving her an odd, rather knowing sort of smile.

"There is no difficulty here, Mrs Somerville," he said at last. "A banker's vaults are not some Aladdin's cave merely awaiting an 'Open Sesame' before they yield. There is a simple and infallible way to get a thousand pounds from any of us. Shall I tell you?"

She nodded. "Please."

"Show us eleven hundred."

She frowned in bewilderment.

"If your land-owning friend," he went on, "has mortgaged every last acre of farmland, then he has milked the cow dry. The only way he can get more value out of it is to change its nature – turn his valueless farmland into a housing estate or a site for a factory, or a golf course . . . a racetrack . . . anything that looks like yielding a better twenty-year return than poor old farming. Then he'll find the bankers beating a path to his door." He beamed at her. "And as for your other friend – what does he do, by the way? I presume this mysterious invention of his is not yet earning him . . ."

"He works for a well-known engineering firm."

"Ah, then without doubt his best course is to interest his employers in his ideas."

"He wishes to 'go it alone' is his phrase."

"Then his path *will* be difficult."

Crownfield's distinctly cavalier, not to say supercilious, behaviour puzzled Julia. It ran quite contrary to his reputation – and to the promise of his benign and dignified exterior.

The banker, grinning as if he had nimbly avoided a dozen traps, went on, "In a curious way I have just given rather similar advice to Mr Deeping, Alexander Deeping. Do you know him?"

"Quite well," Julia could not resist saying. "In fact, we are close neighbours." The answer merely broadened the other's smile.

"Yes, I was sure you did. In case you fear I am in the habit of betraying a client's confidence, I hasten to add that he consulted me in connection with a play he is writing, some points of financial practice, not his own private affairs."

Julia nodded politely. "So, the answers to my friends' problems are simple – in effect, each must prove to his banker that he doesn't need to borrow a penny, whereupon he will instantly be lent all he requires."

He gave a little chuckle. "The world has never been otherwise, Mrs Somerville. Now are you quite sure there's nothing *else* you wish to discuss with me?"

She raised her eyebrows at what she took to be a rather crude way to speed the parting guest.

"Your husband," he went on with a knowing grin, "he wouldn't by any chance be lying in a coma at home while your family's engineering business falls to rack and ruin?"

"I *beg* your pardon!" Outrage and fear fought within her. Had Crimmond discovered something dreadful and passed it on to this alarming man?

"While you," Crownfield continued, now enjoying the joke hugely, "have come here willing to do anything – but *anything* – to save the day. Isn't that what you really came here to tell me?"

"Mr Crownfield!" She rose and prepared for a hurried departure. Quite clearly the fellow was unhinged in one or two respects. "In the circumstances your question is in the worst possible taste."

"Oh, spare me that," he said pleasantly. "It's quite exploded, you know. Tell your friend Deeping I may be a fool in many ways, but hardly such a fool as he – and you – seem to take me for. At least you had the sense to see it at once and switch to this quite convincing story about your land-owning and inventor friends."

She realized then that, far from being unhinged, he laboured under some genuine delusion concerning her and Deeping. Quite by chance Dear Lexy must have said something that led Crownfield to believe her appearance here was completely factitious – part of some plot or practical joke. She also saw it would be futile to try to convince him otherwise; the best she might achieve would be to badger him into an insincere apology. Her wisest course was to retire as soon as possible and try to learn from Deeping exactly what had passed between him and Crownfield. Fortunately, the opportunity would soon arise.

The moment Mrs Somerville left the office, doubts began to assail Douglas Crownfield. All through their interview he was aware of some small piece of information lodged at the back of his mind, something that concerned her; but for the life of him he could not recall it. What really set him thinking was the fact that his remarks, which he had expected would cause her to laugh and confess Deeping's little plot, had merely bewildered her. Deeping *had* sent her, no doubt of that, but perhaps he had revealed only part of the script – the part which read: "Go in and plead with the man." Perhaps Deeping had taken advantage of some quite genuine distress on her part?

If that were Deeping's game, he had chosen well. Julia Somerville was not a conventional beauty. Handsome, certainly . . . interesting, good-looking, attractive . . . a host of other words rose to mind, but not beautiful – until something troubled her. Then, within moments, a wonderfully haunting transformation came over her. She developed an aura of vulnerability that men, especially a man like Crownfield – secure, kindly, and rich – find hard to resist. Crownfield knew it, of course. He was, after all, no stranger to such affairs. So, as he tried to resettle his mind upon the ordinary business of the day, and found it instead returning again and again to the appealing Julia Somerville, he knew precisely what was happening to him. Once more he could not help wondering whether Dear Lexy had planned it so.

Oh, damn all irresponsible artists! Didn't they understand you couldn't play fast and loose with the serious things of life?

He picked up his phone. "Would you see if Mr Deeping has arrived home yet?" he asked.

A minute or so later he was again talking to Dear Lexy. After a few bridging remarks he observed, casually, "What a charming woman that Mrs Somerville is. I didn't know you knew her."

The embarrassed silence at the other end confirmed Deeping's guilt – even without his belated response: "Did she tell you that?"

"I'm afraid so, old chap."

"Well, come to that" – Deeping recovered somewhat – "I didn't know *you* knew her, either."

"But I don't." Crownfield suddenly realized Deeping's mistake. He laughed. "Caught you, my old friend! Did you think we were her bankers?"

After another bewildered pause Lexy came back: "Their firm's, surely? Somerville & Sons. The engineering people. He had that awful accident last year, remember?"

There was a sudden hollow where Crownfield's stomach ought to have been. Desperately he tried to recall his exact words to Julia.

"I don't blame you," Lexy added playfully.

Crownfield sighed. "I'm sure you think you're being very clever, Deeping, but I give you my word I've never set eyes on her, nor even heard of her, before today."

"Then, of course, I accept your assurance," Deeping replied, writing the words, *Convincing liar – v. understated* among the character notes he was even then compiling. Suddenly he remembered what Julia had said as she skilfully extracted that cheque. He challenged Crownfield with it: "And I suppose you've never heard of the Society for the Promotion of Responsible Parenthood, either."

"As a matter of fact, I have," the banker replied triumphantly. "They have an account at our Notting Hill branch."

"So now tell me you don't know that Julia Somerville is their founder and chairwoman!"

That was it! That was the awkward fact at the back of his mind. Oh *double*-damn all irresponsible artists. Now thoroughly sick at heart, Crownfield shouted down the phone, "It's not funny, Deeping. It's just *not!*" And he rang off.

As the earpiece curved down toward its cradle he heard Deeping, still jubilantly amused (about what? about what?), saying, "Well tried, Crownfield, old chap!"

Furiously he stabbed the button that summoned his secretary. "Get in touch with Crimmond at once," he barked. "Concerning Mrs Somerville and the SPRP. I want copies of all recent correspondence, memoranda – any transaction of any kind whatever. And as soon as possible, please."

"Would this be more urgent than your letter to the Bank of England, sir?" the poor fellow asked nervously. For Mr Crownfield to be in such a rage was rare. "I've very nearly finished the first . . ."

"Yes," he roared. "It's even more urgent than that!"

CHAPTER FOURTEEN

A DAY OR SO later Julia plucked up the courage to meet Crimmond and learn the result of his inquiry with Wallis & Thorn. The manager told her that the reply had not been encouraging, but his tone conveyed more. He probably intended to keep his doubts to himself, and he probably thought he had succeeded. He did not know how alert Julia was to the slightest nuance, nor how well she could mask her awareness of it. But when Crimmond had learned that Mr Crownfield himself was taking an interest in the matter, he knew it had assumed a more-than-routine importance, and something of that knowledge conveyed itself to Julia, despite his most practised efforts at concealment. She seized on it quickly and pressed him but he shut down like a clam, leaving her even more worried than the news itself warranted.

By now she could hardly bring herself to speak to George. She had never felt so lonely. To whom could she turn? Max had worries enough of his own; his warning about Baring had made her wary of confiding anything further there; and matters were now too serious to be solved by general chats with Captain Harcourt. Besides, it was all guesswork and feeling, so far. What were the facts?

Her ignorance was the chief problem. In the middle of her meeting with Douglas Crownfield, while she was trying to summarize Max's situation or describe Baring's prospects, she had become painfully aware how little she knew of any of it. Even in the matter of owning and managing land, which had been her family's "business" since the year dot (though most of her forebears would have hated to hear it so described), even that was a closed book to her. And as for the business of engineering . . . she might as well have tried to talk about brain surgery or the National Debt. Crownfield had spotted her ignorance at once, which had led him to assume she was a fake, part of some strange practical joke of Deeping's. She cringed now whenever she thought of that fine-looking gentleman and what opinion he must have formed of her. She had thought about Crownfield rather a lot during the last couple of days.

And then there was Sidney Gold. He would never have spoken so blatantly if he was not sure of his ground.

The dread that some financial disaster was about to strike – a dread that was merely increased by her awareness of her own ignorance – drove her to a desperate measure.

Or did it? Perhaps that is too pat, too rational an explanation. Certainly other, less easily definable forces were goading her, too. Julia was not the sort of person who could discover something amiss and leave it so. She often wished she were. She would see something wrong and she'd try to close her mind to it, hoping it would sort itself out. Occasionally life was kind and the problem would, indeed, resolve itself; but if it did not, the pressures would build until she had to act, almost regardless of the consequences to her own best interests. So perhaps she was beginning to stir with an idea that had been planted in her mind (entirely without her being aware of it) by Captain Harcourt some time previously – the idea that she herself might be the caretaker-proprietor of Somerville's until young Robert grew up and matured sufficiently to take on his father's mantle.

If George had died in that accident, she would have done so without a second thought; but now perhaps the unthinkable was just beginning to stir in her mind, beneath the level of conscious decision: She might also take on that role even while George was alive!

George's own behaviour around that time would certainly have encouraged such a development. The transformation Julia had mentioned to Max continued. Matters came to a head when Nurse Ivory handed in her notice. She pleaded family reasons but it was obvious to Julia that something distasteful had occurred, involving George. She pressed the woman on the matter and eventually she admitted something of the sort: "I know it sounds absurd, Mrs Somerville," she said shamefacedly. "I mean, even if we're not specially trained to deal with . . . certain suggestions from our men patients, we soon learn how to cope. And here's a patient who can't lift hand nor finger, and yet, just by speaking . . ." She gave a baffled shrug.

"What sort of things? Or would you rather not say?"

"I'd rather not say."

She hardly needed to, Julia thought as she watched the woman go.

That evening, without the slightest twinge of conscience, she took a taxi to Forge Lane and "borrowed" the company's accounts. She told Tredwell, the night watchman, that Mr Somerville had asked her to pick up certain papers. He said he was sure he hoped the Guv'nor was better.

All she thought at the time was that his phrasing was a little odd; later it struck her as a strange thing to say altogether. But by then she was in her office at the SPRP, working furiously to produce a trial balance.

After half an hour she was startled by Captain Harcourt, who burst into her room. "Oh!" He was taken aback, too. "It's you, Mrs Somerville."

She smiled. "Did you think we had burglars?"

"I've never known you come back of an evening. I just happened by . . ."

He was trying to see what books she had on her desk. Her first thought was to cover them, or escort him tactfully elsewhere, but then she told herself that if she couldn't trust him, there was no one in all the world whom she could. Besides, she had to confide in someone.

"These are Somerville's accounts, Captain Harcourt. My husband knows nothing of this. I may leave you to guess what doubts and worries have driven me to something that goes against every grain of my upbringing and nature."

He nodded sympathetically. "I left my pipe in my room." He turned toward the door.

"May I ask for your help?" she went on.

"Help?" He eyed her uncertainly.

"Just assure me I haven't gone mad – or committed some absolutely elementary accounting blunder." Her hands invited him to sit in her chair.

"If you wish it, Mrs Somerville." He was not at all as reluctant as she had expected. In fact, from the moment he committed himself he was all eagerness. He totalled several columns, saw that his sums agreed with hers, and then accepted all her calculations. After that it was just a matter of looking at the trial balance and seeing what story it told. To anyone with half an eye for figures this one shrieked like the damned.

"Last year's balance was bad enough," she observed, laying it in front of him.

"Mind you" – he clutched at a straw – "gentlemen are notoriously slow payers. Ask any tailor. Ten years is nothing for bills to be outstanding."

"But tailors allow for that when they set their prices. In fact, I'm sure any sensible coachbuilder does the same. And if you're turning out a steady thirty vehicles a year, it doesn't matter if the ones you're presently being paid for are the ones you did ten years ago, as long as your price allowed for the lag. But when you're expanding, when you're doing *sixty* vehicles this year and the armoured cars you were building ten years ago have long been paid for . . . well, it doesn't need a Mr Micawber to work it out."

He tapped the "Sundry Creditors" column. "Surely some of these fellows will soon start turning nasty – unless the entire industry is working on extended credit."

"Even then it's hardly a happy position."

He frowned at the page and tugged his lip. She asked what he had noticed. "Some of these debtors," he replied, "they're not gentlemen-owners of hand-built cars."

"No. That's the jobbing-engineering side of the business. But it's all lumped into a single set of books. One simply cannot discover whether it's profitable or not. It could be making the most ghastly loss."

She did not add that there were half a dozen further enterprises within the firm – all those pet researches of George's – which had so far failed to earn a penny. How much had they added to present liabilities? Again, it was impossible to say because no separate accounts were maintained.

"So," the captain summed up, "you aren't going mad, Mrs Somerville. Nor, I'm sorry to say, have you made any elementary accounting blunders."

"Shall I tell you the most worrying thing of all?" she replied. "This handwriting." She laid a finger on the neat columns of figures, the copperplate words beside them.

"Eh?" He thought she was seeking refuge in a joke.

"I'm quite serious. Look at it – what does it tell you?"

"The fellow certainly writes a neat hand."

"But that's about all. There's subservience in every letter. This man would have been counting the silver back into the vaults while the *Titanic* was sinking."

Harcourt chuckled. "You think you can tell that just from his handwriting?"

She closed the book and added in a brisker tone, "It's perfectly clear to me that no one down there at Forge Lane can stand up to my husband and do for him what you do for me." She smiled.

His eyebrows shot up.

"You restrain my wilder ideas, Captain Harcourt. You're the sheet anchor of this drifting ship. But no one ever says to my husband, 'You can do it, Guv'nor, but it'll set you back four hundred' . . . or whatever. He has the first and last word on everything."

The Captain surveyed her craftily. "No one?"

"I know what you're driving at."

"Is it so impossible?"

She gave a hopeless shrug. "How would I even suggest it?" She began to gather up the papers, taking care to extract her own jottings from among them. "I'm terribly afraid that our affairs will have to reach some kind of open crisis before any such change could be made – and even then . . ." Again that hopeless shrug.

When she returned the books to the offices, Tredwell let her in once more. She pulled a face and said, "I did a most stupid thing. I don't know whether these are the right papers at all. Fortunately my husband was asleep when I returned home, so I'll just pop these back and if he asks, I'll say I assumed he didn't want them after all. Don't let anyone know what a fool I am, will you. I didn't come here at all, eh?"

He was flattered to join her conspiracy, especially when she told him how beautifully he was keeping the Somerville family grave.

As she was on the point of leaving, a further thought struck her. "Oh, by the way," she added. "Why did you say earlier that you hoped the Guv'nor was better? Was he not well today?"

"That's what they said, Mrs Somerville. That's why he left early."

"Ah, I see. Well, whatever it was he seemed cheerful enough this evening."

She was remembering George's protestation: "I don't *need* a replacement for Nurse Ivory. Miss Davis is better than the lot of them put together."

"Was that Mr Baring's light I saw?" she asked. She was fishing; she hadn't actually noticed any light down there.

"Who else, madam!" he replied.

She looked angrily at her watch, to hide her pleasure, and said, as if she really could not spare the time, "I suppose I'd better go and see him. He promised Master Robert a book on model planes and he keeps forgetting to give it to the Guv'nor." She took the accounts with her. "Perhaps he'll also be able to tell me if these are the right books," she added.

"You promised Master Robert a book on model planes and you keep forgetting to give it to the Guv'nor," she told Eliot even before she was through the doorway of his icy cabin.

"Right!" he laughed.

Then she told him her real purpose at Forge Lane that evening. As he listened he grew more and more solemn. "May I see?" He held out his hand toward the books.

Like Captain Harcourt he checked one or two columns and then

106

accepted her addition. "So," he remarked after he had studied the balances. "Now you have chapter and verse. What can you do?"

"Very little, I fear. Until the crisis comes out into the open."

He raised his hands in the same hopeless gesture he had used in trying to describe the physical layout of the works, that first day they had met. "You see, it may all be lies. Not deliberate lies but sloppy lies. The accounts are spread through so many offices, God alone knows how many debtors just get lost. Creditors are another matter. They send angry reminders. But debtors could just lie doggo and let the debt go out of time."

She had hoped against hope for comfort; instead, he added fresh terrors to those that already beset her. "What can one do?"

He shrugged. "I guess you could sneak back, nights, and just slog your way through . . ." His voice tailed off. "It'd take months." He looked keenly at her. "Why not just make a clean breast of it to the Guv'nor?"

She shook her head. Their eyes dwelled in each other's for a long moment.

"That bad, eh?" he said at last.

She frowned. "Have you noticed?"

He smiled awkwardly. "Well . . . talking of making a clean breast – I'm afraid you and your brother Max must have assumed I'd left that stable at Allbury when you stood outside the window and . . ." A little tilt to his eyebrows conveyed the rest.

She felt the colour rising to her face. All the conventional things she might say flashed through her mind.

Seeing her confusion he said, "I'll buy Max's advice."

She had not heard the idiom before; she was still working it out when he added, "I mean I wouldn't want a mere *affaire*, Julia."

She reached forward and took his hand. "Cold," she said in surprise – having meant to say something much more romantic.

"You know the old saying."

"I'm not . . . I mean, I couldn't . . . this isn't a good time, my dear."

"I know. I wasn't going to bring it up at all. I'm sorry I did – except it's maybe better to be straight from the start."

"Oh, it is. It is." She reached up with her lips and gave him a short, unhurried kiss on the cheek. Even that stirred her dangerously. "Where were we?" she asked as she drew away.

"If we can't tell the Guv'nor, I guess we wait for Wallis & Thorn to make some open move. Generally there's a month or two between that and the actual drop of the ax."

She let a silence grow before she looked up at him and said, "To be honest, Eliot, d'you think there's much of a future in hand-built cars for a small, luxury clientèle?"

He began to make comforting sounds, so she added, ". . . as

compared with, say, aeroplanes?"

The comforting sounds died in his throat.

"In other words," she went on, "do you perhaps see common cause with me in discovering the truth about this firm of ours?"

"The Guv'nor will be . . ."

"I wasn't thinking so much of him. The fact is, I may have found a buyer – in an odd sort of way." And she told him about Sidney Gold. "If it came to a sale, forced or voluntary, I'd hate to see it go for a fraction of its true worth."

"No, you'd want its full price."

"More." She sighed. "No. That sounds awful."

"Not to me."

"It's not that I'm greedy, you understand. It's just that . . ." She shrugged at the hopelessness of trying to explain it. "It's the same with most things in my life. I never seem to get everything that I just know must be there. No matter what. Even in little things. People tell me jokes and I'm sure I only see half the point."

"And in big things?"

"The same. I thought the SPRP would be all I wanted. I'm not saying it isn't, mind – and yet it doesn't seem to *do* as much or offer me as much as I once hoped it would. Things are very simple when all you do is just *want* them. But when you get them you find yourself thinking . . . I don't know. There must be more! That's what I end up thinking always. I say, I do sound awful! Pay no attention."

All the while she spoke he was watching her shrewdly, weighing her up. "Tell me," he said at last. "When it comes to making decisions, would you say you're spur-of-the-moment or plan-it-carefully?"

"Both," she replied without hesitation. "You're talking about big decisions? Not . . . buying a hat or picking a menu?"

He nodded. "I don't see how you can be both."

"I mean, I worry at things – if I know I'm going to face an important choice, I keep picking at it in my mind for days beforehand. But even if I make up my mind, it doesn't necessarily *stay* made up. It sometimes infuriates my colleagues at the . . . George can't stand it. He likes to say, 'We've made our decision, girlie, now let's stick to it.' But I say what's the point of sticking to it, I mean no matter how logical and thorough you were beforehand, why stick to it if it turns out you were wrong? Or if circumstances change? Why are you smiling?"

"I guess it's all part of the same thing. You talk about wanting certain things, and working to achieve them, and then when you succeed, they aren't what you expected. This feeling that there's . . . more. Something missing."

"But isn't that true of most people?"

"Unh-*unh!* Absolutely not. Most people wouldn't be honest enough to face up to it. They'd take the Guv'nor's line. They'd say to themselves, 'This is what you always wanted, man. Now you've got it – enjoy!' They'd wilfully blind themselves to the . . . to whatever it is you find missing." He laughed. "I'll tell you one thing, Boss. You're going to be . . ."

Suddenly he stopped. The dismay in his eyes suggested he had been about to overstep the mark – not some generally accepted social mark but a private boundary of his own. He smiled awkwardly.

"What?" she prompted.

"Oh . . ." He started closing the books and stacking them, fussily. "I'll help any way I can. Count me in."

"What were you really going to say?"

"I'll tell you one day. Maybe. As you say – this isn't a good moment."

CHAPTER FIFTEEN

DEEPING HAD GIVEN Crownfield complimentaries, too, out of gratitude for his help, though the banker took it as a modest peace offering. Their boxes were level with each other, on opposite sides of the theatre. Crownfield was not at all surprised to see Julia Somerville with the playwright; that must be her husband in the wheelchair. He bowed to her and she smiled nervously back.

Dear Lexy noticed the exchange and wondered what she saw in the banker. Not his money. She was not the type. Nor, in his experience, anyway, was she at that stage in her marriage where a wife leaps from one kind of fidelity to another, equally binding.

In fact, how available was she? he wondered.

Mrs Crownfield, whose eyes missed nothing, saw the exchange, too. She did not immediately remark upon it but directed her husband's attention to other ladies in the auditorium below and asked who they were. He told her – those he knew – and realized with some amusement that she was casually working her way closer to Deeping's box. At last she described a woman immediately below it.

"She's a Mrs Monroe," he told her. "She's Kleinman's present mistress."

"And the lady with our host?" she asked at last.

"Mrs George Somerville. Julia Somerville. Her husband's in the wheelchair."

"Is she Dear Lexy's mistress?"

Crownfield laughed. "I very much doubt it, my dear. In fact, I doubt she's anyone's mistress." Almost as an afterthought he added, "Yet."

The light dimmed. The curtain rose. And further talk was impossible.

It was a witty piece. Even Julia, who had adored Michael Arlen's "The Green Hat" and shared every moment of its heroine Iris Storm's bitter, brittle odyssey – and had been quite sure she'd hate to see it parodied – was forced to laugh. She understood, though, why it had not enjoyed the huge success of Dear Lexy's other revues, for it was not a kindly skit. All London had raved about the book and Arlen himself had been hailed as the greatest new writer since Thackeray ("or even since Harriet Beecher Stowe!" as a Bright Young Thing on stage gushed about "Michael Ardent," the transparently disguised author). To see their absurd enthusiasm exposed to such pitiless dissection was not what fashionable London called "pleasure."

During the interval Julia remarked to Deeping, "I see Douglas Crownfield over there. And his wife, I presume?"

Deeping glanced toward George, whose attention seemed miles away. "Yes. Would you like an introduction?" He gave what he thought was a conspiratorial smile.

She stared back in surprise. "But I already know him."

"Ah . . ." He floundered.

She, in turn, grew even more bewildered. "You can't have forgotten, surely? You met me at his office. In fact, I have a bone to pick with you about that."

"Really?" He looked apprehensively toward George, who still seemed lost in some reverie.

"Yes. Crownfield behaved most oddly towards me. It was almost as if he suspected I was playing some sort of practical joke on him."

"How strange . . ."

"It grows even stranger. He hinted that you and I were in this joke together. Against him."

"Oh, he spoke about me, did he?"

"Only to say that you had asked him one or two things about banking procedure – in connection with your next play, he added. I wish you'd tell me what it was because I'm sure that's what made him suppose I was in cahoots with you." She smiled encouragingly.

Deeping took the gesture to imply that she was putting on some kind of act for her husband's sake – though *he* seemed as unconcerned as the man in the moon. Her smile also hinted, to a sophisticate who lived on hints and whispers, that she wanted his help in this masquerade. But if only she'd be more specific! "Surely you've known him for some time?" he prompted, studiously not glancing in George's direction.

"Not at all. In fact, that was my first-ever meeting with him, last week. The SPRP has banked with Crownfield's from the beginning, but until now I've only ever dealt with the local man in Notting Hill."

Deeping realized he was face to face with one of the most consummate actresses he had ever met. She ought to be in movies; she understated everything to perfection.

"Do tell me what you spoke to him about?" she went on.

Deeping could not see what she could possibly gain by it but he trusted what he supposed to be her infallible instinct. "Did you happen to read an article by a man called Wallace Baker in *John Bull* several weeks ago?" he asked. "The usual journalistic exaggeration about the famous Missing Generation . . . women having to take on men's work . . . running businesses . . . the embarrassment of asking bankers for loans . . ." He cleared his throat and raised a questioning eyebrow, meaning, *Am I doing it right?* "I just wondered if there was anything in it, that's all."

"Favour for favour, eh?" George barked suddenly. "What did this Crownfield tell you? Does it work?"

"He says it's pure imagination," Deeping answered. "Or, rather, *impure* imagination. Still – it's going to make a smash of a play!" He uttered this warning directly to Julia.

"I'm sure it will," she responded encouragingly, seeing that he clearly expected some kind of comment from her. But beneath the bright surface her thoughts were racing.

She saw it all now. Without George's crude interpretation, she, in her innocence, might not have twigged it for days, but suddenly she realized how it must have appeared to Crownfield. First the playwright, probing for revelations with his sly questions, planting the seeds of exciting possibilities; then his accomplice, putting the notion to a practical test, seeing if those seeds had already begun to germinate.

Fortunately the second act of "The Purple Hat" came to her rescue, for she was sure her confusion would give her away to so perceptive a man as Deeping. What *must* Crownfield think of her! She'd have to see him again – well, even without this utterly shame-making revelation she'd have to see him again, but now it was twice as urgent. She missed a lot of the second half; her imagination was playing variation after variation of that next meeting.

None of them was very satisfactory. The trouble was that this notion of "favour for favour" was now at the centre of her imaginary stage. Even worse was her insight that if that were, indeed, the only way to save her home and children, she would yield to it. But worst of all was the realization that if Crownfield were the Mr Moneybags in question, the prospect was far from repellent to her.

Also, running much deeper within her, beneath these momentary fears and embarrassments, was a new realization. All over the country there must be these hundreds – perhaps thousands – of women who had been forced not just to assume responsibility for their families' businesses but actually to run them. Thoughts of such responsibility had been much on her mind, of course; but the notion of actually managing the firm was new. She must get that *John Bull* article.

When the curtain calls were over and Dear Lexy had done his witty little speech, Julia gave Crownfield a parting smile and a nod across the half-acre of space that separated them.

The banker – and his wife – smiled warmly back. If Julia had been a lip-reader, she'd have seen the woman say, "Well, Douglas, I'd say the Kleinmans have the poorer bargain."

"As usual," her husband conceded with a grin.

A dozen times the following morning Julia's hand reached toward the telephone, hesitated, and withdrew. Then, when she had told herself, yet again, not to be such a ninny and had squared herself for one more attempt, the instrument rang and Mrs Lacy announced that Mr Crownfield was asking to speak to her.

She felt the blood drain from her face as she said, "Put him through."

He spoke in generalities for a while – the play last night and what a splendid occasion it had been – until her blood was calm again. Then he went on, "Forgive me for asking, but am I right in thinking that was your husband in the box with you – in the wheelchair?"

"Yes, that's right." She never knew what else to say. Explain about the accident? Describe how well George had coped? Be light-hearted? Or outdo their solemnity?

"Then I really do owe you the deepest apology, Mrs Somerville."

"I can't for the life of me imagine why."

"Some of the things I said when you came here – quite unwittingly, I do assure you – were, in the circumstances, in the worst possible . . ."

"Please, Mr Crownfield, I do understand. I mean, I realized at once that you . . . that is, Mr Deeping has since told me what he . . . what you . . . oh dear! Would it be possible for me to call on you again?"

"Indeed, yes! Nothing could give me greater . . ."

"You see, I wasn't entirely frank with you. The problems I mentioned are not the important ones for me at the moment. I have something much more serious I'd like to discuss. So . . ."

He interrupted. "I believe I may know something about them already. In fact, I was going to . . ."

"You know?" she asked in surprise.

"Certain inquiries you asked our Mr Crimmond to make? I was going to suggest a meeting."

"Now?"

"It's almost time for lunch."

"Oh, yes, I'm sorry."

He laughed. "No! I meant are you free? Too much to hope for, I suppose? Attractive and vivacious young women are never free for lunch."

She took her cue from him, suddenly changing her tone. "I'll consider it. Where?"

"The Ritz? Shall we say, in half an hour?"

"My favourite," she replied – never having been there in her life. She came from that section of the upper class which prefers not to "go about."

"Will you arrive in that beautiful Daimler you had the other day? You'll put up my stock no end."

"Oh!" The disappointment in her tone was plain. "It's gone back to the works. I'll take a taxi."

"You'll do no such thing. I'll collect you. *A tout à l'heure, madame!*"

Julia could be as surprised (or alarmed, or outraged) as the next woman; but whatever the emotion there was an almost unreachable core of her that remained calm and together. People often wonder what her "secret" is; but there is none. She has always carried that inner confidence with her. For example, when Crownfield rang off she did not, as so many women would, go into a dither about not being dressed for the Ritz, not having the right hairdo . . . nail polish . . . make-up, and so on.

True, she wasn't dressed for the Ritz, and it undoubtedly caused her a momentary ripple of annoyance, but at heart she didn't care a sou for what others might think, and she wasn't going to let worries about it spoil the most exciting surprise in many a month.

So she did the best she could with her hair and face – and suddenly Crownfield was at the door. She had expected a grand car but it was just an ordinary London taxicab, one of the last survivors of those waspish little red Renaults that had flooded onto the streets just before the war.

"Showing its age," he commented as he held open the door for her. "Like me, I fear."

She wondered whether seeing her had suddenly made him aware of their difference in years. "Aren't we all?" she replied.

He chuckled. "Hoist with my own petard!" He gave the directions and climbed in. "It's just that I can't believe my luck, finding what is probably the one hole of the year in your diary."

"Actually, you're lucky finding my *diary,*" she told him. "Until today I felt sure it was lost."

He drew back and looked at her, as if he needed the distance for a proper assessment. "The truth is," he said seriously, "that, having behaved so abominably the other day, I'm lucky you even admit to having a diary."

It was perfectly balanced between a joke and an apology, and it closed the subject between them for ever – as a source of awkwardness, anyway.

Taxis were not then allowed in the royal parks; theirs had to go along by Bayswater to Marble Arch and then work its way down through Grosvenor Square, Berkeley Square, and so into Piccadilly. Crossing by Marble Arch he watched her closely; she knew he was waiting to see whether she looked back toward Connaught Square or not. How astute of him, she thought, to realize that such a gesture, at such a moment, would be significant. She did not turn her head; it seemed to please him. Later she came to realize that he set great store by such little gestures. It was Solomon's kind of wisdom, which could casually suggest hacking a baby in two in order to discover its true mother.

Perhaps that was why he took such care to make his own behaviour *un*predictable. At Grosvenor Square they detoured to avoid some road works. He suddenly pointed out Tallulah Bankhead's house and remarked, "It's a funny thing about this street. It's always had associations with scandalous women. I don't mean notorious women but women who have scandalized men by their superior intellect or outspoken wit. Did you know the famous Bluestockings first met here?"

Moments later, in Berkeley Square, he pointed out Lansdowne House, "where George III signed away the American colonies. And guess who lives there now? Gordon Selfridge of Chicago – sitting in that very same room, no doubt, and planning to acquire all England in time."

It struck her that, far from being unpredictable, he was like a suave man-about-town who, having consented to squire his little niece around, and having found her a great deal more nubile than he remembered her, was suddenly at a loss what to do about it.

Moments later the taxi dropped them at the Ritz. She strolled through its doors as if she came there every day.

But when they met up again, having visited their respective cloakrooms, she asked, "Have I a right to be enjoying myself like this? I'm sure Crimmond's inquiries discovered naught for my comfort."

"Do you want to talk about that now?" He led the way through the restaurant, where the head waiter greeted him by name, shook him by the hand, and led them at once to *his* table; not by a flicker of an eyelid did the man indicate that her dress was somewhat . . . well, not exactly dowdy but *ordinary* for this grand place. Not that she needed such a reminder; the great looking glasses at each end of the salon were enough.

Crownfield must have noticed her rapid survey of the other women present. With something of a sneer he observed, "Any day now we'll read of a girl being arrested for masquerading in feminine attire – like that poor vicar last week."

She gave him a grateful smile, brief enough to show she appreciated his thoughtfulness more than the reassurance itself, and then asked him, "Do you always shake the head waiter by the hand?" It was something no other Englishman would dream of doing.

"Always." He chuckled. "And, as a result, I am remembered by name, and accorded *my* table, at many more establishments than my patronage warrants. I asked you just now if you wished to discuss our inquiries?"

"I don't, of course, but I suppose we ought to."

He gave a single nod of assent.

"Is it . . . very bad?" she ventured.

The cocktail waiter approached.

"Hello, Frederick. What's good today?" Crownfield asked.

The waiter grinned. "The latest is the Lloyd George, sir. Drink too many and you begin to see *two* Liberal Parties instead of one!"

They laughed. "Try a manhattan," Crownfield suggested. "Frederick mixes the best in London."

He let her take her first sip before he went on. "It's good news in a sense."

"In what sense? That is heavenly." She took another sip.

"In the sense that it is accurate, complete, and up to date."

"I see. You mean in every other sense it's bad."

"I'm afraid so. Tell me how much you already know. What did Crimmond tell you?" He meant, of course, *How much do you remember?* It was a test.

They ordered their meal. Crownfield had expected her to let him choose for both of them; her independence did not annoy him; he simply noted it in his mental card index as another fact about her.

She told him what Crimmond had reported, and also the situation the books had revealed. "Since then," she added, "I've managed to make a fairly random check of just a few hundred of what must be thousands of documents, stored here there and everywhere, and I've discovered more than a dozen debtors not recorded in the accounts."

He closed his eyes and pursed his lips. "And I know how much time it takes to prove a negative thing like that. A *dozen,* you say?" He shook his head.

"I just wonder if somehow Sidney Gold knows about it? He's so eager to acquire the firm, you know. And wouldn't he be happy to discover it was worth double, after buying it at book value! What have you learned about him? Crimmond told me next to nothing about that."

"May I say something improper to you, Mrs Somerville?" His eyes twinkled at seeing her confusion but he spared her a reply by adding at once: "I believe Somerville's should find a new banker. I'm as sure as can be that Sidney Gold has an informer inside Wallis & Thorn. Whether or not he knows about these unrecorded assets is another matter, of course. But even so he knows too much for the good of your husband's firm."

She smiled. "Your suggestion would only be improper if you added a rider that we move to *your* bank."

"Exactly – which is why I left it to you. Oh – may we always combine so harmoniously when improper suggestions are made! But seriously though, your bank *is* going to call in the loan this week, just as Gold predicted. Until a couple of days ago, only four directors and a secretary knew it, one of whom must therefore be Sidney's man. Much too highly placed for comfort."

She paused before saying, "Alternatively, we could stay with them a while longer and feed them misleading information."

He caught his breath and then laughed. "You constantly surprise me. Have you given this so much thought already? I mean, why was that suggestion so ready to hand?"

Her tone pooh-poohed any pretension to shrewdness. "It's exactly what I did last year when my housekeeper suspected the cook was going to walk out on us three hours before an important dinner party, unless she got a five-shilling rise. So we buttered her up no end . . . told her how utterly indispensable she was, and so on – and got her replacement ready at an hour's notice. So when she downed tools we just smiled sweetly and hoped it would be convenient to have all her belongings out of the house by six?" She chuckled. "I'm sure your world of business, for all its manly intrigues, would seem plain sailing to any woman who's managed a large household."

He took her seriously. "Not to mention running a large national charity," he mused aloud.

She gave a tense little shiver. "You're stirring up one of my nightmares, Mr Crownfield."

He raised an eyebrow. "You have many?"

She bit her lip, poised awkwardly between wanting, on the one hand, to confess and, on the other, to make light of it.

"Well," he went on briskly. "You must have formed some outlines of plans for saving your husband's firm?"

She shrugged, reluctant to voice ideas that, to a man of his experience, would probably seem childish. But his eyes encouraged her.

"Obviously," she ventured, "the first thing we must do is change our accounting system so that we know how much profit or loss each bit of the firm is making."

He nodded approvingly. "And your husband – will he ..?"

"He'll fight the very idea. He'd hate to learn that his three favourite schemes are losing the most money."

"Would you try to talk him into it?"

She told him then about a small legacy her mother had left her – and how, upon certain conditions, she might be willing to apply it to the rescue of Somerville's.

As she spoke she noticed a subtle transformation come over him. He relaxed. He grew even more affable. It was almost as if she were proposing to rescue his bank rather than Somerville's. And then it struck her: That was, indeed, the case. Until this moment he had been prepared to put up the necessary funds himself. All the other implications of that – following on what Deeping had told her about his interview at the bank – dawned on her, too. She was flattered, and more than a little thrilled.

The hors d'oeuvres trolley appeared. When they had finished their selection he murmured, "Was it Oscar Wilde – how long will it be before we can say his name without lowering our voices – was it he who said that a question of some delicacy usually turns out to be a question of considerable *in*delicacy? I'm afraid I must next ask a question of some delicacy, my dear. The conditions your lawyers or financial advisors must lay down before you can prudently commit your own money may impose severe strains on your marriage. The question then arises – what sort of a marriage is it, anyway?"

He expected this bluntness to shock the truth out of her. To his surprise she merely repeated flatly, "What sort of a marriage is it anyway?"

"I see." He moved swiftly to the next question. "Bearing in mind that, given the nature of your husband's affliction, you could soon become the sole proprietor – if only as caretaker for your son – you don't think that, despite your present criticisms, you might then feel some sort of sentimental obligation to maintain things just as they are? A sacred trust, as it were?"

"Most certainly not."

"You already have ideas of your own, then?"

She had ideas of Baring's, of course, but she didn't want to admit as much – not yet, anyway. She adopted them without a blush.

She surprised herself, not only at how much she remembered but also at how convincingly she was able to reproduce it in her own kind of language. Indeed, by the time she had finished she could no longer have said how much was due to Baring and how much was truly her own.

Crownfield, whose opinion of her had been steadily rising over the past hour, was even more impressed. She brought him back to earth with her conclusion: "But, of course, until we know our true present position, all these are mere pipe dreams."

A bevy of waiters came with the main course; cold salmon for him, tournedos Rossini for her. "A cold fish and a red-blooded eater of meat," he commented wryly.

"We make a good pair then," she countered.

Their eyes met. He almost took her up on the hinted offer but instead postponed his response with a smile. She felt sure it was only a postponement. It seemed, then, that she might choose her own meal if it amused her, but not the hour nor the form of her seduction; that illusion must be left to him.

Their conversation, with its many amusing asides, turned what had started as a flirtation into the beginning of a deeper friendship. The glow of it lasted right through the meal and on into the taxi ride to Connaught Square. As they approached her home he asked, out of the blue, if she had since read the Wallace Baker article that had so excited Dear Lexy, and which, indirectly, had led to the luncheon they had just enjoyed. She admitted she had not but added that Lexy had summarized it for her in embarrassing detail.

He gave a satisfied smile. "Then may I say, Mrs Somerville, that one of the hardest moments of my life came when I had to decline the role our playwright friend had allotted me in his romantic drama."

He watched calmly to see the effect of his words upon her. She descended from his taxi and closed the door before she turned to reply. Through the open window she said, "I should so hate to be a playwright, Mr Crownfield. Wouldn't you? The minute you leave the theatre the actors are rewriting your script behind your back."

"Ah! Is that what you're doing – rewriting Dear Lexy's script behind his back?"

She gave him a catlike grin.

"Because it's only fair to warn you," he went on, "that if I were to be offered the identical role in a different script – revised, let us say, by *you* – then I should not only be delighted, I should be honoured, to accept it."

CHAPTER SIXTEEN

WALLIS & THORN DROPPED their bombshell on the Thursday of the following week, just as Crownfield – and Sidney Gold – had predicted. Despite her long anticipation of it, despite all rational arguments to the contrary, the news terrified her. Her mind could not relinquish its images of poverty – the mean streets of Dalston, the bare-board floors, the eternal smell of cabbages and drains, drunkards reeling through the fog from one feeble gaslamp to the next . . . And all the while she had to go on smiling, pretending to George that she knew nothing of what was happening out there in the big, manly world of business.

For days he went on as if nothing were amiss, but he pulled such a long face and sighed so many sighs that she saw he was aiming at a kind of inverse confession – that is, she would have to badger it out of him. So she fought back her fears and played along.

When it was finally out, she continued the charade. She was calm and "magnificent" and everything a wife of her stiff-upper-lip background ought to be. And all the while she was watching him like a hawk.

These next few minutes would reveal which he considered the more important – his business or his wife and children. Her mother's legacy would be very much in his mind – in both their minds. Would he ask for that money outright? Would he, more cunningly, make it impossible for her to withhold it? Or would he honourably wait for her to make the offer?

"It can't be your fault," she assured him. "After all the years you ran the firm so successfully. It must be Opie and the others – they've let you down."

He was almost tempted, but some remnant of public-school honour, or perhaps an instinct for self-preservation, held him back, "No, girlie, it *is* my fault. I've overreached. Ambition, you see. Too much to do, too little time to do it in."

"What nonsense, George. Doctor Jordan says you'll live for years. Look, are you sure the books are *right*? All our assets – are you sure they're all properly recorded? Are all the valuations . . ."

"D'you think I haven't had that checked?" He looked like a hunted creature. She knew him well enough to know he was neither lying nor covering a half-truth. So he was either served by incompetents or by shiftless idlers who knew he'd never check the books himself.

"I wanted to be sure you and the children would be provided for," he explained.

She hesitated before she answered. "We shouldn't be entirely destitute."

He frowned, none too convincingly. "Oh . . . that. Yes. I'd forgotten. Or not forgotten but I always thought *your* money would go for Lydia's dowry."

"Well then," she answered brightly, "perhaps it's just as well the days of the dowry have gone for ever."

She held her breath while he wrestled with himself. The struggle ended with a morose chuckle. "Bloody ironical, eh?"

"What is?"

"Oh . . . nothing." He sighed once more.

Again she let the silence grow until it forced him to say, "That's all it would need . . ." He caught her eye and changed tack. "No. Of course not. It would be out of the question."

Here it was then.

"Absolutely out of the question," he repeated, so firmly that for a moment he convinced her. But then he added "Eh?" to let her know that a few more shoves would do it.

She was free of him at last – morally, spiritually – as she had long been physically free. It was not a freedom she had especially sought; it had been forced upon her. She had to accept it, and, accepting it, had to use it, too.

"Perhaps," she offered a compromise, "if we merely let Wallis & Thorn know we intend to use my legacy . . . perhaps they'd stay their hand long enough for us to raise the wind in the proper commercial way?"

He knew how slim that chance was but, believing the hook to be at the other end of the line, he decided to play her at that for a day or two. "Who manages the funds?" he asked. "Is it still with your parents' bank – Coutts, wasn't it?"

"Not any more. Funnily enough I transferred it all to Crownfield's just . . . well, recently. He's the SPRP banker – the man I was talking to Dear Lexy about, remember? We owe Deeping a dinner, by the way. I know! Let's throw a party – a super-big party. Rumours are bound to start circulating. We'll just knock them on the head."

"*Throw* a party?" he echoed her distastefully. "Where do you pick up such vulgar Americanisms, girlie?"

The following day she shortened the line. "Crownfield's proving just a mite sticky," she told George. "I thought he'd agree as a simple matter of course."

"But?" She could see the fear whiten his face.

"Well, he raises no objection in principle but – it's only common prudence, I suppose – he'd like to see the firm's books . . ."

"Out of the question!" George barked at once.

She frowned. "He wouldn't find anything wrong, would he?"

"Of course not!"

He was beginning to develop what she called privately his "curry face." She girded herself for the explosion. "Have you mentioned the possibility of this rescue to Wallis & Thorn yet?" she asked.

"Oh, very likely, I must say!"

"Good. That's one thing less to worry about."

"Why?" His anger was tinged with puzzlement.

"Well, dear, you know what a tiny village the City is. Someone's bound to say he hears Somerville's are in trouble – and someone else is bound to add that rescue was offered but George Somerville refused to open his books. However, if Wallis & Thorn don't even know . . ."

"Dammit, girlie, it's not up to Crownfield – or any other bloody outsider – to say whether that money is available or not. You have absolute discretion over it."

"I know that, dear – of *course*. And as far as I'm concerned, the money is already pledged to the firm. But don't you see? That only makes it even more likely that Crownfield will drop a hint here and there?"

"No, I don't see it," he answered grumpily.

"Look at it from his point of view. He asks to see a firm's books and is met with point blank refusal – which can only arouse the worst possible suspicion. And then his client, me, against his strongest advice, puts every last penny into the firm – and loses it . . ."

"But it won't be lost. For the love of God, girlie, whose side . . ."

"I know that, and you know it, too. But *Crownfield* doesn't – and it's his thoughts I'm trying to follow. If I lost every penny, fellow bankers would be bound to dig him in the ribs and ask what sort of advice he's giving these days. So, out of self-protection, he'd have to cover himself by dropping a hint or two now."

"You seem to know a lot about banking suddenly!"

"I know about human nature, my dear."

He snorted. "So much for their famous pledge of confidentiality!"

"Crownfield needn't *say* a word. In banking circles, I'm sure, a single wink, a finger laid against the nose, a doubtful murmur – these are enough. Why *couldn't* he look at the books, George? There honestly isn't anything murky is there?"

"He wouldn't understand."

To her surprise, George's anger had subsided to a grumpy resentment; she realized that, in his mind, he had already conceded the unthinkable. Here was an unsuspected soft side to the man. Her confidence climbed a further degree.

"Understand what?"

"The way our clients take years to settle their accounts."

She laughed as she gave him the peg on which to hang his concession: "That's his trade, dear. It's in his blood."

The following morning the books were delivered to Crownfield's. Julia left the SPRP early, intending to have a sandwich lunch with the banker and plot their next moves in the light of whatever he had discovered in the accounts. She walked south toward Bayswater, where the chance of a taxi was best; but at the corner of Pembridge Gardens a familiar Rolls-Royce, gold plated where others had chrome, came to an unexpected halt. The chauffeur sprang out and held open the passenger door.

She had a moment of panic, being unable to remember her most recent role with him. Ah yes – Worried Mother Fighting for Home and Children.

He, for his part, was Bland Uncle Sidney again. "Allow me to offer you a lift, Mrs Somerville. You took me by surprise. It's a bit early for you."

"Thank you, but I am meeting a friend for lunch in Marylebone High Street."

Crownfield's bank was just three streets beyond that, in Cavendish Square.

"That's good – and bad," he remarked. "But hop in. I'll take you there."

The interior reeked of some kind of cloying spice. As the car set off he added, "It's good because it gives us more time for a chat."

"And bad?"

"Oh" – he laughed – "it's too close to Harley Street – the Valley of the Shadow of Death." He tapped his chest. "They keep pestering me for an engine overhaul."

"You have some trouble with your heart?"

"Naah!" He was jovially scornful. "There's many as think I ain't got no heart – but you know better. Anyway, the dickey bird says you're going to rescue Somerville's with your own money. Tsk! Tsk! Tsk!" He shook his head sadly.

The suddenness of the accusation caught her off balance. Her face betrayed her; she could see the satisfaction in his eyes – satisfaction that he'd got it out of her, but also anger that it was true.

So George, despite his denial, must have dropped a hint or two to Wallis & Thorn . . . Never mind. She'd consider the implications of that later. For the moment she had to deal with Gold – and with what her face had confirmed as fact. "I could see no other way," she explained.

"I told you the other way. I thought we was agreed . . ."

"Yes, of course – I mean I couldn't see any other way to bring it about, what we agreed."

He gave an exasperated little laugh of disbelief. "Beats me. I offer to pay over the odds for the firm on condition you'll talk your old man into a quick sale. So the only way you can see – correct me if I got it wrong – the only way you can see to talk him round is to pour enough geld in to make the sale unnecessary! Or so you think."

"What are you implying – 'So I think'?"

His tone was withering. "No amount of money is going to save Somerville's, my dear. In your heart you know it. Fair enough – you'll put off the evil day for another . . . what? Three . . . four years? But in the end the same bad management will cause the same bad situation. Only it's not the same, is it! 'Cos this time good ol' Sidney Gold ain't standin' by with a fistful of readies, is he! No, he's gone and bought out Hooper's or Mulliner's and he's taking the trade from under your noses."

They were travelling up Sussex Gardens; she forced herself not to glance toward Eliot's lodgings there.

He cleared his throat. " I hope you're not getting silly ideas, Mrs Somerville. I'm not raising my bid, you know."

"As you haven't actually made a bid, that's easily promised."

They were crossing the Edgware Road. "I'll give you fifty thou'," he said quietly, "lock, stock, and barrel – by which I mean mostly your goodwill. You've not got much else to trade."

The size of the offer surprised her but she managed to look disappointed. "You'll have to do a great deal better than that," she tried.

"No I won't," he continued in the same quiet, amused voice. "Two weeks from now you'll be glad to take thirty." He shifted his weight and added – as if it had only just struck him – "Of course, if you do make this small loan, you'll insist on being given power of attorney?"

"I beg your pardon?" The subject had naturally cropped up in her discussions with Crownfield – and, indeed, with Eliot; both had agreed it should be her minimum condition for parting with the money. But why was Sidney Gold so interested?

"Attorney?" she asked vaguely. "But George and I have the same attorney."

"No! *Power* of attorney. That means . . . oh, never mind. Get someone to explain. Crownfield'll understand." He grinned. "That is where you're going?"

She pulled a rueful face. "No use trying to pull the wool over your eyes, Mr Gold."

"Millions have tried," he answered complacently.

She was sure she'd never mentioned Crownfield to him. Why was he flaunting his knowledge of her private life like this? To intimidate her, perhaps. "Power of attorney . . ." She repeated the phrase a couple of times, as if she'd forget it otherwise.

They pulled up in Wigmore Street, at the corner of the square, out of sight of Crownfield's offices. "There's just the off chance someone might recognize this little runabout of mine," Gold explained. "Just remember one thing – no one is to know of my offer, except the clever little gel who's going to come out of this trailing clouds of glory. No banks. No lawyers. No one. If word leaks out, *everything's* off. And that includes the kid gloves."

She stood there, doing her best to appear lost and defenceless, until the last flash of gold marked his turning into Regent Street.

CHAPTER SEVENTEEN

DURING THOSE FIRST three months of 1926 George showed a most variable interest in his firm; or, more charitably, his interest remained as intense as ever but it had to divide the day with a new regime set by Imogen Davis, who was now his sole nurse, round the clock. She started taking him home at lunchtime, something he had never done before; it was "for a nap," he explained. The hour of his return to Forge Lane grew later and later until, as often as not, his only afternoon presence was a disembodied voice on the telephone. Then would come an attack of conscience and for a day or two he would stay on at the works until well after the evening hooter. And then the whole cycle would begin again.

Julia was in two minds at these developments. To her surprise, her initial anger toward "the Davis creature" and what she suspected was going on between her and George began to wane, tempered by a quite novel feeling of liberation. It was unconnected with finance or the daily round; he had never stinted her money, nor had he ever taken a bossy sort of interest in her comings and goings. Rather, it was emotional. Throughout her married life she had always included George in her thoughts and decisions. If she looked at a new hat or frock, and liked it, her second thought was always, *I wonder if George would think so, too?* If she read an amusing item in the papers, she'd say to herself, "I must remember to show that to him." Almost every thought, great or trivial, contained some reference to George. She belonged to him – not in the sense that he owned her, but in the sense in which she "belonged" to London or to the SPRP. And it was that sense of belonging from which she now felt liberated.

Perhaps fortunately, the firm's financial crisis gave her little chance to follow up this change in her emotional life. She dropped all her activities except the SPRP, and spent every spare hour of her evenings at Forge Lane, trying to restore some order to the books. She would have dearly loved to sack the entire accounts staff, about whom the kindest that could be said was that they were incompetent and lazy – especially the chief, a man called Huxtable. With his blunted nose, fleshy lips, receding chin, sleek hide, and swelling paunch, he reminded Julia of nothing so much as a circus sealion – especially as he had a disconcerting habit of placing the backs of his hands together, in front of that belly, and interleaving his fingers as he rubbed them up and down. She longed to grasp those flippers and clap them together, still back-to-back, saying, "Look – *that's* the way the other sealions do it."

Ironically, after some six weeks of delving, she discovered that Somerville & Son were not verging on insolvency – were nowhere near it, in fact – and thus the pledge of her own small inheritance was not needed.

"I can see exactly what's going to happen," she told Eliot, who, as he had promised, often joined in these evening hunting parties. "A great sigh of relief from George, a pat on the head to me, no assignment of my money, no power of attorney . . . and then it'll start all over again." She looked uncertainly up at him and added, "I don't think this is *quite* the time to tell George the happy news, do you?"

He leaped nimbly over a few awkward replies – but implied them nonetheless in his response: "Does the Guv'nor's will contain some standard clause about revoking any powers of attorney granted during his lifetime?"

"No," she answered – revealing that she had already checked.

"Then I agree absolutely." He flashed her a smile that turned her over. "This is not the time to spread that sort of good news."

"I feel the most awful jesuit," she said. "But you're right."

It amused him to see how swiftly she had transferred half of her decision to him.

She started packing up the books. "I'm not going to dig any deeper. We know enough already."

"In particular," he pointed out, "we know the balance sheets are concocted in such a way that none of these unrecorded assets show up. I mean, the accounts *look* complete. Maybe the auditors should have picked up on it, but when it's a wholly owned family company . . . anyway, what it means is that Somerville's will have to sweep out its own stables here."

"Yes, that's the only thing that remains. All the other papers are ready. The power of attorney is stamped and registered, all it needs is George's signature. The only other thing is that he must agree to a proper accounting system before I put in my money." She pulled a glum face. "And that'll be hardest of all – believe you me."

"I do. I do."

As they walked out by the main gate, Eliot suggested a stroll along the towpath to Kilburn Lane, at the far end of the cemetery. She could pick up a cab there.

The afternoon rain had died away; it was now late twilight in a clearing sky, with a third-quarter moon rising among wisps of silvery cloud. On the far side of Scrubs Lane, in the forecourt of the Mitre pub, stood a van that had been converted to make a mobile fish-and-chip fryer.

"That's Florrie's," he declared in surprise.

Julia's surprise was greater. "You know those people?"

"Her usual pitch is at Paddington Green. I suggested she should try her luck out here, too." He turned to her with sudden eagerness as they crossed the road. "May I be even bolder and invite you to dine?"

"Why not? Try anything once."

He stopped in front of the serving hatch and gave their order: "Two Lillian Gish tonight, Florrie, and make that a spanner's worth of chips."

Florrie dropped a brief grin in Julia's direction. "Evening, Mr Baring. You was right about this pitch, I must say." Now she studied Julia more closely. "Brought the mother-of-pearl out for a bit of tommy-tucker, have we?"

"My pitch-and-toss, no less," Eliot told her impressively.

And Florrie was impressed. "My, my," she remarked.

He produced a pound note. The woman's face fell. "A lost-and-found – ain't you got nothing smaller?"

While he was delving in his pockets Julia drew a shilling from her purse – a bob, in everyday English. "Will a door-knob do?" she asked sweetly, in best Belgravian.

Florrie laughed as she took the coin. "One in the mince-pie for you, my lad," she told Eliot, who was shaking liberal gouts of vinegar and salt over their supper.

"Can't teach you a thing," he pretended to grumble as they walked away.

"I used to know them all once," she explained. "Theresa Ashbury taught me them, just after the war." The smell of fish and chips, especially with the vinegar rising off them, brought it all back vividly. She gave an involuntary shiver.

"I'm sorry. Are you cold?" he asked, misunderstanding.

"Nope." But she took the arm he had half offered.

To avoid a somewhat merry party emerging from the pub they had gone the long way round the van. When they turned back to call out a goodnight to Florrie, Julia's eye caught sight of the coachbuilder's plate, which was rivetted to the bodywork below the back door. By long habit she stooped to read it.

"Hah!" she cried. "Just look who we have here!"

Gold's Commercial Bodies, it read.

They went down the steps to the Mitre Wharf, which led, in turn, to the towpath. "These fish are still red hot," he said. "Shall we start in on the chips?"

Ladylike instincts she could not suppress forced her to glance guiltily over her shoulder before she took the first crisp finger of deep-fried potato. "I've never done this in my life," she observed. "Well – once. But, oh, my father was furious!"

"Eating fish and chips out of newspaper, out of doors, in the dark – that's easily half the joy of living in England."

After her first bite of fish, when the crisp batter coating mixed on her palate with the soft, white flesh, she had to agree; she could not remember when she had last eaten anything so wonderfully scrumptious.

"Apropos Sidney Gold," she remarked. "I don't think he can possibly know about Somerville's accounts – I mean, not in any detail. He must know how sloppy they are, and he probably suspects there are unrecorded assets lying around for a new broom to sweep up. But I don't see how he could be in any conspiracy."

Eliot did not answer.

"You don't agree?" she prompted.

"I guess I do," he answered reluctantly. "And yet I still worry that he called on you so soon after the Guv'nor's accident – practically in the week he returned full time to Forge Lane. As if he'd been lying in wait until then and suddenly saw everything returning to normal and his chances slipping away. I just don't like unexplained coincidences. And look at the inside dope someone at the bank was feeding him."

"But if there is a conspiracy, Eliot, it's even more sloppy than our accounting system. And Sidney Gold doesn't strike me as being like that."

"I know. That's the argument on the other side. Nothing's ever clear-cut in business, is it. I don't suppose we're ever going to know the truth here. We just have to keep all possibilities *always* in mind. Even the ones we can't openly mention – or not yet."

She swallowed the last of her fish and wiped her fingers into the newspaper before she resumed her hold on his arm. "You're an easy teacher, my dear," she murmured. "Max told me the same thing, only more brutally."

When they had finished the last of the chips he screwed all the papers into a ball, which he held loosely in his free hand. "There's a trash – no, litter basket by the bridge," he said.

"D'you know what I'd like – now we've started on this slumming lark? I'd like to find a nice pub and sit in the public bar and drink a pint of bitter."

"English beer." He spoke in as neutral a tone as he could manage.

"Yes," she teased. "Nice, warm, flat, bitter ale. Fish and chips is only Part One of the course, you know?"

They found a pub in the Harrow Road. The public bar was full of wassailers so they sat in the snug instead, where the fire glowed cheerfully and the volume of the singing was tolerable.

"When all the dust has settled," she began, "when the threat is over and the accounts are straight and it's quite obvious to all that my little contribution wasn't necessary . . ."

"Ho–back a mo," he exclaimed. "Does this come under the heading of keeping all possibilities in mind?"

She nodded. "Let me put it to you directly. The money I'm talking about comes to around twelve thousand. Would that put a full-scale version of the BI into the air?"

She expected incredulity . . . gratitude . . . something; but he was utterly poker faced as he replied, "Sure. Easily. But that wouldn't be the problem. If she performs as well as the model, she's going to rouse a lot of interest – by which I mean orders . . ."

Now it was she who interrupted, wanting to bring him back to her line of thought. "Could you add anything to my twelve?"

"Some. A couple more, maybe – which, with the value of my patents, would come near to matching your twelve. But the value of the patents wouldn't be working capital, which was the point I was coming to. We could end up in the ironical situation that the more wildly successful we were at raking in the orders, the less of our company would we end up actually owning! I mean, we'd have to go to the market for capital, and that would dilute our share."

She felt herself adopting his watchful stance. How odd, she thought, that they could discuss almost anything under the sun, feeling perfectly relaxed; yet as soon as it came to something like this they became a pair of territorial animals jockeying for space. "What would you call wildly successful?" she asked. "Come to that, what would you call moderately successful? Or *un*successful?"

"I guess any order below twelve wouldn't be worth it. Wildly successful would be upwards of a hundred. Realistic would be three to five dozen."

"And the working capital for that many?"

"To make four dozen a year? Say, twenty thousand. But the rule is you should always add fifty percent to whatever you *think* you'll need. And then there's the cost of research on the next plane, or planes. And provision for failures." He sighed. "If we didn't start out

with at least thirty, thirty-five thousand . . . well, w
disaster for quite a few years. And, as I say – a man
would be almost as bad as an abject failure." He laugh
"But why are we talking like this? Haven't we ski
somewhere?"

She shook her head, refusing to join his slightly e
amusement. "Ever since that day we drove down to Allb
I've had no doubt in my mind. If it hadn't been for this f
the accounts, I'd have given George no peace. Your plan
built. It *must* fly."

He looked into her eyes and saw such determination ther
such strength, too – that he wondered whether even she we
aware of its power. It made him shiver. "Wow!" he murn
Then, raising his glass, he added, "Not my plane. Ours."

She smiled, relaxing at last. "Ours," she echoed.

CHAPTER EIGHTEEN

WHATEVER THE routine of Julia's day, she was hardly ever at home in
Connaught Square in the early afternoon – which explained Mrs
Crooke's surprise at seeing her there at a quarter to three; but it did
not explain her alarm.

It was the last Friday in March, 1926. Julia had brought home all
the legal papers, which were finally ready for George's signature: the
power of attorney, the acceptance of her assignment, and the one
that was going to send him through the ceiling – his agreement to
reorganize the accounts department.

"Oh, Mrs Somerville!" the housekeeper exclaimed. "We didn't
expect you home so soon."

"Ah, well, it's these documents, you see. They must be signed
today. Is my husband in?"

"No." The reply was a little too quick, a little too brusque. "I've
just been up there and his door is locked. That's a sign . . ."

"Locked?" Julia echoed in astonishment. "But we've never locked
any . . ."

"They'd only be down the road in Hyde Park. They always lock it

hen they . . . when they go out. Yes – Speakers' Corner. The
aster loves to hear the speakers all, er, speaking away. That's
here they'll be."

By now Julia could hardly fail to be aware of the poor woman's
iscomfort. The door *was* no doubt locked. But that George and the
Davis creature were listening to the speakers in Hyde Park was as
ikely as snow in August. "Oh, how vexing!" she exclaimed. "Perhaps I'll just slip upstairs and put these on his desk." She tapped the
documents and smiled affably. "Lend me your keys, there's a good
soul. I'll return them at once."

"Oh, but let me do it for you, madam," she volunteered, turning
even paler. "You could pop down to the park – such a lovely day for
a change – and fetch him back. I'm sure you'll find them at Speakers'
. . ."

Her voice tailed off. She was going to break down. Julia saw no
point in pressing her to an open confession of scandal. "Is Miss Lydia
with them?" she asked suddenly.

The relief was enormous as Mrs Crooke informed her that the girl
was in her schoolroom.

"I'll see her first, then," Julia said. "Perhaps they'll be back by the
time I'm done."

She went up to the schoolroom, trying with little success *not* to
picture her husband and . . . and that . . . no word strong enough
occurred to her. She realized she had passed beyond sorrow. All she
could feel was anger. She stood a moment before the schoolroom
door, counting it down.

She found Lydia and Miss Nightingale, her new governess, working their way through the strong German verbs. They were as
surprised as Mrs Crooke had been. But the governess showed no
alarm. Was she better at concealment than the housekeeper, or was
the knowledge of George's treachery restricted, even in so small a
household?

"Would I be interrupting something terribly important?" Julia
asked.

"No!" Lydia answered emphatically.

Miss Nightingale said sweetly, "We can always extend the lesson."

"I've been thinking about our conversation the other day. Have
you mentioned it to Lydia?"

The governess nodded.

"About going away to school?" Lydia asked. "I don't want to."

Julia smiled encouragingly. "Don't worry, darling. It won't happen against your will. But I just wonder if you've really thought
about it. Not this year, but perhaps next. When you reach twelve,
say. Wouldn't you like to spread your wings then? Go away like
Robert, and make more friends?"

Lydia glanced up at Miss Nightingale before she replied. "I have all the friends I need here in Bayswater. And around Allbury. D'you want to know how many? I counted them. Three bosom friends, thirteen close ones, nine sort-of . . . and oodles on nodding acquaintance. Both Miss Nightingale and I agree that school is unlikely to provide more – and, in any case, do I need more?"

The two women smiled at each other. The governess raised her eyebrows as if to say, *This battle is yours.*

Julia said, "I suppose I should have known better than to ask. If you want something, you jolly well make sure we know about it. So – having demolished me – you can return to pitting your strength against the German verbs once more."

"Oh, I shouldn't mind discussing it just a little bit," Lydia responded hastily.

But her mother merely grinned back as she closed the door behind her.

She returned downstairs to find a much calmer Mrs Crooke waiting with the news that the master and Miss Davis had just returned from the park.

"Oh splendid," Julia said. "Perhaps you'd be good enough to come up with me? I need two witnesses to these signatures."

Imogen Davis was reading Conrad's "Victory" out loud. George was all affability. "Well, well, girlie – what a nice surprise!"

"I hope this humour lasts," she remarked as she stooped to kiss his forehead. No perfume, no telltale dab of lipstick betrayed him.

"Oh?" He was instantly more wary.

"Rest easy. It's only the document Wallis & Thorn have been waiting to see all these weeks." She laid it on the drawing pad before him.

He glanced up at Imogen, who put his specially adapted fountain pen between his teeth. "Where?" he asked, as clearly as the mouthful allowed.

"There, just below my signature." Julia's hand pinned one margin, Imogen's the other. Julia noticed the faintest little wrinkles on her own, none on the girl's. Viewed from above, George's nodding head appeared to be kissing both.

Julia could not help glancing toward Imogen, who stared back with eyes that were strangely troubled. The girl looked away again only because George had finished and she had to wipe the drool off the pen.

He took advantage of the action to ask what the other documents were.

"One is the dreaded power of attorney," Julia replied. "And I hope we're not going to take over all that."

George growled but she could tell it was a mere token; he'd sign. "The other," she went on, "is an accounting agreement. It's mentioned in the document you've just . . ."

"A what?" he asked, this time with genuine anger.

She opened the assignment and found the relevant paragraph – hoping to cloak its horror in legal impersonality. "The assignee further agrees," she quoted, "to institute such normal and well established accounting procedures as shall be required from time to time by the assignor or her financial advisers and especially as set forth in the accompanying schedule." She laid the paper aside. "That's the one you now have to . . ."

"You bitch!" he said quietly.

"Mr Somerville!" exploded Mrs Crooke, but Julia's glance quelled her.

Imogen closed her eyes and shrivelled, as if she wished to vanish.

With thin-lipped calm Julia told him, "You must be feeling a little overwrought, my dear. Perhaps it would be better if . . ."

"I know what you want," he snapped. "Complete financial control."

"Nothing could be further from . . ."

"Oh yes! You want to hold the purse-strings."

"George, we can hardly discuss it in these . . ."

"Well you shan't, and that's that. I'm not signing."

She shrugged. "Then Wallace & Thorn will be sending in the receiver tomorrow." She began gathering up the papers.

Never had his paralysis been more galling to him. She could see how he longed to snatch them from her.

"Not now they won't," he crowed. "We've both signed."

"But the money can't be transferred until these other two documents have also been signed. That's what I've been trying to . . ."

"Then to hell with us!" he stormed. "Go ahead – drag us down. See if I care! I'm damned if I'm going to have you and that banker peering over my shoulder at every turn. I'd rather . . ."

"Listen, George. I don't know whether this is quite the time to tell you, but during these past weeks I've discovered several thousand pounds' worth of unrecorded debtors, who . . ."

"Oh, splendid! Isn't that just what we need!"

"Debtors are people who owe us money! You see how little you know about it! Now if I can discover . . ."

"I'll show you!" he ranted. "I'll sign! Oh yes, I'll sign." He turned to Imogen and roared, "Pen, you little fool! Pen!"

Trancelike she replaced the pen between his teeth.

They waited for him to sign but he stared at the paper as if he had lost his fox. Then he said, "No, no. Not this. The other document." He was still speaking around the pen, so they had a struggle to follow him.

"No!" Imogen protested.

"What other document?" Julia asked.

"Just get it!" George screamed, letting the pen fall from his lips. Ink spattered over the power of attorney.

Julia ran to wet a flannel in the dressing room, to soak up the worst of it. By the time she returned, George was signing another document. It, too, was plainly of legal origin.

"What is all this?" she asked coldly.

George chuckled.

A miserable Imogen explained: "It appoints me a trustee of Somerville & Son, Mrs Somerville – a joint trustee with yourself, in the event of Mr Somerville's death. It's his idea. I want no part of it."

George finished his scrawl, looked up at her in triumph, and then, instead of signing the power of attorney, made several vicious slashes at it with the pen.

Julia no longer cared. "You are a dirty little shit, George." Her voice was hardly pitched above a whisper but the word hit all three hearers like a thunderclap. "And you always have been."

"Which says a great deal for your taste in marrying me!" he sneered, recovering swiftly. The pen dropped to his lap. Mechanically Imogen picked it up.

"You have deceived me."

"Can you wonder?"

"From the first year of our marriage you have deceived me."

"I have *not!*" He was furious once again, thinking she meant he had been unfaithful.

"I can prove it," she told him.

"I'd like to see you try."

"You remember those water colours I painted?"

"Water colours?" He screwed up his face as if in pain. "What are you drivelling on about? What's unfaithful about . . ."

"I painted a pair of water colours – which you took to the office. Later you told me some famous collector had offered to buy them."

"And so he did."

"Don't, George." She almost pleaded. "Don't lie to me now. The time for lying has gone."

His scream rose to a fury. "But he *did,* I tell you. He bought them. I brought you home the money."

"This famous, anonymous collector!"

"I'll even tell you his name. It was Lord Berners."

If she had not actually discovered the discarded paintings herself, her confidence would have been dented at that point. Berners *was* a client of Somerville's; they had, in fact, installed a complete grand piano in one of his Rolls-Royces. And he was also a noted collector. George's use of him carried every conviction – especially when he added, "Go on. Telephone him now. He's in that address book on the bureau. Ask him yourself."

She went to the bureau, but not to find Lord Berners's number.

Instead she opened the bottom drawer and took out the pair of water colours, which she then laid before him.

Give him his due, he didn't turn a hair. "Fake," he snorted. "They must be. You've just painted a second pair." He stared at her with contempt. "My God! The lengths you'll go to! All this is staged, isn't it – and you dare to call me a dirty little . . ."

"George. Before you damn yourself utterly, let me tell you I rescued these paintings from the rubbish you turned out of your office that day I went to Forge Lane."

"Liar!" he shrieked, suddenly losing his temper. "I know your game, you bitch. You want to tar me with every . . . Look! I'll show you . . ."

He had turned a bright, purplish-red. His whole head was shivering. He looked up at her, eyes filled with the most awful malevolence. Then an astonishing change came over him. His face went slack. His head slumped into the cradle of his useless shoulders. The hatred fled from his eyes as they turned upward, seeking her. When they found her they softened at once, filled with a mute pleading. He moaned a single, barely audible word; it could have been "wifey."

"George!" she cried out in alarm, dropping to her knees at his side.

The eyes continued their upward scan and vanished beneath his quivering lids. Then his head slumped forward and she knew that he was dead.

"George?" she whispered, touching him in a kind of awe, finding no life in that lolling skull.

She rose to her feet. She heard herself swallow and felt the clench of her larynx as if they had been two separate events. "Gone," she murmured.

Imogen Davis was clutching a piece of paper; it was, of course, the deed that created her a joint trustee.

That picture, more than anything, restored Julia to a sense of the present, of present dangers, present imperatives. She did not for one moment believe the girl's disavowals.

One by one she removed the mountain of pillows that had helped sustain George in an upright posture. Galvanized by this action, Mrs Crooke said, "I'll phone for the doctor."

"No," Julia told her calmly as she laid George flat. "That can wait." To Davis she added, "It's not valid, you know. It needs witnesses."

The woman came out of her trance, looked down at the document, and gave a single, mirthless laugh. Without a word, she held it dramatically toward Julia and tore it in two – or rather, started to do so.

But Julia stopped her, leaping forward with a cry of, "No!"

Both women looked at her in surprise.

"He may have made a codicil to his will," she explained hastily, seizing the first likely (or least unlikely) reason that came to hand. "He may have mentioned this trust. It would complicate things if you destroyed that. Listen, Miss Davis" – she spoke in a more placatory tone now – "we're none of us in any condition to . . . well, to make irrevocable decisions like that, just at this moment. Let's simply try to stay calm, shall we?"

Imogen handed her the half-torn document. "Whatever you want, I'll do," she said.

Yes, Julia thought coldly, *if my only protector had just died, I'd hope to be as quick-thinking as you obviously are.* "Thank you," she said affably.

Mrs Crooke had meanwhile retrieved the power of attorney. She glanced at it, smiled, laid it before her mistress. "That looks remarkably like a signature to me, madam," she observed.

And so it did. Three or four of those wild slashes had made brief contact with the paper, forming a vee on its side, followed by a sort of zigzag; with a bit of goodwill they could be interpreted as a paralyzed and dying man's attempt at a *G* and an *S*. Two undoubted signatures from unimpeachable witnesses would confirm it.

Julia gave Miss Davis an even warmer smile.

The girl took up the pen and witnessed the "signature" without a murmur; Mrs Crooke followed suit.

Then they did the same for the assignment, the first document George had genuinely signed.

As soon as it was done Julia returned the water colours to their drawer, saying, "Well now, Miss Davis, you'll probably be happier to leave us as soon as you can?"

Imogen's mouth fell wide open. "But, madam – I *belong* here." She looked down at George. Tears were in her eyes. For the first time, the fact of his death seemed to strike her. "I belong here," she repeated in a whisper.

"Your work is . . . done," Julia told her.

The girl dropped to her knees, put her arms about George, and burst into tears. "He was my friend." The words, filled with pain, were squeezed out between her sobs.

Mrs Crooke touched her arm gently. "It would be best," she murmured.

Julia could take no more. She could not understand what prevented her from speaking out, venting all her anger on the little slut. "I must call Doctor Jordan," she said. "And tell the children."

Her eyes met the housekeeper's and she inclined her head toward Imogen; Mrs Crooke nodded. The maid would be gone before Julia returned.

Lydia knew. One look at her mother's eyes and she knew. She shook her head, rose, opened her mouth, floated across the room to Julia's outstretched arms; her lips formed the word "no!" but there was only silence.

Her hug was so tight, so desperate, that for a moment Julia could not breathe. Miss Nightingale slipped away, unnoticed.

But the child had to hear it in words, too, of course. As the rack of her grief began to ease, she disinterred her damp face from her mother's ruined dress and stammered, "Is he . . . did he?"

Julia squatted on her heels, bringing her eyes on a level with Lydia's. "He was at peace," she said. "There was no pain. He spoke about you, and me . . . how much he loved us all . . ."

The lies choked her. Lydia waited and at last shyly touched her arm. "What can we do?" she asked.

It was such an all-embracing question, so filled with reverberations. "Remember him." Julia found herself able to smile at last. "For always. Remember him with love and gratitude."

CHAPTER NINETEEN

THE FUNERAL TOOK place on the following Monday; the burial was in the family plot at All Souls cemetery, Kensal Green. It was a family affair, too – George's real family being the world of engineering and hand-built cars. Julia had no idea it was so large. Its members introduced themselves solemnly, one after the other – "Fuller of James Young" . . . "Marsden of Rolls-Royce" . . . like ambassadors from so many medieval baronies. Each spoke a word or two about the high esteem in which the industry had held her husband. For the children's sake she was glad; for her own part she found the enforced deception hard to sustain. As the coffin was lowered into the grave, she hugged the youngsters to her and borrowed some of their abiding grief; but her own true feeling was a passing anger that George had left her so little to mourn.

At length there came "Gold of Gold's Commercial Bodies," whose knowing grin and extra-warm handshake brought a refreshing touch of honesty to the day. When the formal part of the affair was done and the group was breaking up and moving off, he came close again and risked the comment: "Vultures" – with a barely perceptible nod toward his confrères. "Did you get the power of attorney?" He was sweating.

She nodded. "Call on me tomorrow."

There was also the contingent from Forge Lane – the entire work force. Rumour had been rife for weeks; the firm's troubles could have been no secret there. Behind their mourning, which was genuine, she could sense the rising panic.

She left Robert and Lydia with Miss Nightingale and went over to join Eliot, who was talking with Crownfield.

"That can only be Sidney Gold," Eliot commented.

"Wasting no time," she told him.

Crownfield, who had also never seen the man, turned and studied him with interest.

"I have a feeling that he may try and spring some proposal on me," she added.

"Not here, surely?" Eliot was scandalized.

"He seems in quite a nervous state."

"I'll stay with you." He took her arm – a gesture that abruptly curtailed Crownfield's perusal of the fat little man.

Eliot's touch sent a shiver through Julia; she longed to pack everyone away and just bury herself in his giant embrace. But behind her immediate longing she felt an unexpected caution. The business had grown important, too – not as a simple matter of duty but in the same visceral way as her longing for Eliot. She did not yet know it, but she was developing a new measure of her own stature in the world.

She smiled at him and lightly disengaged her arm. "I'd be grateful if you'd both take Max home and wait for me there. If Gold wants to bring matters to a head today . . . well, I wouldn't mind getting it over and done with. We have so much to do in the weeks ahead and he could become an awful pest."

The two men exchanged glances; this was not quite the Julia Somerville they knew.

When she had shaken the last sympathetic hand, and stood the traditional few moments alone beside the grave ("plucky little woman," the departing mourners told one another), she turned and made her way toward her children, a wan little group in the gathering twilight, held in Miss Nightingale's protective aura.

The sight of them in that cheerless dusk tugged at her heart. *They don't really need me, either,* she thought in a moment of panic. She had given them so little of her time. There were so many other demands on her . . .

I will be a better mother to you now, she promised.

Sidney Gold could not wait, of course. Even before he had set out for the funeral he had determined, somehow, to force a decision soon; the sight of all his competitors gathered around Julia, all in black like the vultures of his metaphor, made him even more desperate. Also, he had certain private information that made it imperative.

As that sad little family group moved toward the gate he stepped out from behind a tree and called her name. She turned in surprise. He beckoned her to him. She told Miss Nightingale to go on and wait in the car with the children.

"Tomorrow," she reminded him as she drew near.

He shook his head. "You don't know what's already in the post."

She frowned.

"Your attempted rescue" – he gave an awkward shrug, distancing himself from the news – "it didn't work. Wallis & Thorn are putting in the receivers tomorrow morning."

She turned and gazed at George's grave, mainly to hide her face from Gold while she absorbed the news.

"No help from there, gel," he commented brutally. "That's what put the wind up the bank, I expect. You'll be knee-deep in final demands by the second post."

"They wasted no time," she said bitterly. Damn it! She had expected at least a week of grace. A week was all she needed, too.

"No sentiment in business."

"Nor honour, it seems." Her voice broke. "They *promised.*"

"They don't know the meaning of the word," he agreed blandly. "I'm the one who remembers promises. Let me drive you home."

She hardly heard him. This news changed everything.

"Don't worry." He expanded genially. "It's all taken care of. You haven't a single worry in all the world."

They began to catch up on the children, who were just going out by the gate.

"Bless their dear little hearts," he murmured.

"We'll follow you home," she called out to Miss Nightingale as she entered the gold-plated monster; again that cloying odour of spice.

"I brought an agreement for sale with me," he told her, switching on the interior lamp. "Two copies. You can sign away your problems now."

The cut-crystal lamp glass threw a bright mesh over both of them, and upon the document he now put into her hand.

She stared down at it. What a supreme temptation it was. Fifty-thousand pounds in the bank by tomorrow! She could wash her hands of the whole Somerville mess and Neville Aero-Engineering (she already had the name) could rise at once, a phoenix from those sordid ashes. At one stroke of the pen! And they'd have at least twice the working capital they'd need.

And what sweet revenge on George . . .

But no. That train of thought died before it started. There was no revenge on George; his very behaviour had killed the woman who could even think in such terms. His neglect of the business, the hazards to which he had exposed his home and children – these had awakened a new Julia and faced her with a challenge that made the very idea of revenge too trivial to contemplate.

She folded the document, unread, and passed it back to him. "I shan't be selling Somerville's, Mr Gold. But you may drive me home, and on the way I shall endeavour to explain why."

The momentum of his greed brushed aside her words. "But it's the only way out for you," he insisted, thrusting the document back. In the same breath he told his chauffeur to drive on.

"Thirty-two, Connaught Square," Julia added before she turned to Sidney Gold. "If what you say is true," she began, "and you've been so remarkably well informed until now that I must assume it is, then I shall find a receiver awaiting me at Forge Lane tomorrow morning."

He pointed at the document on her lap and drew breath to speak. But she went on. "What you cannot know, Mr Gold – because it has taken me weeks of close study to discover it – is that the firm is far healthier than the books reveal. I'm quite confident that before the morning is out, the man from Wallis & Thorn will be packing his bags and advising the bank to . . ."

Gold gave a desperately jovial laugh. "Not a chance, gel! Not a hope in hell."

"If you'll just be patient, I'll explain." She smiled sympathetically. "I know how galling it is to be balked of your wishes at the last moment, just when you're sure that everything's in your favour . . ."

But even now, when he must surely be aware that his estimate of her had gone disastrously wrong, even now he was hardly listening. His eyes kept straying toward an old Gladstone bag that lay at his feet. At last he could bear it no longer. Oblivious to what she was saying, he stooped and lifted it to his lap.

"Look!" he cried as he sprang the catch and upended it. A shower of banknotes – huge, crisp, white fivers, done up in bundles – spilled over the seat between them. "All yours," he added.

She gazed at it in amazement, then at him, then past him, out through the window at the people scurrying by. It was a poor district, North Kensington. If humanity were running true to form, nine out of ten of those passers-by were being eaten alive with worries over the rent, the next meal, the tallyman. What would they think if they knew that this absurdly vulgar car was purring through their midst with the lifetime wages of an entire local street casually spilled between its two passengers?

"Is that what fifty thousand pounds looks like?" she asked flatly.

"Thirty," he corrected. "Fifty was weeks ago. I told you it'd drop. After tomorrow . . ." He picked up a single bundle and shrugged. "Something like that, if you was lucky – and I was still in this generous mood."

How could she penetrate that armour-plated confidence? "Actually," she told him, "a cheque would have been far more impressive. Cash on this sort of scale is considered rather vulgar, you know."

He was furious, of course; but she saw that she had at last halted his attempt to play out the charade.

"D'you really want to own Somerville's?" she asked. "Or do you want to make a lot of money? Which is your real ambition?"

He was experienced enough in business to know that fury is rarely negotiable; already he was replacing it with a wary sort of anger. "Go on," he barked. "Why?"

She began packing away the bundles of notes. "During the years that you've been longing to – how did you put it? – get into the high-class end of the trade, things have been changing, you know? Well, of course you know. But perhaps you don't realize how much. After my husband's accident I was compelled to take a far deeper interest in the business than he wished – well, than either of us wished, to be frank. But there it was. I had little choice. And I discovered to my horror that his knowledge of finance hardly extended beyond the Day Book. And, naturally, that gang of spongers he called our accounts department took full advantage of it! They don't know it yet but from tomorrow they're finished. However, that's by the way."

She wanted him to know that if he had, in fact, been party to the shenanigans, that particular game was up. His watchful gaze told her nothing. She went on: "I hope you won't think it boastful of me to say that I probably have a better idea of Somerville's finances than anyone else connected with the firm. I don't just mean the ledgers and balances, I'm talking about the way things have gone ever since the war." She gave him a brief, weary smile. "I'm not talking about the writing in the books, Mr Gold, but the writing on the wall."

He gulped. If there was a single moment when his estimate of her underwent a complete reversal, that was it. He offered no further argument. "Go on," he breathed.

She dropped the last bundle into the bag and snapped the catch. "You'll probably think I'm being an idiot. I mean, it's hard to say what the luxury coachbuilding side of Somerville's is actually worth, now that my husband's no longer there. But" – she patted the bag – "it's certainly not more than this. So, as you can imagine, I'm exceedingly tempted to separate it out from the rest of the chaos and allow you to buy it for that."

His eyes brightened. "Well, then . . ."

She held up a finger. "Except for two things. In the first place, the trade is shrinking. There's nothing anyone can do about it. It is dying a natural death. And I know it's dreadfully unbusinesslike of me but I'd feel I was cheating you."

He laughed. "And in the second place?"

"I know of a much better investment for you. It would make you twice as rich in half the time."

He tried to laugh again but the conviction in her eyes killed it. He saw in her an almost fanatical assurance that she was in touch with things that had eluded him. "Such as?" he asked in a voice little above a whisper.

They had arrived at Connaught Square. "You did say number thirty-two, madam?" the chauffeur asked.

"That's right – just down to this next corner." She turned back to Sidney Gold and, on an impulse, said, "Why not come to Forge Lane tomorrow? Lunchtime, shall we say? If I'm right, the receiver will have left by then."

"If not?" He licked his lips.

She pushed the bag against his thigh and grinned. "Bring a chequebook anyway."

CHAPTER TWENTY

MAX, CROWNFIELD, AND ELIOT were waiting in the drawing room. "Oh good," she said as she popped her head round the door. "Bear with me just a minute longer. I must go to the children first. Do pour yourselves drinks."

Upstairs she changed her dress and went straight to the old playroom. Thank God for young appetites! They were tucking into hot buttered crumpets dripping with bloater paste and Marmite – Robert heartily, Lydia a little shamefacedly once she saw her mother.

"Well, dears . . ." she began, touching them, running her fingers in their hair.

Lydia, conscious of what must look like their greed, explained, "We have to carry on just as Daddy would have wished it."

"That's right, darling." She turned to Robert. "I'll run you back to school tomorrow."

"It's all right, Mater. Uncle Max is taking me back to Allbury this evening. He can run me over there tomorrow."

"Oh," she said, adding a belated, "Good." She wanted to talk to him, to tell him something of what was happening with the firm . . .

not to be alarmed at anything he might hear, and so on.

Her disappointment made her pause. Had she intended these confidences for his good – or to quell her own conscience? It was his future, after all . . .

No! She checked herself angrily. It was all their futures.

A subtler unease overtook these thoughts: Had she wanted to share her conscience with Robert because he was now the man of the house – and all her upbringing had taught her to lean on the man of the house?

"Perhaps it's as well for you to go with Uncle Max," she told him.

A maid stood just within the doorway and cleared her throat. "Please madam, begging pardon for disturbing you but Mr Neville sends to know . . ."

"Yes. Tell them I'm on my way. Thank you." She turned back to the children. "Listen, darlings – well, you, Lydia, really – because Robert will be away. I have such a load of things to do these next few days – out at the works . . . seeing the lawyers . . . you've no idea. So you will just be terribly terribly patient with me and not worry if I miss tucking you in one or two nights."

"Yes, of course," Lydia exclaimed. Her mild exasperation, heedless of the hurt it gave, betrayed her youth – implying that this guilt-ridden love in her mother's heart was mere fussing.

"Aren't you hungry?" Robert asked. The question was prompted not so much by concern for her as a fear that she might share their dwindling stock of crumpets.

"Ravenous!" She smiled. "But I have people waiting in the drawing room." She went back downstairs.

At the door she paused. She had a sudden mental picture of the three men standing there, beyond the oak . . . turning at the sound of her entry, staring at her. And the void between them and her – in that mental image – was suddenly more than just a few yards of carpet; it was an emptiness that used to be filled by George. Husband George. Head-of-household George. Proprietor-of-Somerville's George . . . shaper-of-her-life George.

That space cried out to be filled. And each of those men, in their different ways, would have the idea at the back of his mind that he was the one to do it. Not entirely, of course, but to some degree. Crownfield most of all; Max the least. But they would all be thinking it. She felt the pressure like some weird radiation, pouring toward her, even through the door.

It was the last thing on earth she felt like doing at that moment but she knew she would have to disabuse them of any such notion. No one was going to fill that void. This was a new situation and they were all going to have to find new roles within it.

She reached for the doorknob – and faltered yet again. Never had she felt so isolated, so vulnerable, so desperately in need of an arm about her, a shoulder to lean on. She drew a deep breath and squared herself to it.

"Well?" It was Crownfield who spoke but the question was in all their eyes.

Here goes, she thought. "Such an odd little man! He tipped thirty thousand pounds into my lap, all in bundles of fivers, and thrust a deed of sale into my hands to sign." She shook her head, as if even this brief summary had made the memory less real. "I suppose it's the way he's always behaved."

"And?" Eliot prompted.

She came out of her reverie. "Oh, I told him that a cheque is generally more impressive than cash – north of the Thames, anyway."

"But did you sign?" Max asked. The others must have been talking about it, putting him in the picture.

"Oh, very likely! No. I told him I knew of a far better investment and asked him to lunch with us at Forge Lane tomorrow. Oh – he claims that Wallis & Thorn are putting in a receiver. I say, Baring – be a dear and mix me a good stiff manhattan."

But Eliot did not move.

"Receiver?" Max echoed.

She nodded and turned to Crownfield. "I think I can quickly convince him that the firm is worth around eighty thousand – and that within a week we can get out bills for about a fifth of that. We'll sacrifice some goodwill, of course. But goodwill that depends on *not* pressing for payment is a bit dubious anyway. Should be all right, wouldn't you say?"

She left Crownfield to mull over the question while she repeated her request to Eliot, who this time complied.

Crownfield shrugged, unwilling to second-guess a fellow banker. "That's really up to Wallis & Thorn."

"But if it were up to you?"

He grinned. "Are you saying it might be?"

She took the cocktail and toasted the banker. "Almost certainly. It would really rather depend on your answer."

He chewed his lip, tense with indecision. She turned to Eliot, but was unprepared for her body's reaction. Her flesh suddenly tingled with the nearness of him. Some profound instinct warned her, *not yet – and especially not tonight.* But how was she going to stop herself? She felt as if something were pulling her apart inside.

Crownfield said, "My immediate response is that I'll send someone to join you tomorrow – if I may? You can convince him at the same time. My more considered response will depend on the outcome there."

"That seems reasonable." She was amazed at being able to sound so calm – and at the blindness of these men.

She crossed the room and sat beside her brother. "Two more burials," he grunted, "and you'll need a new family plot. I suppose you know that?"

She touched his hand fondly. "It almost certainly won't be my problem, dear." Made safe by distance she turned again to Eliot. "How soon could you get together a respectable looking prospectus for a company to build the BI?"

"A week?" he replied. "It would depend on the printer."

"And if it were handwritten? I mean, we could say to someone – Sidney Gold, for instance – that it was about to be sent off to the printer. He'd feel privileged."

"A day, then." Eliot pulled a dubious face. "But I wouldn't offer that man a share."

"Nor would I! But what about him offering us a loan? Would you turn down a loan? Fixed term, of course."

"What's in your mind?" Crownfield interjected.

"What's in my mind is that the tax man probably has no knowledge of that thirty thousand in cash. So Sidney Gold's chances of investing it must be pretty limited. I'm only thinking out loud, mind you."

Crownfield chuckled at her cunning, but he raised the obvious objection: "How would it legally return to him?"

"Still thinking out loud," she warned. "Suppose we divide Somerville & Son into its three obvious parts – engineering, marine, and coachbuilding. And suppose we form a new aero company." Her gesture included Eliot in this. "And the aero company acquires the three Somerville companies and then offers a contract to Sidney Gold to manage the coachbuilding one. Lion's share of the profits, et cetera. The loan could be returned to him, bit by bit over the years, as bonuses of various kinds. I know that in the real world it probably wouldn't be anything like as simple as that, but cleverer minds than mine could iron out the wrinkles in it, I'm sure. The main thing is – it would be legal, wouldn't it? On our side, I mean?"

Crownfield drew a shallow breath and expelled it sharply. "Have you just thought of all this?"

She shook her head. "My dear – for months now I've thought of little else but Somerville's and the BI – and Sidney Gold, reeking of funny money in the wings. Of course, he may not like it one bit. We mustn't rely on it."

Watching her, Baring was fascinated. Moments ago she had made him almost melt with desire – and she had felt it, too. He was sure of it. And yet look at her now! An entirely new fire seemed to burn within her, extinguishing something that had seemed hot enough to consume them both. He was irresistibly reminded of his father. Both could change from one kind of enthusiast to another in moments. Both had that strange mixture of charm and ruthlessness. Both had

144

minds as bright as buttons, yet neither was at all interested in abstract ideas; nor was either of them particularly self-aware – or, in other words, self-critical. Yes – neither was inhibited by that steady trickle of self-criticism which dogs most of the human race. He, Eliot, was beginning to suspect that, lacking such qualities, he was cut out for only modest success in business – on his own, at least.

"What's the alternative?" he asked.

She began to relax; her manner grew less brittle. Over the last five minutes both men had started to cede the initiative to her – only slightly, but at least the move was in the right direction. "Under George's will," she explained, "I have a life interest in part of the firm's income. I dare say I might find an astute banker somewhere who'd let me parley that into a guarantee to an aero company – just until it was on its feet?"

Crownfield nodded vigorously. "That sounds a much better idea to me."

"Me, too," Eliot chimed in.

She tipped her head sideways in reluctant concession. "And yet – vulgar or not – thirty thousand pounds, in cash and begging for a home . . . it did look rather scrumptious!"

Max stood up abruptly. "Got to get that boy back to school," he barked.

Julia, with a smile of apology to the other two, saw him out into the hall, where she sent a maid to go and fetch Robert.

"This Sidney Gold business," Max ventured.

"Yes?"

He shook his head. "Stay out of the hands of the Jews. This Crownfield fellow – he's not one of them, is he?"

She sighed. "Don't be tedious, darling. And I haven't forgotten your own pressing needs, but it'll take a good month to get Somerville's solvent again and I can't do anything before that. Can you hold the fort until then?"

"Going to have to, aren't I."

"I'm afraid so. Cheer up – at least we know there's money in the offing. George could have left us in a much worse pickle."

Robert came and she kissed him goodbye; for once he did not shrink from her, playing the manly chap. Max gave her an unwonted hug, too. She suspected it had less to do with any sensitivity toward her than with a desire to set the boy at his ease for having let the side down in that way. She promised to pop down to Hertfordshire and see them soon.

She returned to the other two in the drawing room. Crownfield immediately asked what was the hurry to build the BI.

The question was directed to her but Eliot answered. "It's the Hun," he said. "Now the ban on Germany's airplane industry is definitely being lifted, Junkers and Dornier and the rest will go home and just cream the European market. And it doesn't look as if England'll even try to stop them."

"Imperial Airways isn't allowed to buy foreign," Crownfield reminded him.

"Right." He grinned. "So who gets the best of both worlds?"

To prevent the occasion from becoming a full business meeting, for which she was not emotionally prepared, she turned to Baring. "I think we ought to have that prospectus ready by lunchtime tomorrow – whether or not we show it to Sidney Gold."

He took the hint and rose to go. "I'll need to start in on it right away."

She saw him to the front door, where she gave him a quick, almost sisterly kiss. "You're wonderful," she murmured.

"You too. You'll be okay – you know – tonight?"

For a moment her resolve weakened, but she steeled herself and replied, "I'll get our future banker to take me out to dinner. I don't think he realizes yet how lucky he is that we've chosen him."

When she returned to the drawing room Crownfield pulled a sour face and remarked, "Did you hear what that fellow said – 'start *in on it*'! What are they doing to our beautiful language?"

She sat beside him and gently laid a hand on his arm. "What are *we* going to do with this beautiful evening?"

"Ah." He grew tense at once.

"Take me somewhere we can dance, Crownfield. I want to dance and dance."

"Of course." He relaxed and laid his hand reassuringly over hers.

Almost at once she began to regret her impulse. "Only make it somewhere discreet. I don't want to open the morning papers and find nasty little paragraphs full of merry-widow jokes."

He rose to his feet, taking her with him. "I know a very discreet little hotel up the Thames at Maidenhead."

He took a suite; the management seemed to know him quite well. The dance floor was six-by-eight of carpet between the heavily curtained window and the bedroom door – a double door, which stood wide open. The orchestra was a wind-up gramophone. There was a plate of smoked-salmon sandwiches and a Bollinger '13 stood in ice.

The misgivings she had felt the moment she suggested this tryst had now hardened into a conviction that the whole idea was a mistake. Through the open doors to the bedroom she could see the bed, not turned down as if for a pair of sleepers but draped in a caramel-coloured art silk and mottled with cushions. Pink and brown tassels hung motionless in air that was too warm for a fully-clothed body.

"Oh!" she gasped and fanned her face.

146

"Shall I open a window?" he asked with a sardonic grin that expected the answer no.

"Please!" she said gratefully.

His face fell but he complied.

The gramophone had a tungsten needle that did not require changing with each new record. They danced to Ambrose and Jack Hylton and the Savoy Orpheans. His dancing was lithe and fluent, so easy to follow that she soon relaxed and let herself be led; but part of her remained alert for the slightest impulsion toward that invitingly open bedroom door.

He was puzzled that she no longer gave out any signals, especially after the brazenness of her suggestion back in Connaught Square; so, like the cautious banker he was, he bided his time and let her control the flow of champagne. To his chagrin she drank only sparingly.

"A waltz?" he suggested after about an hour had passed.

"Mmmm."

She danced with the glass in her hand. It was a sedate English tune but he treated it as if it were Viennese, turning around and around, forcing her to finish the drink rather sooner than she had intended.

Her head was spinning. As they drew near the bedroom door, the last remnant of her caution alerted her to what was happening. Their present turn had brought them to the edge of the opening; the next would place them just beyond its centre, from where a slight change of angle would carry her over the threshold.

She took an extra-wide step that put her almost against the farther door. Now he had to make a reverse turn to get her back where he wanted her. She followed – but then pretended to think he was about to do a second reverse turn to bring them into their regular circuit. He had no choice but to follow.

Later, in the final reprise, he tried once more to take her over that threshold; but she was ready now and kept him gently in the ante-room. Not a word was spoken, except in the language of their bodies.

When the dance ended he tried something more direct. "Hoo!" he cried, passing a token hand across his brow. "Where *do* you get all your energy from?"

She saw at once where the gambit might lead – mate in three if she were careless. If he could bring their talk around to a direct proposition, she doubted she could be so hard as to refuse – if only to spare him the humiliation.

"Oh, poor man," she said, all tender and contrite. "I forget. I forget." And, seizing up a chair, she placed it beneath him before he could protest that that was not at all what he had meant. Then, while he was refilling her glass and thinking of ways to recover the initiative, she took up a second chair and drew it close to his – seemingly unaware that it also stood four-square in the doorway to the bedroom.

And there it remained for the rest of the evening, a form of refusal that Crownfield could take as a mere postponement – and therefore accept without loss of dignity.

Midnight came soon enough, and then the exhaustion of the day's events, both emotional and physical, overcame her. They finished the champagne as they hurtled back to London down the Great West Road. She watched the headlights eat up the miles as she stretched luxuriously in the deep upholstery of the passenger seat. Suddenly she felt very good, as if she had passed some obscure test.

In all those hours neither of them had spoken of business matters but when they drew near Notting Hill he remarked, "You're hoping to take quite a hand in the firm from now on, then?"

She chuckled. "Does that worry you?"

"Not at all. I hope I can help. You mustn't feel afraid to ask. *Anything* – anything at all. I mean, I hope you look upon me as something more than just your banker."

"Silly!" She squeezed his arm.

After a pause he went on, "I suppose you realize you're jumping in at the deep end?"

She closed her eyes, not really wanting to talk about it, and murmured, "Are we discussing Somerville's? Or Sidney Gold?" And then she added, "Or us?"

He refused the bait. "Mainly Somerville's. D'you think you'll be equal to it?"

"It'd be a bit late for me to be asking myself that!" She glanced at him and then reached a finger to his lips. "When the street light's in front, your smile is kindly," she said. "But lit from overhead it's cruel. D'you know that?"

"Equivocation – it seems to be in the very air tonight."

She lowered her hand to his arm and gave it a gentle squeeze – the nearest she could bring herself to an apology. "Why are you smiling, anyway?"

"I was just thinking. Most men never ask themselves, either – about being equal to their business. They just do it because life expects it of them."

The way my brother and your son died in the war, she thought; but what she said was, "Thinking only slows me up."

"Hoo hoo! Dangerous words if ever I heard them!"

"George thought endlessly about the business – but not very sensibly."

"What d'you call sensibly, then?"

"He never had time to think out the long term. He was always . . ." She made blinkers of her hands beside her eyes. "You know? He never grasped the shape of the business. He knew all its little byways far too well."

"And you think you can see its shape?"

"Yes."

"Care to tell me?"

"Oh, it's sort of long and silvery, with flat bits sticking out each side . . ."

He frowned in bewilderment.

". . . and propellers."

He laughed. "Dammit! I'm not going to send anyone to Forge Lane tomorrow. I'm coming there myself."

She was instantly on her guard. "Don't you trust me to deal with Sidney Gold?"

"Of course I do. It's nothing like that. But you've roused my curiosity. And even worse" – he gave her an awkward, sidelong glance – "you've made me realize how long it is since I got ink on my fingers. Not head-office ink, you understand, but the real vintage stuff."

She laughed. "Well, thank you, Crownfield. You're the sweetest banker I ever knew."

"More than just a banker," he reminded her.

Arrived in Connaught Square he leaned over and gave her a brief farewell kiss. "Good night, Crownfield," she whispered.

"Good night, Somerville," he murmured in reply.

CHAPTER TWENTY-ONE

RECEIVERS ARE ACCOUNTANTS with fangs; and – as all the world knows – accountants wear starched collars and shiny suits; they are myopic and fussy, and need a dentist. Before they start work they produce a vast stock of pens and pencils, in several colours, which they line up with mathematical precision. They have nervous tics, high-pitched voices, common accents, and bald heads.

All of which explains why it took Julia several seconds to register the fact that Mr St John Brunty was, indeed, the dreaded receiver – and at least a minute more to believe it. For St John Brunty resembled nothing so much as a happy refugee from some literary outfit in Bloomsbury. He stood as tall as Eliot but had the mein of an aesthetic lion; his long, straight hair framed the right half of his face in a perfect oval, and when he nodded, the ends of it tickled his neck. His pale brows beetled over deep-set eyes that never rested. His nose was long and aquiline and his lips beautifully chiselled. The words they uttered were the purest Oxford English; and he possessed a vocabulary a don might envy. His hands were large as shovels but their long, exquisite fingers emphasized only their delicacy; he waved them frequently as he spoke – not in a florid, italianate sort of way but with a conductor's precision. He was as slender as a faun.

Oh yes – he also wore Harris tweeds and a turtleneck sweater.

Crownfield took even longer to believe it; in fact, he slipped out and telephoned the man's office before he would accept his word.

Brunty showed not the slightest desire to see the books. He asked first to be taken on a tour of the works, which he completed at breakneck pace. He fired off a multitude of questions in every shop, each of them to the point; and in between he outdid even Julia at her best in drawing out the history of the firm and the Somerville family. Baring's private shed and the model of the BI were of especial interest – as, indeed, were the sheds where George's pet projects were being pursued with undiminished vigour.

Crownfield drew a dangerously impressed Julia to one side when the tour was over and they were returning to the main accounts office. "Beware of this fellow," he warned. "Remember Uriah Heep – how his 'umbleness masked a towering ambition? Well, this fellow's bohemianism does the same."

Julia accepted the caution for a while, but the man was so charming that she could not make it stick. Anyway, he'd soon be gone.

She had come to Forge Lane early that morning, partly because she had woken at six, so blissfully happy that she had to get out for fear the servants, or Lydia, would notice; but mainly it had been to allow her time to mark the unrecorded debtors – or those she had so far discovered – and present them to him in one convincing cluster.

He inserted his delicate fingers into the marked pages with a dancer's grace. As he scanned the evidence his free left arm swung, lemur-like, over his head to allow the fingers to sweep back his long, lank hair – which, of course, fell forward again at once.

"Full many a gem of purest ray serene!" he quoted after scanning the first half-dozen. He smiled up at Julia. "And have you plumbed each dark, unfathomed cave in this ocean of yours, Mrs Somerville?"

She shook her head. "I gave up when I had discovered enough to know that we were trading with a great margin of solvency, Mr Brunty." She stressed the point.

He nodded, judiciously pursing his eyes and lips. "Very wise – if true. Not that I doubt your *word,* of course."

"I think if we left you alone for an hour, here with all the books, you would not doubt my competence or judgement, either."

Everything he said seemed to be a trial of something obscure within her, something he alone could pin down. But, while that made her uncomfortable, his response to her answers had the opposite effect, for he somehow conveyed that she had passed the assay (if assay it was).

When she left the room she felt as if she were about to collapse, not being aware until then how tense he had made her feel.

"Whooo! He's like a cross-country run," she exclaimed.

"Over an army assault course with live ammo," Crownfield added. "I tell you, beware."

"You're not saying it's a mask for incompetence? Or slovenliness?"

"Oh, certainly not."

"Well then, that's all that matters – to us." Julia turned to Eliot. "D'you think he's dangerous?"

He shrugged. "He doesn't bother me. Shall we run through our prospectus while we're waiting?"

Crownfield expected a situation in which the two of them presented *their* idea to him; he was surprised to find Julia even more critical than he was – not in a carping manner, but with the passion of a loving parent who wants *her* child to excel. She questioned everything, down to the most niggling detail. For instance, Eliot had drawn a diagram to represent the lift provided by the wings at different speeds and angles; it was a series of coloured bars that grew longer as the lift increased.

"Why are they horizontal?" she asked.

"Because that's the way the paper's ruled."

"But lift is vertical," she objected. "It would mean much more if you redrew them vertically." She turned the paper sideways. "See?"

He pulled a face, suggesting she was being much too fussy.

She pressed a finger into his ribs. "Most of the people looking at this will have tiny brains – like me."

Watching them, Crownfield began to wonder whether Eliot were her lover as well as her business partner. Was that why her mood had changed so suddenly last night? Not that he minded in the least, he assured himself at once. He and Matty, his wife, prided themselves on their liberation from any taint of Victorianism. Still, it would be intriguing to know.

If he was jealous of anyone, it was of Julia herself. At this moment in her life she was enjoying one of the rarest privileges on earth – the chance to found an exciting new business of one's own choice, and with more than enough capital to back it. Most people had such dreams at some time; most died with them unfulfilled.

Banking had its good points, of course. It was certainly not devoid of human interest. But until yesterday, when he had first seen these two youngsters together, talking about their dream . . . and now again this morning, arguing, worrying over every little detail . . . until now he had not known the excitement of making real *things*.

This prospectus was actually meaningless – a sheaf of fancy paper cobbled together to hoodwink people like himself, the cautious men with the moneybags. When this plane flew, as it most certainly would, not one nut or bolt would be owed to this morning's exercise in wishful thinking. Everything would be due to their burning faith, to the zeal that was going to keep them working until they dropped. Faith, zeal, intelligence, stubbornness, stamina – those were the headings of their real prospectus. And, whether Julia and Eliot were lovers or not, he was jealous of them both for their ample share in all those qualities.

Brunty came looking for them. "Who are your auditors?" he asked.

Julia shrugged. "I had nothing to do with the firm until recently, but as far as I can discover we seem to have had different ones each year. My husband never got on with them."

"I can well believe it. I expect he got on famously with this man Huxtable."

"Have you reached any conclusions?" Crownfield asked.

Brunty grinned. "Yes, there's nothing so expensive as a superfluous receiver, is there. My conclusion – or the one I shall convey to the bank – is that your entire accounts department and I should leave at once, and that I alone should return in two weeks. By which time a new broom might have swept most of it clean."

"So you agree we're solvent?" Julia asked.

He was trying to read the prospectus, while appearing not to. "No doubt about it," he muttered absently.

Eliot chuckled and slid the papers toward him. "The more, the merrier," he commented. "You may just know someone with money to lend."

Julia looked at her watch. "Sidney Gold should be here by now," she said in annoyance.

Brunty skimmed it once and then read it thoroughly. Crownfield watched him intensely. Julia said something about arranging for lunch and plucked Eliot with her.

"What d'you think?" she murmured, tilting her head slightly toward Brunty.

"Ask him to stay to lunch," he suggested. "Go to work on him."

When it became clear that Sidney Gold was not going to keep the appointment (not that he had ever said he would), they asked Brunty to join them instead. And Julia went to work on him with all her skill.

He was thirty-one years old, married, with one child – a boy of three. They lived in Hampstead (which made Crownfield's ears prick up, for that was where he lived, too). His wife was an occasional cellist with the Queen's Hall orchestra.

"And have you got any hobbies?"

"Hobbies?" He repeated the word with vague distaste.

"Well, what do you do with your spare time?"

"Ah! You mean what am I really? What do I do when I'm not in this business disguise?" He gestured at his tweeds and the rollneck pullover. "Then I put on a very smart suit and play the piano in a quartet with my wife and two friends."

"Professionally?" Crownfield asked.

"We, ah, charge."

When she had asked every question that a comparative stranger could decently ask a fellow human, Julia concluded: "Forgive me for saying this, Mr Brunty, but you are very far from being anyone's picture of a typical receiver – or, indeed, accountant of any kind. Is it actually what you would choose to do – given a free rein?"

He laughed and rubbed his hands together. "Mrs Somerville, if you are thinking of offering me, first, the job of putting your accounts here in order, and then (assuming I prove satisfactory at it) the more challenging career of managing the financial and legal sides of your new enterprise . . . then I might as well tell you – I have already decided to accept." He beamed at each in turn.

CHAPTER TWENTY-TWO

THANKS TO St John Brunty, the BI took shape about twice as fast as anyone had dared dream. He was more than an efficient accountant, more even than a good finance director. He knew nothing about aeroplanes, nothing about engineering, nothing about industry (or so he often claimed); and yet it was to him that Julia and Eliot carried their ideas; he was the silent umpire at all their arguments. He never seemed to contribute much of his own – certainly never anything so positive as a decision – and yet they came away with resolutions and insights that had not been there before He was the ideal sounding board for all those ideas, both great and absurd, that are the lifeblood of any business.

His was the role Julia had hoped Crownfield would play. But

Crownfield, angry that Julia had ignored his advice about Brunty, contented himself with providing the firm's capital (on the foot of Julia's life interest in Somerville's profits), and had then withdrawn from day-to-day contact with any of them.

"We shall have trouble with him one day," Brunty predicted.

Julia asked why.

"Because our way of doing business (by which I mean, of course, *your* way) is diametrically opposed to his. The only audience you care about, Mrs Somerville, sits inside your own head. Not so with Crownfield. His audience is God, or Tradition, or the City. You'd be satisfied with any strategy just as long as it wins. Crownfield wants *the best possible* winning strategy. Everything he does is for the record, the official biography. If he went into business, he'd probably fail, you know. That's why he's so fascinated by you."

The violinist in Brunty's semi-professional quartet was an estate agent, and it was through him that Neville Aero-Engineering acquired the site for its new aircraft factory at Dollis Hill, just beyond the northern fringe of London and only a mile or so from the aerodrome at Hendon. The place had formerly been a coal yard, so most of it was open space, graced with a thick layer of black dust. But there were two empty shells of buildings, which they turned into a temporary office and the first of several workshops. They reorganized Somerville & Son into its three logical branches: Somerville Motors, which continued in the coachbuilding line at Forge Lane; Somerville Engineering, the jobbing-engineering business – which had, in fact, proved by far its most profitable element, and which they moved to Dollis Hill; and Somerville Marine, whose sale to Thorneycroft brought in all the capital they needed to reorganize the Forge Lane works along rational lines. George's "pet projects" simply fell into abeyance. The drawings and prototypes were locked away in plan chests and cupboards at Dollis Hill, and the men were absorbed into the workshops.

It may seem strange that, at a time when they were almost desperate to start the new business, their first act was to revive a bit of the old – that is, Somerville Engineering. But they realized how urgent it was to generate a bit of cash. A brand new 24-seat airliner, due to fly sometime next year *if* it gets its certificate, does little to pay next week's wages.

They were proud of the fact that they did their first bit of jobbing on the very day they moved in. True, it was only a broken bicycle chain – Julia it was who found the tearful young lad trudging five miles home to Barnet; but, professionals as they were, they charged him for the repair – a full penny, which can be seen to this day, polished bright and set in concrete in the entrance hall, with the legend: TALL OAKS FROM LITTLE ACORNS GROW.

Brunty had put two thousand of his own into Neville's. "I could put more," he told his new partners in his disarmingly offhand way, "but that's all I'd feel justified in risking at this stage." The same detachment permeated everything he did at Dollis Hill. On the stroke of five every evening, no matter what excitements or crises might be under way, he laid down his pen and went home.

Meanwhile, Julia and Eliot worked like slaves, supervising the installation of the machinery, kitting out the offices, and setting up the design room and blueprinting equipment. After a month or so, when she looked ready to drop from fatigue, he put her coat over her shoulders, though it was still midmorning, clasped it to her like a straitjacket, with the words, "Come on, Boss. This morning we've got *important* work to do."

But she squirmed out of his grip, picked up a memo that her secretary had just dropped in her in-tray, skimmed it swiftly, and replied, "Sorry, but it'll have to wait. There's a crisis about installing the new vertical milling lathe (whatever that is)."

He took the paper from her and, without reading it, let it fall to her desk. "Let me tell you the one big secret of good management – the one they never taught us in college. When we get back this evening, there'll be two more memos here on top of that one. The topmost one will say: 'That trouble with the milling lathe? Forget it. Problem solved.' The middle one will say: 'That trouble with the lathe – I think I see an answer.' Take my word."

"But what's the secret in that?"

"The secret is to hire good people and vanish when there's trouble." He herded her toward the door.

"But what . . ." she asked, still reluctant to yield, "could possibly be more . . ."

"You'll see. It's high time you learned what this-hyar outfit of ours is all about."

Her half-guesses were confirmed when, a few minutes later, he swung his little Alvis onto the new road to Hendon.

"Seriously," he told her, "you must learn to delegate more. You'll kill yourself at this rate."

"I'll try," she promised.

They bounced around the landing field, pausing to let a Pup go taxiing ahead of them to the fuel pumps. "Rory McRory," Eliot informed her. "The all-time lunatic of the air."

"Why d'you say that?"

As if in answer, McRory, who was only a couple of hundred yards short of the nearest petrol pump, decided that taxiing was too slow for him. He revved up, took off, and landed again almost immediately – but still with too much impulse to halt in time. He sideswiped the pump and slewed around, seemingly undamaged. The pump teetered and fell. All around the airfield people held their breath, waiting for the flames. But none came.

"What a man!" Eliot laughed. "A couple of years back he flew that thing through a railway tunnel on the line to Bury. How he didn't kill himself . . ." He shook his head. "Anyway, he ran out of gas and crash landed in Bury high street. A dear old lady there thought he was in shock. Actually he was just hung over, but she stoked up her fire and set him right beside it. He sat there and sweat till the dye from his flying suit ran down him in rivers."

"Why didn't he take it off?"

"He only had pajamas underneath. It was early Sunday morning – he hadn't even had breakfast. He was stained donkey-brown for weeks. I tell you – some of the people you meet here!"

They drew to a halt outside one of the smaller hangars. "Nervous?" he asked.

She wasn't going to admit it. "You're not crazy like that," she commented hopefully.

"A lot of people would say it's crazy to be messing around with airplanes at all – even in the way of business, I mean. My father, for one."

"Yes, but physically reckless. Daredevil. Madcap. You're not like that." She helped push aside the huge doors.

"I guess I'm second generation," he replied. "The same thing happened with cars. Those early automobilists were kind of maniacs, too." He opened a locker just inside the doorway and took out a Sidcup suit. "Put this on. You can find a dark corner somewhere. I'll go log us out."

He was away about five minutes. She felt manly, gladiatorial inside the leather suit – also a bit of a fake. While she waited she strolled around aimlessly.

The hangar was crowded with planes of all shapes and sizes – a forest of struts and spars and wire; it reminded her of that room filled with fossil skeletons at the Natural History Museum. Each individual plane was dwarfed by the enclosure. If they seemed small here, she pondered, what puny things they must be in the horizon-to-horizon vastness out there. Her stomach fell away inside her.

When he returned he, too, was in flying gear. She had never seen him like that before, so heroic. Her heart began to dance. He looked her over with approval before he pointed out his own machine, an Avro 504K, which had actually been built at Grahame White's factory here in Hendon. He lifted the tailwheel clear of the ground; as always his physical strength excited her. "Push anywhere you see a rib."

"Talking of those early automobilists," she remarked as they inched the machine toward the doorway, "if they were maniacs of anything it was of patience. My father drove me to London once, it must have been soon after the turn of the century. He had a very upright old Benz, a real boneshaker. We had eleven punctures going up and fifteen coming back. All my early motoring memories are of sitting becalmed in country lanes, enjoying the silence and birdsong, while someone went to hire a horse to tow us home. He always joked that *two*-seater was a misprint for *tow*-seater." The comparison suddenly struck her. "What do we do if this thing suddenly breaks down hundreds of feet up there?"

"It won't." His grin was confident as he braced the wheel with chocks.

"Yes, but if?"

"What we do is look around for a cream-puff factory – there are usually several – and we pick the biggest."

She sighed and began a critical inspection of the machine, now that it was out in full daylight. The doped-fabric skin, the bolted covers over the engine, and, in the cockpit, the polished brass control knobs and levers and things . . . the very lettering on the dials – there were far too many parallels with prewar motor cars for her to feel happy with jokes and bland assurances. Above all she wished he hadn't talked of *crash* landing in Bury high street. He helped her in and then climbed into the cockpit behind her; she felt terribly exposed. Why couldn't it be like riding pillion on a motor bike, with her sitting behind?

A passing mechanic didn't even ask if they wanted a swing; he stopped and waited while Eliot hovered over Julia, telling her how to tighten the straps. The flying helmet, which had been lying casually on the front seat, smelled of leather, oil, pomade – everything but fear. The fit was snug and more reassuring than anything Eliot might have said.

"Plug in that cable there," he advised, "and if you want to talk to me, there's a mike in the pig's snout." He waggled a cone-shaped lump of leather that dangled from one of the cheek flaps.

"Is this *your* plane?" she asked. "I mean not hired or anything."

"It's my own." He settled in the rear cockpit. "Bought it two weeks back," a crackly voice added in her ears.

She wondered why he'd bothered to equip it so lavishly for two and then realized it was for her. She felt inordinately pleased.

She tried the intercom. "Why am I in front?" she asked.

"The instructor needs to see what blunders the learner is making," he explained.

Before she grasped the implications of that, the joystick in front of her started to move. "Grab a-hold," the intercom commanded. And while she followed the movements that disembodied voice, which seemed to be located inside her skull, said things like, "descend, climb, bank and turn . . ." When it came to "rudder," bits of the floor moved. It concluded with, "Okay, now you're familiar with that. See? Nothing to it."

After a moment he spoke again. She thought he said, "See that leather to your right?"

"Leather?" she queried.

"Okay – *leever,* if you insist. That's the throttle – more gas, less gas, okay?"

He must then have nodded toward the waiting mechanic, for the man sprang into action and swung the propeller, and again . . . and again.

"Ah, so that's what we do when it conks out at five hundred feet," she called over the intercom.

"Damn – I was saving it as a surprise."

The lever hunted up and down the scale until at last the engine fired. The sudden roar was deafening, despite the muffling effect of the flying cap and earphones; it was like standing amidst half a dozen racers at Brooklands.

The mechanic ran a short way backward, giving the thumbs-up. The engine was quick to heat. Eliot throttled back while the man walked in again and pulled away the chocks. Now nothing – or no physical impediment – lay between them and the wide blue yonder.

The revs climbed until they began to inch forward; the moment they started moving, all her fear drained away. Action was the grave of all her misgivings.

What little wind there was lifted the airfield sock fitfully toward the southeast. They taxied to the nearer, southern, end of the field and put the thin, watery sun behind them.

"Ready?" he called.

"Don't ask. Just go!"

The motor rose to an earsplitting roar. The backwash, which had been a breeze, turned into a full gale as the machine leaped eagerly forward over the grass. "See?" His voice was now a reedy crackle. "She comes complete with her own headwind."

Details of the near terrain blurred in horizontal streaks. Faster and faster they went, yet still they seemed earthbound. Then came a sudden change, which took a moment or two to identify; she realized that the deep thrumming note of the wheels had stopped. They were airborne at last.

They began gaining on their own shadow, which soon fell away beneath them. The stick came toward her and suddenly there was nothing but sky ahead. Looking sideways she could see the roofs of the houses, smoke from the chimneys curled gently downwind, like seaweed in a tidal pool. The "ocean of the air," an image beloved of airmen, was suddenly made visible.

Higher they climbed, while she watched the bird's-eye view turn into a coloured map. Cars became indistinguishable from one another. People turned into ants. They were passing over a lot of houses.

"Where are we?" she asked.

"Don't you recognize it?"

The sun was ahead and to the left, so they were pointing almost due south. That and the canal gave it away. The randomness below took on a familiar order. There was the cemetery . . . Scrubs Lane, the railways, the huts and sheds that were now Somerville Motors, some half demolished, others half built. And below her, somewhere in that grove of trees, was the clay that had once been George Somerville. She tested herself for some emotion, but the distance, the antlike quality of the people, precisely mirrored her feelings. The calendar might record it as only months ago; to her it was already a previous life.

Eliot banked in a long, slow arc, veering southward over Wormwood Scrubs – both the park and the prison – the old exhibition grounds at White City, Shepherd's Bush Green, the vast new exhibition halls of Olympia and Earl's Court, looking like hangars for Zeppelins . . . and on over Fulham and Chelsea to the Thames. It amazed her to see how exactly the streets and buildings conformed to the familiar maps of London; when you were down there among it all, trying to use those same maps while driving through an unfamiliar quarter, you'd swear the draughtsmen were bungling fools.

The other surprise was the *greenness* of the city. It wasn't just the huge expanses of the royal parks, nor even the smaller squares; it was the individual gardens before and behind almost every house.

When they reached the Thames he turned sharply left and flew eastwards, downriver. He also shed some of their altitude until the maplike view gave way to the most wonderful toyland in all the world. As they skimmed over the buildings – the huge power station at Battersea, the Tate Gallery . . . the Palace at Lambeth . . . the whole of Westminster and Whitehall . . . and on toward St Paul's floating majestically above the city . . . she had to keep reminding herself that these were not perfect scale models but the actual buildings themselves.

Even when they reached the Tower of London and he turned north again, continuing their long anticlockwise tour of northern London, she was still on familiar ground, for here was the East End, most of whose pinched, drab streets she and Theresa Ashbury had trudged on SPRP business.

"You know where we are?" Eliot asked.

"Indeed I do."

But it was true only in the most general sense. How indistinguishable they were, those endlessly duplicate back-to-back houses! She could pick out the main thoroughfares, the ancient highways that had once carried Roman legions to and from Londinium, but the modern streets between them were like the teeth of a broken comb.

When he picked up the line of the River Lea she guessed his intention, for if they followed it upstream, almost due north, it would bring them twenty-odd miles to Ware. The journey, which took a car the best part of an hour, lasted under twenty minutes. If she had any lingering doubts at the wisdom of switching from cars to planes, that answered them.

But how vast London was growing! They did not fly clear of the built-up area until they reached Tottenham, about seven miles out. When they were once more over green fields, now spattered with reservoirs and glasshouses, he suggested, "Why don't you fly her a piece?"

"No!" she shrieked by reflex, but in the same breath she added, "D'you think I dare?"

"Grab a-hold of the stick. Have you got it?"

"Yes." She held her breath, too.

"All yours, Boss. Just keep her straight and level."

At first she did not believe him. They were in calm air and level flight. Every control rested in its neutral position. Only when she pulled the stick hesitantly toward her and saw the horizon drop away did she know it was true.

"Keep her there," Eliot told her. "A bit steeper."

"But we're climbing!"

"You'll see."

The rush of wind steadily declined in force. The engine began to labour.

"Feel anything?" he asked. "Move the stick about."

Gingerly she complied.

"More!" he called, and waggled it for her.

"It doesn't seem to make any difference."

"Right! Make a note of it."

The entire machine felt as if it were somehow sagging in the sky. Then one wing began to dip. Immediately Eliot thrust the joystick forward.

She felt as if her innards were still some hundred feet above them but as the plane fell it gathered speed and the controls began again to bite.

"That's called *stalling*," he told her. "Learn to recognize it. It's the big killer."

He let her do it a couple of times more, until it became almost instinctive to thrust the stick forward; then he set her on to simple weaving, which brought them all the way to Ware.

"Who taught you to fly?" she asked.

"An out-and-out charlatan. Later I found he'd only done three hours himself. I learned with a manual in one hand and the stick in the other."

"And your heart in your mouth, I should think."

"Right!"

He took the plane on the last few miles to Allbury, where they

circled the estate a couple of times.

"Can't you find a field?" she asked. "They all look pretty fl
me."

"I was thinking the same," he replied. "It's wonderful."

He picked the field on the little ridge above the house and set
down gently. Over lunch Max told them Crownfield was the gr
est banker since the early days of Lombardy. (He did not know
Julia and Neville's were his secret guarantors, of course.) The wh
place was looking cared-for once more and the spring ploughii
though late, was all complete.

"I see young Dolly's landed quite a good part in some bally pla
Max commented as they were strolling back to the plane.

"Good heavens!" Julia tried to joke about it. "Is the theatre st
going, then? Is there still a West End . . . night clubs . . . all that?"

He nodded glumly.

She became serious. "Oh, Max – what am I to do? I swore t
myself that I'd let her make the first move this time."

"May I butt in?" Eliot asked. "Not knowing your sister, of cours
– but could it be she's waiting for a big success? Or any kind o
success? Then she could meet you more on level terms."

"I told you so," Max said.

Julia stared at him in astonishment. "You did no such thing!"

"No, no." He grew testy. "That's what she'd be able to say. I
think Baring's right."

"Well then." Julia's shrug closed the topic. "We shall just have to
redouble our prayers for the dear girl."

Eliot allowed her to pull back the joystick at the moment of
takeoff. By the time they landed at Hendon she had acquired an
addiction. They manhandled the plane back into the hangar, to the
space it had occupied that morning.

Was it only that morning, she wondered in amazement? Since then
she had begun a new life. She clung to one of the wing struts and,
closing her eyes, leaned her cheek against its varnished surface.
"Beautiful . . . beautiful," she murmured.

"Beautiful," he echoed from very near.

She looked up to find him only inches away.

She closed her eyes once more, opened her lips, and lifted her face
to his. That long moment flowed out of – was continuous with – her
earlier intoxication with flying. He was a radiant sky-god and this
was another kind of flying, light-bodied and soaring.

Their lips broke contact. He took her head in his hands and stared
deep into her eyes. But she could not look at him for his beauty
roused her too keenly. She hugged him close and laid her head
against his throat.

"How about it?" he asked.

"About what?"

"You know – us. I didn't want to intrude myself. But you've been pretty open. You haven't pretended to a grief you don't . . . you know. So I just wondered."

"Well . . ." She tried to think what she could say that he wouldn't be able to take as a veiled commitment. "You've been so wonderful to me, Eliot. If you hadn't been there, if we didn't have all this, I mean, the company and flying and everything, I'd have been so . . . *angry* these past months, so bitter and . . ."

"Angry?" The word surprised him.

"I was a good wife, Eliot."

"Sure you were." He was still mystified.

"Yet I don't think George ever . . . I mean, he was in my mind for a large part of every day. But I don't believe he ever thought of me at all. I was just 'wifey.' That's what he called me." She shivered at the echoes of the word, at the memory that she had once found it endearing. "And at the end . . ."

"What?"

"You know that girl who looked after him – Imogen Davis?"

He held her tight. "Don't distress yourself, honey. I know about that."

"They were having . . . you can't call it an *affaire*. An *affaire* has at least some spark of romance. They were . . . just . . ."

"I see why you said anger."

"No, I was angry because I couldn't mourn him properly – because he took with him all the things that love should leave behind."

He held her tight awhile and then murmured, "Okay. I understand."

After another silence she added, "I'm still not quite ready."

"Sure." His lips, grazing her ear, her neck, made her instantly regret the finality of words, all words.

"I wanted to kiss you that very first day," he told her. "D'you remember it?"

"Mmmm." She kissed him lightly and broke free. "You didn't know how to deal with me at all."

"Well maybe I was getting confusing signals. I'll tell you one thing that puzzled me – those paintings you found among all that garbage. They meant something, didn't they. I never felt anyone's mood change quicker."

She explained their significance to him.

"Wow!" he exclaimed, flinching.

"George denied it to the end, of course," she added. "He even accused me of faking copies. He didn't know the first thing about me."

They began to stroll back to his car.

"I can't begin to tell you how grateful I am for . . . today, Eliot," she sighed.

"Aw . . ." He shrugged and cleared his throat uncomfortably.

"I can confess it now. I was beginning to have doubts about . . . well, you know – the wisdom of getting so involved in the business. I mean, the reason I've immersed myself . . ." She gave up and started a new tack. "I shouldn't be fretting about vertical milling machines. It's absurd. I fell into the same trap as George – trying to do everything. *Be* everything. That's why today was so valuable." She turned to see if he understood.

He nodded, smiled lazily, like a cat.

"You knew it, too," she accused. "Mind you, I still can't say what I ought to be doing."

"It'll come."

"Yes. Somehow today I felt near to knowing it. Oh yes, I'm sure it'll come."

When they were in the car and on their way back to Dollis Hill, she took up their earlier conversation. "Talking of those water colours, funnily enough, I found them again only last week. In fact, I brought them to the office to hang them up. I had them mounted in one large frame – to cover the wall safe, I thought. There's an old wall safe just lying about in one of the cellars at Allbury."

"Oh, well that shows how observant I am. I didn't even see them. I'm sorry."

She laughed. "No. I forgot to do it. But I will, the minute we get back. If George's ghost ever came spooking around . . . what a snub, eh!"

Ten minutes later they arrived back at the works – where, naturally, the vertical milling lathe had been installed perfectly, despite their absence. "What a lot I learned today," she told him. "How to manage a company. How to fly . . ."

"How to fend off a rash suitor in the nicest possible way," he added.

She glanced hastily up and down the corridor and promised, "Soon, my dear."

But lessons were not yet over. She had just hung the pictures when Mrs Henderson, George's former secretary, who had transferred here from Forge Lane, came in. She saw the two paintings and gasped. "Boss! Where did you find those?"

Julia spun in surprise; she saw the woman had turned almost scarlet. "D'you recognize them?" she asked.

"Oh . . . yes." She was all flustered. "Hyde Park aren't they?"

"No, I mean have you seen them before?"

"Why . . . no."

It was the most transparent lie. Julia smiled, "I think I've already guessed the truth, Mrs Henderson."

"I knew it." The woman slumped. "I knew it would all come out one day." She stared hard at Julia. "You know what really happened?

And you aren't cross?"

"I was extremely cross at the time. But . . ." She shrugged. "Wounds have a habit of healing, eh? Tell me – exactly."

"Well – it was a long, long time ago. I was ashamed as soon as . . . you know . . . and I've been deeply ashamed ever since."

"Oh, it was hardly your fault, Mrs Henderson."

"It was *all* my fault. The Guv'nor was so proud of them. So proud of you. And when he offered it – the first one you painted – when he offered it to Lord Berners and got refused, he was so crestfallen. But it was I who made up the lie. I told him Lord Berners had returned and bought it after all. I just explained he was a bit embarrassed at dealing with the Guv'nor, so I'd taken it on myself to sell them. Thank God the Guv'nor died never knowing the truth. He crowed about it for months."

Julia felt sick. "How did you raise the five pounds?" she asked. "That must have been a couple of weeks' wages then."

"We had a whip round. Then when you painted the second one and he asked me to offer that to his lordship, too! You can imagine. Thank heaven you stopped at that or we'd all have been broke." Her rich laugh carried her to the door, where, however, she turned solemn again. "The Guv'nor – he never knew, did he?"

"No. He died believing your story."

When the woman had gone, Julia put out the lights and sat at her desk. "Oh George," she whispered. A large, hot slug of a salty tear crawled down her cheek. "Oh George, I'm *sorry!*"

There was a movement in the room. Her hair stood on end. Her flesh crawled. "Who . . ." she faltered.

"It's me, honey," Eliot said. "Are you okay? Where's the switch?"

"No! Leave it dark. Oh, Eliot – it's so awful!" She burst into tears.

"Darling . . . oh, darling." He came swiftly to her and lifted her out of her chair into his enormous embrace.

Never had she wanted him, or any man, quite so desperately. "Now!" she whispered. Her voice was reedy, shivery. Her heart was all over the place. As they peeled off each other's clothes she thought she would faint with so much longing, with all that saved-up desire.

He was marvellous – big, eager, firm, gentle . . . and loving. Above all, he was loving. And for that she yielded to him without reserve.

When it was over, when she had gathered her scattered wits and feelings, she asked, "Let me spend tonight with you? Don't let me be alone tonight?"

"What is it? What's happened to you? Is it anything to do with . . . flying today?"

As they climbed back into their clothes she told him the story, just as Mrs Henderson had told it to her. She broke down again before she finished but he had the gist of it. He put his arms around her and caressed her gently until her grief worked itself out.

"I was so sure," she said bitterly.

He let her talk. Standing there in the dark, he gave her scope to say it all. "Oh Eliot, that poor man! How little I tried to understand him . . . I mean – when he rejected me like that . . ." She fell silent.

After a while she went on, "I was so sure he did it deliberately – threw away those paintings, I mean. I was so sure he had that sort of contempt for me – little wifey and all that."

"He did deceive you with Imogen," Eliot reminded her gently.

"But why? That's what I've never faced – why? How can I ever judge him again?"

"Because not to judge people – even the dead, or maybe especially the dead – is just a different form of contempt."

"But look where it's led me – judging him like that."

"It's led you to realize that on at least one occasion you were wrong. Okay, there may be others. Other occasions, I mean. But d'you think you were always wrong – just because of this one time?"

"It wasn't just *one* time, my dear. It was *the* time. The final time. His rage at being accused . . . I . . . I'm the one who . . ." She broke down again.

"You can't quite say it, can you?" he asked calmly. "Not because it's too awful, but because it's not true. Look, suppose that particular bout of anger hadn't been the one to kill him. Are you saying there wouldn't have been others? Just think of all the anger he was going to feel over the weeks to come. Or are you trying to claim you'd just have torn up all those bits of paper and let him have carte blanche?"

She did not reply.

"Come on," he urged.

"If I'd known it would kill him – yes, I would."

He chuckled. "Well now that's something else. *'If I had known!'* That puts you in the same class as any motorist who ever had an accident in which a pedestrian had the misfortune to die."

Still she said nothing, but he felt a sort of relaxation in her.

"And anyway, you're not alone," he murmured. "We're all in there somewhere."

At last she could speak.

She raised her lips to his ear and she whispered, "I love you."

CHAPTER TWENTY-THREE

IT WAS BRUNTY who finally helped her discover her true role at Neville's. For a while she thought that, as she knew a bit about accounts and (by now) a bit about workshop practice, she could act as a kind of liaison between those two important branches of the firm. But neither Eliot nor Brunty would agree to it. In fact, Eliot brought in a college friend of his, a Canadian called Tom Murgatroyd, to be what he called "cost comptroller" and what Brunty called "progress chaser." Tom kept the tightest rein on all workshop costs as well as on the flow of every job through the factory. After watching him just one day she knew she could never have done it. The workers, untroubled by such niceties as the 49th parallel, called him the "Yankee Scroogedriver."

"And they call *me* Boss," she complained to Brunty. "But what does it mean?"

He, ever ready to lay down his pen – which he did with a lordly grandeur – said, "I've always thought of it as a pet name for the real world."

She gave him a puzzled frown.

"Yes," he insisted. "Take the rest of us – the specialists. Despite our talents, each of us works in his own kind of vacuum. For instance, papers flow across my desk here; I read them; and then I reach a decision. But this desk could just as easily be at the north pole for all the difference it would make to the quality of my decision."

"Maybe, but it's different with Baring," she pointed out.

"Is it? His work is essentially a battle with the physical constraints of the universe – the laws of physics, if you like. He has to find ways of persuading certain organized lumps of matter to give more output for less input, to do it more reliably, to wear out more slowly . . . and so on. But that kind of battle could just as easily be carried on at a laboratory bench in some university. D'you see my point? In a way it's only *coincidentally* going on here at Neville's."

His demeanour suggested that he'd answered all her worries.

She gave an ironic laugh. "You speak of the real world? In the real world, I'm something of a curiosity. I meet it all the time at dinner parties – a female boss of such a technical business. People can't believe it. And nor can I sometimes."

"How d'you deal with it?"

"Oh, I've evolved a stock answer by now. I say, 'If you asked me to check the clearance on a poppet valve, I wouldn't even know what size sledgehammer to use. But I do know why the clearance is important – more or less.'" She chuckled. "And d'you know, I've actually had one shocked engineer reply: 'No, no! You shouldn't use a sledgehammer.'" She pulled a face. "That's the real world for you."

"Not at all – if I may say so. The real world is *not* one in which people check poppet valves, or shave twenty seconds off the time taken to ream out an oil galley, or decide to get out of gilt-edged and stay liquid. That's a *play* world, which is why we wear such funny clothes for it. The real world is where a rich wife wakes up one morning with a whim to *fly* to Paris instead of taking that slow, grubby old boat-train. And if Neville's doesn't succeed in *that* world, then Baring and Murgatroyd and Crownfield and St John Brunty might just as well go off and play marbles."

She laughed, thinking he was being perverse, as usual. The truth of his words did not dawn on her until, a week or so later, she described her maiden flight with Baring to Crownfield. The banker listened with interest and then let fall some casual remark about being able to understand how a bomber pilot can be so offhand about dropping high-explosive indiscriminately on people: "because to him they aren't people. Just ants."

She asked when he had experienced flying and he told her he had, in fact, flown to Amsterdam the previous week, to a trade fair in which one of the bank's customers was heavily involved.

Naturally she began at once to ply him with questions – which air company, what planes, how many seats, was it comfortable, who were his fellow passengers, what made them decide to fly rather than take the ferry? And so on.

He had to admit that while waiting at the Croydon Airport he had buried his face in the *Financial News,* and on the plane his attention had been equally divided between a pair of company reports and a pair of legs that belonged to a night-club singer from Rio.

"Good lord, Crownfield, anyone would think you had no connection with the business at all!"

"I fail to see," he answered loftily, "how my turning myself into a sort of aviational Sherlock Holmes would in any way affect the advice I might give to you or the decisions I might take. Why don't you do your own sleuthing?"

And there it was. Brunty's advice without the fancy topping.

The following Friday, the last in July, she and Eliot were whisked in an Imperial Airways limousine to the Croydon Airport, where they waited half an hour for the "City of Birmingham" – a brand new Armstrong Whitworth Argosy, to take them on the "Silver Wing" service to Paris. "Silver Wing," at four guineas single, was extremely First Class. Other flights, at four pounds, were just standard First Class. The comparable boat-train ticket, she noted in her commercial diary of the journey, was three pounds.

While they waited, a receptionist went around checking their names against a list. Julia, reading upside down, saw that Lady de Reszke, Baron Doiney, and a certain H. Latham Esq. were of their party.

"I wonder if that's the Hubert Latham who was always crashing his aeroplanes?" Julia murmured quietly to Eliot. "Before the war. Every time his rescuers found him, the newspapers always reported that he was 'discovered calmly smoking a cigarette.' It became a music-hall joke. Every petty adulterer, caught in the act, was always 'discovered calmly smoking a cigarette.'"

"Talking of newspapers," Baring replied in equally muted tones, "and in that same general area – did you see that girl? When she finished checking all our names she handed the carbon to a furtive little guy who looked mighty like a reporter."

"Oh, but the press get all the passenger lists."

"They *what?*"

"Shh! Didn't you know?"

"Did you?"

"Well," she replied, "I often see the names in the papers, and I've never imagined the reporters had to stow away to get them."

He lowered his voice still further. "But . . . what about the risk? Us, I mean – it's like announcing we're off to Paris for the weekend."

"Baring's at the top of the list. Somerville's near the bottom."

"But people can put one and one together."

"And make two. They'd make two *hundred* if my name were on today's list and yours on tomorrow's. Besides, I don't know how it is in America but you should learn one thing about England: No one cares a fig what a widow with a couple of children does."

She turned to him, only to find a look of faint surprise on his face. "What now?" she asked.

"Oh, nothing. It's just when you say 'a widow with two children,' I mean, it's a whole different part of your life. The part I never get to see. You're pretty amazing."

She looked at him coolly, unable to accept the compliment. "Guilty. That's more my word for it. I feel I neglect poor Lydia dreadfully. Robert has Max, of course. And being away at school."

"D'you think Lydia shares your opinion?"

After a silence she said, "Oh, let's talk about something else." But then, almost immediately, she added, "All this nonsense about emancipated women – I think my mother was a jolly sight more emancipated than any of us nowadays. I mean, I used to see her for about ten minutes every day." She turned to Eliot as if these revelations were almost as new to her as they were to him. "And do you know – I never for one moment doubted her love for me or felt insecure and all the things they go on about in books ad nauseam."

"Lydia is one of the luckiest little girls in England. What are you worried about?"

"Not spending enough time with her."

"Sackcloth does not become you. I much prefer the Chanel suit we are certainly going to buy tomorrow morning. Tell me what you think of our fellow passengers. Only don't look up. This is a memory test."

She played along. Running her mental eye clockwise around the room, she said: "Those three are obviously businessmen. The woman next to them is a film star, or would-be, a night-club singer from Rio, probably. I wonder if Lydia would like to go to that wonderful freedom school everyone's talking about – Sunny Dale, is it? Some name like that."

"Who's next to the night-club singer from Rio?"

"It's run by that man, Neil something. He wrote that splendid book about problem children. Not that Lydia's a problem child. But they take in normal children, too."

"Hey." Eliot touched her arm. "Remember me?"

She laughed. "Sorry. I think I'll talk to her about it. I'm sure it's her sort of place. The fat little man next to the night-club woman is obviously a German. And judging by his camera, I'd say he's spying for Junkers. The couple are on their second honeymoon. The man next to them is Baron Doiney, I feel sure. Next to him . . . something in Grand Opera, don't you think? The two smart lawyers are going out to advise the French Government on ways to avoid repaying the British War Loan . . ."

"I'll risk saying it again," he interrupted. "You're amazing."

"Don't be absurd. I'm making it all up."

"Yes, but it fits. Age, sex, type – it fits. I could never do that."

"It's no secret. I don't clutter my head with foot-pounds-per-cubic-second or parties-of-the-first-part, so there's plenty of room for fancies to rattle around. And guilt. I'm tired of sitting here. Let's go out and see how they load the baggage."

The Junkers spy took advantage of their lead and followed them out. He stood a little way off and began snapping as if the film were free.

"By God he *is* spying for Junkers!" Julia said.

Eliot chuckled. "Hey – what if *everyone* on this trip is spying for rival airlines or manufacturers! Or everybody on every trip. Suppose there's no real market at all! Like this thriller I'm reading where the baddies are anarchists but it turns out that every single one of them is actually working for the secret service and there's no real gang at all."

Out on the tarmac apron some porters were stacking mailbags in the hold, which was tucked behind the passenger cabin. Every bag had its weight written on a label, which the pilot checked before telling them where to stow it. When the work was complete he locked the door – and checked it twice.

"That's the gentleman who pays the rent," he remarked affably as he joined them. "The Postmaster General." He gave the Junker spy a cheery wink and then nodded to a couple of mechanics, who set about starting up the three engines. "We'll just let her warm up a bit," he added, "and then we'll be off. Nice clear day for navigation."

"We're the profit, then?" Julia suggested.

"The cream, ma'am."

One engine roared into life. They had to raise their voices.

"What's she like to fly?" Eliot asked.

"Bit of a crate. She only had her maiden flight in service last Monday. She's not bad with the wind up her tail, but *against* the wind – well, I've watched buses and cars down on the roads overtaking me. The ashtrays are more streamlined than she is – but she's steady and dependable, I'll say that."

The two other engines had now added their roar and further conversation was impossible. The passengers were invited to join the aircraft at that moment. The cabin resembled a long railway carriage of a distinctly narrow gauge, furnished by a designer of suburban tennis clubs – all wickerwork chairs and tables, ranged down its length. Magazines and ashtrays were dotted here and there; the pilot was right about the streamlining. Julia chose a copy of *Passing Show* for herself and offered *Ikarus* to the German spy. He pulled a face and told her, in a perfect Welsh accent, "Not my cup of tea, I'm afraid." He then introduced himself as David Morgan and added self-consciously that he was the pilot's brother-in-law; he waggled the camera – "Taking a few snaps for my wife's family album, see."

Surreptitiously Julia placed her foot firmly on Eliot's toe cap and squashed it.

A narrow door at the front of the cabin gave access to the open cockpit where the pilot sat. It was used almost incessantly by a freckle-faced schoolboy (or so he seemed) known as the "Observer." His main job appeared to be to observe the passengers, smile enormous encouragement at them, and (as it later transpired) collect the sickbags. Shortly after takeoff, while the pilot was still seeking out the railway line to Dover, this young lad had quite a bit of collecting to do, for those huge, sail-like wings put the craft at the mercy of every stray up- and down-draught.

But all was well again when, an hour or so later, they soared out over the white cliffs at that curious half-and-half altitude where, although you can just about discern individual waves on the face of the sea, you are too high to notice any movement. Ships were coloured toys at the points of white arrows upon that frozen surface of wrinkled glass.

These wonders kept everyone's eyes down until they were well out to sea. Eliot saw it first. "Unh-oh," he murmured in her ear. "I've just remembered the second good reason why we shouldn't be in the same plane."

Julia followed his gaze. A six-foot streak of flame was pouring downwind from the starboard engine. She gripped his arm and tried not to remember that, apart from the metal of the engine itself and a few yards of staywire, everything out there was fuel to a flame like that.

The freckled cherub saw her gesture and glanced to starboard, too. The freckles darkened as his skin turned white. He dived through the cockpit door.

Moments later, to a chorus of surprise from the passengers, the tail slewed to starboard, causing the craft to yaw about ten degrees to its flight path. Then they, too, noticed the flames.

The night-club singer from Rio screamed. The two smart lawyers shot to their feet and grabbed the edge of the luggage rack. Everyone else just stared – except for the brother-in-law, who went on remorselessly filling the family album. "Don't worry," he told everyone cheerfully, "if anyone can get us down safely, it's Dicky."

The Observer returned. If his skin had earlier gone chalk-white it was now almost translucent. He stared sorrowfully around, gave a brave but wan little smile, raised his fists, thumbs-down, and dunked them a couple of times. Then he fixed his eyes on the damaged engine.

Spontaneously, everyone rose to their feet and, clutching the luggage rack, turned to look at that same spot; the boy's fatalistic gesture had the extraordinary effect of calming them.

"I'll just never understand the English," Eliot mused. He stared again at the engine. "Looks like he's cut the gas at least."

The propeller was free-milling. The tongue of flame had grown visibly shorter but now the tip of it was curling down against the canvas of the wing. The pilot must have seen it, too, for he put the plane into a moderate dive. The increased airflow stretched the flame again and unstuck it from the wing surface.

Julia estimated their height at two thousand feet, or even less; their lives now depended on which gave out first – their altitude, or the petrol that was still, somehow trickling into that engine.

Ships were now bigger than toys; you could peer down their funnels and discern their rigging. You could see the waves moving.

"Is that the French coast?" she asked, pressing her cheek to the window and squinting forward.

"Unless they moved it," he replied with a laugh he would have done better not to attempt.

Until then Julia had been confident of living; suddenly, in that ghastly attempt at cheer, she heard the knell of death. "How well do these Argosies pancake in water?" she asked.

His expression revealed a vain search for some encouraging way of saying, "dreadfully." At length he just shrugged. "So-so."

The ships had passengers now, and deck cargo. The waves were capped with white horses. And still the fire guttered on.

"Why doesn't he climb and try again?" one of the businessmen asked.

Julia almost answered him. She knew enough about airflow by now to realize that any attempt to climb would stick that flame to the wing like glue. Eliot, who had a born teacher somewhere inside him, was about to offer the explanation when she caught his eye. "That engine's got to run out of fuel soon, surely?" she asked.

"Any second," he answered.

The ships' passengers had faces now – and arms. They were waving gaily at the bold plane, swooping so low. To Julia's surprise, she found herself waving back. Everyone was waving back. One of the businessmen began to laugh, "They're probably filled with envy of us!"

The laugh developed an hysterical edge.

At last the plane ran out of altitude. Fifty feet above the waves she levelled out. Now, with nothing to lose, the pilot "poured on the coals," and the two remaining engines roared to their maximum. Everyone felt the surge of power, and once more dared to hope. If they could make it to a beach somewhere . . .

She felt her grip tighten on Eliot's arm; that vast, lean strength of his had never seemed so reassuring. They all watched in horrified fascination as the wing caught fire. Eliot disengaged his hand and put an arm around her.

It was the end. Nothing else would lead him into such an open display of tenderness. She put her arms about him and waited calmly for the last seconds of her life to pass by. Held tight in his arms like that, she felt extraordinarily calm and happy. For once, thoughts of her children did not intrude; she and Eliot were the last two children in the world.

But then, with a swiftness that was almost savage, her resignation yielded to a bitter anger – at fate, at God himself. It was suddenly intolerable that Life, having so recently revealed its many possibilities to her, should now snatch them away so brutally, so casually . . . so *pointlessly*.

A cheer went up and she opened her eyes to discover that the flame had at long last been extinguished. In its place was a strange kind of gray tongue, a "flame" of smoke, that licked backward off the trailing edge; oddly, it was even more sinister than its fiery parent had been. A new sense of horror gripped them all as they realized that the menace, far from dying, had merely changed its form – and only its outward form at that. Eliot glanced at the kid. "Better tell your pilot," he suggested. "Maybe he can't see it."

But at once it became clear that the pilot had seen it – and from out there in his open-air cockpit he had seen something else, too, for the plane turned sharply to port. Eliot craned his neck, eagerly scanning each new strip of horizon as the turn brought it into view. "Well . . . jumping jiminy!" he said at last.

"What?" she asked.

"Brace yourself!" His grasp tightened.

The plane was suddenly buffetted from every quarter.

"Hold tight!" the Observer shouted, quite redundantly.

"It's probably the only shower in the whole English Channel today," Eliot marvelled. "And there it is – oh, you beauty!"

Julia relaxed her hug and turned to look out of the window, but rain was lashing the glass, obscuring the view completely. They were like fish in an aquarium tank. But they all cheered to the echo, for the rivers that ran across the glazing must also be running down the burning wing. Seconds later they were out again in the gleaming sunshine, which, as the ripples smoothed themselves upon the glass, revealed the burned patch, black, charred, glistening – and beautifully, wonderfully, dead.

But the pilot was taking no chances. He did a full, tight turn, and made one more pass through the shower before he banked and headed again for France. The light canvas ripping panels in the roof turned – in the words of the old air traveller's joke – to dripping panels, but no one complained.

They found a gap in the cliffs near St Valéry and soon put down in a field. The engines died and the silence was filled with one great collective sigh at their deliverance.

The pilot appeared and was given the ovation of his lifetime, but he cut it short with a wave of his hand. "Sorry about that spot of bother back there," he said. "I don't know whether any of you noticed, but we had a tiny hole in one of the exhausts. We'll just bung it up with chewing gum and be on our way again." He turned to his colleague. "Come on, Ginger – do your stuff. You know the drill."

Everyone piled out onto the grass. They all had to touch the burned patch. Eliot took out his pocket knife, selected the spike, and jabbed hard at the wooden frame beneath the charring. "Pretty sound," he called to the pilot. The man waved his acknowledgment and went on with what he was doing – which, to everyone's surprise, was painting out the legend IMPERIAL AIRWAYS and the much larger G–EBLO along the side of the fuselage. Ginger was doing the same along the other flank.

"My dear man, what *is* the point of that?" asked the second-honeymooning wife.

"Standing orders, madam." The pilot laughed. "The Paris papers, you see, will pay fairly well for snapshots of British planes enjoying a forced landing."

Everyone laughed, a little too loud and too long. To cheat death was hilarious enough, but to combine it with biffing those froggy newspapers was exquisite.

The moment they were rendered anonymous, Ginger got out a pair of snips and cut the paint tin down one side. Then he cut away the top rim and the whole of the bottom, leaving a flat sheet of metal. The pilot, meanwhile, had gone to the edge of the field; he returned with a handful of clay from the ditch and an angry farmer at his heels. But the man calmed down on receiving the company's standard envelope, containing more than adequate compensation for his trampled grass. He became genial enough to pull out a hip flask of Calvados and share a couple of noisy swigs with the pilot – whose knuckles, Julia now noticed, were cut and bleeding.

When the peasant had gone they smeared the clay on the sheet of metal, bent it around the holed exhaust tube, and bound it with stout, galvanized wire.

"Does this often happen?" Julia asked as the pilot snipped off the ragged ends.

He shook his head. "First time for me. It's usually either the water or the fuel. Chewing gum and insulating tape – that's our standard repair kit. This is sheer improvisation. Not bad, what?"

"Your hand?" she asked. "How did you do that?"

He glanced casually at them. "Oh, in that squall of rain back there. The stick was banging all over the cockpit. My own fault for removing my gloves."

The patch held all the way to Orly. Not a single passenger stayed behind in Normandy to follow on by rail. By the time they touched down they all felt like veterans. Looking about her, Julia thought, *The rich will put up with any extreme of discomfort or danger as long as they're assured it's beyond the pocket of the poor.*

The night-club singer from Rio was engulfed in a sea of children, shepherded by a fussy paterfamilias – Parisians every inch. The pair of smart lawyers now flew their own true colours, too – a brace of undergraduates to whom the idea of a spree in Gay Paree had once, in the mellow afterglow of a club supper, seemed quite spiffing.

Julia gave Eliot an acid smile. "Aren't I amazing?" she asked.

He didn't bat an eyelid. "To me," he said.

"I'll say one thing," she conceded. "I know a heck of a lot more about our business than I did this morning."

* * *

The brush with death, the closeness of their bodies throughout that incident, had made them hungry for each other as never before. Their hotel was a quiet, family affair in one of the quaint little streets that meander around the hill below Sacré Coeur. As soon as the room was theirs they locked the door and raced out of their clothes and into each other's arms. She had not made love so impetuously, so hungrily, since George's honeymoon (for that was how she still thought of it). Now that she was free of his strange regime, free to writhe and press herself against her lover, to move with him, to come with him – and show it – she was furious at the waste of those years, the still, silent servitude he had enforced on her and the dutiful yielding she had accepted as the real thing.

She made up for it that weekend, though. On Sunday afternoon, before their evening flight home, they went to bed one last time – and could do no more than lie there and laugh at themselves, at the gap between desire and performance.

"He's given us his all," Eliot murmured, looking down at himself.

"You've been marvellous, darling," she told him.

"Have I?" he asked. There was a nervous edge to the question.

"Yes," she affirmed.

"I wondered."

"But why? Haven't I said it often enough?"

"It's not that." He sighed. "I keep remembering what you once told me about yourself – how when you finally get something you wanted, it's not . . . it only seems like you got half of it."

She relaxed back into his arms. "Well I can't think of a single thing more I'd want from you, my darling."

But he was still tense. "Not even . . ." He shrugged. "No, I guess not."

"Eliot!"

"What?"

"You always *do* that! You say a tantalizing half of what's on your mind and then . . . what's your word for it? Clam up. Only you're not a clam, you're an oyster. For God's sake – cast your pearls!"

"Sorry," he intoned.

"No you're not. But if you were about to say what I think you were about to say, then let me tell you – I'm not ready for more than this. I can't . . . My life is too . . ." She clutched at her forehead in exasperation. "I'm just not ready. All right?"

He lay completely immobile.

"What now?" she asked.

He gave a dry laugh. "I'm just so dumb. I don't deserve you."

"Oh dear, Eliot. Somewhere between all these extremes isn't there a nice, comfy, dry little patch where you can just curl up and rest awhile?"

"It's just that I love you so much."

"And I love you, too. Isn't that enough?"

She kissed him hard, but – such is the power of suggestion – it now began to seem *not* enough.

CHAPTER TWENTY-FOUR

ELIOT BARING HAD a joke, which relied on the fact that the word schedule is pronounced "skedule" by his countrymen and "shedule" by the rest of the English-speaking world. "A *skedule*," he claimed, "is a *shedule* that actually delivers."

When the Baring One was ready in the early spring of 1927, just fifty weeks after the financial go-ahead was clear, he said it so often that the engineers at Neville's modified a little asbestos hut on the site, labelling the door: KEEP OUT – CHIEF DESIGNER'S GLOATING CHAM-BER. On the wall inside they pasted a map of America, a postcard view of the Statue of Liberty, and a list of shipping agents. But they also gave him his due – he had, indeed, organized the work with an efficiency undreamed of in the old Somerville days – he and Tommy Murgatroyd.

Crownfield was impressed – and he was not easily taken that way. "Those boys have saved you at least five and possibly ten thousand pounds," he told Julia.

Baring pooh-poohed the compliment, but only because he was trying to acquire English habits.

She was still an avid reader of literary romances, which surprised her. At the back of her mind she had always imagined that if a real-life passion of this intensity ever seized her, she'd lose her taste for what seemed like its substitute. But no; the relaxation of a mindless plunge into Daisy, or Sheila Kaye-Smith, or Juanita Savage was as necessary as ever. After a day at her desk, or flying, or at the SPRP (which she still kept up, though she was looking for someone to take over her more mundane functions), she found that a long mental soak in those vaguely steamy pages did for her mind what a good Turkish bath did for her body.

But both kinds of romance, literary and real, shared one thing in common: They mixed poorly with business. She and Eliot could be cat and dog during working hours; and the steamy novels stayed hidden in the wall safe behind the water-colour views of Hyde Park. In fact, they were the only valuables in there – and, like her drinks cabinet, it was never opened until after six of an evening.

Since her love affair with Baring had grown so strong, her relationship with Crownfield had turned into no more than a mild flirtation. He chafed, of course, not being sure about Eliot and being too proud to inquire. But what else could she do, she asked herself?

She saw the humour of the situation, of course. Both men were romantic heroes of a kind. Let Daisy get her simplifying hands on either and what would they become? Crownfield – sophisticated, charming, urbane, courteous, wise, tender, thoughtful, responsive to all her moods – it was all true, too. He was all of those things. And Baring – the young he-man, absurdly good-looking, gifted, and above all an aviator, the dream-hero of the age. Both men were fascinated by her. Both were marvellous lovers – at least, Crownfield would be, she felt sure (not that Daisy would have dwelled on such qualities but her readers would have known what she meant). Between the flattering attentions of the one and the passion she shared with the other, she ought to have been living one unbroken romantic idyll.

Why did it not feel like that, she wondered?

The answer lay somewhere within her; she was still waiting for that extra something. More! There must be more – it was that old feeling creeping back again.

Also, to be sure, there was Dear Lexy, who had started as a potential lover and was now turning into the staunchest of friends. He was, of course, the third romantic type, easily recognizable from her leisure-time reading – artistic, debonair, sensitive, lionized, *au fait* with every amusing scandal, always centre-stage. To him, too, she was someone very special. With him she could enjoy a true romance – and she did.

Deeping himself wanted something less ethereal than that. Julia in her early thirties was more attractive and vivacious by the day. Now she was no longer just "George Somerville's wife," or "whatsername with those two darling kiddies across the square," she was discovering that men found her fascinating, sought her company, canvassed her opinion, valued her approval. She was exactly the sort of ornament Deeping would have loved to wear, even if she had been no more attractive than the back end of the average London bus.

His own, rather simplistic, explanation for his failure to bring their romance to consummation went back to the weeks before George's death. He misread her devotion to her crippled husband and so, when the blow fell, offered himself as a sort of idealized older brother – *slightly* older, he would stress – in which role she gratefully accepted him. And there he was, frozen in the part for the foreseeable future.

Be that as it may, Dear Lexy was then putting the finishing touches to "Business Affaires," his finest play to date. In it, Edgar Luscombe, the banker, begins by lending Samantha Drysdale, inheritor of the family sawmills, more money than the business justifies – in return for which he demands and gets The Favour (as the Lord Chamberlain, censor of England's thespian morals, insisted they call it). At the final curtain, a slave to his passion, he has ruined the bank, himself, and her.

By the time he delivered the script, Lexy no longer saw the relationship between his Samantha and Edgar as Julia's to Crownfield. He knew, because she boasted of it to him, how she and Eliot and Brunty had raised the wind at Neville's. And yet he held in his safe the "confession" that Wallace Baker had concocted and which he still could not avoid equating with her and Crownfield – perhaps at some earlier stage in their lives. He could not help but use her for his heroine.

Edgar, as James Agate pointed out at the time, is simply Faust in modern dress; Samantha, by contrast – he added – "is the pure creation of Mr Deeping's genius." It was a judgement that caused many a smile among Julia's friends. Samantha was modelled so shamelessly after Julia that Crownfield, though relieved at finding nothing of himself in Edgar, was appalled. But Dear Lexy had been clever. He actually quoted Julia verbatim in several places. The best-known is where Samantha, in ironic comment on the charitable efforts of certain West End hostesses, proposes to form "an East End Ladies' Association to clothe the poor, half-naked creatures of Mayfair, to improve their insanitary diet by weaning them off paté and champagne, and to establish a crêche in Belgravia where young Society women may safely leave their babies instead of being compelled to entrust them to careless servants whenever heartless capitalism whips them to the Theatre, Ascot, and the villa at Cap d'Antibes." Another is where she says, "Just because ex-army officers and other gentlemen nowadays sell motor cars, it doesn't signify that the *general* morality of the trade has been lowered." Julia, once she began to move in Lexy's circle, showed a wit as sharp as any among them.

As a result, every time some *kind* friend suggested to Julia that Samantha was modelled after her – and didn't she object? – Julia, thinking she knew exactly which bits the friend had in mind, replied that, if anything, she was rather flattered.

The First Night of "Business Affaires" fell a week or two before the BI was due to take its maiden test flight; both events being in April, 1927. There was a bit of a last-minute panic when Tallulah Bankhead, who played Samantha, and Sir Francis Laking (who was always identified by the papers as "her young friend") were involved in a car crash in Kent; but it later appeared she was uninjured and she made it to the dress rehearsal on time though rather disgruntled because they had had to walk several miles for help.

Lexy knew he had a winner the moment the final curtain fell on that rehearsal. So to the First Night he invited everybody he could think of. Julia knew his circle fairly well by then, so few of the guests needed explanation, even when they were not already household names – the Prince of Wales and Mrs Dudley Ward; Ramsay Macdonald; Winston Churchill, who was then Chancellor of the Exchequer and busy organizing the nation's disastrous return to the gold standard; Lady Cunard, who had just begun asking people to call her Emerald; Lord Castlerosse, the *Sunday Express* gossip columnist; Cecil Beaton and a brace of Sitwells (Edith and Osbert, perhaps? – they were always so interchangeable in public); Oswald Mosley, the new Labour MP for Smethwick, and his wife, Lady Cynthia, one of several prominent socialist aristocrats . . . oh, and so many more. Evelyn Waugh, not yet published but a Bright Young Thing (Elsa Lanchester wangled his complimentary, in fact), failed to attend; he had had an accident with a pen nib, resulting in a poisoned finger ("Thus confirming what many of us had begun to fear," as Patrick Balfour commented when recalling the event many years later); but Wells was there, and so was a forgiving Michael Arlen.

A few names on that list were, however, new to Julia and she insisted that Lexy tell her all about them – which he did with his usual relish.

"Poor Fresca! She was reared in the hothouse of Victorian sentiment and then exposed too soon to the frosts of Swedish and Russian novels. I sent her in to dinner once with Tom Eliot. My dear, he simply *loathed* her! D'you think I should invite him, too?"

"Lady Ashley? Surely you remember all that brouhaha, a couple of months ago? She was Sylvia Hawkes, the actress. The Earl of Shaftesbury issued a statement – 'My son is most definitely *not* marrying Miss Hawkes.' And next day he did! Actually, I've only invited her to annoy Winston, because young Randolph was sniffing around dear Sylvia for weeks. Won't it be delicious?"

"Ah, Yvna Duplessis! A darling little creature, but such a snob! You remember when greyhound racing was all the rage, and the fuss about the cruelty of forcing dogs to chase the electric hare? Well, someone put about the story that Yvna Duplessis and Laura Corrigan were seen chasing an electric *lion* along Knightsbridge – and Yvna lost because she kept stopping to explain to people that her father and the lion's father had been at school together. People are too, too cruel. I'd forgotten that story. It's worth a brief revival, don't you think?"

"Isn't Laura Corrigan coming?" Julia asked.

"Alas, no." He grinned. "Into each life a little rain must fall. We can't have everything. Mustn't be greedy."

Everyone grinned when Laura Corrigan's name came up. She was the (would-be) "leading Society hostess" who, on her first arrival from New York made the famous gaffe about the Dardanelles – "No, I haven't met them yet but I have so many letters of introduction to them. They sound swell people." After that it was a twelve-month open season on poor Laura Corrigan.

Before we leave the Who's Who of that grand evening, it should be added that the name of Wallace Baker, too, was on the list. He was not then so eminent a hack that he would have been included as a matter of course; it was Lexy's own exquisite humour to put the fellow down there, just to study Julia's response. If she even noticed the name, it can only have been with utter indifference; after all, they had never met. Her cool reaction must have confirmed his opinion that here was one of the most consummate actresses of the age.

It was one of those glittering occasions that people speak of for a decade. Her Majesty's Theatre, from the stalls to the gods, was one sea of chiffon and diamonds. Those who were not there have been compelled to pretend they were. Those who were conspicuously not there have been compelled even further into fantasy. For instance, Evelyn Waugh's absurd pretence, later in life, that he was a recluse, or some kind of rural gentleman, can be traced directly back to his early excuses for absence on that night.

When the curtain rang triumphantly down, the calls and speeches lasted more than half an hour; the stage groaned under floral tributes, at least half of them from the Earl of Lonsdale, it seemed.

Afterwards, in the green room, Darling Noël complained that, having been elsewhere on *important* business, he had arrived late, without his ticket, and the management had at first refused to admit him. "They pretended not to know who I was," he said.

"And who *were* you?" Lexy asked – a victory sweeter to him than the whole triumphant evening.

On the crest of it he swept his immediate party out to the Embassy Club in Old Bond Street, the original home of soft lights and sweet music. He bought a single gardenia from the one-legged man in the entrance tunnel and gave it to Julia, a mark of favouritism that was not lost on the company. Nor, indeed, on Julia.

The Prince was already there, with Mrs Dudley Ward and the Duff Coopers; the Mountbattens joined them for a while. When Dear Lexy led his party in, the whole royal table rose and clapped – which forced the entire company to follow suit. Lexy almost wept.

Churchill and the enigmatic Brendan Bracken were at a nearby table with several empty chairs; they beckoned the playwright and his party over. Another table was added and soon the talk was flowing like wine (and so was the wine).

Wallace Baker, camouflaged by Lexy's sly invitation, was secretly covering the affair for Lady Eleanor Smith's column in the *Weekly Dispatch*, she being at Cap Ferrat with Lady Grey of Fallodon's party. Years later, of course, Eleanor became a romantic novelist and one of Julia's great favourites. But that was not the only coincidence associated with that evening. Another was the fact that Baker was squiring Dolly Savile, entirely unaware that her real name was Dolly Neville or that she had any connection with Julia. In fact, he was more than squiring her (an ambiguous usage at the best of times), for this was the night on which he had given her a diamond ring he could ill afford and asked her to share a life of which the same general judgement might be made. And she had giddily, blissfully accepted.

Those were the years when actors and actresses considered themselves gentlefolk, while true ladies and gentlemen tried hard to ape actors and actresses. Dolly was the best of both camps – a blue-blooded woman *and* a very fine performer. From Baker's point of view she was the ideal companion. Not only was she good company, she also knew absolutely everybody. On that night, for instance, she sat there calling out the names while he wrote them down surreptitiously beneath the table. She would tease him by dropping little nuggets he could not possibly use – "That's Martin Fausse-Delauney with Madge Drysdale. She absolutely worships the ground he walks on – provided he can prove clear title, of course" – that sort of thing.

"And who is the handsome lady with Dear Lexy?" Baker asked. "Now talking to Churchill."

Dolly had been so conscientious, going around the room in strict rotation so as not to miss anyone, that she hadn't noticed. "Good God!" she exclaimed. "What is *she* doing here?"

"Who is she?" he repeated, even more eager to know.

"My sister, Julia Somerville. My *elder* sister. Would you call her handsome?" She studied her sibling critically. "She's improved." It came as a reluctant concession.

"Could you get us squeezed in at that table?" he begged.

"Someone told me she was going about with Dear Lexy but I thought it was exaggeration – just neighbours meeting et cetera."

"Let's go and talk to her, eh?"

She pulled a face. "Her husband kicked the bucket last year. A ghastly man – George Somerville. Why does every man called George have bad breath and an Oedipus complex? He used to call her 'girlie' and 'wifey' – my God!"

"Could you?" he pleaded.

"The thing is, you see, I never got in touch or anything. I rather went wild after the war and we sort of drifted apart. She was very disapproving. But if she's here with Dear Lexy . . . well, she must have changed since dear *husbandey* shuffled off the mortal coil."

"Aren't you curious to find out?" Baker tempted her.

She came to a decision. "Stay behind me all the way," she ordered. "If I look like bolting, shoot me in the back."

They wove among the tables, Baker smiling just *over* people's heads to give the impression he knew simply everybody else, and Dolly pretending not to notice her sweet little barbs sticking out of most of the flesh they passed. As they drew near Churchill's table, Julia looked casually up and, still listening to him, stared straight at Baker. It was a moment neither of them ever forgot – though for different reasons.

What is it about falling in love? Take Baker. By any rational calculation, Dolly was his ideal partner. She shared his cynical humour, his debonair way with life's responsibilities, his aversion to bed around midnight and his love of it until midday – all the things that Julia abhorred. He had, moreover, just proposed to Dolly and been accepted by her – and thereby counted himself the happiest man in the room.

Yet in that one meeting of their eyes, all these considerations were set at naught. He knew, in that very first instant, he knew that here was the partner he had really been seeking all these years. And he also knew there was not a thing he could do about it.

And Julia? With her it was not so clear cut. She certainly noticed Wallace Baker. There was that little *frisson* of something between them – whatever it is that, sometimes . . . rarely, ripens into love. While he was around she was aware of him. Well, she was made uncomfortable by him; that is the most one could honestly say about her response. It certainly was not negative.

Dolly, walking ahead, saw nothing of all this. "Why Mr Chancellor!" she cried gaily. The wave of her hand took in Churchill, the champagne, the cigars, the caviare – all items that were highly taxed. "Do you simply *never* stop working?"

Everyone laughed, except Julia, who suddenly recognized her sister, didn't believe her eyes, looked again, and then gave a little, well-bred cry of delight.

Their reunion was very English upper-class, full of well-wells and how-extraordinarys and almost-no-touching. Then Baker was introduced.

Dolly whispered to Julia, "My fiancé," and surreptitiously showed off the ring. "I hope you'll be terribly happy, dear. He looks charming," Julia told her. From that moment on she avoided even looking in Wallace's direction. He, for his part, swiftly melted into the background and resumed his work for Lady Eleanor and her column.

Almost at once he had proof of Julia's qualities. Someone farther down the table, a man, was talking about Mrs Corrigan and he repeated her gaffe about the Dardanelles. It was a more serious gaffe in its own right; one just did not mention the Dardanelles – or Gallipoli – in Churchill's presence.

There was, of course, a ghastly hush. But Julia stepped in at once with, "Oh, but have you heard the latest Corrigan story?"

If it had been the oldest Corrigan story in the world – like her calling her *pied-à-terre* her *ventre-à-terre* – everyone would still have laughed and blessed her; but this really was the latest.

"She dined at Lady Cunard's last Tuesday," Julia explained. "Emerald sent her in with George Moore, who – wicked man – thought he'd have a little fun at her expense. 'Mrs Corrigan,' said he, 'do you know that of all the sexual perversions I find chastity the least comprehensible!'"

Everyone roared with laughter and leaned forward, eager to learn what the unfortunate Corrigan could possibly have replied to that.

"Poor Laura," Julia went on. "She suffered from three immediate disadvantages. In the first place she hadn't the vaguest idea what Moore was talking about. In the second place her simple, fundamentalist soul was quite certain it was indecent. And thirdly, she knew he was a Great Writer whom she could not possibly offend."

Julia paused and glanced around, promising more with her smile but saying nothing.

"Well? What did she say?" someone asked with a strangled shriek.

"She said, 'Golly, Mr Moore, I guess I'll just have to think that one over'!"

The whole table collapsed in helpless laughter. Wallace Baker was one of the few who saw Churchill reach across and lay his hand on Julia's arm. Their eyes met and he twinkled at her with that puckish charm of his. He knew damned well what she had just done; and, whatever else one may say of him, he admired a nimble mind and he remembered acts of kindness.

As the laughter died Julia could not avoid turning to see how Wallace Baker had taken it. Her sudden movement impelled Dolly to look, too.

What she discovered, in her fiancé's eyes, broke her heart; for Wallace was the first – and, as far as she was concerned, the only – love of her life.

CHAPTER TWENTY-FIVE

"THE FACT IS," St John Brunty declared, "we simply are not a rational tribe, we business folk."

He was talking about the problems no one had foreseen when Neville's chose the site at Dollis Hill.

"We camp along the fringes of a land called Hysteria. We intoxicate ourselves with that heady brew called Myth, which, naturally, gives us a hangover. And to cure it we call in these witch doctors – who, for some curious reason, can only go about in pairs. Organization and Method. Time and Motion. Research and Development. These terrible-twin medicos claim to have graduated from some college called Scientific Method. But, actually, the potions they prescribe are just the hair of the dog that originally bit the patient. And that hound's name is Controlled Chaos, sired by Panic out of Lossmaker. The Tribal God of us business folk, as everyone knows, is Money – which means we're indifferent to it almost all the time and only appreciate it when we're in trouble. Ask any god. Furthermore . . ."

"Brunty," Julia said, drawing out the final syllable with ominous intonation.

"Sorry," he replied. "Sorry. My speech for the Institute dinner tomorrow night."

She started in alarm. "You're not going to talk about . . . *our* problem here, I hope?"

He beamed at her, reassuringly. "Believe me, dear Boss, I'm not short of a few hundred other examples, none of them remotely connected with Neville's."

The problem was that the prototype B1 was made at the factory and then had to be partially stripped, loaded onto big, expensive transporters, and then reassembled a couple of miles away at Hendon, where it would undergo its trials. The cost for a single prototype was bearable, but if every production model were made that way, it would add significantly to its price.

"You see," Eliot tried to excuse it, mainly to himself, "we thought

184

we stood a good chance of buying that long strip of land to the west of us here. We'd have had a better runway then than de Havilland."

The de Havilland works were just across the Edgware Road. That had been the other advantage of the site – the ready availability of labour and of all those small suppliers and services that spring up around big industries.

"It's nobody's fault." Julia tried to soothe him. "How could anyone have known that the Metropolitan Water Board had earmarked the site for a reservoir? The really annoying part is that it probably won't be built for the next half century."

"D'you know Lord Berners?" Brunty asked suddenly. They were gathered in Julia's office and his eye flickered briefly toward the water colours; it could have been a coincidence.

"What about him?" Julia asked. "Does it have any bearing on all this?"

"Oh, very much so. He's a great collector, as I'm sure you know. And whenever he visits the Bond Street galleries he's likely to spend several hundred thousand pounds. Then on his way home he gets the most frightful attacks of conscience, you see – which he salves by saying to his butler as he steps from his car, 'Just biscuits and water for dinner tonight, Hethers.' Or whatever the fellow's called."

"Well?" they both asked.

"Well, this Dollis Hill site was our 'biscuits and water,' you see. Don't you remember what astronomical sums we'd just spent on new machines and tools and vast stocks of duralumin?"

"It could be a blessing in disguise," Eliot ventured.

"In what way?" Julia asked. After St John Brunty's helpful contribution she was ready for any comfort.

"How many planes a year could we build here – at full stretch? A dozen? But if this baby's the winner I think it is, we could be called upon for ten times that number. In which case, we'd have to split the work up anyway. We'd then manufacture our components and engines here at Dollis Hill, but we'd make the airframes in a new, much bigger place alongside Hendon. And actually" – he smiled, warming to his theme and discovering its virtues like flowers in the hedgerow – "that's right. It's the right way. Internal combustion skills are readily available here in North London. But the assembly skills are new. We'd have to train those people anyway. It's exactly what Armstrong-Whitworth do. So" – the smile turned to a laugh – "every day in every way we're getting better and better and better."

"Marvellous," Brunty said admiringly. "We paint ourselves into a corner. Then we look at it closely and say it isn't a corner after all. It's a barn door!"

Even before the prototype was fully reassembled at Hendon, it became a centre of pilgrimage. Pilots, mechanics, groundsmen – anyone who had the slightest business with aircraft and who happened to be at the airfield, dropped by to see it for themselves. There was an unvarying ritual; enter, stop, gape, frown, advance, look increasingly suspicious, draw close, pause, raise incredulous hand, touch gingerly, push harder, laugh in disbelief, give her a slap, listen to the echo, laugh again, and shout, "Tin, by jove! She's made of bloody tin!"

Metal-skinned aircraft were actually nothing new. Junkers had built one in Germany before the war and their FI3 all-metal passenger plane was now in regular service with Luft Hansa. But its duralumin skin, being corrugated for strength, caused the most terrible drag. Baring called them "flying grain elevators." Their performance was no better than their wood-and-fabric rivals. So all-metal planes *seemed* a failure.

Baring's idea, though, was to strengthen the skin not by corrugations but by stretching it over the underlying frame, which, in his case, was also of metal. In this way the skin itself took some of the stresses of flight and he could afford to make that underlying framework lighter. Even this idea wasn't new. Shorts had made a stressed-skin single-seater biplane back in 1920, and Adolf Rohrbach built flying boats using the technique. But no one had ever tried it on a single-wing machine designed for three engines and up to two dozen passengers. The wingspan was over a hundred feet and there wasn't a supporting strut or spar in sight. The undercarriage could also be winched up into the main fuselage – a feature which had previously been seen only in single-seater racing planes.

In short, the only "revolution" in the BI was that it gathered a number of previous revolutions into a single airframe; by Eliot's lights, the design was very conservative.

The response of the English was an eye-opener to him. "I knew this was a land of *old* fogeys," he complained, "but until now I never knew how young they start being old. For God's sake – how long has the aircraft industry been around, anyway? Yet they stroll into the hangar – youngsters of our age – look her over, and shake their heads like senile old judges and bleat about *tradition!* I'll bet the day the first-ever airplane flew from British soil they formed an Old Aviators' Club with its own tie and cuff links and a constitution and rule book back-dated fifty years. It must be something in the water."

What especially irked him was the criticism of his cabin for the pilot. In Europe and America you couldn't sell a plane with an open cockpit – not an airliner. But Britain's Imperial Airways still insisted that its pilots should sit out there in all weathers, just like the coachmen of old. Bully for tradition!

After sitting through one of his diatribes Brunty took Julia aside and told her, "Someone really ought to explain to him about the English, you know. How we hate winners and all that. And when we do win – the extraordinary pains we take to make it look accidental. I mean the one thing we loathe and detest is the man who sets out to win, plans the way he'll do it, and then single-mindedly pursues that plan, come what may. Don't you agree?"

Julia nodded glumly. She had a dispiriting premonition that the reactions of the young fogeys at Hendon were the merest sample of disappointments to come. "It's not going to be easy," she answered.

"Don't I know! Americans have made such a god of success. It's their Eighth Deadly Sin – and they pursue it more avidly than the other seven put together. Give a New York hostess a choice between seating a wildly successful child murderer or a failed saint and she'd chew a hole in her cheek before making up her mind."

So, while the BI took shape at Hendon, she began a subtle course of education for its designer. For instance, once, flying over Hertford toward Ware, she pointed out a large country house. "That's Tewin End. It used to belong to the Duke of Ancaster before the title went extinct."

"It looks lived-in," he commented, taking up the bait.

"Yes. I don't know their name. Funny thing that – they're one of our nearest neighbours and I don't even know their name! *She* made him buy the place – no doubt imagining she'd become the local queen bee. He's something terribly successful in refrigerated meat, I think. Pots and pots of money. They must be the richest people in the county but she's quite ghastly. No one ever calls on them."

She hoped that the steady flow of such casual comments would eventually have their effect.

Julia often flew up to that part of the country, to Allbury, where one field was now kept mown as a permanent landing strip. Two low circuits got rid of the livestock and then she could put down. Sometimes she went with Eliot, sometimes solo, for she not only had her pilot's licence by now, she even had her own plane – one of the new de Havilland DH60 Moths, a two-seater.

On the morning after the First Night of "Business Affaires" Dolly decided to call on her sister – to celebrate their reunion, she explained. They had all danced until dawn, so she expected to find Julia just rising. In fact, Julia had not even gone to bed; instead she had taken a Turkish bath, put on a new face, and gone directly to Dollis Hill. She returned to Connaught Square just as her sister was preparing to leave in disappointment. Their greetings, being private, were less inhibited than they had been the previous night. When they were done, Julia said, "Just let me phone the SPRP and tell them I'll pop in tomorrow instead, and then I'll take you to see the wonder of the age at Hendon."

Dolly checked her watch and said that would be lovely. On the way they talked only of safe childhood memories, studiously avoiding the recent years – and most particularly the events of the previous evening. It surprised Dolly to discover that Julia was not in the least bit dull and solemn; it pleased Julia to learn that Dolly had a serious, responsible side to her after all. Neither of them mentioned Wallace Baker.

"You've changed," Dolly told her.

Julia shook her head. "I don't think so."

"Well, you must admit that George Somerville's wife would never have turned up at the Embassy Club like that."

"Oh . . . George knew Lexy, you know . . ."

"Don't quibble, Ju."

"All right. Perhaps I've changed a bit. But only those who haven't seen me for years would notice."

Dolly tossed her head. "I knew that had to come. Well, all right – I'm sorry. I know I really ought to have . . ."

"No, no, I'm glad. Honestly. Seeing you now, meeting you again, I think you did absolutely the right thing. I should have had more sense. I ought to have left you alone."

Dolly eyed her warily. "Why d'you say that? I mean, I agree, but I don't see why you . . ."

"What you did, darling, was a very brave thing – running away like that. I mean, think of all the girls we know who tried it and just fell flat on their faces."

"Backs, actually," Dolly said nonchalantly.

Julia laughed. "But not you. You went on fighting to prove you were right and we were all wrong. And now you've succeeded. This part in *Mrs Warren's Profession* – Vivie Warren – that is definite, isn't it?"

Dolly turned to her, full of surprise. "I can't believe it's you, saying all this! You, of all people!"

"Well." Julia dug her gently with her elbow. "Don't ever let us lose touch again, eh? Not like that."

Dolly was immediately wary once more – remembering that look in Wallace Baker's eyes last night. "It's not easy," she warned. "The theatre is so demanding."

"So is business, darling. Let's just promise to try, eh?"

Dolly agreed, rather guardedly. "There is one teeny thing . . ." she started to say, just as they turned off the road and into the aerodrome.

"Yes?" Julia prompted.

"Oh. Nothing important. I mean, it'll keep. Is this your aircraft factory?"

"No, this is mostly Avro's. Are you dreaming? I pointed out *our* factory a couple of miles back."

Dolly gave a guilty laugh. "I sometimes think I *am* dreaming." She stretched, catlike, holding out her left hand, waggling the finger that held the engagement ring. "I still can't believe it."

"It is beautiful. He must be doing well."

"He hocked himself to the gills for it. No, I mean I can't believe he chose me."

"He's the lucky one, darling. And he knows it, I'm sure."

In the BI's hangar they were just fitting the third engine, which was a geared Rolls-Royce Condor. (That was for the prototype, of course. Alan Hackett, whom Somerville's had originally poached from Jaguar, was still developing the Savage I for the production model.) The sisters watched for about as long as anyone can reasonably watch six men bolt several hundredweight of metal into a prepared cowling, then Dolly remarked that it was "absolutely deevy, dahling," and looked at her watch again.

"Let's lunch with Max," Julia suggested, all off-hand.

"Oh, I'd adore that but we'd never get there and back in time. I've got this horribilino matinée at half-past two."

Julia led her to the back of the hangar, where the Moth stood, serviced and ready as always.

Dolly grasped the idea at once and took it almost without flinching. "What did I have for breakfast?" she asked. "Isn't that the unwritten motto of aviation? Never eat once what you'd hate the world to see twice."

When Julia helped her to strap in, she said, "Actually, *my* motto is eat, drink, and be merry for today we die. We're doing this the wrong way round."

But once they were airborne the wonder of it touched her and she forgot the jokes. She sat entranced all the way to Allbury. The green touch of Spring was on every tree and blade of grass.

Max came running out, as he always did, the moment he heard Julia's plane. He was waiting at the gate by the time they had taxied back to the start of the runway, ready for takeoff again. He waved, but his arm faltered when he saw Dolly.

"Damn," Julia exclaimed. "He's recognized you. You should have kept the helmet on. I wanted to see his face."

"I wonder what his first words will be?" Dolly asked; her heart was thumping away like mad.

"With Max it could be anything. He might pretend not to know you at all. He might pretend he's been meeting you every week."

"What an odd bunch we are, eh? D'you think it's true about blood going bad after so many generations? Max is definitely a bit . . . you know."

"There's nothing wrong with my blood."

"Yes, but women don't count."

Max drew near enough to speak. "Thought it might be you, Dolly. Had a dream about you last night. We had to fell that big fir tree down at Stiggins Weir and all the labourers ran away, leaving just you and me."

His two sisters burst out laughing. He stared at them in disgust and said, "Oh lord – still at it? Giggle, giggle, giggle!"

Dolly put her arms around him and gave an apologetic hug. "We haven't long, darling," she warned. "I have a matinée."

They began walking back toward the house. "The thing about that tree," Max went on, "is that it was rotten from root to crown. We didn't need to fell it. We stood there and crumbled the trunk to compost with our fingers. And you said, 'Those men will be furious to learn they ran from such easy work.' God, but I felt depressed when I woke up."

"Well you would, wouldn't you," Dolly told him. Their stroll had brought them to the edge of the field, where the view sloped gently down toward Allbury. "It can't be easy – having to cope with symbols like that."

Max looked at her, uncertain as to whether she meant his dream or the house.

"You should sell up here, Max. Take chambers in London. It's much more your sort of place than this. What d'you find to *do* all day?"

He shrugged. "Keep the place going, you know."

"Yes, but going from what to what? You should sell to Ju here. Her blood's better than yours. Come to London where we can *see* you sometimes."

Julia saw that her sister was being provocative, teasing Max, as she always had done, and yet she had hit upon an important truth. The sole reason Max was at Allbury was that he was the oldest, and now the only, male heir. From birth he had been told this house and estate was his destiny. But in every other way he was the least fitted of them all to manage the place.

"It's quite a thought, Max," Julia suggested.

A sour grunt closed the conversation.

Julia turned to her sister. "Show him," she said.

"Show me what?"

Dolly stretched out her left hand, making the diamonds sparkle in the noonday sun.

"Oh God," he moaned in disgust. "I suppose that means I'll have to give you away? Nancy boys mincing all over the house. *He's* not a pansy, I hope?"

Dolly laughed and flung her arms around him again, lifting both legs off the ground. "Oh Max!" she cried.

Back on her own two feet she grew serious once more. "In point of fact, he's not in the theatre at all. He's Wallace Baker, the journalist. You must have heard of him."

"A bloody scribbler, eh?"

"That's exactly what he calls himself. You and he'll get on famously." She swiped off a dandelion head, one of the first of the year. "I hope we all do."

"You'll love him, Max," Julia said. "He and Dolly are absolutely made for each other."

Dolly took her arm as the three of them walked down the slope.

Their pot-luck lunch was cold game pie, cheese, pickles, and beer, which came by the barrel from McMullen's brewery in Hertford. Afterwards they wandered through the empty, dusty rooms and relived memories of their different childhoods there. Max was affable and calm – and yet Julia, who now knew him better than anyone, was left with an uneasy feeling all was not well. However, there was no time to probe; Dolly had to be back for her matinée.

As they drove up to the West End, Dolly casually asked her sister, "D'you suppose you'll ever marry again, Ju?"

"I often wonder. There's no terribly pressing need. I'm still rather enjoying the freedom of it."

"I don't blame you!"

Julia laughed. "Yes, you never did like George, did you. How odd that you saw through him at once and I didn't – until almost near the very end. Insights like that can happen in a flash, can't they – the moment you meet a person."

Dolly avoided the comment. "So there's no Mr Right in the offing?"

"Too many!"

Dolly looked at her in delight. "Honestly?"

Julia grinned back and gave a most knowing nod.

After that, Dolly was as happy as a skylark.

Julia, who was by now feeling the lack of sleep, took the rest of the day off. She saw most of the performance, including all four of Dolly's scenes. She assuaged her puritan guilt with the certain-sure prediction that next week, with the test flight of the B1, the very idea of "an afternoon off" would pass into blessed memory.

Just as she was leaving the theatre a furtive little man in a threadbare raincoat came up to her and mumbled, "Mrs Julia Somerville?"

"Yes?" She backed off a little.

He thrust a large manilla envelope into her hands and melted swiftly into the crowd.

Bewildered, she turned it over. "Hook, Hook, and Hook," read the embossed letters on the back. "Solicitors at Law."

She tore it open and, after a couple of quick scans through its half-dozen pages, saw that it requested her response to certain charges of failing to establish a trust as stipulated in her late husband's will. If no satisfactory reply were forthcoming, it warned, the complainant would have no choice but to apply for an attachment of the entire assets of Neville Aero-Engineering.

The complainant was Imogen Davis, described as trustee.

As Julia's gaze lifted from the paper she saw, in the corner of her eye, a familiar flash of gold disappearing up Shaftesbury Avenue.

PART THREE

THE AMAZON OF THE AIR

CHAPTER TWENTY-SIX

OR A DAY or two Julia did nothing about the letter – not even consult her own lawyers. Her instincts told her this was not at heart a legal problem. If she had not seen that gold-plated Rolls-Royce disappearing up Shaftesbury Avenue, she might have assumed it was a personal, Imogen Davis problem; now she concentrated her thoughts on Sidney Gold.

She ought to have followed up his non-appearance at Forge Lane the day after the funeral. True, he might have had no interest in her tempting-sounding proposal, but he was not so uncouth as to send no word at all. She should have taken that as a sign that she had offended him.

Was it her sneer at the vulgarity of offering so much cash? Probably. That, coupled with the offhand way she had dashed his hopes – especially when she must have seemed so encouraging at their earlier meetings . . . Yes, putting one and one and one together, it did add up. She had not been terribly bright.

Even so, how had he discovered Imogen Davis?

George's will. He must have gone to Somerset House and read George's will as soon as it was probated. He'd have seen the codicil and started wondering who this Imogen Davis might be. Good lord, that must mean he still had some hopes of acquiring Somerville Motors!

Julia remembered now that, when tidying up George's room, the morning after his death, she and Mrs Crooke had searched high and low for the document Imogen had half-torn up, the one appointing her trustee. Its absence hadn't seemed to matter at the time because George's signature had not been witnessed – or, strictly speaking, the two witnesses, herself and Mrs Crooke, had never signed.

Julia was on the point of asking her own lawyers what difference that might make when it struck her that, here, too, the problem was not legal but personal. The legal niceties were of no importance. The fact was, she could never allow a public dispute over that document.

The filth that might emerge! She had no choice but to establish this wretched trust and accept the Davis creature as a fellow trustee. Could she steel herself to do it so charmingly that the girl would then become useless to Sidney Gold?

She needed to talk about it with someone. Immediately she thought of Dolly, but there was no reply from her flat. She called her agent and learned that Miss Savile was on tour.

Eliot, then? No – that threat to attach the assets would worry him, even though it was utterly empty; and with the maiden flight of the BI only days away, this kind of problem was the last thing he needed.

Brunty? Somehow, no. Ever since he had casually dropped Lord Berners's name and glanced at her famous water colours, she had felt a mild distrust of Brunty. It was probably unfair of her. Such a trivial event on which to hang so much; most likely it had been pure coincidence. And yet . . . and yet.

Her confidant would have to be Crownfield. She'd leave out the bit about the attachment of the assets, she decided.

They arranged to meet in the cocktail lounge at the Ritz and then take luncheon together. But she had not been there five minutes when her name was paged; the message was to ring Crownfield's office.

His secretary answered. He told her that Crownfield was extremely sorry but his son (the one who wasn't quite all there, she remembered) had suffered a minor accident; nothing serious, but they had taken him into hospital and Crownfield had naturally gone to see him. Would tomorrow do instead?

Julia promised to call him that evening.

She put down the phone and turned around, only to find that Wallace Baker was standing directly behind her.

"I heard the pageboy going round asking for you," he explained. "It seemed curmudgeonly not to say hello."

"Oh . . . hello." She was all confusion. She offered her hand, withdrew it, offered it again. "I, er" – she pointed to the phone – "That was . . . how are you, anyway?"

"Broke." He grinned. "But very happy. Dolly and I got hitched the day before yesterday. Special licence."

"Oh, congratulations! I'm *so* pleased for both of you. Shouldn't you be on your honeymoon?"

"We're saving up for it. Sometime around 1935 at our present rate. You and I are sister- and brother-in-law now, you realize? May I buy you a drink to celebrate?"

"Oh . . . please." It annoyed her to seem flustered like this, when there was so little cause. "Are you waiting for someone?"

"I've just interviewed a woman who actually saw Countess de Janzé shoot Raymond de Trafford."

"How exciting. You must tell me all about it."

"In fact, the pageboy thought she was you – which is how I heard."

"Extraordinary."

They'd just have a quick drink, she decided.

"Were you going on to lunch somewhere?" he asked.

"No, I was meeting my banker here, but that was him cancelling. Why don't you ring Dolly and both of you join me? My treat."

Then she remembered that Dolly was away on tour – which, unfortunately, left the rest of the invitation in limbo. "Well, it'll still be my treat," she had to say. "We must celebrate this, er, this marvellous . . . thing."

"Well, thank you. I'm in no position to refuse. Ah . . . do I call you Julia now?"

"It would be ridiculous not to . . . Wallace?"

He nodded. "A manhattan, isn't it?"

"How did you know?" But it pleased her that he did.

"At the Embassy Club the other night."

"Ah yes." There seemed nothing to add. She said, "You and Dolly were pretty quick off the mark. She said nothing about it when we went down to Allbury the other day."

"Dear me," he answered with jocular sarcasm. "And you and she are such marvels at keeping in touch!"

Julia's frozen mask made him sharply aware he had blundered. "Actually," he laughed, trying to recruit the smile back into her face, "I think that's what prompted it, your trip down to Allbury. You have a brother – Max? – who threatened to give her away? That was enough."

Julia was only slightly mollified. "Yes, you're lucky not to have met Max before the great event," she said. "He'd have played the heavy paterfamilias."

Her tone suggested he would not have withstood Max's inquisition; but, far from being insulted, he seemed merely amused at the idea.

For a moment their eyes locked. It was so brief that later she could not be sure of it, yet she felt she had recognized in him that quality of *otherness* which always excited her in a man – a vigilant hardness that was both menacing and thrilling at the same time. He glanced casually around the room and when his gaze returned to her, it was gone. The everyday mask was back in place. She now felt sure it was a mask, though.

They talked of one thing and another until it was time to go into the dining room. Then as they opened their menus, he said out of the blue, "You don't seem so carefree as you were the other night."

She gave an awkward shrug; he watched the skin beside her fingernails grow white. "Some problem?" he asked.

She turned to the wrong page of the menu, to put his face at the very edge of her field of view. But even there his eyes had an almost hypnotic grip on her. "You ask as a journalist?" she responded. "Or as a member of the family?"

He chuckled. "As a good listener, actually. Try me."

To her own amazement she told him everything. He heard her out, almost without interruption; only when she leaped ahead of her tale, or assumed Dolly had told him things that, in fact, she had not, did he throw in a question. When she had finished she knew he could have repeated it all, practically word for word.

For a long while he said nothing. She tried examining him objectively, looking for safe, familiar compartments in which to pack him away. He was good looking, in an intellectual sort of fashion; but that only added to the mystery she was now beginning to make of him – a mystery his eyes did nothing to resolve. During her recital, they had encouraged her with their kindliness and understanding; but now that he was distracted, or turned inward upon his own thoughts, she glimpsed once more that steely hardness which had so unnerved her. She gave up the attempt and fell instead to wondering if he was really as unsuccessful as he liked to claim. His name was beginning to appear in quite a few places.

"She's the clue to it," he observed at length. "Imogen Davis, not Sidney Gold. You're right there. Tell me if I'm prying too deep, but you seemed to imply that some kind of canoodling was going on between her and your husband?" Without even looking for confirmation – in fact, keeping his eyes studiously upon his own, well-manicured hands – he went straight on: "With the man paralyzed from the neck down, it must have been fairly innocuous?"

"Unfaithfulness . . ." She paused awkwardly but saw no other way of expressing it. ". . . I mean, it doesn't have to be physical."

He smiled at her hesitation, as if they now shared a secret. The implication angered her but he saw it at once and looked away, letting the reverberations die. "What did she really want?" he asked, all businesslike again. "You say she worked for him practically round the clock. Did it ever seem she was doing it merely in hope of a legacy?"

"No. I have to give her that. She really seemed devoted."

"She can hardly have been doing it for a few snatched kisses."

Again Julia had reluctantly to concede its unlikelihood.

"Well what can it be, then?" he asked. "How did she take his death?"

Julia began to wish she'd picked a less perceptive confidant. "It's not easy for me," she explained.

"Is it meant to be?" He smiled but offered no easy exit.

"I mean it's not easy because I have to confess she was . . . she took it much harder than I did. She was heartbroken while I was just

. . . I couldn't feel anything. I was numb." A sudden memory opened up to her. "She fell to her knees and put her arms around him and said she *belonged.*"

"To him?"

"No. To the house. To us – to the family, I suppose. Yes, that's what she meant. She belonged to the family."

After a silence he asked, "D'you really need me to tell you any more, Julia? Because there's one question I'm dying to put."

"Oh?" She looked up with interest.

"Yes. Do you always shake the head waiter by the hand when you enter a restaurant?"

She laughed and explained.

She was grateful for the skill with which he had led her to the point where she could supply her own advice. Yet, paradoxically – or precisely because he had seemed to show her that she had really known all along what to do – she now began to resent having told him anything about it.

"Actually," she said, "talking of Crownfield and that lunch we had here, I have a bone to pick with you."

"Oh?" His smile was guarded; he had already divined that her playful tone was more assumed than real.

"Yes. His invitation was by way of apology for some rather boorish behaviour on his part – behaviour occasioned entirely by the fact that I seemed to be acting out a fantasy that *you* had sold to Dear Lexy."

His smile wavered.

"Lexy and Crownfield are old friends," she added. "Of course he went at once to see him."

Wallace shrugged with genuine incomprehension.

"You can't have forgotten," she insisted.

"Well, of course I remember very well selling about ten thousand words of pure fantasy to the man. Highest-paid work I ever . . ."

"But none of the details?"

"Not a sausage. D'you mean names and things? I don't remember any names. It was all about war widows having to stand in for . . ."

"They weren't all war widows, were they?"

She saw an uncomfortable memory beginning to stir within him. "There was one," she prompted, "whom Lexy called Samantha Drysdale . . . I don't know what you called her but you said her husband died after an accident at the family engineering works."

He closed his eyes. "Oh, God."

"Were you going out with Dolly then?" she asked brutally.

The implication smarted. "I've known your sister for years."

"That doesn't quite answer the question, does it?"

"She never mentioned you. I mean . . ."

"I'm sorry, Wallace, I simply can't believe that."

"No. Of course she *mentioned* you – all of you. What I meant was that she never said a word about George, the accident . . . all that."

"You just read it in the papers, eh?"

"Family's important to you – I can see that. But not to her, and not to me. Or not in the same way. We just didn't talk about that sort of thing."

"*Did* you read it in the papers?"

He looked trapped. "I suppose I must have. But never for one moment did I connect it with . . ." He laughed, as a way of abandoning the line onto which she had manipulated him. "Anyway, it brought you two good friends. Would you ever have done more than smile at Lexy across the square? Would you have been present at the First Night but for that? Or sat at Churchill's table? What did you think of him, by the way? I know he was highly impressed by you."

Something in his tone suggested he had actually discussed the incident with Churchill. "D'you know him?" she asked at once, burying her annoyance for the moment.

It caught him off guard. "I . . . we . . ." He sat back and gave her a rueful glance, as if she had caught him out – or, more precisely, as if he had decided to let it appear so. "I know *of* him – is what I meant to imply. But I could see he was impressed. The ease with which you covered up that woman's gaffe about the Dardanelles."

"Pure fluke," she said. "Someone told me that particular Laura Corrigan story during the interval – Patrick Balfour, I think it was. Talking of flukes, how was it that you and Dolly just happened to be there, too?"

He gave her an oddly challenging look, smiling and frowning at the same time. "Are you actually *trying* to pick a quarrel with me, Julia?" he asked.

"Of course not," she assured him crossly. And then she had to spend the rest of the meal proving it – much to her own (though supremely well disguised) annoyance.

Later, when they were standing outside in that long, cool colonnade, about to part, he asked, "You wouldn't be going Fleet Street way, by any chance?"

She was, as it happened – give or take a mile – but she pointed vaguely in the opposite direction and said, "I'm sorry, no."

"Well then, we'll meet again soon enough, I suppose," he said, as if awarding himself a consolation.

"Will we? Oh yes, I suppose so."

He laughed awkwardly. "Anyway, thank you for a splendid lunch."

"Not at all. Give my love to Dolly."

"It's good that you're seeing each other again."

Julia glanced at her wristwatch. "I really must fly, Wallace."

"Yes, of course. Forgive me."

They shook hands and parted.

Her car was around the corner in St James's. She had just bought a new Lancia – the seventh-series Lambda, the finest car Vincenzo Lancia ever built. That was around the time when her addiction to what she called "thoroughbred" cars began – though perhaps it had always been there, masked, so to speak, by her marriage into the Somerville business. In less than fifteen minutes, that long, sleek thoroughbred, bright blue with a red stripe, carried her from Piccadilly to the City College of the SPRP. If Imogen Davis were the key to her present problems, the person to see was Theresa Ashbury.

It ought to have been the purest pleasure, that drive; but she could not shake off the memory of Wallace Baker. What was it about him that angered her so? The fact that she could not pin it down only added to her fury. She sought distraction in the passing streets, but they were of little comfort. A century ago the houses of Islington must have been rather fine. But as the city pushed its greener fringes outward, first to Highbury, then onward to Finsbury and Tottenham, this older suburb had come down in the world. Though never a slum it nonetheless carried all the drab marks of lives spent in cheeseparing and making do – teetering on the edge of that poverty which always made Julia shudder. She was glad when the college came into view.

Theresa was at the courtyard gate, counting sacks of coal as the merchant emptied them into the chute; she had her own steelyard out there, too, and made him reweigh each sack.

"Such a fuss about a pound of coal!" the man was saying in disgust as Julia approached.

"Funny how they're all a pound light! If I was to give you tuppence short on every quid, you'd soon holler!" Theresa commented with a wink at Julia. "You're quite the stranger, Mrs Somerville," she added.

Julia nodded. "To everything but trouble."

Theresa smiled, not truly believing her. "What now?"

Julia inclined her head toward the merchant. "Is he local?"

The other nodded. Julia made small talk, waiting for the man to leave. She asked where the Gunner was. At the vegetable plot, to be sure. A good year for it? Not bad at all. Couldn't grumble. Seen worse.

Theresa proudly showed her the new Austin Seven the SPRP had bought her. "It's changed my life," she said. Then she laughed. "The Gunner calls it an Australian Seven. Isn't he a caution!"

The last sack was tipped. "Correct to the penny," Theresa told the man as she handed over the payment. She tucked the receipt in her sleeve.

As the cart drew away up Wharf Road, a couple of urchins tried to steal a ride under the overhang of the tailgate. But a practised flick of the whip dislodged them, and they stood there, rubbing themselves and yelling imprecations.

"D'you remember a Mrs Davis?" Julia asked. "She must have been among the earliest of our students. A Mrs Consuelo Davis."

As soon as she heard the first name Theresa laughed. "Her! I'll say!"

"Is she still alive?"

Theresa pointed a finger eastward. "Used to live three streets that way – corner of Shepherdess Walk and Forston Street."

"But not any more?"

She shook her head. "They had to put her away." She tapped her forehead.

"Oh dear, I'm sorry to hear that."

"No harm in her. Funny you should mention it, but I called on her not long back. She's in a home near Friern Barnet and I can go that way to Ware, see." She laughed at the memory. "She thinks she *owns* the place. A very grand old gentleman's house. 'Oh, Mrs Ashbury,' she says, 'they've not paid me my rent, you know.' And she watches all the staff like they was her own servants. Told the gardener to search one of the nurses – 'maid,' she called her. 'She's carrying out a leg of lamb under them skirts,' she says." Again she laughed. "Poor thing. She fancies she's back in her days of glory."

Julia made an effort to join in the mirth. The descent from affluence to poverty was terrifying enough, but the thought that it might bring madness in its train . . .

"As a matter of fact," she said. "I was more interested in the daughter."

"Imogen?" Theresa raised her eyebrows in laconic comment on the name.

Julia nodded and went on briefly to explain why.

Theresa shook her head. "You should ought to of told me this before, Mrs Somerville. I could of saved you a lot of bother."

"You obviously know the girl?"

Theresa held her hand about thirty inches above the cobblestones of the yard. "Since she was so high."

"Tell me about her."

They went indoors, where Theresa made a fresh pot of tea. As she refilled the kettle she spoke of the Imogen she had known – which was after the family's collapse into poverty, of course. "Everyone said she took it the best, but I'm not so sure. Granted she was always cheerful, but she was one of them kids as always wanted to be older than what she was. Know what I mean? In Infants she hung about the Juniors. In Juniors you couldn't keep her out of Seniors. She'd nick older girls' clothes off the line and try them on. And she rolled up old stockings to give herself swellings before nature obliged."

Julia could not suppress the thought that, in many ways, the young Imogen Davis sounded remarkably like the young Julia Neville.

Theresa was laughing at another memory. "When the Fresh Air League took them on that outing in the war, to Southend – she can't of been more'n ten – old Canon Thirkettle, he asked her what she wanted to be when she grew up. 'Lord Chief Justice of England!' says she. Straight up. 'Lord Chief Justice of England!' Poor man didn't know what to say to that. He just laughed and give her a threepenny bit. Oh, I can see her now, slipping her little hand into his and leading him off down the pier to spend that threepence. She had sauce, see, even then."

"Was she good at her lessons?" Julia asked.

The tilt of the head was ambiguous. "She was bright enough. No doubting that. But when she got up thirteen, fourteen, she was always in trouble. Shepherdess Board School, they almost kicked her out. That was just before the mother come to us." She half-stood and peered across the table. "You want a drop more tea in that?"

Julia pushed the cup toward her. "Are you talking about serious trouble now?"

"Not what they'd call serious round 'ere. She was up before the beaks more'n once, I know. She come *that* close to the reformatory. Somehow she always could talk herself out of it. Always the little lady. Very refined in her speech. But then, once she started to fill out and that, she changed completely. Funny how that often happens, innit. 'Course, she'd left school by then, but she went to see old Canon Thirkettle – he always had a soft spot for her. Retired by then, he was – but he got her took in at that domestic college up Alma Road, bit of a snooty place. And he got some charity to stump up the fees." Her eyes narrowed as a new memory came to her. "Funny thing about that. According to her mum, it wasn't the Canon's idea, it was hers. Imogen's, I mean. She knew of the place long before. Set her heart on it, that's what her mum said."

"And she also found the way to get there." Julia smiled. "D'you know, Mrs Ashbury, the first day young Imogen came to Connaught Square, I took a liking to her. And the strange thing is, I begin to feel it again now. Perhaps not actual liking, but certainly a kind of admiration. In spite of everything."

Theresa nodded reluctantly. "Yeah, I know what you mean. Still and all . . ."

Julia agreed. "Yes – still and all, as you say."

"D'you want to pop out and see the mother? I've got the address in the office."

"I think not. There's too much risk. Word of it might get back to the girl."

"Or is there anything I might find out? I mean, she's got her memory and all that."

Still Julia shook her head. "In fact, you've given me such a marvellously clear picture, I think I know exactly what to do."

CHAPTER TWENTY-SEVEN

SHORTLY AFTER HER conversation with Theresa, Julia was lunching with Dear Lexy – this time at the Savoy. Actually, she was showing off the new Lancia. He played his part well, gushing like a paid puffer, though, in truth, cars and planes and all things mechanical bored him stiff. Comfort and reliability were his only demands; you could keep your v4s and your coil suspensions and your fin-cooled brakes. But he took his cue from Julia's eyes and voice, and he made the appropriate responses. Fortunately her knowledge of those mysteries, though it was inevitably increasing by the month, was still of a dilettante kind, and the conversation soon wandered down more interesting avenues.

Julia described her troubles with Imogen Davis, including her recent conversation with Theresa Ashbury. She did not, however, mention her lunch with Wallace Baker.

Lexy listened gravely and then asked why she was telling him all this.

"Because I don't want to bother Baring with it just now. Every day there's some little postponement of our maiden flight – it's just been put off again this morning. And the only other person I could tell would be Crownfield – and I know exactly what he'd say. 'Don't try anything clever. Go by the book.' I don't know what it is about that man. I suppose all bankers are the same. They know everything there is to know about business – except how to do it."

"Harem eunuchs," Lexy commented as he gazed about, seeking familiar faces. "They know what to do. They see it done every day. But!"

She laughed. "Everything Crownfield does is like setting an example. He's the world's greatest example-setter. He won't take any risks. And he behaves as if we had all the time we could wish for."

Lexy gave a sympathetic nod and let her talk on.

"That's it, really: *time*. We never have enough. For us it's always too late already. We should have done everything last week. The only reason we didn't was we were too busy doing what we ought to have done the week before. Anyway" – she smiled – "that's why I can't discuss this affair with Crownfield."

"So. Let me get this right. You suspect Sidney Gold's behind it all, but really it's little Imogen you're trying to nobble, eh?" He rubbed his hands, becoming genuinely interested. "How will you set about it?"

She nodded morosely. "That's the point, Lexy. I don't even know where she lives these days."

"I know a good inquiry agent. Track her down in no time."

She gave his arm a squeeze. "Dear Lexy. As a matter of fact, I've already done that. Funny little man called Sefton Storey. But he's only been on it since last Monday. And even when I find her, what do I say?"

A party of distinguished people entered at that moment, including several members of the government. She only half-heard Lexy saying, "Well, we know the two most important things about her: She passionately wants to be included in whatever's going on and she has this absolute dread of poverty."

She turned to him briefly and gave a rueful smile. "I know. I can't help it. But how astute of you to spot it."

Lexy frowned in bewilderment; but Julia was still staring toward the door. Now, however, her eyes were wide with surprise.

"What's up?" he asked.

"It can't be! It must be autosuggestion but I'll swear I just saw the woman herself go by out there. Hang on a mo."

She rose and walked swiftly to the door. Outside she glanced up and down the corridor, seeking the pale green that the Davis apparition had been wearing. She caught the merest flash of it at the turn of the stairway leading down to the foyer. Heads turned as she took the steps two at a time, not quite running but striding out in a most unladylike way.

The figure in green, seen from behind, certainly looked like Imogen. "Miss Davis?" Julia asked when she had drawn within a few paces.

The girl spun round and stared in surprise at her former mistress – not least because Julia was saying, "I'm so glad it's you."

Imogen's eyes made a rapid survey of the foyer, as if seeking help. Who was she with? Julia wondered. And why was she here?

And that green dress was pure silk, too. And so was the matching hat.

"I really do think we ought to talk," Julia went on. "Don't you agree it would be in both our interests?"

"No!" was the peremptory answer as she backed away.

It was Lexy who saved the occasion, Lexy at his suave and charming best. "Oh, forgive me," he cooed as he caught up with Julia; his tone switched nimbly from delight to embarrassment. "I thought you were Connie Hale." He stared at Imogen as if he'd made a gaffe and wanted her to rescue him.

Connie Hale was a good name to pick; not only was she then at the height of her fame as a revue artiste, she did – as Julia now realized – bear a passing resemblance to Imogen. "No, this is Miss Imogen Davis," she explained, stepping in smoothly. "Miss Davis, allow me to present Alexander Deeping."

Lexy swept up the girl's hand and raised it to his lips. "But you surely are on the stage, Miss Davis?" he asked.

The transformation that came over Imogen was astonishing. She relaxed, she smiled, she let her gloved hand linger in Deeping's while, with the other, she patted her shingled hair and caressed the lobe of her ear.

Julia saw at once that there would never be a better moment. "We were just about to order luncheon," she said. "Do say you'll join us, Miss Davis?"

"Oh, how delicious!" Lexy murmured, working her over with his twinkling, *genius* eyes.

"Well . . ." She was uncertain. "I don't know."

"Don't say you've already eaten?" Lexy spoke as if her confirmation would desolate him.

A radiant smile flagged her decision. "Well, I thank you," she said and turned again toward the stair. Lexy offered his arm. "Are you staying here?" he asked.

"No. I have a friend who is." It sounded like the truth.

An extra place was swiftly laid and a further menu brought. Julia watched Imogen's eyes as they ran up and down the list; did all that culinary French mean anything to her? Perhaps they covered it at the domestic college. The girl, meanwhile, was basking in a delicate shower of compliments from Lexy.

But she could not avoid Julia's eyes for ever. At last they met, each over the top of a menu. Imogen's wavered for a moment and then held steady.

"It really is an extraordinary stroke of luck, running into you like this," Julia remarked as she folded her menu and laid it down. Then, turning to Lexy, she added, "I ought to explain." She gave Imogen a brief, reassuring nod. "Miss Davis is the daughter of someone connected with the sprp. She stayed with us in Connaught Square – it must be a couple of years ago now. In fact" – the memory appeared to strike her at that moment – "she arrived on the very day of poor George's accident." Another nod at Imogen. "Providence again, you see, my dear."

Imogen just stared at her, open-mouthed. The waiter came and took their orders. Imogen had no trouble with the French. Lexy ordered a bottle of Chablis.

Julia continued with her revisionist explanation. "Miss Davis was extraordinarily helpful to George. I doubt any man ever had more devoted care. She was secretary, reader, nurse, companion . . . I can't tell you the half of it. And George spoke so highly of her. In fact, in his will he made her a kind of trustee – a joint trustee with me – of the Somerville business until Robert comes of age."

"But how extraordinary," Lexy exclaimed, as if it were, indeed, news to him.

Julia laughed. "It came as a bit of a surprise at the time, I must confess. In fact" – she turned to Imogen, who was now hanging on every word – "I have a little bone to pick with you about that. You mustn't think he intended it as a sort of sentimental gesture, you know. When George did things like that, he was entirely in earnest. So you should take the compliment as he meant it – quite seriously – and not go around avoiding me and the business."

Beneath the table she gave Lexy a nudge and murmured, "Isn't that C.B. over there?"

It cost him a great effort to rise and say, "So it is. I must just have a word with him. Do excuse me."

"What's all this?" Imogen asked the moment they were alone. "Got you scared, have I?"

Julia framed a denial and then changed her mind. "As a matter of fact – yes. You have. But not in the way you think. You're playing with a loaded gun, and I'm afraid it may go off in your hand."

"But what's all this . . . sweetness?" She shivered in distaste. "I haven't forgotten how you kicked me out, you know. You just couldn't wait. So I know you don't really . . ."

"All right, Miss Davis. Cards on the table. I don't *like* you any more than I ever did. But we can be civilized about that, surely – especially when we have so much of common interest."

Imogen gave a single laugh of scorn. "Us?"

"Indeed. Look at it from a purely business point of view. Forget any personal feeling you may have about me. Just think of your daily bread and where it's going to come from – and, above all, which side it's buttered on. I'm sure Sidney Gold's somewhere behind all this. I don't know how he imagines it's serving his interests, but I *know* it's not serving yours. D'you suppose he'll care tuppence about you afterwards?"

There was a knowing gleam in Imogen's eye. "Oh, he'll care!"

"Enough to put it in writing?" Julia asked. "With witnesses?"

She saw it dented the girl's composure, but not enough to prevent the sneer: "And what would you put in writing, then?"

"But that's the whole point," Julia answered, unruffled. "It already is in writing. You are a trustee. If you want that deed of yours witnessed, Mrs Crooke and I will gladly come to your lawyers' offices and sign it. But it's only a formality. With or without it, I accept you as a trustee. I" – she steeled herself to say it – "I want you back where you *belong!*"

Imogen was speechless with surprise.

Julia went on hastily, "Here's Lexy coming back now. We'll talk more when he's gone. But just ask yourself this – how much milk can a dead cow give? For such an astute and ambitious young woman, I really am surprised you haven't already worked it out." She turned to Lexy as he rejoined them. "We've just decided to hold a meeting of the trustees of Somerville's immediately after this luncheon."

Lexy gazed fondly from one to the other. "Women nowadays," he said. "I don't know. Engineering, indeed! Look" – he turned exclusively to Imogen – "I'm throwing a little party tonight. Just thirty or forty friends, most of them quite vile. A pretty girl like you would really help it swing. Do say you'll come?"

Julia considered he was overdoing it, but he touched that nerve in Imogen. All through the meal he continued to work his charm.

When Lexy had gone, the smiles faded and the tough talk began. Imogen said she'd consider – not consent to, but consider – dropping "her" action (that is, ditching Sidney Gold) if Somerville & Son was brought back out of limbo and made the owner of Neville's and of the two remaining Somerville firms; further, she wanted a seat on Somerville's board at a salary of £500 a year.

Julia shook her head. "Think again!" Neville's was her own creation, capitalized mainly out of her own money, and she was damned if she'd see it all pass to Robert when he came of age. "But," she added, "Neville's holds the two Somerville companies in trust for Robert. You, as trustee, could be seated on the main Neville board – where you'd be much closer to the heart of things. You'd have a vote on anything that affected Somerville's. The salary would be, say, two hundred?"

"Five hundred or nothing," she came back at once.

Sadly rather than stubbornly, Julia pointed out, "My own salary is only two hundred and fifty. The directors of even our largest and most established aeroplane companies wouldn't draw more than four hundred. *Someone,* I'm sorry to say, has been making you impossible promises. Draw what conclusion you like from it."

And that was where they left it. "At least," she said to Lexy when, on the morning after the party, she told him of the conversation, "we're each of us looking the right way – toward one another."

The word "right" stirred childhood's conscience. She realized that, from the moment she had spotted Davis at the Savoy, she had thought only of what was right for Neville's. What would her old governess, Miss Creen, make of it – coming to terms with a greedy little wanton like Imogen Davis?

Lexy grinned sheepishly. "I'm sorry to say this, but I quite like the girl."

"So I noticed."

He grew serious. "Don't let emotion blind you, darling – understandable though it would be. She's no empty headed young flibbertigibbet. She made one or two quite shrewd little comments last night. You'll have to watch your step with her."

The last person Julia expected to find waiting to see her at Dollis Hill, that same morning after Lexy's party, was Sidney Gold, as truculently india-rubber as ever. "You done well," he commented, running his eye over the premises and grinning. "A lot of good money went into this place, I can see."

Much against her will Julia could not avoid a smile. "You don't change," she told him.

"How was the Savoy?" he asked.

Later, Julia could only thank her stars that some instinct prevented her from replying, "So she told you!" or "I wondered how long it would take her to inform you" – something that would implicate Imogen. The words were on her tongue but in that split second before their utterance she changed her mind and said, "You see – you still know it all."

He laughed as if to suggest it was just a joke for old times' sake and really he had changed quite a bit. As if to reinforce that message he added, "No mystery this time. My boy works there. Randolph Gold. Nice name, innit?"

She raised her eyebrows.

"Yeah," he went on. "I didn't think you'd know that. He's assistant to the manager. Makes a few bob on the side tipping off the gentlemen of the press about who's buying meals for who. Have a decko at today's *Standard* – all about Dear Lexy lunching Mrs Julia Somerville, attractive widow and heiress to the famous coachbuilding firm." He chuckled. "Two and two make five."

"Today's *Standard* or last year's?" she asked. "Mr Deeping and I lunch there quite often." She wondered why he made no mention of Imogen. "Did you get it from the paper, then?"

He shook his head. "Straight from the horse's mouth. He's a good lad, my Randolph."

"Then he surely told you about the third member of our party?" she ventured.

He frowned, but more in disbelief than in annoyance that his boy might have told him less than the whole truth. Julia realized that — for whatever reason — Randolph Gold had, indeed, kept back from his father the news that an important ally had broken bread with the enemy. She grinned, as if to suggest she had only been teasing.

"Ha!" He pointed a finger at her and chuckled. "Clever! Yes, I'd forgotten how clever you can be."

"As a matter of fact" – she laid the groundwork of the lie that Gold junior was going to have to tell his father – "we *were* three for a time. Connie Hale's understudy joined us over coffee. I forget her name. However, it would have spoiled the gossip story, I suppose. Anyway, you haven't struggled out to Dollis Hill just to tell me you already know what's in today's newspapers."

He grew serious at once. "Quite right, Mrs Somerville. I come to suggest a truce."

"Oh? I had no idea we were at war."

He waved a hand about his head as if shooing off a cloud of gnats. "Come off it, gel!" he snapped. "You know what I'm on about. You know Imogen Davis wouldn't have the guts to do what she's done, not on her own. You know I'm the one behind it all."

"How interesting." Julia was suddenly quiet and watchful.

"Well, I was thinking, like – we've both passed a lot of water under the bridge since last we met. We're both uglier and wiser – or, in your case, more bootiful and wiser but it's the same difference. Anyway, I was thinking, where's the point in what we're doing? We're only helping put a lot of lawyers' kids through good schools. And to me that's not what life's all about. Don't you think?"

"Certainly not." Julia wondered why someone so utterly awful could, at the same time, be so fascinating; she hung on every word.

"No, you see. You're like me underneath it all." He leaned forward earnestly. "We should be together, you and me. We shouldn't be fighting each other."

"Well, as I say, I had no idea we *were* fighting each other. Am I allowed to ask what it's all about?"

"Me being stupid." He touched his breast and spread his hands in benediction. "That's what it's all about. My trouble – this is it, now – my trouble is that if there's two ways of doing something, one straight, the other a bit dodgy, I don't even consider the straight one. Soon as I saw as how the Davis gel might have a bit of a hold over you, well, I couldn't help myself. I had to use her."

"In what way, Mr Gold? I mean, I still have no idea of your purpose."

"I'm coming to that. The minute I walked in 'ere, into your factory, I knew I should of tried the straight way. Which reminds me – talking of walking in – was that the new Lancia I seen you drive up in? Not the *seventh* series, is it?"

Julia fell for it, of course; the temperature of her office rose from a watchful frigidity to a relaxing mildness while they discussed the merits of the "finest-ever Lancia."

"Well," she said at length – and curtly, as she realized what she had let happen – "what was your idea? This 'truce,' or whatever you call it?"

He sighed and put his fingertips together, the way clergymen do when, in the midst of jolly company, they regretfully have to mention God. "Let's just wipe the slate clean," he suggested. "This is the way I see it. You're lumbered with Miss Davis. No way round that, thanks to poor old Somerville's will. But suppose she hadn't got there the way she did, eh? Suppose it was all regular and straight – her a close friend of the family or something – you'd give her a seat on the board, I dare say?"

Julia was by now confused. *Had* Imogen been talking to him or not? If so, it must have been within the last few hours – for she had been at Lexy's party until dawn. And in that case, why had she not also mentioned the meeting at the Savoy? Why did she – and Gold junior – keep that from him? It all came back to the puzzle of what Imogen had actually been doing there.

She decided that, improbable as it may seem, Imogen *had* mentioned at least their conversation to Sidney Gold.

But then Gold immediately threw everything back into doubt by adding: "You'd pay her about a hundred and fifty a year, I suppose – something like that?" And when Julia frowned he quickly amended it to, "A ton, anyway – surely?"

These suggestions, far more modest than Imogen's, made it seem most improbable that she had said anything to him.

Perhaps it was the other way round, then? Perhaps he had spoken these thoughts aloud to Imogen at some time? Yes! And then she, seizing the chance yesterday, had jumped the gun on him in order to raise the salary. Now that made more sense.

Gold was waiting for her response.

"It's possible," she conceded.

"Well, in that case" – he was Jolly Uncle again for a moment – "I'm sure I could persuade her to drop the action. Mind you – a salary of a ton and a half would make it certain."

"I'd even consider that," Julia allowed. "But what's in it for you?" She laughed. "I always seem to be asking that question, don't I."

"Me?" He tried to look modest. "I'm just a humble follower where greater minds have led." He pointed at her. "You've got the right idea. There's a bigger future in aeroplanes than what there is in hand-made cars for toffs. I don't want Somerville Motors no more. I want to get my nose into the airframe business."

She chuckled, not at the idea but at the long and tortured path that had led him to this simple conclusion.

He misunderstood. "Listen – don't think I couldn't do the work. I had a peep round your shops here before you come, 's'matter of fact. I couldn't believe my luck. It's all metal. I thought aeroplanes was all wood and wire. Well, I've got lads can bend metal the way you only dream about it. I asked your top man – the big Canadian they're all scared of. I don't want to get no one into no trouble, mind, but I asked him, 'What happens,' I says, 'if, when you've bent up a spar or something and it comes out a few thou' too big or too small?' Know what he told me?"

She shook her head.

"He said, 'They change the drawings in the office.'" Gold laughed. He had two flashy new teeth to back up his name. "Well that would never happen down at Gold's Commercial Bodies, believe you me. We can bend metal to half a thou' – no sweat. So tell me, gel – are you interested?"

"You'd want a contract?" she asked at once.

He nodded. "I'd deserve it, too. Don't you believe me? Listen – I could still use Imogen Davis to force you to it – the dodgy way. But I'm saying forget all that. I'm good enough to do it the straight way." Briefly he covered his eyes with his hands, as if in shame. "My life! Can this be Sidney Gold?"

"I'll think about it," she told him.

He looked up in delight. "Seriously?"

"Very. In fact, I'll show you how much. May I send my chief designer down with some drawings and we'll see if you can make good your boast?"

He fished out his card, the commercial one.

"I still have the last one you gave me," she told him with a smile.

"There!" he crowed. "Didn't I say it at the time? 'You never know!' Wasn't them my very words?"

When he had gone she went to the drawing office to tell Eliot.

"What's the matter?" he asked the moment he saw her expression.

"I don't know if I've just done the wisest – or the most foolish – action of my life," she replied.

CHAPTER TWENTY-EIGHT

ONE OF JULIA'S amusements was to imagine what sort of animal people would be if they hadn't been born human. Churchill, for instance, would have been a bulldog, Charlie Chaplin a raccoon, Theda Bara a cobra. It was a mixture of character and physical appearances.

By both criteria Sefton Storey, the inquiry agent, was a ferret, with his beady eyes and hatchet face and his habit of sniffing as he spoke. Even the way he would dive into his notebook and trawl its pages for facts had a ferret-like intensity. After a week of ferreting out the life of Miss Imogen Davis he reported: – that subject was born at The Laurels, Acton Ave, Turnham Green, on Monday, 6 November, 1905, and was subsequently reared at 3 Forston Rd, Hoxton. After elementary and board school she had attended the Alma Rd Domestic College, gaining a certificate with honours. She had since held a number of domestic posts, all with good character. – that subject presently resided in rented accommodation of superior quality (viz. furnished, and with bath and telephone) at 13 Maiden Lane, Covent Garden. – that subject held no regular position but was seen to visit the cocktail bar at the Savoy Hotel on most days at around noon, where she . . .

He paused, seeming reluctant to continue.

Julia could not resist the chance to shine. "Yes, it's all right, Mr Storey. I happen to know why she goes there."

He looked at her in some surprise. "You do?"

Julia nodded. "Luck, I'm afraid, not cleverness. Did you follow her inside?"

Another dive into the sea of words. "On Monday, Tuesday . . . Friday and Saturday." He cleared his throat. "Sunday was a day of rest, as you might say. For her, I mean."

"Well on Wednesday, and quite by chance, I happened to be lunching at the Savoy with a friend of mine, and I saw her there. We spoke, in fact."

"And she told you why she goes there?" he asked, still more than somewhat surprised.

"Of course not." Julia laughed. "No – it was the father of the young gentleman in question – he let it slip when I mentioned it to him the following day."

"Well!" Storey seemed bewildered.

"Randolph Gold." She was pleased to be one up on him. "One of the Under-Managers there. I suspect that Miss Davis and he are . . ."

Comprehension dawned. "So that's it! I knew it had to be something like that. Under-Manager, eh? She's flying high."

"Oh, she's ambitious."

"Usually it's a backhander to the barman. So!" He snapped shut his notebook with something like relief. "Now that you know where she lives – and *how* she lives – I expect you've no further use for me?"

"Happily, no. She's withdrawing her threats. But tell me one thing – she didn't go south of the river at all?" Julia rose to see him to the door.

"No." He shook his head knowingly. "They're two different

territories – north of the river, south of the river."

"Yes, indeed. My husband used to say they're two different countries."

When he had gone she took up his written report. The paper was green, the same cool green as the silk dress Davis had been wearing. Corruption's disguise.

She sighed. There was something corrupt in all this business. You could hedge it around with excuses – *they* started it; they were the attackers, she was only defending; the intention was good, however dubious the means – but in the end it was corrupt.

She felt suddenly reluctant even to hold the papers in her hands. She knew she ought to read them, not once but many times, searching for weaknesses in the woman, shames to exploit. The creature whose life was here laid bare had threatened the firm. She might still have ideas in that direction, for she had certainly spoken with great bitterness. And here was the ammunition to stop her. But still Julia could not read.

Her father would have burned these papers without hesitation. Her mother, too. Or perhaps not? Her mother was always more ambiguous; she'd have asked someone else to read them and then she'd have quizzed every last morsel out of the hapless victim. But neither would have read a word themselves.

Had they more morality, that generation? Perhaps they could afford it. No, to tell the truth, the only difference was that they did their dirty work at a clean distance. They bought shares in a firm and took the dividend and never troubled to inquire how many dark deeds of this kind were happening "down there." For them, commercial morality began and ended with the statutes – minimum wages, minimum hours for children, and so forth. But if they had sat at this desk, with their own fortunes depending on it – not to mention the livelihood of several hundred workers – they'd have commissioned reports like this. And they'd have read them without a qualm.

But even as she reached this comforting conclusion it was undermined by a suspicion that her father, at least, would rather have gone broke than compromise his notion of honour.

She glanced reluctantly at the first few paragraphs and saw that they merely repeated what he had told her. No need to go through all that again, she thought with relief. She knew it already.

She took up the papers and considered the waste-paper basket. But Brunty came in at that moment with some accounts to initial and so she stuffed the report hastily into her safe, the one behind the Hyde Park water colours. And then she forgot the whole business.

It was a frantic sort of week; the BI was ready at last and would definitely, but definitely, make its maiden flight on Friday. Baring was spending almost every hour at Hendon, of course, sometimes working straight round the clock. On that particular day, however, he happened to be at Dollis Hill just as she was packing up to go home.

"Who was the little guy with the long nose – this morning?" he asked.

"You have good spies."

"No, I happened to be here."

She confessed then, all the things she had tried to keep from worrying him. "You don't mind, I hope?" she concluded.

"Not in the least. I'm grateful. So what did the guy find out?"

"Nothing I didn't know already – but entirely by chance, I must admit. If I hadn't bumped into the Davis creature at the Savoy, I wouldn't have had a notion. So it wasn't wasted."

"She was hanging around us at Hendon this morning. I didn't recognize her at first. She's changed. She told me you knew and it was all okay."

Julia gave a sour smile. "I thought she'd waste no time – the minute she withdrew the action. Listen, Eliot, my dear, that's exactly the sort of thing we've got to guard against. She's probably harmless. A waif and stray who's looking for somewhere to belong. But she may actually be the enemy, or the enemy within."

"Are you implying there's an enemy without?"

"Sidney Gold. Again, this may be absurd . . ."

"Oh, I don't think so. Not from what you've just said. What's he ever done to earn our trust? No, we have to behave as if she's his Trojan horse."

"Oh, good. As long as we're agreed." After a short pause she added, "I don't know what we can do about it, mind. We can't just stop her turning up . . . I mean, I don't want to."

"Absolutely not. Everything on the surface should seem all smooth and friendly."

"But we must utterly, utterly get into the habit of not leaving documents lying around and not saying things she could carry back to her master . . ."

"Sure. I'll tell Brunty, too. Mind you – if Sidney's craftsmen are as good as his boast, we'll be subcontracting work out to him! It seems kind of screwy."

"It's a devious game we're being forced to play, my dear. Believe me, I'm only too aware of the risks. But there's so much I don't know. I have to let them get close, so as to find out."

"It's another no–choice choice," he agreed glumly. "If she's to be a trustee and a director, we simply have to win her to our side."

Julia broke into a slow smile. "One thing I've always admired about you, Eliot – your loyal use of the word *we*. She's not a bad looker."

"Oh no!" he exclaimed in alarm.

"And she's bright. A lot of young men found her very good company that night at Lexy's." Her eyes danced. "I'd be terribly understanding."

"Absolutely not."

"Naturally I'm not pressing for an immediate decision."

"Forget it. I'll give the same answer next year. Anyway . . ." He rose and shambled awkwardly to the window. "I love you."

Her heart sank. "Oh, darling! Don't be so solemn. Can't you tell when I'm joking?"

For a while he was silent; his breathing clouded her windowpane, frosting out the darkened workshop beyond. "I've thought about it rather a lot, lately. Because . . ." He swallowed. "Because of Friday, I guess."

"Oh, Eliot!" She rose and went to him. "I didn't mean to be horrible." She slipped her arms about him and hugged him hard.

He did not at once relax. "There isn't anyone else, is there?"

"Of course not. Who could there possibly be?" When he did not reply she asked, "Do I behave as if there's someone else?"

He sighed. "I guess not. I've just been overworking."

She wanted to make love, there and then, but she could feel the exhaustion in him. "That's certainly true," she agreed. "I tell you what – let's go and swim in Jermyn Street and . . . see how the evening goes from there?"

He had a million things to check on the B1, but she prevailed. She almost made it company policy: For the next three nights, until the maiden flight, he was going to sleep normal hours and do all the normal things any young test pilot would do – like dancing at night spots and getting his picture in the papers.

As they locked up and left, she remarked, "Talking of leaving documents lying around and picking up useful inside information – we probably have more time than we thought to develop the Savage One."

"Oh?" Eliot took her arm as they walked among the silent machines.

"Yes. While I was at the Air Ministry the other day, talking to the Big White Chief himself, it . . . er, came to my notice that Rolls-Royce had sent in a memo pointing out that their engineering is so amazingly advanced that no ordinary mechanic could possibly service the Condor. It could be tackled only by Rolls-Royce-trained engineers." She chuckled. "They must have thought it would guarantee them work from here to eternity. But d'you know what Trenchard had scribbled over it? *No more Condors!* One in the eye for Royce!"

"You're sure it was Trenchard?"

"I'd know that handwriting in the dark."

"A bit of a warning for us," he commented. "It's the sort of thing any proud father might say."

"Also I think we may be able to hold Royce to a very keen price for a job lot of Condors that will soon have no home!"

Laughing, they climbed aboard the Lancia. Things were so much easier in the dark. She turned to him, her heart beating double, her stomach already falling away inside her. He took her head in his hands and ran his fingernails over her scalp until it nearly drove her wild. And all the time his marvellous lips crushed hers, grew soft, moved, parted . . .

When the emotion had run its course she pressed the starter and pointed the mascot at the bright glow of London. Must there be more? she wondered, as five metres of bright blue metal whispered down the Edgware Road.

After a swim at Jermyn Street, they dined at Chez Victor and went on to dance at Taglioni, two of the best night spots of the Twenties. Modern youngsters, who know only the dullness of Quaglino's and the Café de Paris, can have no idea of the sparkle and gaiety of London's nightlife then. By midnight Eliot was exhausted, though Julia was game for another hour or two. However, his plea that the BI needed him fell on the most receptive ears in London, and she saw him to his taxi almost without complaint. "I have a little unfinished business myself," she admitted.

She drove straight to the Savoy, where she asked if Mr Randolph Gold were still on duty.

Inside every fat man, they say, is a thin one struggling to get out. Sidney Gold was chubby rather than fat, but if there were a slim man within him, then, give or take a couple of decades, Randolph was it. In his black tie and tails he was also the very image of a lounge lizard, especially with that sleek, dark hair and his bright, roving eye. Julia understood how an impressionable girl like Imogen might have fallen for him.

"Mrs Somerville – how very pleasant to meet you at last, madam!" He did not offer his hand until she held out hers. Then he shook it warmly. "My father has told me so much about you." His accent was polished rather than genuine. A bit like Imogen's, in fact.

"And naturally you believe it." She laughed.

He did not quite know how to take that. The smiles – of which he had a variety – never left his face; and yet he was full of unease. He kept looking toward the stair, also the main entrance door. "Is it against the rules to hobnob with patrons?" she asked.

"Indeed, no, not at all." He glanced at the clock above the porters' desk. "Is there some particular matter, may I inquire?"

"Do you have a private office?"

"I'm not sure now, whether . . ."

"Your father called on me recently."

His demeanour changed at once. With a quick shift of smiles he led her to a cubbyhole beside the telephone room. It contained a chair and two tables – also a shelf filled with ledgers, blank registration forms, packs of playing cards . . . In a corner stood a sand bucket and shovel and a first-aid chest. "Bit of a dumping ground, I'm afraid," he commented, moving aside a broken umbrella so as to pull out a chair for her. "My father, you said?" He seated himself opposite.

"Yes. He told me you work here – which was how he knew that Mr Deeping and I took lunch upstairs the other day."

Alarm invaded his eyes. "I never dreamed he'd call on you."

"No, I'm sure you didn't. I almost put my foot in it."

He glanced at her sharply. "Almost?" he asked. There was hope in the lift of his eyebrow.

"I think you should be frank with me," she went on. "He obviously knew nothing about the fact that Miss Davis was also there." She smiled. "Yet I can see it's not news to *you*. Why didn't you tell him?"

His grin turned roguish, and yet his unease persisted. "I have my reasons, Mrs Somerville. Please don't think me rude."

She thought it time for plain speaking. "I believe I can guess, Mr Gold. You and this young woman have fallen for each other. Your father knows nothing of it and would be displeased if he were to find out. If I may say so, I think you're unwise to deceive him. Miss Davis has as many faces as the moon. He's bound to hear of it."

Young Gold's response was illuminating. Julia expected him to leap to the defence of his lady love; but not at all. He gave a savage grin and replied, "I hope he does. But not yet." A cheery nod of the head promised Gold senior a brutal surprise when that day came.

All Julia's invisible feelers were now out, straining for more. Either this lad had no idea what a hard man his father was, or (just as interesting) he had some kind of emotional or family sway that, in a crisis, would thwart his father's determination. Either way, here, perhaps, was Sidney Gold's Achilles heel.

"Rather you than me," she commented. "He's not the man to cross."

The young fellow laughed as if she'd made an enormous joke. Then, seeing her bewilderment, he asked, "Don't you know what you did to him?"

"Well, of course I do."

"No. I mean . . ." He tapped his heart. "He'd walk through fire for you."

Now it was she who laughed. "Mr Gold! Come, come!"

"I don't mean *love*." He spoke the word as if it were tainted. "I mean it's the only way he can salvage his pride. Surely you can see that? He was master of the game since he could talk. He was so sure of getting his hands on Somerville's – you were putty in his hands, he said. And then you just walked away with it! What else can he do, except . . ."

"You speak as if you disapprove?"

"Of course I do. He's a strong man gone soft. He'll lose the business. There'll be nothing left to come to me."

Julia felt all her certainties dissolving again. "You won't make me drop my guard," she warned. "We may be on the point of doing business with your father – lots of it, if he's as good as he claims – but I shall never, never trust him."

Randy Gold smiled. "I'm sure he knows that. After all, that's where he starts with everybody!" He cocked his head. "But you're surely joking – I hope – about doing business with him?"

Ignoring the question, she eyed him shrewdly. "What you've told me gives me more than a passing interest in *your* plans, too, young man. Don't you think we'd better start pooling our information?"

"Maybe." He nodded warily. "What did the old fellow want?"

"Peace. He came with a peace offering. I wasn't joking. Gold's Commercial Bodies may soon be building airframes for my company – or parts of airframes . . ."

"It's a trick," he interrupted.

"Well, thank you for that warning!" She laughed. "Incidentally, did Miss Davis tell you what she and I discussed the other day at lunch?"

He blinked at the rapidity with which she could change the subject; then he nodded. "You're wasting your time trying to plead with that one. There's only one language she understands." He stroked the palm of his hand.

So not only were they not lovers, they were not even frank with each other – at least, Davis clearly hadn't been frank with him. Swiftly Julia returned to his other weak flank – his obsession with his inheritance. "That wasn't your father's only purpose, by the way – building airframes. He, too, has plans for Miss Davis. He suggests I should appoint her to the board of my company."

The young man laughed, as if the very idea were preposterous.

Her heart fell. What incompetents these two youngsters were; they left their lies around like unexploded bombs; they trusted their luck but not each other. She felt alarmed at having to deal with them at all – yet what other choice had she?

Firmly she told him, "It would be only natural. She's a trustee, after all."

"You'd be mad," he snapped.

"I'm afraid the madness was my husband's. The trustee thing was his idea. But I can't just ignore the situation. It won't pack up and go away. Look at the trouble she's already caused."

He leaned across the table, solemn for once, and asked, "You want to stop her at that game?" He tapped his chest. "Randy Gold's your man."

So he didn't even know she'd withdrawn the action! She provoked him with an amused glance. "I think *Sidney* Gold may have different ideas. Let's not be hasty. Tell me, would it upset your plans for Miss Davis if she were to get this seat on the board?"

He puckered his lips and inhaled deeply through his nose. Then he remembered to smile. "Depends what's in it. For her, I mean. As I said, money's all that talks there."

She tested out the lower figure first. "A ton and a half – that was how your father put it."

He laughed, but not at his father's quaint expression. He laughed at the pitiful size of it.

"Something more like two hundred?" she tried.

He shrugged. "Whatever you think, Mrs Somerville. If *that's* all we're talking about, it can hardly upset the apple cart here, can it? What's it involve – one meeting a year?"

She nodded warily. "We do have to hold an annual general meeting – by law."

"There you are, then. If that's the way the old man wants to play – why not? Least said, soonest mended, eh?"

She rose to go. This conversation had given her food for a month of thought. Before leaving she told him the little cover-up story about Connie Hale's understudy, just in case his father checked.

All the way home the questions churned. Were the two Golds, father and son, a fiendishly clever pair – the father pretending to dote on his son, who, in turn, pretended to loathe the old man? In other words, was Randy intended as the genuine Trojan horse and Imogen only the feint?

And if Randy and the girl were not lovers, what was the connection between them? Why did she go to the Savoy to see him every day? She must be his mistress. That would certainly be in keeping with her character. (And it would also explain Sefton Storey's hesitation when that delicate point arose.) But would young Randolph pay her enough to buy such expensive silk dresses? In that case, he must have money of his own. Surely a trainee manager couldn't earn more than forty pounds a year, cash in hand? Yes, he must have money of his own – otherwise how could he sneer at a salary of two hundred?

Also, don't forget that Sidney Gold must be paying her something, too. Knowing nothing of his son's involvement, he'd assume he was keeping her, at least while she might be useful to him. One way and another, there'd be enough to buy silk dresses.

As Julia coasted silently into the mews behind Connaught Square a great weariness filled her. So many unknowns. So much to learn.

Too much, it seemed, at times.

She switched off the motor and sat in the dark awhile, trying to think of Eliot.

CHAPTER TWENTY-NINE

IT WAS MAX'S idea to bring Robert. Julia had taken Lydia out of Summerhill for the day, where the curriculum was so free and easy, but she had thought Haileybury, with its more military approach to such things, might object. Max, however, had talked Robert's housemaster round.

Neither youngster would ever forget that day – the one on which all their future prospects quite literally got off the ground. For the rest of the world that early summer of 1927 was marked by Charles Lindbergh's solo transatlantic flight and, some two weeks later, Clarence Chamberlin's less publicized but historically more significant flight from America to Germany with a passenger aboard. But for Eliot Baring and the three Somervilles – indeed, for everyone connected with Neville Aero-Engineering – Friday the 27th of May, neatly sandwiched between the two historic flights, was *the* great moment of history.

No one who was there that day would ever forget it. Not only Crownfield but also Dear Lexy was present. Even to his untutored and uninterested eye the Baring 1 looked like the first of a new kind of aeroplane, smooth and streamlined and shiny. It may have been the gift of hindsight but Lydia always claimed that was her first and strongest impression. From the day Julia took up flying, Lydia knew that she, too, was going to be a pilot. Her mother was her first heroine – soon to be joined by the Duchess of Bedford, then Ruth Nicholls, Amy Johnson, Amelia Earhart . . . and a long list of great women aviators. The one after whom she modelled herself most closely, however, was Sophia Heath, the Englishwoman who, having browbeaten the Olympic Committee into allowing women athletes, had turned her guns on the International Commission for Air Navigation and their absurd ban on women commercial pilots. She never won an athletics event and she never flew an aviation first; but she qualified in meteorology, navigation, aeroplane construction, the theory of flight, and engine fitting – and then she went on to pass the physical and mental aptitude tests for a commercial pilot's licence, deliberately choosing the time of her period, "just to show them." Her single-minded, unspectacular dedication truly inspired Lydia.

Even then, at the age of twelve, Lydia knew every plane in the sky – not only what they looked like but their dimensions, engines, pedigree, and performance. She was the despair of her brother, who tried to keep up for a while and then abandoned the laurels to her. His was the usual sort of young boy's knowledge – twenty-percent half-digested fact sandwiched in eighty-percent bluster. Lydia plagued the life out of poor Eliot, wanting to learn the most recondite details of the machine's construction. "If ever you want an innocent-looking little spy," he advised Julia, "she's the one."

He did the taxiing and tail-up trials at six-thirty that morning; Julia sat in the engineer's seat behind him. The plane handled beautifully; at the very end, without warning Julia, he took off, flew a couple of seconds at about six feet of altitude, and put her down again. After they had taxied back to the apron she leaned forward, pulled aside his flying helmet, and kissed him on the neck. "Thank you for that," she murmured. They had made the maiden flight together.

Walking back to the canteen for breakfast, though, he seemed less ebullient than she had expected.

"Tired?" she asked.

He seemed about to deny it, but then he answered, "Probably."

All her caution came alive. "What is it?"

"Oh . . ." He made awkward circles with his hands. "I thought I detected a little instability while we were airborne."

"A little bit of a cross-breeze?" she suggested.

"Yeah – must have been."

Both avoided looking (or looking obviously) at the windsock, which hung limp from its mast.

She went on, "And we were only just above stalling speed."

"Sure. That was it. No doubt."

After a pause she said, "Darling, you wouldn't take any foolish risks, would you."

He put an arm round her waist and laughed.

"Because I'd go out of my mind," she added. "Because you are all the world to me."

He slowed down. After a silence he told her, "You should say it more often." Then, after a further pause: "And in more everyday circumstances."

She put her hand over his and squeezed it to her tightly. "I know," she said.

Eliot was torn between his two selves that day. His newer, English personality would keep stressing that there was nothing in the least bit revolutionary or new about the machine . . . it was already ten years out of date . . . and the real credit for this or that feature should go to Mitchell or Junker or Rohrbach; and all the while his American, toot-your-own-horn personality chafed under this shower of modest half-truths.

But that native streak could not be entirely suppressed. It showed in the way he organized the event. Back home, no doubt, even though it was a private affair confined to the company's staff and friends, there'd have been a brass band and those girls who jump up and down while juggling sticks. As if he knew it would be a red-letter day in the company annals, Eliot had printed a souvenir programme, promising takeoff at 11.45 am, and then listing the "manoeuvers" (the spelling itself revealing the conflicts within!) that the plane would perform. It amounted to half an hour of climbs, banks, turns, and descents, culminating in a flypast, thirty feet above ground level, at stall angle, "where the high-lift coefficient of the modified Göttingen aerofoil will be demonstrated to advantage."

The production was like one of those modern plays where the sound effects begin even before curtain-up. In this case it was the ear-shattering roar of three Rolls-Royce Condors at full revs *inside* the hangar. How the structure withstood the assault no one knew. At the height of it, just when everyone was thinking that no natural machine could be responsible for such thunder, Baring throttled back and the hangar doors like theatre curtains drew apart to reveal the new machine in all its burnished glory. Lexy swears that in siting the hangar, Eliot had calculated the precise angle of the sun at that moment, for it positively bathed the whizzing propellers on nose and wing in its radiance, leaving the rest of the fuselage in inky mystery.

The wheel chocks had already been removed, so the moment the revs began again to climb, the B1 inched forward out of the dark; it resembled some great polished insect shedding the last remnants of its cocoon. The cheering was drowned by the roar of those three mighty engines as the plane went swiftly past. With confidence confirmed by that morning's trials, Eliot moved directly to the end of the field and lined up for a take-off across the least muddy strip he could find.

The two youngsters were beside themselves. "Is that *ours?*" they kept asking their mother. "Have we really made that?"

To them it was magic, even though they had visited Dollis Hill and Hendon and seen the wonder as it grew. That had been mere stage scenery. The enchantment did not exist until it all came together in this gleaming, thundering dragon.

Eliot barely paused. Again the roar crescendoed until, at its climax, the B1 leaped forward over the turf. Soon it was hurtling over undulations that shook the wings and gave them a hint of a flapping motion, like a bird's. In just over a quarter of a mile she was airborne. This time the cheer drowned out the by now distant roar of the Condors. The undercarriage, though retractable, was left extended for this maiden flight.

"By jove," Max enthused as he watched her do a tight turn over the airfield, "she's exactly like those snaps you took of her out at Allbury."

Julia, who had thought the same thing even as the machine was gathering speed for takeoff, was still waiting for her heart to start beating again. Her face ached from a smile she forced there. In reality she was sick with dread, watching for the faintest sign of the trouble he had hinted at earlier that morning. It did not help to know that Eliot was a good enough pilot to disguise any but the severest defect.

Later, when the instability of the B1 had been cured (and could therefore be admitted) Lydia explained to anyone who'd listen that the Göttingen aerofoil ("that Götterdämmerung wing shape," as Brunty always called it) was chosen to accommodate the fuel tanks. "But it suffered from intrinsic instability because it had greater destabilizing CP travel than was normal. The Hawker Horsley had similar trouble two years earlier," she would add airily. "But Eliot thought that was because it was a biplane. Only a pilot of his outstanding capability could have kept that crate in the air at that angle."

Be that as it may, the B1 performed exactly as the souvenir programme promised, and Julia felt able to relax a little. At last the "manoeuvers" were completed, including that near-lethal flypast at the stall angle; she rose again, did her final landing circuit and a perfect touch-down before taxiing to the wildly cheering spectators at the edge of the field. As a final bit of swank Eliot parked her with the wheels (invisible to him in the cockpit) slap-bang on the apron line.

Of course, everybody wanted a ride then, but the instability ruled that out. Eliot made some excuse about doing the test first with sacks of potatoes. Crownfield and Deeping were not as crestfallen as they pretended to be. They cried *Oh dear!* along with the rest, but their thoughts turned happily to the celebratory luncheon waiting for the whole party at Wheeler's in the Strand.

Julia soon found a moment alone with Eliot. "Well?" she asked. "Was she as good as she looked?"

He made a so-so gesture with one hand. "We need to add a touch of torsional stability."

"In other words, she could have fallen out of the sky."

He grinned. "But she didn't."

"Oh, Eliot!" She both laughed and frowned, clenching her fists and squaring up to him like a boxer.

He laughed too, clipping her jaw gently with his great southpaw.

She had the devil's own job persuading him to join them at Wheeler's, but she insisted – "for the look of the thing." He gave orders to dismantle the wings at once, and of course he wanted to stay and help. Every minute counted, for the instability was serious.

"Now that she's flown, what are you going to call her?" she asked, hoping to distract him as she steered him toward her car.

But he was still looking back over his shoulder. "If Gold's men really can work to half a thou'," he said, "this is when we're going to need them."

"What name?" she pressed

"If we'd finished our own wind tunnel just a month earlier . . ."

"The name!"

". . . the one at Farnborough is just . . ."

"Eliot, I'll strangle you. You haven't even bothered to think of a name, have you!" She bundled him into the back of her car and climbed in beside him. Julia turned to beckon the children, too, but saw with dismay that Robert was already handing Imogen Davis into Max's car, his prewar Vauxhall Prince Henry. Max had clearly taken a liking to the girl; during the test flight they had been chatting like old friends. And, since Robert took so much pattern from his uncle, this had caused him to look at the former nursery maid with new (not to say fresh) eyes. There was now a joking sort of rivalry springing up between the pair of them over her.

"I did actually consider a name," Eliot was saying. "But it's probably awful."

"Well?" she had to prompt.

"What about 'Fleet'?" he asked hesitantly.

"The Neville Fleet . . ." Julia murmured experimentally. "I flew to Rome in a Neville Fleet."

"Fleet also means swift," he pointed out.

Nobody denied it.

"I said it was awful," he told them.

"What about 'Allbury'?" Julia suggested. "Fly to Delhi in a Neville Allbury!"

Nobody cheered.

"You could call it 'Fleet*liner*,' couldn't you?" Lydia told them. Since going to Summerhill she had lost all her inhibitions about joining in grown-up conversations.

"And pray how did you go to Paris, my dear?" she asked – answering herself with arch solemnity: "Oh, by Fleetliner, don't you know."

Of the thousands of people who later spoke such words in earnest, how many would believe that the name had such casual origins?

CHAPTER THIRTY

IT SAYS MUCH for Baring's humility that, having poured so much scorn on the slotted-wing concept pioneered by Handley-Page ("a dead-end in the search for stability at low airspeed"), it was, nonetheless, the first remedy he tried in the firm's new wind tunnel at Dollis Hill. Later generations will find it hard to realize what a desperate search that was, not just with the Fleetliner but with almost every plane then in service. The previous year alone some 340 aircraft had fallen out of Britain's skies, mostly because once they stalled they developed an uncontrollable spinning-in. When a plane started that spiral, her ailerons lost their "bite" and she became unsteerable. Every week, somewhere in England, a pilot died waggling his joystick in a futile attempt to regain control.

Handley-Page's answer in their biplanes was the famous "slotted wing." Then the Royal Aircraft Establishment at Farnborough improved on the idea. They linked the normal aileron to a leading-edge slot that could open and close. This produced less drag in normal flight.

Baring tested models of both, though in his engineering bones he knew they were lash-up expedients rather than true solutions. But he also tested variations based on Antony Fokker's "stable cantilever wing," as in the FVII, which was then in service with KLM. Like the Fleetliner, it was a single-winged plane – though the Fokker wing was high while the Fleetliner's was low. Instinct told Eliot that if he gave the wings a sharper backsweep than in the FVII – more like that extraordinary experimental plane the Pterodactyl, designed by Graham Hill at Westland – and at the same time brought the centre of gravity forward, he might not only cure the original fault but produce even less drag.

And so, indeed, it proved – at least, insofar as the wind tunnel could prove anything. Now they had to reshape the prototype Fleetliner and go aloft again.

If she had been made in wood, they would have had to rebuild her more or less from scratch. But with metal it was possible to weld in the extra gussets at the wing stubs, stretch new metal skin over them, and make the necessary adjustments to the centre of gravity, all without sacrifice of strength; and, amazingly, the job was completed just inside the month. The skilled benders of Gold's Commercial Bodies earned not only their laurels but also a hideous amount of overtime – and the certainty of future contracts.

There were other modifications, too. Wind tunnel tests on the propellers showed that, though highly efficient at takeoff, they were lamentable while cruising. Baring changed them for the French Ratier type in which the pitch can be adjusted high for takeoff, after which it automatically falls back to low for cruising. He also enlarged the air intake and redesigned the radiator grilles – there were dozens of minor "mods" of that kind, all completed while the wings were being rehung.

So, on Thursday, 30th June, the redesigned prototype, now looking every inch like the Fleetliner you see in all the aeroplane books, flew again.

There was a mere handful of spectators – Julia and a few other senior people from Dollis Hill – to watch her take off and go once more through her paces. Again, Baring made it look easy. Not until he landed and she saw the mixture of relief and exhilaration in his eyes did she realize how wide a gap there is between a successful test in the wind tunnel and a successful flight with the real machine. By way of final approval he invited them all aboard for "a short flip" – a lap of honour over north London.

Never mind "over north London," Julia was over the moon. This was the moment of which she had dreamed ever since that dreary autumn day, almost two years before, when Eliot had invited her into his hut at Forge Lane and showed her the original test model. And she had thought it no more than a glorified hobby! But here it was – the new world, barely glimpsed then, now all about her.

The most astonishing thing about the takeoff was the acceleration. The Argosy and the DH66, aboard both of which she had flown several times by then, had no more acceleration than your average bus. But the three Condors and the sleek lines gave this new plane the feel of a sports car. The seat pressed against her back as forcefully as if she were taking off in her own Moth; indeed, the pressure made the ribs of the wickerwork distinctly uncomfortable.

We've done it! she told herself as the ground rumble ceased and she saw their dwindling shadow fall away to the north. *We've actually made a real live aeroplane!*

But the joy was short lived. Now that the day had arrived it did not seem like the culmination of anything. Quite the opposite, in fact; all she could think of was the work that remained to be done before this flying test rig became a regular "liner" of the air.

She realized it would always be so. Every day would have its goals; every morrow its achievements, in an endless succession. Problems and solutions would always recede before them, promising an ultimate Achievement that would never materialize. In philosophical mood Baring would agree that there must be ultimate limits – a speed beyond which materials would melt like meteors entering the atmosphere . . . stresses that would crack the strongest and most subtle alloys . . . fuels whose speed of combustion set limits to the power they could deliver . . . and so on. But his very tone of voice implied that none of them would ever see the day; for as long as they lived they would be rolling the rock up that hill. Were they therefore to be pitied or envied? She imagined herself sitting in that ultimate air liner, the man-made meteor, with no further progress possible (beyond, say, changing the colour scheme) and she decided that on the whole they were to be envied their mere 100 mph machines and the problem of reaching 120.

Even so, she reminded herself, that was not to say colour schemes and other "fripperies" were as yet unimportant. She sat at one of the Fleetliner's windows (which were circular, like portholes, to distribute the stresses in the outer skin more evenly) and tried to imagine herself a passenger. How could she make the inside of this aircraft look utterly different from the inside of any other? True, almost all the others – and certainly all the passenger planes in service with Imperial Airways – had square bodies; the Fleetliner was more of a tube, or a tall oblong with rounded-off corners. Baring's idea was to square it off inside. This would restore the traditional, railway-carriage appearance, to reassure the customers, and also provide useful space between the inner and outer skins for the control wires and electricity and things. Julia now had second thoughts: Keep the two-skins idea, but round off at least the ceiling corners. That would gain an extra six inches. What then?

As they circled over Hendon and Cricklewood, flaunting themselves to their competitors at de Havilland (none of whom, of course, would later admit to seeing them at all), she planned the interior down to the smallest detail. Her inspiration, as is obvious to anyone familiar with both, was the new decor at the Savoy Grill, which was considered the very avant garde of interiors.

That evening she stole into the children's old nursery (and it gave her a little pang to realize that already one could talk of their *old* nursery) and rummaged around for their water-colour sets. Lydia must have taken hers to Summerhill, but Robert's were there, almost unused. She was quite pleased with the result, which she took to Dollis Hill next day. Everyone said they were divine, but she did not go short of reminders that there was a big difference between a five-minute sketch and a working drawing you could hand out in the upholstery shop.

And here was Eliot suggesting an accelerated building programme for two more Fleetliners and the immediate commissioning of another eight . . . and meanwhile some high-up in the Royal Navy, who had been at Hendon yesterday, thought the plane would make a pretty fine long-distance spotter . . . which raised the whole question of military applications. With very little modification the Fleetliner would also make a better bomber for the RAF than anything in present service, or even on the drawing board. So what did she think?

With a sigh she put away her sketches. There would obviously be no time to develop them. And yet, as she knew from the old Somerville days, a Rolls-Royce car, in general, may sell on its superior engineering, but many a *particular* sale has hinged on the colour and feel of the upholstery. It was important, too. Not for the first time – not even for the hundredth – she wondered how to split herself into half a dozen Julias.

In fact, she already had the answer, though she did not realize it until, a few days later, she went to a party at the Crownfields' home in Hampstead.

CHAPTER THIRTY-ONE

CROWNFIELD'S HOUSE, like most houses in Flask Walk, was quietly assertive, dignified, aloof. It was protected from the gaze of the vulgar by a high wall of red brick, unnecessarily supplemented by a thicket of dark green cypress – the kind that flaunts great bundles of dead-looking twigs. "Like a witches' car park," Max commented as he held open the gate for his two sisters. Wallace Baker was covering King Fuad's visit and unable to come; Julia noticed that, since their accidental meeting at the Ritz, her brother-in-law was always "on an assignment" whenever the possibility arose of their meeting at some arranged function.

The pathway up to the house was flanked by the sort of shrubs that *know* they are always on official and public display – laurel, aucuba, and bay – around whose leaf-soured feet violets, crocuses, and even Irish moss simply wilt and die. It was a bright July evening. Up on Hampstead Heath, where the three had just been walking, shirt-sleeved lovers were strolling arm in arm, while youngsters tried in vain to launch their kites on a breeze that would not raise thistledown. Yet here it was almost chill.

Dolly had been invited because it was she who first introduced Julia to the Honourable Jasper Torode, the "artist" at the centre of tonight's festivities; in fairness the invitation ought to have gone to Lexy, not Dolly, for it was at one of his parties that the introduction took place.

They were an unlikely pair to hit it off, "Jass and Ju." He was a mixture of such impossible opposites – a socialist aristocrat, a rich bohemian, a widely talked-about artist who had never held an exhibition, and a self-proclaimed (not to say self-trumpeted) bisexual. Even the name by which most people knew him – Young Jass – was a misnomer; he was the most wrinkled and balding *young* man Julia had ever seen. (However, let us not be catty; for a man in his mid-forties he wasn't so dusty, either.) She ought to have disliked him at sight, yet she did not.

At Lexy's party he had been holding forth, wittily but with little substance, about the triumph of modernism. When Julia had heard enough, she interrupted, in that disingenuous manner of hers, "Oh, I get so sick of Modern – one has to keep replacing it every year."

It was one of her test sentences, like the one about adjusting poppet valves with a sledgehammer. For a moment he teetered on the verge of taking her seriously; then he laughed. And that was when Dolly had made their introduction.

Dancing was one sure way to Julia's favour, and Jass was a fine dancer. Jog Trot, Vampire, Missouri Walk, Hesitation, Elfrida, Camel Walk, and, naturally, the Charleston – he did them all superbly. That evening they had danced together so much that his regular partner, Yvonne Norton, stormed out in a huff; true, he and Yvonne had never much cared for each other, but that was beside the point; girls did not pick their dancing partners on the trivial grounds that they *liked* each other.

From Lexy's they had gone on to the Café Anglais (which is still today as it was then, except that dear old Rex Evans is no longer there, singing about white mice and snowballs and the wrong end of his horse), and there she persuaded him to be slightly more serious about himself and his ambitions.

He was actually, as far as she could make out, a kind of artists' agent. "My lads and lasses," he called them. The last real painting he himself had done was just after the war, when he moved from rich house to rich house (all belonging to friends and acquaintances) painting fake Chinese tapestries on their walls.

"Ghastly homes," he sneered. "Was it less than ten years ago? All that wistful lavender, faded lilac . . . white, mauve, pink . . . and crammed with vile Jacobean cottagey furniture. I used to sneak in jazz cushions and futuristic lamp shades." He giggled. "My time bombs."

He pretended to be crestfallen. "But what can one lone crusader do against the forces of Philistia? Even when that man is Jasper Torode. Vile gave way to viler – pickled panelling, walnut furniture, Spanish ironwork, Italian bric-à-brac. Surely you're not too young to remember it, Ju, dear?"

Julia was trying *not* to remember that it was the sort of interior she herself had commissioned only last year. The varnish still squeaked.

"But!" He brightened. "Silver lining time. It was all genuine."

"By which you mean expensive." Julia knew it. The bills were still arriving.

He gave a Cheshire cat's grin. "Comfortable livings for bright young things with an artistic bent. Especially if they have an out-and-out genius to represent them."

"And that's what you do – you and your lads and lasses?"

"*Did*, dear. I'm talking about last year. That particular party's over. *Genuine* genuine is out."

"And what's in?"

"Fake genuine," he told her solemnly. "Connemara marble made to look like Italian plaster. Beech panelling, scratched and limed and stained until you'd swear it was oak. Parana pine shelves with *knots!* Doesn't it sound exquisitely decadent?"

Suspicion gripped Julia. "Would this be the same Connemara marble and beech panelling you installed only last year?"

"Oh, quick!" He chuckled. "No wonder you're in business. No wonder you're *still* in business. Yes – of course it is."

Then Julia remembered that Crownfield had recently complained about Matty's wanting the whole house done up yet again – though it had only been finished eighteen months ago. And that, to make no more tale of it, was why they were all forgathered in Flask Walk this fine evening in July.

Even while they were paying their respects to their host and hostess they were commandeered by Jasper, who had to show them everything himself. He was dressed in a green velvet suit straight out of the Gay Nineties – "Torode of Torode Hall," he explained. "Please don't say you like it."

On the bare wooden doors an extra grain had been added to the one nature had put there; plaster panels had been marbled; marble shelves had been painted with a deep white lustre to mimic alabaster; in the bathroom, black drapes banished the sun so that pale-blue "daylight" lamps could, in turn, banish the artificial night. Reality was not banished, however – or not exactly; it merely found itself at a perpetual Mad Hatter's party in which everything had "moved on" and was pretending to be something else.

"Oh, Dolly," Jasper implored, "be a pet. Trip up to the telephone kiosk at the tube station and ring us here. No one, simply no one, can find the phone! Aren't I a brute?"

But while she was taking down the number the apparatus began to ring and they were able to trace it to what looked like a collected set of Milton's poems in their original seventeenth-century bindings; in fact, it was only the bindings, stuck on to the door of a little mahogany cabinet in the bookshelf. Everyone laughed.

"I was fearfully lucky to find the set," Jasper gushed. "Apparently original Miltons are getting frightfully rare."

Max, already appalled enough at Jass himself, was outraged at this vandalism. "What did you do with the pages?" he asked.

Jasper turned on him gratefully. "Thank God for a man who cares! None of these philistines, sir, would dream of inquiring. The original and priceless pages have, of course, been re-bound within *fake* original bindings." He pulled one volume from the shelf above the secret telephone cabinet and handed it to Max. "Superb craftsmanship, what?"

The telephone caller, whom no one had bothered to answer, gave up – accidentally joining the appreciative silence that momentarily reigned.

When the hubbub resumed, Crownfield murmured in Julia's ear, "Dear Somerville, I can't begin to tell you how grateful I am to you, not merely for discovering this creature, but for introducing him into the bosom of my family."

"Oh?" She pretended to be surprised. "Is Mrs Crownfield not pleased?"

"She's ecstatic, of course. When are you letting him loose at Connaught Square?"

She passed it off with a laugh but she could see he was not as playful as he was pretending to be.

Refreshments were on a buffet, to allow uninterrupted dancing in the dining room – where the parquet floor had been painted to look like a Roman mosaic. There were three musicians, piano, saxophone, and drums, who seemed to know all the latest tunes. Julia danced with everyone; only when the trio rested did she take something light from the buffet and find someone to talk to.

More usually, they found her. That was about the time when Princess Löwenstein-Wertheim was preparing for a "wrong-way" transatlantic flight (that is, Europe to America, against the wind) in a Fokker VII powered by Bristol Jupiter engines. She herself was to be the sole passenger; the pilots were old friends of the princess, Leslie Hamilton and F.F. Minchin. Everyone wanted to know Julia's opinion of the venture.

She privately thought it ill-advised but would never have said so; there was an unwritten law among aeroplane people that one didn't pour cold water – in public – on any venture, however lunatic. All flying was heroic, all aviators intrepid, and all promoters – like the princess – angels. Julia skilfully answered a different question – not whether this particular flight was wise but whether "people," from the princess to the airlines in general, were wise to employ so many ex-RAF types. Neither Hamilton nor Minchin had been able to settle to civilian flying. She knew Minchin fairly well, a kindly, charming man but one for whom any routine was the kiss of death – perhaps literally so in his case, for he was the pilot responsible for the endurance tests on the original Jupiter engines. As later experience showed, his conduct of the trials had been a mite casual. It was probably engine failure that led to the deaths of all three, somewhere in mid-Atlantic, later that year. Even then, a month before their departure, Julia must have suspected their chances were slim for she said, "Perhaps they miss the zest of combat and so need ventures like this to supply it."

"And the princess?" Crownfield asked with a definite edge to his voice.

"Risk is no longer a male preserve," she reminded him.

"Ah," he exclaimed, as if she had unwittingly made an important concession. "Do you think a woman is capable of distinguishing risk from . . . folly?"

She laughed, for she knew well enough what he was driving at. "But one woman's risk *is* another man's folly," she pointed out.

Everyone else took it as a sexual innuendo – with particular reference to Crownfield and some private knowledge she must have gleaned about him. And the man's anger at losing this obscure skirmish seemed only to confirm their supposition.

There were several other occasions that evening when Crownfield made some rather barbed comment of that kind. They mystified most of his guests, for, although his remarks seemed perfectly general in character, Mrs Somerville responded to each one as if it carried some particular reference, too; and she was obviously giving as good as she got. Crownfield retired wounded each time, yet could not let it rest; he had to keep returning for one more go.

At last, during a soft, sentimental waltz, Jasper Torode murmured into her ear, "This banker friend of yours, our esteemed host – he will pay up, won't he?"

"Why do you ask?"

"He seems to have it in for you. I wondered if it was because you were the one who introduced me to him? Maybe he thinks my price is a bit steep?"

She laughed. Only a few hours earlier, up on the heath, Max had asked Dolly if playing Vivie Warren in the Shaw revival had changed her outlook on life – meaning, of course, had it made her more sympathetic toward Unfortunate Women, and all that sort of thing. But Dolly had replied, "Of course it has. I'm getting offered buckets of serious roles now, not just your endless drawing-room comedies, thank you very much." The total self-absorption of artistic people always delighted Julia.

"It wouldn't be too-too risible," Jasper warned.

"I wasn't laughing at that. I don't think you need worry about being bilked of your fee."

His relief was enormous, but not absolute. "You can't deny he's got his needle into you for *something*."

"Don't you worry your pretty little head about that, Jass, dear. It's just that he doesn't approve of my business methods. Well, I don't much care for his taste in cravats – so we're about equal."

He stared at her with enlarged respect. People who could be as cavalier with their banker as she had been with Crownfield were clearly seeded far above him. "When do I start on *your* house?" he asked. "It will be my chef d'oeuvre."

A thought flitted through her mind and vanished. Something he could do. But she couldn't think clearly at this party. "When I run out of tidbits like this to toss your way" – she waved an airy hand about her. *Business promises,* as she called them – that is, promises you keep only if it truly suits you – were second nature to her by then.

Crownfield came up to them at that moment and pointed out that the painted mosaic was being scuffed off the floor, in quite large flakes, by all these dancing feet. Jasper was magnificent. Anyone with the slightest bit of soul, he remarked, could see that was precisely the intention. The floor was to be forever poised between its two personalities – the honest rustic of wood and the metropolitan sophisticate of fake mosaic. "You have the only schizophrenic dance floor in London," he boasted. But when Crownfield had gone muttering away, he added in Julia's ear, "Except for Lady Blesdale's. I seem to remember a similar spot of bother there. They don't move in the same circle, I hope?"

"Hardly."

In the small hours, when the party began to thin, and the trio was replaced by a rather magnificent gramophone, Crownfield at last took her onto the floor. The tune was from "No, No Nanette" – one of the records he had played at Maidenhead that very first night. Was he deliberately reminding her of it now, as an ironic backdrop to the harshness of his words?

"You're turning shallow, Somerville," he snapped. "These people you've taken up with, they're not worthy of you."

"If you mean the unspeakable Jass, Crownfield, have a care. He's going to design the interior of the world's finest air liner." It was pure inspiration, concealed from her until that moment by the ideal mental secretary who organizes her chaotic mental desk. But it was also the perfect answer to her problem. "He doesn't know it yet, of course. I'm telling all the important people first."

She felt him stiffen with anger. "You do it deliberately," he accused, forcing himself to be calm.

"With deliberation." She spoke as if it were a correction.

He was silent for several circuits, and though he danced with his usual suppleness, she could feel the resentment eating away at him. "What is it?" she asked at length.

"You're not really going to get him to design the Fleetliner?"

"I'm afraid I am."

"But what d'you *see* in him?"

An odd question, she thought – for Crownfield, anyway. Could it be jealousy?

"Talent," she replied. "Also, he has time on his hands and I haven't."

"And he *amuses* you no doubt?"

"He does. But no more than that."

The implication that he might be jealous, and that she was soothing him on the point, only infuriated him more. She started to lose her patience with him.

"You surround yourself with traitors and sycophants," he sneered.

"And nincompoops. But I can understand why you omit them."

He positively radiated his fury – and a sense of menace she had never felt in him before. A cautionary voice within warned her not to go further, not to push him to the brink; this man, it said, would make no trivial enemy.

"D'you remember this tune?" she asked, caressing him with her voice.

It almost worked. He faltered, lost the rhythm for a second; but then his momentum sustained him. "You're riding for a fall," he answered.

Her patience snapped. "Can't you just come out with it, man? Why are you behaving like a bear with a sore head?"

He chewed his cheek in silence for a while. Then he told her, "I've only just heard about the letter from Hook & Co."

Julia did not immediately connect the name with Imogen's writ – which was, in any case, several archaeological layers deep in her mind by now. Her bewilderment seemed contrived to Crownfield, for he had thought of nothing else all day.

"Oh that!" she said at last.

"Yes, that. And don't try to . . ."

"But it was about a million years ago, and it's all come to nothing. Unless you know something I don't. Is it something fresh?"

His lips twitched angrily. "The fact that it came to nothing is neither here nor there. I don't give a fig about Imogen Davis or the writ or anything like that. What infuriates me is the cavalier way you went about dealing with it."

"Well, I certainly wasn't going to allow it to come out in open court. Look, let's go out for a stroll. I can't dance and talk like this."

"No!" He glanced toward the door. It was almost as if he were afraid. For the rest of their conversation he made great efforts to curb his annoyance, none of them wildly successful.

"What was wrong with the way I handled it?" she challenged.

"How would you have kept it out of court?"

"Bit late to ask me now, don't you think?"

"Ah!" Understanding dawned. "You're all upset because I acted without consulting you! Look, I just happened to bump into the Davis creature one lunchtime . . ."

"Yet another of your amazing coincidences!"

"I don't know what you may mean by that. Ask Lexy. He was there."

"And had it not been for this wonderfully accidental meeting, you *would* have consulted me? And the rest of the board? Is that what you're saying?"

She wriggled uncomfortably. "Probably. How do I know?"

"Just as you've consulted us over hiring Torode?"

"I've only just thought of that one."

"Oh, Somerville!" His anger was getting the better of him once more. "I could name half a dozen recent decisions of yours – all of which we only heard about afterwards, and usually by accident."

"That's not fair. I've made not one single decision outside my own area of responsibility. Anyway, the rest of you are all too busy."

"That's why we sacrifice certain special hours. They are known as board meetings."

"But if I wait until then . . . well, everything's moved on. A board meeting is a way of freezing a decision not of reaching it."

He gave up at that. "You cannot be carried for ever," he told her.

There were a dozen possible replies to that but she bit her tongue on them all. Desperately she sought some way to change the subject. "That was terrible about Jimmy White," she ventured.

White was a financier, a millionaire, who had been badly hit by Churchill's insane return to the gold standard. He had been found dead at his racing stables a couple of weeks earlier. Then it had come out that he had swallowed prussic acid and inhaled chloroform – of all the vile ways to go. Julia had been taking lunch at the Savoy Grill on the day it happened; the news caused pandemonium there. In his suicide note he had written: "The world is nothing but a human cauldron of greed. My soul is sickened by the homage paid to wealth."

For some reason Crownfield assumed that her introduction of the topic was a deliberate commentary on his trade as financier and an obscure slur on him in particular. He stopped dead in mid-glide. Unconsciously she must have been expecting it for she stopped, too, without even a momentary imbalance.

He was absolutely livid – shivering with fury – but not even then did she imagine he would rant and storm. She had never seen him in such a mood, at least, not at such an extremity, and yet she knew he would always modulate his voice; he would speak the most vicious words as if they were mere formal courtesies. He'd break your spirit, but never the china.

"You," he said icily. Then he just stared at her, breathing deep to cool his fury.

"Yes?"

His eyes roamed over her face, as if seeing things he had never noticed before. "It's time you were taught a lesson," he told her. He was in control again; the words were as casual as if he'd said it was time she got a new hat.

Her jaw shot up, but she saw the ghost of a smile touch his lips. A cruel smile. And such arrogant lips, too. How had she never seen it before?

Her worst response would be anger. Now it was she who fought to stay calm. She was afraid to lose his support as her banker, but she was not afraid of him; above all, he had to understand that. "Listen, Crownfield," she warned. "You may try me as a friend, and I will tolerate a great deal. But never make the mistake of trying me as an enemy."

He turned on his heel and walked from the room.

Within moments, Matty Crownfield was at Julia's side; she must have observed – and perhaps even overheard – some or all of their exchange. "You mustn't take too much notice of Crownfield, my dear," she chortled. "He's just a teeny bit furious about what dear Jass has done to this house."

"Oh? I'm sorry to hear that, Mrs Crownfield. And what about you?" Julia was dubious of the woman's affability. Beneath that urbane exterior she sensed an aggression equal to her husband's. Perhaps they'd had a furious row just before the party began?

"Oh, I'm doubly delighted, Mrs Somerville." She gave a wicked grin. "Have you noticed the paint on the parquet floor downstairs?"

"But that's intentional," Julia began loyally.

The other laughed and waved a dismissive hand. "I know. I've heard that bit. Also," she went on in the same brittle tone, "he does worry rather a lot about your affairs, you know – unnecessarily, I'm sure."

"He thinks I'm too impatient, I know. And he's probably right."

"Is that the latest word for it?" Matty asked.

An awful truth suddenly dawned on Julia: This woman suspected that Crownfield was her lover. The consternation must have shown in her face – which Matty would naturally misinterpret. Indeed, her next words were, "You mustn't take us for one of your simple bourgeois couples, my dear. We do, after all, choose to live in

Hampstead, not Surbiton. As to our *plaisirs d'amour,* Crownfield and I keep each other completely informed – I might almost say regaled. Good heavens, he would never deceive me on so important a subject. He's a perfect gentleman – don't you agree?"

This was more than suspicion. It was knowledge, flaunted like a banner. But why? Did Crownfield and his wife have constant *affaires,* and joke about them all? And had he then been unable to admit that, for some reason, he was unable to conduct one with her, Julia? Had he, instead, boasted of a conquest?

She felt defiled beyond measure. And yet, even then, when the feeling was at its most intense, she saw there was nothing she could say to dent the woman's overweening complaisance.

Julia did not speak of it often; yet her occasional references to it – at other important moments in her life – showed what a scar it left. She even mentioned it to the man she eventually married. They were strolling out of Hyde Park one evening, out into the Bayswater Road. And there, working away in perfect harmony, was an Italian organ grinder with a dark and roguish eye; beside him stood his wife, a magnificently dignified singer. But there was a third member of that musical party – a prettified monkey on a chain. "That's how I felt," she said, pointing at the sorry little creature. "And for no reason," she added in anguish, clenching a fist and pressing it against her chin. "For no reason!"

CHAPTER THIRTY-TWO

BRUNTY WAS UNUSUALLY silent as he listened to Julia's retelling of the events at Flask Walk. She strode around his office, waving her hands, angrily reliving each moment. But toward the end she realized that the decision they now faced was purely commercial; it would not be enhanced by compounding it with her emotions, however justifiable. She forced herself to calm down somewhat. "So, all in all," she concluded, "I suppose we'd better prepare to find another banker." She looked at him and shrugged, trying to provoke him into giving straight advice for once.

Still he kept his peace.

"Well?" She had to prompt him at last.

"I don't suppose many books by Sir James Jeans come your way?" he asked.

"Brunty – I do hope this is going to be useful."

"He claims that every time a flea hops or a baby throws a rattle out of its pram, the resulting displacement of matter has a gravitational effect throughout the universe. Don't you find that awesome? The stars are moved by it, if only to an infinitesimal degree, even at the uttermost limits of space and time."

Julia folded her arms and fixed him with a stare.

"And yet," he went on, "even if two entire galaxies collided, there isn't a device anywhere on earth sensitive enough to measure the effect."

"From which you conclude?" she asked icily.

"From which I conclude that we are rather looking down the wrong end of the telescope here."

"Therefore?" she almost shouted. "We stay with Crownfield or we move to another bank?"

"This tiff of yours – was it like two galaxies colliding? Or . . ."

"It wasn't a tiff of ours. It was a tiff of his. And do stop going on about galaxies."

"Or a baby throwing his rattle out of the pram?"

"Yes. Yes. Yes. Whatever you like."

"Then why bother speculating about its effect? We should ask ourselves instead whether a hostile Crownfield on the board might not actually be a bit of an improvement?"

She smiled and sat down opposite him. "All right. Now I *am* listening."

"Somerville's under your late husband would have been a better company, don't you agree, if there had been regular board meetings at which one or two members had been ever so slightly hostile?"

"Crownfield won't be 'ever so slightly' hostile. But I see your point."

"I'd say the same is true of all companies where the single largest shareholder also has day-to-day control."

"I said I do see the point," she told him, rather thin-lipped.

He let her consider it awhile. "However," she continued at last, "it doesn't add up to an overwhelming reason for staying with our present bank. Funny thing – I imagined you'd leap at the chance to move."

He did not smile. "At any other time I would have. It's most unfortunate that it's happened just now."

"Ah!" She pounced. "So there are other – and better – reasons for staying with the man! You just wanted to get in your dig against me. The one-woman band and all that. Your usual."

He tilted his head, conceding the point – this time with the ghost of a smile. "Concerning the man himself, Boss, my feelings are neutral. But, as you know, I don't think his bank is the right one for us. We need someone who's happier with risks, and whose hair doesn't turn white when the market changes overnight – as our market does. However, what if we get a couple of dozen orders in the next four weeks? Could we . . ."

"I wouldn't mind the chance!" She laughed.

"Oh, it could happen. And we just wouldn't have time to educate a new set of bankers – especially as we'd first have to convince them there was nothing fishy about leaving Crownfield at such a moment."

"So your advice is to stay? God, Crownfield's going to die of bewilderment!"

"We stay until *we* decide when to throw the rattle out of the pram."

"For a moment I thought you were going to say '. . . the baby out with the bathwater'!"

Brunty's stock within the firm rose enormously over the following weeks as his caution – and more especially his reason for it – proved well founded. Neville's did, indeed, receive "a couple of dozen orders" – and more.

The first of the new, redesigned Fleetliners was still in assembly when Paul Deterle of KLM called by. He had tested the JU13 and the DH66 and could not choose between them; but one look at the Fleetliner and the decision was made – four hours at the controls of the prototype merely confirmed it. Its C of A, or certificate of airworthiness, was due within the month. As soon as possible after it came through, he wanted four machines for KLM – the first four off the line.

Suddenly, the way these things do, everything started to happen. Within a week of the KLM order, Hanno Schwartz of Luft Hansa was in London, wanting to know what all the excitement was about. He impressed Julia enormously by stepping out of his plane in an ordinary business suit; the only sign that he was actually the pilot was a simple flying helmet. "It's the way all flying will one day be," he told her – so confidently that she resolved she herself would always fly in an everyday suit after that.

He impressed her even more with his order, which was for a dozen machines. The fact that the Fleetliner could easily convert into a bomber was no doubt important. The Versailles treaty forbade Germany to develop any warlike capabilities, so all her civilian planes were designed for rapid military conversion.

The following month's *Ikarus* carried one of the most enthusiastic articles ever written about a new plane. Someone in Fleet Street with a working knowledge of German must have picked it up because next day Imperial Airways was being canvassed for its opinion of the Fleetliner – and, of course, it didn't have one, never having seen the machine. The papers had a field day. Two foreign airlines had already placed orders, yet Imperial Airways, whose employees visited de Havilland's at Stag Lane almost every week, had never thought to cross the Edgware Road and see what Neville's were up to on the other side! (In fact, the press was wrong in thinking there were only two foreign airlines involved; by then there were unconfirmed orders from America, Argentina, Egypt, and the Balkans, too. Every postal delivery brought at least one fresh inquiry.)

In most of this brouhaha the names of Eliot Baring and Neville's were prominent; no one seemed to have cottoned on to the fact that an astonishing woman called Julia Somerville was there at the heart of it all. It annoyed no one more than Wallace Baker.

Day after day he waited for the penny to drop. The *Chronicle* came close. They mentioned her as the firm's owner, but explained her away as the widow of George Somerville, "the engineer who had seemed set to become one of the leading lights of his generation until the accident that so cruelly shortened his life." The impression was given that George had been the inspiration behind the enterprise.

At last Wallace could bear it no longer. He called a friend on *Vogue* to see if they'd be interested in an interview of some depth with Julia, explaining the truth behind the excitement. But the woman felt it was too hot; someone on the dailies would surely tumble to it over the next few days, which would leave *Vogue* looking scooped. Baker had known it all along, of course. He had been hoping for a tip-off fee, while they sent a staff reporter to do the actual work. He did not want to meet Julia again, having no stomach for such complications in his life. But, as always with his tribe, the journalist overcame the private man; he phoned Tommy Newman on the *Daily Express* and got himself commissioned to do a feature. He rang Julia the following morning.

"An interview?" she exclaimed. "What for? What is there to talk about?"

"You? Neville's? British aviation . . . whatever."

There was a long pause before she replied. "Very well. I suppose it has to be, sooner or later. And rather you than anyone else, Wallace."

"Could I come out now? Me and one photographer."

"No!" she replied at once. "In fact, it won't be possible at all this week . . ."

"Oh dear, Julia, that's a pity. I also have to be away from tomorrow. It really ought to be this week, you know. Nothing's more volatile than today's news. Are you sure?"

"Didn't Dolly tell you?"

"Tell me what? She's so frantic over this new thing at Drury Lane,

I've hardly seen her since . . ."

"Ah! Otherwise I'm sure she would have. Anyway, it's the tenth anniversary of our brother's death. One of us ought to mark it. She can't go because of . . ."

"No, she hasn't mentioned that. Or of course I wouldn't have dreamed of . . . look, do forgive me. I must have seemed awfully . . ."

". . . and Max has some regimental thing of his own at Ypres. Nothing to forgive, my dear. But you do see – it'll have to be next week."

"Yes, of course. I'll call you next week."

The day was thundery, unsettled and dull. At the town of Albert-sur-Ancre, a tributary of the Somme, she stopped to confirm her directions to the military cemetery at Thiepval. The owner of the garage was English, an ex-officer; Julia had met him on an earlier visit. Even if she hadn't known his background, the sign would have told her: "Cars for hire, Fr2 per kilometre. Captain Edward Winter, ex-London Scottish Regiment, proprietor."

"Somerville-bodied, eh?" he commented as he ran his eyes admiringly over the car. She was driving the works Rolls-Royce, which had, in fact, been Bill's, before he joined up. It seemed appropriate.

Winter added: "I used to go and watch old George Somerville racing at Brooklands, you know. And then Le Mans when we settled here. That was tragic, what happened to him."

Julia felt she had no choice then but to introduce herself. The man turned pale. "Then I think I know why you're here, Mrs Somerville. I met your brother, briefly . . . in fact, we shared the same mess for three weeks, not a dozen miles up the road here during the push towards Bapaume."

The very name chilled her. It was during the mopping up, after the line had settled down just short of Bapaume, that Bill had been killed. "I'm afraid he never mentioned you, Captain Winter," she apologized. "But then he never wrote of the war at all, or not in that way."

"I can imagine the sort of letters he wrote, Mrs Somerville. He often mentioned you, all his family. No one who met him ever forgot him, you know. He was a . . ." He glanced at his watch, then up and down the almost deserted road. "Nothing much doing to-day," he remarked in a different tone, as if he were arguing with himself. Then he looked at her again. "I take it you know where the grave is?"

Julia nodded. "But would you think it impertinent of me if I asked you whether I may return here, after I've visited it? I would so like to hear whatever you can remember about him."

"Would you think it impertinent of me," he countered, "if I were to suggest that I accompany you there now?" Then, seeing the unwillingness in her eyes, he added, "I have other comrades lying up there. I wouldn't intrude, you understand, but I could tell you about Bill as we go."

As they drove up the west bank of the Ancre, through the rolling and still scarred countryside of Picardy, they passed several signs to Thiepval. At the first she slowed down. "Shouldn't I go that way?" she asked.

"I'd like to show you something else first."

"Tell me about Bill." So far they had talked only in generalities, establishing fragile bridgeheads for heavier assaults on grief and memory; she knew he had been waiting for the invitation.

"The war changed everyone who fought in it," he said, "certainly those who survived a whole year – and Bill survived, what, three?"

"Jolly nearly."

"Some, of course, went mad. Oddly enough, they made the best sort of soldier. I don't mean raving. In fact, they were very quiet usually, utterly calm. But as you got to know them you realized that some part of their mind had been destroyed. They weren't afraid of dying because in a way they already had. That ought to tell us something about war, don't you think? Especially when the talk turns to glory. Anyway, the reason I'm telling you this is that when I first met your brother, I imagined he was one of those."

She thought briefly of Max. "Were you and Bill in the line together?" she asked.

"No, as it happens. We were both convalescing. He had a wound in the foot and I had a bit of scrap metal in the shoulder. Nothing serious – not what we called 'a Blighty one'." He chuckled. "How antique it sounds already. We were up the line a bit, towards Arras. That's where I got to know him. He was quite a philosopher, your brother." He sank into reverie.

"What sort of things did he say?" Julia asked at length.

"Oh, quite ordinary things, I suppose. When I say philosopher I don't mean he tore into Hegel and Descartes. It wasn't what he said but the way he said it – and the circumstances." He thought for a moment and then went on. "My most vivid memory of him was one evening" – he glanced around at the sky and the trees – "must have been a little earlier in the year than this . . ."

He broke off and put his hand to his eyes. "Of course it must! This is the anniversary week of his death, isn't it." He sighed angrily.

"It must be hard," Julia told him gently. "Remembering such details out of all that chaos."

He perked up again and smiled at her. "Not half as hard as forgetting! Yes, it must have been around the middle of June because news of the slaughter at Messines and Hill Sixty was just beginning to filter down the line. Bill and I went for a stroll up a little hill, just

243

outside Avesnes. We watched the sun go down. And then came that strange sort of twilight in which you could almost believe there was no such thing as war. We'd met someone on the way up who'd told us of . . . I don't know how many tens of thousands killed that day. We didn't speak much after that but on our way back down Bill turned to me and said, 'Eddy, old chap, this must never be allowed to happen again.' But, you know . . ."

There was a catch in his voice. He paused to collect himself. "It sounds a very ordinary thing to say, doesn't it. That's what I mean. Back in 1915 it was the sort of thing everyone said. But there weren't many old hands left by 1917 who talked like that. It's what we were fighting for, of course, though we'd all forgotten it by then. But he hadn't. He somehow kept that flame burning. When he spoke, you know, when he said that – *it must never be allowed to happen again* – he looked at me as if he thought I could prevent it. Or, rather, as if he thought *we* could prevent it. People like us." He shook his head sadly, knowing he had conveyed only a trivial portion of that experience. "I'll never forget it, anyway."

"Thank you," Julia managed to say, grateful that she had the discipline of driving to hold her together.

They were passing through Beaucourt on the main road to Bapaume. Suddenly he told her, "Turn left here and take the first right, just a little way up the road." As a new quarter of the sky came into view he added, "Those clouds look threatening."

At the edge of the village they saw a ruined windmill, half a mile away to the north. "That's it," he said. "Bill's company HQ."

Without a word he managed to convey, too, that it was where Bill had died. She realized he was giving her an easy exit; she could draw up here, gaze at it from this safe distance, thank him, and turn back for Thiepval. She kept her foot lightly on the accelerator. They passed a lorry that had burned out a dozen years ago, too rusty now even to identify.

They stopped at the nearest point to the mill and got out. To their left, on the opposite side of the road, stood a small clump of trees; from somewhere behind it a cow bellowed to be milked. The breeze soughed among the leaves and birds sang in mild alarm.

Julia felt a moment of panic. She turned from the mill and stared into the woodland. The trunks were scarred with bullet holes and shrapnel wounds. The ones beside the road had curious horizontal blazes at about knee height. She went across for a closer look.

"Wagon axles," Winter explained, stooping slightly and miming their passing with his clenched fist. There was a distant rumble of thunder but, beyond holding up a finger and giving her an ironic smile, he passed no remark upon it.

They recrossed the road and went into the mill yard; only the rusting hinges showed where the gate had once been. The yard was a forest of weeds but Winter trampled a path for her. At the doorway two almost unrecognizable rifles and a small heap of tin helmets somehow confirmed the building's military demise. The rubble of the roof and upper floors lay everywhere, inside as well as out. The sappers' lean-to shelter of corrugated iron and turf was still intact, supporting a lanky, sky-seeking colony of yarrow, antirrhinums, and other wildflowers.

"The shell must have burst immediately overhead," Winter said. "Bill was doing some observation up there on the parapet." He pointed to an arrangement of scaffolding on the opposite wall.

She could see it now, quite vividly. Bill standing up there, his eyes glued to the trench periscope . . . the sudden, unbelievably loud explosion overhead, the deadly rain of shrapnel . . . his body reeling back . . . falling . . .

She was out in the yard again, alone; she could hear Winter rooting around inside the mill. There was another rumble of thunder, more distant this time. Beyond the coppice the unmilked cow was still bellowing.

She was composed once more and drying her tears by the time he emerged. He was holding up an earthenware cruik. "Look at this – an old SRD rum jar. I wonder where they liberated that?" All the while he questioned her with his eyes, asking how she was and whether he had done right to bring her here.

She smiled and let her gaze wander over the ruined stones. "Thank you, Captain Winter," she told him. "Somehow the real thing, however awful, is never so bad as one's imagination."

"Good-oh." His relief was almost palpable.

"One can't quite let it rest until one knows," she added.

He pursed his lips and dipped his head in agreement.

"You yourself weren't actually here?" she prompted as they climbed back into the car.

"No. But I knew Bill's adjutant at that time, Louis Skinner – Loopy Skinner, we all called him. He survived that one."

"But not the war?"

She meant, would it be possible to meet him? She did a three-point turn, using the mill yard, and set off again toward the main road.

"He's in Thiepval, too," Winter replied. "Our best way there now is to turn toward Bapaume and cross the river at Miraumont."

When they finally reached the cemetery and she saw all those thousands of gravestones, forming rows and columns and diagonals in every direction, she turned to him and asked, "Would you stay with me?"

He nodded. "May I offer you my arm?"

She accepted the support gratefully.

"It's a strange thing," he mused. "All this year, ever since I heard that Plumer was going to open the new memorial at the Menin Gate,

I planned to shut the garage and attend that ceremony. It was only yesterday, in fact, wasn't it? Yes. I felt I somehow owed it to all those who never found a grave. Did you hear Plumer on the wireless? 'He is not missing. He is here!' That caught it exactly. And yet, when the moment came, something stopped me."

"One can only take so much, I suppose," she offered.

"That's what I thought at the time. But now I wonder. Did some Power keep me here . . . so that this meeting of ours could happen?" He gave a dry laugh. "I don't believe in that sort of thing."

"Sometimes," she replied diplomatically, "it's hard not to."

When they reached Bill's grave he said, "Loopy's just over there," and left her alone again. But the catharsis of that morning had taken her beyond the sort of grief that tears can assuage. What she felt growing within her now was something indissoluble and altogether stronger. She laid the wreath she had brought with her. The greenery, already beginning to wither, had been picked yesterday at Allbury; the flowers she had bought that morning in Amiens. There was nothing else to do. The local employees of the Imperial War Graves Commission kept the place immaculate. It was hard to avoid the cynical reflection that a government which had sent so many young men to die in mud and gore was now seeking absolution by honouring the remains with such meticulous reverence. She stood and spoke to the grave, as if Bill were actually sitting there, pipe in hand and that gentle, laconic smile on his lips.

"This must never be allowed to happen again," she declared, looking around at the row upon row of stones. "If we owe you nothing else, my darling, darling brothers, we owe you that."

She went to join Winter and repeated her pledge, in silence, at Louis Skinner's graveside. Their return walk took them past Bill's plot once more; there, Winter paused awhile in prayer. The inscription on the stone began, "Here lies all that can die of William Neville . . ."

Winter drew her attention to it. "That wording has always impressed me," he remarked. "It's so exactly right for Bill."

"Our older brother Max insisted on it," she explained. "The War Office sent us an invoice for the extra wording. Three shillings and threepence! And d'you know, they wouldn't do it until we paid up."

Her father had sent five pounds and told them to use the rest in defraying the cost of similar requests from those whose families could afford to give their sons' lives but not thirty-nine pence.

"Yes, I can believe it," Winter commented. "They showed us every sympathy short of actual compassion."

"It's odd that you should have mentioned the Menin Gate Memorial just now," she went on. "That's where Max is today – or was, yesterday."

"Half the Empire was there, I should think – of our generation, anyway."

They took the direct road back to Albert. As they were drawing near its outskirts, a dark-blue Renault approaching them flashed its headlights.

"That's one of my hire cars," Winter exclaimed. "Gosh, I hope nothing's gone wrong."

Julia slowed to a halt. The other came on, also decelerating. When the distance between them was down to a few dozen yards, Winter muttered, "I can't say I recognize the driver."

"I can," Julia told him. "It's my brother-in-law, Wallace Baker."

There was a wide marble bench near Bill's grave. They sat on it while she told Wallace all that she had learned that morning. He could not take his eyes off her.

"The odd thing is that I've met Captain Winter at least once before – the last time I was here, in 1924. I stopped to buy petrol and we had a brief chat. I suppose the same would have happened today if I hadn't been in Bill's old car."

"It's obviously made a huge impression on you."

"It's changed everything, Wallace. At last – at long, long last – the war is over for me. In fact, all wars are over – for me."

He raised his eyebrows. "Quite a claim."

"You'll see," she promised, but she would explain no further. "I'm ravenous," she said, looking at her watch. "My goodness, it'll soon be time for dinner. Where are you staying?"

He shrugged. "Nowhere yet. You?"

"Nor me."

There was a moment of awkwardness.

"Choices," he ventured, standing up.

Unaccountably, her heart began to race. She thought of half a dozen things to say but all of them seemed trite, unworthy of the occasion. But what occasion? Why should it be at all special?

"Let's stop all this beating about the bush," he said somewhere in the silent crannies of his mind. "You must have realized long ago that I'm in love with you."

"Oh, Wallace, please don't," she would almost certainly begin.

And then? What would he tell her then?

He turned and looked at her; his whole body seemed to be on fire, burning to let the truth come out.

She loved him, too. Inwardly he felt quite sure of that. And earlier this week, as soon as he had realized that her slightly ambiguous words about marking the anniversary of Bill's death meant she was coming here, he persuaded himself that if only he could contrive some such meeting as this, it would open her eyes to her real feelings . . . and then a new chapter could begin between them.

Perhaps it might have happened that way, but who could imagine that she would first meet Edward Winter – and all that flowed from that?

An inner voice – conscience? or a journalist's instinct for people? – warned him that it might now be years before she was ready to face the truth. Indeed, by then it might no longer even be the truth. In those circumstances – and in that awful place, where sacrifice was in the very air – what else could he do but retire, dissemble, cheat himself, lie for her peace of mind?

"Actually," he confessed, "I'm catching the night boat from Calais, but we could have an early dinner and get this interview out of the way, and then I needn't plague you next week?"

Surprisingly enough, considering the harrowing day it had been, that evening was one of the most pleasant she had experienced in a long time. Wallace was more charming than she had ever known him; all his old awkwardness had gone. Instead, he was genial, sophisticated . . . the most marvellous company altogether.

"We should have done this a long time ago," she remarked toward the end of it.

"Done what?"

"Oops!" She put her hand guiltily to her mouth. "I keep forgetting this is also an interview. I must guard my tongue."

He tapped his notebook. "Look – it's closed. That means it's no longer an interview. Time for all your indiscretions!" He leaned forward in jocular eagerness.

"Very well." She licked her lip playfully. "You must admit you've always behaved as if you've had just a teeny little bit of a pash for me. Be honest now. Ever since that night at the Embassy Club."

"Have I?" He grinned disingenuously even as he felt his heart fall away inside him.

"Not that I was aware of it, mind," she added. "Except through Dolly. She behaved as if I . . . well, anyway, it was her response that made me aware of it. I don't know what you may have said to her . . ."

He drew breath to protest.

"And I don't want to know." She quelled him. "Anyway, that's not what I started to say. The thing is, we should never have had that absurd argument."

He frowned. "I don't even remember it."

"Of course you do – when we ran into each other at the Ritz. You interviewed the Countess de Janzé. I remember it distinctly. And we snapped at each other all the way through lunch."

"Your memory's obviously in much better order than mine, Julia. What was this argument about?"

"Oh, it hardly matters now. That's what I wanted to say. We should have made it up long ago. Just look what a splendid time we're having!"

Never once did his smile waver, though he thought his heart would break.

After a brief silence she added, "What a shame we're both so busy!"

She drove him up to Calais and they took the night ferry together, she in her cabin, he at the bar. But he still looked fresh as paint next morning when they drove onward to London and a brief date with the photographer.

During that journey, she asked him how long he'd been a columnist.

"Oh, hardly a columnist," he replied modestly. "I'm just a journalist. To be given a column is quite an achievement. I'm still working my way up toward that eminence."

She took these disavowals with a grain of salt. "Is it hard?" she asked.

"It is for me. Some writers are born to it, the rest of us just have to work."

His piece, fifteen-hundred words as lean as their author, appeared, complete with suitably flattering photos, in next morning's *Express*.

"Aeroplane Amazon in a Coco Chanel suit," was the rather cumbersome title the sub had chosen. "Other women may fly planes, but she builds them," trumpeted the four-column stock head. She loved it and rang Dolly up to tell her what a clever man she had married.

The gossip writers were onto it at once, of course. Soon she couldn't dine out or go to a night club without the fact being reported in half a dozen papers next day. Wallace got no phone calls thanking him for that – just a cable, saying: SOME ARE BORN COLUMNISTS STOP SOME ACHIEVE COLUMNS STOP SOME HAVE CALUMNY THRUST UPON THEM! He had an ironic call from Lexy when a picture in the *Tatler* was captioned, "Mrs Julia Somerville enjoying a quip with Mr Alexander Deeping." Not many could force Dear Lexy down to second mention.

By Christmas there can have been few people in the country who did not know her name and what she looked like. She was recognized in the street. She was high on everybody's guest list. Complimentary tickets to events great and obscure poured in, along with invitations to speak, to launch ships of a modest size, cut ribbons, judge flower shows . . . babies . . . gala floats . . . homemade jam.

But there was one way in which her interview with Wallace Baker served her ill. The man was just too honourable. When he put his notebook away, it meant she was off the record; but he was rare among journalists. So, when – early in the following year, January 1928 – she announced one of the most surprising and controversial decisions of her career, the news of it came out in a most unfortunate way.

CHAPTER THIRTY-THREE

CROWNFIELD DID NOT open his paper until he was in the company car, actually on the way to Dollis Hill for the Neville's monthly board meeting. He read the brief item three times: AEROPLANE COMPANY SHUNS WAR ORDERS – and still could not believe it. He told the driver to draw up directly outside the drawing office. But Eliot had anticipated him; stamping his feet against the cold, he was waiting in the lobby. The moment he caught sight of the banker he came out and climbed into the car. "You've seen it," he said, noticing the paper.

"Just this minute. I can hardly believe my eyes. Is it true?"

"She didn't intend it to be announced in this way." He waved a hand toward the paper. "She says . . ."

"Never mind what she says – I take it the report is accurate?"

Eliot nodded.

"Can Neville's possibly survive?" Crownfield asked.

The other eased his collar. "You see, the thing is, I kind of half go along with her. You'd understand if . . . I mean, commercially it's probably not the snappiest decision, and yet . . ." He looked at his watch. "We'll be late."

"Have you spoken to Brunty? What does he say?"

"He's against it."

"Strongly?"

Eliot nodded. "For him, anyway."

The banker leaned forward and told the driver to go on to the main door.

The atmosphere within the boardroom was sizzling. Julia, looking harassed, fretted with a ragged cuticle all the way through the minutes of the previous meeting. When Max sought consent to sign them, nobody – for once – objected.

First on the agenda was an emergency item: the report in that day's *Sketch*.

Crownfield leaped in at once, asking Julia if it were true.

She licked her lips and looked round the circle of stony faces, feeling very much at bay. "It is a true account of my feelings," she replied. "But, naturally, I did not intend the man to print it."

"You made a press announcement and yet did not intend . . ."

"I didn't exactly *announce* it. If you must know, Crownfield, Baring and I flew to Paris on Friday, to conclude our business with Péchiney. We stayed on for the weekend, and when we returned on Sunday – yesterday – I was waylaid at Croydon by that reporter, and, well, I just happened to mention it to him. If you'll just . . ."

". . . never for one moment believing he'd be so dastardly as to print it!" Crownfield sneered. "D'you really expect us to believe that your assiduous flirtation with the Fourth Estate has taught you nothing?"

Julia sighed. "The man had closed his notebook by the time I told him that."

"He had his notebook closed!" Crownfield offered her defence to the others in theatrical disbelief.

Julia persisted: "There were heaps of other things I told him – while he had his book open, scribbling away – but, of course, he didn't print any of that. They never do. I mean I didn't just state baldly that we'd never . . ."

"Here's another novel defence!" Crownfield cut in once more. "An informer might equally justify himself for giving away one secret on the grounds that, in point of fact, he gave away ten!"

Julia appealed to Max, who, with a weary smile, drawled, "A better defence might be that prosecuting counsel kept interrupting."

Crownfield gave an apologetic chuckle. "Do I sound like prosecuting counsel? I'm sorry." He grinned expectantly at Julia but she held her silence, forcing him to say, "Do please go on. What other unminuted decisions did you impart to this reporter?"

"He asked where I had been and I told him. Not about Péchiney, of course."

Crownfield could not help interjecting: "But about Coco Chanel, perhaps?"

There was a flinty challenge in her eye. "Actually – as I was about to tell you just now – Baring and I visited the war cemeteries." She turned to Max. "Including Thiepval." Her gaze fell; she rearranged her blotter and papers as she added, "In fact, we visited quite a few – cemetery after cemetery after cemetery. Not all five hundred of them, of course, but quite a few – right down to Cambrai."

Crownfield shifted uncomfortably at the word; his son Algernon was buried at Cambrai. He glanced toward Eliot, who nodded gravely.

"Yes." Her voice had gone very quiet. "We laid a wreath there, too, Crownfield. And said a prayer." Her eyes would not release him. "And as we stood there, looking this way and that, seeing those stone crosses vanish almost to the horizon in every direction, it occurred to me that prayers were not enough. D'you remember how they're arranged – so that wherever you stand, they seem to radiate away from you? I mean, wherever you stand, you're at the centre? And I suddenly thought, 'That's right – we *are* at the centre. Everyone who comes here is deliberately *put* at the centre.' You must know what I mean." She looked around that circle of faces. The others were hardly breathing. "When you're there, when you're actually standing there, you can't walk away from it. You try, but every time you look around, you're still at the heart of it. All that carnage. All that . . . senseless slaughter. All those poor, dead young men. Those Williams and Algernons – and Berts and Freds. What would we not give to have them back with us? I'd give the whole of Neville's, ten times over, to have just one of them back among the living." Her voice almost broke but she rallied and, turning gently to Crownfield, asked, "What's your answer? The government must do something? The League of Nations must act? That's what people usually say. And while they dither, we're excused!"

He let out his breath as if she had rammed him in the solar plexus. "Not quite according to Queensberry rules, Somerville," he complained.

"And did Queensberry rules save them? But I'll tell you this – the Neville rules might. I'm sorry it emerged in the way it has. I've learned a costly lesson there. But I tender no apologies for the decision itself – which I now have to tell you is absolute: We shall make no machines of war. If enough ordinary business people like us abide by such a code, we might just save the next crop of Bills and Algies from . . . being butchered. Except their names won't be Bill and Algy, they'll be Robert and" – she turned to include Brunty – "Frank." And then, with a sigh, she added, "And probably Lydia, too, by then."

She stared around the table defiantly.

Poor Crownfield. The moral high ground is usually an island afloat in a sea of syrup; its capture is sticky work. He did his best. "Such decisions," he commented, "are of little value unless the world knows about them."

Julia fell for it. "And now they do, don't they."

He smiled. "Then my original point is vindicated. This was no accidental blurting-out of some as yet only half-formulated decision. Mrs Somerville obviously made up her mind quite firmly and landed at Croydon already determined . . ."

"May I cut in here," Eliot asked. "I share my partner's sentiments. I hope that goes without saying. Indeed, I'm sure we all share them. But – as I've told her – I don't think her decision is the practical one. I don't believe the next war will be *fought* in the skies. I'm firmly convinced it will be *prevented* there."

"May the chair cast a pearl?" Max asked. "The next war is already prevented. There'll never be another like the last, and I'll tell you why. Because three-quarters of the House of Commons fought in the trenches. They remember the generals' incessant cry for more men. And now they see that the generals (the same ghastly crew, for the most part) are still at it – and the air marshals, too. Only now it's not more young lives they want but more equipment, more tanks, more guns, more planes. The problem is, the House don't hear them. The House is deafened by ancient gunfire. It's our problem, too. The amount of profit to be made out of military orders for aeroplanes wouldn't keep a dog in fleas. We're fighting here over a bone with no meat left on it – and even then they cut the bone in half each year."

"What are you saying, Max?" Julia asked impatiently. "That this whole meeting is a pointless storm in a teacup?"

He shook his head. "I didn't say there'd be no more wars, Ju. Only no more wars like the Kaiser's war. But hang it, woman, John Bull's got to keep a salvo or two in his locker, eh? Or the dagoes will trample all over us. What about when you can't go out for a spin in your Moth, or your new Isotta-Fraschini, because there's no petrol in the pumps – because the Bolsheviks have nobbled all the wogs in Persia? And no lovely cotton frocks to wear, because Gandhi's gang has been stirring up the go-downs in Bombay? And no coffee for breakfast, because the niggers . . ."

Julia grew angry. "You're suggesting we should supply aircraft to make it possible to bomb or machine-gun defenceless tribesmen and dock-porters, just so that . . ."

"No, no, no!" Max was growing short-tempered, too. "I said nothing about bombs or machine-guns. That's my point – that sort of war's a thing of the past. It could be done quite humanely, with the absolute minimum of bloodshed. All you need do is assemble the villagers and then tip their chief's favourite son out at four hundred feet without a parachute. Bob's your uncle. They'd be back in the fields in no time, singing away from dawn to dusk."

"Oh, come on, Max!" Crownfield did not welcome this kind of support.

"Put on a bit of a firework display first, to make sure everyone was watching. Buffy Frobisher was telling me all about it at the club."

Julia was appalled. "You mean it's already happening?"

Eliot drummed the table with his fingertips. "At the risk of usurping the function of the chair . . ." he began.

"According to Buffy," Max answered his sister, "we're trying it out in Africa at the moment. And one or two places in Arabia."

She stared at him aghast.

"Not every *day*," he added reassuringly.

". . . we are straying from the point," Eliot insisted. "What about you, Brunty? You've contributed nothing yet."

The finance director gave an apologetic tilt of his head. "There's very little one can say. Our managing director, with the proxies she holds in her children's names, has the majority of the votes. The function of this board is really advisory." He flung his pencil down with a regal flourish. "True, we can exercise certain ultimate sanctions – legal moves if we suspected that something fishy were afoot, or . . ."

"I trust you're hinting at no such thing," Julia said ominously.

He fended off the suggestion with a smile. "Or, if our disagreements are honourable but deep-felt, we can resort to mass resignation, a word in the ear of our favourite journalist, et cetera. So, the real question for this meeting is: How many of those sanctions are we prepared to risk?"

"We?" Crownfield asked.

"Those who feel strongly on the issue."

"And are you among them?"

Brunty smiled as if the suggestion were absurd. "Risk is surely the word on everyone's mind? Even for well-established competitors like de Havilland and Shorts, aeroplane making is a risky venture. A new company with a single airworthy machine to its name is already something of an outsider in the survival stakes. Rumours of a divided board would be just so many nails in its coffin. So, without wishing to be too dramatic, we at this meeting hold between us something akin to a fragile piece of porcelain, rather than the robust bits of engineering we're more used to considering. Whoever risks its breakage will really be trusting the others to catch it as it falls." He beamed at one and all. "A trivial point, I know. But worth making, I feel."

After a dense silence Max turned to Imogen. "I know you have no formal standing here, Miss Davis, but perhaps you have an opinion?"

Imogen looked uncomfortably around. "Does anyone know the cost of this decision?"

"In lives?" Julia asked swiftly, before Crownfield's grin could turn to laughter.

Baring stepped in. "The actual cost, in the short term, isn't too serious," he pointed out. "Taking just the military possibilities, we've been talking about an initial order of four for the RAF, plus a possible two for the navy – all for role-evaluation."

"So the lost profit is under a thousand pounds." Julia's tone was airy, begging for Next Business. Damn that Davis creature!

"We could expect follow-up orders for at least two dozen more." Baring enunciated the facts in his usual crisp voice. "Then there's what one might call the recruitment multiplier, which means that other armed services would almost certainly follow suit, mostly in the empire but also South America, Turkey, Japan . . . say, fourfold.

So in fact we're looking at lost orders for a hundred-twenty planes."

"*Potentially* lost orders." Julia was by now several shades paler; she'd had no idea that military orders might amount to so much. No, the truth was, she hadn't *wanted* to know.

Eliot continued: "Then there's the question of economy of scale. Shall we ask Tom Murgatroyd in? He could tell us the extra profit per unit we might generate if the order book swelled by . . ."

"We can take it for granted," Julia cut in brusquely. "It would be up around twenty pounds per plane."

"On *every* plane." Eliot was remorseless. "The civilian ones, too. Of course, my partner, as the principal shareholder, has every right to forgo profits approaching twenty-thousand pounds . . ."

"I'm glad that's acknowledged," Julia cut in.

". . . but I believe the board should minute the decision."

Crownfield sank his head in his hands.

Max prodded him with a pencil. "Don't agree?" he asked.

The banker's only hope now was Imogen. He turned to her. "You, young lady, seem to have .sked the most pertinent question of the day," he prompted. "How do you feel about it?"

"It's hardly for me to say," she ventured timidly. "I was only a kid in the war, but even so, I know what's made Mrs Somerville think as she does. Wouldn't it be best to work out *exactly* what it could cost and then see if there isn't some sort of half-way?"

"How can there be a half-way?" Julia asked sharply.

Imogen made all the submissive moves she knew. "Well – where's the harm in a plane out over the sea looking for U-boats? Or flying round Scotland training navigators? I mean, there *are* military planes that don't carry guns or bombs."

It seemed a good point at which to leave it for another day.

"Little vixen!" Julia said to Lexy when she described the meeting to him that evening. "Butter wouldn't melt in her mouth."

Deeping had by then met Imogen several times and had had plenty of chances to size her up. "You don't think you could possibly be just a teeny bit wrong about her?" he asked. "Might she not be a victim, rather than a villain?"

"George's victim," Julia commented sarcastically. "Sidney Gold's victim. And now Lexy Deeping's victim? I don't think! Obviously she only needs to flutter those eyelashes and . . ."

"Yes, they are rather gorgeous," he allowed. Then he looked at her speculatively. "I don't suppose you *can* see it. In fact, you're probably the very last person one ought to expect to . . ."

"See what? All I see is an ambitious, grasping . . ."

"Just hang on a mo. Forget her. Let's talk about you."

"Oh, yes please!" She grinned.

"I'm serious. Tell me – when did you first come out? No – perhaps that's a bit ungallant."

"I'll tell you. It was just before the war."

"D'you remember those balls – Lady Ellesmere's? The Grosvenors? Can you remember how you felt? Picture yourself now – you're in your first proper ball gown . . . you're walking up the steps. The house is ablaze with lights. You can hear the music – and the laughter. No, it's not laughter, it's that peculiar braying noise the English aristocracy makes on its own stamping ground – you know what I mean. And you're outside there in the dark, approaching it for the very first time. Remember?"

She had her eyes closed by now, and she was smiling. "Oh, yes!"

"How d'you feel?"

"Thrilled."

"Nervous?"

"Of course."

"Terrified, perhaps?"

She opened her eyes in surprise. "Not at all."

"Never? Not even for the most fleeting moment?"

She shook her head, bewildered by the suggestion.

He laughed. "There you are. Tell me, what does terrify you?"

"Bats. Large, hairy spiders . . ."

"No, I mean social occasions. Talking to large audiences? Up before the beaks for speeding? Being presented to their majesties? Anything?"

"I feel apprehensive, I suppose . . ."

"You have been presented at court?"

"Of course."

He laughed and stabbed a finger at her. "There you are: *of course.* Of course you've been presented at court. Of course you were at Lady Ellesmere's ball – and not as a gatecrasher, either. There's nowhere from which you've ever felt excluded, is there."

She tried to think of some such place or occasion. Now she knew a thing or two about the business she realized that George had always excluded her. But the feeling was entirely retrospective; at the time she hadn't experienced it at all. Anyway, it didn't sound as if that was what Lexy meant.

He, meanwhile, was continuing: "Until we met, you and I, you'd never gone about in the West End, had you. You never frequented night clubs. You hardly ever dined out – certainly not in places where they had cabaret and dancing."

"No. That's true."

"Yet look how you've taken to it. I watched you the first night I took you to the Blue Lantern. Remember – one of David Tennant's parties? I saw you stroll into the thick of it as if you'd been coming there every night of your life."

"It's all very interesting, Lexy dear, but I don't quite see what point you're making."

"In a way that *is* my point: You don't see it. Well, if you really want to see it, you just watch young Imogen next time she's in our party and we go to a night club or somewhere."

"Why don't you shorten the suspense for me and tell me what I'll see?"

"I don't suppose you'll see a thing. What you ought to see is a frightened young girl who desperately wants to belong and yet never will. Even worse – she *knows* it in her heart of hearts. You can't even begin to imagine what that must be like, can you."

"She should have stayed where she belongs, then."

He closed his eyes, smiled forgivingly, shook his head. "That's nowhere. She was always an outsider, even at home. You know her story as well as I do. Theoretically she's one of *us*. In fact, we're just a vision, a vision she invented for herself down there in Islington or wherever it was. Where did she get her raw material? From a middle-class reading primer at school? Some trashy servants' magazine?" He gave a wicked grin. "Perhaps she met *you*, my dear, at the SPRP, and began hero-worshipping you from afar!"

Julia lurched forward and grabbed his arm. "Christ, Lexy! Don't!"

He chuckled. "Something anyway put that vision there and spoiled her for the contented style of life. You call her ambitious. I say she's driven, whipped, haunted by that vision – despairing that she'll ever find the knack – the one you possess without even knowing it. You and she are at the very opposite ends of that spectrum of assurance, of . . . *belongingness,* or whatever you want to call it. You'll never understand her."

His very smugness forced Julia to try. She remembered images Theresa had conveyed. Child Imogen slipping her hand into Canon Thirkettle's, compelling such affection by her vulnerability that even years later he went in to bat for her. Young Imogen pressing her pale, strained face against the railings of the college in Alma Road, desperate to be allowed in. And then there was nurserymaid Imogen, on that very first day in Connaught Square, offering more than a servant's loyalty while George lay paralyzed on the morning-room carpet . . .

She shook her head irritably, annoyed that Deeping had forced this insight upon her. He, meanwhile, was saying: "I know you think she seduced George . . ."

"Well, I don't believe she was averse to the idea!"

"You were there from the start? You saw her modesty yield at his first little push? Come on, darling – you have no idea how long he had to work on her, what subtle arguments he used . . ."

"George was about as subtle as a helping of curry."

"Don't evade the point. Above all, you don't know why she gave in. You once told me you didn't think it was for pleasure."

"No, it was for power – which, indeed, she got by it."

He tilted his head and smiled wearily. "It's as simple as that, eh? We don't need to ask ourselves, power for what?"

She frowned.

"Let me put it another way. Why are you in business? For money, of course. But is it as simple as that? Money for what? Not for its own sake. Doesn't it occur to you that she doesn't want power for its own sake, either? Nor to threaten your business. Nor even to threaten *you*. She hoped it would be the key – the *entrée* – the thing she can never find."

"Damn you!" Julia said, and meant it. "Running the business is hard enough as it is. I need fixed points on my map, not this . . . field of shifting values."

But he was remorseless. "Poor little Imogen! So much love to give and no one to value it – because, of course, she cannot go the right way about giving it. I say!" Suddenly his tone changed. The essential artist reasserted itself. "Don't you feel there's rather a spiffing little two-hander in it? Fay Compton as the girl, all warm and frustrated. And who for the man? Some cold fish, cold and masterful – Ernest Thesiger! Eh? Oh yes! I'll start on it tomorrow." He beamed seraphically, hardly remembering what they had been discussing – or remembering just enough to say, "God bless little Imogen, after all!"

CHAPTER THIRTY-FOUR

THE FLEETLINER, with Jasper Torode's *Savoyard* interior, marked the start of a new period in air travel. Until then, passenger planes were wartime machines in civilian clothing. They gave the distinct impression that the bomb racks had only just been dismantled to make room for the wicker chairs and tables. The Germans, theoretically free to design purely civilian planes, were in the worst bind of all, for their air ministry insisted that every civilian passenger aircraft be capable of conversion to a bomber within thirty minutes. Their interiors suggested railway coaches rather than "the transport of the future." But the moment people stepped aboard a Fleetliner something within them said, "Yes! This is what I always thought it would be like."

Even Crownfield grudgingly admitted that the unspeakable Jass's design probably sold more planes than the Rolls-Royce engines or the stressed duralumin skin or even the sub-stall stability. By May, when the firm's accounting year ended, they had taken confirmed orders for five dozen aircraft. They were, in fact, *too* successful. Dollis Hill and Hendon had enough capacity to build three frames a month – five with double shifts. If they had been able to find enough skilled men, they'd have worked three shifts, round the clock.

They had to put most of the business out to subcontractors. The work of forming the curved duralumin skin was very like the bending of steel or aluminium sheet for car bodies. Not just Somerville Motors but most of the famous names in coachbuilding – Mulliner, Hooper, James Young, and so on – acquired a profitable little sideline, forming the complex parts of the Fleetliner skin. Indeed, they were ideally suited to the work for at that time the chrome plating on a Rolls-Royce was not electroplated but wrapped by hand and then soldered. Stretching a relatively thick duralumin skin over any form, no matter how complex, held little challenge to such craftsmen.

"If Sidney Gold hadn't approached us first, last year, we'd probably be on our knees in front of him now," Eliot joked.

And indeed, Gold's company was suffering the same strains as Neville's; he, too, had to farm out the simpler work, though the final welding and assembly remained with his craftsmen. (As an historical sidelight – to show how the Fleetliner soaked up the skills of the nation: When Westland started using welded tubular steel that same year, they had to send workers to Holland to be trained; their only welders until then had been a small gang of semi-skilled women.)

The strain on the senior personnel of both companies was intense. They divided all their time between checking their subcontractors' work and readjusting the schedules to cope with the chaotic flow of materials. It was the sort of nightmare that couldn't be allowed to go on. The firm would simply have to recapitalize and (yet again) find larger premises. Unfortunately, nobody had time to step back and take care of it. Even Julia was out there on the shop floor in her dungarees, micrometer in one hand, clipboard in the other (and, despite her aching back and throbbing head, loving every minute of it).

In such circumstances, the question of developing a military version of the plane was entirely theoretical, no matter what Julia had decided. There were, of course, approaches, not just from the Air Ministry but from the RAE at Farnborough, too; they were especially interested in Baring's modification of the Göttingen aerofoil, for the question of near-stall stability was still the hottest thing in the whole field of aviation. Julia let them have the original prototype to play with for a couple of months; but when the RAF wanted a production machine "for evaluation," she was able, quite truthfully, to point to a huge backlog of orders already on the books. They sent a brace of pilots over from Martlesham and the reports they brought back only increased the service chiefs' eagerness to get a plane of their own.

Trenchard himself was furious, of course. Other British aircraft manufacturers would go through hoops to secure an Air Ministry contract; to insist on fulfilling an order from Luft Hansa, the national airline of the defeated enemy – not to mention orders for a handful of other *foreign* companies – before even accepting one from the RAF was as close to treason as makes no difference. His instinct for people, however, warned him not to tackle Julia directly. Instead, he called up Crownfield.

Though it was the cautious banker rather than the the resentful ex-would-be-lover who took the call, Crownfield knew better than to try to laugh off Julia's well publicized pacifism. Instead, he put the best gloss he could upon it: "I blame myself," he confessed. "It was I who brought up the subject of a military version at the last board meeting. I didn't know it at the time, but Mrs Somerville had only just returned from visiting her brother's grave at one of the war cemeteries. Worst possible time, of course. I felt at once the way her mood was going and so postponed further discussion before any decision could get set in concrete. Leave it with me. I'll sort her out – only it'll take time. You know yourself how strong-minded she is."

Crownfield rang around Julia's acquaintance, seeking her weak points, where she might be vulnerable to pressure. Brunty gave away nothing, beyond the assurance that he was doing what he could from within. Sidney Gold proved more promising in the end, though to start with he simply laughed. "Change that woman's mind?" he sneered. "Take my advice – get in some practice on the weather, first!" However, he later suggested that a little bit of chipping away, especially from the rear, might eventually work the trick. "While she's busy fixing trip wires all round her bloody Fleetliner, see if you can't get the army to approach the other companies – Somerville Motors and the engineering one. I mean Somerville Motors built your actual armoured cars in the Kaiser's war. But I wouldn't start with nothing warlike, mind. Modify a shock absorber or something what she won't even understand. Get old Trenchard to twist someone's arm up the War Office. They could lay it on. Chip away, see? Softly, softly catchee monkey."

Fate must have had a crossed line and heard every word, for not long after that – though in a quite unconnected sequence of events – a certain Miss Davenport, the membership secretary of the Society of Women Engineers, wrote to Julia asking her if she would consider joining. Julia, too busy even to dictate a reply, picked up the phone and went into her poppet-valve and sledgehammer routine. Miss Davenport laughed; they got talking; and Julia ended up inviting her to Dollis Hill the following day. During the course of showing her round they came across a bin of oddments that had been moved from the Forge Lane works but had never got sorted any further. Among them was the prototype of the high-pressure universal hydraulic joint that had been one of George's pet projects.

Miss Davenport grew quite excited and asked if the original drawings had survived. Julia took her to the plan chest where all the archive material from those days was stored. Miss Davenport riffled through it briefly and almost had a fit.

"It's Tutankhamen's tomb," she enthused as she turned over blueprint after blueprint. "You mean, these are just lying here gathering dust?"

"Our minds have rather been elsewhere," Julia pointed out.

"Yes but even so!" She waved at the drawings as if their mere existence were proof enough of incredible value.

The following week Hannah Dawson, member of the Institution of British Engineers – and, to be sure, of the Society of Women Engineers – was appointed managing director of Somerville Engineering, at a salary of £410 a year. She took up her post immediately. She brought one contract with her – from the navy, as it happened. They had been trying to develop a universal high-pressure pipeline joint. Dawson Engineering, Hannah's father's firm, had been heavily involved, but after his death the Admiralty diehards had been uneasy about trusting further development to a firm now run by a woman.

"They wouldn't have minded *your* sort of set up in the least, Mrs Somerville. If I'd stayed in the office and put a man in charge of the workshops . . . fine. But a woman with oil behind the fingernails – horrors!"

Julia, herself in dungarees at that moment, clenched her fists to hide her nails. "I can just imagine it," she said. However, she knew exactly why the naval gentlemen had balked. Hannah Dawson was five foot four, blonde, blue-eyed, rising fifty, and looked as if one puff of wind would carry her off.

"And it wasn't just the navy," the woman continued. "It was all the men who were used to dealing with my father. Nobody said anything, of course. Their smiles were six feet wide and their manners impeccable. But somehow the work just fell away to a trickle."

"You still own the firm?" Julia asked, thinking it might be going cheap.

She shook her head. "I sold out while it was still worth something – to a man who can't even get his associate membership! Heigh-ho! But, with your late husband's high-pressure joint in mind, I think I can persuade the navy to let me bring their contract with me."

She spoke as if it were such a feather in her cap that Julia could not raise her usual objections to military work. "What exactly would it *do* on a ship?" she asked.

"It's supposed to be 'hush-hush,' as they call it. They'd fit a number of them to a submarine hull, you see? In a knock-out recess. Then if it were damaged, lying on the sea bed, they could pump in fresh air, water, fuel, hydraulic power . . ."

For such humanitarian work, how could Julia possibly object! She glanced up at the water colours of Hyde Park. Did she not owe this tribute to that unlaid ghost? The thin end of the wedge was in.

The Admiralty was so delighted with the high-pressure joint, and the apparent speed with which the difficulties had been solved, that they came back with a few more problems in search of solutions; nothing very warlike, of course – anything of a direct military nature tended to be kept within the service, anyway. They wanted an improved gyro-compass bearing, a faster servo mechanism for their stabilizers, and a rethink of the central-locking system on watertight hatches. Again there was little to which Julia could honestly object.

"Nothing to it," Hannah commented when they had gone – having maintained quite the opposite while they were still there.

"What I don't understand," Julia remarked, "is why they're so keen to work with you here when, before, they couldn't get away fast enough."

Neither woman knew that Trenchard had been talking to friends at both the Admiralty and the War Office. Hannah's explanation was that the name of Somerville was enough to overcome any doubts. "I mean, after Rolls-Royce . . . well! Also, look at this." She pointed around at what was by now quite a large and bustling aeroplane factory. "It's a far cry from my dad's old shed on the Kingston bypass!"

If the naval jobs did not excite Hannah, it was quite another story with the designs she kept unearthing in George's neglected plan chest – especially the independent four-wheel suspension with which he had hoped to achieve his ambition of moving the radiator forward of the front axle. She thought Julia had been quite wrong to keep the coachwork business merely ticking over – to stop all innovation at Somerville Motors – and she made no bones about it. Julia was left feeling she had been distinctly thoughtless.

"However, the way forward is clear," Hannah concluded. "The craftsmen can continue at Forge Lane, but the innovation and forward-looking engineering can resume here at Dollis Hill. In fact, we could even set ourselves up as part-laboratory, part-design workshop for the car industry in general. We have the sort of skills they're only starting to acquire, and the capital equipment. How many car makers have a wind tunnel, for instance? Not one, as far as I know."

Before the year was out, Julia was wondering how they had ever managed without Hannah Dawson. And, looking at the half-year balance sheet, she wondered how they had managed without the income from the revitalized Somerville companies, too. By then the armed services were accounting for almost a quarter of their turnover; but still none of it was for any direct, warlike application.

That August the RAF held its second annual test of the country's air defences – a trial of strength between the bombers of "Eastland" (a thinly disguised Germany) and the interceptors of "Westland" (Britain, not the aeroplane maker). Reports released to the press were bright and breezy, with copious thanks to the landowners who allowed searchlights on to their property and to the civilians who looked after the flares on emergency landing grounds. The tone of amateurish muddling through was terribly-terribly English.

But, as Eliot was quick to point out (and he never lost a chance to let Julia know how parlous the country's air defences were), almost every plane taking part was of a type that had flown a full decade earlier, during the Great War. "And though they're lyrical about the daylight raids," he added, "you'll notice they're very careful not to say how many *night* bombers got through."

Sir Philip Sassoon made a similar point when he invited both Julia and Baring to lunch at the House of Commons; he was then Under-Secretary of State for Air. He was (if one may be excused a pun) disarmingly frank, saying that he couldn't understand why the press had let his ministry off so lightly. "If you read between the lines of the official summary, you can see that we'd sustain losses of up to fifty fighters a day – even against an enemy as poorly equipped as ourselves."

But he did not labour the point, especially as Britain had just signed the Kellogg Pact outlawing war between civilized nations. In fact, he spent most of the meal asking them what they knew about the German aircraft industry – in effect, recruiting them as informers on a casual, "keep-us-in-touch" basis. He had no doubt got wind of the recent agreement between Neville's and Messerschmidt to build the Fleetliner under licence in Germany, using Daimler-Benz engines. De Havilland, facing similar problems with the incredible success of the Gypsy Moth, which was now pouring out of their Stag Lane works at more than one a day, had set up subsidiaries in North America and throughout the empire. Neville's, lacking the necessary capital, had to turn to licensing agreements instead.

Only toward the end of the meal did Sir Philip revive his earlier theme. "Even if we were to nationalize every aeroplane factory in the land," he remarked, "and devote all their resources to military aircraft, it's doubtful that we could keep pace with our expected wastage during the early weeks of a future war."

"Artful devil!" Julia commented to Eliot on their way back to Dollis Hill. "That was really the whole point of our meeting, you realize? He just wanted to make it clear that, in the likelihood of war, the government would nationalize Neville's and all our fine principles would count for nothing."

"And doesn't that thought worry you?" Eliot asked.

She shook her head. "Popular opinion would force them to hand it back. Everyone's so sure that the next war will start where the last left off and that Germany will be the enemy once again. Well, the Germans have too much respect for private property. Neither their air force nor ours would bomb civilian or private commercial premises. My goodness, just think of all the people in England who own businesses and land in Germany! They wouldn't tolerate it if the RAF went over and smashed it up. So when we talk about targets for bombers, we're only talking about each other's military installations, and they'd all be in ruins inside a month. And a good thing, too! Anyway, there's never going to be another war, so there's no point in discussing it."

A few weeks later the RAF itself accidentally dampened Eliot's keenness for military orders. The Air Ministry announced that in future all planes except fighters were to be fitted with slotted wings, to improve their stability. Since the Fleetliner needed no such "improvement," but would not have been exempted from the ruling, he became a half-convert to Julia's point of view.

In any case, he was now working day and night on a new design. Despite the success of the Fleetliner, it worried everyone that they were a one-plane company. The temptation was to remain in the field of large passenger- or freight-carrying machines, where they already had such a good name. But Eliot, looking at de Havilland's success with the Moth (literally, with the Stag Lane works just across the Edgware Road from Neville's), thought he could do better.

It was a risky thought. Fairey, Westland, Short, A.V. Roe, and Armstrong-Whitworth had all toyed with it and had either backed away or burned their fingers. The Moth that Julia had bought for close on £1,000 a couple of years earlier could now be had for £650, a price that could be sustained only by building in huge numbers. Rivals had to come in at fifty or so pounds under the Moth and hope to build up their sales over the years.

"In other words, we'd have to absorb serious losses – *planned* losses – for a considerable time," Julia commented. "I don't like the sound of that."

But when she learned that Crownfield, for once, agreed, she changed her tune. The entire aircraft business was a gamble, she pointed out. Success and risk went hand in hand . . . and so on. Julia at her bombastic best. It was, in fact, Eliot himself who persuaded the banker to give his guarded approval. The Moth, he pointed out, was all expensive curves. True, they were cheaper to make now that the plane was being sold in high volume, but it should be possible to design a plane with much cheaper curves, without sacrificing any aerodynamic qualities.

"What is a cheap curve?" Crownfield wanted to know.

"In a word – symmetry," Eliot told him. "A plane in which you could take the right wing, turn it over, and use it as the left wing would be cheaper than one in which each wing was unique. Ditto for all the other parts. If we have five jigs instead of fifty . . ." He did not need to finish the sentence.

"What about a name for it?" Imogen asked when the matter was formally raised at the next board meeting. "Should we send for Miss Lydia?"

But Eliot, grinning straight at Julia, said, "I think we already have the name. I'd like to propose the *Amazon?*"

CHAPTER THIRTY-FIVE

THE FIRST SKETCHES of the Amazon were put to paper at the beginning of January, 1929; the full-size test machine completed her taxiing and tail-up runs a mere nine weeks later, in the early part of March. And then the troubles started.

The Amazon was a high-wing monoplane with fixed undercarriage. Eliot wanted experience with this arrangement mainly for the sake of the next big plane he intended to build. The Fleetliner had been aimed at European and imperial routes, where skilled technicians were always available. But there was a big market opening up in what the Australians call "outback" routes, where the nearest mechanic probably spends most of his life shoeing horses. A big, safe, simple, rugged plane was what they wanted, with none of your variable-pitch propellers and retractable undercarriages, thanks very much. The Amazon, though designed as a profitable aeroplane in its own right, doubled as a flying test bed of his ideas for that much larger machine.

The problem lay in his basic requirement that its parts should be interchangeable, especially the wings. It did not result in the most aerodynamic shape and version after version failed in the wind tunnel. Eliot tried everything. He learned more about aerodynamics – especially about that elusive quality, *lift* – in those few months than at any other time in his life; but still the answer evaded him.

Meanwhile, Somerville's own Savage I engine, which Alan Hackett had finished the year before, had been handed straight back to him for further development in a supercharged version. This work was finished before Baring arrived at the definitive shape of the Amazon. The Savage 1 was an 8-cylinder V-type engine of 245 hp; it was built in two identical 4-cylinder blocks. By some stroke of genius, Baring realized that one of those blocks gave exactly the power he needed for the Amazon – around 120 hp. So there was a further saving in costs, since the same engine would serve for both the Neville aircraft.

The Savage Half, as they called it, was not supercharged and so could be tested at once. Chiefly, it had to undergo sky trials. Running it so many hundred hours on a test bench would convince nobody; it had to be up there at all altitudes and weathers. So, as the Amazon was still having teething troubles, they fitted it into a Moth frame – the new G-AAAA model with the enclosed coupé cabin – and Julia volunteered to fly it for the necessary few hundred hours. It suited her well because the SPRP was then expanding to Manchester, Liverpool, Leeds, and Glasgow, so she would have been doing a lot of flying anyway. But before two weeks were out she realized she had volunteered for the most boring job in the entire aircraft industry – sitting for hour after hour, listening to the unwavering (you hope) drone of an engine.

Then inspiration struck her. Where else in the whole universe was there a place more private than the cockpit of an aeroplane! So she put "The Charming City" by Ella Rosewarne Stevens between brown paper covers, wrote, *Savage Half Operating Manual – Strictly Confidential* upon it, and whiled away many a dull hour at two thousand feet. "Circassian Slave" . . . "Marigold's Summer Heaven" . . . "Proud Beauty of Versailles" – just about the whole Romantic section of the Boots' circulating library at Golders Green did temporary service as the operating manual for the Savage Half during that idyllic summer of 1929.

In the school holidays she took one or other of the children with her, as a treat. Actually, Robert had only a couple of "flips"; he was away most of the time, at OTC camp, then at VPS camp, and then at Allbury, where he helped with the haymaking. He showed a curious lack of interest in flying; Lydia claimed it was because too many women were becoming famous at it. She achieved the lion's share of flights. Though only fourteen she was already a good little pilot, quite proficient enough to land and take off without her mother's hands on the instructor's controls.

Like her mother she seemed to have a natural aptitude for it. The first couple of times, flying as passenger, she let her hands follow Julia's movements. Then she asked if she could take over, to which her mother had agreed, heart in mouth, hands a fraction of an inch off the stick. And from then on she had picked up the knack almost effortlessly. Once, while doing a few circuits and bumps at Hendon, she stalled during the takeoff phase. The hardest thing in a stall is to push that joystick forward when all your instincts are to pull it back and pray for lift. To do so when you're just ten feet off the ground is something that tests the mettle of even the finest pilot. But Lydia rammed it forward without a moment's hesitation, pushing the throttle to full revs simultaneously; it was Julia who had to fight the impulse to haul back. The sudden roar of the engine turned heads all over the aerodrome. It was amazing no one had a heart attack, for they saw the port wingtip actually graze the field. Everyone expected the plane to go cartwheeling down the runway, turning itself into matchwood. But by some miracle the tip sheared and the remnant of the wing held. For a moment or two the plane lurched wildly, hanging from the sky by sheer willpower and prayer; then the props got a grip and they wallowed upward just in time to clear the hangars on the western edge of the field. By tradition Lydia had to carry the damaged wingtip around for two weeks, but everyone said it was a badge of honour rather than a punishment.

No one was more proud of her than Julia. Through their shared passion for flying, mother and daughter formed bonds that summer which were to endure all their lives. But what pleased Julia even more, if that were possible, was Lydia's maturity, which seemed to grow as fast as her skills in the air.

"Your father would have been so proud of you," she told the girl one evening, when her two weeks of lugging the wingtip around were done with. Julia had always striven not to pass on her own jaundiced views of George.

Lydia said nothing, but her look of incredulity spoke volumes. Her mother never tried that easy sort of white lie again.

It was the season of air shows and pageants, so they saw thousands of aircraft and, more important, dozens of different types, during those months. Everywhere they went people crowded around the Moth to raise the cowling and peer at the Savage Half and ask pointed questions.

Lydia was in seventh heaven. She met all her heroes and heroines – Louis Paget, Sholto Douglas, Portal . . . also Sophie Heath, and that flamboyant Irish peeress Lady Heath (no relation), who was adored by the Americans but considered too loud by the English; they vastly preferred the quiet and dreamy Lady Bailey (who had flown to South Africa "without the foggiest idea what that outside ring on my compass was for"). No mere autograph hunter, Lydia buttonholed them all. The conversation would go something like:

HERO (or HEROINE): So you're Mrs Somerville's girl. And what wonders has Neville's in store for us next? Is it true you're building a rival to the Moth?

LYDIA: Yes. Mr Baring's adapting Fritz Koolhoven's idea – the one he used in the Baboon trainer in the war.

HERO: Ah . . . yes. Yes . . . quite so.

LYDIA: Only he's been trying to make the wings interchangeable, too.

HERO: Oh *that* Koolhoven. Yes, I remember now. Interchangeable wings, eh? How does he get enough lift?

LYDIA: Exactly! Especially as it's a high-wing monoplane. Personally, I don't think he'll do it. He'll have to settle for parallel-sided true aerofoils with detachable wingtips, so that he can interchange without flipping.

HERO: Bless my soul! It sounds as if you'll be the first to fly it, too?

LYDIA: Oh, I wish I could be!

The admiration in her eyes showed them how their exploits had stirred the imagination of at least one member of the rising generation.

She also managed to log (unofficially and illegally, of course) an amazing number of flying hours. And she saw lots of fascinating old-time planes that would otherwise have remained just photographs in books. For years after, she talked ecstatically of an ancient BE2e at Hadleigh, and an RAF-powered SE5 at Canterbury.

Apart from the public displays, they also called several times at the Air Ministry's testing field at Martlesham, where something of interest was always going on. There was no nonsense in those days about doing preliminary circuits and waiting for people to fire Very lights before you could land; if the field was clear, down you went.

On one visit they saw an astonishing demonstration of the tiny Blackburn Lincock, the ultra-light fighter capable of 150 mph. Some of its manoeuvres had never been seen (nor even been possible) before – a half loop with a sharp turn while upside-down, for instance, and a half roll that ended a hundred feet or more higher than it started. Every pilot loved it, and great indeed was Lydia's mortification that she was too young to have a go herself. Julia managed an upward spin of three turns, which would have been impossible in any other plane at that time.

Baring's joking prediction that Lydia would make a grand little spy came true at those meetings, especially at Martlesham. No one paid the slightest attention to a leggy young schoolgirl with her hair in pigtails, wandering around humming the latest Al Bowlly and looking oh-so-bored. But her eye – even the corner of it – was marvellous at detail; and of course many of the machines in the hangars were half stripped, to see how well they had tolerated the stresses of test flight. Lydia would spend the return journey filling her little sketch book with drawings of strut junctions, rafwire stays, engine bushings, and lattice spars. These she would discuss earnestly with Baring, who would tell her what to sharpen her eyes for next time.

Representatives of other companies tried to spy on Neville's, of course – not always with Lydia's kind of success. Arthur Thomson, who at that time sold planes for the Gnat Aero Co., once crept into the Neville hangars at Hendon to try to glean details of the Savage Half. He confessed it years later, to the amusement of everyone but Julia (this was at a party in 1936, to launch the prototype of the low-wing Amazon IV). He had the great good fortune, he said, to find the operating manual lying casually in the cockpit. He opened it eagerly, but all he learned was that Anna Mallard, a tender girl of rose and apricot, whose eyes were luminous and dreaming, had a face like a flower that has glowed all day, now folding for sleep.

Gosh! he thought. *If this isn't the best disguise ever for a technical manual.*

He flipped to the middle where he felt sure he'd find the real guff, and read: "Under the thick skin of Simon Medlicott's neck his blood burned darkly."

Everybody laughed – except Julia. He stared at her with those great, lugubrious eyes and said, "It was a brilliant code, Mrs Somerville. I never did break it."

Baring's final solution for the Amazon wing was very much as Lydia had suggested (though, naturally, she had picked up the idea from him as he fought aloud to avoid such a compromise). By then, so much time had been lost that he had to go for a type of wing already tested and in service. He chose the "twisted-cantilever" type, not only because he had seen it flying successfully in the DH77 most of the previous year, but also because he found a paper by Otto Glauert setting out the mathematics of it in detail, which saved weeks of trial and error in the wind tunnel. He was so pleased with the result that he tried to call Glauert and tell him the good news – only to discover that the poor fellow had been accidentally killed the previous year, walking on Farnborough Heath while some workmen were dynamiting tree stumps.

Baring's decision to compromise was vindicated not long afterwards by what happened to another designer, Oliver Simmonds. He left Supermarine to found his own small company and build the Spartan, priced at £620 and aimed at the Gipsy Moth market, too. Spartan was a biplane in which all four wings were interchangeable – also the struts, bracing wires, ailerons, fins, tailplanes, rudders . . .

everything. It was a brilliant design but, despite the easy maintenance and low price, no more than four dozen were ever built and Simmonds Aircraft Ltd soon folded. Eliot always quoted his own failure as the one that saved Neville's.

As soon as the Amazon (in its final, successful form) had undergone her taxiing and tail-up runs, they fitted the Savage Half, which had almost completed its trials, and tested both together. The verdict, as all the world now knows, was that they had at last produced a splendid little two-seater. It was a joy to handle. Landing was almost automatic, with no tendency to balloon. The stall was virtually harmless and a pilot had to work hard to get it to spin; and even then, as soon as the controls were returned to central position, it corrected itself at once. The two seats, in tandem, were as close as possible and directly over the centre of gravity, which meant that it could be flown solo without the need for compensating ballast – a feature the flying clubs all appreciated.

The absence of a bottom wing gave pilot and passenger a marvellous view, too. Julia, flying alone now, could not resist having a crack at the world altitude record of 19,980 feet, set the previous summer by Geoffrey de Havilland and his wife in their own Gipsy Moth. She got the Amazon above 19,500 feet with plenty of poke to spare but had to give up because of icing in the carburettors; in fact, she windmilled down below 1,000 feet before she got reignition! She never admitted that at the time. The following week, however, she did beat Hubert Broad's endurance record (also set in a Gipsy Moth the previous year) of 24 hours on 68 gallons. They changed the carburettors and fitted overload tanks to give 80 gallons capacity. In the 24 hours she flew a circuit from London by way of Land's End and Inverness, a distance of over 1500 miles; she landed with 13 gallons of petrol to spare, beating Broad by one gallon. She was furious then that she hadn't arranged to do the flight in a straight line – London to Athens, for instance – as she'd easily have taken the world distance record, too.

She was all set to try it the following week when Crownfield suddenly decided to call in Max's mortgage. The blow could not have fallen at a worse moment in the company's history – and the banker knew it, of course.

CHAPTER THIRTY-SIX

THE TEMPTATION WAS to go storming down to Cavendish Square and march directly into Crownfield's office; no doubt he, thinking he knew Julia well enough by now, expected such a response. The suspicion alone was enough to give her pause.

Instead, she spent days she could ill afford sorting out with Max what had gone wrong. There were, of course, extravagances.

"Three dozen magnums of *Moët et Chandon* and four pounds of Beluga caviare, delivered by Fortnum & Mason to the Boxing Day meet of the Ware Foxhounds . . ." She read the bills in tones of utter disbelief. "What on earth were you thinking of, Max?"

He shifted uncomfortably. "To tell the truth, I was going to shoot myself at the kill. Let the hounds break me up instead of the fox. Go out in style, I thought."

"Style!" She waved a hand at the disorder of bills. "That's what all this is about, isn't it. You imagine you're some White Russian prince."

"Then, while we were drawing the second covert, someone gave me a tip for Cunard shares." He uttered a single, hollow laugh.

"But that's only one example. Look at this!" She picked up another bill. "Why are you still buying guns from Purdey? Aren't the other five pairs . . ."

"Brace! Anyway, the others weren't made for me. You wouldn't understand."

"Made for you or not, you've done well enough with them, over the seasons."

"If you must know, they were ordered a couple of years ago, when things were a bit different."

"No they weren't, Max. They've never been any different. You've always tried to live like a lord on the income of a farmer."

"I've lived like a Neville – which is better than any lord."

She sighed and shook her head. "So what do we do? I think Dolly has the right idea. You'd better find a place in London and . . ."

"Sell up?" He became apoplectic with rage, showering spittle and swearing he would not do it.

The trouble was, she could not ask him to do it, either.

Now, of course, she felt even less ready to confront Crownfield. She sought the advice of St. John Brunty.

"I know it's not strictly company business," she began, "except insofar as we are my brother's guarantors. By the way, never let him know that. It'd shatter him. He thinks Allbury's worth the loan on its own merits. But what d'you suggest we do about it now?"

He rolled his pencil to the far edge of his desk and, in the same flourish, pulled his hair back over his ear; of course it fell again, immediately. "I believe the answer to that lies in a deeper question, Boss," he replied. "What does Crownfield really want?" He eyed her shrewdly. "That man must feel pretty sure of our custom."

She pricked up her ears; one always had to read Brunty's remarks obliquely. "You mean we could safely move to another bank now?"

His eyes gave away nothing. "Why do we stay with Crownfield's? That's the question. They're not really a merchant bank, you know. They're not geared to our sort of risk. In ten years' time, perhaps, when we're up among the big fellows, Crownfield's would probably be ideal. They're used to well-established industrial clients, not little terriers like us. I think we *worry* the man."

She laughed. "You mean *I* worry him. Well, that's hardly news."

He did not join her laughter. "You see – by calling in this mortgage . . . I think he's waving a flag of warning. It's our credit, not Allbury's, that worries him."

She felt there must be more to it than that but she wanted to hear how Brunty developed this line. "Then let's put his mind at rest," she suggested. "D'you think you could do me a brief financial statement? Something stronger than the usual balance-sheet snish-snish – which he must know backwards, anyway. What I need is a projection of our profits over the next twelve months, say."

Brunty leaned back in his chair, tugging at his lip.

She added, "So that he'll see we *could* easily go to another bank."

He did not take up that point. "The projection," he told her, "is of course extremely rosy."

"Well then."

He began to soap his hands uncomfortably. "It is our present position that is . . . how shall I put it?" His expression said it was the kindest word he could choose: "Parlous?"

She felt a sudden, icy twist of fear. *Parlous!*

"In point of fact," he went on, "I don't suppose many other banks would have carried us even this long."

"But that seems to contradict what you were saying earlier."

"Does it? I was mainly asking why we stay with him. Why he indulges us in our expansionary . . ."

"Indulges? Good God, Brunty, we are going to make that man's fortune – and our own, of course."

He smiled. His head wove this way and that, as if dodging bullets. "But just at this moment we are . . . very delicately stretched."

She couldn't believe he was talking about Neville's. "But the Amazon is a howling success. So is the Fleetliner. Our order book is full for *years* ahead. We've never had so much . . ."

"Exactly. What you're proving is that we *have to* expand. We've outgrown Hendon, just as we outgrew Dollis Hill. What we need is several hundred acres of flat countryside and twenty to thirty thousand quid to put up hangars and workshops." He tilted his head apologetically. "And we really ought to have started six months ago."

"We have reserved five thousand," she reminded him. "That would buy the land."

Maddeningly enough, it would also bail out Max, though she did not say so.

"And put up circus tents for hangars?" he suggested. "I wonder if one could?"

She shook her head. "I shall just have to go and browbeat it out of the man."

"I know what he'll say."

"What? Start accepting military orders?"

"No! As if we hadn't a big enough crisis with the orders we've got! No, he'll say what he's said at several recent board meetings. Float the company. We are already so drastically undercapitalized it's a miracle we're still in existence."

"Never!" she exclaimed.

He gave a sphynx's smile.

"I suppose you agree with him?" she challenged.

"You mean if I were writing a textbook on commercial finance and this were one of the examples? Yes, I'm afraid I would. But, of course, this isn't a textbook, and really we're not even talking about business finance. We're talking about business *people*. It's what textbooks always leave out. The world of business is full of people. And some of them would rather go to the wall than go to the market."

He reached for his discarded pencil, smiling at her as if at the ineffable sadness of everything. She slept very little that night.

She passed the following morning at the SPRP, finishing in time for an early lunch – if only she had an appetite. She decided to walk through the park and so up Piccadilly to the Ritz; perhaps that might help. It was one of those gorgeous, cold, brilliantly sunny, English winter days, with the sky so blue it almost hurt the eyes. All of London lay about her, gold and majestic – and utterly indifferent to the triumphs or tragedies of those who might presume to own it or claim it as theirs. It was the very worst sort of day on which to face such problems as now confronted Neville's.

Hers was a situation shot through with ironies, none of which escaped Julia. A confident, good-looking young woman, elegant without being voguish, raising many an interested eyebrow as she strode beneath the bare-boughed trees, she felt nonetheless like an outcast, a lost and frightened wanderer in an alien landscape. Objectively she knew it was absurd, yet she did not dare turn round for fear of . . . for the fear that never ceased to dog her days: poverty. Always at her back she felt the spectre of poverty. Argument was powerless against it.

How she wished she had never taken up Theresa's challenge, never forced herself to experience what had, ever since that time, been her most dreaded nightmare. There in Hyde Park, at the heart of six hundred acres of green space, all she could feel about her were the grimy brick streets, the weeping, fungus-sprouting walls, the mean little tombs of Dalston.

There was no comfort in her present affluence. Every week the papers carried stories that revealed how hollow such comfort would be. She had lost count of the numbers of rich people who had gone smash lately. Aristocrats with lands and titles that went back to time immemorial – wasn't one of them selling fruit off a barrow in Covent Garden? And another was living on the dole in Liverpool. And the businesses that were going bust every day – people having to get rid of their houses, cars, servants . . . everything, and go and live in some wretched little backwater, or even abroad. The mills of fear did not lack for grist in 1929.

She walked along the banks of the Serpentine, actually turning over in her mind the very thing she had always dismissed as impossible – this notion of going public. Why, she asked herself, was she so bitterly opposed to it? The subject had never arisen in George's lifetime, so it could not be one of his leftover prejudices. Nor was there any tradition, one way or the other, in her own family; they were landowners, to whom "going public" meant opening one's house to Sunday trippers. So it must lie within her, this fanatical, deep-seated urge not to divide and share out what was hers, hers, hers. Yet perhaps it was in her Neville blood. Indeed, the family motto ran: *Rem familiarem conservare!* which they had always translated as *Hold fast to what is thine!*

For her, "thine" had once meant George; for Max it meant Allbury. Perhaps this was the generation in which the Nevilles came unstuck?

As a moth to a candle flame her mind kept returning to the thought of the five thousand pounds she held in reserve for the new factory site. She was even then negotiating with the owner of an ailing foundry in Enfield – all that remained was to persuade the neighbouring farmer to part with fifty-odd acres. But nothing was signed. The money was available for Max if she so chose.

Would its loss really damage the firm? Perhaps Brunty was being too pessimistic. Yes, there was something of the civil servant in him – the sort of man who knows you can never be faulted for pouring cold water on an idea. If she bailed Max out with the five thousand, she could justify it because it would get the liability of the guarantee off Neville's back. Then, if she could inspire Brunty to put his name to a list of rosy prospects – his very words for it, after all – then she could go to another bank. Or at least show Crownfield she had a good enough case to go elsewhere . . .

Not until she left the park and started up Piccadilly did the real answer strike her – in all its horror.

"No!" she called out aloud, causing amusement or alarm among several passers-by.

Insidiously the thought seeped back, and this time she could not shut it out: She should buy Allbury herself – for Neville's – and build the factory there. Two hundred and fifty acres of flat, high ground! Hadn't Eliot commented on it the moment he first saw it from the air?

But no, it was unthinkable. It would kill Max.

Well, come to that, it would kill Max to have to leave Allbury anyway.

Time and again she beat back this vile, horrible plan; and yet it would not die. It just waited patiently for each storm to blow over and then it would rise and present itself once more. In the end she realized it was unanswerable.

At that moment she saw Max himself, walking toward his club, the In and Out, on the far side of the street. Dear Max, striding out in his British warm, with his bowler hat and his rolled umbrella, with all the cares of the world upon him and not one of them showing. She felt a sudden lump in her throat. It wasn't simply to do with Max, but with the very fabric and quality of England and everything she held dear. It was all there – that secret homeland which she loved so much. In him. In that pale London sunshine. In the stones of Piccadilly. In his very stride. All the things that money could never even know, much less buy.

Even when she realized it was not, after all, Max but some other ex-army officer in another British warm and another bowler hat . . . even then, the insight remained. She could not turn Max out – not until she had exhausted all other hopes, however slim.

She discovered she still had no appetite. In any case, lunchtime would soon be over. Her only wish was to have the matter out with Crownfield, once and for all. She determined to go to him immediately, and simply talk to him, man to man – try to make him see the business through her eyes. If she succeeded, he could not possibly refuse. For, if Eliot believed passionately in planes and flying, she burned with a corresponding zeal for aviation, for the industry itself.

If that man could only see the future as she saw it, oh so clearly, he could not possibly refuse.

She took a taxi to Cavendish Square, where she was shown immediately into Crownfield's office. "No need for this," she told him, brandishing his letter calling in the loan. "I've sorted Max out. There'll be no further trouble."

Even as she spoke she knew she might have thought of half a dozen better openings; it was just that the man brought out all her belligerence.

His eyes narrowed. "That wasn't really the problem, Somerville."

Just to hear her name on his lips, in that lighthearted style they had assumed on the night of George's funeral, revived old feelings. Everything had been so full of hope then, so *possible*. She lost her concentration for a moment. "No," she said. "The problem is you don't even begin to understand me, or the aircraft business . . . nothing."

"Understand?" He laughed. "You speak as if you had some sort of coherent strategy! Philosophy, even."

"I do," she objected. "What you mean is I don't have yours."

His eyes narrowed. This was not the sort of conversation she usually sparked off. He tried to return to familiar ground. "I expected you here some days ago."

"I haven't been skulking away from you, if that's what you're . . . I had things to do."

"Including a bit of thinking, I hope?"

"A lot – especially about Neville's" – she waved her hands awkwardly, aware how unused she was to putting such things into words – "the industry, the future. That's what I'd like to . . . I just wish you could – I mean I wish we were on the same side, Crownfield. I wish we were still . . ." She looked down – then quickly up at him again. "I do miss our old friendship," she added gently.

His watchful gaze softened for a moment. "I miss you, too, my dear."

The loudest word between them – *but* – remained unspoken.

"D'you think I oppose you for opposition's sake?" he asked. "I want nothing more than to be on the same side, as you call it. It's only when you behave as if you're the first person in the world ever to have discovered this thing called *business* and you're the only one who knows the rules."

She closed her eyes, feeling the discussion slipping down the same muddy banks as so many others. Even so, she could not help saying it: "I've discovered this thing called *my* business. I may not be able to talk about it like Eliot, with his master's degree and all that – or you, with all your years of experience."

"Good girl! You obviously have been thinking." He drew breath to take over the conversation.

"But," she insisted, "I do have a picture, a very clear picture, of Neville's. I know the way it ought to be. The way it can be. The way it will be."

"Then if it's as clear as all that, why can't you . . ."

"It's only clear when something happens that feels wrong. Or something threatens it. And then I know it at once. I mean" – she snapped her fingers – "like that. I just know what feels right and what's wrong."

"Oh dear." He shook his head sadly. "I'm only listening because I know what you're really like – shrewd, clever, determined, and a born leader. I'm not saying those things to flatter you – just to explain why, if I were any other banker in London, sitting listening to such a farrago of mystical drivel, I'd be reaching for the little button under my desk by now. But do go on!"

She saw that, for some reason, he was trying to provoke her anger; and yet it was too clumsy, too obvious for him. Perhaps he only wished her to think it? Then what was his real purpose?

She pointed to his letter again. "What was in your mind when you sent that?" she asked. "You don't simply want the mortgage repaid. You're trying to make me do something – or see the light, or something. What d'you really want? I'll tell you, you've achieved one thing: I am ready to listen."

"Penny on the drum?"

"A guinea on the drum if you want."

He sighed. "What I really want is for Julia Somerville somehow to lose her skull-and-crossbones vision of the world." He laughed at having put it so succinctly. "As an asset to Neville's its value must be nil – if not actually negative. I grant it served the firm well for the first few months, but now . . ." He shook his head and shrugged.

She closed her eyes wearily and said, "It is a risk-taking trade, you know."

"All business is."

"I don't know about *all* business . . ."

"Exactly!"

". . . but I do know about the aircraft business. No one, absolutely no one, has ever succeeded at it by shunning risk, playing cautious. You think I'm wayward and capricious, don't you. You think my decision on military aircraft is pure feminine caprice."

He shrugged uncomfortably.

"Well, I admit it has an emotional core. But so does your behaviour towards me, so don't pocket my admission too smugly."

"Are you implying there are good practical reasons for turning down so much profit – for being the *only* manufacturer who . . ."

"The only English manufacturer – yes. Let's pin this thing down once and for all. The Germans are doing better than us – and with no reliance at all on military orders. Because, of course, the treaty forbids them. So, as a result, they build for the *market*. But we – I mean the other English plane makers, not Neville's – the English build for the latest Air Ministry spec – which is written by civil servants and therefore always at least four years on the wrong side of cautious. Why else d'you imagine all English planes *look* so bloody obsolete?"

He was about to interject, but she had the bit between her teeth. "When I was down at Martlesham one day this summer, someone made a rather grisly joke. He said, 'If a pilot who died in the Great War were to come back to life this afternoon, he could jump into any plane here and fly it without a moment's tuition.' And by God, Crownfield, he was right! And why? Same answer. Because every plane in this country is designed to meet those blasted Air Ministry specs. We – Neville's – are the only exception. All right – life is tough without profits from military orders – I can't argue that. But if we can only weather this first crisis (and let me remind you, it's a crisis of success, not failure), then just you watch us streak ahead of the others! We'll leave them standing – or, rather, twitching, in their bureaucratic noose!"

The banker let his head sink despairingly in his hands. Then he looked abruptly at her. "For heaven's sake, Somerville – do you ever listen to yourself?"

"I hoped you were doing the listening."

"I was. And do you know what I heard? What I always hear from you – the song of an incorrigible bloody freebooter! You haven't the slightest desire to run a business along ordinary lines, with common prudence and simple wisdom. Well this time" – he leaned forward to pass her hat and gloves – "you're bloody well going to learn. If you came here hoping to get this foreclosure postponed – request re-fused!" Like a fussy border official in some Ruritanian republic he thumped the table twice, putting an official stamp on an imaginary document.

"Just six months?" she asked. She had meant it as a genuine last request but it came out subtly different. It came out as if she were offering him a last chance not to be such a fool – not to risk being defeated by her.

He heard it and stirred uneasily. He had hoped for a return to more amicable relations between them – but on his terms. There was a harder tone than he intended in his reply: "This time you've no way out. I'll allow you two weeks to admit it."

She went straight round to Lexy's, where she found the great man in bed with a sinusitis. "The smell of the tea room at the Savoy will cure that," she told him brusquely, throwing his clothes at him. "I forgot my lunch. We'll have a slap-up high tea."

Actually it was her account of the battle with Crownfield that revived him. His fingers itched to get it all down verbatim.

"It's a clash of two different philosophies," she summarized grandly when she had done. They were at the Savoy by now, waiting for their food in pleasant anticipation.

"Don't give yourself airs," he replied dourly. "It's just two different ways of getting out of bed in the morning. What are you proposing to do?"

"I haven't the foggiest notion. All I know is that if Crownfield forces me to go public, I'm finished." She tapped her breast. "In here. Neville's is still too young, too small. We have to stay nimble. I'm . . . it's like leaping across stepping stones in a mountain torrent. I couldn't do it with Sinbad the Shareholder on my back." A wistful look came into her eyes. "God, I wish I'd said that to Crownfield. I just can't think of the right words when I'm with him. Why does he have such an effect on me?"

Kindly Lexy desisted from pointing out that it was actually Sinbad who had carried the Old Man of the Sea. "What's the last thing in the world that he'd expect you to do?" he asked.

She grinned. "Heaven only knows. Ask Sidney Gold for a loan?" She laughed at the very idea.

He joined in. "You're surely not considering it?"

She shrugged. "I can only say I'm rejecting nothing at this stage." Her eyes narrowed. "I might even tap you, my dear."

He pulled out his cheque book and tossed it in front of her. "You write, I'll sign," he promised.

He meant it, too. Such impulsive generosity, so close to her own heart, moved her deeply. She passed it back. "I should have known," she told him. "Thank you, Lexy darling. You're the best man friend I've ever had."

"Sell *me* the shares, then. You can buy them back at will."

She shook her head.

"Why not?"

Her smile was shy, reluctant, at first, but then it grew impish. "Actually, of all the people I know, you're probably the one who'd understand it best. I can't take up your offer for the simple reason that it's too easy – like finding a secret hoard of money suddenly. It wouldn't be . . . satisfying. When I beat Douglas Crownfield, I want to do it by turning his own cleverness against him. You do understand, don't you? Say you do?"

He beamed. "You're an artist," he said, paying her the highest compliment he knew.

They dropped the topic for the rest of the meal but when they reached the Madeira and Turkish cigarettes he came back to it. "How will you turn Crownfield's cleverness against him?" he asked.

"I'm trying to avoid thinking about it," she replied.

"Why so?"

"Because his cleverness is to point Max and Allbury at me, like a loaded pistol. He's daring me to pull the trigger."

He didn't see her point.

She sighed. "Whatever I do, it'll have to involve Allbury. Max will never forgive me. He has no idea I'm his guarantor. What's Dolly doing these days? We seem to have lost touch since she married whatsizname – Wallace Baker." Suddenly she looked at the door and said in quite a different tone, "Good heavens! Is Imogen Davis still coming here to see young Gold? I'd forgotten all about that."

Lexy spun around and gazed toward the door.

"She went on up the stairs," Julia explained. "Sorry. What were we talking about? Oh yes – Dolly."

"Dolly's at Wyndham's, doing about as well in *her* firmament as your Fleetliner is in yours. Why?"

Julia gave an even deeper sigh. "Because she will somehow have to persuade Max that this cup of poison in my hands is actually his passport to a new and better life – away from Allbury."

CHAPTER THIRTY-SEVEN

ALLBURY HAD NEVER seemed so beautiful. *It's doing it deliberately,* Julia thought. *It knows.*

She made several reluctant circuits of the landing field, unable to rid her mind of the image of a vulture, soaring above the African plain.

Dolly's voice came over the intercom: "All those times we've made remarks about how we could really put down in *any* of the fields!"

"I know. It never occurred to me, I swear it. Not that Max will ever believe me."

"There he is now. Does it matter what he believes? Why d'you worry so much? He's jolly lucky to get out with something to salvage. God, you've given him *months* to see reason. I say, are you thinking of landing sometime today?"

Grimly Julia banked, dethrottled the engine, and came into the final approach. By now Max could judge her landings to the nearest yard; he stood no more than half a dozen paces from the point where she came to rest. His grin was broad but both sisters could read the terror in his eyes.

Was it too much to ask – a dispensation from the ordinary demands of life, a safe-conduct through this trivial corner of history?

"Poor bugger!" Dolly's last comment came over the intercom.

Julia cut the engine. When she slid back the canopy, the small sounds of an English summer afternoon emerged from hiding – the popping of distant shotguns at the clay-pigeon butts, the oiled whine of gears in twisting lanes, the ting-a-ling of the Walls ice-cream man, the stop-me-and-buy-one. Julia held on to each moment, not *as if* it were the last but because it was, indeed, the last: Max's last afternoon of unchallenged tenure here; her last landing as a visitor, her last care*free* survey of her native fields. For Allbury was now hers.

She was using the coupé version of the Amazon, so the only flying gear she wore was the helmet, and that only for the intercom. She eased it off with the crook of her thumb and tossed it back into the cockpit as she clambered out. Then she ran a loving hand over the doped-fabric skin – anything to avoid having to turn and face Max.

"Has either of you heard from Agnes?" he asked.

The sisters exchanged glances and said no. Julia added, "Have you?"

"No."

"Well why did you bring it up?"

He shrugged. "I just thought it would be nice if she were here now. All four of us together. Here in the old place."

They strolled in silence toward the house. "It doesn't take long," Dolly offered.

Max turned to look at the Amazon.

"No," Dolly explained. "I mean nature." She waved a hand toward the sea of thistles that crowded the landing strip.

Max lost interest. Julia was watching him closely, trying to gauge his mood. Their eyes met at last. He frowned and asked "Well?"

"We've managed a *kind* of rescue," she replied.

"That's an ominous emphasis."

She wished the next five minutes could just flash by, take them as read; she wanted to be on the far side of the coming storm.

They had reached the gate into the field that sloped gently down toward the house. Max began to untie the twine that held it closed (and upright, for both hinges were rotted), but his sisters leaned upon it and stared out over the sunstruck landscape. "Divinissimo!" Dolly murmured.

"Three bloody valleys!" Max commented morosely; his eyes were fixed upon the house.

Julia frowned at him inquiringly.

"The roof," he explained. "Leaks like a sieve. That storm the other night. D'you know what *Rem familiarem conservare* really means? Maintain the family property. I could tell you about maintenance. Fancy building a roof with three valleys. Archer should have been shot – or Sir Ralph for employing him."

To Max even the most distant forebear was almost a contemporary. Julia's heart grew heavier yet. How could she uproot him from this special soil? While he was here, a dear but dying England lived. All those things at which it was now so fashionable to scoff – family, tradition, inheritance . . . all the ancient values, they *were* Max. Take him from that stony soil and what monster of luxuriance might not begin to unfold within him? And what of Allbury, too? Its history would survive, of course, but only in penny books sold to Sunday trippers. Julia shuddered. Never! She would never let it come to that.

"Looks perfect from here," Dolly commented, unwilling to be shaken from her mood. Then she laughed. "Actually, I used to think the architect was a brother-and-sister team called William and Mary. The way people always called it a perfect William and Mary house."

"We'd have done better to lose the war," Max added, as if the remark followed naturally from his criticism of the architect. "Lose the war, see our currency vanish into the skies . . . smash the lot and then rebuild. You watch Germany now."

Julia cleared her throat. "To put it in a nutshell," she began, glancing at her brother for some sign of encouragement.

"Some nut," he commented, still not taking his eyes off the house.

"Some shell!" Dolly laughed – and then remembered it was a shell that had carried off poor Bill.

"Crownfield, as you know, was the mortgagor."

"Bloody Jew," Max grumbled.

"I say, is he?" Dolly asked with interest. In her world, Jews were Angels.

Julia shook her head wearily. "Not for two generations past."

Max said, "He's living proof that communion wine *doesn't* turn into Christian blood. You should read some of the fascist literature, you know."

"If he's a living proof of anything, it's that when it comes to tolerance and fair play . . ." Julia clapped a hand to her mouth, halting her own flow. "No," she went on, in a less argumentative tone. "I'm not going to get caught up in one of your inane Jew-baiting discussions. Apart from which, what makes you suppose Jesus's blood wasn't Jewish, too?"

Silence returned.

"Anyway?" Max prompted after a while. The sinews in his hand were white where he gripped the gate rail.

"Anyway, the money from the mortgage was supposed to be treated as working capital, not income."

"Yes. Ha ha. Have your little dig. We all know what a wizard accountant you've become, Ju, dear."

"It's not a *little* dig, it's the whole bloody point, Max. That money was supposed to modernize the home farm, not go on caviare and Purdey guns."

He stared at her pityingly. "You've caught the infection. Money, money, money – bisch-nisch! The point of owning a country estate is to live like the owner of a country estate, not like some blasted parvenu with his nose in the books all day. It's got nothing to do with red ink and black ink."

"Oh?" Julia asked scornfully. "And whose job is it to take care of all that, then?"

"Why d'you bother?" Dolly asked. "Just *tell* him."

"It's the banks' job, and always has been." His brain took in what Dolly had said. He turned to her. "Tell me what?"

Dolly looked at Julia, who sighed and explained, "Very well. If you really want to know – Neville Aero-Engineering has bought out Crownfield's interest in Allbury." It seemed the kindest gloss to put upon the truth.

Max stared at her. Slowly his incredulity turned to joy. She drew breath to explain further but he took off his deerstalker and flung it high in the air. "Y e e e o w!" He leaped and caught it. "You were teasing," he accused blissfully. "Good old Ju!"

"Wait," Dolly warned.

"But if she now holds the mortgage . . ." he began.

"Not me," Julia corrected. "Neville's."

He smiled, as if he thought she were just being pedantic.

"We had two choices, Max, dear," she went on. "In fact, we still do. Nothing irrevocable has yet been signed. I'm in exactly the same dilemma as the bank was. We can either sell up Allbury as a bankrupt estate, or . . . well, what d'you think the 'or' might be?"

He had no hesitation. "Carry it, of course – as a matter of family honour and duty. Surely you can afford it now? Perhaps I was a bit hard on Crownfield. After all, why should he do that? But if *you're* holding the mortgage . . ." He beamed happily, believing the rest of the sentence was too obvious to need saying.

"Yes. Now that I'm holding the mortgage I have to persuade my board that it's a good investment."

"Persuade them? Just bloody well tell them."

"Minority shareholders have legal rights, you know."

"Eliot Baring? Just tell him no more night exercises."

"Oh?" Dolly turned on Julia in delighted surprise. "Are you sleeping with Eliot? Good God – I always thought it was Lexy."

Her picayune sophistication angered Julia into a snapped reply: "I'll sleep with anyone I want."

She had meant it as a general comment; to her dismay she saw that her sister took it as a particular threat. Even angrier now, she turned on Max. "And as for you, you can't keep anything, it seems – neither accounts nor confidences."

"Nor Allbury," he added. "Whatever we hold dearest in life" – he glanced briefly at Dolly – "you'll steal it from us. You're an evil, grasping woman."

Julia felt the panic rising within her. Dolly must at some time have blurted out to Max her fears about Wallace. The little idiot.

Fight fire with fire was all she could think.

"Steal?" she echoed scornfully. "I suppose it isn't theft when you borrow five thousand on the understanding you'll modernize the farm and then go and spend it on caviare and . . ."

"What's that to you?" he barked. "It wasn't your money."

Julia glanced at Dolly; the lift of her eyebrows asked, *Tell him?*

Dolly, now adrift in the ocean of her own fears, shook her head, more in bewilderment than as a considered response.

Max noted the exchange and asked angrily what was going on.

Julia sighed. "It doesn't matter." She gave him a wan smile and her tone became businesslike, crisp. "Listen – you're lucky, really. I only hope you can see it. The reason why Neville's had enough cash to put up was . . ."

". . . you've been selling planes like geese at Christmas," Max interrupted.

". . . was that we had certain reserves set aside for acquiring a new site. D'you understand what I'm saying?"

"Perfectly." Max grinned as if all their harsh words had never been spoken. "Cheer up! It won't take a million years to scrape up another few thou'. Just sell more planes."

"And where do we build them? That's my point, Max. We need land. Can't you put one and one together? You've run out of money; all you have is land. We've run out of land; all we've got is money. Can I possibly make it clearer than that?" She turned and surveyed the fields.

He followed her gaze. His dented euphoria vanished, replaced by stark incredulity. He looked deep into her eyes and shook his head, a man stunned.

Slowly, hating herself, feeling like a whole pack of traitors, she nodded.

Dolly began to remember some of the lines she and Julia had prepared. "You'll love it in London, Max," she enthused.

He ignored her. "Here?" he asked, running his eyes in one dazed sweep of the skyline.

"As I said – you . . . we – we still have the choice. If you'd prefer a clean break – let it all go smash, as you hinted just now – there is an alternative. You could sell out to a spec builder. D'you know Wally Larkin – the fellow who put up that vile monstrosity for himself in Hoddesdon? He's made an approach to us."

"To you? Why to you?"

"Never mind why. That's the choice. You choose."

"I've already told you my choice," he replied truculently. "Leave things as they are. Find another site for your factory. I can't believe that's beyond your powers. Not if you *really* wanted to."

Julia sighed. In a way it was true, of course. If, for instance, Max had only a year to live, and everyone knew it but him, she'd wangle it somehow to let him live out that time in contented ignorance. But that was precisely the trouble. In actuarial probability, Max had almost two score years yet to run, during which time – at his present rate of spending – he'd let the best part of seventy thousand pounds trickle through his fingers. And at the end of it all, she'd still be standing here, asking him to choose between this or that awful fate for Allbury.

She could give him no answer beyond a further shake of her head.

"Please?" he begged, sinking to his knees and starting to waddle toward her.

"Max!" Dolly shrieked, embarrassed beyond measure.

His absurd gesture collapsed. He sank back on his heels. "It's funny that Allbury was a good enough pledge until last week. What's so different between last week and now? Not the size of the debt, anyway."

"How can you be so bloody naïve?" Dolly asked furiously.

He looked at her in surprise.

"Dolly – no," Julia cautioned. "Please don't. And Max – do get up."

His trouser legs were plastered in dust and thistledown.

"He ought to be told," Dolly said.

"What?" Max looked from one to the other in bewilderment, spectator to a battle between the eyes.

"Dolly," Julia said quietly. "Be quite sure in your own mind – as to why you're . . ."

"It's time for realism," she snapped.

"Are you really such a devotee of realism? Or are you trying to get at me?"

"Why should I want to get at you?" Dolly gave a toss of her head.

Julia merely stared at her.

At last Dolly could not bear the strain. She turned to Max and blurted out, "The fact is, brother dear, Allbury alone couldn't possibly secure a mortgage above a thousand, not with things as they are."

"That's not what Crownfield said," he countered.

Julia realized it would come better (or slightly less badly) as a confession from her, rather than as a revelation from Dolly. "Crownfield said what I asked him to say. He advanced the money on the security of Neville's. It had nothing to do with Allbury."

It was the moment she had dreaded all that year. But she had ignored the one most important rule in dealing with Max: Never try to predict what he'll do. Far from exploding, he turned to her in delight and chortled, "You mean Allbury's free of debt after all?"

Dolly stamped her heel – almost silently in the soft ground – and strode away.

"Let her go," Julia commented. "She's not much help, I'm afraid."

"What d'you suppose Father would say if he were here now?" Max asked. His calm, after her expectations of a storm, seemed eery.

"I don't suppose he'd understand it – any more than you can."

"He wouldn't understand *you*."

She shook her head. "It's the world, Max. His entire world – and yours, I fear. It's gone. Dead. It died . . . where Bill died. How you managed to come through it unscathed . . ."

"Hardly!" he protested, touching a few of his scars.

"I mean your mind's unscathed. You can't see how the world has changed."

"You're not going to do it, are you, Ju?"

"The ironical thing is that the first Nevilles would probably understand it perfectly. They were merchants, commercial . . ."

"You are going to. By God, you *are!*"

"The rot set in later."

For a long moment Max stared silently at the house. Dolly, who had walked a great, aimless circle, came back and put herself between them. "Well?" she asked.

Max stirred. "I suppose you'll tear the house down," he grumbled.

"Not at all. You could go on living here," Julia offered, hoping he'd have the sense to refuse. "If you like, we'll treat the debt as a mortgage – over forty years. And Neville's will lease the rest of the estate. That would leave you with around six hundred a year to live on."

"And how could I manage on only six hundred?"

"Ask your neighbours. They all do – much less, most of them."

It was absurdly generous, of course; the mortgage itself was more than five times the value of the house, and a rent that would leave him six hundred clear was far too generous. But it would never have occurred to Max to work such things out for himself; all he saw was that he'd wake up tomorrow owning nothing but an overmortgaged five-acre site with an ancient, leaking house upon it. "Go to the devil!" he roared.

Julia suppressed a sigh of relief. Now that everything was out in the open between them she felt quite calm. "I'll live in the west wing," she told him. "The rest will make good offices. Nothing will be demolished."

He was barely listening. "If you do this thing, Ju," he said in a voice all the more menacing for being so quiet, "it's the end of you and me."

"You'll see it differently in time," she told him.

"I'll get my own back," he went on. "I don't know how . . ."

"For Christ's sake, Max!" Dolly exploded. "Can't you get it into your thick skull that but for Ju, you'd be out on your ear and bankrupt? Thanks to her, you'll be free of this millstone and have money to spend."

Max just stared at her coolly, waiting for her to finish. Then he turned to Julia and added, "I'll find a way."

Julia smiled at him with a confidence she did not feel. "No you won't, my dear. You'll take a decent set of rooms in London – with Fritz to look after you. You'll spend your days in the club. You'll motor down to friends at the weekends and hunt and shoot to your heart's content. And a year from now you'll thank me for making it possible."

He gave her a look of utter contempt and, with an agility astonishing for his age and build, reached down and swung himself, legs-high, over the rickety gate. Then, without a backward glance, he set off downhill toward the house.

"D'you think he will?" Dolly asked dubiously.

"Probably not," her sister answered grimly. "It's how all great families die out. They stick in the mud while the tide moves on." She turned her back on the house and let her eyes wander across the fields and hedgerows. "I hope he doesn't hang on here. This must be an airfield by the autumn."

She was talking in this calm, almost brutal way so as to put some distance between herself and her own confused emotions. Her thoughts kept returning to the fiendish way Max – in just a few words, a lift of an eyebrow, an inflexion of his voice – had driven a wedge between his two sisters.

Dolly said, "It must be dreadful to have to be so ruthless."

"But I'm not," she protested, as if she were talking about the landscape. In her mind's eye, the trees were already tumbling, but she went on: "Max was so wrong. I don't want to take anything from him – from either of you."

"Only if you have to, eh?"

"Oh, damn him!" Julia exclaimed as she walked away.

She meant Max, of course, but Dolly failed to understand that.

Max went straight indoors, flung his hat at the hall table, missed, and stormed on upstairs to his bedroom. There at the window, with a full view of the gate where Julia had just ended his life and the whole Neville connection with Allbury (for he no longer considered her to be of the blood), stood Imogen Davis.

"Well?" she asked.

"I owe you an apology," he replied. "You were right."

PART FOUR

THE EAGLES ARE GATHERING

CHAPTER THIRTY-EIGHT

MAX SIMPLY WALKED out of Allbury. He didn't even carry a spare shirt. Julia assumed he took his toothbrush because none was left behind; his toothbrush and his Vauxhall Prince Henry. But everything else was just abandoned. She had to get Pickford's to come and pack the lot before taking it into storage. It was no trivial task, either, for Max threw away nothing. Ancient visiting cards, back numbers of *The Boy's Own Paper,* a gold tooth he had knocked out of a senior's mouth in an assault-at-arms at Haileybury in 1899, a hot plug from an old Benz Victoria – they and fifty thousand equally useless items were all preserved, along with the rare old books, the ancestral portraits, the now tarnished silver, and all the other heirlooms that any family would keep. There was even a set of five suitcases that, by some fiendish Victorian ingenuity, could be put together to make a light horse carriage.

"Sling the lot. It's all rubbish," Dolly advised. "It's his own stupid fault for just walking out."

But Julia – stung by Max's taunt that she was an evil, grasping woman, and needing to disprove it to Dolly above all – insisted that every item be listed and that the foreman from the repository should sign for each crate and tea chest as he accepted it. He, a veteran of quarrelsome old families being forced out of their ancestral lairs, did not raise an eyebrow.

It took six weeks and cost a fortune. Even so, all the larger, heavier items were simply stacked in one of the barns, which was then boarded up and padlocked; they ranged from a broken Lewis machine gun to a reversible plough for a long-vanished steam engine.

Max, true to his word, refused to see Julia, but Dolly relayed all the news to him. "You're loopy to go out like this, darling," she scolded. "We could have had a scrumptious auction, made oodles of oof, and all gone for a super autumn on the Riviera. Agnes could have flown up from Kenya. Instead it's costing Ju a king's ransom and you're stuck with Fritz in this vile little cubbyhole in Earl's

Court. Such a waste!"

It was, actually, rather a grand set of rooms – two floors and the servants' attics, the entire upper half of a house off Gloucester Road, part of a terrace that had been built in Edwardian days for a grandeur that none of its tenants had ever quite achieved. The prosperous rentiers at whom it had been aimed, and who would have flocked there in the days of the carriage, took advantage of its horseless replacement and moved on to Chelsea and Kew. A despairing builder had sold the terrace off for boarding houses, so Max's single occupancy of so many chambers was actually a small step of reversion toward the original dream. The neighbours called him squire.

Julia did very little of the packing herself, but Thelma, the maid of all work whom she had once discovered mending the front door window, was a splendid deputy, so much so that Julia decided to retain her as housekeeper when Allbury House became the offices of Neville Aero-Engineering.

For the rest of the time she was up the hill in oilskins and gumboots, supervising the removal of the hedgerows and the levelling of the few small ridges and hollows that marred an otherwise perfect airfield. Or, rather, it would have been perfect had this not been glacial sand-and-gravel country, liable to the sudden appearance of what are locally called "moneyholes." These are cavities that form within a hill of sand and gravel as it settles over the millennia; grain by grain, almost, the roof drops upon the floor so that the cavity acts as a kind of bubble, taking centuries to rise to the surface. Some are small enough to give a man a minor fright when he drops into one up to his waist; others can dump a tractor and plough at the pit of a thirty-foot crater.

In the few years of their existence, farm tractors had discovered more moneyholes in Hertfordshire than all the men and beasts to tread that county's turf since Domesday. And if that were true of a two-ton tractor, what of a twenty-ton plane? One whopper of a moneyhole was breached and filled that autumn at Allbury, and several minor ones as well. It worried them all as they stood at the rim of the overnight crater and imagined a Fleetliner half buried in it. A geologist advised them to drill a number of holes in a circular pattern about the landing field, pack the bottoms with explosive, plug them, and "give the whole moraine a hearty shaking." It cost a three-week delay and over two hundred pounds and produced nothing. Good news, they decided – until the geologist said, as he pocketed his fee, "Of course, we might simply have disturbed a cavity that would otherwise have been safe for another ten thousand years."

Inexorably, though, the Neville airfield took shape. Julia was quite determined once she set herself at a task. Beloved fields and hedgerows, each of them rich in childhood (and, indeed, ancestral) memories, cared for down the centuries, named and tithed in the parish registers – all vanished for ever as the hilltop became a prairie of mud; two fields alone were left, hedgeless but unploughed, as a temporary landing strip until the reseeded turf grew green once more.

Dolly watched her sister in a kind of horrified fascination. As the plough cut through a field where malting barley had lately stood, she remarked, "That's where you first tasted cider. Don't you remember? Papa brought it out and wouldn't let me have any. And Agnes kissed Tim Barnicoat from the village for a dare."

"Happy times," Julia replied absently, checking for dips in the terrain, which were much easier to spot in the wake of the plough.

"Doesn't it make you sad?" Dolly asked.

She shook her head. "I expect when the first Norman baron laid waste the forest to create these fields, a pair of charcoal burner's daughters probably stood here and mourned the loss of *their* childhood haunts."

"But it *is* sad. When we're gone, no one will ever know the life that went on here. Someone should write it down."

"So that it could moulder away in a tea chest at Pickford's," Julia commented.

And while this work proceeded, the nightmare of assembling Fleetliners from bits made all over the Home Counties went on at Dollis Hill – not to mention gearing up to produce Amazons in quantity. But by the spring of 1930 the new airfield was a deceptively firm-looking green. Then, heart-in-mouth, they put a mighty steam roller over it, north and south, then east and west, to produce the firm turf they needed for their huge planes. No new moneyhole was revealed.

By then, too, the great hangars and assembly sheds were complete down to the last arc light and rolling bay. At once, they transferred the Amazon production line to Allbury. Only eight craftsmen moved out from London with it, most of them being housed in tied cottages belonging to the old estate. The plane did not call for many skills beyond the reach of carpenters and smiths, so most of the new work force was recruited locally. Production was soon up to four a week, all of which helped to bring in sorely needed cash.

Lydia, now fifteen, approved of the changes at Allbury. Her Uncle Max, remote, bluff, idiosyncratic, had always seemed rather frightening, and visits to Allbury had ranked among trips to the dentist and the school outfitter in her scale of desirable pastimes. But now the place was transformed: a gracious country home with exciting gardens full of secret places and, just up the hill and most thrilling of all, an aircraft factory with its own private airfield. And all of it presided over, indeed, owned by, a mother she adored – a mother who was as crazy about flying as she was and who couldn't say no to anything, within reason, because she wanted to do it, and share the thrill of it, with an identical passion.

Inside the house, too, there were new wonders. Gone were the old hunting trophies – the stags' heads, the Bengal tiger, and the charging rhino that "must have hit the wall at a fair lick." (That had been George's joke to the children; Lydia had believed it for years and always wondered did they sever the neck on this side or the far side of the wall – because the rest of the animal wasn't there and the plaster work was perfectly restored.) Gone, too, were the ancient ancestors and the muddled histories it had been a duty to learn; from the fastidious-looking Sacheverel and his roguish wife Margaret to thrice-married William, the family Bluebeard – those piercing Neville eyes that had stared down upon the generations now had nothing to quiz but the ventilated gloom of a Pickford's repository.

And in their stead were the most marvellous machines. There was a thing called Gestetner, whose handle she was sometimes allowed to turn; it was just like a printing machine except that it made copies of typewriting – and it had a pale, waxy correcting fluid she could pretend was nail varnish. And there were typewriters with two-coloured ribbons and strange devices like ¶ and @ that you could use for patterns. And a blueprint machine that would make copies of anything you drew on tracing paper . . . and draughting boards where you could draw straight lines and angles and any sort of curve you wanted. Allbury had become an utter paradise.

Her brother Robert could not have disagreed more violently. Now seventeen, he was old enough to be allowed beyond junior school bounds, and he used the privilege to cycle over from Haileybury and grumble at every little change. Thinking to win him over, Julia took him up for several flights, but all he did was point out other flat areas in the locality that would have made equally good sites for the Neville factory. It frightened Julia to see how like his father he was growing, even in the tiniest detail. George had had a particular way of scratching his left eyebrow with the nail of his middle finger before making a joke. Robert must often have seen it, of course, but never in the five years since George died had he done it himself – until now. Was it imitation? Or did such unconscious usages pass down by heredity? It was a chilling thought that Robert might be doomed in his seed to become his father.

She watched him drift away from her, and from his sister . . . drift willingly into Max's dubious sphere. Exeats and holidays, once spent at Allbury by overwhelming preference, were now passed in Earl's Court. All he could think of was military uniforms and "biffing the Bolsheviks" – obsessions of Max's, to be sure. Later, Max joined up with Sir Oswald Mosley – "the Leader." Then it was all black shirts and the regeneration of the Empire, saving it from the clutches of the international Jewish-Bolshevist conspiracy.

They found a new superman, too – the fiery and charismatic Adolf Hitler. Robert set to and learned German, or enough of its more rabid parts of speech to enable him to follow *der Führer's* outpourings without the interpolated comments of the British press, which were far too lukewarm for him and his uncle; Max, of course, spoke the language fluently. The boy could hardly wait for the school holidays to come round; for now every possible day was spent in Germany, at one of their youth camps or rallies. He became such a *bore* about it all.

Julia knew she ought to do something, but no one could tell her what. The consensus seemed to be that most adolescent sons went through these troublesome phases and that it was all part of growing up, and at least he was getting a bit of discipline; parental attempts to shorten the process and open their eyes to reality generally did more harm than good.

Neville's was far too busy for her to do anything other than accept the advice gratefully. And, to be quite honest, one had to admit he came back bronzed and fit and full of beans. His spots cleared up. He never loafed around, smoking and looking furtive, the way most young lads do. He kept his room – and his clothes, and his person – absurdly neat and clean. Perhaps, all in all, it would do more good than harm – if he could manage to grow out of it in the end . . .

At the back of her mind Julia had anticipated that the pressure at Dollis Hill would begin to ease once the move to Allbury began; indeed, she had been hoping for a time of consolidation – firming up their already considerable achievements and making a rather slow and considered assessment of their future. In a purely negative sense it was true. If they hadn't moved the Amazon out into the country, life at Dollis Hill would have been intolerable. But demand for the Fleetliner continued to burgeon and its production swiftly ate up each newly available inch.

"Nothing will change here even when Allbury's going flat out," Baring warned morosely one day when, yet again, they had to scour their neck of northwest London for space to hold their stocks.

That same day, Alan Hackett and Hannah Dawson came to Julia in great excitement. They had just put the finishing touches to their joint design for a revolutionary new engine built largely of aluminium. It would, they said, increase the thrust-per-pound ratio by over a third. But there were worries about corrosion. All they wanted was about eight (for which Julia read sixteen) thousand pounds to develop it.

Meanwhile, St John Brunty was pressing her to set up licensing arrangements for Australia, Canada, South Africa, and the Middle East; their ever-lengthening delivery times were losing them business.

Also there was the "outback" plane, the Bushmaster, as they had decided to call it. Wind-tunnel work on the scaled-up version of the Amazon wing was almost completed and a go-ahead on the prototype would soon be needed – but where could they build it?

And the ordinary work of Somerville Engineering was still expanding under Hannah Dawson's competent guidance. The navy, impressed by the results they had already achieved, wanted them to bid on a number of more routine contracts, where speed and efficiency rather than brilliance were required – all those details that call for scaling up or scaling down and other minor modifications whenever a vessel is redesigned. "But they also need an engineering eye on the job," Hannah explained to Julia. "Some sixth sense that'll say, 'Watch out – if you make it that small, you'll run into trouble here and here.' And, of course, they also need someone who's able to deal with it."

"But you're the only one who could do that," Julia objected. "It sounds like a waste of your talents."

Hannah shrugged. "In a way, yes. But it's just the sort of bread-and-butter work we might need in a lean time. The armed forces could easily cut down on a lot of new plans, but they'll always have to keep these more humdrum things ticking over, no matter what. And it wouldn't all land up on my plate. There are two lads here I'd like to promote, both working like billy-oh *and* going to evening classes. And perhaps, if the work looked like being regular, we could take on a couple of qualified engineers?"

And then there was Sidney Gold complaining that drawings were being altered without any prior consultation . . . and some days his blokes were working like slaves and other days just sitting round with nothing to do – or no stock to do it with . . .

And Crownfield, still smarting from her "cleverness" at using the money earmarked for expansion to solve the Allbury problem as well, was going for her every chance he got, pressing her to raise more capital "the proper way."

And St John Brunty, running with hare and hounds, as usual.

And Max – refusing to sign papers, refusing to take phone calls, refusing to agree to anything – even when it was outrageously in his own favour.

And then they found dry rot in the wing Julia proposed to use as her country flat.

And Messerschmidt wanted to extend the existing licensing agreement.

And Junker wanted to set up a meeting.

And Curtiss in America had asked Eliot's parents a string of searching questions.

And there was still the SPRP . . .

And . . . all at once it dawned on Julia that those periods of retrenchment, those longed-for hours of quiet contemplation where the future could be faced in a calm and reasoning frame of mind – would never materialize. It was all a pipe dream, a mirage that would recede before her as swiftly as she advanced to embrace it. There would *never* be any peace. Each new achievement would raise the pressure to complete next year's prototypes and design the ones that would follow a year later.

No – six months later! For the pace would accelerate. At the moment she could just about keep all the daily business of the firm in her head; but the time was fast approaching when that would no longer be possible. A year or two from now, even at their present, financially constricted rate of expansion, important things could happen inside Neville's that she would not hear of for days or even weeks. It would then no longer be possible to hold a working model of the firm in her head. What was she preparing to put in its place?

Nothing. Neville's would be like the dinosaur which got so big that its cold-blooded nervous system took four seconds to tell its brain that some passing carnivore had just bitten its tail off.

The necessary reorganization called for more formal structures than she cared to contemplate, administrative structures that reeked of bureaucracy and divided power . . . empires within empires and all the cankers that she could see eating out the guts of other businesses. She had a horror of them all – and yet she could not escape the logic that dictated their creation. She had not yet found a way to adopt Eliot's advice on the day of her first flight: Learn how to delegate!

Still, she was lucky with Eliot, she realized. Brilliant but utterly lacking in ambition, at least of that empire-building kind. That's what she needed – a stable full of brilliant non-empire-builders. Then she might loosen the reins.

But then look at Hannah Dawson; an empire builder if ever one breathed. She wanted to build Somerville Engineering into the biggest and best in the field. Yet that was all right. If the empire were self-contained enough, as in her case it was, the ambition did no harm. The trouble began when Finance fought Production and both ganged up on Design – that sort of thing, all within the same firm.

"Just hire an assassin to shoot them every three years," Lexy suggested when she tried explaining the problem to him.

It was then the summer of 1932, the year the Bushmaster went into simultaneous production on three continents – the year when Julia's all-in-my-head style of management was proving to be the biggest single constraint upon the company's onward march. Indeed, if the effects of the Wall Street Crash had not finally worked their way through to the economies of Europe, the expansionist pressure on Neville's would have been so great that something must have exploded.

Lexy, who no longer vied with Darling Noël but contentedly occupied the gap between him and Shaw, had watched Julia winding up to that eruption all year.

"Come on," he said at last, when he could bear it no longer. "It's a super day. I have a new launch to try out. I'll get them to bring it down to Westminster pier and we'll go up to Kew Gardens for the day."

She began to protest, listing all the things she had to do. But he was adamant. "When was your last day off – I mean, really off?"

She couldn't remember.

"Westminster pier in half an hour, then," he commanded.

CHAPTER THIRTY-NINE

EVEN IN THE HEART of London, a luxury launch on the Thames is as private a place as any aircraft cabin; and if its engine is a well-bred little Parson's steam turbine, it's a great deal more restful, too. Lexy's *Marina* was actually newly refitted rather than plain new; she had the razor bows and the general lines of a prewar vessel, elegant and thoroughbred, not the streamlined, modernistic thing Julia had pictured at his first mention of it. Below deck, her old Somerville eye approved of the brass and mahogany, the plush Edwardian upholstery and the cut glass.

"You're growing decidedly mellow, my darling," she told him. "It's not at all the sort of launch I imagined you getting."

"It belonged to a Baron von Stael," he replied, handing her a manhattan. "D'you want to stay down here or go back on deck?"

She sipped it gratefully, pointing upward. She relished the cold liquor before she added, "There's an old love affair I want to resume. Such ages since we broke it off . . ."

He frowned in amused bewilderment.

"Me and the *sun,* you goose."

She lay at full length in a divanlike seat of teak and woven cane, basking in the hot caress of an unclouded morning. A gay canvas windbreak turned aside the breezes off the bow; only the gentlest eddies crept around the fringe to play lightly with her hair.

Lexy, unable to take his eyes off her, sat beside her – though under the shade of a personal awning – and regretted for the hundredth time that he had not declared his love for her years ago. Now, of course, it was far too late. "You'll burn," he warned. "You're as pale as a prisoner."

"Ten minutes won't hurt."

After a silence he remarked, "Your drink'll boil."

"Mmmm."

An even longer silence. "Make yourself at home," he said.

She chuckled and opened one eye. "Just five minutes, eh? Then I promise – up sunshades and I'm all yours."

They slid past the Tate, then Vauxhall Bridge. He timed her to the second. They were approaching the brewery as he cleared his throat and put a fresh cocktail down beside her, making the ice tinkle with an aggressive invitation.

"Five minutes," she murmured reproachfully.

"Up already." He was spreading the awning above her.

She sat half upright with a heavy sigh. "That's life. D'you notice how, in plays on the wireless, people are always 'going away for a good long think'?"

"It's a lie," he told her solemnly. "Or bad writing – which is the same thing. What they really want to do is spout a soliloquy close to the microphone – but they realize that people would only laugh if they tried it in company."

She grinned. "Yes, but I mean – the whole notion of 'a good long think' – stepping out of life for a while . . . I mean, there's nowhere you can step out of life. And in novels they're always crossing the Atlantic and landing in New York – speaking of which, this is the best manhattan you've ever mixed for me – and all their worries have been magically straightened out in five days 'away from it all.' Baloney, as Eliot says."

He toasted her, sardonically. "Shall I *freshen that drink,* as Eliot says?"

By habit she started to say no, but then thought, *why not?* She passed him the glass. "I should get a launch," she murmured, gazing at the sunlit river bank. "God, it's so peaceful. There's twelve million people around us and yet here we are, perfectly alone."

He handed her the refreshed glass. "Except for the crew."

She hadn't even considered them. "Thank you for insisting," she said. "I had no idea I needed this break so much."

"Are things so fraught?" he prompted. "D'you want sunglasses? You shouldn't pucker your eyes like that. You'll get wrinkles." Without waiting for a reply he pulled a spare pair from his blazer pocket and passed them to her.

She accepted the offer almost as if it were slightly risqué. "Oh, mollycoddle me all day," she begged. "You always know exactly what I want. We should have got married, you and I."

He licked his lips uncertainly, not wanting to pile seriousness on her humour – but not wanting, either, to suggest he found the idea absurd. "Well . . ." He glanced playfully at his watch – and wished he hadn't given her the means of hiding her eyes.

"No." She looked away and became serious. "Marriage just wrecks one's life. If we'd married, we wouldn't even be on speaking terms by now."

After a pause he asked, "D'you mean you'll never marry again?"

"I can't begin to imagine the man."

Oddly enough, she thought not of Eliot but of Wallace Baker. Forbidden fruit!

"Nothing like George, I'm sure," Lexy was saying. "Not that I knew him all that well, but I often wondered what you ever saw in him."

She shook her head absently, as at some long-dead folly. Then she gave a single short laugh and added, "Blame literature."

They were approaching Barnes Common, where a hot breeze came straight off the new-mown grass. That fragrance, more than anything else, brought it all back to her, impelled her into a rush of total recall. "I'd just read 'Jane Eyre', and you know how it finishes? The opening words of the last chapter – 'Reader, I married him!' – something like that. And I thought, after everything she'd suffered, how splendid . . ."

"And him," Lexy pointed out. "He suffered, too."

"Yes, but part of him always seemed to relish it."

"And you don't think the same was true of her?"

Julia didn't want to face that complication. "Anyway," she continued hastily, "it seemed like the ultimate reward for all she'd endured. I went around for days . . . I couldn't get the idea out of my mind, that marriage was a marvellous reward for a woman. And then George proposed to me. And it was like being offered the reward all at once."

Lexy shook his head. "I don't believe you were ever that shallow."

"No, of course, there was everything else. People telling me what a marvellous *catch* I'd made, how *wise* I was. Also I did love George, or the George I thought I knew. And he adored me. When every fingerpost in the forest agrees on the way out, it's very hard for a young girl to say, 'Thank you, but I'd rather blaze a trail of my own.'" Her smile begged his agreement.

"What is the name of that forest?" he mused.

"Something frightful."

For a long, painful moment each of them teetered on the verge of confession – the sort that does not reveal its nature until one is fully committed to its utterance. She drew back first, saying, "Anyway, what I mean is I can't imagine my wanting to marry the sort of man

who'd want to marry the sort of woman who leads my sort of life
. . . if you can follow all that?"

"Sort of," he allowed. "What would be so wrong with him?"

They veered to avoid an eight, rowing their guts out. As they
drew level the cox shouted, "Easy all!" and the exhausted oars
flopped to the oily-calm surface, sending a flotilla of ducks scurrying
for the bank. Looking into their happy, weary faces, Julia could
almost feel the gratitude that bathed their muscles. The one rowing
at stroke winked and blew her a kiss; she toasted him with her glass.
Their slave driver on the towpath began shouting criticisms down
his megaphone and then one of the piers of Hammersmith Bridge
slid across the scene, like a curtain. "End of Act One," she murmured.

She suddenly realized that this was where the Boat Race started;
she hadn't been on this part of the Thames since she was thirteen,
when Max was in the crew. A different Max in another world.

They came out into the sun once more. Lexy did not press his
question. "Hungry?" he asked.

She shook her head. "Not yet."

"Churchill's a lot better this morning," he went on. "According to
the *Telegraph.*"

"Yes, it sounded like a close thing. Max Beaverbrook was very
worried. I dined there the other night."

"Beaverbrook's taken quite a liking to you."

"He couldn't stand me once upon a time – my decision about
military aircraft, you know. He's such a jingo. But now we're
spawning little Neville companies throughout the empire, he thinks I
can't be all bad. Wallace Baker actually brought us together."

Lexy chuckled. "It seems to be his second trade – bringing people
together."

There was a pause before Julia said, "Yes."

"He's the Beaver's blue-eyed boy at the moment. He must be
doing very well."

"I hope so – for Dolly's sake. I think she rather carried him a year
or two. Talking of the Beaver, I fancy he wanted Churchill to meet
me. Together, they hope to . . ."

"But you've already met Churchill. Don't you remember – at the
Embassy Club after the First Night of . . ."

"Well, of course *I* remember. But Churchill wouldn't."

"I'll bet he does." A further memory struck him. "Oddly enough,
Wallace Baker was there, too. Wasn't that the night he and Dolly got
engaged? Yes."

She nodded absently, staring into her empty glass.

"Odd sort of bloke. He has that journalist's knack of turning up –
of being there."

"Being where?" She came out of her reverie.

"Wherever he's wanted."

"Oh, yes, I suppose he has."

"D'you see much of him at all?"

She shook her head, not casually but as if she were shaking off water. "Anyway," she went on, reverting to their former conversation, "I don't know why the Beaver thinks Churchill would be so persuasive. His political career is over, surely?"

Lexy gave a vague nod of assent. Memories of that First Night began to stir him. "Oh, wasn't the theatre *fun* in the Twenties!" he gushed with sudden enthusiasm. "And the night spots . . . where's it all gone, eh?"

"It's Wallace's famous missing generation," she offered. "Now we really are missing them. God, if Bill were only alive now, he'd have sorted out Max ages ago. *My* Max, I mean. All this fascist nonsense."

They moored in the backwater behind Brentford Ait and walked across the bridge to Kew Gardens.

"It's absurd to come all this way to do something one could do just as easily in Connaught Square," she remarked, "but I simply cannot help it." And, choosing the lightly dappled shade of an acacia tree, she spread their rug and, stretching herself full length, fell almost at once asleep. In her last conscious moments she was aware of his hands lifting her head and slipping something soft – his blazer? – beneath it.

He sat there, trying to sketch her in the little notebook he always carried. He had a talent for swift caricature; he could flay Darling Noël in six lines. But give him fifty more to play with and he'd turn it into a sculptor's armature. Not that it worried him today; all he wanted was the excuse to look at Julia and indulge his fantasy.

An hour later she awoke, feeling more relaxed than she had done in years. Arm in arm they went back to the launch, where the steward had set out *the* most marvellous lunch – half a dozen oysters, followed by a Waldorf salad with salmon mousse, followed by fresh strawberries and cream – all helped down by a Franken Spätlese and the superb 1922 Château Rieussec. It was two o'clock and the temperature was in the nineties.

"Mmmm!" she murmured, closing her eyes and stretching luxuriously. "There's not an ache in my body. This mixture of breeze and heat is . . . just perfect. I know there are a million worries at the back of my mind but at this moment I can't recall one of them." She surveyed the table, almost regretfully. "Even without such a lunch as that, I would have to say this is one of the best days of my life."

He basked in the praise. "Shall we go on up to Hampton Court?" he suggested.

Her eyes lit up. "I haven't been there since we took Lydia, when she was ten – the year George had his accident. I thought the maze would terrify her. It frightened me at that age. But we had to drag her away. Yes, do let's go to Hampton Court."

They lowered the windbreak now, being in need of the breeze, and sat on the foredeck sipping tiny cups of Turkish coffee, without which Julia would have gone straight back to sleep.

"Could you retire now, Lexy?" she asked. "I mean, could you just live off investments and things?"

He nodded.

"So could I." She hid her hand in the folds of her skirt and crossed her fingers. Neville's finances were never so definite as to warrant such an assertion. "D'you realize – we could live like this every day. Aren't we fools?"

He shook his head. "I'd just sit here and write plays anyway – and then fret that no one was calling me to say how marvellous." He lowered his face, mock-accusingly. "You'd be the same."

She grinned. "The nice thing about artists is that they needn't be ashamed of enjoying their trade. Soldiers and judges and civil servants and so on have to talk of duty and service to the community and self-sacrifice, snish-snish."

"And business people, too."

"Oh yes, we thunder away with the worst of them."

"Are you saying it's not true?"

She shrugged. "I don't know about them, but let me tell you" – she lowered her voice and leaned toward him – "I'm as passionately nuts about making aeroplanes . . . flying aeroplanes as any artist who ever lived. When I see a new crate of ours take off for the very first time . . . well, it's better than your old cocaine. I think of all the sweat and heartache – which isn't just physical labour, but grubbing for money and . . . oh, listening to bloody trade unionists snivelling away and . . ." She became incoherent, trying to convey the sheer bloodiness of her business. "Anyway – it's worth it. Just as you *are* your plays, so I am all the aeroplanes we make."

"So there!" He slapped his wrist.

She laughed. "I know! I didn't mean it like that. I started out to say something quite different. What were we talking about? Oh yes – what we'd become if they took our life's work away from us." She grew sad all at once. "Well – just look at Max. He wasn't so bad when he had the weight of history – and the expectations of all his neighbours – to keep him in check. But now!"

Lexy disagreed strongly. "Max was always mad. Not that he's alone. Far from it." He gave a theatrical shiver. "Our century is turning very nasty in its middle age, my dear. And we had such hopes of it, too, when it was young."

"I'm thirty-nine next week," she told him, as if it somehow confirmed his gloom.

He was at once all smiles. "But you didn't say! Oh, we must have the grandest . . ."

"We must have the grandest silence on the whole subject – thank you very kindly. If you so much as breathe a word . . ." She slit her throat with her finger.

"It's a marvellous age to be," he assured her. "The threshold of forty! You're going to adore it."

"Promise?" she insisted. "Not a word?"

He shrugged. "If you wish it. But you do surprise me."

She raised an eyebrow.

"I'd have said that you, you above all people, would have embraced it openly – taken it in both hands – told all the world."

She stared at him in disbelief.

"Women are so wrong to think that aging's the end of the world. It's a good thing you have bright eyes and silky skin and lustrous hair at twenty – because, by God, there's very little else to be said for you then."

"So why did you warn me of wrinkles this morning?"

He slapped his own wrist. "Because I'm a conventional fool. Actually, I'm devoted to your wrinkles. I could wish you had . . ."

"Could we please change the subject, Lexy dear?" she said menacingly. "I feel the most awful fit of jumping-overboard coming on."

He refilled her coffee cup, watching her closely, challenging her not to laugh.

Eventually she gave way, fighting to keep the coffee in its cup. "Light me a cigarette," she begged. "One of your nice, gold, Turkish things."

She puffed contentedly and peace settled on them once again. The muted roar of Teddington weir could be heard in the distance – the point beyond which the Thames ceases to be tidal.

They tied up at Hampton Court but bought no ticket for the state apartments. Julia just wanted to walk around the gardens. "I couldn't face all those heavy gilt frames and that clumsy brickwork," she explained. "Not on such a day as this."

They went straight around to the eastern side of the palace and strolled up the banks of the Long Water.

"What of little Imogen Davis these days?" Lexy asked. "I send her the odd invitation – to the larger parties, you know – but she never comes."

"But she's living with Max – didn't you know? That's part of the whole bloodiness of everything."

"Oh really?" He cleared his throat. "I'll bet Randy Gold is pleased!"

"And the father. Actually, it's her influence on Robert I fear the most. He's so impressionable. He's going to inherit Somerville Motors in just over four years' time – and he hasn't the first idea about business, or managing people, or . . . anything." Briefly she took his arm, to dramatize her need to steady herself more than for genuine support. "Never mind. It's not one of this year's battles."

"And what are they, may I ask?"

She gave a hollow laugh. "You see – like the shadows of evening they reach forward to engulf us. We can't escape them."

But she did not tell him what they were. She clung to her noontide illusions for as long as she possibly could.

CHAPTER FORTY

THE RULE AGAINST military sales only ever flew on one wing. True, no Neville aeroplane of the early Thirties was built in a military version (or not by Neville's – one Arab sheik, assisted by a gleeful 30 Squadron RAF, modified a flight of Amazons for use in desert reconnaissance and interception, with wing-mounted Vickers machine guns). But Neville patents inevitably found themselves under licence in other makers' warplanes, for the aircraft world handled patents quite differently from any other branch of engineering.

American planemakers actually pooled all of their patents. In Europe, things were never quite so organized but licences (usually in the form of cross-licences) were never refused, even between the fiercest competitors – the reason being that if *everything* on a new plane had to be tested, it would take so long that the machine would be obsolete even before it gained its C of A. Even Eliot's most advanced designs involved taking out licences on dozens of systems patented by other firms; as he explained, "There's no sense reinventing fire and the wheel each time." Those firms naturally sought cross-licences on Neville's patents, too.

So on either continent there was no practical way of ensuring that Neville's efforts did not promote the warlike ambitions of any country – short of giving up the business and going into . . . well, what? Brunty offered a five-pound prize to anyone who could come up with an industry whose products did not directly or indirectly aid the military. Nobody won it.

Then there was Baring Instrumentation. Because of Eliot's prejudice against the slotted wing, he had poured a lot of the firm's efforts into "pilot's assisters," as Julia preferred to call them; he would have liked "robot pilots" or "blind-flying aids," but she felt neither term would inspire the confidence of the flying public. Eventually, of course, they came to be known as "autopilots," which, for some reason, the flying public accepted happily. Eliot's assisters were gyroscopes of various kinds, coupled to devices to show how the plane was pitching, rolling, yawing, or deviating from the true horizon. Their great advantage over their competition was that they did not need to incorporate a turn indicator. This improved their accuracy to the point where they were useful in real flight (as opposed to specially rigged sales-promotion "flips"). Naturally they were soon in great demand around the world.

So much so that a new company, Baring Instrumentation, was formed to handle their sales. Its slogan was, "For your true bearings call Baring's." Its foremost customers, too, were the makers of warplanes.

In many ways, then, Neville's pacifism was a leaking old tub. Perhaps for that reason, pressure from official quarters eased. Lord Beaverbrook stopped chiding Julia for her lack of patriotism, not just privately but in editorials in the *Express,* too. Lord Trenchard (as he became in 1930) no longer spoke of the firm's "unfortunate policy" on every possible occasion. And routine sniping from all and sundry at the Air Ministry no longer cluttered their communications. It was not long, however, before Julia began to suspect that the reasons lay deeper than that.

Despite the assurances of politicians, and the strong antiwar sentiment of the day, Britain's "hidden government," that clique of permanent officials and standing committees who actually run the country (with only minor interference from parliament) were increasingly convinced that the Great War had not been fought to its conclusion – simply to the exhaustion of its participants. The bell for Round Two would ring before long and, as before, it would be the Germanic nations against Britain and France – with question marks now hanging over Italy and Russia. Julia realized that those far-sighted gentlemen might consider it expedient for Neville's to maintain its close commercial links with Messerschmidt, Junker, and Focke-Wulf – not least for the valuable information they thereby acquired.

The man most responsible for maintaining those German ties was a soft-spoken young Irishman called Mickey McHugh. He had originally been Alan Hackett's assistant during the development of the Savage 4, the famous Vortex engine, where his quiet geniality had proved deceptive. His dedication to any work he undertook was an obsession that bordered on mania. He had come to Julia's notice very early, when Hackett told her, "I don't know what it is about that fellow. We convene what we hope will be a perfectly ordinary production meeting where we'll spend ten to fifteen minutes bringing each other up to date . . . and then suddenly he'll get his teeth into some little thing that doesn't smell quite right and . . . well, I'll give you an example. At a meeting last month he just happened to notice that Terry Watts, who's developing the gear trains, had ordered about twice as much of a certain alloy bar as usual. So, of course, Mickey asks why. And it turns out that the shafts kept on shearing between certain velocities. And blow me if we weren't still sitting around that table two hours later, worrying that problem to death. We all left feeling like wet dishcloths – but *inspired*." He tapped his head. "Up here. No one slept much that night, I can tell you. But come the dawn and we had it solved. He's like a little terrier. He just won't let things go. And yet so quiet!"

Such a man was too good to keep as a mere technical assistant. When the Vortex finally went into production, Mickey McHugh became a second pair of eyes and ears to Julia. Naturally, such a brief took him far beyond the firm's boundaries. With his immense knowledge of engines he was the ideal man to convey Neville's ideas to any receptive listener. In fact, designers in other firms would often ring him up for an opinion about competitors' products, too – so he'd even get to know what was going on in the drawing offices of de Havilland's, Shorts, and others. Julia nearly had a fit when she heard him advising George Carter at de Havilland to use Napier's new engine, the Rapier, for the DH77.

"Sure, we've nothing for them," he explained to her. "He's looking for a lightweight three-fifty horsepower job."

A year or so later, however, she had cause to suspect his seeming altruism. The Rapier-powered DH77 proved no match for its rival, the Kestrel-powered Hornet from Hawker-Siddeley. Of course, it was a small loss to de Havilland but it was the death knell for Napier's in the aero-engine business. The Rapier engine had been their last chance. Frank Halford, their chief engineer, was now desperately trying to upgrade it to around 800 hp, where it would compete with similar-size motors from Rolls-Royce and Bristol – a job he would have started months earlier had it not been for the chink of hope offered by the de Havilland contract. Had Mickey McHugh foreseen all that? If so, he'd be a dangerous man *not* to have on one's own team.

Mickey clocked up so much mileage that his special all-weather Amazon became a flying test bench, and thus roving advertisement, for many of the firm's ideas. He was often down at Martlesham among the latest bombers and fighters (many still secret), where his opinion was always listened to eagerly. The same was true among the flying boats at Felixstowe, or with the RAE at Farnborough – and even in the most secret place of all, the base of the Schneider Trophy team at Calshot. The morning might find him supping a dram of his favourite malt with that sturdy little ball of fire, Ernest Hives of Rolls-Royce – or some other great man within the industry; and come the afternoon you might as easily spot him in some remote squadron workshop, bending over a recalcitrant engine with a humble RAF mechanic. From the top of the industry to the bottom, the quiet, cheerful Irishman was welcomed with a smile.

And in Germany, too, where Neville's had so many connections, the same smile from the same general range of people invariably met him – at Dornier in Friedrichshafen, at Messerschmidt in Regensburg, or Heinkel in Warnemünde . . . Mickey knew them all. He was thus the natural person for her to turn to when her misgivings about Neville's became acute. But that was after Hannah Dawson had shown her the solution.

She had spent the evening down at some provincial theatre in Reading, where Lexy had invited her to see Wilfred Lawson as John Brown (the antislavery hero whose "soul goes marching on") in the pre-West End tryout of "Gallows Glorious." Actually, she had only consented to the outing so as to show off her new Bugatti 41 Royale, Coupé de Ville. It wasn't their sort of play at all, but Lexy wanted Lawson for the lead in his new masterpiece, "Nest of Vipers." They found the story crude and the production melodramatic, but Lawson had an energy and a sincerity that, given the theme, disturbed them both. Even as she drove them home she knew she would not easily find sleep that night. So, stopping at Connaught Square only to drop off Lexy and change out of evening dress, she drove on to Dollis Hill. Mickey McHugh had written her a report on his recent gleanings at the Schneider Trophy team and she had forgotten to carry it home with her.

On her way through the works – it was by then gone midnight – she heard a small sound from Hannah Dawson's office. On investigation she found Hannah herself there, working in a tiny pool of light over her desk. She looked up at Julia, smiled, and said wearily, "Do we ever truly leave school, I wonder?" She was elbow-deep in books and papers on the subject of stainless steel. "I thought I knew everything about it when we did the wet liners for the straight-six. Then a simple little question from Mr Baring, about possibly cladding an aeroplane with stainless instead of duralumin, and . . ." She tapped her head as people tap sauce bottles to extract the last drop. "Hopeless! And he's bound to ask me tomorrow."

"It's very good of you," Julia commented as she sat down and offered Hannah a cigarette. "Why not simply tell him there are only so many hours in a day?"

Hannah answered with a rueful grin. "I made such a play of my superior knowledge, I'm afraid. I can just see the smirk on his face if I had to confess failure."

"I know exactly what you mean." After a short silence she added,

"D'you know what a man told me at dinner the other night? He said, 'Speaking for myself, I'd rather employ a first-rate woman than a fourth-rate man – any day.' I'm sure he imagined he was being outrageously feminist."

Hannah sighed. "That's exactly it. We're not aware of it most of the time, are we – but it's there. All the time. It's there. We have to be first rate to be deemed the equal of a fourth-rate man." There was a despondency in her eyes that hinted at a loss she could no longer measure. "Anyway" – she began to close the books and stack them with a pyramid-builder's precision – "I can at least point him at the answer. He may do the slogging for himself."

"Hear hear. But isn't it awful when you're on the trail of something like that and you just can't let it go?"

Hannah, catching the whiff of confidentialities on the air, said, "Oh?"

Julia went on. "With engineering problems you almost always know what it is. I mean, sooner or later, you'll find a book or a paper that will, as you say, point you at the answer. There should be books like that for business."

Hannah nodded, and waited.

"But business is magic, not science."

After another short pause Hannah prompted, "Is it any particular problem?"

Julia shrugged. "I just don't know. It's as if my nerves don't end here any more." She tapped her fingertips. "Instead, they seem to extend outwards into every part of the business." Her brow knitted as she sought examples. "You know how you can get those vague aches . . . you can't see anything or even feel anything wrong, and yet they just won't go away."

Hannah tapped the ash off her cigarette and returned her calm, collected gaze to Julia, who explained, "That's how I feel about Neville's at the moment, only it's even more vague than that. I can't even say where the ache is, and yet there's a sense of . . ." She sighed at being unable to find the word. "Something about to go wrong."

"Menace?" Hannah offered.

"I feel we're vulnerable. Like Little Red Riding Hood starting through the forest. There's a wolf somewhere. When we started – well, of course, you weren't here then, but you must know it from your own experience. We were too small for anyone to bother about. It was a wonderful time in a way – I mean, we were so free. But now the little wildcat is turning into a lumbering great . . . dinosaur or something. A ponderous creature with enough meat on it to awaken the interest of every carnivore in the jungle." She chain-lit a new cigarette. "And just look who's steering this fat, juicy creature – why, it's only a woman, who – even if she's first rate – is (as we now know) only equivalent to a fourth-rate man. A dotty woman who makes idiotic decisions like staying out of military sales." She shivered dramatically. "Yes, I feel vulnerable."

She stubbed out the new cigarette and began to pace the carpet. "Are these just night terrors? We saw a very disturbing play tonight."

Hannah considered her reply. At length she said, "It's not magic, though, Mrs Somerville. It's still science. Or half-science, anyway. Biology."

Julia looked at her with interest.

Hannah rose and started to amble toward the door, speaking as she came. "What do animals do when they don't want to be devoured? They run faster. Or they grow thick armour. Or take to camouflage. Or become even fiercer than the thing that's after them. Or make themselves poisonous or evil-tasting. I'm sure all those strategies have business equivalents."

Julia, holding open the door for her, laughed. "Miss Dawson, I think a veil has fallen from my eyes. Thank heavens you knew slightly less than you thought about stainless steel!" She switched off the corridor light and walked beside Hannah among the lathes and machines.

Hannah asked, "Yes, but which strategy is for us?"

"Ah, we shall have to see."

The following morning she was there before the hourly paid men and only ten minutes after Mickey McHugh, whom she found deep in files of German correspondence. He was not his usual placid self.

"We lost three sales last month," he told her. "Entirely because Dornier's production slipped behind schedule again."

"That's the fourth time in twelve months, isn't it?"

"God, I've lost count. They're not the only ones. You'd think none of them really want to work for us any more. Lord knows why. Haven't we put enough clothes on German backs?"

"You were there recently?" Julia prompted.

"Last month," he agreed. Then, fixing her with his eye, he added, "I got the quarest feeling, altogether. You remember when we caught that young apprentice – Duggan – machining out model plane engines after hours?"

Julia gave a rueful smile. "We slipped badly there. We should never have sacked him. You know he's now an extremely successful maker of . . ."

"Yes, but you remember that look on him? Sweet as a linnet and smiling like God's gift to gaiety? Well, that was Herr Doktor Schumacher of Dornier, too. And the rest. They're up to something behind our backs. I know it."

"Perhaps they'd treat us with more respect if we had a factory of our own over there?"

He stared at her in astonishment, for he had made the very same suggestion more than once, only to have it turned down out of hand. "We'll stay small and unencumbered," she would say. "Small and ready to jump." Now all he said was, "Do you know something I don't, Mrs Somerville?"

"I don't know anything. But I feel . . ." And she went on to summarize her conversation with Hannah the previous night.

He saw it at once. "We're not big enough to beat them yet – not blow for blow. But we are big enough to be leaned on – isn't that the truth of it. Any one of the big fellas could soon force us into agreements and cartels – or bury us if we won't play the game."

"But if we had a separate outfit in Germany . . ." She smiled, letting the obvious conclusion hang.

He laughed. "Indeed, yes!"

"Have you a firm in mind? Someone ready to sell? We've no time to start from scratch."

"I think I know just our man. One Peter Rosenheim. I'm sure I've mentioned the firm before? Segelflug Hessen?"

"Gliders!"

"Well, they make airframes generally. Very good ones, too. Give me a month and I'll bring it to point of sale. You may put Berlin in your diary for mid-February."

CHAPTER FORTY-ONE

JULIA FLEW THE prototype version of the Fleetliner Mark III to Berlin. Eliot and Mickey McHugh came with her, of course, plus a couple of engineers in the development team. She had to navigate her own way; they spent every minute of the flight taking measurements and making various adjustments. She put down at Hanover, 150 miles short of their destination, to give them the chance to fit shorter-reach plugs and tweak the carburettor settings; the Mark III was the first of the series to have only two engines, the thousand-horsepower Somerville Maelstroms, one on each wing and nothing on the nose. It was still a low-wing monoplane, though the point of attachment had crept a little way up the fuselage, or, rather, the underbelly had grown downward to produce the same effect. As Mickey had once drily commented, Eliot Baring had learned a lot about aircraft design since Dornier had taken up the Fleetliner licence.

Smaller than the previous two marks, it was also an enormous commercial improvement, for it could carry up to twenty passengers in heated comfort, cruising at 195 mph. The interior was again by Jasper Torode, who, to Julia's relief and Crownfield's chagrin (and, indeed, to his own surprise), had got out of domestic work and was now a successful and much-sought-after interior designer of luxury liners, restaurants, and hotels.

Planes from Neville's could refuel at Hanover by arrangement with Messerschmidt, on that firm's account; Julia now took advantage of the facility. As they returned to the machine, having cleared customs and registered their flight plan onward to Berlin, she remarked, "D'you know, I can't remember the last time I flew any Neville plane purely for pleasure."

"If it's fun you're seeking," Eliot began . . . and he finished the sentence with a nod toward dark banks of cloud that were massing on the eastern horizon.

Snow was, indeed, forecast, and not before time. The year 1933, just eight weeks old, had so far been uncommonly mild.

Thanks to the latest in Baring instruments she could, in fact, navigate blind all the way; but to be on the safe side she followed a southerly curve that would take them over Brunswick and Magdeburg, whose lights would, in an emergency, give better landmarks than the smaller towns and villages along the direct railway line between Hanover and Berlin. The leading snowclouds were low, but by the time the Fleetliner was over the Elbe at Magdeburg, the weather was "banked up solid" to 30,000 feet and they plunged from watery sunshine into the gloom of late twilight.

Now they really were flying blind. She called Berlin; remote-controlled radio was another new feature with the Mark III. The operator at Tempelhof advised her to turn back. The cloudbase was down to 300 metres, he said, and there was already a powdering of snow on the runway. He did, however, admit that the fall had eased off and it was not snowing at the moment. She decided to go on.

After a while Eliot came forward and watched the instruments over her shoulder. "Want to turn around?" he asked. "We could still beat this back to Cologne."

She grinned as she answered, never once taking her eyes off the panel, "Let's surprise those blasé Berliners – or don't you trust your own instruments?"

He smiled at the thought. "I'd better watch, then." He sat in the observer seat, behind her and to one side. He spent as much time watching her as the panel – telling himself how useless it was to go on feeling this way about her, wishing she would do something, say something, to liberate him.

"Talking of trust, you certainly can't trust your feelings, can you," she commented.

"Pardon?"

"Without that artificial horizon I'm sure I'd fly this thing steadily downwards at about two degrees. At least – if I close my eyes and try to fly by my own sense of horizon, that's what I tend to do." She glanced toward him – then past him. And her smile faded.

He followed her gaze and saw that ice was beginning to form along the wings.

"Damn!" she exclaimed. "The cloudbase must have lifted. I'll have to go down."

He checked the time. "Any idea where we are?" he asked casually.

"I'll tell you in a mo'," she joked. They were now in a steady descent, trying to get below the layer of supercooled rain – which was the cause of the icing.

"Are you serious?" he asked, a good deal less casually.

She had a map on her lap but there was a better one in her head. "Coming up over Brandenburg," she replied. "About thirty-five minutes to Berlin."

Moments later she was able to add, "What did I say!"

They had broken through the cloudbase at 900 feet and there, not a mile ahead lay the town.

"How d'you know it's Brandenburg?" he asked.

She looked at him in exasperation. "There's the Marienberg – where you caught that butterfly and said something rather sweet to me, if you recall? Not to mention the Ober-Havel and the Unter-Havel and the cathedral. Would you like me to go right down and point out our bedroom at the Schwarzer Adler?"

He grinned. "I guess not. Okay – it's Brandenburg. I can even hear the concertos now. D'you know which road out of town?"

She glanced at the wings and saw that the ice had melted. "I have a better idea," she told him. "Hold onto your hat!" And she pulled back the stick.

Almost immediately they were back in the cloud, but this time they were climbing fast through the icing layer, up, up, into the snow.

"Hey!" Eliot protested.

She passed him the map. "Give me the exact bearing of Tempelhof from Brandenburg. Let's sell these disbelieving Germans some instruments."

He broke into a slow grin as he began measuring her bearing for her.

"I mean," she added, "they're not to know we came down for a fix at Brandenburg, are they? I told them we lost visibility back over Magdeburg somewhere."

"Eight-two, ten," he told her. "That's from Brandenburg cathedral to . . ."

"To the midline of the runway, I hope!"

She levelled at 8,000 feet. Small flurries of snow cluttered the windscreen but the wipers coped.

Around Potsdam the snowfall petered out. "This'll be the leading edge of the let-up Tempelhof mentioned," she said. "Let's hope it lasts all the way."

They remained in thick cloud. She switched off the wipers and held up crossed fingers. But the respite was short-lived. About five minutes before landing – if her reckoning and Baring's instruments were any good – they ran into a blizzard. The snow was so heavy against the wipers that Eliot had to reach under the panel and assist them by hand – something (he made a mental note) that would not have been possible in the production version as presently planned.

By then Julia was committed to the final descent – five degrees on a steady bearing of eighty-two. In silence they watched the altimeter wind its way inexorably down. *Did you put in the right offset for Berlin?* he wanted to ask. And, *what correction did you make for this weather?* The barometer must be down to 730 mm at sea level out there.

At a thousand feet they were still in thick cloud. "This is beginning to look as if it goes down all the way to grass," she remarked. "Thank God we refuelled. And to think I almost decided not to." She glanced briefly toward him. "What have you got to smile at?"

"I was remembering a time when, on a beautiful sunny day and in clear blue skies, you shrieked at the merest suggestion you might take the stick."

Eight hundred feet – and still nothing but gray snow flurries all around.

"You misheard," she told him with mock primness. "I never shriek." But it pleased her to realize that he had not offered to take the controls; it was an unvoiced tribute to her skill. She was, after all, one of the very few women in England with a Class B Transport licence. On paper – and in reality, now – she outclassed him as a pilot.

Mickey McHugh joined them. "Have ye seen a white cat?" he asked, peering earnestly forward. *Jesus!* he thought, catching sight of the altimeter.

They were at six hundred and still cocooned in a world of gray. It was in all their minds that, only a couple of weeks earlier, Bert Hinckler, one of the finest pilots ever, had vanished over Italy in just such a snowstorm.

"Wouldn't you level off?" Eliot suggested hesitantly.

"If I do, we'll overshoot." She kept strictly to her planned descent.

The two men, hardly daring to breathe, watched the visor for any sign of the city. Eliot changed hands and urged the wipers with even greater vigour.

314

As they dipped below five hundred and still nothing was visible even Julia was ready to admit defeat. But part of her urged, *go on!* The result was that she pulled the plane into no more than level flight while she debated with herself.

"Well I vote we go back," Mickey volunteered, to no one in particular.

Julia, agreeing with him at last, gave it full throttle and pulled back on the stick. But at that moment they hit an air pocket and dropped almost a hundred feet in little over a second. Fortunately her previous manoeuvre put them in exactly the right attitude to recover swiftly.

And suddenly there it was! Spread out before them was the mighty city of Berlin and – most beautiful sight of all – directly ahead rose the unmistakable silhouette of Tempelhof Berg.

"By all the holy!" Mickey cried out. "We'd not better that with rails beneath us all the way from Allbury."

She turned and mocked him coolly. "Oh ye of little faith! Now look at Baring – he knew his instruments would get us through, didn't you, old chap?"

Eliot gulped and nodded.

If the Fleetliner had put down only half an hour later, it would have pancaked in the snow; even so, the machine slewed wildly down the runway and had to be flown almost to its halting place. Taxiing was tricky through the uneven drifts but Julia managed to bring them within a hundred yards of the hangar apron; there a tractor fitted with snowchains towed them easily inside its shelter.

As they drew close she recognized it. "We can't go in there," she said. "Surely that's where they keep Lilienthal's glider?"

But the historic old machine was no longer there.

"And Lilienthal himself not dead two weeks," Mickey commented, patting Eliot on the back. "So much for fame, old boy!"

Their reception was little short of reverential. Not that there was any shortage of skilled navigators among the German airmen; indeed, there were at least half a dozen present who, given a sextant, a good chronometer and compass – and a starry night – could fly from Berlin to England and set down in a specified *field,* never mind airport. But in weather like this they wouldn't even take off for a quick suicide.

"How did you do it?" everyone was asking.

The three from Neville's were nonchalance itself.

"Oh, with the proper instruments it's child's play."

"In fact, we quite often land blind – using our latest pilot's assisters, of course"

"What – no sextant?"

"Only for when the assisters fail – which has never happened yet."

The two engineers remained on board, where a sleeping cabin had been rigged for them. They would take turns to guard the plane's secrets and work on the various modifications Baring would now decree for their journey home.

Julia and the two men went directly to their usual hotel, the Kaiserhof in the Zeitenplatz. There Mickey (but only Mickey) was surprised to find he was not expected to share with Eliot.

They dined early, then Eliot returned to the airport to brief the engineers on tomorrow's work; he had the suspicion that he himself might not be rising too early. Julia and Mickey went out to one of the cafés along Unter den Linden, where they had arranged to meet Neville's full-time German agent, Theo Ecker. The snow had stopped falling and workers were out sanding the roads; every inch of the footpath had been swept clear by shopkeepers or janitors of the adjacent buildings, most of which, along the Wilhelmstrasse, anyway, were government buildings.

But which government? Julia wondered; there had been so many these past few years. First Brüning had gone, then von Papen, and now, only a couple of weeks ago, General Schleicher. How long would this new man Adolf Hitler last? The country seemed to be plunging back into chaos. It was a queer time, indeed, to be thinking of setting up shop here.

Nonetheless, the city itself seemed more prosperous and feverish than ever. The Linden was filled with smart cars carrying elegant, fur-clad ladies and fat men in evening dress to all the usual luxury rendezvous. The wail of the saxophone was everywhere, threading its way through the laughter and the aroma of cigars.

"Give me London any day," Julia said, to ward off the unpatriotic comparisons hovering at the edge of her thoughts. "A truly imperial city, eh? All this is so . . . manufactured. Theatrical scenery – that's all it is, you know."

McHugh agreed offhandedly but did not tell her that similar thoughts had crossed his mind about London when he first arrived there, fresh from Dublin.

"And all these uniforms!" she added scornfully. "It's high time these Germans grew up."

Ecker was waiting for them at his usual table in the Bauer café. It had a good view of the door and of the street outside. "You heard we'd landed, then?" Julia remarked as he stood to greet them.

"All Berlin heard it, madame," he replied as he kissed her hand. "It was on the wireless even – miracle landing in blizzard. Of course they say it was a pure fluke."

Julia's hackles rose at once. "Is it too late to get an advertisement in tomorrow's papers?" she asked.

He looked at his watch. "Just text. They couldn't make a block."

Five minutes later a kitchen porter was on his way to three newspaper offices with an advertisement stating that the Fleetliner's only luck was to be equipped with pilot's assisters from Baring Instrumentation – which, by happy chance, could be purchased through one Theo Ecker . . . et cetera.

"And now, dear Theo," Julia asked. "What on earth is going on in this extraordinary country of yours?"

He raised both hands, palms up, in a gesture of shared incomprehension. But he replied: "Not that yours is any less bewildering. These Oxford undergraduates, eh? What about them?"

A couple of weeks earlier the Oxford Union had carried by a majority of 122 the motion, "That this House will in no circumstances fight for King and Country."

Julia bridled at the implied criticism. "They're setting an example to the generals and politicians. If only the students here would do the same! Your Schleichers and Hindenburgs would have to think again. Just look at it!" Her roving eye picked out several tables occupied either by the blackshirted SS or the Brownshirts, the SA.

Theo gave no argument. He knew – because Mickey McHugh had told him – that Julia was angry at her own brother's love affair with the British equivalent of these organizations, Sir Oswald Mosley's Union of Fascists.

"Tell me about Hitler," she said. "We've always treated him as a bit of a joke."

He nodded. "We, too. Until two weeks ago."

"Yes, what happened?"

"Von Papen and Hitler went to Hindenburg in the middle of the night and told him Schleicher was plotting a military coup. Poor old Hindenburg! He's okay before breakfast, they say. After that his mind's gone. And as for the middle of the night . . . well!"

"So he believed them?"

"In a way it was Schleicher's own fault. Months ago he told the old man that Hitler was plotting an uprising, using the Brownshirts. Scum of the earth, of course." Even though the nearest of the uniformed Nazis were well out of earshot, he lowered his voice as he spoke. "But they amount to two and a quarter million men! Schleicher had merely been warning Hindenburg he might have to use the *Wehrmacht*. But all the poor old fool could remember was that Schleicher had told him he'd call out the troops. And so, although Schleicher was still legally chancellor, Hindenburg swore Uncle Adolf into the office, with von Papen as vice chancellor."

Mickey asked, "And does von Papen still imagine he and the president can tame this Hitler?"

Theo shrugged. "It's not so impossible, you know. There are only two other Nazis in the cabinet – one of whom, by the way, is your friend and mine, Captain Hermann Göring . . ."

"So I read. Reich's Minister for Aviation. I want to discuss that, too – but go on."

"I was saying – only three Nazis in the cabinet, against eight on von Papen's side. Not counting Old Father Time."

Julia raised an eyebrow.

Theo explained: "Time is most certainly not on Hitler's side. Nazi popularity is falling. Twelve million in the last election – two million down on the one before. The Reichstag has six hundred deputies. At best Hitler can hope for two hundred and fifty."

"And the communists?" Julia asked.

"A hundred."

"So if he could remove the communists, it'd be only five hundred and he'd stand a chance?"

Theo smiled and shook his head. "He tried that – last week. His stormtroopers marched down to Bülowplatz and ransacked Karl Liebknecht House, the reds' headquarters. They were absolutely sure they'd find treason in every file . . . and they got nothing." His eye wandered to the uniforms at those other tables. "No. Take it from me – Hitler was a product of Germany's defeat . . . the war debt . . . the inflation. He's the man of yesterday. But just look about you. It's a different Germany now. Prosperity is returning. From now on the Nazis can only fade. Or become respectable, which amounts to the same thing."

The waiter brought their coffee and a sinful plate of *Sachertorte*. When he had gone Julia said, "Tell us then about Herr Rosenheim?"

Theo seemed surprised.

"I've seen all the paperwork you sent me. Very good, very thorough – as one would expect. But the *man*. Tell me about the man."

"Will you first tell me one thing, madame? Why this particular firm? You know they make mostly gliders? They have very little to do with powered flight."

Julia encouraged Mickey with her eyes. "It was your choice first, McHugh."

"Mine and Baring's," he agreed. Then, turning to Theo: "Ever since the German gliders swept the board at Biggin Hill a few years ago, we've been very interested in them. We feel they have much to teach us in the way of powered flight, too."

Theo glanced at Julia. "You know it's all been a 'front,' as they call it. Our German gliding clubs are the military without motors. Your amateurs at Biggin Hill were taking on the aces of tomorrow's *Luftwaffe*."

Julia turned to Mickey McHugh. "I hadn't gathered any of this."

He gave a small, noncommittal shrug. "That's why Rosenheim wants to sell. He thinks that phase is over. Dornier and Messerschmidt and Junker have been making military aircraft for at least three years. That's why they're no longer so interested in us. Rosenheim thinks he'll be left with a lot of idle capacity – which is exactly what we're looking for. We're made for each other."

Once again she had the feeling that Mickey was furnishing her with comfortable reasons for doing something that *he* wanted done – and for quite different reasons. Never had she met a man so transparent on the surface, so opaque within.

"And Rosenheim's a Jew?" she asked.

"Yes," Theo replied.

McHugh added, "That's the other reason."

CHAPTER FORTY-TWO

BARING OPENED HIS eyes and found himself staring into Julia's, only inches away. "Oh God," he groaned. "Did I oversleep?"

"We," she corrected. "Haven't we deserved it?" She rubbed his bristly cheek with the tip of her nose and then chuckled. "Hark at me! I've picked up McHugh's habit of answering questions with questions." She snuggled tight against him and added, "Aren't you the living marvel."

His great arms went about her but there was little arousal left in either of them.

"Talking of McHugh," she went on, "what d'you make of him?"

"Hey – what if he goes into my room?"

"Don't worry. He's already left the hotel. He had breakfast at six and went out. That man has a secret life. D'you think he's working for someone – apart from us, I mean?"

"How d'you know all this?" he asked. "I suppose you've been up and about already."

"I tried to phone him about half an hour ago. I went into the sitting room – you looked so angelic. You haven't answered me."

Eliot sighed and turned on his back. She resettled on his chest, listening to his heart and trying to recall when she last felt so relaxed. Not since that day on Lexy's yacht.

He said, "When you say 'working for someone' – do you mean the competition?"

"No."

He was silent awhile. She felt a slight tension growing in him. "Good heavens, Eliot," she exclaimed, "has the same thought occurred to you?"

"Paranoia?" He made it slightly more of a query than a statement. "We spend so much time looking over our shoulders, it gets into the blood."

"Think back carefully – this company of Rosenheim's . . ."

"Segelflug Hessen?"

"Yes. Who suggested it first – you or McHugh?"

After reflection he replied, "It was after Biggin Hill in 1930 – when Kronfeld and Magersuppe wiped the floor with us. You remember that day?"

She remembered Kronfeld, the Austrian, birdlike and sun-bronzed in his immaculately white helmet with the Meyrowitz goggles – which so impressed her that she bought her own pair the very next week. She recalled, too, how he and Magersuppe had stayed up aloft for hours, two German albatrosses soaring over one brief British event after another.

"Sidney Camm was there," she recalled.

"Oh yes. It's beginning to come back now. He looked at the *Wien* and said every designer in England should be forced to study it."

"And didn't Mickey McHugh then say something about Rosenheim and Segeflug Hessen?"

Eliot rose on one elbow, spilling her back onto the sheet. "That's right. He did, too." He straightened the bedclothes over her. "It never occurred to me – but how did he, with his background in automobile engines – how did he know about SH when even I . . . I mean, I don't want to sound like some know-all, but I could have named half a dozen German glider companies. Yet I never heard of SH until that day."

She pulled a dissatisfied face. Now that all the words were out in the open, they didn't seem to amount to much. "Perhaps it is paranoia," she admitted. "After all, he is fanatical about aeroplanes. Always has his nose in *Flight* or *Ikarus* or something. And I've never discovered him snooping in offices where he has no business. And I'll tell you another thing. Hannah Dawson often works late – and you'd never know it because she just has a little pool of light over her desk – I mean, an intruder could walk straight past her office, still thinking he was alone there – and yet she's never mentioned his coming back after hours. Still – it's funny we've both had our doubts."

He scratched the stubble on his chin and prepared to rise. But Julia reached forward and touched his arm. "Just one more thing, my dear."

He looked at her warily.

"Suppose for some reason that we pull back from this German deal. It's going to leave us . . ."

"Is it likely?" He was all ears suddenly.

"No, not at all. But in business one m____
thing. It would leave us still very vuln____
Allbury basket. What would you say t____
company? Not a subsidiary, a fully inde____

"Inside the United States patent cartel?____

"That's a detail, dear."

"It isn't, really – but never mind. This cou____

Her eyes widened with surprise. "It's unli____
quickly. You've been considering it."

He grinned. "Well, I have been thinking of it,____
mentation, as a matter of fact. I was going to raise it____

"Fine. Just as long as I know it's a possibility for Ne____
won't feel McHugh's enthusiasm has pushed us into a____

Now it was she who prepared to rise – and he who stay____
a touch on the arm. "Listen, honey – since this seems to be____
time, perhaps you'll tell me if you have the slightest intentio____
remarrying?"

He saw her eyes go soft with pity, and that was really a____
answer he needed. "Oh, Eliot," she murmured.

"Okay." He leaped briskly from the bed. "I just thought I'd ask.____

"Don't be like that now."

"Like what?"

"What's wrong with our life, just as it is?"

He stared blankly at her as if she had not spoken. "Did I relock the
connecting door? I think I did."

"If we were to marry, we'd risk everything – and for what? That's
the point."

He was hunting in his dressing gown and pyjama pockets for the
key. Their eyes met; hers forced an answer. "It was just a question,"
he said. "I need to know how things stand."

"Every month?"

He found the key and started toward the door. "I don't ask it every
month."

"Often enough, anyway."

He unlocked the door, poked his head forward for a brief peep and
then let the rest of him follow. As he closed it behind him he told
her, "Never again, honey. That I promise you."

It seemed strange to be sitting there in her suite at the Kaiserhof,
buying an entire business, larger than Neville's had been in its first
three years, a business she had never seen, and from a man she had
never before met. True, Mickey McHugh had been to the works,
near Wasserkuppe, many times; and in matters like this she trusted
him absolutely. True, everyone she had spoken to was highly complimentary about the firm, so that, even if what they said were only
half true, the price would still be a bargain. True, too, Peter Rosen-

321

...self was an extremely pleasant and able young man. Yet it
...ot seem right.
...ooked at her watch. Not yet ten. "Is there an air-taxi service
...n?" she asked. "There must be."
...u wish to go somewhere?" Rosenheim asked.
...ow far is Wasserkuppe from here?"
... smiled. "Ah, you wish to see the works?"

Mickey was surprised (which he ought to have been for she had
...er assured him she wouldn't need to see the place), he hid it well.
...ctually," he said, "it's in Rhön, about a hundred and fifty miles to
...e southwest."

"Two hundred forty kilometres," Rosenheim confirmed. "But
here's no need for a taxi, you know. I have my own plane, a Dornier
DO10." He looked at her as if she should know it.

She shook her head.

"They only built two. It's a . . . *Jagdflugzeug*, what's that?"

"Fighter," Mickey translated.

"That's it. I got one. It will get us to Rhön in less than an hour."
He turned to Mickey. "But it's only a two-seater, you know."

"You can take the taxi," she suggested to McHugh. "The weather
looks good."

He stared at her. "What are you hoping to see, Boss?"

She shrugged. "I don't know. Obviously I'm not going to make
an exhaustive survey. I'd just like to see the place before I sign the bill
of exchange. I know the time will come – and soon, probably – when
I can't see everything for myself . . . but it's hard to let go."

Rosenheim's nod suggested it was all very reasonable.

"Would you be needing me at all at all, then?" Mickey asked.

"Only if you feel there's something you'd particularly like to point
out to me on the spot."

He shook his head.

"Excellent," Rosenheim said briskly. "If we leave at once we could
even get back in daylight."

He telephoned the airport to have his plane ready. But as soon as
they walked out on the tarmac she sensed trouble. Two dour-
looking men in semi-military raincoats were waiting by his machine,
a sturdy, high-wing monoplane with typical Dornier lines.

"*Um Gotteswillen!*" Rosenheim said under his breath.

"You know them?" she asked.

"A million of them, Mrs Somerville. They are policemen – but
first they are Nazis."

The older of the two, a pasty-faced man running to seed, said,
with a studious politeness that was in itself offensive, "Herr Rosenheim?"

"Yes."

The younger man, quite handsome but with vacant eyes, was

staring at Julia. She glared back until he had to look away.

"There seems to be a little trouble with your papers," the older policeman explained.

"My papers, or the plane's?"

"The plane's, actually. Would you mind accompanying us to the offices? I'm sure we can sort it out."

"I'm supposed to be taking this lady to Rhön. We wish to return before nightfall."

The younger man asked, "Have you any papers, madame?"

"My passport's at the hotel." Julia spoke in German. "But I'm well known to everybody at this airport."

"Come!" the older one snapped and began marching toward the offices. The younger one trotted to join him.

"What's happening?" Julia asked.

"They're bored," Rosenheim explained wearily. "They'll delay me for half an hour, pretending to sort something out, and then they'll let me go – all smiles again. They have nothing better to do. I'm sorry. Can you wait?"

"But why?" she asked. "Don't they know who you are?"

He laughed. "Of course they know who I am, Mrs Somerville. I am a Jew."

She was appalled. But she responded swiftly. "I have an idea. Turn around and walk towards them."

"Please don't try to be clever," he warned.

"All right, I'll wait," she promised.

But when he was half way toward the two men, both of whom had stopped and turned, she called after him, still in German, "Herr Rosenheim – I know the minister for aviation, Captain Hermann Göring. Shall I telephone him and see if we can sort this out more swiftly?"

Rosenheim froze and looked daggers at her.

The older policeman walked back and stood uncomfortably close to her. "What did you say, madame?"

She gave a smile of puzzled innocence. "I am in a great hurry," she explained. "I happen to know Captain Göring – I believe he's also the Speaker of the Reichstag, though I met him at Herr Willy Messerschmidt's house. He told me, 'if ever you have any trouble with the bureaucracy, Frau Somerville, here is my telephone number.'" She began a search of her bag.

"Gnädige Frau!" The man was all smiles again. "This matter is quite trivial. You are obviously in a hurry – and you say you will be returning tonight?"

"This afternoon, I hope." •

"In that case . . ." He stood back and waved them both toward the plane. "I'm sure we can have everything sorted out by then. Gute Reise! Heil Hitler!"

Rosenheim did a meticulous check of the aircraft – not the check of a careful engineer like McHugh but the check of a frightened man. "Do you really know Göring?" he asked.

She looked all about them before she answered. "I met him once. An odd mixture of the fat, the jolly, and the sinister. I don't suppose he'd remember me but he'd certainly know of Neville's. Anyway I thought it worth a shot."

"So there was no card with his number in your handbag?"

"I could still have tried phoning. They're just petty bullies, those two. Show them a little real power and they wilt. I'm surprised you didn't threaten to call someone high up. Surely *you* know Göring? All those gliders you've supplied to the Luftwaffe?"

He said nothing.

"Are you angry with me?" she asked.

He gave a wan smile. "They will take their revenge – sometime, somehow. They never forget."

She waited until he had completed his inspection; then she asked, "Why so careful?"

He grinned ruefully, as if he agreed with a criticism she had not, in fact, implied. "I know! It's absurd. I'm still too useful for them to try any tricks. But you never know. There's always one madman who'd think it exquisitely funny to see a Jew fall out of the sky."

Paranoia, she thought, seemed to be everyone's lot these days.

The barometer had climbed steadily all night and the day was set cold and fair. They took off eastward in a flurry of snow crystals that spun a circular rainbow, or icebow, in their wake. The view of the city, all in white, in sparkling sunshine, was dazzling. She had to admit that it made London seem a rather domestic and amateurish sort of metropolis. Suddenly she remembered that compelling mental snapshot of Max, seen in Piccadilly in just such a wintry brilliance as this. Even though it had turned out to be someone else, imagination had since triumphed over humdrum fact. That unknown warrior had been Max. Max as a way of life. Max as England.

Then she thought of what her brother had actually become – the kind of fellow who'd guffaw at the petty spite she had just witnessed. It filled her with overweening anger at an ideology that was capable of such transformations. And somewhere down there below her was the vile little man responsible for it all. Heil Hitler, indeed!

"Why d'you put up with it?" she barked into the intercom.

It must have been on his mind, too, for he did not ask what she meant. "What's the alternative?" he asked.

They were out over the lakes already. He had not been boasting when he promised they'd be in Rhön in an hour. He banked into an arc that put the sun and wind behind them.

"Now you've sold up, you could go and live abroad. Come to England, why not? With your talent we'd all be fighting for you."

He made no immediate reply.

"Have you other ties that keep you here?" she ventured.

She saw he was pointing downward, with a gesture that took in the snowclad fields, the dark woodlands, the huddled little villages. "It's my fatherland, too," he told her. "Why should they take it from me?"

She remembered how meekly he had been prepared to go along with the two Nazis; his question, in that context, was odd. "Will you fight them for it?" she asked.

There was a pause before he replied, "In my own way."

"D'you think there's going to be a war?"

He laughed, as if he supposed she must be joking.

Exactly fifty-four minutes after takeoff they landed in a private field behind his house in Rhön. His mother did not come down to greet them but waited in her boudoir like royalty. *Like a Swedish princess, actually,* Julia thought as she was ushered into The Presence. Though Frau Rosenheim must have been all of fifty, she was petite, blonde, svelte, and extremely well preserved. Whatever change in fortune or way of life might attend this sale of her son's business, she betrayed not the slightest interest in it, much less anxiety. Her talk was all of fashionable London, Paris, Berlin; she was, Julia considered, the least likely woman one might meet, there in the heart of rural Germany. She at least could surely have no roots here.

But of the son she felt less certain.

They ate a light lunch downstairs. Frau Rosenheim joined them but merely toyed with her food. When she had gone, Julia asked about his father.

"He died in the war." And then, with a smile, he added, "Fighting for our fatherland."

He showed her around the works and then took her up to the launching site at Wasserkuppe. Everything was, of course, exactly as Mickey McHugh had led her to expect it; Peter Rosenheim was plainly much more than just a brilliant glider designer. What Eliot had once said about good engineering also applied to businesses; if they were good, they looked good, too. They had a good feel about them. Segelflug Hessen GMBH had a very good feel. She could sign the bill of exchange with an easy mind.

But now the man himself was even more of a puzzle than ever. It was hard to equate the confident, forceful young fellow who had built up such an enterprise with the meek victim who had been prepared to kowtow to those two bullies at Tempelhof.

They had the wind, such as it was, against them on the return flight; it added eight minutes to their time. As they approached Berlin the lights were being kindled, turning the city, point by twinkling point, into a vast carpet, studded with diamonds. "For this privilege," he called through the intercom, "the emperors of old would have squandered whole armies."

When they landed she suggested he put his plane beside the Fleetliner, where her own people could keep an eye on it. He was pleased to accept. Of the two policemen there was no sign.

They went straight back to the Kaiserhof where they put their signatures to all the necessary instruments without further delay. Then Rosenheim asked the three of them out for an evening on the town. He would return to collect them at eight.

"Well?" McHugh asked Julia as she poured them both a well-earned drink. "And what did you learn that you didn't already know?"

"I wouldn't know where to begin," she told him.

CHAPTER FORTY-THREE

BERLIN, HALT EIN! proclaimed the poster. *Besinne Dich. Dein Tänzer ist der Tod!*

"Who puts up messages like that?" Julia asked in bewilderment.

"The government," Rosenheim told her. "The previous one, of course."

"*Berlin, stop!*" She translated it, feeling she might have missed something. "*Wake up. You're dancing with death!*" It still seemed an odd message, especially for a government to promote.

"It's from a poem by Paul Zech," Rosenheim explained, going on to quote:

"With beastly jaws and vulture claws,
They abandon themselves to the ultimate joy
And dance while the thunder mimes applause.
To the beat of the drum, their lips decoy.
Berlin, awaken! Take hold, take hold!
Oh, can't you see – you dance with gold.

. . . and so on. In each verse we dance with something different until we end up – of course – with Death for our partner."

"Of course," Julia echoed with a shiver. "But not tonight, let's hope."

"No." Rosenheim rubbed his hands. "Tonight we might just be

lucky."

"Why d'you say *we?*" she asked. "Are you a Berliner?"

He grinned. "Tonight we are all Berliners. Well now, let's see. There are places we talk about and patronize and there are places we don't talk about but we patronize them just the same."

"At which of them can we dance?" she asked.

"At all of them, naturally."

She laughed. "Then naturally we'll go to all of them."

"Right!" He turned up his collar and pointed a stiff left arm, hand extended – a curiously military gesture – up the Friedrichstrasse. "To the Café Zielka and then the Schwarze Kater."

She took his other arm and linked with Eliot on her right. As they set off, laughing, she turned and glanced at Mickey McHugh and said, "This is your triumph, you know."

"Sorry, Boss." He laughed, too. "Was I looking miserable?"

"No – just inscrutable."

Her previous taste of Berlin's nightlife had been confined to the theatres and revues; its café society was something new. The city, she now learned, had one small thing in common with London, something that set it apart from both Paris and Vienna: Its night life was dictated by the locals rather than by tourists. So London's was either decorously daring or ferociously fey; where it descended into seediness, it was more sad than vicious, an eternal "morning after." Berlin's by contrast, was an endless "night before" – the next day being Armageddon (for which Berliners had their own pet name: *Amusemang*).

For Julia the evening dissolved in a rapid succession of smoky cellars, sweating bodies, frenetic dancing, opulent salons, cramped tables, cups of coffee, sweetly burning liqueurs, and something truly vile called *Weisse mit Schuss,* which tasted like (and possibly was) beer and raspberry syrup. She soon lost count of the number of places they visited; their names melted in one great blur of unfulfilled promises – black cats, blue monkeys, old Bavarias, bulls on roofs, golden cockerels . . .

Most had cabaret between dances, much of it political. One *Conferancier* told a story of a homosexual law student whose lover was his professor. The older man was trying to guide the younger toward the answer: "because they are of unsound mind." He beamed at the sweet youth and said, "Come, come, now – some people, though proven guilty of assault are acquitted because they are minors . . . others because they acted in self-defence . . . and yet others because they are . . . what? What is the third category that always secures an acquittal?" At which the young man brightened and replied, ". . . because they are *Nazis!*" Everyone laughed, to be sure, but Julia noticed the way they all looked around at their neighbours, almost as if first seeking permission to find the joke funny. The city's nerve was yielding to mere nervousness.

But where the humour avoided those dangers, where it was merely surrealist ("He gave me a kidney punch though my usual drink is a liver cocktail . . ."), the audience joined in and the comedian on the stage became no more than first among equals – the equals being at the tables all around. Even the poorest acts – things that a London audience would have hissed out of town – were tolerated for the chance they gave to the crowd. One such act was a wild-eyed, half-naked girl who must surely have been high on cocaine. She came on, clutching a broken violin bow, and started to leap about in a way that jarred every bone and joint in her skinny little body. In the corner of the stage sat an old Chinaman playing *Bei mir bist du schön* on a wheezing accordion (though it was three choruses before anyone recognized the tune). From the way they glowered at each other, it seemed that they were actually two separate acts, each refusing to yield. Certainly the dance bore no relationship whatever to the music, which finished while the girl was still half-way through her piece.

Ribaldry swiftly supplied a new accompaniment. A respectable-looking man stood up and waved a slip of paper, shouting, "Telegram! Telegram for Fräulein Gebühr!" That was, apparently, the young lady's name, though she paid not the slightest attention.

Everyone laughed. "What's it say? Read it out!"

Fussily he put on pince-nez. "Your lover has shot himself. Your babies have been burned. Your husband has taken his teeth out of pawn and is on his way. Hugs and kisses – your ever-loving Mamma."

Still the girl went galumphing on amidst gales of laughter.

"P.S.," he added. "Please put out the cat when you get home."

"He must be part of the act?" Julia commented.

"No, no. This is Berlin. You watch."

"Augustus, you old Jew!" shouted someone from the back. "Where's your wife tonight?"

A stout old man, seated next to the self-appointed telegraph boy, stood up and rounded on his questioner. "Well at least she's not with you," he cried. "Who is that tempting little beauty at your side?"

The woman in question, who was of no more than average appearance, blushed with pleasure and hit her companion, dragging him back into his seat.

The woman beside Augustus stood up and announced, "Actually, I am here."

The applause was crazy. The wild-eyed thing on the stage saw her chance and fell into a curtsey; even that was incompetent. Someone ran on from back stage and pulled her off. The band came back on and then the very architecture was drowned in a heaving mass of jazz-stirred bodies.

An hour or so later, they had somehow found their way around – or across? Julia could no longer be sure – the Tiergarten and were in a plush establishment called the Café des Westens in the Kurfürstendamm. They were hardly through the door when a complete stranger rounded on Julia and snapped, "Hurry along with that wine, Miss."

She, ready for anything by now, snapped back at him, "You didn't pay me for the last lot yet."

He at once became most apologetic and asked what he owed.

"What was it?" she asked. "Two bottles of Avelsbacher, yes?"

"Er . . . yes."

"Two bottles at 13.75 Marks each is 35.20 – plus ten per cent, comes to 42.45." She held out her hand in a manner that brooked no challenge.

He gave her fifty and said to keep the change. She bought a raffle ticket with it and – several dances and glasses later – won a live monkey (which the management privately bought back for 200).

Later still she found the man who had challenged her over the wine and gave him his fifty back. But he wouldn't take it. He said one dance with her would be a better recompense. He was a poor dancer, though, so she considered he'd got his money's worth.

They were just about to leave when a man rushed in in great excitement and announced that the Reichstag building had burned to the ground.

At first everyone laughed and offered the man drinks for a good try. But then others arrived, repeating the story, and it began to seem as if it might be true.

Mickey McHugh, who had gone to the telephone the moment the first announcement was made, returned and confirmed it – not, curiously enough, to Julia but to Peter Rosenheim.

Suddenly everyone was most dreadfully sober. They searched about them like lost souls; eyes met eyes, but no world-weary Berliner quip lay behind them, ready to be challenged into the open.

"Let's go and see for ourselves," Rosenheim suggested.

He alone seemed quite calm. Eliot thought only of protecting his Julia. Mickey McHugh was deep in some private calculation. "They won't let us near it," he said.

"Not if we go along the streets," she replied. "But perhaps if we approach through the Tiergarten?"

"It's worth a try," Rosenheim agreed.

The park was full of people with the same idea. Moments after they entered it the light, cold, easterly wind brought them the acrid smell of burning and before they were half-way across they could see the glow where it lit the undersides of billowing smoke clouds.

By now they began to meet one or two who, having seen their fill, were on their way home, against the general tide. Avid questions were asked and the word soon spread. The fire had started around nine that evening.

"Just as we went to our first café!" Julia marvelled. "And all the while we've been enjoying ourselves." It seemed incredible that the parliament could have been burning down while they, and so many hundreds of others, had been taking such mindless pleasure, not two miles away.

It had been started by the communists.

No, the Jews.

No, the Nazis themselves . . .

The police had arrested a Dutch Jew called van der Leyden . . .

No, he came from Leyden . . . and he was no Jew but a communist.

Hitler had stood and watched it with tears streaming down his face.

The poor Führer – he'd see justice done.

At last they stood in the throng that had pressed forward among the trees, as close as the police cordon allowed. Ropes had been stretched from tree to tree and the German crowd, suddenly very orderly, determined to be proper, stood in silence and watched democracy's embers die. The façade of the grand old edifice stood, but the heart of it had gone.

Mickey McHugh turned to Julia. "Remember what you said to Theo Ecker?"

She shook her head.

"'If he could get rid of a hundred communists . . . '" he quoted.

"*Dein Tänzer ist der Tod!*" Rosenheim murmured. "The waiting is over."

His unnatural, almost triumphant, calm began to annoy Julia. "It is for you," she snapped. "What about me? I've just bought a business here."

CHAPTER FORTY-FOUR

JULIA WAS RIGHT about Frau Rosenheim. She must have had some money in her son's firm; the moment she got her hands on it, she moved to Paris. But as to Rosenheim himself, Julia was wrong. In her bones she had felt he would stay on in Germany and join the opposition to the Nazis. Yet a few weeks after she returned to London, leaving Mickey McHugh to supervise the transformation of Segelflug Hessen into Neville Flugzeugwerke GMBH, a powered-aircraft works, Peter Rosenheim was knocking at her door, cap in hand.

He had a scheme for a fifty-fifty partnership in building ultra-light sporting planes powered by ordinary motor-cycle engines – capitalizing on his unrivalled understanding of gliders. It appealed to Julia because the idea went against all the conventional wisdom of the past ten years. Ask anyone in the business and he'd assure you that small power plants made for impractical machines. De Havilland's Moth – and, indeed, the Amazon – were considered to be the smallest workable planes. Since then the tendency had been to go bigger, as with the DH Leopard Moth and with one of Neville's latest machines, the four-seater Orinoco, an upgrading of the Amazon intended chiefly for the air-taxi business.

Julia was long enough in the tooth by now to be wary of cranks – and the aircraft industry had an unfair share of them. Technical expertise was no guarantee against the affliction, for every company had its coven of plausible lunatics in the drawing office. If she had not actually seen Rosenheim's factory at Rhön, she might have dismissed him as just another magnificent dreamer. As it was, she started the process that might, in a month or two, lead to the formation of a new company aimed at a market that conventional wisdom said did not exist.

She took him to lunch at the Savoy on the strength of it. Randy Gold, now Special Assistant to the Manager (rather than mere Assistant Manager) spotted her the moment they entered and he ushered them in great style to her favourite table. He spoke like a family

331

friend and quite shamelessly pumped Rosenheim for details of his business – just like his father but without the rascally humour that made it tolerable. To shut him up Julia asked about Imogen Davis.

He gave her a saucy grin. "Oh, your brother put a stop to all that, Mrs Somerville. Still, it was good while it lasted. I can't complain."

At that moment Dolly walked in – and Wallace just behind her. For a second or so Dolly hesitated and Julia knew she was toying with the idea of failing to notice her. But then Wallace waved and nudged his wife, drawing her attention, superfluously, to where it was already anxiously lodged.

"Things must be looking up," Julia commented as they drew near. Rosenheim stood up.

"Haven't you heard?" Dolly replied. "I've got the part."

"The part," Julia repeated flatly.

"*The* part," Wallace explained; he smiled at Rosenheim.

"Oh forgive me." Julia made the introductions and invited the newcomers to join them. The sommelier came to take their order for drinks.

"Compliments of the management," Randy Gold chipped in.

After that it would have seemed churlish for Dolly to demur. Two extra places were conjured up.

Julia thanked Gold junior and said, "*Do* convey my best regards to your father." Her manner suggested *at once!* Reluctantly he went.

"What a creepy-crawly," Dolly remarked.

"Have you ever met him before?" Julia asked Rosenheim.

"Not to my knowledge."

"He seemed extraordinarily keen to learn more about you. I wonder what's on his mind?"

Dolly started explaining to Rosenheim about Sidney Gold and his connection with Neville's; the words came fast and the smile was brittle. Julia let her tell it all, hoping she could talk herself calm again. It would also help if Wallace, bloody fool, could take his eyes off her.

"Tell us about this part," she invited, the moment Dolly finished.

Talking about herself always helped.

"I haven't actually got it yet – or not quite. There's some Broadway angel who has the final nod. But they say it's a bagatelle."

"Oh!" Julia was all excitement. "You're playing a *bagatelle* at last! How marvellous! Isn't that what you've always longed for?"

Dolly frowned and then glanced at Wallace, suspecting joint mockery.

"You forgot to tell her," he explained with the sort of wary gentleness lovers use after a recent quarrel. Then he turned to Julia. "It's the part of a lifetime, actually – the lead in Lexy's 'Héloïse' when it transfers to Broadway." He turned to Rosenheim. "Forgive all this shop-talk."

Julia reached over and squeezed her sister's hand. "Sorry I teased, darling. No wonder you're excited – isn't it the best news ever?"

Dolly, happy again, clutched her husband's arm and said, "I owe it all to this one."

Wallace gave a modest bow. "If you say so."

"All that medieval philosophy – nominalism and realism and stuff. He actually understands it!"

"Be honest, darling," he exclaimed jovially. "We help each other. You've helped me understand a lot, too. For instance, how it feels to be a man like Peter Abélard."

Dolly pretended to take it as a joke – not in the best of taste, perhaps, but nothing more than a joke. Half slipping into the part of Héloïse, she pouted à la parisienne and pinched him just slightly too hard.

Rosenheim adroitly changed the subject; he took up Wallace's earlier comment. "None of this is shop-talk to me," he said. "I have many theatre-friends in Berlin."

Wallace became serious at once – seriously interested, that is. "Ah yes – Berlin. Do tell us."

He meant, of course, the Reichstag fire and its aftermath. The dining room went quiet for several tables around while the two who had actually been there retold their experience – everyone pretending to moments of profound reflection, or studious interest in a wine list that had not changed markedly in years.

Then came the question everyone wanted to ask, especially Julia, who had not been in Germany for the past month: What were things like now?

Rosenheim shrugged and said diffidently, "It's exactly as you would predict if you had no crystal ball and must rely on common sense. First the Nazis suspended the six constitutional freedoms . . ."

"Our papers are saying that the Terror was over in two weeks after the fire," Wallace interpolated.

"It's not true. Every day there are unidentifiable bodies found in the parks of Berlin. Indeed, of every town. No one is safe. Frau Ebert, widow of the first president – her house was turned upside down. Professor Einstein – the same. Looking for explosives, they claimed."

"The fools!" Wallace commented. "Don't they realize he hides all his best explosives in his head?"

Rosenheim laughed grimly. "That's one for the cafés."

"Is it only Jews and communists?" Dolly asked.

"No. *Innocent* people, too," he replied solemnly.

She was chagrined. "I'm sorry, I didn't mean it that way."

He sighed. "No one ever does. It's going to be a bad year for Jews and piebald dogs."

Dolly almost fell into it twice.

"What's your theory?" Wallace asked. "I mean, they did catch this

Dutchman, van der Lubbe, red handed. And he is a communist. And he has set fire to a number of other buildings – and he has confessed to this one."

"I believe he was Satan's gift to the history books of Europe."

"It's all invented?"

"No – it's all true! But no half-crazed republican, wandering around the Reichstag like that – with a box of matches and a bundle of household firelighters – could possibly create such a blaze. I think he boasted beforehand what he was going to do, some Nazi heard him, and then they just followed him around with cans of petrol and their own matchboxes. I'm sure he thinks he did it all – the glory of his career as a fire raiser. He'll go to his death swearing he was alone. As I say – Satan's gift to history."

Wallace licked his lips. "I thought it would just be a showpiece trial. It's beginning to sound as if it might be an interesting one to cover."

Rosenheim was suddenly, and uncharacteristically, eager. "You should. You must. The whole world must be there. I tell you – if God hasn't turned his back on us – he may have one trick to answer Satan. The Nazis declared at once that Ernst Torgler, who was head of the communist bloc in the Reichstag, was in the plot with the Dutchman. They thought he'd try to flee, of course, and that would be his confession of guilt. Instead he gave himself up and demanded a trial. Very astute! They can't try just those two. They'll have to round up a few more. And then the whole case will fall to shreds."

Wallace, who had watched him shrewdly throughout this speech, said, "Forgive me if this seems impertinent, Herr Rosenheim, but may I ask why you've left Germany?"

"Have you seen this morning's papers?" He laughed. "That must seem impertinent to you!"

"You mean this business of boycotting the Jewish shops?"

He nodded. "That's only the beginning."

Wallace's eyebrows politely, but unconvincingly, conceded the point. "The general belief here is that Hitler's simply rewarding the faithful with a brief orgy of Jew-baiting. But once he feels the responsibility of office – starts moving in international circles – he, and even more important, his financial backers, will pull in their horns and start behaving decently."

For once Rosenheim appeared to have no immediate answer. He was silent so long that Julia almost felt she ought to reply for him – something soothing to the effect that Wallace was probably right. But at last the man looked up from his reverie and told them, "It hurts me to say this – especially as a Jew it hurts me. But I believe that the show trial and the persecutions, the arrests, the tortures, the deaths . . . all this is just a diversion. It takes the eyes of the world away from what the Nazis are really doing."

"Which is what?" Julia asked.

He looked at her then, spoke only to her. "Bruno Walter is prevented from conducting at Leipzig and then in Berlin – and every newspaper in the world is full of it. Dornier convert the DO P to military use in public trials in Switzerland and" – he glanced at Wallace – "how many paragraphs did you give it?" He swung back to Julia. "That's what the Nazis are really doing, Mrs Somerville. Day by day by day."

She studied him thoughtfully. "And I suppose," she said at last, "that ultra-light planes would find a useful role among the infantry?"

He gave an expansive, central-European shrug. "I could not have kept it a secret for ever."

Mickey McHugh was furious when he heard of Rosenheim's proposal.

"It puts me in such an impossible position, Boss," he complained. "You've no idea what this new government is like."

"On the contrary, I think I have a better idea than most."

"You're a one-eyed woman in the country of the blind," he replied with a smile – though there was no humour in his eyes.

"I've always admired your frankness, McHugh," she warned.

He reined himself in. "Well, the point is, they're not at all happy at the way we bought out Segelflug Hessen. They had no more use for gliders. In another few weeks they'd have started squeezing Rosenheim out in their own not-too-subtle way. And then . . ."

"You mean we paid more than we needed? We could have got it cheaper if we'd waited?"

McHugh caught her note of sarcasm. "Oh no," he replied at once. "Both Dornier and Heinkel . . ." He paused and then added in quite a different voice, "Well, they were showing mild interest."

The response immediately struck her as odd. He had plainly been going to say that the two German firms were keenly interested – and it would have been all the more credit to him that he had snatched the prize from beneath their noses. So why did he change his mind and complete the sentence in a way that weakened his own case?

And why did she always find herself asking questions like this about Mickey McHugh?

She returned to the original point. "You're saying that the new German government is annoyed with us for buying out Rosenheim at something close to full market value?"

He nodded. "And now, if they hear that Neville's is in some kind of partnership with him – well, we might as well close down at Rhön."

Her face fell. "Is it as serious as that?"

"I'm afraid so, Boss."

She sighed. "In that case, you can convey my assurances to . . .

whoever you like, that Neville's will not be going into partnership with Herr Rosenheim. Furthermore, you will do everything in your power to conform to the wishes of the new German government and assure them of our closest cooperation in any venture they may propose."

She had never seen a man look so relieved, though he did his best to hide it. He furrowed his brow and said, "It's unlike you to make up your mind so quickly, Boss – if I may say so without being accused of unbecoming frankness again."

She grinned as if he had caught her out. "Candidly, I had already decided it."

"Well," he almost sang. "We can make a fortune over there. The German plane makers will be so busy with government orders, we'll have a clear run at the civil field."

"That's the whole idea," she agreed.

The moment he had gone she put through a call to Brown's, where Rosenheim was staying, and left a message for him to call back on her direct line.

At five o'clock the phone rang, but it was not Rosenheim.

"I hope you don't mind, Julia." It took some moments for her to register the voice as Wallace Baker's. "Using your ex-directory number, I mean. Dolly gave it me. I'm calling apropos our most enjoyable lunch last week. I thought I'd let you know that I shall, after all, be covering the arson trial – which opens in Leipzig, by the way, not Berlin. I'm going over for the *Express* group. The Beaver asked me to."

He paused as if he expected some response from her.

"Bully for you," she told him.

"Anyway – I was wondering – things being as they are – whether you'd like me to carry messages either way, or see anyone for you over there?"

She was silent a long while.

"Hello?" he prompted.

"You speak German?" she asked.

"I learned it as a prisoner of war. Bit rusty, but . . ."

Still half-thinking of Mickey McHugh she went on, "As a matter of fact, there is something you might be able to do for me – you better than anyone. But I couldn't possibly tell you over the phone. Can we meet somewhere?"

"I don't suppose you know the French pub in Soho?"

"Indeed I do. I've been there with Lexy."

"I'll see you there."

She looked up the number of the pub and called Brown's again, to leave it for Rosenheim. Then she went out to her car.

Motoring down the Edgware Road she found herself thinking about the quarrel that Wallace and Dolly had made no effort to

336

conceal. It worried her. True, they had survived quarrels before, some of them quite hot. No – *all* of them quite hot. Perhaps that was what worried her now. This present hostility was cool. The heat that might reweld their marriage was simply not there any longer.

All at once she felt it would be wrong, even dangerous, to go through with this rendezvous. She must call the French pub and leave an excuse. Her eye caught the red of a telephone kiosk a couple of hundred yards ahead. She dropped her speed and pulled in just before it. In her distraction she misjudged her distance from the kerb and had to back a little closer – which was how she came to notice the unpretentious little Morris Cowley pulling in about thirty yards behind. Oddly enough, the same vehicle had been parked outside de Havilland's gate as she had driven out of Neville's; she had noticed it as it swung into the Edgware Road behind her.

She fished out her powder compact and, using its mirror, saw that the car contained two well-built men in their thirties. Were they following her, or had she caught Rosenheim's paranoia? She had to know before she made her call.

She walked past the kiosk and into a newsagent's, where she bought a local paper. She pretended to check some item in it as she returned to her car. Then she set off again.

And so did the Cowley.

She turned left at Kilburn and began to weave her way eastward, going by Swiss Cottage toward Regent's Park. The Cowley followed her at what its driver must have considered a discreet distance but her route was such a way-to-nowhere that she could no longer doubt they were tailing her.

Even in imagination she had never faced this situation. In rare, morbid moments she had wondered what it would be like to be followed on foot – by sex fiends or purse snatchers, for instance. But this was not like that. These men were simply keeping her under surveillance. Though they threatened no violence, their leech-like tenacity seemed far more menacing. And her response to that menace, too, was more deeply disturbing than anything she might have predicted.

For the first time in her life she was seized by the terrors of absolute loneliness, an icy panic in the pit of her guts. It had nothing to do with being alone; after all, she was quite used to that. Indeed, she had lately learned to relish it, her man-free self-sufficiency, as the proof that she had at last grown into full maturity. But this loneliness was different. It was a blind, unreasoning terror. Not all the crowds in London could dispel it.

She must shake off these two men. That meant leaving the Bugatti somewhere and trying to lose them in a crowd. On the Tube perhaps. Where was the nearest station? She never used the Tube; the only one she could think of was at Baker Street, on the far side of

Regent's Park. She gave a little laugh of relief as she recalled that old friends of hers, the Fairbairns, lived nearby in Cornwall Terrace; Penelope would be out at this time of day but that wouldn't affect the plan she had in mind.

As she drove around the Outer Circle of the park she fiddled with the ignition and the advance-retard lever until she induced the engine to backfire a couple of times. Then, in seeming disgust, she pulled into Cornwall Terrace and parked outside the Fairbairns, where she rang the bell and left the key with the butler. To her pursuers it would look as if she were arranging for a mechanic to collect the beastly thing. Then she set off on foot for Baker Street.

She walked toward the parked Cowley, giving the two men the incurious stare of a casual passer-by; they were poring over a tourist map of central London. As she turned the corner into Baker Street they got out.

She took the Bakerloo Tube as far as Piccadilly Circus. There was no sign of her two followers but she did not relax until she had left the Tube far behind and was pressing through the crowds into Shaftesbury Avenue; and even then, notwithstanding the throng, that sense of loneliness was almost overpowering still.

It was mid-April. Bulbs were flowering in all the window-boxes; spring was on the wind. The Soho girls were turning out on all the pavements, tapping their heels at the going-home trade. Their hard, incurious eyes assessed her and lost interest almost in the same moment; on that wave of indifference she drifted along the small, rather village-like streets to the French pub.

Wallace Baker was waiting for her; he had even ordered a gin and French, remembering that was what she had had at lunch.

She downed it in one. He raised an eyebrow, but all he said was, "There's been a phone call for you."

She took out a cigarette; as she was tucking the case back into her handbag his lighter snapped into flame at exactly the right position. She inhaled deeply, gratefully. "I think I know who it is." The words raised a smokescreen before her eyes. Wafting it away she asked, "D'you mind? Have you time?"

He pulled the phone toward her and gave her the number. Moments later she was through to Rosenheim. "That business we were talking about," she said. "I'm ringing you to say that, no matter what you may hear to the contrary, we're still on. Keep this entirely to yourself, mind, but 'we' means me in person, not Neville's. When would you like us to meet?"

His response was cautious, not at all enthusiastic.

"Are you free to speak?" she asked.

He laughed then. "Oh yes, nothing like that. To tell the truth, I may have to postpone my plans for a year or so. I've had a very tempting offer of a job in South America."

"That's a long way away," she said neutrally.

"I thought so, too. At least you have a year to think it over . . . discover the market. That's always been your strong point at Neville's – finding the right market."

She wished him bon voyage and good luck. "Short and sweet," she commented to Wallace as she dropped the earpiece back in its cradle.

With a practised hook of his finger he lowered the instrument into its niche behind the bar.

She took out her compact to powder her nose.

"You seem on edge," he told her.

She snapped the compact shut and stared at him in terror. "Those two men," she said, almost in a whisper. "The ones who've just come in."

"I saw them." His eyes did not move from her face. "What about them?"

She told him.

He took no time at all to reach a decision. "Just finish your drink, quietly and slowly, and leave." His smile, his calm, infinitely confident voice filled her with reassurance. "Turn right outside and take the next little alley on your right. Don't look back, okay?"

She nodded. "What are you going to do?"

"Oh, I'll finish my drink, too."

"I mean with them?"

He simply smiled. "Have you noticed them before today?"

"No." His raised eyebrow puzzled her. "Why – have you?"

He nodded. "After our luncheon at the Savoy. The taller one, he was reading a newspaper in the foyer and he followed you and Rosenheim without much effort at concealment. In fact, I wondered if he was a bodyguard."

She shook her head.

"How about Eliot?" he asked bluntly. "Would he hire one without telling you – not wishing to worry you, I mean?"

The implications behind the question were vast. How could he know about Eliot? Had Dolly taunted him with it after Max had blurted it out? "And as for my adorable sister, don't imagine she's pining away for *you!* She's getting all she wants from that hunk of Yankee beef!" Was her name bandied between them like that? Were things so open already?

"It hadn't occurred to me," she confessed. "But I don't think they could be . . . no, I'm sure that's not it." She downed the last of her drink.

"Good enough for me," he told her. "Away you go."

The men took no pains to disguise their pursuit. As she reached the little alleyway she heard the pub door open and close again. She walked the full length of it, straining her ears for the slightest sound –

or the slightest unusual sound over the throb of the city. She was a few paces from the far end when she heard Wallace's cry: "Okay now. Carry on round the block!"

But curiosity got the better of her and she retraced her steps instead. The two men were sprawled among a litter of cardboard boxes and dustbins just inside the entrance to the alley. She stared at them, and then at him, in disbelief. "What did you do to them?" she asked.

"They'll be all right," was all he'd say.

They went back to the pub and resumed the seats they had vacated not three minutes earlier. But in those three minutes her estimate of Wallace Baker had changed drastically. She had thought him a fairly ordinary, decent, medium-everything sort of man. Yet there had always been something about him that had unnerved her, attracted her against her will, and, indeed, her conscience, too. Now she knew why. Beneath his deceptive exterior was that quality of toughness and danger which always exercised such a powerful hold on her. Now she hung on every word he said.

"Nasty thing," he told her. "Being followed. Especially for a woman."

"I'm afraid I panicked. I don't suppose you know what it means?"

"Panic?" He grinned. "It's when buff envelopes saying Westminster Bank drop on your doormat. I don't suppose *you* know what that means!"

"How can you be so calm?"

For a while he stared at his hands. Then, with a dry little chuckle, he told her, "I almost rang through here and cancelled, you know. I must have had a premonition."

"Me too," she murmured softly.

For a long moment their eyes dwelled in each other's. The universe shrank until its limits were around them like a cocoon. The bar and all the people in it . . . Soho, London . . . everything vanished.

Their knees touched; they trembled; his hand closed over hers. And all at once that sense of loneliness became a distant memory.

The world about them began once more to lap at her eyes and ears. "What now?" she asked.

CHAPTER FORTY-FIVE

SHE DID NOT repeat her question. The answer was already spoken in their eyes, in the touch of their hands. It lay on the very air between them.

They finished their drinks at leisure and strolled out into the evening. A small crowd was milling around the entrance to the alleyway, a policeman among them. Wallace took Julia's arm and steered her in the opposite direction. "They were both wearing English tweed, by the way," he told her. "But the tailoring was German, a firm in Berlin."

"Ah."

They did not worry her in the slightest now.

In Old Compton Street he paused before an Italian warehouse-man. "I've nothing in the fridge," he said. "Let's see what strikes our fancy."

Why did he say *"I've* nothing in the fridge," she wondered.

He chose with a discrimination rare among Englishmen – and a frugality that was surely unique in his trade. Was he really so poor or was it just diehard habit? Either way he was the first person to make her feel that poverty might have its romantic side – the poverty of bohemia rather than of Dalston.

"I'll buy the wine," she offered, choosing two bottles of a suitably modest piesporter.

Outside she added, "This is the first time in my life that I've carried any kind of parcel in the street. Where's best for a taxi?"

"Let's walk," he suggested.

"Walk!"

He turned to her. "You've never done that, either?"

She shook her head. "Not when there are taxis around."

It was a night for firsts, but neither of them said it. Suddenly she felt half her age, a young girl in love again.

No, not again. She had never walked anywhere, with any man, in quite this mood of . . . the only word that occurred to her was "fatalism" – blissful fatalism.

In Brewer Street he nudged her and pointed at a huge playbill on the side wall of the Queen's theatre. The name Dolly Savile was at its head.

"She's in all four acts," he remarked.

To Julia it seemed irrelevant – news from a forgotten war. Even if she were assured that Dolly was just ten minutes behind them, would follow them to . . . wherever they were going, would break down the door and catch them *in flagrante,* even so, she would not falter by a single footstep.

"They were probably trailing Rosenheim, not you," he said. "If he's managed to give them the slip, they'd reckon you were the one most likely to lead them back to him."

She laughed happily. "I think they'll try some other lead next time."

At Regent Street she could contain her curiosity no longer. "I thought you lived in Holborn?" she asked.

"I have a room in South Audley Street, too."

Had he and Dolly already split up, then? But why did he say "too," as if the joint home were still intact? She felt an impulse to ask but realized it would change the nature of what was about to happen. She did not want that. Above all, it had to be total, unconditional, heedless of consequences.

Similar reflections must have been on his mind, too, for when they had safely negotiated the traffic and were strolling down Burlington Gardens, he began to tell her of a recent interview with some famous psychiatrist she'd never heard of.

"Nor had I," he confessed wryly. "He has a theory that sounds completely absurd at first, but I've been thinking about it more and more lately and I can't shake it off. It's to do with time – with the extraordinary way it unfolds in our lives."

He was silent for a while, as if there were too many thoughts to marshal. She did not press him.

"At first," he went on, "he wouldn't generalize about it. He just gave me example after example. One that I remember vividly was the story of a patient of his, a woman, who eventually became so disturbed she had to be certified. But he described the process from the woman's childhood onward. And it swiftly became clear that every bit of her madness, which occurred in her sixties, arose out of things that had been done to her in her childhood and teens."

"Cause and effect," Julia suggested.

He chuckled. "Yes. I can feel you're having the same difficulty as I had at first. I kept thinking, *What's so remarkable about all this?* And then it dawned on me – as example followed example – they weren't all so dramatic, of course. But it suddenly struck me that once the cause had operated, the effect was inevitably going to follow. When that poor woman went mad in her sixties, the madness she moved into, as it were, had already been there inside her for the past fifty years. D'you begin to see it? The passage of time made it *look like* her future, but actually it was her past that was waiting there to claim her! So we all move into our futures and what do we find there? Nothing! Only our pasts waiting for us." He shivered. "I keep feeling there's a much bigger thought behind it."

"And you can't quite grasp it?" she asked.

"I don't think I want to. Isn't it bad enough that we are constantly claimed by our own past – just when we're so sure we've got the future in our grasp?"

For a fleeting moment she glimpsed that "bigger thought," the one he shunned. "It makes happiness superfluous," she told him. "And misery, too, of course."

He looked at her in surprise, tinged with admiration; the point had not occurred to him. Then it triggered another memory. "That's what he meant when he said we spend our lives cheering the rising tide and booing its ebb."

Soon they were in Curzon Street. A couple of hundred yards ahead she saw the covered entrance to that maze of narrow lanes and mewses behind the grand houses of Piccadilly, where the opening chapters of "The Green Hat" are set.

"I say," she cried. "D'you mind if we go round through there? Shepherd's Market?"

He looked at her with new interest. "Not at all. Have you any particular reason?"

"I haven't actually been there since just after 'The Green Hat' came out."

As they walked toward the entrance she went on: "I tried to work out which house it was – the one where . . . oh, I've forgotten the story now. But Iris Storm parked her famous yellow Hispano-Suiza outside. They have an extra sort of reality, don't you think, people in books – especially when everyone in London is reading it at the same time. I remember looking at the house and thinking, *I know exactly what happened inside there.* But, of course, it hadn't. I could see it so vividly – every word, every gesture, every thought. And yet it had never happened." She laughed slyly. "Perhaps our psychological past is more like that than we care to believe."

He stared at her and remarked, "You really are amazing, Julia. You'll always find the exit, eh?"

They had reached the old arch. Suddenly he put out a hand to restrain her. "I don't think you should go down there. You should leave that memory intact."

His intensity moved her. "Very well," she agreed and turned away to continue their stroll along Curzon Street.

He was right. Iris Storm – and all those heroines of romances that never were – had no place in the life she was about to enter.

His flat was one half of the former servants' attics of a once-fine house near the southern end of South Audley Street. "The place belongs to some dubious import-export company," he said, to explain the echoing gloom. The grand stairwell had been ruined about a quarter of a century earlier, to judge by the wrought-iron elegance of the hydraulic lift whose installation had caused the damage. It wafted them upward in an eery, nonelectrical silence.

The other half of the attic was tenanted by someone called Elvira; he called out her name as he opened the door but there was no reply. He repeated his call, just to be sure.

"What does she do?" Julia asked.

"She gives parties . . . gets taken away for weekends, holidays. She's the last of the Bright Young Things."

"Is she old?"

"I don't know and I don't care." He turned and took her in his arms.

Their little attic world dissolved in a brief kaleidoscope of impressions: the bed, with its covers hastily thrown over, now unhastily drawn back again; the clock that had stopped at half past two; the cracked ceiling . . .

The crack was ominous. Was this a world that would soon fall in upon them?

But *soon* was another lifespan away. Time was now measured in heartbeats. She closed her eyes and let herself drown in this long, sweet, tender moment. The heat of their bodies melted into the cool of the sheets. His voice at her ear murmured her name, losing it in the thunderous whisper of her pulse. Their desire rose and fused, joining her not just with him but with every part of her self, as well. Their ecstasy was like a detonation of that united flesh. It left them gasping. They saw a moment of death and returned from it unscathed.

It was past eight when the telephone woke them. It was a wrong number but in those few moments Julia had her first real taste of the guilt that was now a third party in her life.

"Are you as hungry as I am?" he asked.

"Probably." She grinned. "But I could also do with a bite to eat."

He did everything; he would not even let her set the table. "Just talk to me," he said.

"What are you going to make?"

"A tasty mess, I hope. I'll vamp it."

"It" was dried fish, rice, chopped egg, fennel, and green pepper. As she watched him – stirring, tasting, adding wine and herbs – earlier questions returned to her, questions that could now be asked; like, "Have you and Dolly split up?"

"Were we ever together?" he replied. "It's an odd thing, you know. We were such good friends. Well, we still are, come to that.

344

We can go out together and have the most marvellous time. We are so suited to each other. Much more" – he gave a rueful grimace – "than you and me, I fear. It seemed such an ideal basis for our sort of lives. Both so busy, both . . . I mean our two lives hardly overlap. But we both work late, have fun late, get up late. And, as I say, we get on famously. But it's not enough, is it?"

"What are we going to do, Wallace?"

"Do we need to do anything?"

"We need to meet, see each other. Don't you want that?"

He closed his eyes as if to shut out pain. "Every minute of the day, every second of the night." He looked at her and smiled. "But that's hardly new. Not for me. Still – that part of it's over."

"What's the next part, then?"

He shrugged. "Whatever it is, let's take it slowly. After all, we both love Dolly, too."

"How does she feel about you?"

"Disillusioned, I'm sure. But love is a terrible habit."

"Never!" Julia said vehemently. "It will never be a habit with me."

He refilled their wine glasses. "Slowly and carefully, eh? Let's just take it one year at a time."

It was an impossible dream but they toasted it in hope.

"Talk to me about yourself," he invited. "All the things you must know I'm dying to hear. Tell me first why the Beaver keeps asking me about you."

"Does he?"

"Every time we meet."

"I dine with them every couple of months but I've never been able to make him out. What d'you think of him?"

"Hah!" He gave a single laugh. "The same as you. He's an impossible man to describe. Just when he's done the most generous thing you ever heard of, he turns round and does the meanest. Thousands hate him – but hundreds don't. And those hundreds will work for him till they drop."

"You among them?"

"For the present. He's a bit like Churchill in that respect, except that Churchill leads from in front, while the Beaver does it from behind."

"I didn't know you knew Churchill."

As he replied he dropped the venetian blinds so as to dim the summer evening, and he lit a candle that was stuck into an old chianti bottle; then he tipped their meal straight from the pans onto their plates. "As a matter of fact I did some of the research for his book on Marlborough. It's coming out soon, and I'll show you the bits I actually wrote. Funnily enough, I was down at Chartwell only yesterday, returning a few things – and, of course, being shown his new Daimler."

Julia smiled at the mention of it; the car had been a gift from Churchill's friends and admirers. "I subscribed to that." She took a mouthful and found it tasted even better than it had smelled. "Oh, you've got the job!" she enthused.

"I enjoy cooking," he replied diffidently. "If that's what you call it." Equally casually he asked, "D'you admire Churchill so much then?"

"Ye-es," she answered with some reluctance.

He pressed her on the point: "Most people would write him off as noisy, shameless, truculent . . . pushing. A sort of intellectual Horatio Bottomley of the upper classes."

"So he is at times."

"All gifts and no character?"

"No, that's too harsh. Much too harsh. Only the snivelling sort of politician who lives for compromise would say that. The man's greatest fault, in my view, is that he's too fond of a scrap. I think he'd drop all his friends rather than give in. But what d'you think? You must know him far better."

"I think he's Saul on his way to Damascus."

"Mind you, I didn't have such a high opinion of him before his speech in the House last March – on the air estimates, you remember? Anyway, how does he like his new car? Did he take you for a spin?"

"Mm-mm." He shook his head. When he had swallowed his mouthful he added, "Come to think of it, you should have been there. It was a meeting of his aeronautical 'gang' – all about warplanes and the frightening pace of German rearmament. They weren't exactly delighted to see me, until he convinced them how harmless I am."

"You? Harmless!" She laughed at the idea. "But what gang is this?"

"No names, of course. You'd probably know them all. Two or three of them had RAF stamped all over their faces – all in mufti, mind – and the rest smelled of aeroplanes, too."

"Well, well," she exclaimed, "the things one learns! Doesn't that explain it. I wondered where he got all his facts. Every one a bullseye."

"That's how it's done. Duplicity everywhere, but all in the national interest."

"Talking of which . . ." She extracted a fishbone and laid it delicately on the side of her plate.

"Ah yes," he said, "the message you wish me to carry to Germany."

She placed her hand on his. "Don't run any risks," she begged.

"No message?" He smiled. "Own up then. You thought you'd die if you didn't see me?"

"I wonder?" Her eyes narrowed. "Perhaps I've been in love with you for quite some time?"

He pooh-poohed the idea. "I think I'd have noticed."

"Yes." She agreed. "We would have known it, wouldn't we. A thing like that . . ."

"Really no messages?" he interrupted.

She sighed. "Not what you'd call a message. But, well, as you are going to Germany anyway, and as you are rather a dab hand at observing people and digging things up . . . no, let me explain the background."

She told him about Neville Flugzeugwerke and Mickey McHugh.

"I wonder," she concluded, "if I gave you his address, could you look him up while you're over there – friend of the family, and so on?"

"And then?"

"Just let me know what you think of him. He's the best manager I've ever known. Absolutely dedicated. Tireless. Snish snish. And yet I get the feeling he's working for someone else as well as Neville's. I'm not alone in that – so don't think I'm turning paranoid – German spies . . . traitors, and so on. But I suspect my wonderful Mr McHugh may be working for the Germans. Don't ask me *which* Germans. As you'll swiftly discover, the place is rife with factions."

He raised his glass. "Consider it done."

"But I mean what I say about not doing anything dangerous, mind."

He laughed. "I'm just bowled over by your amazing foresight. It's surely psychic."

She frowned.

"To set up a business in Germany – which will no doubt require your *frequent* presence in its early stages – and to do it in the month *before* I get sent there on what looks like being a long and fairly easy assignment!" He leaned forward and kissed her tenderly. "To Berlin!" he murmured.

Her lips moved hungrily over his. "To Berlin!" she whispered in reply.

CHAPTER FORTY-SIX

ORDINARY LIFE WENT on in its ordinary way for Julia, despite this shattering change in her life and outlook. She held board meetings, went to dinners, attended to her duties at the SPRP (which were now largely ceremonial), kept all ten fingers on the many different pulses of her life – and no one, she felt sure, would suspect the slightest change in her. Indeed, the only outward variation in her routine was that she went down to Allbury more often at weekends. There she enjoyed long walks through the fields and woodlands with an imaginary Wallace at her side; and she loved to fly, to fill the perfect solitude of flight with dreams which seemed to assure her that her loneliness was finally at an end.

She was aware of the dangers – that she was creating an impossible lover, a Wallace who never was and never could be. Soon she would have to go to Germany and see him. But the spur for such a trip must be found in one of Mickey McHugh's reports; and they were so infuriatingly bland, so reassuring, they gave her no excuse at all. So she bided the hours at Allbury and felt the tensions mounting within her.

The least frequent visitor there, curiously enough, was Theresa Ashbury – though she was in the neighbourhood twice a week. So when Julia saw her Morris Ten come nosing up the drive one Friday evening toward the end of May, she knew it must be something important. She went out to meet her.

To her surprise she found Lydia in the car, too. "Hello, Mrs Ashbury. What's this?" And to her daughter: "Where's your own car?"

"I had to leave it in Ware," Lydia grumbled. "The handbrake still keeps sticking. Somerville Motors is a *dump!* I especially wanted it this weekend."

"Then you should have done the job yourself. *Anyway . . .*" Julia pushed the word against a potential barrage of protest from the girl and turned to Theresa. "It was very good of you, Mrs Ashbury. Will you stay and have a bite to eat now you're here?"

The woman looked at her watch and said yes, thank you, she would. Julia nodded to Lydia. "Go and arrange it, there's a dear."

Theresa cleared her throat. "Actually, Mrs Somerville, I think she'd better stay. She . . ."

But the girl was already skipping indoors with her weekend bag. "I'll see to it and catch you up," she cried. "You tell her if you like, Mrs Ashbury. I shan't mind in the least."

The two women started an aimless stroll about the lawn. "Is it anything serious?" Julia asked.

"Kids!" Theresa replied. "I don't know sometimes. I mean, why did you put Miss Lydia to work in the SPRP offices, eh? To help her, right? Learn about accounts and that."

"Oh dear. Has she done something awful there?"

Theresa shrugged. "Not in that way. I mean, she's not upset nobody, nor pinched the petty cash."

"But there is something? She has that truculent look I know so well."

Theresa gave a sigh. "She'd better tell you herself. I'd only perjure her. I know it's not my place, but if she was my daughter . . . well!"

Lydia joined them at that moment. "Just high tea I told cook. I hope that suits everybody?"

"Mrs Ashbury thinks you'd better tell me yourself."

"I'll go and wait indoors if you like," Theresa offered.

But they prevailed upon her to stay.

Lydia spoke with the deference due to an older generation but her tone conceded not the slightest doubt in what she was saying. "Let me ask you the question that started it all," she began. "There's a new typist there, called Vera Watson. And she turned to me one morning this week and asked where we do our shopping. For food, she meant."

"Cheeky baggage!" Theresa cut in.

Lydia smiled in jovial agreement and went on: "So I explained about housekeepers and things. And she said what if all the staff were ill, or some crisis fell upon us, so that the only one who could do the shopping . . ."

"It's so unlikely, darling," Julia objected.

"Never mind. Just assume it – so that I can get to the point, eh? You're the only one who can do the shopping and you've got some people coming in to dinner. What would you do? Where would you go?"

"What did you tell her?"

"No – you answer it first."

Julia gave the matter some thought. The really honest answer was that she'd go to Harrods or Fortnums, but she suspected that was what Lydia expected her to say. "There's rather a good little Italian warehouseman I know in Soho . . ."

"Oh." Lydia was crestfallen. "Expensive, I'm sure."

"Not at all. In fact, he's so cheap that your Uncle Wallace shops there. And Aunt Dolly, of course."

"Ah! So you know *of* it. You've never actually shopped there." Julia made a noncommittal noise.

Relentless Lydia pressed home: "Have you ever shopped there?"

"Not actually shopped, no."

"Have you ever bought food anywhere? My God, it's like trying to get blood out of a stone."

"All right, darling. I do sometimes buy food and it's usually at Harrods, or sometimes Fortnums. What of it?"

"Hah!" Lydia pounced in triumph. "And why? Why don't you shop around? Compare prices? Look for bargains . . . take your time and make sure you get value for money?"

"I don't see where this is getting us, dear, but – as it seems to fascinate you and little Vera so much – you've just spoken the magic word: time. I don't have time."

Lydia stopped and faced her. "Because?"

"What d'you mean – because?"

"You don't have time because . . . ?"

"Because I'm rather busy earning a hundred times more than I could possibly save by doing all that shopping around and making comparisons."

Theresa was staring at her open-mouthed. Julia asked what was wrong.

"You just wait, Mrs Somerville. She'll tell you."

"Compare your preaching with your practice," Lydia was meanwhile saying. "At the SPRP we tell them not to buy soup in tins but to go down to the butcher's and get bones and then up to the market for the tired greens and then back home to fill the stockpot. And that's a good hour's work. On the other hand, if the woman can open a tin of soup, which is the equivalent in her case of popping into Harrods, then she's got an hour in which – like you – she could be earning."

They both stared at Julia, waiting for the explosion. When nothing happened, Theresa pointed out, "What she's saying, Mrs Somerville, is that grubbing for money is more important, more rewarding, than doing right by your family."

They had reached a seat in a little suntrap among some rhododendrons, which were just coming into flower. The late-afternoon sun was warm and strong. They all sat down and Lydia, to the surprise of the other two, peeled off her stockings and hitched her skirt up to the top of her thighs. She closed her eyes, lay back, and declared, "It's only one example, but it's symptomatic of everything we do at the Society. We take women who could be out in the world earning good money – I mean, things have changed so much since the Great War, you know – we take those women and we teach them to stay

350 hp. They called it the Cyclone. It was designed especially for the Pony, which had come into being, in the usual roundabout way, as a result of gossip, rumour, spying, cries from the market place, and bees in the bonnet up in the drawing office.

Neville's agents around the world, and especially in America, had all spoken of a large and growing market for light mail carriers. Simultaneously, Eliot, who had kept his ear to the ground on several visits to Germany during the time when Mickey McHugh had been negotiating with Peter Rosenheim, had got wind of a scheme to use the Dornier Wal flying boat (the "8.5 t" version, specially strengthened for catapult launching) to carry mail to Brazil. It would fly out to a newly adapted launching ship in mid-ocean, where it would be hoisted aboard, take on fresh fuel and crew, and then be catapulted onward to its destination.

Eliot's idea was that a seaplane version of a much lighter mail carrier could be launched from the deck of a fast liner as it drew within a thousand miles of America, or Europe, and speed the delivery; being a lighter aircraft, it could make do with a short catapult. In fact, the Germans already operated such a system, using Junker Ju46s, but only for letters posted by the ship's passengers. The general postal traffic across the North Atlantic was neatly monopolized by America, France, and Britain, thanks to their happy ownership of the termini and the necessary staging points in Bermuda and the Azores. Also, American law laid down that only American companies could carry US mail – and that, of course, was where Eliot saw his chance.

All these considerations had come together in the specification for a new low-wing monoplane, capable of being built in both sea and land versions, with a new engine that did not need a heavy water-cooling system. To evoke the notion of "express," they called it the Pony – actually, Sea Pony or Land Pony. It was the test version of the latter that Julia was proposing to fly to Cardington that afternoon. Cardington was where the two big airships, the R100 and the R101, had been housed a few years ago, before the disaster. It was now an RAF airfield, but there was always a chance that something interesting might be going on.

Julia was no longer Neville's chief test pilot, official or unofficial; for some years now that role had been filled by Eric Ovenden, who had previously flown for Westland and Armstrong-Whitworth, plus a two-year stint at the RAE in Farnborough. A reserved, taciturn man, he had produced the classic statement: "Testing a plane is like the Dance of the Seven Veils. You have to discover the naughty bits slowly." Friends called him Salome.

"How many veils has Mr Ovenden removed, I wonder?" Lydia asked as she and her mother walked toward the airfield. They would be flying open-cockpit so they wore full gear.

out of the job market . . ."

"But that's not true," Julia protested. "You think your comparison with me is very smart, no doubt. Actually, it's the perfect answer to your own argument. We train women to do the jobs of half a dozen – cook, maid, housekeeper, nanny, governess, and companion."

"And nurse," Theresa added.

"There you are," Julia went on. "Seven jobs in one! Now if any one of the women who goes through our course were capable of earning enough to pay the wages of those seven, then naturally we'd be mad to train her to do all seven jobs herself. Now you tell me honestly – how many women do you know who can earn enough to pay the wages of seven? I suspect you only know one! And she's the one you so cleverly picked on for your example."

Lydia sighed; the beautiful edifice of impregnable argument was tumbling about her. The sun seemed hotter than ever, too. She started unbuttoning her blouse.

Julia glanced uncomfortably around the garden. "Are you going to give us a complete show here or what?" she asked.

Her daughter gave a disgruntled groan but contented herself with tucking the liberated bits of her blouse behind her straps. "All right, I didn't pick a good example. But I still think I have a point. We do train women to stay out of the job market. And that cannot be right."

"But making a home and raising a family – they are jobs. Fulfilling and rewarding jobs."

"Oh yes!" Lydia sneered. "They're so fulfilling and so rewarding that they're the first jobs a woman will pay others to do as soon as she can possibly afford it!"

Julia was beginning to grow angry. "You keep answering your own objections," she pointed out. "The women we work with cannot possibly afford it. They are stuck doing all seven jobs."

"Imprisoned."

"All right. I'll even call it imprisoned if that makes you happy. So what is their choice? Not your choice or my choice, but theirs. They can either do it well and feel proud and self-reliant and fulfilled – or they can make a hash of it and feel ashamed and rotten and failures. Now that's all we do. We're not some grand crusading leviathan. We don't aim to change the world. All we do is take women who find themselves in that prison of poverty and ignorance and we help them to make the best of themselves and their wretched circumstances."

Lydia was now so worked up she forgot her affair with the sun. Rolling down her skirt and buttoning up her blouse, she said, "But the reason they're in such wretched circumstances is that they're not earning enough. Can't you grasp that simple, elementary fact?"

"And again you're wrong. A lot of them are earning. They do all kinds of outwork. You see, you haven't the first idea of . . ."

"Oh, I know all about their outwork! Sixpence a shirt! A farthing a buttonhole! Threepence to address a hundred envelopes! Don't tell me about outwork."

"And what are we supposed to do about that?"

"We could teach them how to organize, for a start."

Theresa gave a snort. "They can go down the Communist Party for that."

"The Communist Party doesn't give a damn about women," Lydia almost shouted in her frustration.

She hadn't meant to snap at Theresa but her unintended rudeness was suddenly too much for her mother. "If you can't hold a civilized discussion," she told the girl, "perhaps it would be better for you to go indoors."

Lydia, keener to make her point than to stand on her dignity, apologized to Theresa, who was annoyed at having to accept it; to her mind Lydia should have been sent indoors long before. The way that posh folk let their children argue back always scandalized her.

The mechanic from the garage in Ware delivered Lydia's car at that moment.

"You was quick," Theresa called out.

"Not really," he answered disparagingly. "It was just the knuckle on the rear linkage. I spread it a bit with a pliers."

"Just ten seconds with a pair of pliers!" Julia commented to her daughter. "It's sloppy, darling. Everything you do is sloppy these days – from maintaining your car to thinking about the SPRP."

"Oh, you're just impossible!" Lydia exploded at last. "You know I'm right and you just won't admit it." And she flounced off toward the house, shouting back at them, "And I don't want any tea, thank you."

Julia turned to the mechanic. "I'm sorry – Mr Ambrose, isn't it?"

He was delighted to be recognized. "No need to apologize, Mrs Somerville. We all go through it, I'm sure."

"Well, it was very good of you to bother. What do I owe you?"

"Oh, I don't hardly like to charge. But" – he licked his lips and took a chance – "I got a cracked block back at the garage. Cast iron, see? If I could bring that up and heat it in one of your pits, I could weld it back, easy?"

Julia told him to bring it up on Monday.

Theresa decided that as Mr Ambrose needed to get back to Ware, she'd take him and not stop for supper after all. "Be firm," was her parting advice.

Julia watched them go and then turned toward the house.

Was she so absolutely right and Lydia so completely wrong? she wondered. Perhaps there was a level of worthwhile income well below anything that would pay all seven deputies? At least one should not dismiss the idea out of hand. One should look into it.

Lydia was no fool, after all. She shouldn't have called her sl

She went up to the girl's room and tapped gently at the do

"Go away!" Lydia screamed. "I hate you."

Julia tried the door and found it locked.

"I wanted to apologize," she said.

There was no reply. Further knocking brought no response. turned and went downstairs.

Next morning hunger brought Lydia down for a rather late bre fast. Cool, offhand, she avoided her mother's eye – waiting fo renewal of the half-offered apology.

"What's on for today, then?" Julia asked casually, as if nothing h passed between them.

"Oh, I don't know. I thought I might take the car and mot down to Freddy Quinton's in Leicestershire. I haven't seen him fo donkey's years. It's his twentieth and I was sort-of half invited."

"Do I know them?"

"He was at Summerhill."

"Ah. Good." Julia ran her eye down the deaths column in *The Times*. "I thought I'd try the new Pony – fly her up to Cardington, perhaps. Ring for more toast, there's an angel."

Lydia's eyes opened wide. "I say – is the Pony ready?"

"She was test-flown all week. Completed her stalling trials yesterday. Passed with flying colours."

Lydia was silent for a while.

Julia checked her watch and remarked, "You will allow enough time to motor down at a reasonable speed, won't you, darling? Even though your brakes are now repaired, you know I hate it when . . ."

"Mummeeee!" her daughter warned.

"Well do leave yourself plenty of time."

After another thoughtful silence Lydia said, "Actually . . ." and then paused.

"Mmmm? I see Max's chum Buffy Frobisher has died. You wouldn't have known them. Vile people."

"Actually . . ." Lydia tried again.

"What, dear?" her mother asked more sharply.

"Actually, I think I might join you in the Pony. Can we go after lunch? I fell a bit behind with my swotting this week."

"Other things on your mind, eh?"

But Lydia offered no concession. Fixing a cool eye on her mother, she added, "Also we can have a good long talk."

The Pony was Neville's latest plane; everything about her was new. She even had a new type of engine from Somerville Engineering. All their previous motors had been water-cooled, in straight or vee formation – drawing on their long experience with cars; but this was a radial air-cooled job with twin ranks of cylinders delivering

Julia consulted her clipboard, where the summary was set out in meticulous detail. "He seems to have lifted them all," she replied. "The only serious warning is against prolonged flying upside down. He says the fuel pump needs modifying."

"Well, that shouldn't cramp our style too much."

"I hope it won't cramp our style at all. I just want a nice sedate flight and no showing off."

"You're getting old," Lydia remarked – and then rather wished she hadn't. She had forgotten that her mother would, in fact, be forty this coming August, less than three months away.

"Thank you." Julia smiled grimly. "Perhaps we'll find time this afternoon to talk about growing up?"

They came around the corner of Number 3 hangar, where the Pony stood, serviced and fuelled, on the apron. "God but she's a beauty!" Lydia exclaimed.

"Did you hear me?"

The daughter sighed and answered, "Y e e e s!"

"It's important, darling," Julia went on. "God knows, the last thing I want is to spoil your youth or put an old head on young shoulders. But Robert will come of age next year, and will be put to work his way through every department of Somerville's. And then at twenty-three he inherits the lot."

Lydia's face went white. She looked around them. "All this?"

"No!" Julia answered crossly. "Do you never pay attention? Only Somerville Motors, plus a fair share of Somerville Engineering. I want everything else – this is what I wanted to talk about – I want you to join me in Neville's and eventually take over the reins."

Lydia swallowed hard and stared at her mother. Julia gestured right and left. Lydia looked around her with new eyes.

"The reason you're working at the SPRP," Julia went on, "is not to undertake root and branch reform – though sensible suggestions, like the one you tried to make yesterday, will be seriously considered if put in a reasonably mature manner. And that's all I want to say about that particular topic. But this is much more important. The reason I sent you there is that I don't know a better place for you to pick up the rudiments of accountancy. Of course, you must have a formal training, too, but it will mean more if you've seen it in action first."

"I know," Lydia replied awkwardly. "I just sort of forgot."

"Exactly. You live from one all-consuming enthusiasm to another. No proportion. It's frightening."

"I'd still rather be at an engineering college. That's what I'm really keen on."

"Ha! A *keen* engineering student who can't be bothered to mend her own handbrake!"

Lydia closed her eyes and counted ten. "Can we finally bury that one?" she asked in a monotone.

They were standing by the Pony now. Its stainless-steel body, burnished bright by the sun, contrasted oddly with the duller dural-skinned wings.

"It's the first time I've seen it all put together," Lydia enthused, forgetting her frustration. "Isn't she beautiful! This is the secret, of course." She ran her hands lovingly along the fairings of the wing roots, where they joined the fuselage; what started as a tiny dip at the front became a pronounced concavity at the trailing edge, like the fluting on a Vauxhall car bonnet. "Eliot really understands the dynamics of it here."

Then, with an impish glance at her mother, she started to explain that the flow at every point along the fairing had to approximate to that at the outlet cone of a venturi . . .

Julia put the palms of her hands over her ears. "You know it means nothing to me."

"What it means to *you* is that you'll get better lift and less drag at lower speeds." She gave the fuselage an affectionate pat. "Even Amy Johnson could land this without buckling anything."

The weekend duty mechanic saw Julia climbing in while Lydia prepared to swing the prop. "I'll do it!" he shouted as he ran across the taxiing strip. "You know about not flying her upside down, Boss?" he asked before he began.

Julia hoisted both thumbs. The engine started on the third swing. She let it warm up for a minute or so and then signalled chocks away. Her heart was pounding like a mad thing. At that moment she would not have traded places with anyone else in the world.

The difference between this new machine and the Amazon was apparent even before takeoff. With the Amazon there was a certain lag between an increase in the throttle and the resultant increase in forward speed; but with the Pony it was immediate, just like a car in low gear. Julia could feel that every ounce of thrust from the propellers was being captured in useful work; she envied her daughter's understanding of a process that, to her, would never be more than intuitive.

As they rose above the airfield Lydia could not help looking back for a birdseye view of the workshops, assembly sheds, and hangars. To think of *owning* it was impossible; she did not even feel her mother actually owned the place. It was a natural feature, like a mountain or a forest; no one could really own such things.

For Julia, the sensation of rightness grew even stronger after they were airborne. Everything about this new plane was firm and tight. You moved the stick and the response was immediate – yet not jerky.

"That's those Simmonds-Corsey cables for you!" Lydia's voice came over the intercom. Then, as an afterthought, "Plus good piloting, of course."

356

Twenty minutes later they were touching down at Cardington – at a mere 38 mph. "I still have lift!" Julia marvelled.

"Did you change trim?" Lydia asked as they walked away from the parking zone.

"I didn't need to."

"That's because . . ."

"No!" Julia shouted. "No. No no . . ." And she stopped her ears and ran away – almost into the arms of a burly security guard, who, having prepared his face and voice to tell them to clear off and what did they think they were doing, had to make a swift accommodation to say: "Why Mrs Somerville! And Miss Somerville! Someone's slipped up. You're not on my list of expected visitors."

"No, it was a spur of the moment idea, Flight Sergeant ah . . ."

Lydia remembered him from a previous visit to Martlesham. "Flight Sergeant North, isn't it? We're just trying out a new crate. Care for a dekko?"

After that he was eating from their hand.

He admired the Pony, genuinely, but told them there was no flying there that weekend. The squadron was stood down and they were all playing polo at Esher.

Lydia suggested they should tootle on to Leicestershire. "The Quintons have a landing strip on their farm," she explained. "And you'd love them."

But Julia decided they'd park the Pony here for an hour or two and go into Bedford, where they could take a boat on the river and have tea. Flight Sergeant North arranged a taxi for them and took their flying gear into safe keeping in the guard room.

The River Ouse at Bedford is too deep for punting, at least in the reaches near the town. They hired a scull at Banham's yard.

"I'd go upriver if I was you, ladies," the boatman advised. "I know it looks nice and broad down there but that's mostly where the clubs do their sprinting."

"I'll row and you steer," Lydia suggested. "We can change over coming back." She set off in fine style.

Up the river, once they were past the brewery, was a mixture of scruffy water meadows fringed by ancient, pollarded willows, suburban back gardens with the romantic weeping variety, and road or railway bridges of every vintage. Julia watched her daughter and felt proud of her strength and coordination. Although the boat was a heavy, clinker-built tub, robust rather than racy, the girl moved it at creditable speed and left satisfyingly energetic "puddles" where her oars had dipped.

Continuous conversation was impossible, though.

"Max would be proud to see this," she told Lydia. "One thing he could never bear was sloppy oarsmanship."

"One of many things," Lydia corrected.

A Bedford School four went by, downstream. Their coach, a senior oarsman on a bicycle, roared into his megaphone, "I never saw anything so shent as you pathetic weeds! By God, here's a *girl* could outrow every man of you! Brace up, house . . . pull together! Give 'er ten, cox."

Julia grinned with pride at the exhausted oarsmen, but she turned back to find Lydia scarlet with fury. "How *dare* he?" she cried. "Did you hear the way he said 'girl'? God, I *loathe* public schools. What possessed you to send Robert to one? No wonder he's turned out the way he is."

In her anger she caught a crab with her left oar and had to steady herself. Julia suggested, "We can moor if you like. Here's a nice sunny bit."

"No. I want to go on. I need to work this off now."

For a few strokes the puddles she left looked more like seething wounds in the water but she soon settled back to her old rhythm. An eight came into view, downriver, and gained on them rapidly – an altogether more disciplined crew. Lydia's eyes challenged their coach to make comparisons but he did not even glance their way.

Five minutes later they came across them again, slumped exhausted over easied oars while their coach told them exactly how awful they were. Julia watched their eyes pick up her daughter's lithe, muscular body and saw an ancient hunger veil them. Yet there was no sudden bristling within her of those automatic defences she remembered in her own mother.

Was she then defective in that way? She remembered another parent saying to her, at an open day at Summerhill, "I honestly don't think it's reasonable to expect a girl to remain a virgin until she marries – not these days. Do you?"

And Julia had heard herself agreeing that, yes, it really was an absurd expectation.

As they drew level Lydia, too, became aware of the boys – and of the fact that their minds were not on what their coach was trying to tell them. Her response amused Julia.

She was studiously indifferent to them, to all her surroundings. You would have sworn she was deep in communion with some watery god. Though her muscles must be tired by now she ignored their protest and moved the oars with the same crisp, vigorous strokes she had showed off to the boatman at Banham's. The wood groaned in the rowlocks as she took each strain; the water responded with a deep, complaining gurgle; the cumbrous vessel shot forward like a greyhound at the slip; and a double thud in perfect synchrony marked the brisk finish of each stroke. In their wake the neat, even whirlpools mocked the lads.

"Yes, Davies," the coach sneered. "Makes you think, eh?"

"It certainly does, sir," Davies answered evenly.

The entire crew broke down in ribald laughter and comment.

"It's crowds, darling," Julia hastened to say. "Girls are just the same in crowds."

They went under the railway bridge just as a train was passing over it; talk was impossible until they were well out the other side. Shortly after that they were in open countryside, where the banks were not staked or shored but left to crumble in reed-filled shallows.

"Watch out for sandbars," Lydia warned.

Black and white cows stared at them through great, incurious eyes from the meadows on either side. Fishermen sat stoically on folding stools, dignifying their passage with the merest nod. Lovers lay entwined, in sunbaked oblivion, among the taller grasses.

"Of course," Lydia went on, as if the conversation had been flowing between them all this while, "you grew up in that public-school world. It's very different for you."

"The public schoolboys of my young days would never have made such comments in the hearing of ladies."

"Yes, but then ladies wouldn't have been dressed like this and they wouldn't have dared show they could row as well as your average male."

"No – but it was my generation who brought about that change. So don't lump me with the Edwardians, thank you very much."

"But you still have *some* Edwardian values – about working for money, for instance. Why shouldn't women be taught to be just as money-grubbing as men? It hasn't done you any harm."

Julia looked at her in surprise. "Money grubbing? Is that really what I seem like to you?"

Lydia rested her oars. Julia steered toward the bank, where she managed to leap ashore and make fast to the root of a sawn-down tree. Her daughter, immediately behind her, put an awkward arm around her and murmured, "Sorreee."

Julia turned and hugged her. "You're in a funny sort of mood these days, darling. What is it?"

The girl just shrugged. "Don't know."

"Because if anything were seriously wrong – you would tell me, wouldn't you?"

"Of course. But there isn't anything. I just feel generally . . . nyaaa."

"Oh my dear, I remember days like that." She released her daughter and sat on the bank, drawing her legs up under her. "Did I do the right thing – telling you about taking over Neville's? Is it going to weigh on you now?"

Lydia sat beside her. Smiling to herself, she kicked off her shoes, peeled off her stockings, and dangled her feet in the water. "No," she answered with a kind of slow, emphatic amusement. "It hasn't sunk in yet, but it's . . . it'll . . . ."

"Give you a new sense of direction, I hope. That was my intention, anyway."

"Something like that."

After an easeful silence Julia went on. "There isn't a young man or anything of that sort, is there? Nothing's upsetting you in that way."

"Not any more."

"Oh?"

There was a pause before Lydia answered. "It was at school." She closed her eyes and breathed out. "God, I thought I'd die when he told me he . . . didn't . . . I mean, there was someone else." Then she produced an elfin grin and added, "Lot of fuss over nothing."

"And you didn't say a word."

"Good thing, too. There was nothing to tell – as it turned out."

"Was his name Quinton, by any chance?"

Her daughter nodded and then, still smiling, resettled herself to face her mother full square. "And what about you – talking of new directions? Are you going to be married to Neville's for ever? Isn't there anyone . . ."

Julia could see her toying with several possible endings to the question, varying between flippant and impertinent. To rescue her (after all, she herself had created the circumstances in which the question became even possible) she echoed, "Will I ever marry again? I don't know. I doubt it, somehow. What would I need to get married for?"

The thought of Wallace filled her with a sudden longing. Did German courts sit on a Saturday? Or was he free – strolling through Leipzig, perhaps, or lying beneath the trees in the Rosenthal, staring into the lake and thinking of her?

"I always hoped you and Eliot might hitch up one day," Lydia was saying in her most casual tone.

Julia smiled indulgently.

Lydia, feeling challenged, asked truculently, "Why not? He's far and away the nicest man *you* know."

Carefully Julia replied, "I'm very fond of him, of course. In some ways I even love him. I'm sure you know that. But we'd be so wrong for each other."

"But why? He'd be so . . ."

"No, listen, darling. All joking apart. This is serious now. I was . . . trapped into marriage with your father. I don't mean he trapped me. Poor man – he was as much a victim of the Edwardian marriage system as anyone. But let me tell you – love is not the most important thing in a marriage. It's not even *enough* for a marriage. Of course, it's got to be there – but it's not enough. The most important thing is to marry someone with whom you won't feel trapped. Perhaps I'm a little unhinged on the subject. We make jokes about all those ghastly committees and so on that now run the SPRP, but they really do make me feel trapped. And it's the same with selling shares in the company . . . all the different ways of getting trapped."

Lydia persisted: "I still don't see how that makes Eliot wrong for you."

"Well . . . just take it from me, it does."

"What you're really saying is that you'll never get married again."

"One should never say never."

Lydia rolled over onto her back, bringing her head almost into her mother's lap. For a while she tried shielding her eyes against the brilliance of the sky, then she gave up and simply closed them. "We never get anywhere when we talk," she complained. Then, with a laugh: "We're a committee of two!"

Julia thought for a while before she replied, "We don't arrive at great and stirring decisions. That's true. But that's not what it's all about."

"The trouble is you never really tell me anything. You distil the wisdom of your two extra decades for me – and don't think I'm ungrateful. But I have no idea what's really going on inside you." She sniffed and added, "If anything."

Tell her? Julia urged herself.

She even drew breath to speak, but all she said was, "I'm trapped in a different way. Perhaps I'll tell you soon."

"Yes, but when?"

"Soon."

CHAPTER FORTY-SEVEN

JULIA'S FIRST EXCUSE to visit Germany came late in the June of that year, when Mickey McHugh reported he was experiencing some minor contractual problems with Dornier at Friedrichshafen. She cabled at once to say she was coming over.

He phoned back to tell her there was no need. "You must have more than enough on your plate, Boss. You may quite safely delegate this to me."

But she insisted it was nothing to do with delegation. "I'm feeling increasingly restless about Germany and I want to see things for myself," she explained. "Naturally, you'll be there, too."

She also phoned Wallace, who was ecstatic at the prospect of meeting again. He'd be waiting for her in Berlin, he promised – at the Kaiserhof. By good fortune he was moving to the capital, anyway. The trial was going badly for the Nazis in Leipzig and they wanted to move it closer to party headquarters. He started to apologize that he'd had no time as yet to meet McHugh, but she cut him short.

"I'll bring him to Berlin with me. It'll provide the ideal camouflage for a casual meeting."

After a pause Wallace asked, "Will he stay at the Kaiserhof, too?"

She laughed. "Don't worry. He always disappears on some mysterious errand or other. In fact, that's part of the problem."

She began to count down the hours.

Toward the end of the meeting with Dornier, just when everyone was making noises of satisfaction and proposing an adjournment for lunch, Dieter Wölfflin turned to her and asked offhandedly, "I don't suppose you'd consider selling Neville Flugzeugwerke, Mrs Somerville?"

As she swung round to look at him her eyes dwelled for a fraction of a second in Mickey McHugh's, long enough for her to read the alarm there. She thought of denying it emphatically, to reassure him, but realized that both men would know how uncharacteristic that was. Instead she smiled and replied, "Try me next year, Herr Wölfflin."

"You wouldn't really, would you, Boss?" McHugh asked later, when they were on their way to Berlin.

"It's up to you, McHugh. You keep the profits rolling, we'll keep the company."

She wanted him to understand that, whatever his *other* game might be, it should not damage the firm.

They checked in early at the Kaiserhof. She had arranged to meet Wallace at seven in the ornate new bar on the ground floor. When she told McHugh he said he couldn't come; he had to "meet a fella" at seven-fifteen; she prevailed upon him at least to say hello.

It was already ten past as they entered the bar. Wallace was sitting with his back to them, holding a cherry on a stick, seeking to get rid of it but being too fastidious to drop it among the cigar butts in the ashtray. "There he is," Julia said.

Mickey McHugh, who had been fretting about the time all the way down in the lift – too much to notice Julia's nervousness – looked once more at his watch and apologized. "I really am sorry, Boss, but I could never have stayed longer than this anyway. I have to meet this man – he's between trains, you see."

She did not press him to stay. Alone again, she tried to creep up on Wallace, who still seemed absorbed in his problem with the cherry.

But then she realized that his gaze was actually upon her – by way of the mirror at the back of the bar. As soon as their eyes met, he turned round and grinned, relaxed and easy as always. "Darling," he said, taking her shivering hands between his.

She raised them to her cheek and smiled at him, too happy to speak.

He lifted his eyes toward the ceiling in unambiguous inquiry.

She shook her head. "I think I'd die. Let me get to know you again – I've invented so many Wallaces these past few centuries."

"It has been an age," he agreed. Then, turning to the barman, he ordered her gin and French.

"Talking of missing people," she added as she took the empty stool beside his, "you just missed Mickey McHugh. He had to . . ."

"Was that him with you at the door just now?"

"Yes." She glanced at the mirror and saw that it gave a perfect view of the entrance and the foyer beyond.

"Useful in most countries," he commented. "Essential in this one."

"I can imagine."

"Well, Julia, if that's your Mickey McHugh, I can tell you one thing about him. You're quite right – he *is* working for someone."

"You've seen him before?"

He nodded. "At Chartwell."

She frowned. The mental leap from some imagined shady corner of Germany to Churchill's house in leafy, rural Kent was too great.

"He was one of the gang – that meeting I told you about."

She breathed out, closed her eyes, and murmured, "Of course!" She kept them closed while she rapidly rearranged her mental card index on Mickey McHugh. Gathering information for Churchill! She really ought to have guessed.

"Why do you say of course?" he asked.

She opened her eyes again. "Because it's so obvious now. Maybe I'm too eager to see conspiracies. I should have realized that he's working for . . ."

Baker's eyes went wide in warning. "I didn't actually name any names, did I. Shall we take our drinks over there?"

Chastened, she followed him to one of the tables. "It's so easy to forget."

"Don't I know it. I could bite my tongue off twice a day." He sat down not quite opposite her, as if a third party might join them soon.

"Oh, Wallace, how I've missed you," she murmured.

He nodded and, fishing in his pocket, pulled out a tattered Luft Hansa ticket. "I can't tell you the number of times I had to stop myself from using that!"

"Every minute was such . . ."

"It's over, darling." He leaned forward and squeezed her arm. "The torment will begin again soon enough."

"I can't go on like this much longer."

"I haven't been able to say a word to Dolly – because of being here, you see. And then she's off to America soon."

"I feel something will burst."

"Let's just relax tonight and tomorrow – and we'll face the problem on Sunday. Okay?"

She pulled herself together, gave him a brave smile, and nodded with far more assurance than she felt.

"Oh" – he reverted to a more businesslike tone, as if a third party really had joined them – "before I forget: I saw your brother yesterday."

"Max?"

"Didn't you know he was here?"

"Well, I knew he came over last month – to bring Robert to one of these wretched Nazi *Strength through Joy* camps. But I didn't know he stayed on. You're sure it was him?"

He nodded. "In Ku-damm. He was with a group of SS officers."

"It sounds like Max, all right."

Watching her carefully he added, "I rather think Robert was with him. Yesterday, I mean."

"Oh, God!" All her joy crumpled. "Why don't the pair of them just apply for German nationality and have done with it? They practically *live* over here as it is."

"I hate having to tell you – but you wouldn't have thanked me for keeping it back."

"No." She reached over and squeezed his arm. "Of course not, darling. You were quite right to say it." She leaned back, sipped her drink, and then stared into its depths. "The question is, what do I do about it?"

"D'you feel you ought to do anything? They're a pair of political virgins. It's as good a way as any of opening their . . . eyes."

"To be honest," she said slowly, "I'm a little frightened of Robert."

"He would be . . . twenty-odd now?"

She shook her head. "Twenty exactly. Lydia's almost nineteen."

"He looked older yesterday."

"That's because he scowls so much."

"And what exactly frightens you – his being mixed up with . . ."

"No. He frightens me because he's so dreadfully like his father. We've never talked about George, have we?"

"Dolly's told me her view." A sardonic lift of one eyebrow added an unspoken, *for what that's worth!*

"You see, George and I – and you, too, I suppose – we were brought up in a world where everyone knew that men and women

364

could never be friends. We could be extremely friend*ly* but not actual friends. Men had their friends. Women had theirs. Anything else was grotesque. Or suspect, anyway. Men and women who tried to be real friends were considered . . . well, pretty odd."

He nodded. "Or liars."

"Exactly. But then, in the Twenties, we discovered for ourselves that that was all wrong. Real, authentic friendships are possible. So . . ."

"You don't think that's still a bit of a dream?"

"No!" The suggestion surprised her. "Do you?"

"I'm sorry. I shouldn't have interrupted. How does this affect Robert?"

For a moment she had lost her thread; she picked it up again, uncertain of precisely where she had dropped it. "At least we've brought our children up to believe that such friendships are possible. Whether or not we're deceiving them, time alone will tell. But Robert behaves . . . well, as if it's all passed him completely by. He's exactly like all those young Edwardian gentlemen of our youth."

He pointed to her empty glass. "Can the Beaver refill that for you?"

She laughed. "No, thanks all the same. But can Neville Flugzeug-werke take the *Express's* most distinguished correspondent out to dine somewhere?"

He accepted with a grateful dip of the head.

"Somewhere very elegant and respectable," she added. "Last time I sampled the other side of this city's night-life, and they went and burned down their parliament behind my back."

The pair of them strolled arm in arm around the cold, bright streets, enjoying the contact and working up an appetite, teasing it by saying, "what about here . . . or here?" at every likely or unlikely café. In a little *Gasse* off the Linden she saw an antique brooch, in the window of a jeweller's shop. "That would suit Lydia," she remarked, making a note of the place.

Eventually they settled for the Künstler Café. "On my first visit to Berlin," she told him as they went inside, "when we were just starting talks with Messerschmidt, I came here. I heard Erich Weinert delicately tearing the poor old Weimar Republic to shreds."

"If they could only take back all those twittering jokes, those barbed little words," he commented drily, "I'll bet they'd eat them, every single one. The Nazis' road to power was paved with jokes like that."

There was dancing, of course, and a musical cabaret, and even a *Conferancier* who told a string of passable, though strictly apolitical jokes; but the waspish old sparkle had died. The wasps themselves – those who had not fled abroad – were all being re-educated in the concentration camps, along with the socialists, pacifists, and other deviants whose stings needed drawing.

Wallace was a good dancer, solid and moderately inventive without being flashy. They enjoyed several "spins" before they sat down to order their meal, but she found she was unable to abandon herself to the thrill of such close and vital contact with him. Her worries about Robert still haunted her – together with the rather bizarre thought that, for all she knew, they could be within a hundred yards of each other at that very moment.

He sensed it, of course. As soon as they returned to their table he assured her, "If Robert has a spark of decency in him – which of course he has – a whole furnace full, I should imagine – then he's going to get his eyes opened here. I honestly don't think you need worry."

"Are things really bad? You're not just trying to . . ."

"You remember what Rosenheim was telling us? I owe him an apology. I thought he was putting it on a bit. But he wasn't. I mean things are so bad that the Nazis often have to announce disciplinary measures against their own enthusiasts. Only last week Göring had to say that six Brownshirts had been shot for exceeding their orders. Communists and republicans and Jews all get beaten up daily. Is that the sort of thing your son would applaud?"

"I suppose not." She smiled gratefully, feeling slightly comforted. She would have felt a great deal easier if she could have said the same of her lunatic brother. "I think what frightens me is that there's the same terrible anger in him as I can see in Max. It's even more terrible in one so young. Sort of contained . . . and yet so strong."

"Is there any reason for it, would you say?"

She looked glum. "I don't know what the Davis creature may have told him about his father's death. She was in the room at the time . . ." Julia closed her eyes a moment, breathed once or twice, half sighing.

"You needn't tell me, you know, darling. Not if you'd rather . . ."

"No, it's not that. I'd like you to know." And she went on to describe the events surrounding George's death in as much detail as she could remember.

Throughout her story he was on the edge of his seat, never for a moment taking his eyes off her. At the end he reached over and held her hand. "Now you know," she concluded, grateful for his touch.

"More than that – now I understand. But, honestly, d'you think Davis has told Robert any of it? Why would she paint such a poor picture of herself?" He removed his hand from hers to light her cigarette.

"I'm sure it'd be a highly partisan version – as, indeed, the version I've just given you may be." After a pause she added, "Perhaps if I'd married again . . ."

He looked up at her sharply.

She smiled. "But, of course, I couldn't." She puffed her cigarette to life. "Even so, I think I may have failed him as a mother. A boy like Robert needs a man to model himself upon. That's why he's so thick with Max."

He drew deeply on his own cigarette and blew the smoke upward, among the dark shadows and the soft lights; ghostly remnants of it clung to every word as he asked, "How did the boy take his father's illness?"

She realized suddenly that he was far and away the most perceptive man she had ever met. "Can't you guess?"

He grinned. "I'd say he probably couldn't take it at all – just turned his back on it as much as he could." His eyebrows questioned her.

She nodded. "It cut poor George to the quick, of course."

"So young Robert is reachable," he pointed out. "Even if not by reason. What I mean is he's not deaf to circumstance." He grinned again. "I keep assuring you of the same thing in different words."

She accepted his comfort at last and forced herself to a deliberate gaiety. "I didn't want to talk about any of that. Let's drop it. Tell me what you've been doing. I've read all your reports about the trial, of course. But what else?"

He laid down his cigarette and took her face briefly between his hands. "I thought of this," he murmured, staring deep into her eyes. "And dreamed of it. And longed for it." He closed his eyes and let his hands fall. "Oh, Julia – I've been like a sick adolescent."

"I know . . ." she began.

"People our age aren't supposed to feel like this, are they? Unable to eat . . . churning over inside all the time." An incredulous light came into his eye. "Good God – I've even felt *jealous!*"

She swallowed against the lump in her throat. "I was so afraid people would notice."

"Oh, I was afraid I'd actually go and blurt it out to everyone. It's my trade, after all."

She chuckled, remembering her talk with Lydia on the river bank. "No, I passed that test all right."

Once again she gathered herself. "I wish you'd stop bringing me to the point of ruining my mascara. Can't you save all this until we're in bed? Just tell me normal things – your normal day. Anything normal."

"In Hitler's Germany? Impossible." He thought for a moment and then went on, "But I'll tell you an interesting encounter I had. Trotsky's son was here in Berlin recently, partly to see his mad sister and partly in connection with some discredited Soviet painters they want to exhibit. I asked him how his father viewed the arts in general – what was the artist's role in the class struggle? After all, we know Joe Stalin's view only too well. He said that according to Trotsky the artist can bypass the logic of materialism. The artist can be in direct touch with truth – or what seems like truth – and he must be free to express it. We can always argue about it later, about whether it's really true or not; but that mustn't interfere with the artist's freedom to have his say."

"One can understand why Stalin wants him dead."

Wallace leaned forward and spoke earnestly. "But don't you see, Julia? What Trotsky's saying is so utterly banal and trivial . . . it only takes on meaning in the awful world we've somehow allowed to grow up around us. And this is the point: What are we to say about the banality of a world in which such a windy little truism can shine out like a beacon of revealed truth? Trotsky has a tenth-rate mind, but in Soviet terms and Nazi terms he's a towering genius. God, what an age!"

He looked into her eyes and then suddenly burst out laughing. "Sorry! You didn't quite mean that sort of thing either, did you." He scratched his head diffidently and added, "I get carried away sometimes. Why don't you tell me about London and what's really happening there. Is there anything in this business with Ernest Simpson's wife – did the Prince of Wales really give her that orchid? It was all over the papers here, but not a word in the British rags. And is Honor Guinness serious about marrying Chips Channon? Is all that sort of thing really going on still?" There was something close to desperation in his humour.

"It really is still going on," she assured him.

"God help us," he murmured.

CHAPTER FORTY-EIGHT

THE FOLLOWING AFTERNOON Wallace had to file his copy for an hour or so down at the agency, so Julia went to buy the beautiful little brooch she had earmarked for Lydia. When she found the shop she marvelled that they had come across it at all in their quite aimless wandering. Kleine Kirchgasse was a small cul-de-sac off Unter den Linden, on the northern side; the shop of Abraham Wiechert, once jeweller to the court of the old Kaiser, was to the left, near the blind end. The lovely brooch was still there, but the graffiti were new: *Kauft nicht beim Juden!* and a crudely drawn star of David. She ignored it and went inside, where she found herself the only customer.

The external façade was unchanged from prewar days but the interior had been completely modernized, all in glass and chrome and stainless steel. Wiechert himself served her, a small, courteous man who, with a few more inches, might have passed for Crownfield's younger brother.

"Can't you wash that filth off?" she asked, nodding toward the window.

He tilted his head apologetically. "It would be unwise."

"I'll do it for you, if you like. They won't touch me. Just give me whatever will do the job."

The apology grew firmer, more steely. "Madame is too kind, but it would only make matters worse. Was there anything in particular you wished to see?"

As soon as he started handling his wares, he placed a pair of pince-nez on the very tip of his nose and immediately gained a couple of decades. He still had all his courtly instincts, though, and skilfully talked Julia up through not one but two previously unthinkable price barriers. The piece she finally decided upon was not the little brooch at all but a platinum aeroplane propeller studded with amethysts.

After she had paid he promised to have it delivered to her hotel strongroom and was just taking down the details when the door was kicked open and there came the sound of studded boots on the marble floor – boots being scuffed deliberately, so as to scratch the stone.

Julia resisted the impulse to turn around. New instincts took over as her eyes sought among the reflections in the mirror-backed cases behind Herr Wiechert. With no surprise she saw two black-uniformed SS officers, one tall, one of average height. Behind them, still at the door, stood a corporal and at least one other.

"Listen, Jew," the shorter one drawled, "I want a pair of gold earrings, cheap. If I get them at cost, we might just forget to make a slight mess of your shop."

In a further reflection Julia saw that someone outside, a civilian, was renewing and embellishing the slogan and adding a swastika. A pair of civilians, in fact. She had looked away to spare the jeweller what embarrassment she could. She returned to the scene to find him staring coolly at the officer who had spoken. "As a patriotic German," he began . . .

But he got no further. With lightning speed the other officer slapped him hard with the back of his gloved hand. The pince-nez somersaulted over the counter and landed near the door. Whether or not they broke then was immaterial, for the corporal made a deliberately clumsy effort to retrieve them, in the course of which he ground them to splinters. All three laughed. The taller officer turned to Julia, plainly expecting her to share their amusement. With a speed no less than his she slapped his face as hard as she could.

"You are filth," she told him in the shocked silence that followed.

Wiechert, in great distress himself by now, put a futile arm across the broad glass expanse of his counter, managing to intrude only his hand between her and the officer. "Please, madame, do not try to involve yourself. It truly does not help." To the officers he explained, "She is English, sirs. Ignore her impertinence. She does not understand our modern ways."

"English?" echoed the shorter one. "She has a damnably Jewish look to me."

The words seemed to wake his comrade from out of his shock. "A Jewess?" he roared and, seizing Julia by her lapels, thrust her backward, causing her to lose her balance and fall against a showcase at the back of the street window, breaking its glass. She did not feel it cut her but she saw the blood where it smeared the remaining shards. She reeled groggily as she tried to rise. The glass made further cuts in her forearm. Then the officer was standing over her, kicking her in the ribs, calling her a filthy Jewess.

Someone came bursting in at the door and shouted "Jew!"

Someone behind him added, "Mummy!"

And then she realized that the first cry had not been *Jew* but *Ju!*

Max and Robert stood in horror at the door. The grinning corporal slapped them heartily on the back.

Her fading consciousness seemed to split into equal halves. In one, the melée continued at the same crazy pace; the officer went on kicking her; Wiechert, still imprisoned behind his counter, went on protesting; the shorter officer tried to smash the glass top with his riding crop – but to no avail. In the other half everything froze. Her eyes met those of her brother and son. She was beyond crying "Now! See! Look!" but her eyes shrieked it for her.

It was Robert who dashed forward and swung his paint pot at the officer. A long streak of primrose yellow fell upon the man, covering him from the shiny peak of his cap to his brightly burnished boots. It was the last thing Julia saw before she passed out. But as she spun down, down through that dark, her only thought was of Wallace.

She did not regain consciousness until the following night. Robert was at her bedside, dozing in a chair. She herself was floating between sleep and wakefulness but one good sight of him in the low-wattage lamplight tipped the balance into alertness – indeed, alarm. She tried to turn toward him and at once became aware of her many injuries. Her ribs felt as if a strong man were kneading them with knuckledusters; there were sharp, shooting pains, like needles, at the back and side of her neck; and her left arm throbbed and ached. The agony drew a small, involuntary cry from her.

Robert came awake at once. "Mummy?"

"Mmmm." She opened her eyes but this time made no attempt to move. "What time is it, darling? Come where I can see you."

A moment later she wished she had not asked. One of his eyes was closed, the other black and blue. His lip was cut and swollen and one half of his face was swathed in a dressing. "Oh, my poor boy," she cried, raising her unwounded arm to caress his cheek.

"Never mind me," he said. "I'm just walking wounded. Uncle Max is in the next room, you know. How about you? It must be awfully sore?"

"Max? Is he badly hurt?"

"You should see the others. They shot one of them – the tall one, Oberleutnant Schwarz." He reached across the bed – to straighten the covering, she supposed. But he put a finger into her lightly clenched fist and asked, "Can you feel anything?"

She squeezed him as hard as the pain allowed.

"Thank God for that," he exclaimed. "They were worried you might have lost the use of that arm."

"Good Lord. Was it cut so deep?"

"Don't!" He clenched his eyes against some awful image.

After a silence she asked, "Robert, what were you doing there in the first place?"

He withdrew his finger and sat back, outside her field of view, saying nothing.

"Were you actually *with* those . . . those beasts?" she asked.

"I didn't think it would be like that," he replied at last.

"What *did* you think, then?"

"They promised me it was just, you know, painting slogans."

"And that would have been all right, would it?"

Again he was silent. Slowly, riding the pain, she turned her head until she could see him. Tears were running down his face but he made no sound of weeping. "I was filling the star, the Jewish star, with the yellow paint" – he mimed it, re-enacting the horror of each moment – "and suddenly there, framed inside the bit I was about to fill, there was my . . . there were you." He clenched his teeth, forcing the words out between them. "And I *saw* the glass go into your neck and that swine kicking you. I *saw* it!" He broke down completely at that.

"Oh darling!" She cursed her wounds and the pain that imprisoned her.

After a while he mastered himself. The compulsion to talk still gripped him. "There's more. It was awful." He spoke calmly now, little above a whisper, and in a tone of awe – ghastly awe – as if he still could not quite believe it all. "A little girl came into the shop,

371

while they were beating Max and kicking him. She must have been Wiechert's daughter. Or the caretaker's – someone living above the shop, anyway. It doesn't matter whose. She was only a toddler. And Müller, the corporal, just picked her up and threw her back outside. Like . . . like a bundle of butcher's meat."

He fell silent, struggling to prevent himself from breaking down again.

Julia hated what she had to do next, yet knew she had no choice. She let the silence return and then, speaking with deliberate care, she said, "When your last suit came back from Achille Serre, there was the usual envelope full of things from your pockets. Among them was an essay in your hand. It began, 'A Jew is for me an object of physical disgust. I vomit when I see one . . . ' Do you . . ."

"It wasn't an essay," he mumbled. "It was a translation from something Dr Goebbels wrote. Uncle Max asked me to translate it for the Leader – I mean" – he shook his head angrily – "for Mosley." It was the first time she had heard him pronounce the name with the disgust most Englishmen gave it. "I didn't hand it over to him because of Lady Mosley's death and all that."

"Well, at least it wasn't something you thought up off your own bat. Did you agree with it? I tell you, *I* almost vomited when I found it."

He knelt at her bedside and kissed her. "It's over, Mummy," he whispered. "There's no need now to . . . just don't keep rubbing it in."

That kiss, more than anything he said, warmed her to him again. "And what about your Uncle Max?"

"I don't know. He's still unconscious." Quickly he added, "They say he's not in danger."

"It'll be the first time in his life, then."

Against his will – and mood – Robert laughed.

"What about the jeweller – Herr Wiechert? Has anyone been back to see him?"

"Mr Baker went. In fact, you've only just missed him. He's been here most of the time, too. And Mr McHugh, on and off. Anyway, when he got to the shop he found everything was cleared up. All the broken glass replaced . . . everything."

"And the little girl?"

"She's in hospital, too. They have to be in a separate wing, the Jews. D'you mind if I sit up again? This position . . ."

"No, do."

"I should tell someone you've come to. Are you hungry?"

"No, let's just . . . stay here and talk."

"Ueeergh!" He gave an anti-parental groan that came straight out of his childhood.

"Not about the past," she told him. "If you wish to close that and start afresh, then I'll only applaud. But there's also the future, isn't there. Tell me your thoughts on that."

"Well," he exclaimed with the least enthusiastic snort she had ever heard. "Daddy left all that mapped out for me, didn't he."

She considered several responses before saying, "I think you're doing him an injustice, darling – if I read your tone aright. Of course, it would have pleased him to see you sitting behind the Guv'nor's desk at Somerville's. But he'd never have let that pleasure stand in the way of your own choice of career. Just because he put his wishes in his will, don't treat them as if it were holy writ. What would you really like to do?"

He could not let go of his grudge. "I don't see that I have much choice."

"Wouldn't you much rather go into the army?"

He stopped breathing.

"Don't make me try and turn my head, there's a dear. Just answer."

"I can't believe I heard what you just said."

"The army? Why not? You could enlist in Uncle Max's old . . ."

By now he was laughing with disbelief. "You? The great pacifist? Telling me – why not join the army!"

"Yes, well," she answered quietly, "you're not the only one who's been forced to revise some cherished beliefs. There is a new evil in the world. What we saw in that shop the other day – that's not some little carbuncle on the body of Europe. It's not something we can simply allow to fester for a few months and then lance it and all will be well. It's a cancer. And if we don't fight it, it'll consume us all. Look what it almost did to you."

He sat there in stunned silence; even now he could hardly believe it. "You're saying you honestly wouldn't mind my joining up?"

"I'd be proud, my darling. And you haven't given me much lately to . . . well, well, never mind. I'd be proud to see you in khaki."

"And what about Somerville's?"

"Nothing simpler. You'd be the owner, and Miss Dawson would go on being your managing director."

He let out a gasp of wonder at the way his world had so totally rearranged itself in such short order.

"Could you go next door and see what news of Uncle Max?" she asked.

The next time she awoke it was daylight and the room was full of flowers. Wallace was at her side. Their eyes met. "God, you gave us a scare," he told her.

She closed her eyes again and smiled. It hurt even more now she was no longer half-drugged by sleep. There was a dull, hot pain at the side and back of her neck, and her arm was throbbing even more furiously. He slipped his index finger into her lightly clenched fist.

She squeezed back. "Robert did all that."

He gave out an enormous sigh of relief. "They were so afraid you might be paralyzed in that arm." He shifted his chair to where she could see him without moving anything more than her eyes. "Shall I ask if you're allowed to sit up?"

"No." Again that instinctive shake of the head – nipped in the bud of pain. This was going to be awful. "All these flowers," she murmured, rolling her eyes to take in as much of the room as she could.

"There's a bouquet from Reichsminister Hermann Göring – with a note regretting the incident and saying that the officer in question has been shot. Robert threw it out but Mickey McHugh insisted on putting it back. Robert's asleep now, by the way. He didn't rest until he knew you were all right."

"Is that what I am?" she chuckled.

For a while she just lay there, thinking his calm English voice was the most comforting and restful music she had ever heard.

"Shall I go and let someone know you've come round again?" he asked.

"In a mo. First, just go on telling me what's happened, what day it is . . . what people are doing."

His finger was still in her grasp. He tried to move it but she clutched even tighter. "You've been asleep . . . ah . . . the best part of thirty hours. Eliot Baring's on his way here with Lydia."

"Oh, they shouldn't. Has Max come round yet?"

"Yes – and eaten heartily. You must surely be hungry?"

"Soon. How is the old boy?"

"Pretty battered, you know. But his love affair with National Socialism is over at long last. I think the book-burning started the process . . ." His recital petered out. "Oh God, Julia, if you had died, I don't know what I'd have done."

"I knew I wouldn't," she replied. "I thought of you. As I lost consciousness, I could only think of you."

His one-finger grip tightened in her hand.

"Who sent the other flowers?" she asked.

"Your head will burst its bandages. They're from the Beaver, and Churchill, and Trenchard, and . . . oh, there's half a dozen House of Commons names there. Everyone at the SPRP, of course. Actually, I've made a list – having nothing better to do in the long watches of the night."

"Oh, Wallace – I do love you. But here . . . aren't you supposed to be covering the trial?"

"I'm managing that, too – somehow."

"Tell me about it? Tell me anything. Just talk."

"It's pretty much as Rosenheim predicted. This Bulgarian communist, Dimitrov, is walking circles around the prosecution. The whole show has degenerated into a rearguard action to prevent too much damaging information from emerging in open court. Dimitrov's the only man on record to have made Fat Hermann go red with anger in public."

"Talking of him – d'you really suppose they shot that SS officer – the one in the shop?"

There was a slight pause before he answered. "Well, he is certainly dead."

She froze as the true meaning of his words sank in. "Wallace – no!"

"And God help the sergeant if they don't post him out quick."

His voice was so calm and even; it was far more chilling than if he had put the normal emphasis upon the words.

"Oh, Wallace. I don't . . . I mean, I can't . . ."

"No one can do that sort of thing to you and get away with it." Bitterness crept in as he added, "The trouble is, my darling, it's the way of the whole party – not just one or two wild men among them. They will all have to be dealt with." He tickled her finger gently. "You do understand what I'm saying, eh?"

"Yes," she sighed.

She had a light lunch. The doctor came and gave her another Prontosil injection. She asked him how long she might expect to be detained in hospital but he refused to be drawn. As he left he barked, "Heil Hitler!" It was fast becoming the standard salutation among those who cherished their families and future.

When she awoke again it was evening. The lowering sun was streaming in through her windows, which were almost fully open; outside she could hear birdsong, the splash of water, children laughing.

And beside her: Max, half-whistling, half-breathing an *Enigma Variation* that Elgar somehow forgot to compose.

She did not need to turn her head. "Well, Max," she said.

"Quite. Yes, indeed." He went on with his tune.

Dammit, she thought. *I'm not going to make it easy for him.*

"It's a bloody shambles," he said.

I wasn't ruthless, not really. Just firm. I had to be – for his own good.

After another lengthy piece of sub-Elgar, he added, "D'you know – they burn *books!*"

On the other hand . . . No! Don't weaken.

"I told Goebbels and he promised he'd put a stop to it."

Just tell him you're sorry – what would it cost?

"In my opinion, the man's a professional liar. You see, Ju, the real problem is the Hun. Can't change his spots. Fascism's wasted on the Hun."

"Max . . ." she began

"It *ought* to be safe with the English. Fascism, I mean. But we've got our own Hunnish beasts. They've wrecked it in England, too."

"Max – I'm sorry." She let out the rest of her breath in one great rush. "There!"

Silence. She could almost hear the rusty cogs squeaking in his brain. He knew what she meant but he pretended to have misunderstood her. "Can't be helped," he replied philosophically. "Mosley's too dynamic. That's the root of it. If we had that little twerp . . . who's that Labour chappie who talks like a dentist's drill? If we had him in charge of . . ." He relapsed into silence and then added, in a tone much less ebullient, "Actually, old thing, I'm the one who should say sorry."

Penitence sat on Max about as well as the average infantry adjutant can sit a horse. Whatever the rights or wrongs of the case, his apology served only to make Julia feel as spiritually uncomfortable as she already was in the flesh. "Well, we've both said it," she told him. "Let's leave it at that. Shall we start seeing you down at Allbury again? The place doesn't somehow . . ."

"I say – steady in the line! Give it time, eh?"

"Oh yes – time." Julia sighed. "For two days – or whatever it's been – I'd forgotten such a thing even existed."

"Anyway." He cleared his throat. "I've found it in my heart to forgive you. Make do with that."

He rose and shambled back to his own room. On the way he must have passed Mickey McHugh, for, the very next moment, the door opened again and the man himself popped his head in. "God, that's grand," he chirped on seeing her awake. "Here's me head and this is the rest of me." He advanced toward her, smiling broadly.

"Sit yourself down, McHugh," she invited.

"That was an atrocious business, Boss. They say you were lucky, bad as it is."

"Other names for it have occurred to me. Tell me, now . . ."

He grinned. "I have a wee nip of the hard stuff that I'd never miss."

"Save it for my brother. Tell me, while we're alone, how important is Neville Flugzeugwerke to . . . er – *us?*"

He froze. He stared at her for what seemed an age and then asked, conversationally, "Did our friend Mr Baker tell you about his last little jaunt down in Kent?"

She grinned. "He told me enough to prompt my question."

"I see." He chewed his lip in annoyance. "Well, it's pretty important. That's not just my opinion."

"Good. That's what I thought you'd say. I just wanted you to know that the board of Neville's is very pleased with your work here in Germany. And as long as it continues to be so satisfactory – to *all* the parties involved – we would have no intention of accepting this offer from Dornier, or anyone else – unless, of course, you advised it?"

His annoyance turned to a grim kind of satisfaction. He plainly did not enjoy knowing that his game was rumbled, but he was glad she was able to be so cautious, especially in circumstances where a mere civilian might be pardoned for imagining they were alone. "No doubt we'll have to sell one day," he conceded. "And I'd waste not a second in telling you. We certainly wouldn't lose money by it."

"Good."

"Our pacifist policy is an important element in our success – of course, you realize that."

"I can foresee no change in that as far as *Neville's* is concerned."

He caught the implied qualification. His eyes narrowed but he said nothing.

She continued, "Did someone tell me Mr Baring is on his way here?"

McHugh checked his watch. "He should be here within the hour. He's flying in with Miss Lydia."

"So I heard, yes."

"He was on the point of sailing for America, you remember."

"I do. He was going to 'stall' this aviation company in Massachusetts, as he puts it. I hesitate to say this, yet in a ghastly way, a lot of good may have come out of my present circumstances – may Herr Wiechert forgive me for saying so. But I've been so impressed by what I see here in Germany – I mean, it's made such a marked impression on me, if you follow? – that I think we need to give a different answer to the Worcester Aircraft Corporation."

"We won't stall them any more?"

"I think stalling is the last thing one should do where aircraft are involved. *Any kind* of aircraft." She smiled. Even that hurt.

CHAPTER FORTY-NINE

"IT MUST BE understood that this is in no sense a meeting of the board of Neville's." Crownfield stared in turn at his fellow directors – Eliot, Brunty, Imogen, and Hannah Dawson.

"I'm glad that's made clear," Hannah commented.

"Yes," the banker went on. "The reason we're lunching here at the bank, rather than at Dollis Hill as is our usual custom, is that I, in a sense, sail under two flags – Neville's and Neville's bankers – and it is the latter pennant that you should imagine to be fluttering at the stern today."

There was a small ripple of laughter.

"Do the gentlemen mind if we smoke?" Hannah asked.

"My! *There's* a significant reversal," Crownfield commented. He took out his own case and offered it around, but people were already helping themselves from the boxes on the table. "I think our first bit of informal business should be to sign a well-wishers' card to our esteemed managing director and her brother, who, as I said earlier, are making such a magnificent recovery."

He took the card from a drawer in the table and started it on its way.

"Yes," Eliot remarked as he added his signature and a few *x*s, "even during the day or so that Lydia and I were there, she was fantastic. And when I called the hospital a couple of hours ago, they told me she'll be allowed up today and could be out next week."

"Oh?" Crownfield looked puzzled. "I mean – oh!" Now he seemed pleased. "I must have spoken to somebody else. They said two weeks at the earliest. Still – either way, time marches on and certain decisions are pressing. And, as I say, although this is not an official board meeting, I felt it my duty to bring up to date those directors still in harness. Someone will then have to fly to Berlin to talk to the Boss, who, as always, will have the final word."

"I'm going over to see her again soon," Eliot told him. "The Massachusetts deal is pretty well squared up now – I mean, we've reached the point where we've got to face them over a table."

The banker nodded. "That's one of the things, of course. However, some fairly intricate financial juggling is involved, so perhaps you wouldn't mind if Brunty goes to Germany with you?"

"Delighted." Eliot grinned at Brunty.

Brunty smiled at Crownfield, who took it as a signal to proceed. "Let's start, then, with the Massachusetts deal. The idea, as you know, is for Neville's to acquire the Worcester Aircraft Corporation. Now WAC enjoys a fine reputation and had a good trading history until the Wall Street Crash, which found them over-committed and" – he looked round with a twinkle in his eye – "under-capitalized, a word familiar to us all, I think!"

"Is that still the case?" Hannah asked Eliot.

"'Fraid so." He nodded dourly.

"You can see why some fancy footwork is called for in *our* department," Brunty commented. "A chronically under-capitalized British company is about to take over a temporarily under-capitalized American one."

"Can it be done?" Imogen asked.

"I can't deny it's risky. Especially when you look at our other commitments, which" – he turned to Crownfield – "is your next point, I imagine?"

The banker smiled. "My next dozen points, I should think. The Pony is proving an immense success in both its sea and land versions. Orders far exceed our present capacity. The question is, how do we satisfy them? We said goodbye to a lot of profit when we entered into those licensing arrangements for the Fleetliner, the Bushmaster, and the Amazon."

"And the Orinoco," Eliot added.

"Indeed yes. So shall we yet again . . ."

Hannah grew impatient. "Listen, Crownfield, this is a tediously familiar melody. We all know the arguments in favour of increasing our capital by means of a share flotation. And probably we all agree that it's something we ought to do in an ideal world." She glanced around the table. "But we also know the Boss hates the very idea. So aren't we wasting our breath?"

"Not necessarily, Dawson." It was Eliot who answered. "I've discussed this with Brunty and we think we see a way – without treading on the Boss's susceptibilities in the slightest degree. It all hinges on this Worcester deal. However, perhaps Brunty should tell us about it. I just threw in the original suggestion. He's the one who's developed it."

Brunty, who became more not less professorial with the passing years, leaned back in his chair and stared at the ceiling. "As Baring says, it all hinges on the Worcester deal. The Boss's hatred of diluting her ownership of Neville's is more than understandable. I for one have always supported her in it. But the same arguments can hardly apply to WAC. So our idea is that as soon as we've bought the company we float it on Wall Street. When it's known that WAC is now owned by Neville's and will be building virtually all of Neville's planes for the American markets, then . . ."

"Except for the Argentine," Imogen objected.

Crownfield frowned and looked at Brunty, who said, "She's right, but it's a quibble. Let's not get bogged down in detail, eh? The point is that as soon as it's known what a rosy future there is for WAC its value will rise to – we think – about double what we shall pay for it. In round figures just under forty percent of the equity will recoup our entire purchase price."

"You mean we acquire the company for nothing?" Hannah asked.

"No. We just get the remaining sixty percent of it for nothing. But that's not all. They have certain other assets – land mainly – I won't bore you with details. They could all be sold off without harming the aero side of the business."

"In short," Crownfield interpolated, "by the end of the year WAC could be awash with cash."

"But Neville's can't just appropriate it," Hannah objected – think-

379

ing she saw their purpose.

The two moneymen grinned. "There's nothing to stop WAC from making advance payments on parts, engines, sub-assemblies . . . all the things it's going to be buying from Neville's in future. Also inter-company loans. Leave it to us – we can move the money legally and ethically to Neville's."

"Can we put figures on it yet?" Eliot asked.

"Hold tight, everyone." Crownfield beamed. "If sterling stays close to three dollars seventy-five, Neville's could easily find itself with around sixty thousand pounds in cash by the end of the year."

"For nothing!" Hannah laughed.

"Not quite that," Crownfield objected. "In a sense the money's there now but only Neville's can get at it. In short, this plan allows the Boss to capitalize the Neville name without selling a penny of actual Neville equity. I believe the idea will appeal to her."

Hannah cleared her throat. "Before we get carried away with euphoria, one thing should be said. We've all chafed from time to time at our perennial shortage of working capital. And financial wizards with only one tenth of your skills, Brunty, could show exactly where and how it's done harm to Neville's. But what is just as true – though no one can prove it so easily – is that the Boss's way of managing this firm has run circles around more orthodox theorists." She studiously avoided looking toward Crownfield. "For example, her decision not to build military aircraft looked utterly suicidal at the time. And yet – by keeping free of the dreaded 'Air Ministry spec' – Neville's has consistently stayed four or five years ahead of the crowd. I know that's not always a good thing. After all, Rolls-Royce's motto is, *Never be first*. But in our case, who can deny that it has brought us from nowhere to the very forefront of the industry in just six or seven years?" She turned to Eliot. "I know most of the technical credit for that is yours, old boy. But if the Boss had insisted on designing everything so as to meet the latest spec, would *any* of our planes ever have flown?" She smiled. "Sorry. I didn't mean to go on. But I thought it ought to be said."

"Indeed, indeed," Crownfield was murmuring. Eliot's thoughtful silence worried him; he sought hastily for a counter-argument. "On the other hand, neither of our technical directors needs me to tell them that the control settings that will cause a plane to rise above the clouds are quite different from the settings needed to keep it there. There comes a time when negative tactics – avoiding official specs, refusing to go public, and so on – do more harm than good. However, we're all of us on the same side here. We've found a way of satisfying all our apparently conflicting wishes."

Eliot returned to an earlier point. "Sixty thousand pounds is a whole lot more than I expected."

The banker nodded gravely. "Officially we're saying fifty, to err on the side of caution."

"I'd like to see the figures, even so."

Brunty looked at Crownfield, who smiled and answered, "Of course. Brunty can show them to you on your way to Berlin. Well!" He stubbed out his cigarette and rubbed his hands. "That was the good news. The rest is not so cheerful, I'm afraid."

"The rest" proved to be a list of developments to which Neville's was committed, or soon would be if they decided not to license the Pony but to build all the planes themselves. "In short," Brunty summarized it for them some twenty minutes later, "if we don't achieve that magical fifty thou' via WAC, we'll be in dire trouble . . . far worse than anything we've yet tried to weather."

On which sombrely hopeful note the meeting broke up.

Brunty stayed behind "to dot a few *i*s and cross a *t* or two," he explained.

As soon as they were alone Crownfield asked, "Your figures – they will pass Baring's scrutiny?"

Brunty grinned. "You're talking about my masterpiece."

The other relaxed somewhat. "And yet you're sure there's no hope whatever of actually reaching fifty thou'?"

"We won't get within sight of twenty, man – trust me."

Crownfield relaxed completely at this assurance. He soaped his hands again. "We've got her this time, my friend. She'll be so overbalanced, she's bound to fall." He saw Brunty frown and corrected it to: "Fall in with our much more rational plans for Neville's, I mean."

The accountant was only partly appeased. "See here, Crownfield, I hope there's nothing personal in this? True, we're working behind the Boss's back – but we both know it's entirely for her own good, and for the good of Neville's. She'll be furious, of course, but when it's over, she'll be thanking us."

"Quite," Crownfield replied, seeking to appear chastened. "I couldn't agree more. She will make a wonderful chairman of the new company – just as *you* are going to be a superb managing director." His amusement bubbled up again. "I say, what about little Hannah Dawson, eh? Trying to tell us that Julia Somerville's the greatest gift to industry since the invention of fire and the wheel. Trust a pair of females to stick together! I'm only surprised young Imogen didn't add her soprano bleating to the chorus." A further thought struck him. "By the way, what was that about excluding the Argentine?"

"Oh, it'll probably come to nothing. Some chum of hers or Max's has got together with Peter Rosenheim – the man who sold us Segelflug Hessen, you remember. He's designed a high-altitude cargo plane that could work in the Andes. They were going to build it themselves in the Argentine, but now they want to license Neville's instead."

Crownfield was happy again. "So Neville's is to stretch itself in yet one more direction! Good-good."

Again, his ebullience worried Brunty. "Don't underestimate the Boss, Crownfield," he warned. "On a good day she's pretty magnificent."

"In the dusk with the light behind her!"

"No, truly."

Crownfield gave a sour smile and shook his head. "I thought so once – during her first year in the saddle. I was brought up to believe that women in business were like Dr Johnson's dog walking on its hind legs. And she seemed to disprove all that. But, it was all a flash in the pan. Managing director? She couldn't manage to roll eggs downhill. She just lurches from one emotional female intuition to another – some of which, more by luck than good judgement, happen to pay off. No, take my word for it – when we've forced her to go public with Neville's – when we've got our wild young moorland filly between the shafts, shareholders on one side, banks on the other . . ." He seemed to lose the thread of his own argument.

Brunty finished it for him: "Then, by God, she'll pull the firm forward at the smartest pace you ever saw! You put it so exactly, Crownfield. That's the only reason I'm willing to go behind her back like this."

"Ye-es," Crownfield observed. "Something like that, anyway."

Julia was out of hospital before Eliot and Brunty arrived in Berlin; indeed, she was out of the Kaiserhof, too. They found her at the old Germania instead.

"I didn't notice it before," she explained, "but the Kaiserhof is almost the Nazis' own hotel – swarming with them. The Oberkellner actually pointed out with pride that I was sitting at the very table where Goebbels, Göring, and Hess waited for the Führer to come back from Hindenburg clutching the chancellor's seals of office in his grubby little hands." She shivered. "I moved here within the hour. So!" She smiled. "Thank you for your cards and letters. They did more for my recovery than all the Prontosil in Germany. How many crises have come and gone at Neville's while I've been idling here?"

It was their cue to explain their ingenious scheme for capitalizing the Neville name without issuing a single share. Needless to say, Julia required a great deal of convincing. It was only when the alternatives were canvassed – the need to postpone several projects and, yet again, to license other firms to produce the Pony – that she began to cave in.

Then Brunty made the mistake of pushing a little too hard. "You really ought to make up your mind this week, Boss," he warned.

Eliot saw it at once. "Not at all," he assured her, looking daggers at the accountant. "I won't be in Worcester, Massachusetts, until three weeks today. We have that long. But not much longer, Boss," he cautioned with a smile. "We'd lose momentum. The acquisition will get good coverage and we ought to build on it at once."

Still Julia was doubtful. "Fifty thousand pounds seems extraordinarily high," she remarked.

Eliot nodded. "I felt the same. But I've been through Brunty's figures every which way and they check out okay."

"Well," Brunty looked at his watch, "I must leave it with you. I'm flying back tonight as there's so much to do – and my wife has told me not to dare return without" – he fished a list from his pocket – "something called a Catty Cruiser doll?"

"Käte Kruse?" Julia asked. "Oh, they're lovely – in a rather Germanic sort of way." And she told him where to find the best selection.

When they were alone she and Eliot went for a stroll around the old city.

"You're looking so much better than when I saw you last," he told her.

"Those first few days seem like a dream now. A nightmare. I don't think I could face constant pain, you know."

"I wanted to go out and shoot everyone in a black uniform." He smashed one great fist into the palm of his other hand.

She thought of Wallace's quiet confession. "The chance will come soon enough, I fear."

He pricked up his ears. "Did I just hear what I think I just heard?"

She took his arm. "I didn't want to say anything while Brunty was there, but I have plans for WAC. I almost told you last time but I just needed to think about it a bit more."

"Plans?"

"Yes. I don't know whether they'll affect your scheme for floating the company?"

"What are they?"

"This having to lie in bed – so far from the daily round at Neville's – it's been a blessing in disguise, you know."

"You do surprise me." He chuckled. "Solitary thinking never was your forte."

"Oh, but I haven't been alone. Wallace Baker – you know, Dolly's husband? – he's covering the Reichstag Fire Trial for Beaverbrook. Anyway, he's popped in from time to time to jolly me along. He knows so much about Europe . . . France, Germany . . . the way everything's going. I hate to admit it – I've had my head in the sand these last few years." She laughed and squeezed his arm until he protested. "Don't you *dare* tell Crownfield I ever said any such thing! But anyway," she became serious again, "the question is: How many designs for military planes have you been piling up in secret behind my back?"

"None," was the laconic reply.

"Really?"

"Honest injun."

"Oh, Eliot – that *is* loyalty."

"My middle name, honey." He hugged her arm.

She veered away from the line he offered. "How soon could we get a model of a fast one-seater interceptor into the wind tunnel?"

He shrugged. "I shall have to check on the latest batch of Air Ministry specs. I'm a bit out of touch on . . ."

"Oh no!" she said vehemently. "I'm not lifting my head out of *my* sand and sticking it straight back into *theirs!* You just ask Mickey McHugh what he saw at Rechlin last time he was there – and what Messerschmidt and Dornier are up to. No, the interceptor that's capable of knocking the *Luftwaffe* out of the sky won't owe a single *rivet* to any Air Ministry spec. That is still holy writ as far as Neville's is concerned."

"To what, then?"

She disengaged her arm and raised it to tap his hat with her finger. "To what's inside there. I'll set you a challenge, Eliot. In five years from now, I'd like to fly at a sustained speed of four hundred and fifty miles an hour."

He gave a low whistle. "Just forwards, I hope."

She drew a deep breath before she spoke her next words. "The hardest part of all, my dear, is that I'd like you to stay on in Massachusetts and do it all there at WAC."

He stopped in his tracks. Reluctantly she turned to him and saw that the blood had drained from his face. "Leave?" he asked.

She nodded miserably.

"Just . . . go?" He stared at the buildings about them, followed the traffic aimlessly with his eyes, as if he had that moment woken up from a long sleep.

"You see," she tried to explain, "I don't want any direct connection between Neville's name and warplanes. It's to do with . . ."

"Julia!" His eyes were filled with a mute plea.

She steeled herself and went on: "Our business here in Germany would suffer if . . ."

"You know that's not it!" he exclaimed.

"Oh, my dear." Her lip trembled. "Please don't make it any harder. Surely you know by now that I'm never . . . that we're just not . . ." She choked on her own words and had to look away. "It would be better for both of us," she murmured.

"There's someone else." His words were like gunfire behind her.

She turned to him again. "Whether there is or not, it doesn't make any . . ."

"There *is* someone else. My God, I didn't believe it! Who is it? It's someone here in Germany."

After a silence he added, "You see, you can't deny it."

She sighed. "There's no one else in *that* sense."

"Oh? What other sense is there?"

She turned and took a step back toward the hotel. "All right told him, "there is someone. But he's already married. What's he's very fond of his wife – and so am I . . ."

"You mean you know her?"

She nodded. "I'm afraid so. Neither of us is willing to hurt not for all the world. So, if you mean 'someone else' in the sense we're going to run off and get married tomorrow, then . . . answer's no. Nothing's going to change. Nothing's ever going change. Except that I can't bear to deceive you any longer."

"Any longer?" The echo was filled with anger. "How long has been going on then?"

"In his case, from the very moment we met, which was" – sl closed her eyes as if it might lessen the pain – "in April, 1927."

"And in your case?"

"Maybe since then, too. I don't know. But I'm sure about *now.*"

"God, I think I'll go out of my mind! You're saying you've deceived me all that time?"

"No! Not consciously. Please listen, my dear . . ."

"To what?" He turned and walked angrily away from her. "To the lies behind the lies?"

She ran and caught up with him, plucking at his sleeve as she begged him to stop and listen. "It's not at all the way it must seem."

But he would not stop. Still striding out he rounded on her and snarled, "Just leave me be! Leave me alone! I don't ever want to see you again."

PART FIVE

OUT OF A CLEAR BLUE SKY

CHAPTER FIFTY

SHE HAD BEEN crying. Wallace Baker saw it at once. His first thought was that she had suffered some further unpleasantness with the Nazis. When she explained, he was relieved – and even said cheerfully, "Well, thank heavens the truth is out at last."

"Oh, but I didn't mention any names," she told him quickly. "Not even the smallest hint."

His face fell. "You didn't?"

"You mean you want it all to come out? In spite of what it would do to Dolly?"

He sighed. "I suppose not." He put his arms about her and hugged her for reassurance.

"Eliot flew back with Brunty this evening. They probably haven't landed yet. I should have gone with them. I can't let him go to America in this mood."

"I'm finishing up in Berlin this week," he told her. "The trial has degenerated into a farce and the Beaver agrees there's no point hanging on. Shall we take off for a holiday? I'll dash back and say bon voyage to Dolly, then we could . . . what – pinch someone's yacht and go pottering about the Aegean? There's a super midnight-sun cruise from Bergen around the north of Norway. Or what about Leningrad? I've never seen the Hermitage . . ."

Each suggestion sounded more enticing than the last but she knew that, even on the most idyllic holiday in the world, she'd not be at peace until she had made it up with Eliot. "The thing is," she said, "I know him. I know that stubborn streak. After all, it's what makes him such a wonderful designer of planes. But there's only about ten days left before he sails. He can hold out that long easily. He wouldn't give me a chance."

Wallace chuckled. "Take an earlier boat and be there to greet him in New York."

"Well, that's the other thing. Brunty and Eliot have cooked up a scheme to raise money on Wall Street."

"A good one?"

She looked at him uncertainly. "It's almost too good, Wallace. I think I have to go over there and sniff the breeze for myself." She broke into a slow grin. "Now if I only knew which boat he was sailing on . . ."

It was, of course, the easiest thing in the world to find out. Within an hour of her return to Dollis Hill, Mrs Henderson, her secretary, had learned from Eliot's secretary that he was sailing on the next crossing of the *Mauretania*.

"The only problem," she told Wallace that evening, "is that every cabin and stateroom is booked. My only hope is a last-minute cancellation."

With a Cheshire cat's grin he picked up the phone and dialled a number from memory. To her surprise his next words were, "Lord Beaverbrook, please. This is Wallace Baker." And then, after some general newspaper chat: "Listen, Max – I was just thinking that – what with the Nazi rally in Nuremberg next week and then . . . you what? . . . Oh, well, yes, I suppose I could. Damn – I walked into that one, didn't I! . . . Yes, yes – I haven't even unpacked my German dictionary yet. Okay. Anyway, what with that and then Bernard Baruch coming over to see Churchill the week after – I don't suppose you'll have much need for your suite on the *Mauretania*, will you?" After a pause he went on. "As a matter of fact, it's for an old friend of yours. Let me pass you over to her."

Julia took the handset. "Max? It's Julia Somerville. Listen – this is entirely Baker's idea. I didn't even know you had a suite on the . . ."

"It's yours from this moment, my dear," rasped the familiar Canadian voice at the other end. "You'll get the necessary papers in tomorrow afternoon's delivery. And just let me know when you wish to come back."

"Oh, dear Max. That is so good of you – and so very characteristic. For various reasons I *have to* go on that sailing and would you believe it – every single cabin . . ."

"Not another word, Julia. It needs an airing." He chuckled. "You know the system, now? Have you crossed the Atlantic before?"

"No, I'm ashamed to say."

"Well, a normal first-class ticket includes all meals in the first-class dining room. But swell people dine à la carte in the grill and pay for it. *Really* swell people never leave their staterooms and have all meals brought in."

"And I suppose the really-*really* swell people buy a ticket but don't actually travel at all!" She had meant it as a joke but then it struck her. "Like *you*, you old fox!"

"Now you have it. Bon voyage!"

"Listen, Max – there's so much to tell you. A lot of things are happening and even more are about to happen. Keep me a lunch free in the last week of September and I promise I'll set your ears alight."

She rang off and returned the phone to its little table. Then she sat on Wallace's lap and put her arms around him. "Oh darling, you're so competent . . . and organized and . . . knowing. And wise." She kissed his ear. "And out of reach."

"And in love with you," he murmured.

"What are we going to do? I feel everything's coming to the boil."

Suddenly she sat bolt upright and exclaimed, in quite a different voice. "My God! Dolly! Lexy – Héloïse – New York!"

Smiling, he pulled her back into his arms; running his lips up and down the side of her neck he murmured, "She's booked on the *Oceanic*. Would you mind awfully if I spend the next hour or two telling you how much I'll miss you?"

When Julia heard that Beaverbrook's staterooms included three bedrooms she decided to take Lydia and Robert, too. Robert would be joining his regiment soon and this would be his last chance of a good holiday for some years. Lydia, her mother felt, should start to be *in* on things, and there was nothing like jumping in at the deep end. They were down on the passenger list under the surname of Perceval, her mother's maiden name; she explained it to them as a matter of commercial secrecy. They left Southampton for Cherbourg on the last Friday in August.

The *Mauretania* and her ill-fated sister, *Lusitania*, had always been called "The Incomparables." Other great liners were described as floating grand hotels, but the word "palaces" was reserved for these two jewels of the Cunard fleet. *Lusitania*, all white enamel and gold, had been considered slightly more elegant than *Mauretania*, with her traditional interior of carved oak, mahogany, and cut glass; but *Lusitania*, whose sinking by a German U-boat had brought America into the Great War, had lain drowned these last eighteen years off the coast of County Cork, and ever since then the surviving sister had been peerless on the ocean. Her post-war refit had added every modern convenience to the never-to-be-repeated elegance of the Edwardian original.

Everyone aboard knew she was probably in the last year or two of her life. Work on the *Queen Mary*, which had been halted by the economic blizzard in 1931, would restart soon; and then there'd be no room in the same fleet for a 26-year-old ship, no matter how elegant.

Julia and the two youngsters stood on the promenade deck, throwing paper streamers at the crowds on the quayside. She had not mentioned that Eliot would be on board and she did her best not to hunt around for him, not even with her eyes. She rather hoped one of the youngsters would find him first; he could hardly be churlish with them.

Soon a thousand bright streaks of colour, arcing from brilliant sunshine into the warm darks of the overshadowed dock, enmeshed a sea of upturned faces. The band played its heart out as the fussy little tugs pushed and hauled at her 40,000 tons. At first they produced nothing but a wrath of white water. Then "Look! Look!" came the cry as the streamers grew taut and one by one began to snap. If they had been chains of bondage the redoubled cheers could not have been louder – and they grew louder still as sunlight ousted the shade. Soon their arms grew weary with the waving and they rested on the rail, contenting themselves with an occasional token flutter – until the ants who had been people merged into the general coloration of the shore.

By now the ship's own turbines were reducing the work of the tugs to light steering and correction. And then at last she was independent of them altogether, out in the Solent and ploughing a salt-white furrow toward the Channel and France. Looking down at her vast sides, at the black, foam-mottled water slipping aft with no more fuss or noise than you'd expect from a small launch – from Lexy's *Marina,* say – on a choppy estuary, Julia was lifted into a sudden awareness of the magic of a long sea voyage. It is a magic that, though especially powerful at the moment of embarkation, is never exhausted and which lingers for months, even when every detail of the trip itself is long forgotten.

If Eliot was there at that traditional leave-taking, none of them noticed him. At dinner time Julia glanced around the grill, observed no Eliot, and suggested, "Let's just see what the first-class dining room offers."

"Scrooge," Lydia muttered.

But the menu was as good as any at the Ritz or the Savoy, and the sea was calm, the music sweet, the lights warm and subdued; they soon forgot that, in terms of the *Mauretania,* this was slumming. They were just about to begin their main course when Robert nudged his sister and nodded toward a table behind their mother.

Lydia exclaimed, "Good heavens. Look who it is!"

Julia smiled at them both and murmured, "I've been waiting for this. Pretend we haven't seen him – I mean, let him discover us."

Brother and sister exchanged puzzled glances. "Dearest Mama," Lydia said, "*who* do you think is sitting three tables behind you?"

"Isn't it Uncle Eliot?"

The two youngsters laughed.

"Who is it then?"

"Aunt Dolly!" they whispered in unison.

Julia's heart fell.

The other two were still encouraging each other to laugh; but then Robert broke it off. "Just a mo," he exclaimed. "The mater must be turning psychic in her old age. Look who's just joined Aunt Dolly!"

CHAPTER FIFTY-ONE

LYDIA STARED moodily at the sea. The Atlantic Ocean was a fraud. For three days it had just sat there, bright and shimmering, stirred only by the gentlest swell. You weren't even aware of it unless you took a fix on the horizon against the rails at the bow; then you could see a tiny, ponderous rise and fall, no more than three cycles per minute.

"Haven't you finished yet?" she asked as she stood up to move her deck chair away from a threatening shadow.

Julia took a sip of grenadilla before she answered; she held it briefly toward the deck steward for more ice. "What's the hurry?" she responded. "I thought you said it was all tosh."

"Well, so it is. But there's nothing else to read."

"There's a whole library full of books."

The fresh ice made a deliciously chill tinkle in the glass.

Lydia sat down again and stretched herself in the sun. "I just want something mindless. Anyway, I thought you said you'd read that one last year."

"I keep getting that feeling I did, and then something new happens and I begin to doubt it."

"It's all displacement, you know," Lydia observed.

"Displacement," her mother echoed absent-mindedly.

Petalis, the Flower of the Veldt, was about to be devoured by a lion, and craggy big-game hunter Bill Carter was coming to her rescue. In *real* life (insofar as the word had any meaning between those pages) he was a rich Canadian businessman.

"Yes, displacement." Lydia was disappointed that her challenge had fallen so flat.

It was the Canadian bit that bothered Julia; if craggy Carter had been a rich American businessman, she'd have been sure she'd read it before. He was such a *bad* businessman, so debonair and careless. She spent most of the book having fantasies in which she walked off with all his trade – in a setting that was half prairie, half Rocky Mountain. If she'd had those same fantasies in an equally improbable mixture of

Manhattan and the Grand Canyon, she'd have remembered it.

Anyway, the lion was terrifyingly authentic.

"A poor substitute for the real thing," Lydia added.

"If you keep up this chatter, we'll reach New York before you inherit this book."

Actually, Julia thought. *If she keeps up this chatter I'll have to pass it on to her and admit I've got eleven others inside.*

"Goodness, what a tragedy," Lydia replied.

Julia closed the book with a sigh. "In other words, you want to talk."

"Not if you don't"

"It depends what about."

"Well, what d'you think?"

"Eliot and Dolly?"

"Hooray!"

"What of them?"

"Don't you think they behaved a little . . . well – sort of odd when they spotted us at dinner last night?"

Julia had already decided what gloss to put on it. She smiled. "You're much too perceptive for someone your age, darling. Keep it under your hat but Uncle Eliot and I have had a bit of a quarrel. He's furious with me for taking this trip at all. He says I can't delegate. I have to do it all myself. It must seem to everyone else that I don't trust him – especially when the whole Worcester deal is his 'baby,' as he calls it." She gave a long-suffering smile. "I can't say I blame him – even though that's not at all what I'm coming over for."

"Does he know that – I mean, have you told him?"

"I've hardly had the chance yet."

"What *are* you coming over for?"

"The thing I was telling you about – floating WAC on Wall Street and selling off some of its secondary assets. Brunty and Eliot think it'll raise something like a hundred and eighty thousand dollars. I find that very hard to believe. And I'm not someone like Crownfield, who could sit deep in a cave somewhere, looking at papers and making decisions. I have to see things for myself. That's why I'm coming over."

Lydia screwed up her face. "But surely it's easy enough to tell him that? It's hardly taken a minute."

"It's a bit more complicated, darling."

"I wonder if this is *too* soon?" Lydia mused.

"What d'you mean?"

"On the river at Bedford, remember? You said you'd tell me soon."

"Oh dear." Julia screwed up her eyes and rubbed her forehead. "There's one awful thing about promises."

After a silence Lydia pressed, "Well, is it?"

"When you were younger," Julia spoke hesitantly, "did you ever feel . . . sort of neglected?"

"Good lord, no. Why?"

"I always felt guilty about that."

"There were times when I hated you, of course."

"Of course? Why of course?"

"Oh . . . you just seemed so perfect at everything. You always knew the right thing to say. Mrs Crookes said you're the perfect mistress of a household. And you remember Miss Nightingale – my last governess before Summerhill? I think she worshipped you from afar."

"Oh really, Lydia!"

"It's true. When you took over Somerville's and started Neville's and all that. She said you were the New Woman. And all I could do was smile and sit there *hating* you and *hating* you." She warmed to her theme as the memory returned. "I just seethed with it."

"But you never said a word!"

"There was nothing I could do, nowhere I could turn. You'd been everywhere before me and done it better."

"What about engineering?"

Lydia gave an ironic chuckle. "Yes, isn't that a marvellous thing for a girl to excel at! It means so much to the world in general. 'D'you know, my dear, my poor ignorant mother has no idea of the difference between a fully-floated and a semi-floated half-shaft!' Doesn't that sound . . ."

Julia bridled at the accusation. "As a matter of fact, I do."

"*Aaaargh!*" Lydia pretended to tear out her hair.

"Sorry!" Julia was all contrition. She touched her daughter's arm, hesitantly, withdrew . . . touched it again. "Sorry! You're right. Oh dear!"

"And when I fell in love and made such a mess of it . . . and there you were, supremely above all that sort of thing. Uncle Eliot at your feet and Uncle Lexy just adoring you – and the way Mr Crownfield treats you. They'd all just eat out of your hand and you can say *pfff!* to all of them!"

She ran out of steam. Into the silence that followed Julia said, "If you'll just hold your horses for five minutes, I'll tell you exactly how perfect and infallible and self-sufficient your mother really is. Obviously it's not too soon."

She told of her first love affair, with a lad from Ware, which had been a disaster from beginning to end. She described the shallowness of her feelings and ideas at the time she had married George. She revealed the utterly stupid and irrational fears of poverty that had haunted her since the days of Theresa Ashbury's challenge. She told of the grievous error she had made about the two little water colours, and how it had contributed to George's death. She spoke of her emotional confusion at the time of the funeral and how it had led her almost to throw herself at Crownfield and how only his instincts as a gentleman had saved her. She listed a number of serious errors she had made in managing the business, any one of which could have combined with a run of bad luck to ruin them – the greatest of all being her edict against military work. "Good intentions have nothing to do with so-called perfection, you see," she added.

"But I think my greatest error of all has been Uncle Eliot," she concluded. "I only hope I haven't spoiled his life."

And she explained that, too.

"It's a great burden of *perfection* to have to carry through life," she summed up.

Lydia bit her lip, sniffed, blinked rapidly. She could say nothing; she just took her mother's hand and stroked it. But after a while she found her voice again. "And now there's no one to help with the carrying?"

Julia grinned. "Now I didn't say that. I was only telling you of my *mistakes.*"

"Ah!" The smile returned to her daughter's face – an expectant smile at that.

But Julia shook her head. "Soon," she promised. And she tossed her "Petalis, Flower of the Veldt."

At that same moment, farther down the deck, Eliot and Dolly, having just been eliminated from the quoits tournament, were stretched full length, soaking up the ozone.

"What will they say about a suntanned Héloïse?" he asked.

She lay with her eyes closed and drawled, "If they say anything at all, it'll be about what marvellous make-up Leichner do these days."

"You mean Paul Robeson could play Desdemona?"

She gave a dirty chuckle. "I wouldn't like to be the one to suggest the necessary surgery to him."

"No, but that's the challenge, isn't it? Think how excited Lon Chaney must have been when they told him he'd been picked for the Hunchback – and how awful it'd have been if they'd scoured America for a real hunchback with an acting diploma. Isn't that right? The illusion itself is the important bit?"

After a pause she said, "Yes. Illusion and reality. You'd think that someone who spends her life trading in both would know the difference."

He let a silence grow and then asked, "Are you ever going to tell me?"

"Tell you what?" she responded lightly.

"Ever since you called me and asked would I mind if you changed your booking to this ship, I've had this feeling that you wish to . . . or need to . . ."

"How close are you to Julia?" Dolly asked suddenly.

"That's a good question."

"You see – *you're* keeping something back, too."

He raised himself on one elbow. "Like for instance what? She obviously doesn't trust me to do this deal with Worcester – that's all I meant."

The look in Dolly's eyes was almost of contempt. "All right, Eliot," she sighed. "If you say so."

He saw he had almost lost her – and in the same instant he realized, suddenly, how much he wanted to talk about it. And more than that – he wanted to talk to her.

"You're right," he admitted. "It's just foolish pride. The fact is, your sister and I have had a sort of on-off *affaire* for . . . well, to be honest, since before George died."

"*Before* he died?" Dolly was astounded. "Honestly? Prim old Ju? I can't believe it."

"Not in a physical sense. I mean, physically we didn't even kiss or touch each other until . . . oh, a month or more after the funeral. But" – he tapped his skull – "in the white, anglo-saxon protestant sense of the word, yes, she was unfaithful. And now it's over." He lay back again and let the sun soak into his skin.

"Well, there's my secret," he added after a while. "What's yours? A lot more interesting, I imagine."

For a long while she said nothing. Then, in a flat, faraway tone, she observed, "I thought I had only one. Now it seems I have two."

"Tell me either of them," he encouraged her. "I don't mind."

"You will, you know," she assured him. "Just let me think about it a bit, eh? I'll try and . . . well, let's come up on deck after dinner."

That evening she took their liqueurs on deck; he slipped below to her cabin to fetch her wrap. He found her near the stern, making fiery trails among the stars with the glowing tip of her cigarette. "Perfect," she told him. "In six seconds I shall start to feel the first little twinge of a draught."

He slipped the mink jacket around her shoulders and bent to retrieve their glasses, which were in the scupper at her feet.

He kindled his cigarette from hers and for a while they leaned on the rail, side by side, in easeful silence.

"In such a night," she murmured at last, "stood Dido with a willow in her hand upon the wild sea-banks, and waft her love to come again to Carthage. In such a night Medea gathered the enchanted herbs that did renew old Æson . . ."

"In such a night," he interrupted, "Troilus methinks mounted the Troyan walls, and sighed his soul toward the Grecian tents, where Cressid lay that night."

"Well, well!" she exclaimed.

"You picked lucky," he told her. "We did 'The Merchant' when I was at Harvard. You didn't know I was once a thespian, eh?"

She grew serious again. "One of many things I didn't know, it seems."

He leaned on the rail beside her, their arms just touching, puffing his cigarette, watching the sparks dance downward, and he fought his impulse to prompt her.

At last she said, "If I don't tell you, Eliot, I'll go mad. You spoke this afternoon about a lingering *affaire* between you and Julia. Did you ever think it might ripen into marriage?"

He shrugged. "I hoped, of course."

She drew deeply on her cigarette and let it out in an explosive puff, without inhaling. "You hoped against hope then," she intoned flatly.

"Did Julia ever tell you that?"

"Of course not. I knew nothing about you and her until today. No – I know it was hopeless because I've known, all these years, who she's really in love with."

"Oh."

Dolly frowned and turned to him. "You don't sound too-too surprised?"

"No. In Berlin, you see – well, she mentioned something about it. She said she'd been in love – or *might* have been in love, I don't know – with some man ever since . . . oh God, she even mentioned the date."

"April the twenty-ninth, nineteen twenty-seven," Dolly intoned. Her voice caught on the decade and broke on the year.

Suddenly the hair rose on Eliot's neck. "For heaven's sake . . ." he whispered, staring at her in horror.

"Mmmm." Now she could not speak at all.

He closed his eyes. "Oh, Dolly!"

At that she burst into tears. His glass fell into the sea. He took hers and let it follow. Then he put his great arms around her and hugged her until she gasped.

"Don't stop," she begged when he relaxed a little.

He held her tight then until the sobbing died down. Her first words as she freed herself slightly, still within his embrace, were, "Did you notice? I didn't wear mascara tonight."

"Don't, Dolly," he murmured.

"What?"

"Pull that brittle shell about you again."

"I've worn it so long."

"I can just imagine."

"No you . . . well, come to think of it, I suppose you can, now. We've been rowing the same boat all this time, old friend." She closed her eyes again and leaned gratefully against his broad chest. "I'm glad you know at last. I mean, I'm glad it's *you* who knows. You're the only one. Apart, of course from . . . you know."

He began to caress her fur, gently.

"D'you still love her?" she asked.

"Of course." After a pause he added, "And you? You still carry a torch for him?"

"Of course."

Then she said, "If your hands are cold, it's warm under the mink."

His hands were already warm but he accepted the invitation.

"Carry a torch," she echoed, "that's a good phrase. Is it your own?"

"Unh unh – standard American."

She eased her feet gently and asked, "Your torch – is it every bit as bright as it ever was?"

He cleared his throat awkwardly. "Maybe not."

"Nor mine," she volunteered when he failed to ask. "I think I was a fool ever to have married Wallace."

"I've felt foolish ever since she told me."

"I think they tried, you know. I mean really tried – not to . . . *do* anything about it."

"On the other hand," he allowed, "give her her due – she's never encouraged me to think that marriage might be on the cards. She's always talked about needing her freedom."

"Except maybe this year," Dolly added. "Perhaps, with them both being in Berlin, and that awful business with the Nazis . . ."

There was a silence, which he was the first to break. "It's very hard to give up a dream like that, though – don't you find?"

She thought it over. "Perhaps not. Perhaps the first stage is to realize that's all it ever was – just a dream."

She snuggled against him. He misunderstood and asked if she was beginning to feel cold.

So she had to tell him. "D'you know what I feel, Eliot? I feel that a teeny weeny little shipboard romance would do both of us the world of good."

CHAPTER FIFTY-TWO

ON THE DAY the *Mauretania* berthed in New York, Randy Gold
waylaid Imogen Davis on her morning walk to the corner shop. At
first she tried to pretend she hadn't seen him but he fell in beside her
and took her arm. "Time for another little chat," he said.

She stared at him evenly. "I can't think why. The last one was
quite pointless."

He grinned. "I forgot to mention one or two things. That's why
I've come back."

"I'm not in the least bit interested in your plans to build aeroplanes. As I told you, neither Mr Neville nor I have that sort of
influence with his sister."

"Ah, but that's not what I'm after. Where can we go for a chat?"

"There's no more money," she warned him. "You had the lot."

He laughed. "It's not money I want – well, not yours. What about
that teashop over there?"

She followed him across the street. Time was when he had meant
all the world to her, when he was the only person who cared a damn
whether she lived or died, when to do what she had done for him had
seemed not nearly good enough to repay his love. Now it seemed
like another life.

The shop was almost deserted. He chose a table by the window, as
far as possible from two old dears who were gossiping at the back.
When the waitress had left them alone with their tea she said,
"You've persuaded Neville's to keep back the Argentine territory. I
had nothing to do with that – so what more d'you think I can
achieve? This is pointless."

He ignored her. "You can wander more or less as you please
around Neville's, can't you?" he asked.

"I'm not going to break the law," she responded swiftly.

He grinned and rocked his outspread hand uncertainly. "Nearly. I
wouldn't like to argue it."

"I don't want to know, Randy."

"That's not quite right, my love. What you mean is you don't

400

want *people* to know – about you."

"Mr Neville knows already."

He looked at her with genuine admiration. "That took guts." Th
ingratiating grin returned. "But what about the sister, eh – the gre
Julia Somerville herself? I'll bet she doesn't know."

Imogen looked at him uncertainly, wondering whether to risk th
bluff. But he went on, "No – she'd bounce you out of that trustee
ship before your feet could touch the ground. Goodbye director'
salary . . . goodbye seat on the board. You'd be little Miss Nobod)
once again. Worse – you'd have your reputation for company." He
smiled pleasantly, as if he were doing her an enormous favour. "No,
I reckon you'd cooperate quite a bit to keep her from knowing the
truth about you."

Now that he'd given her something to face, she faced it calmly.
"And what about you, Randy, darling? Whore may not be the nicest
word, but I reckon pimp is a lot worse."

His grin did not waver. "I'm not hearing this," he warned. "You
can't possibly be threatening me." He raised a hand and caressed her
cheek lightly once or twice. "Beautiful," he murmured. "You really
must look after this gorgeous skin."

She lost the battle of the eyes. "What d'you want?" she asked.
"Not that I'm promising, mind you."

He was rummaging in his briefcase but he stopped and fixed her
with that gaze again. "No, I'm the one who promises, love. You're
the one who performs." He winked. "Just like old times." He pulled
out a Leica camera. "Find her books," he told her as he passed it
over, "the Neville company books, the real ones, and photograph
them. Just the last two years. Okay?"

"But I wouldn't know the first thing about it," she protested.

"'Course you would. Big firms like that – they all work on double
sets of books. She's got a safe somewhere with the real set hidden
away. Just root about. You'll find it."

Peter Rosenheim did not enjoy having Mr Randolph Gold for a
partner. He would trust him about half as far as he could throw him.
But Mr Randolph Gold had come to him with the commission of a
lifetime – to design and build a high-altitude cargo plane to work in
the Andes. No other powered plane would use his skills as a glider
designer half so well.

The paymaster was an Argentinian millionaire called Thomas
Morgan, who already operated a fleet of road trucks. When he came
to London he always stayed at the Savoy, which was how Gold came
to know him. Rosenheim would far rather have worked directly for
Morgan. There was no need whatever for young Gold. True, he had
a little money, but no business experience – least of all in aviation.
His ignorance was monumental. But he seemed to have some kind of

a hold over Morgan. At any rate, the Argentinian insisted that everything had to be done through Gold.

The one point Rosenheim kept drumming home to the greedy and ambitious young man was that, even by pooling their resources, they hadn't nearly enough to start any kind of aeroplane assembly line. All he'd sold had been a glider factory in Germany – and his mother had taken her half of the profit. What was left would pay for the design and a prototype, but it would take thousands more to build the production models.

Mr Randolph Gold would merely smile that sickeningly confident smile and say, "Leave that to me. I'll get it when the time comes."

"I must know where from," Rosenheim insisted at last. "You're asking me to invest several months of my life – never mind the cash. I must have some assurance."

Reluctantly, Gold conceded. "What's the only aeroplane company that you *know* I know?" he asked with a lopsided grin.

Rosenheim was astonished. "But I thought of Neville's, and then I thought it couldn't possibly be them because you'd have said. Why *didn't* you say? I know Julia Somerville very well indeed."

"Ah, but it's not as simple as that, old chap. My father's firm, Gold's Commercial Bodies, does all Neville's specialist welding and metal bending. And according to him, I haven't got what it takes to run his sort of business. So I just want to show him, see?"

"What do I say if I meet her?" Rosenheim protested. "She'll think it damned odd if I say nothing and then a week or so later . . ."

Randy's impatience began to show through his professional cordiality. "Just take it from me – there are reasons to say nothing just yet. The word is that Neville's may shortly be in no position to refuse any kind of an offer – as long as there's enough cash in advance on the table. They'd even do it at cost. And cash in advance is the one thing Morgan's got."

It was so unusually frank it was almost convincing. Only a German Jew who had built his business during the Nazis' rise to power would have continued to suspect the young man's reasons for choosing Neville's.

Max sat at his window watching some loitering workmen pretending to mend a leaking water main.

The pointless idleness of the working class infuriated him. All right, fascism wasn't the answer, but the country needed *some* kind of discipline. Idleness was the prerogative of those who could appreciate it – use it constructively. Go on like this and before you could turn over in bed everyone would be claiming it as a right.

Perhaps the Russians had the answer: Tell the buggers they already owned the earth and everything in it, assure them their government was working thirty-six hours a day exclusively for them, warn them

about the wolves over the border – and, hey presto, you had them where the pharaohs had the Israelites! You wouldn't find slackers like this on the streets of Moscow.

He turned to Imogen, who was darning a pair of his socks. "D'you remember a meeting at the Central Hall once – a fat little cove with teeth like a buck rabbit who bored the stuffing out of us talking about some Russian . . . Plinkoff – some name like that?"

"They all bored the stuffing out of me," she told him.

"Yes, but this man must have had diplomas in it. Plekhanov! That was the name."

"What about him, anyway?"

"Next time you're down at the library, see if he ever wrote any books in English. Plekhanov, I mean."

"And bring them home, if he did?"

"Yes. Of course."

"Heigh-ho!" she sighed.

"What does that mean?"

"It means here we go again! Why don't you pop down to your club?"

"It's not the same since Buffy went."

After a silence she said, "As if there weren't enough to worry about."

He turned and stared at her in surprise.

"You weren't there," she reminded him. "It was while you were in hospital in Berlin. Crownfield had us all to lunch, all the directors who were in London then, and mainly it was about Baring's and Brunty's idea for the Worcester company, but he also read out a list of all the other things we're doing, or starting on, or planning."

"Who – Crownfield?"

"Yes."

"Well, that's his usual monthly moan at Julia."

"Only this time there was more, and it was bigger, and . . . and even Miss Dawson was worried. And Eliot Baring, too. So it wasn't *just* the usual."

Max grew thoughtful.

Imogen pressed home the point. "Everything now depends – this was what Baring and Brunty both said – it all depends on getting a good price when Neville's floats the American company. Crownfield spoke of sixty thousand pounds . . ."

"Fifty, surely?"

"That was just to be on the safe side. But the point was that if we don't raise that fifty, we'll have to sell shares in Neville's."

He shrugged. "I've always thought Julia was absurdly negative on that point, you know," he observed blandly.

"Shareholders vote in the board of directors," she reminded him tactfully. "Your sister might not be so free to make you chairman, not automatically. Nor would a trustee like me be so sure of a seat. That's my main worry."

Max had turned white as chalk. She let him digest his thoughts in silence. At length he asked, "You'd never leave me, would you?"

She dropped everything and went to his side, where she put her arms about him and hugged him fiercely.

"Can't see why you stay," he muttered.

"Because I love you."

"Can't see that, either."

"Because you care for me. You know everything about me, Max, and you still care. You've given me the only real home I've ever known. I only need to look at you and I *feel* like someone." She kissed his neck. "That's why I worry, too."

He sighed. "Not much we can do about it."

"We could be prepared," she said slowly.

"For what? Living on bread and cheese and kisses?"

She returned to her chair and picked up her darning again. "Have you noticed one strange thing about your sister?"

"Lots!"

"No – I mean, as you say, we've often had these dire warnings before, from Crownfield and Brunty. And always, at the last minute, she manages to pull the rabbit out of the hat. Somehow she finds the money from somewhere."

He cleared his throat. "Careful in the trenches! Bit of a sore point, that."

"But look what happened. That's a very good example. Crownfield's always wanted Neville's to issue shares, right? On that particular occasion he tried to use the mortgage on Allbury to force her to it. So what did she do? She used money he didn't know about – or forgot, or something – to get round it." Casually she added, "You don't suppose she's got a special reserve fund hidden away somewhere, do you? Just to outwit Crownfield if he ever tries it again."

"Wouldn't put it past her."

"The thing is, where would she keep the records of it? I'm sure there'd be nothing at Connaught Square. I mean, Mrs Crooke has duplicate keys to everything, including the jewelry safe in the bedroom and the silver safe in the old butler's pantry."

"A safe deposit somewhere?" Max suggested.

Imogen shook her head. "Every time she wanted to make an entry she'd have to go there specially. People would see. Someone would notice it, sooner or later. Then there'd be talk – which is the last thing she'd want. No, I think it must be in the safe in her office at Dollis Hill."

He frowned. "I don't remember ever seeing such a thing."

"It's buried in the wall, hidden behind the two paintings of Hyde Park. She's absolutely fanatical about keeping it locked, too. She won't even have it open, Mrs Henderson says, if there's anyone else in the room."

"Well, there you are, then."

"The thing is, darling – I wonder if you know anything about it? The plate on the door says it was made in Ware."

His eyes lit up. "Can you describe it?"

"I went out and had a look at it today. It was made in 1892 by a Ware firm called Branfoot and Son . . ."

He laughed. "About so big? Keyhole in the middle, covered by a sort of formal rosette decoration in brass?"

To each detail she nodded.

"But that's the one from Allbury. She must have taken it there." A crafty look crept into his eyes. "And you think that's where she keeps the accounts? The real ones?"

"Exactly."

"But I still have a key for that! It was on my fob when I walked out. God, the number of times I almost threw it away, too!"

He held it up for her delighted inspection. Its toughened steel, polished down the years in his pocket, gleamed in the afternoon sun. "D'you want me to come out there with you?" he asked.

"I'll be less conspicuous on my own."

He was reluctant to leave all the work – and danger – to her but in the end she convinced him.

CHAPTER FIFTY-THREE

SINCE THE MOVE to Allbury, some years ago, the works at Dollis Hill had been completely taken over by Somerville Engineering. Now that there was no need to manipulate large sections of airframe, the site had been almost completely covered by buildings, each one being added as the need for it had arisen. Indeed, to Julia's discomfiture, it resembled nothing so much as a re-creation of the old Forge Lane site in modern industrial style. *But no one could have guessed how quickly we'd expand,* she would assure herself – knowing that George and his father could have offered exactly the same excuse for their higgledy-piggledy empire.

Though Imogen was both trustee and director, she had no actual office within the building; but she did "own" a cupboard in the directors' dining room, which was off the board room, which, in turn, was just down the corridor from Julia's office. It contained a hipflask of Scotch for Max and emergency things for her, like spare stockings and reserve make-up; also a random accumulation of agendas and reports, the debris of past board meetings, which every now and then she gathered up and threw away. She thus had a sort of entrée to the building, which enabled her to go in and out unchallenged.

On this particular late-September day, she decided to pay her call about an hour after the final knocking-off time, which, in the drawing office, was six o'clock; it was late enough to stand a good chance of finding the place empty except for the night watchmen, yet not so late as to evoke comment. True, Hannah Dawson often worked through the evening, but Imogen had established a pattern lately of turning up around seven or eight, not too often, and going through the company suggestions book, perusing the odd catalogue "for Mr Neville," and stopping by Hannah's office for a brief chat – in general, taking the kind of intelligent lay interest in the firm she had tried to show in the early days, before 'the Boss' made it clear she wasn't wanted.

The one sure way of hurting Imogen was to make it clear she wasn't wanted.

She bade a by-now-customary good evening to Tredwell, the gatekeeper, and another to Joe Gordon, one of the night watchmen, as she threaded her way among the buildings to the main offices. There she had to run a gauntlet of silent lathes and milling machines in an air sweetened by the cloying aroma of cutting oil. At the far end, the blacksmiths' forges still glowed with the last embers of their daily fire.

For once, Hannah Dawson had gone home early. At least, no light glowed beyond the frosted glass of her door. Imogen went straight to the drawing office, where she had previously noticed two shrouded lamps that would provide perfect illumination for her photography. She carried them to the directors' dining room. The camera was already there, having been brought in earlier that day. All that now remained was to open the safe and take out that elusive set of books.

A sudden twinge of fear gripped her. While she had been setting everything up, the activity itself had kept her calm. Also, there was nothing irrevocable about it, and nothing that was positively criminal. But the moment she turned the key to unlock the safe she would be committing an indisputable felony; then there would be no going back.

Perhaps she had left the key behind? She could always return tomorrow.

Her heart sank as she found it, ornate and already somewhat accusing, where she had put it earlier.

She picked it up, tried to think of a prayer, tried *not* to think of a prayer, and set off for Julia's office. It was unlocked, of course. That was her style. And anyway, what need to lock it when all the real secrets were in that safe.

BRANFOOT AND SON, WARE, 1892. She read the rubric half a dozen times before she slipped the key into its hole and turned it. Her heartbeat thundered in her throat and ears.

Engineering traditions die hard. The lock turned as easily and silently as it had on the day of its first greasing.

When the dark interior – surprisingly near-empty – loomed before her, Imogen's courage failed. She turned and went back across the room to the door, where she looked up and down the passage, straining her eyes and ears for something that would give her honourable cause to abandon this work and come back some other day.

But there was nothing.

She thought of Randy, of what he had threatened. She thought of Julia Somerville's probable reaction. And then she returned to the yawning safe and began to remove its contents.

Randy had asked for books. Well, the safe held plenty of *them*. She extracted them one by one – in mounting bewilderment.

"Desire of my Heart" . . .

"Desert Passions" . . .

"The Barbary Flame" . . .

"Wanton Flower of the Garden" . . .

There were about a dozen of them all told.

At first Imogen thought the covers must be some kind of disguise. But no. In page after riffled page, eyes melted, bosoms heaved, blood burned darkly – and weak female hearts fluttered in the grip of sweet and overpowering passions.

Perhaps it was some kind of code? Or were the accounts slipped into a pocket inside the hard cover – like the maps in those guide books?

Again no. These were the actual books in their original, published form – and Imogen could not doubt it for at least four of them were duplicated on her own shelves at home. She even remembered the plot of one of them, "Wanton Flower of the Garden," which was all about Nell Gwynne's days as a whore in Covent Garden.

She piled them neatly on the desk and turned again to the safe.

A little jar of toffees came next. Imogen unwrapped one and popped it into her mouth, ready to spit it out if it contained a surprise. But it proved to be a perfectly ordinary toffee.

Next came an old cigar box containing fifty pounds in assorted notes.

Then a silver-framed photograph of Julia's parents in front of Allbury; Max had the identical one. She remembered now – it always stood on the Boss's desk when she was here. And, yes, there was George. And, finally, there were the two children; it was a long time since either of them had looked like that.

Poor George! She took the photograph to where the light was a little stronger. He had needed her – and he cared about her, too. No matter what any of them said, she had given him a happiness no one else could have brought – certainly not the Boss. All right, maybe that was more George's fault than hers, but it was still a fact.

She returned it to the empty safe and began to repack the other items, beginning with the silver-framed photo of Max's parents.

All the planning, all the sweat, all that fear – and all for nothing!

The frame would not go back all the way. She cursed herself – it had been *on* the bottom shelf, not under it. She must be more careful.

But something was catching it there. She slipped her hand in between the shelf and the floor of the safe – a gap too narrow to hold even one ledger, let alone the three or four she expected. With the tip of her fingers she felt . . . something soft and papery.

She took a foot rule from the desk and began to pry it forward. It came with agonizing slowness, something quite large, though thin . . . something of paper . . .

Her elation soared. She had found the missing "books" after all – except that they were loose leaves in an envelope. In fact, as she could now see, it was a large manilla envelope. Quite plain. No writing of any kind upon it. In triumph she carried it to the desk and switched on the reading lamp.

Before she perused it she made one further trip to the door. It would be dreadful to be balked of her prize now, in the very moment of her triumph. Still there was no sound. She returned to the desk, picked up the envelope, and tipped its contents into the pool of light.

And then, just for a moment, the entire day seemed to go out of joint. Instead of the expected scrawl, the rows and columns of items and figures and subtotals and totals and carried-forwards . . . there was her own name: Miss Imogen Davis.

Subject: Miss Imogen Davis, it proclaimed.

And beneath it: *Report of surveillance by Sidney Sefton* . . . dated in March, 1927. Her eyes scanned the spilled pages: "Subject was born at The Laurels, Acton Ave, Turnham Green, on Monday, 6 November, 1905, and was subsequently reared at 3 Forston Rd . . . elementary and board school . . . Alma Rd Domestic College, gaining a certificate with honours . . .

Imogen's blood began to boil. *The bitch!* she thought. *She had me dodged!*

She read on: "Subject presently resides in rented accommodation of superior quality (viz. furnished, and with bath and telephone) at

13 Maiden Lane, Covent Garden."

Suddenly she dropped the paper as though it scalded her – not only dropped it but turned it face down upon all the others. Her heart was racing like a fluttering bird. If this piece of slime, this Sefton Storey, had dodged her from Maiden Lane . . .

Sick with dread she watched her leaden fingers pick up the page and turn it over. Her helpless eyes sought the place where she had broken off: "Subject holds no regular position but was seen to visit the cocktail bar at the Savoy Hotel on most days at around noon, where she . . ."

Imogen bit her lip. *Dear God, no. Please – no!*

". . . where she struck up acquaintance with men and later accompanied them to their rooms. (Details in Appendix A.)"

Now she knew the worst a fatalistic calm descended on her. Feeling no emotion at all, she pushed the papers this way and that, seeking something that said *Appendix A*. She found it soon enough – and there it all was: one week of her shame chronicled in obsessive detail. The names of the men – names she herself had not even known, their room numbers, the time she entered, the time she left, the dates . . . it was all there.

And suddenly it struck her: *Julia Somerville has known all this for the past six years!*

Six and a half, actually.

She checked the date of the report and found it had been written – and presumably delivered – at the very moment when her solicitors had sent that threatening letter. Mrs Somerville could have used it then and the entire case would have collapsed! There had been no need to accept the slightest compromise – much less to appoint her to the board or tolerate her there all these years.

Now she felt more wretched than at any time in her life. She thought back over the past years – the hostile things she had said, the opposition she had posed; and to think that at any time the object of her enmity could have tossed this slim envelope upon the table and ended it for ever.

It would have ended her life, no doubt of that.

She gathered the papers up, intending to put them back where they had lain so securely for the past years. But then it struck her that people did sometimes fall under buses, and other people would then come along and clear up after them . . . so, all in all, it might be best if Sefton Storey's report were destroyed for ever.

She remembered the blacksmiths' forges.

Back through the silent factory she went. The smithy was the part of the works that fascinated her most. She loved to see the glowing steel being forged and shaped or given its final temper, so she knew where the switches to the bellows were, even in that gloom.

The noise of the motors starting up roused Hannah Dawson from her books. She leaped to her feet and crossed swiftly to the door, where, at a sharply oblique angle, she could just see the smithy. And there she halted. One of the fires was flaring brightly – far too brightly for glowing coals. And by its light she saw a young woman, feeding sheet after sheet of paper to the flames. Almost immediately she recognized her as Imogen Davis.

Hannah retreated into the comparative shadow of her room, puzzled to see what the girl would do when she had finished.

She was certainly thorough, for she picked up one of the smiths' rakes and riddled the ashes of the paper into the coke and charcoal, making sure no piece large enough for reconstruction might survive. Then she turned and made her way back up the shops, toward the Boss's office and the directors' suite.

Hannah gave her time to settle to it and then tiptoed after her. But she need not have bothered. She heard Imogen sobbing even before she had gained the corridor; then she strode out without caution.

She found the girl sitting at the Boss's desk, writing a note and crying her heart out, all at the same time. For quite a while Imogen did not notice her, standing there in the darkened doorway; it gave Hannah time to scan the rest of the room. The picture had been taken down and the wall safe lay wide open. There was a pile of books on the desk, and a couple of framed photographs – the silver ones that were usually locked away whenever the Boss went on her travels. Apart from that, everything seemed as usual.

"Why, Miss Davis!" she exclaimed at last.

Imogen glanced up, startled out of her wits. When she saw it was Miss Dawson she broke down completely. Hannah came forward to comfort her, asking what ever was the matter. Imogen, her head buried deep in her hands, used her elbows to push forward the note she had been writing.

It read: "Miss Dawson – I must see you. Please, this is urgent. I don't know who else to turn to . . ." It finished there.

Her heart melted. She looked down at the girl, who seemed set to sob out the next hour, and then turned again to the door.

"Don't go away," she called over her shoulder – feeling rather foolish but not knowing what else to say.

Moments later she returned, carrying her thermos flask of tea, the one she always had made up by the canteen whenever she intended working late. She took some cups from one of the cupboards and found a box of sugar lumps out in the secretary's desk.

These reassuringly everyday activities had given Imogen time to collect herself. The sobbing had dwindled to those involuntary sounds, something between a hiccup and a sniffle.

"I'm here quicker than you thought," the older woman began encouragingly. "Did you surprise some burglars or what?" Deliberately she did not turn on the main lights, leaving only the soft pool upon the desk.

For a moment it looked as if the girl would start weeping all over again but she mastered it and squared herself to the inevitable confession. She revealed everything, what Randy Gold had asked her to do, and Max and the spare key. The only thing she kept back was her discovery of the Storey report. She sipped at her hot, sweet tea as she spoke, and it visibly revived her. Toward the end she even took Hannah through to the dining room and showed her the photographic apparatus, all set out.

"And did you find these alleged books?" Hannah asked as they returned to the Boss's office.

Imogen pointed dramatically at the pile of romantic novels. "That's all that was in there. Them and the photos. Oh, and fifty pounds and that tin of toffees."

Hannah pulled the pile of books into the light, saw their titles, and smiled. "Dear, dear Boss!" she murmured affectionately.

"Did you know about them?" Imogen asked.

"My dear, everyone knows about them. Or everyone here. Why she tries to keep it such a deep, dark secret is a mystery – as if it were something shameful." She smiled at Imogen, whose answering smile was weakened by those last two words.

"And you found nothing else?" Hannah continued.

There was an edge to the question that made Imogen pause; but in the end she gave a firm shake of the head. "Nothing."

Hannah could feel the tension in the girl; it almost sent feelers out into the air between them. She let it develop before she asked, "Then what was it you were burning in the forge?"

Imogen, about to drink her tea, set the cup down again. A new tear trembled on the rim of one eye. "I did find something else," she said flatly.

Hannah nodded. And waited.

"I discovered that Mrs Somerville is one of the most . . ." She seemed to lose the thread of the sentence. "A saint," she added at length. "There's no way round it."

"And that was what you burned? That evidence was in there?"

She shook her head. "It's not what you think." She stared straight at the woman then. "Listen. I've never been too much of a . . . not what you might call her staunchest ally in board meetings and that, would you say?"

"You've generally taken the same line as Mr Neville," the other agreed tactfully.

"I've generally opposed her. I've generally been a thorn in her side – be honest, now."

"Yes, I suppose one could say that."

"Well let me tell you – for the last six years and more, Mrs Somerville has had in that safe the evidence . . . I mean certain writings that . . . if . . . well, put it like this – she could have finished me. I mean *finished* me. And she never used it."

Hannah's face hardened. "And now you've made sure she never can."

"I just didn't want it to fall into the wrong hands."

The sneer did not leave Hannah's lips.

"Listen!" Imogen said with rising desperation. "Look – if she was ever going to use it, she would have. Right? I mean, God knows I gave her chances enough!" Her eyes fell and she added bitterly, "If I told you what it was, you'd understand."

Once again Hannah softened. There was an odd intensity in the girl, something that assured her that now, if never before, she was telling the truth. "So it boils down to one question – what do you propose to do about young Gold?"

Imogen slumped. "I hadn't thought. I mean, I haven't had time. When does the Boss get back?"

"Next week." Hannah considered the situation a moment and added, "You could tell him what you found – even take a photograph back . . . Or you could say it wasn't here and therefore she must have taken it with her – and so you'll have to try again sometime after next week."

"And then let Mrs Somerville decide what to do about it."

Hannah broke into a broad grin. "Good girl!" she exclaimed, patting her arm. "Good girl! That's what I was waiting to hear."

Pleased at the way things had turned out, she rose and strolled over to the safe. "I don't suppose such secret books exist at all," she mused. "It would take a mind like Sidney Gold's to think it all up."

"Sidney?" Imogen was startled.

"Well, you don't believe he's not behind his son, do you? I wonder if he could be right?" And she ran her hands deep into each of the shelves, for all the world as if appreciating their maker's craftsmanship.

CHAPTER FIFTY-FOUR

AMERICA NEEDS MORE PROHIBITION, said a fly poster on a wall near Battery Park. *For God's sake!* someone had scrawled across it. *We aren't even using what we've got.* Julia remembered the posters she had seen in Berlin. Different people, different mood.

She felt it odd to arrive in a city she had never visited before and yet to find it so familiar. There were dozens of things that ought to have been peculiar or novel – the yellow taxicabs, the steam that gushed from under the "sidewalks" and streets, so that the whole city seemed to be built on a flattened volcano, the shoeshine boys, beggars, policemen carrying guns, men trundling huge racks of clothes through the streets, Negroes, automats, drug stores, soda fountains, streets laid out on graph paper, and, of course, the office towers that soared to blot out the sky. But the only real surprise in the whole lot was the yellow of the cabs; everything else was exactly as Hollywood had been portraying it to the world over the past decade and more. New York had become everyone's fantasy capital; the big surprise was to discover it was real, after all.

However, no celluloid anticipation could dim the wonder of the view from the top of the two-year-old Empire State Building. True, they picked a lucky day. Eliot told them he'd never seen the air so clear – and the only New Yorker (or the only one who would admit to it) up there on the observation deck agreed. "Yorktown Heights and that bridge," he added. "I never saw them from here before."

"It's what one has always wanted to do as a pilot," Lydia commented. "Stop the plane and just look and look."

"One good howitzer and you could pick off the whole city," Robert murmured, looking to see his mother's reaction.

"One good fighter-bomber and you'd be squelched," she told him.

He winked at Eliot. "At least she's picking up the lingo."

Eliot shot him with a finger. "She'd win that battle, too," he warned.

When the others went up to Massachusetts, Robert stayed in the city, ostensibly under the wing of Dolly and Lexy but actually under the feathers of any chorus girl who fluttered the smallest invitation.

"He is so *Edwardian!*" Lydia commented in disgust as she drove with her mother and Eliot to Idlewild. Oddly enough, it was their first commercial flight in a DC1. They compared notes avidly and came to the reluctant conclusion that the Fleetliner IV needed a lot more work if it was to stay in the field.

The final negotiations with the Worcester Aircraft Co. were really just a formality – a few niggling details. Eliot had prepared the ground well. The most surprising thing about them was that they took place not at the firm's offices nor in one of the city hotels but actually at the home of Dennis Moore, the company president. Moreover, they were disguised as a sort of sideshow or preliminary to the apparent main event of the day – a tennis tournament.

"You look surprised," Moore said to her. "I know what it is. I've done a lot of business in Europe. You get to see plenty of grand hotels but never the inside of a person's home – even people I've dealt with for years."

"Oh, I hope we don't seem stand-offish," Julia replied. "There's just a sort of thing among us that we don't bring business home. Army officers don't talk shop in the mess. And in the gentlemen's clubs nobody talks business. Even the pubs, you know, have a private bar for business deals. It's just a different tradition."

And indeed it is, she thought as her eye roved over the groups seated around the tennis court, all dressed for the game, either waiting to go on or having just come off. From the way they were talking to one another, leaning forward, poking at arms and ribs with their fingers, staring deep into an opponent's eye – they weren't discussing the weather or who's whose; those gestures of hand and body were sculpting tracts of housing, planting skyscrapers, smoothing the path of a new thruway. This was Eliot's country, she thought. He understood these rituals.

"Let me know when you'd like us to get our heads together," Moore told her, as if he were tactfully filling a gap left by her ignorance of the local etiquette.

She came to a sudden decision. "I think this is Baring's show, Mr Moore. He and I were up quite late last night, going through it all. My only real question of any substance was whether the ten per cent referred to in paragraph twenty-seven was ten per cent of the gross profit or after deductions. I know the sum involved is petty but paragraphs like that have a way of turning into precedents for later dealings where much larger sums are involved. So . . ."

"Oh – forgive me for interrupting, but that isn't a problem. I don't think we ever meant it to be ten per cent of the gross. That's just sloppy wording. We'll lick that into shape."

She laughed. "Well, I didn't mean it to be quite so easy, Mr

Moore. But there it is – that's nice. What I was going to say was I'd prefer this whole show to be Eliot's. I'll just come and sign when I'm needed."

American friendliness seemed so genuine to her; that was a danger, not a bonus. In England, you were never sure whether friendliness was real or a sort of noblesse oblige, so you returned it in kind and kept up your guard. But here she could feel herself being sucked into it, warmed by it, and even – despite the brief exposure – growing dependent upon it.

"If that's the way you want it," he said uncertainly.

Was he doubting her courage? Her aptitude? She felt she should nail those possibilities. "Really, I suppose, I think it's important for you to understand that I trust Baring to the utmost degree. Knowing that, you'll feel much happier working with him, won't you?"

"Ah! Yes indeed." The admiration in his eyes showed he had not considered the point. "I can see how Neville's acquired such an outstanding team, Mrs Somerville."

And you'd probably be right, she thought wryly, *if only I were the sort of person who can work out things like that in advance – instead of leaving it to the inspiration of the moment.*

While the final negotiations proceeded, in the best American tradition, in a smoke-filled back room, Julia and Lydia sat beside the tennis court, watching the latest round of the tournament, and talking with their hostess and friends. The earliest tinge of the fall was on the leaves. Everyone said it was a shame they couldn't stay another three weeks; it was going to be a beauty this year. Her love of classic cars was legendary – or at least it had been mentioned in the New York gossip columns at the time the *Mauretania* docked. A Mr O'Laughlin, described as a "re-altor," invited her for a spin that evening in his Franklin Series 17.

"With the twelve-cylinder air-cooled engine?" she asked excitedly.

"The last of the line," he affirmed.

"Why d'you say that?"

"Oh, they've done a Brodie – like your W.O. Bentley." His hand dived from a great height. "It's these terrible times."

He looked as if he'd never in all his life known even one terrible day. But then didn't they all?

"We've seen the last Pierce Arrow, too," someone else said.

"The last Stutz," put in another.

"The last Cord."

"No, Cord'll pull through."

That's what cords are for, Lydia thought. She just sat there and let the talk wash over her; the way people expressed things, the words they chose, were fascinating.

At last someone came out to tell Julia that all was ready for signing. She stood and beckoned Lydia to come with her. But then,

just as she was about to take the first step toward the house, something – almost a physical pressure – turned her aside and set her at a
right angle to it. Her daughter, a little bewildered, fell in beside her.

"It's this way, Mrs Somerville," the minion called.

"I shan't be a second." She sent him back with a cheerful wave.

"Why this?" Lydia asked.

"I don't know. I just felt a sudden misgiving. Let's walk once
round the court and see if it goes away."

"Golly!" The girl was awestruck at the sudden possibilities before
them. "But you can't go back on it now."

"Never think that, darling. Until there's a signature, there's nothing to go back on. Until there's a signature, you're free."

There was a pause before Lydia asked, "And after it, Uncle Eliot is
free?"

Julia sighed. "Yes."

"This *thing* that's going on between him and Aunt Dolly – it's
more than just a shipboard romance, you know."

"I know."

"Well, what about poor Uncle Wallace? It's hardly fair on him."

"I wonder – if we took some of these acorns back with us, would
they grow in England?"

"Mummeee!"

"People have to take their own chances, dear. Falling in love is
taking a chance. Getting married is taking an even bigger chance."

"But even so – I mean, it's awful to think he doesn't even know it's
started. We know and he doesn't. Don't you feel guilty?"

Julia gave an awkward laugh. "There are still times, you know,
when I'm tempted to say you'll understand so much more in a year
or two."

"You'd better not!"

"I know. So what I'll say instead is that Uncle Wallace can certainly take care of himself." She stooped and picked up a few acorns.
"Red oaks and white oaks, they call them. They are different from
ours, aren't they."

"More pointy leaves. I still can't help feeling sorry for Uncle
Wallace."

They turned at the far end of the tennis court. "Gosh, this is rude,"
Julia said. "I must go in to them. Listen – I'll explain it all, soon."
Would the girl recognize it as the same *soon?* "But don't worry about
the Bakers – either of them. It's working out for the best." Her stride
lengthened. "I must go in!"

"Go on! You're impressing them no end with your nonchalance."

"Is that the name for it?" She laughed. "When I was young we
called it butterflies in the tummy."

Dolly's opening-night performance in the title role of Lexy's

"Héloïse" was the best she had ever given. Part of the magic of the theatre is that you know instantly when you are witnessing something truly great. With music, books, poetry – even with paintings – you may reasonably ask for time to consider your verdict; but with a dramatic performance such consideration has no place. You find yourself a witness to greatness and it plucks that instantaneous response from you. If it doesn't, you are dead, and all the thinking time in the world cannot revive you.

The first-night audience certainly felt it. In that moment before the curtain falls, when the walls of her convent cell have mysteriously dissolved on the air and poor Héloïse stands utterly alone on a pitch-black stage, when she raises her eyes and transforms the spotlight into the finger of a dire and vengeful God, when she gives out that unbelievably animal howl, so full of pain and rage and yet so triumphantly defiant, there was not a person in the house who doubted they had all witnessed one of the truly legendary moments of the modern theatre. The curtain calls went on and on and on – even after Dolly, and then Lionel Barrymore, her Abélard, and finally Lexy himself, had given their speeches.

It took an hour even to reach Dolly's dressing room. While they shuffled their feet on that slow progress it seemed to Julia that Eliot was not as cheerful as he ought to have been; in fact, he was downright lugubrious. She tried arousing him with comments on Dolly's performance but it only seemed to make him worse. Lydia noticed it, too. "Come on," she said, plucking her brother's sleeve. "This is useless. You and I will go ahead to the Biltmore and see that everything's all right for the party." She gave her mother a wink.

"Oh, I don't mind staying here," Robert replied. But she closed her ears to his protests and hauled him off.

"Cheer up," Julia cajoled Eliot when they were alone (in a Manhattanish sense of the word). "You've negotiated one of the best deals in the history of the aircraft industry and you've just seen a bit of theatrical legend. I ought to be hauling you down off the ceiling."

"There seems nothing to say," he responded. "All those times together – you and me – and now there's nothing to say."

"That's just not true. But even if it were – so what?"

"I just feel it ought to mean more than it seems to now. When you told me – that time in Berlin – I really thought everything had come to an end. Life and everything. And yet now . . ." He shrugged. "It makes you distrust your own feelings." Their eyes met. "Of course," he added, "your feelings never wavered."

"I didn't lie to you, Eliot. Don't try and suggest I'm made of stone. I never once said – I never even hinted – that it was more than it was. Are we going to end on a quarrel?"

His smile was sad. "I guess not."

"Try this," she suggested. "If Dolly and you had met before either

Wallace or I came into your lives, you'd now be either planning or remembering your seventh wedding anniversary. Think of it in that light. These last seven years have been a slight mistake, that's all. Dolly's being much more sensible than you. She told me she knows she was wrong to have gone ahead with her marriage to Wallace when she knew in her heart of hearts she'd already lost him."

"You and he were wrong, too."

"Of course we were. We should have been ruthless about it. We shouldn't have stepped back and looked the other way, pretending nothing had happened. All that was wrong."

The woman in line ahead of them could bear it no longer; she just had to turn around, oh so casually, to see who was there – and to get a good look at these parting lovers. When their eyes met, Julia explained, "We write romantic novels in partnership. We always wile away time with variations on the current chapter."

"Oh!" The woman laughed in confusion. "Well, it's going to be a good one – I can just feel it." She looked the pair of them over. "Tell me," she asked Julia. "Do you always say the sensible things and he says the things 'most any man would say?"

Eliot laughed at last. "My God, you're absolutely right," he assured her.

The party at the Biltmore was one long cavalcade of well wishers and good timers. Everyone was waiting for the papers, of course, though few doubted that the reviewers would rave . . . but still, you couldn't be too careful. Sol Halberstein was there from MGM and so was Twentieth Century's Art Drucker; they all made encouraging noises but they stopped just short of anything that even the best lawyer could pick up on. Only one man there had the courage of his own judgement – Morton Eustis. Dolly, of course, had read every one of his "The Artist Attacks His Part" articles in *Theatre Arts Monthly*. "My dear," he told her, "I want to devote an entire feature to you – unless, that is, you have some objection?"

Before midnight, spies on each of the papers were phoning through, reading from galleys. Willy Frasch, the theatre manager, sat there white-faced, looking as if he could hardly take it in, repeating, "yeah . . . yeah . . ." endlessly. "Roses all the way," he murmured in a stunned voice as he cradled the earpiece again. "Lexy, didn't I always say I love ya? Well, I love ya!"

Twenty minutes later the galleys arrived by cab, and Hollywood pounced. But by then there was already a surge for the door. The Biltmore was suddenly too plush, too respectable; the music too mellow; the lighting too gorgeous. Someone mentioned the Onyx where Joe Sullivan played piano and drinking was communal. Dolly found herself trying to talk deals over her shoulder with Mack Read, her agent, who, in turn, was having to shout over an increasing distance with Halberstein and Drucker – and, indeed, others. In the last minute, while cabs were scooping them up like a meat slicer, she caught sight of Eliot.

"Here!" she yelled.

"It's impossible!" he cried back.

"Kick and bite!" she advised, but just then a huge Cadillac pulled up and several dozen eager hands willed her inside. She barely had time to cry, "The Onyx!"

It was a walk-up speakeasy on the north side of Fifty-second Street. Joe Helbock, who ran it, liked jazz and served *the* most delicious steaks. The beer, the most drinkable that Julia had tasted since coming to America, was fifteen cents a pint.

"That's the best beer since Berlin," she told Eliot. "Not that I'd want to make any other comparisons."

"Drink deep," Helbock advised. "They're gonna repeal Prohibition, and that's the end of good hooch everywhere."

The piano was marvellous. She rocked her head to the beat and smothered all thought of tomorrow.

Dolly arrived an hour later. She seemed to have acquired half a dozen lackeys, each carrying armfuls of newspapers. There were so many good bits that people got tired of reading them out. Then it was drinks all round again and Joe Sullivan played a nice, jumpy version of *Conquering Hero,* which, while he had their attention, he modulated back into two old favourites, *I'm gonna stomp, Mr Henry Lee* and *That's a serious thing.*

In fact, he made a mistake, because once the reviews were read everybody wanted to go on somewhere else. One of those untenured professors who spring up in the over-fertile night-soil of jazz remarked, casually, that those two tunes were written by Eddie Condon, which was where Joe Sullivan learned them because he was in on the session.

Someone else said, "Condon's playing with the Mound City Blue Blowers at the Stork Club right this minute."

"Can't be," put in a third. "They closed it."

"That was in Ancient Rome already. It's reopened at Fifty-first and Park."

It was too close for anyone to resist the temptation.

"Have you seen Lydia or Robert?" Julia asked Dolly in a brief moment when the surging tides of people brought them close enough together. "I thought they were following you."

"Yes. We went to some place in the Village called Nick's. They met a Norwegian who said he knew a lot of buffet flats in Harlem."

She turned to Eliot for some explanation, but he was already threading his way to Dolly's side, and the distance between them was increasing. "It just means liquor and music," he called back.

They had already passed the bend in the stair; by the time she reached it, they were out of sight. She gazed about her and saw not a single face she knew. But they were all smiling, all happy, all intent on the next pleasure. That vicious despair, which would have been the most noticeable thing in a Berlin crowd, was nowhere evident.

So she gave herself up to this benign tide, drifting toward the Stork Club. *It's freedom of a kind,* she thought.

But in all that ambiguous lighting there was a face she had missed. A moment later a familiar London voice murmured in her ear, "A thorn by any other name would be as sore a grief."

"Lexy!" She turned and threw her arms about him. "I looked for you. Were you up there?"

"Only just arrived, old darling. Met Dolly on the way in. She's not the only one who's . . . er, 'talking turkey,' as they call it."

"Oh, I'm so glad for you. People forget it's your night, too."

"Not the ones who matter, fortunately."

They were down in the street by now, with space around them. He went on, "Eliot tells me you've been having your own successes?"

"We haven't done too badly."

"I was wondering – d'you feel like a bit of a break when all this is over?"

She was intrigued. "What had you in mind?"

"Well, the *Marina's* in Venice at the moment. What about joining her there and doing a long, leisurely cruise down the Adriatic and around the Greek islands?"

"Oh, Lexy, it sounds absolute heaven."

He linked arms with her. "So you'll come?"

She hugged his arm. "That's the most wonderful thing about you," she said. "You're always *there*." But realism asserted itself, too, and she felt bound to add, "Mind you, I have no idea what horrors may be awaiting me in London."

CHAPTER FIFTY-FIVE

It SHOULD HAVE been more triumphant, somehow, that voyage home. Neville's no longer had all its eggs in one basket; and, though still small in comparison with giants like Junker, de Havilland, or Douglas, it was too big now to be pushed around. In a few years' time, given no more than normal luck, their WAC subsidiary would have made up all their lost ground in military applications, and that could place them at least among the top half dozen plane makers in the world. Yet Julia felt deflated.

Robert had stayed in New York, where he found that his English accent and upper-class manner was like an open sesame to unbelievable delights. He had worked it out that, if he survived the adventure, he could catch the *Oceanic* home and still be in time to join his new regiment. So Lydia and her mother had the Beaver's staterooms to themselves. Lydia, who had already had two late nights, decided to stay in and wash her hair.

Julia offered to dry it.

"Is anything the matter?" the girl asked from under the towel. "You don't seem on top of the world."

"Perhaps I'm not. You remember I told you my reason for going to America?"

"You mean about having to see things for yourself?"

"Yes. Well I've done it now – and I just don't understand how Brunty arrives at his figure of fifty thousand pounds. He grossly overestimates the likely rise of WAC's shares. And the other assets won't fetch anything like their book value."

"And yet Uncle Eliot thought the figures were all right."

"Not after he'd been there a couple of days. He was just out of touch with the way prices have fallen. In charity, I suppose we have to say the same of Brunty."

Lydia stood up straight and pulled back the edge of the towel. "Is it so serious, then?"

"Very. We shall be left looking for thirty thousand pounds. Crownfield is going to have a field day."

"Where do we usually get money?"

"We borrow it from the future. But we've already done as much as we can in that direction."

"And we have no reserves?"

"It's the old, old story, I'm afraid: They've all been used up in the purchase of WAC."

Lydia had never seen her mother so worried. She leaned toward her and gave her a kiss. "You'll do it," she soothed. "You always have done."

Julia smiled thinly. "I feel a little short on magic."

"Something will turn up."

"Me and Mr Micawber!" She pulled the towel back over the girl's head and resumed her drying. "Also there's another little cloud on the horizon."

"Uncle Wallace," came the muffled voice from under the material.

"Eh? Oh no. Dolly must be the one to tell him that. No, I'm talking about a little bit of SPRP business – not unconnected with you, as a matter of fact. It would seem that your modest proposal has found favour with the committee. And . . ."

"Oh good!"

"It would be but for one small thing – I mean, one very large thing. Theresa Ashbury has decided she cannot accept the change in policy and has tendered her resignation."

"Oh no!" Again the shocked face peeped out between the folds of her towel, eyes full of concern.

"It makes me wonder if I shouldn't retire, too."

Lydia relaxed and smiled indulgently. "You can't possibly do that. Cheer up! Your real trouble, you know, is that you're stuck here and all this is happening over there where you can't get at it. You wait – once we reach Southampton and you can throw yourself into the thick of it all again, things will look very different."

Julia kissed her on the forehead and began combing out her damp locks. "Bless you," she murmured.

The day before landfall she received a cable. It was from Peter Rosenheim, saying he'd be meeting her in Southampton.

"We may joke about Mr Micawber," Julia remarked as she passed it over to her daughter, "but I have the feeling that something has just turned up."

Whether Rosenheim represented salvation or not, the main excitement of that landfall, for Julia, was to see her new 8-litre Bentley waiting at the quayside. When it had first been shown at Olympia, three years earlier – before W.O.'s sad bankruptcy – she had thought it too sporting. More recently, however, she had seen Jack Buchanan's original saloon driving down the Mall and, though she considered that version too heavy-looking, she had realized what a

superb sedanca de ville it could make. A little stretching of the chassis
. . . a slight lowering of the profile . . . she did a rough sketch and
left the problem with Somerville Motors. That had been about four
months before she left for America.

And now there it was in the Cunard park, gleaming black and
scintillating Bayard red, every regal inch of it. Even before the
Mauretania docked she could see it waiting – and Strong beside it,
polishing, polishing.

The customs formalities dragged; her greetings to Peter Rosenheim were rushed; there was room only for the Bentley in her mind.

"The Guv'nor would have been proud of this one, Boss," Strong
told her as he led them toward it. "And proud of you, too. Look at
the lines of her!"

A lot of classic cars appear elegant only from a distance; they are
designed for theatrical effect. Close to, some clumsiness of proportion or unresolved detail lets them down. But with this there was not
a feature, not a line, not an angle that Julia would have altered. They
stood and admired it in holy silence.

"Do I gather that you had some hand in her design?" Rosenheim
asked.

He had come down by train and Julia, to kill two birds, had
invited him to drive back to London with her.

"I did a sketch," she told him. "The real work was done, I
imagine, by Tony Crossthwaite and Michael Devaney at Somerville's."

All Lydia wanted was to see under the bonnet. She and Strong
were buried there for several minutes while Julia and Rosenheim sat
in the back and talked – and drank iced cocktails. One lovely surprise
awaited her there – a bouquet of roses and a note: "In the hope they
might not wither – W.B."

All the heaviness seemed to lift from her. "Such a nice man," she
remarked as she tucked them on the rear-window ledge out of
harm's way.

Such a nice man who can make you blush like that! Rosenheim
thought.

"Well now," she turned to him.

"You had a good voyage, then?" he asked.

"We had a very successful trip. Tell me, what's been going on
while I was away? Why this urgency to see me?"

"What was it your sister called him – the creepy-crawly?"

"Randolph Gold?" she asked at once.

Her quickness delighted him. "Tell me some things about him.
For instance, what exactly is the relationship between him and his
father?"

Julia thought back to the only time she had ever discussed the
matter with Gold junior. "I got the impression," she replied, "that

the son is none too happy at being shut out of the family business. He's a strange man, old Sidney Gold. People call him a shark and a crook – and worse."

"Yes, I've heard."

"Actually, I think he's only ever wanted to be a big, respected, honourable man. But he was always looking for a short cut. However, that's another story. To get back to young Randolph. The original reason he, the father, didn't want the son to join him, is that the business in those days was about as straight as a banana. He wanted something better for the boy – and 'better,' to him, meant the Savoy, one of the world's great hotels, where he'd mingle with the high-born and the powerful and generally learn to rise above his humble origins. Unfortunately, all it seems to have done is corrupt the lad. And that, paradoxically, is why (in my view, anyway) our Sidney won't have his son within ten miles of the family business – because it is *now* thoroughly straight and decent. And that, in turn, I may say, is almost entirely due to his contracts with Neville's."

Lydia joined them at that moment and they set off for London.

"Who are the flowers from?" she asked, looking at Rosenheim. "You?"

He shook his head. "Alas."

"Uncle Wallace sent them," her mother told her. "Such a sweet thought. He arranged our stateroom with Max Beaverbrook, of course. That's how he knew." She turned to Rosenheim. "And come to think of it, you met him the day we lunched at the Savoy – when Randy Gold did all that eavesdropping and Dolly called him the creepy-crawly. Have you met him since?"

"Only in print. I read all his articles on the trial. I think he must be quite a remarkable man?"

"Is he? I suppose he is." She turned to Lydia. "Would you say he is, dear?"

"Yes, of course." Lydia was trying to hide her surprise; she could not remember the last time she had seen her mother's ears turn such a bright pink.

"But never mind all that," Julia went on. "What d'you think of my beautiful Bentley! I could kick myself for not having at least tried the standard saloon while W.O. was still in business."

The silent comfort of the huge car was astonishing. As they wended their stylish way through the city of Southampton, she summarized her discussion with Rosenheim for Lydia's benefit. It gave him the chance to think.

"How certain are you," he asked at length, "that the father *is* reluctant to take the son in?"

"Pretty certain. I've mentioned it once or twice – you know, comments like when shall I have the pleasure of dealing with young Randolph – the usual sort of fishing. And there's always been that uncomfortable gleam in the man's eye."

"I don't suppose it's anything you'd ever talk about with Randolph?"

She hesitated before she admitted, "It did arise once, some years ago. I was surprised to learn how contemptuous he was of his father – thought he'd gone soft, thought he wouldn't last, and things like that. He spoke as if he'd kick his father out one day and take everything over."

"Hah!" Rosenheim gave a single, decisive handclap. "I think you're right. And I fear that – in some way – I've been drawn into this plot of his."

"If so, it puts you in an awkward position with me," she pointed out.

He looked hurt. "I don't see that. I've put all my cards on the table. Indeed, I came here to warn you. I've held back nothing."

She smiled placatingly. "I didn't mean it in that way, Herr Rosenheim. But if we are to plan our future moves together – to make sure we aren't just pawns in his game – then my next question to you, logically, should be, 'How much money are you going to put on the table?' But perhaps that's something you, quite properly, wouldn't wish to . . ."

"Oh!" He waved the words away. "To hell with such negotiating niceties. It's not *my* money, after all. I just wish Randy Gold out of it. I want only you and me and Morgan working together. So I'll tell you gladly: Our offer would be around twenty-five thousand pounds."

"For ten aircraft! C.i.f. Argentina! There's no profit in that."

"But that's what I was telling you. Young Mr Gold seems to have private information that you're in some sort of jam – or will be – where you'll leap at the offer just to get the cash. It's 'cash on the nail' – is that the expression? Cash in advance?"

Julia saw her daughter's head turn abruptly toward her; by way of object lesson to the girl, she did not move her own by a fraction of an inch. And all she said was, "How interesting."

"It could be," Rosenheim added. "At first I thought his only purpose was to drive a hard bargain. But now, from what you tell me, I think he wishes to use that money against his father. That's his real game."

They dropped Rosenheim off in Chiswick. A couple of Nazi thugs were going around London looking for him, he explained. So far he'd given them the slip.

Mother and daughter arrived back in Connaught Square in mid-afternoon, only to find the most unlikely deputation waiting: Hannah Dawson and Imogen Davis. Between them they revealed the entire story behind Imogen's debut as a safe-breaker.

Julia was absolutely furious; but when it became clear that nobody was actually going to mention the literary discoveries, she grew somewhat calmer.

"So what did you tell young Mr Gold?" she asked.

Hannah explained. "We put everything back in the safe and took a few snapshots of it."

"And I told him you must have carried the ledgers with you," Imogen added.

"Ledgers!" Julia exploded. "It's so absurd."

"The real question," Lydia pointed out, "is what will Randolph Gold do now?" She looked inquiringly toward Imogen.

The woman shook her head. "He didn't even explain why he wanted copies in the first place. He never does."

Lydia turned to her mother and asked, "Cards on the table?"

Julia stood and walked over to the window, where she fiddled with her rings and stared at the empty square. "I hate these conspiracies," she muttered at last.

"We only know of one," Lydia reminded her.

"Yes, but things are falling into place – other bits of the picture. God help me, I even end up suspecting Peter Rosenheim."

"Good Lord!" Lydia cried.

"Business has rules," Julia explained. "People who break them put themselves under suspicion."

"What rule did he break?"

"He began with his final offer. He gave it all away." She turned to Hannah Dawson. "Apparently this Argentinian, Morgan, is willing to put up twenty-five thou', cash in advance."

Hannah whistled."

"Precisely," Julia said. "But why did Rosenheim rush down to Southampton to tell me – making sure it was the first thing I heard when I got back?"

"But he explained that," Lydia pointed out. "He suspects Randy Gold's up to no good and he wants us to know he's not party to it. Don't you believe him?"

Julia dipped her head reluctantly. "Ninety per cent – perhaps even ninety-nine. But it would be foolish to ignore other possibilities. For instance – he tells me about this cash. We make our plans on the assumption it's coming. Then at the last minute there's some small problem. But now we're in deep trouble – vulnerable to all sorts of pressure – and no time left to rescue ourselves."

Imogen saw a point. "Randy would say we can have the money if we cut out Gold's Commercial Bodies."

Lydia laughed at the absurdity of the suggestion – until she saw her mother nodding. "And then he'd go to his father and say, 'Take me into partnership with you and I'll drop that demand.' Miss Davis is right, darling." She sighed. "Of course there are other possibilities."

Hannah chimed in. "Can we be sure Crownfield's nothing to do with it?"

Julia looked at her sharply. "Why d'you say that?"

"He was so full of himself at that unofficial board meeting at his offices – while you were in Germany, Boss. When he went through the list of all our commitments – all the new capital we were going to need – well, he did his best to seem all businesslike and solemn but you could tell he was just bubbling with pleasure inside." She turned to Imogen. "Didn't you think so?"

"Definitely."

"And it would suit his books no end," Julia explained to her daughter. "If we were in the sort of trouble I described, we'd have no choice but to sell off shares. Crownfield would crawl on broken glass to achieve that. And if Crownfield's in, can Brunty be out? You see – where does one . . ."

"I've never absolutely trusted that man," Hannah observed.

"Well, we mustn't confuse eccentricity with disloyalty. Anyway, why stop at Brunty? It's not impossible that Sidney Gold's actually the man behind it all."

Lydia frowned. "But how?"

"Just suppose that he and his boy are only pretending to fall out. They provoke Rosenheim – who remains quite innocent of what's really happening – they provoke him into telling us part of the story . . . enough for us to work out that Randy wants to get a stranglehold on his dad. So we think poor Sidney's an innocent victim and start making overtures to him. D'you see? Before we discover our error, we could end up with Sidney Gold as a partner! And then Gold's Commercial Bodies would be assured of work for as long as planes fill the skies. Very neat. My point is – once you start seeing conspiracies, you see them everywhere."

"Well, *I've* told the truth," Imogen asserted.

Julia looked at her evenly. "And I believe you. Not that I have any hard evidence, mind, but" – she tapped her breast – "I believe you here."

"And now we're all thoroughly confused," Lydia complained. "If everyone's in a plot against us, what do we *do?*"

They all looked to Julia, who remarked, "You'd be amazed how many answers to business problems are to be found in simple domestic practices. Any housewife could tell us what to do next: We stir the pot and see what floats to the surface."

There were smiles all round. Hannah asked, "Who's got the spoon?"

"She has." Julia nodded toward a somewhat surprised Imogen. "Did you return the young man's camera?" she asked.

"No. He said wait until you come back – have another go then."

"Good. Well, since he's so keen to feast himself on ledgers, let's cook up a special edition, just for him!"

Before they set off for Dollis Hill, Julia went upstairs to change. First she put Wallace's roses in water and stood the vase on her dressing table. "In the hope they might not wither," she quoted; and only then did she realize it was an allusion to the song, *Drink to me only with thine eyes.*

The thought of seeing Wallace again almost overwhelmed her. To close the door on the world and all its sordid, stupid greed . . . to be alone with him in that quiet little room, lying in his arms . . . sharing his wine, his simple fare . . . talking about everything under the sun . . . hearing his calm, confident voice.

Her hand went to the phone; her fingers dialled his number. He answered in person.

"Darling?" she said.

He laughed in delight. "I sent thee late a rosy wreath?"

"And you have no idea what you started."

"Why?"

"Because now I crave a drink divine."

"Oh." He was crestfallen. "Now? That would be a little difficult."

She laughed. "Don't worry. It would be more than a little difficult here, it would be abso–bloody–lutely impossible. But that's life. I just had to hear your voice again. Can we meet this evening?"

"Usual time and place. Hey listen – great news!"

"What?"

He paused and then said, "I love you."

She laughed. "And I love you. It's great, but it's not news."

"But it is," he insisted. "That's the most astonishing thing. For seven long years I've been waiting for it to turn a little brown at the edges and it never does. It stays as fresh as ever. It's new every day. Brand new! I . . . I can't get over it."

She blinked back tears of happiness. "Tonight," she promised and rang off.

He was right. It did feel new, every day. Absolutely, utterly new.

She was just brushing her hair when the door opened and closed behind her; she looked up to see Imogen standing there. "May I talk to you, please, Mrs Somerville?" she asked.

"What about?"

"I'm sure you know what about." Not waiting for any invitation she crossed the room and took the hairbrush out of Julia's astonished hand. She began at once to brush her former mistress's hair, talking to her at the same time via the looking glass. "It's about what was in that safe – the thing we didn't mention downstairs."

Julia turned red with anger. "How dare you! If you must know, I confiscated them from some wretched little flibberty-gibbet of a typist. Good heavens – you surely don't imagine . . ."

But Imogen was not even listening. "You could have ruined me," she went on. "At any moment these past six years, you had in that safe the power to destroy me entirely. When I think of the times I crossed you and said hurtful things about you – well I tremble, and that's all about it. So I just want you to know that I think" – her voice fluttered almost out of control – "I think you're the nicest . . . best . . . ever . . ." She swallowed audibly. There were tears in her eyes.

Julia sat in dumbstruck embarrassment, having not the faintest idea what the girl was talking about.

"Anyway . . ." Imogen sniffed up a miniature ocean. "I just wanted you to know how much I regret everything I ever did to harm you. I know I can never expect your forgiveness. But you can expect my support and help in anything, in any way I can. Just call on me."

She dropped the hairbrush in her embarrassment and began a hasty retreat to the door. She had almost reached it when she stopped, hit her own forehead with the butt of her palm, and exclaimed, "Look at me – all at sixes and sevens!" And she reached in her handbag to pull out what looked like a box of chocolates, all wrapped up as a present. She took two steps to the bed and laid them on the corner of the counterpane. "These are my own two favourites," she said. "I hope you haven't already read them."

Julia watched in absorbed fascination, unable to think of a thing to say.

At the door Imogen turned one final time. "I don't suppose you could say you forgive me just a little bit?" she asked. There were fresh tears ready to fall. "No," she added glumly. "Why should you?"

She had turned to go before Julia found her voice. "Miss Davis?"

Imogen reappeared in the dark rectangle of the doorway.

"What you've owned up to today – that took some courage. I greatly respect you for that. Also, I know you've helped my brother, not once but twice, through most difficult episodes in his life." She gave an awkward little laugh. "And I suppose I have to be fair and tell you that . . . with regard to what happened in this house more than seven years ago now . . . I believe you were much less to blame than my husband."

For a while Imogen stood there, uncertain what to say. She just shook her head in a dazed kind of wonder. "Knowing what you do about me," she murmured, "you can still say that!"

Left alone, Julia racked her brains to think what on earth it could be that Davis assumed she knew – something scurrilous . . . and connected with that safe. It made no sense.

Abstractedly she opened the wrapping on the present the woman had left. It proved to contain two books. The first was "Petalis and the Mountains of the Moon," the sequel to "Flower of the Veldt," which she had been longing to read ever since the voyage out on the

Mauretania. And the other was "Jane Eyre." Inside the cover of each was an inscription: *To Mrs Julia Somerville with profound gratitude from Imogen Davis.*

Inside the Charlotte Brontë was an ornate sticker saying *Alma Road College of Domestic Science – presented to Miss Imogen Davis – Best Fish Dish,* 1923.

Julia, close to tears herself by now, hugged the book to her and wondered how she was going to cope with this sudden outpouring of love from one poor, bewildered, vulnerable woman who had never in her life felt anything other than an outcast.

And all in the middle of a crisis that threatened to bring her own world down about her.

CHAPTER FIFTY-SIX

ON THE WAY to Dollis Hill, Julia suddenly cried "Eureka!" It startled Lydia, who had been remembering her mother's pleasant confusion at getting roses from Wallace Baker, and was trying hard *not* to draw the obvious conclusion.

"Eureka what?" she asked irritably.

"Oh . . . nothing, really," her mother replied. Then, seeing that would not do, she added, "Well, I just realized that, with these fake accounts, if we make it seem we're in *too* deep a hole, then we shan't see Randy for dust."

"And what if we make it seem that we're just groaning with cash?" Lydia asked.

"I'm not sure. Let me think about that."

In fact, what she thought about was the discovery that had prompted her outburst. It wasn't so much a discovery as a memory, something she had buried and refused to recall since the day it had happened. But now she saw it again, quite clearly: The admirably nondescript, melt-in-a-crowd figure of Sefton Storey.

She could see him mumbling his way through his report as if the disclosure of its contents, even to the client who commissioned them, were somehow a breach of trust. She recalled her impatience . . . how she had already, by chance, discovered it all, anyway . . .

and his relief at not having to recapitulate that long, tedious rigma-role. And then she remembered the thing itself – a large, plain, manilla envelope in which it was all set out, one meticulous step after another. *Subject: Miss Imogen Davis.*

Clearly, she had not "discovered it all."

The moment she arrived at her office, even before she said hello to Brunty, she opened her safe and thrust her fingers as far as they would reach into that narrow space. Finding nothing, she concluded that it must have been pushed to the back. As she went to her desk to get the ruler she saw that Hannah Dawson was standing at the door. "Where's Lydia?" Hannah asked.

"I think she's talking to Tony Crossthwaite about her Part One," Julia replied.

Hannah nodded toward the safe. "What was the shameful secret, eh?"

Julia blushed. "I know how it must seem. Candidly, I'd forgotten the books were even there. I confiscated them . . ."

"No, no, no," the other cut in impatiently. "The documents Miss Davis burned." She frowned. "Didn't she tell you about it back in Connaught Square? I thought that's why she went privately up to your room." She jerked her thumb in the direction of Julia's home, or, rather, she jerked it vaguely over her shoulder – a form of navigational sloppiness that always irritated Julia.

"Connaught Square is that way, actually," she pointed out. It also gave her a necessary second or two for thought. "She mentioned it in passing," she went on. "But she didn't tell me that *you* knew."

"Oh? But that's how I caught her. She carried it through to the forge and burned it – although by then I think she'd already decided you're the bee's knees. I'd love to know what it was – some informa-tion that would have destroyed her, she said, if ever you'd revealed it."

Julia smiled. "She's an avid reader of sentimental fiction, you know. Rather like the little typist I confiscated those books from last summer. I had no idea they were still there. I don't suppose you'd know anyone who'd like to take them off my hands?"

Hannah grinned wickedly. "To be honest, I'm rather partial to that sort of reading myself. After a hard day here, it's exactly what I need. You really ought to try one sometime, Boss. You'd be very pleasantly surprised. But yes, thanks very much, I'd be delighted to take them off your hands."

And so Julia had to suffer the sight of the cream of her collection being carried off in triumph – and a damnably *knowing* triumph – by, of all people, solid, sensible Miss Dawson, fellow of two learned societies.

Brunty reached the car park on his homeward way before he saw the Boss's new Bentley and realized she must be in her office. He broke his invariable routine and went back to see her.

He almost caught them at it, cooking the books. Fortunately he stopped in the outer office for a word with Mrs Henderson, giving Julia time to forestall him.

"Brunty! How good to see you! I've just this minute arrived. I was on my way to . . . oh, but you're off home, I see. Let me walk you to your car."

He didn't demur. "Good trip?" he asked. "I saw all your cables – and there have been several more from Baring. All pretty bullish."

"Oh, well," she said brightly. "Nothing much to add then."

They emerged into the evening sun. She breathed deeply and murmured, "Oh, London!"

He cleared his throat. "You didn't, er, chat with anyone in Wall Street?"

"Oh lots!" She laughed. "Actually, I should put a flea in your ear about that."

"Oh?"

"You've obviously no idea how depressed things still are over there. It's as bad as here. I'm afraid the flotation of wac won't bring in anything like the estimated amount – nor the sale of the so-called assets."

"So-called?" He swallowed audibly.

"We'll be lucky to see twenty thou' at this end when all the expenses are met."

It stopped him in his tracks. "But Baring also agreed . . ."

"Yes, well, we're all a little out of touch. It wasn't my idea, as you know. And fortunately I never placed any great reliance on it."

"But we were absolutely counting on that money, Boss. I'm desperately sorry if I've misled . . ." He shook his head in disbelief. "I must recheck everything tomorrow."

She gave his arm a reassuring squeeze and pushed him gently onward. "By all means. But anything from that quarter will be a bonus. We can manage without."

"Can we? How?"

"Oh . . . things in the pipeline, as they say. I'll tell you tomorrow."

Three inquiring faces greeted her return to the office.

"I hope I found a second spoon," she told them.

"I wish there was something I could do," Imogen sighed.

Julia, suddenly remembering they had had no lunch, said, "Well there is, my dear. Something *only* you can do." And she led her out to the cupboard where the spare keys to the canteen were kept. "You can pop across to the kitchens and cook us the Best Fish Dish of nineteen *thirty*-three."

CHAPTER FIFTY-SEVEN

WALLACE WAS CHECKING his watch for the third time as she arrived. "Oh darling, I'm so sorry." She put a hand on his shoulder to keep him seated. "But just let me tell you what a day I had."

She kissed him briefly, full on the lips. Seeing his surprise, she told him, "We hardly need hide it any longer."

That thought prompted another: "Oh, when I saw Dolly on the boat I nearly died! Especially as we were so sure she was on the *Oceanic*. But it all worked out for the best. How are you?"

He passed her her drink. "Never better. I had a good day, too." She knocked the gin back.

"On an empty stomach?" he asked.

She shook her head. "I've just eaten." Then, seeing his disappointment, she added, "But that was to make up for lunch. Don't worry, I'll be hungry again in an hour – and it'll take that long to tell you."

The barman put the refill an inch from her fingers. She nodded her thanks and then slipped her hand into Wallace's. "I missed you," she murmured. "Sometimes I thought I'd just chuck it all in and catch the next boat back. You're a dangerous man. Can we go on a holiday together?"

He smiled.

Realism overcame her. "No! There's too much of a crisis at Neville's. But a weekend. What about a weekend together?" She closed her eyes and luxuriated in the very sound of it.

"Of course." He squeezed her hand and let it go. "Tell me about your day. Tell me everything since you left."

It took about half an hour. Lover and journalist vied in the questions he asked; between the two roles he dug out everything – including things she had not realized she knew.

She refused another drink, being lightheaded enough already. "Let's go," she suggested. When they were outside she asked, "Do we need to buy food?"

He linked hands and answered, "Nope."

It was dusk. Old Compton Street was thick with whores – "brasses," in the local idiom. Their clients were like fat bumble bees, droning mechanically from flower to flower. The ritual was invariable: quick mutual inspection (for vastly different motives) – heads close together – a mutter of, "a dollar . . . ten bob . . . a quid," depending on a lightning estimate – then he'd either turn on his heel or they'd walk off, not quite side-by-side.

Julia wondered what it must be like to be walking along a street with a man, going to do what she and Wallace were going to do, yet *not* feeling that thrilling, melting excitement about it.

"Shades of Imogen," he commented drily. Then, seeing the puzzlement in her eyes, he added, "You mean, you hadn't worked that out?"

She stopped and stared at him.

He laughed. "What else *could* it be?"

She gave a silent whistle. "But poor Max – he must be told."

"I'm sure he knows, Julia." He took her hand again. "You are an enigma, you know. So quick in some ways – so blind in others."

"I'm not quick in anything," she said. "Except perhaps commerce."

He laughed and looked back along Old Compton Street. "And that's not commerce?"

But when they were in Brewer Street he picked up his own words: "Actually, in Imogen's case, I doubt very much whether it was commerce. I think she did it for Randy Gold. I'll bet she gave him every penny."

"I was just thinking about him – some of the things he said. They make sense now." She leaned her head against his shoulder. "Oh, Wallace, I wish I could *see* things like you. I'm either warm or freezing about people. I've been so unjust to poor Imogen all these years – even though she thinks I've been a saint. But you're just cool. That's what I need – especially at this moment – a cool eye."

When he did not reply she chided, "You're supposed to make an offer. That was an invitation."

"Let me think about it," he replied. "The last thing you need this week is someone who promises what he cannot deliver." Then, after the briefest pause, he added, "About our weekend."

"Yes?"

"It just so happens that I have to pop down to Chartwell this Saturday to see Churchill. There's a pub in Westerham called The Limpsfield Poacher – an old coaching inn with candlelight and four-poster beds and . . . very romantic. We could motor down on Friday afternoon?"

"Mmmm!" She closed her eyes and swung her legs as if she were already walking through the autumnal stubble. "I'll take my sketchbook. It's years since I did any drawing."

They made love and slept and made love and slept until almost midnight. Then she put together a salad while he cooked a couple of *omelettes aux fines herbes*.

"Dolly says she'll get a Nevada divorce," he remarked casually. "No names need be stated."

"Yes, she mentioned something like that to me before I left."

"D'you think she and Eliot will marry?"

"I'm sure they will." Julia laughed. "And I'll tell you why. In the cab on the way to the Cunard pier Eliot dropped a remark about possibly moving WAC to California. Of course it was all to do with the climate and cheap migrant labour and real-estate prices . . ."

". . . and not a word about a possible Hollywood career for Dolly!"

"Hole in one!" She sighed. "Oh I do hope they'll be happy. They're much more suited to each other than they were to either of us."

"So – here's to us!" He turned out her omelette and passed her a glass of hock, raising his own to the toast.

"And meanwhile my problem looms larger every minute."

He tucked in heartily. "I don't think you even know what your problem is."

"And you do?"

He stared at her a moment, as if sizing her up. Then he said, "I didn't tell you how I spent my morning. It may seem to have no relevance but it has. I did an interview for the *Burlington Magazine* with a rising young sculptor called Henry Moore. He used to – why are you smiling? D'you know him?"

"No, it was just the coincidence. The president of WAC is called Moore." She laughed. "Sorry – that really *does* have no relevance. Go on. This Henry Moore used to . . . what?"

"He used to teach at the Royal College. Now he's at the Chelsea."

"And what did he say?"

He shook his head. "That's not the important part. He's very down to earth. It's like talking to a shepherd or a gardener. It was what he *did* that was so fascinating. All during our conversation he held this piece of clay in his hands, twisting it and turning it, this way and that – the way old men sit and whittle a bit of wood. Except that when he'd finished . . . there was this." He reached across to the sideboard and took up a small biscuit tin. He opened it gently to reveal a wad of damp cloth, which he peeled back with great care. And suddenly she saw revealed a perfectly formed human leg, about six inches long. A classical male leg.

She reached her hands forward but he warned her, "I don't want to touch it until I get a friend of mine, a dental mechanic, to make a plaster cast. But isn't it perfect? Look at the tension in some of the muscles and the relaxation in others. Here. And here. It's incredible!

435

And he was doing this – hardly looking at it even – all the while he was talking to me. And at the end I told him that was one of the most amazing things I ever saw, and d'you know what he replied?"

"What?"

"He just stared at his fingers and he said, 'It's down there in those fellows by now.' Isn't that perfect? That'll be my test from now on, to tell true art from the bogus – is it all in the head still, or is it down there, where it really belongs – in the fingers?"

She thought he had completed the point of his tale but he leaned forward and continued, "And then in the taxi on the way back, knowing you'd already landed at Southampton, and thinking about meeting you again, it suddenly occurred to me that that's the way you function. Your approach to business is artistic. I mean it's in your very bones. You do it as naturally and effortlessly as Henry Moore did this." He wrapped it up carefully and put it back in its box.

"Is that my problem?" she asked.

"No. Your problem is that you can't accept you have this gift."

He sipped his wine, letting her think it over, before he added, "Mind you, you're not the only one. Crownfield has exactly the same difficulty."

She drew breath to comment and then thought better of it. "No," she murmured. "You go on. Tell me about Crownfield."

"In the beginning," he explained, "when it looked as if you were just a caretaker for your son and, in any case, Somerville's was small beer – high in reputation, I know, but small beer by the standards of modern industry . . . during all that early phase, Crownfield thought it highly amusing that you, a mere woman, should be in charge. But when you, in effect, stood on your own hands and lifted yourself to your present heights . . ."

"From which it's a long fall down, I may say!"

". . . and what is more, did it against Crownfield's express advice to the contrary, you began to present an intolerable threat to him."

Her heart fell. "Are you saying you think Crownfield's behind it all?"

He shook his head. "Possibly not. But taking a longer view of it, I honestly believe he will not rest until he has you neatly trussed up in a nice, tidy, limited company."

She sighed. "I'm sure you're right. But if I don't manage something soon, there may not be a long term to worry about. What am I going to do in the next seven days?"

"I don't know," he replied mildly. "Chiefly I don't know enough about the people concerned."

"Can I help?" She was thinking in terms of inviting him to lunch with them.

"You can indeed." He grinned. "You can trust me."

"In what way?"

"Leave me to do a bit of digging? You've told me all I need to know – pointed me in all the right directions. D'you now trust me enough to stand back and not ask questions for a day or two?"

"Nothing . . . er . . ." She was trying to think of a nice word for "violent."

He knew what she meant though, and merely laughed. "Good God, darling – if *that's* all you think I'm good for, it becomes even more important."

But she was not completely mollified. She swallowed the last of her egg and washed it down with wine. "More than five hundred people's livelihoods depend on that trust, Wallace."

"Oh, my darling!" He reached across and took her head between his hands. "Much, much more than that."

CHAPTER FIFTY-EIGHT

DESPITE ALL THE claims on her time the following day, Julia realized she had to go and see Theresa Ashbury. She set off soon after lunch. Although she visited the college in Islington several times a year, she soon realized that familiarity had blunted her awareness of the place – indeed, of that entire district of London, where the years of the trade depression had left so dire a mark.

Her way took her up the Pentonville Road, on past the Angel and into the City Road, then finally into Coalbrooke Row. And in all that journey she did not see a single newly painted window frame or door. Broken panes were stuffed with yellowing newsprint or tacked over with flattened biscuit tins. Men stood in morose clusters at every corner, watching the huge Bentley sweep by, watching stray dogs snap at the brewers' horses, watching the clouds as they massed in autumnal skies, watching the years turning – watching, with their great, incurious eyes, anything that moved, however slowly.

She recoiled from the very sight of it, fixing her eyes on the road ahead – trying to turn everything else into mere backcloth. She had forgotten what the images of poverty could do to her – or, rather, she had believed herself beyond it now. But then she remembered that, by next Tuesday, she was somehow going to have to find about twenty thousand pounds – and at the moment she could hardly rake together a quarter of that sum.

The grand sedanca de ville came to a ghostly halt in the yard of the City College. Theresa was at the door before Strong could get to it. "I thought you'd be here today," she commented grimly.

"I came as soon as I could."

"Shall I put the kettle on?"

For some reason Julia found she could not face going inside. She had not yet alighted, so she moved back to allow room for Theresa and asked, "Would you mind if we just drove around?"

Theresa's eyes lit up. "I'll never say no to a ride in one of these. Let me get my hat."

"You don't need a hat."

But she had already vanished. "I can't go out them gates without something on my head," she said when she returned.

"Where to, Boss?" Strong asked.

"Anywhere. Just drive about."

Theresa did a little buttock jig in the seat, like a child on a treat. But as they pulled out of the yard she became serious again. "In case I forget," she said, "poor old Mrs Davis, that Imogen's mother – she died this morning, you know."

"Oh dear, no, I didn't. Oh, the poor girl! She was with me yesterday and there was no hint of it."

"Poor girl?" Theresa looked at her askance. "That's a new tune."

Julia gave a confessional sort of smile. "We've, er . . . we see more eye to eye, now. She's been the salvation of my brother Max. When did it happen? This morning, you said?"

"Yes. Nice and peaceful, seemingly. In her sleep. Best thing, really. The funeral's tomorrow in Friern Barnet."

"That's quick."

"Nothing to delay it – no other relatives nor nothing."

"Well I'll go. She must have someone to support her at a time like that."

Theresa was full of admiration. "It's more than I'd do, I tell you."

Stoke Newington, the Balls Pond Road, Hoxton, Hackney . . . the Bentley whispered at the pace of a mourner-less funeral through those drab, working-class slums that lay to the north of the City's golden square mile.

"I haven't been down some of these streets for years," Theresa remarked. She stared out through the windows like a foreign visitor.

Julia was surprised. "I thought this was our trawling ground."

The other shook her head sadly. "They don't want to know us – not your real labouring classes. All they want now is money. Cash. 'The only housekeeping as pays,' they say, 'is all up West.' There's a whole army goes out from here, every morning. Not just to houses

438

but to offices and all."

"So who comes to us?"

"Tradesmen's wives and daughters, mostly. And clerks. The working class that fancies itself as middle class."

"I had no idea."

Strong's voice came through the speaking tube, startling them slightly. "I think this is the place, ladies."

Julia recognized it before Theresa, funnily enough. "That's the little house I rented when we had our wager. Good Lord, it's not changed one bit."

As if in a dream she climbed out and stood on the narrow pavement, staring at the anonymous façade that had been "home" to her – and to how many hundreds of tenants? Theresa joined her. After a moment's silence she turned to seek out her own old home. But she took no more than half a dozen paces toward it before she spun on her heel and came back. "There's no point," she said. "There's nothing there any more."

Julia peered up the street, thinking she meant the house had been demolished.

"No," Theresa went on. "Nothing of us. It's all moved on."

But for Julia it was not "moving on." Indeed, it was all coming back – not just the sights and sounds but the whole flavour of that age: the end of the war, the girls being displaced from the factories because the men wanted "their" jobs back . . . that bewildered, resentful return to the domestic hearth . . . the dashed hopes as the Land Fit For Heroes turned into a playground for war profiteers . . .

"It's all moved on," Theresa repeated in her ear. "I hope you weren't thinking of trying to talk me out of it, Mrs Somerville?"

Julia shook her head.

As they got back into the car, Theresa added, "They were miserable days – and yet we were happy."

"Let's go back to Islington, Strong," Julia said. And then, to Theresa, as they set off: "We make an odd pair, you and I, my dear. Seeing that wretched house again has brought it all back to me. On the face of it, I won our wager, yet I've always felt that you taught me ten times as much as you may have learned in return. And it's the same with the society. People talk of it as *my* society, yet I've always thought of it as yours – ten times more than it's mine. I can't imagine it without you – but I can also see that we may have had our day. What are you going to do instead? I can't think you'll be idle."

Theresa roared with laughter. "Idle – that's rich! No" – she became serious again – "it's not so much what I'd like to do now as what the Gunner wishes. I've had my innings – and a more loyal supporter I couldn't have hoped for. I'd say it's time to give him a bit of consideration."

"And does he have anything in mind? You know I'll help if it's a question of that."

Theresa looked at her in surprise, which was quickly masked by an impish smile. "You wouldn't like to go partners in a roadhouse, I suppose?" Her laugh declared the suggestion to be a joke, but the eye was watchful.

"How much of a partner?" Julia asked cautiously.

"About eight hundred. We've got twelve hundred saved and the place he's got his eye on is seventeen – leaving three for stock and working capital. The Gunner wants to borrow the rest but you know my views on that!"

"This is an actual place?"

She nodded. "It's called The Dovecote, on the Brighton road. It does a very good class of trade."

"All right. We'll go and see it next week. Next Thursday or Friday, eh? And if I approve, I'll go in with you."

"D'you mean it?" Theresa looked at her with a kind of trepidation, as if she feared that everything might vanish on the stroke of midnight.

"Only if I approve, mind." Julia pretended to be severe. "And I'd expect you to buy me out over a period – ten years, say."

They both knew she was talking about an interest-free loan. Theresa wanted to hug her but the odd kind of formal friendship between them, though it was far more intense than many that were superficially warmer, made it impossible. "Oh," she stammered, all flustered, clawing at Julia's sleeve with an uncertain hand. "I never meant . . . I never expected . . ."

But Julia could see that her mind's eye was already measuring The Dovecote for carpets and curtains.

CHAPTER FIFTY-NINE

IMOGEN WAS THE only mourner, Julia the only witness, at the burial of Mrs Davis, which took place in the Great Northern Cemetery, just outside Southgate. There was no outward display of grief, merely a fitting solemnity. Julia had money ready for the sexton in case Imogen forgot. But the woman "saw them all right" and then thanked the vicar – who, incongruously, turned and thanked Julia for coming.

"He took the words out of my mouth, Mrs Somerville," Imogen said brightly as they fell in beside each other on their way to the gate. "It was more than good of you to come. All this way, too."

"It was so quick. I hadn't even time to write you a note. I'm so sorry that it's happened. Was it completely unexpected?"

"Not especially. I mean, it's been on the cards for years. It was a happy release for her. Did Mrs Ashbury tell you? I asked them to ring her."

"Yes."

"She probably also told you about Mum's trouble – thinking she owned the place and all that. She was even going to sue them for rent. She got very crotchety about it towards the end." She drew a deep breath and expelled it sharply – not so much a sigh as a closing of the subject.

But Julia did not take the meaning quickly enough. She was already saying, "It's awful, isn't it – knowing you're in the front line now? I remember feeling it when my parents died, within a month of each other." Then, with a change of tone, "How did you come out here? Can I offer you a lift back?"

Imogen accepted gratefully. She had come out by train the previous evening and stayed overnight at the home in Friern Barnet. Julia asked if she'd like to collect her things but she said she'd drive out one evening next week and sort through her mother's bits and pieces. She couldn't face it now.

"I thought Max might be here," Julia remarked as soon as they were settled in the car.

"He says death is a bourgeois event. Let the dead bury their dead."

"No point in asking what that means, I suppose? There never was."

"Search me!" Imogen laughed; but then she added more seriously, "I suppose it means he's a bit frightened of it."

"Not for any reason?"

Imogen shook her head. She opened her handbag, peered inside, and then closed it again.

"What were you thinking of doing for lunch?" Julia asked. "Or perhaps you're not hungry?"

The other hesitated before she replied, "I was wondering how to ask you. Could you *bear* to have lunch with me . . ."

"Imogen!" Julia answered testily.

"I'd understand if not. Only there's something I want to tell you – or think I ought to tell you." She peered inside her bag again, and once more snapped it shut.

"Let's see if there's a café open at Alexandra Palace," Julia suggested. The glass division was down, so Strong needed no second bidding. He parked the car at the hillcrest and walked back along the lane to Muswell Hill, where he said he had an uncle. The two women went down into the park and discovered that one of the caféterias was serving soup and sandwiches.

It was a bright autumn day, warm where there was shelter from the breeze. They carried their selection to a wooden gazebo, which, though well below the crown of the hill, gave a commanding view of much of north London – all the way down to St Paul's, six miles away. Surrounded by rhododendrons and backed with bark siding, it formed a perfect little suntrap.

Julia had brought the gin from the Bentley's cocktail cabinet. "D'you want to liven up your orange juice?" she asked.

Imogen nodded and replied, "I don't usually." She opened her bag and pulled out an envelope, all in one movement. "Let's get it over and done with," she went on. "I wrote that last night. I was going to call at Dollis Hill on my way back and leave it for you."

The letter inside read:

> Dear Mrs Somerville,
> I enclose a letter from my solicitor to Mr Randolph Gold. If it is of any service to you, please feel free to use it as you will. I know he is trying to use our company to further his struggle against his father. I'm sure you can stop him with this.
> Thanks again for all your goodness to me,
> Your obliged and humble,
> Imogen Davis.

The solicitor's letter requested the reimbursement of £7,000, "the proceeds of our client's earnings over two years between 1926 and 1928, which were criminally sequestered by you." It went on to say that under certain conditions, which were not specified, Imogen was prepared to withdraw the action and had appointed Mrs Julia Somerville to negotiate on her behalf. And it concluded with the assertion that, if Mrs Somerville could not be satisfied, "our client intends to pursue this matter through the civil courts, at which point it will become necessary to name both her trade and yours."

Julia was in a turmoil as she folded the papers and replaced them in the envelope. Imogen, watching her keenly, said, "You're going to say no. I can see it in your face. But please – before you do, just think of . . ." Alternatives paralyzed her for a moment. She finished, in a tired voice: "Just think of me."

Julia handed her back the letter. "I am thinking of you. I couldn't possibly use this."

"Even though he's using you? And Morgan, and Rosenheim – he'd use anyone, just to harm his dad."

"I know that, my dear. But even if he were out to destroy Neville's – which isn't remotely likely, I may say – even then, I couldn't use those letters. I couldn't do that to you."

"You just shut me out all the time," she exploded bitterly. "How can I ever undo the wrong I did you?"

"You can't, I'm afraid. Time has already done the job for you. I wish you knew how hard it is for me to remember those days now. Tell me – what d'you think you did that demands this endless wallowing in guilt?"

The slight note of scorn had its intended effect. Imogen bridled and sat several degrees more upright. "You know jolly well," she said.

"Really? I'll tell you what I do know." Julia was cheerfully belligerent now that she was no longer talking to a bit of wet cloth. "I know that George was a distinctly odd person. Somewhere along life's way he'd picked up the lunatic notion that 'gentlewomen don't move' – as Lord Curzon put it – whereas every other woman is fairly panting for those pleasures."

When she saw Imogen begin to nod her agreement she relented enough to smile. "I also know that my resentment of you – understandable though it may have been at the time – was not very understanding. I allowed it to blind me. I thought I was the only victim. But now I think we both were – victims. And, in an odd sort of way, so was poor George. Good heavens, Imogen" – she shook her head in puzzlement – "it was all so long ago, I honestly can't remember much of it now at all. Why d'you want to keep it so fresh, poisoning your life like this?"

"I don't!" There was anguish in her voice, as if Julia had utterly missed the point.

"Well there you are, then." Julia was determined to keep the argument in her court. She put the letter back on the table, near Imogen. "I'm more touched than I can say by this, but I simply couldn't use it. I couldn't let you sacrifice yourself." She gave a single laugh. "I should think being with Max is sacrifice enough for one lifetime from any mortal! Why don't you make him marry you?"

Whatever Imogen had been going to say deserted her at that question; she simply stared at Julia, open-mouthed.

"Don't tell me you couldn't, if you put your mind to it."

Again that shake of the head, implying that Julia hadn't merely got the wrong end of the stick but the wrong stick altogether. "It's what he wants," she replied. "He keeps on at it, but it's me who says no."

Julia gave an inverted smile. "Well, that's understandable, I suppose."

"No!" Imogen tore out some imaginary hair. "I thought, if he married me . . . well . . . I thought you'd never speak to him again. Giving me your name – Neville. Then I thought he'd turn against me in the end. So I've always said no."

Julia almost asked her if it was what she really wanted in life, if she wasn't simply marrying Max for the sake of belonging somewhere. But then it occurred to her that the woman's need to belong was so overwhelming that all other emotions were trivial in comparison. Indeed, the boot was on the other foot. If Imogen said she was marrying for love, the proper question to ask her would be, "Yes but are you sure you'll ever *belong* with this man?"

She said, "Well you go straight home and tell him you've changed your mind."

"And you honestly don't . . . I mean you wouldn't . . ."

"Listen – just think of this: Max and Dolly and I had no choice about being Nevilles. But if you want the name, and if hard work and devotion and" – she prodded the letter an inch or two nearer the woman – "willingness to sacrifice yourself are any sort of qualification – well, by God, you've earned it! I should feel proud you'd freely chosen to join the clan."

"Oh, Mrs Somerville . . ." She stammered. There were tears ready to fall.

"I think it had better be Julia from now on, don't you?"

Imogen looked away, uncomfortable at having to dab her eyes. "I never did that for my mum," she commented morosely.

Julia, who was not going to have herself promoted, replied, "Yes, there are some kinds of grief that 'do lie too deep for tears.' I didn't weep for George until I discovered he wasn't, after all, lying to me about those water colours."

Imogen stared at her aghast. Julia knew she was thinking, *But for heaven's sake – that's what killed him!*

"It took me a long time to get over that," she said. And she went on to tell the story as Mrs Henderson had unravelled it.

"Are they the same ones – in your office now?" Imogen asked. "The ones over the safe?"

Julia nodded.

"And I didn't even recognize them," she remarked gloomily.

"Imogen!" Julia punched her playfully and laughed. "Stop it, for God's sake! You've always got to go one worse, haven't you! I never knew anyone like it."

Imogen's shock turned quickly to laughter. "You wouldn't have a drop more gin, would you?" she asked. Then shyly she added, "Julia?"

There was a brief silence while they tucked into their sandwiches.

"Put that letter away, there's a dear," Julia asked.

As Imogen popped it into her bag she asked, "You're not just saying it because you've already got a better answer – and you don't want to be under any obligation to me?"

"Better answer!" Julia repeated ironically. "At the moment I don't have any answer at all."

CHAPTER SIXTY

THE POACHER WAS an old coaching inn on the cross route from Dover and Canterbury to the western home counties; nowadays most of its passing custom came by car along the north-south roads between London and the coast. It offered candlelight meals and four-poster beds, just as Wallace had promised; and yet in other ways it was not quite the idyll he remembered.

A traditional English inn will go to almost any lengths to adapt to changing times and a new clientèle – as long as the requisite altera-tions are only skin deep and will cost no more than a few pence. So, although it endures a sort of perpetual vandalism, the result is always splendidly reversible. For instance, at that very moment the Poacher's fifteenth-century oak beams, which had been plastered over by the Victorians, were now being discovered again – and stained black to demonstrate their long exposure to smoke. Repro-duction horse brasses were nailed upon them to revive the warm sentiments attached to the name "coaching," even though the genu-ine coaches themselves were mouldering to dust in the stables across the yard. Meanwhile, the bedroom fires that had actually warmed the original coach parties had all been newly tiled in antique designs you might see in any unfinished bungalow in Metroland. Thus – eternally poised between a confused past and an unguessable future – the Poacher stood four-square upon tradition.

Traditional, too, was its inability to decide whether it were *really* a small hotel or a private house. It boasted only three bedrooms for guests (large rooms, it is true, for each had been able to accommo-date travelling parties of a dozen or so, sleeping in common). The family and staff occupied the remaining two dozen rooms. A guest who strayed even slightly out of bounds could easily find himself in the heart of a family quarrel, or in a silent bathroom filled with the tokens of permanent occupation – toothbrushes, shaving sticks, sec-ond-best dressing gowns. Throw open a window and you were awash with all those noises that hotels contrive to keep from their guests – kitchen laughter, the scraping of beer crates, Radio Luxembourg dispelling the boredom of the split-duty waitress.

Julia loved it from the moment she crossed the threshold. The public bar had sawdust on the floor; the saloon was filled with Windsor chairs and black oak tables polished to confusion with lavender-scented beeswax. Unnecessary fires transformed intruders into guests and dared them to go back outside.

"Care for a stroll before supper?" Wallace asked.

"In a mo. Let's just sit here and have a drink first. I haven't been in a real English pub since . . . I don't know when."

She drank Bass; he stuck to his usual Guinness – or, rather, it stuck to him, in a thin line along his top lip, making him look like a bad attempt at Ramon Navarro.

She stretched luxuriously. "A whole long weekend!" she purred.

"Except tomorrow," he reminded her.

"Aren't you going to tell me anything?"

He stared at her a long while, smiling a little. "Yes. I'll tell you one thing straight away," he said at last. "I changed my mind about seeing Churchill. I rang him up, explained about coming down here with you . . ."

"You didn't!"

"Why ever not? Anyway, I was about to ask if we could join them for lunch on Sunday when he came out with the suggestion himself."

"Ah. So you'll be here tomorrow after all?"

He grinned. "That depends."

"On what?"

"I'll tell you when we go for our walk. Or, rather, I'll ask you."

She finished her drink, more quickly than she would have liked. Ten minutes later, having meanwhile changed into sensible country things, they were striding toward the hills, west of the village. Their path rose out of a pool of shadow into the setting sun, whose blood-red light reached horizontally in among the trees, giving the wood-land the air of a fantastic kingdom, all on fire. Above them, among thin autumnal branches, the first stars were shining.

"Have you ever been up here before?" she asked.

She meant with another woman, of course, but, if he understood, he ignored it. "Only when I came down to work with Churchill."

"Yes, whereabouts is Chartwell?"

He pointed vaguely away to their left.

They sat in silence on a fallen log at the farther edge of the wood and watched the sun go down. She edged her hand along the log until it met his, flat on the rain-bleached curve of it. She slipped her fingers beneath it and closed her eyes, doubling the red of the twilight.

She felt him move. His other hand darkened that sinking fire for a moment and then touched her cheek. Her free hand rose of its own accord and held him there. They turned their faces inward, cheekbone to cheekbone, nose to nose, and finally lips to lips – yearning to yearning.

"Will you marry me, Julia?" he asked as they drew apart again.

For reply she showered his face and neck with kisses – brief, urgent, breathless kisses. "Oh, Wallace – isn't this absurd?"

"What?"

"We're both in our forties, for heaven's sake."

He leaned into her, caressing her neck and cheek with his lips. "If we're not still doing this in another forty years . . ." he whispered.

"Then what?"

"I don't know. It's not even possible to contemplate."

For some reason she remembered Lexy's offer of a cruise in the Aegean. She must ring him and decline, she told herself; but in her inmost heart she knew that was not at all why she had remembered it at this particular moment. The prompting had come from a dying Julia, clutching about herself the shroud of a vanishing freedom. *One more day,* she promised herself – that other self.

She straightened up, pulled a little apart from him. "You were going to tell me what you've learned so far?"

As always, he knew precisely what to push and what to leave. He gave one brief laugh, whispered through his nose.

An immense calm filled the space around them.

The final crimson wafer of the sun was nipped into a fleeting mirage before it vanished entirely. As at a signal they rose to go.

"I've been gathering material about you for a piece in *Vogue,*" he remarked. "They're starting a series to be called 'Woman in the News'."

"But I'm not in the news – anyway, why didn't you tell me?"

"I was going to wait until you'd settled back into things again, after Germany and then America. They don't want it for at least a couple of months. But then I thought what a perfect excuse it gave me for going round to Crownfield and Brunty and so on – hoping for the odd hint or indiscretion."

"Good idea."

"The reason I called Churchill was that I felt time was short and I ought to see Sidney Gold – which I've arranged for tomorrow lunchtime. My question was, would you be upset if I were to take a slightly more active part than I first planned? I know how you *love* delegating things."

She stiffened. "What sort of active part? Give me an example."

"What I'm thinking of is something like this. If we're right in our guess that Randy wants to get a full-nelson on his dad, then he can't have done it yet. If he had, we'd have heard the squeals even at this distance." He turned to her. "How d'you think our Sidney's going to respond?"

"He'll come and ask me not to play Randy's game."

"And you'll tell him you have very little choice – because of needing that cash."

"He's a resourceful man, Wallace. We needn't worry about Sidney. He'll find a way out – or round. Or probably under."

"So you'd rather I did nothing? Don't you realize you're delegating the decision to Sidney Gold?"

"Don't keep on and on. Anyway, it's not true. I'm leaving his business to him because I know he's well able. I can only delegate things that *I* could do."

"You can still stir the pot. For instance, when I see Sidney tomorrow, I could drop hints about what we think his son is up to."

She thought it over a moment. "Perhaps I'd better come with you," she suggested.

He was wise enough not to respond immediately. When they drew in sight of the Poacher she cried, "Good Lord, that's Lydia's car."

It was standing on the forecourt.

Their pace quickened. By the time they reached the inn they were almost running. But the person waiting to greet them at the door was not Lydia, it was Peter Rosenheim. Julia called out a greeting and asked him where the girl was; but she herself came to the door at that moment, carrying two pints of bitter.

"Damn! Caught in the act," she cried jovially. "I put them on your bill, actually, and told them we'd be four to dinner. I hope you don't mind? In fact, I know you won't – not when you hear the news we've brought." She craned over her brimming glass and gave her mother a kiss.

"How did you manage to find us?" Julia asked quietly.

Lydia giggled and, fondling her mother's ear gently, as though it were delicate silk, answered, "If you really must know, it was because these turned pink."

Julia frowned in bewilderment.

Lydia checked that the two men were absorbed in their own conversation and then started feeding clues: "At Southampton . . . new Bentley . . . back seat . . . bunch of roses . . ."

"Ah!" Comprehension dawned; she smiled guiltily and bit her lip. "And did my ears really . . . Heavens, I hope Herr Rosenheim didn't notice."

"I'm afraid he did, old thing. When we'd drawn an absolute blank on all the places you might have been – and you've no idea how many there are until you try a thing like that – anyway, he turned to me and said, 'what about Wallace Baker – the man who sent your mother roses at Southampton and made her *glow* with pleasure?' Isn't he sweet!"

"You're not shocked?"

"Mummeee! I went to Summerhill, for heaven's sake."

"Why this desperate urgency to find us, anyway?"

"I think we must all be together for that." She half turned. "Oy! Gentlemen – are you ready to take us in to dinner?"

"Darling!" Julia laughed to mask her annoyance. "Wallace and I are dressing for dinner."

"No you're not," Lydia shot back confidently. "There honestly isn't time. Anyway, we're the only guests expected, so it hardly matters."

Rosenheim added, "I'm afraid she's right, Mrs Somerville. Time is rather pressing."

Dinner was a three-choice table d'hôte; they all picked oxtail soup and jugged hare.

"Now!" Julia turned to Lydia.

The girl looked at Rosenheim, who began their tale with a question: "I presume, Mrs Somerville, that even in the few days you've been back you've had several discussions with Brunty about the impending cash crisis at Neville's?"

Julia gave an intrigued sort of smile. "Not so. In fact, I had one very brief chat with him on the evening I got back – just while I walked him to his car. He has an absolute fetish about never staying late."

"May I ask what you told him? I have a very good reason . . ."

"Of course you may. I don't remember the exact words but I was rather offhand, nonchalant, you know. I told him that his and Baring's scheme would be lucky to raise even half of what we need – but fortunately I'd never relied on it and I had, in fact, found the money elsewhere."

"And was he pleased?"

"Skeptical would be a better word. He wanted to know how, so I said I'd tell him next day – the day before yesterday, in fact. But I didn't. I waited, deliberately, for him to come and see me. But he never came. Then there was SPRP business . . . then the funeral . . . and then we came down here . . ."

"Leaving a false trail to Berkshire," Lydia complained.

"Sonia's an old, old friend. She'd have got in touch with me if you'd said . . ."

"No she wouldn't. Because her phone's out of order."

Rosenheim cleared his throat delicately.

"Sorry!" Julia turned back to him. "You were saying? Oh yes – Brunty. Yes, he never came to see me."

He nodded as if she had confirmed his thoughts. "In fact," he went on, "it's fairly clear he went instead to Crownfield. We can only guess what they discussed but they must have realized that your only source of cash on that scale would be Morgan, working through Randy Gold."

"What we *think* happened," Lydia took over impatiently, "is that

Crownfield told Brunty to speak to Randy Gold and get the truth from the horse's mouth. But Brunty had never met Gold junior – so it could've been a bit embarrassing to go and ask him fairly searching questions like that. I mean, he'd no longer have the excuse that you were away in America. However, he has met Peter here a couple of times . . ."

Julia's eyebrows shot up at her daughter's use of Rosenheim's first name but no one else seemed to notice – particularly not the man himself.

". . . and so it must have seemed easier to get in touch with him."

Rosenheim interjected: "He obviously has no idea of the real relationship between me and my so-called partner!"

Julia chuckled. "So he phoned you instead."

"No – he called in person! This morning. And no beating around the bushes, either. Half a dozen innocent little questions, and there in among them – how big will Morgan's down payment be?"

"Which you naturally refused to tell him."

"At first, yes." Rosenheim smiled. "But I must also think quickly, especially after what you told me on the road back from Southampton. First I thought I'll tell him. Why not – I had already told you. Then I thought no – let him hear it from you. So I denied there would be any down payment at all, apart from the necessary minimum to make the contract enforceable."

"And then," Lydia took over, her eyes glowing with the promise of a climax, "he must have gone straight to Crownfield, who must have panicked."

"Never!" Julia told her. "That man may do many things, but he'll never panic."

"You tell me the right word for it, then. He's seeking a court order of sequestration on the assets of Neville's. He has a lien on some of the property – is that the right word?"

Julia felt her blood turning chill. "Crownfield?" she asked.

"Crownfield."

She turned to Rosenheim, who nodded confirmation.

"He's tired of the old waiting game," Wallace suggested.

"Or," Lydia pointed out, "he and Brunty were so confident we'd be in trouble when WAC failed to provide enough cash that they've already started to move. And, having started, they can't go back." She looked at Rosenheim as she spoke. Julia realized he must be the source of this insight; they must have talked of nothing else on the way down.

She turned to Wallace. "You were right," she told him. "We daren't now leave it to time and Sidney Gold. We must get together with him – close ranks."

He agreed. "Call him now," he suggested.

"No. Not with Sidney. I need to be there. I need to see his eyes,

watch his hands. It's much too delicate to manage o\
phone."

Lydia was aghast. "But you can't go and see him."

"Why ever not?"

"Because it's your most obvious move. You know what a meticu
lous planner Crownfield is. He'll have worked that out. He's bound
to have people waiting for you and following Sidney Gold wherever
he goes."

Julia laughed. "What of it? What can they do? You're surely not
suggesting . . ."

"What they can do, Mother dear," the girl cut in, "is hand you a
bit of paper that will freeze all of Neville's assets. Your freedom to
move depends on one thing and one thing only: You have to avoid
them. The minute that bit of paper's in your hands, you're done for!"
She looked around the otherwise empty dining room. "You simply
have to stay where they'll have the devil's own job finding you."

"Well *you* managed it," Julia pointed out scornfully.

"We had privileged information." Lydia casually stroked her own
car and grinned.

For ten more minutes the battle of wills raged between them. Julia
tried every argument she could think of but Lydia was always ready
with a better answer. Watching and listening, Peter Rosenheim was
reminded of a wily angler and a fierce, fighting trout, a scornful
veteran of a dozen hooks, never before netted.

But Julia was netted this time. The conclusion was inescapable: At
the moment both Crownfield and Brunty believed she knew nothing
about their writ; they must think she'd go breezing in to Dollis Hill,
or her lawyers, or (if worried) to Sidney Gold; all they had to do was
watch and wait. And as long as she kept them waiting like that,
they'd make no further move – which left the secret initiative with
her.

At last she turned in resentful acquiescence to Wallace Baker and
asked: "Your interview with Sidney Gold . . . tell me your plan
again?"

Later she asked Lydia what her intentions might be.

"You have the open-cockpit Amazon at Hendon, haven't you?"
the girl asked.

Julia nodded warily.

"Well." She licked her lips. "We can be back in town before
midnight. If I could just borrow your white helmet and the Meyrowitz goggles, it's a full moon and a clear sky, I could fly down to
Freddy Quinton's place in Leicestershire. That would send them off
on a wild goose chase on Monday!"

"But you can't land at night – I mean, what if the moon went
behind clouds?"

"His father's put floodlights on their landing strip."

can't just drop in on them. They may have a house party
voice tailed off at the sight of Lydia's smile. "You've
arranged it all, haven't you."
xcept for getting the Amazon out. I shan't phone until I get to
ndon town, so even if someone does let Crownfield's men know,
they'll arrive too late."

Julia gave an angry sigh of vexation. "I don't know. What d'you
think, Wallace?"

"Oh," he replied laconically. "I think it must be marvellous to find
yourself surrounded by such resourceful and competent friends."

CHAPTER SIXTY-ONE

JULIA WALLOWED IN the bath, turning the hot tap on and off with her
toes, until the landlord's wife came to the end of the passage and
shouted rather pointedly, "I can't, Len. You'll have to wait. Someone's been and gone and used up all the hot water."

An equally leisurely session at her dressing table meant that she did
not emerge until eleven, by which time the woman, who had been
waiting with glee to inform her that breakfast was "orf," had to
admit that tea, coffee, and sandwiches were now "on"; she had no
choice, for the fact was blazoned at both ends of the forecourt. Half
an hour later, Julia set out in that vaguely southward direction which
Wallace had indicated last evening. "I shall probably be out for
luncheon," she told landlord Len.

She did not, however, intend to call on the Churchills. This was
really an aimless walk, a walk for walking's sake – or, rather, for the
sake of keeping her mind off the dreadful things that might be
happening out there in the real world . . . and herself powerless to
intervene. A distant prospect of Chartwell (which, in fact, she had
seen only in photographs) would at least give her stroll, and her day,
some focal point. Then she could go on to discover old churches,
scenic views, and sketch them in her book.

It was a bright, crisp morning, what was left of it, with not a cloud
in the sky. A road sweeper was burning leaves at the end of the
village street. The smoke rose to just above rooftop height and then

hung in a horizontal layer, so exactly like a water-colour wash that she longed, as she had not longed in years, to open her sketchbook at once.

The man gave her directions to a road that ran past Chartwell and afforded a good view of the estate. She set off at a brisk walk. She was twenty years old again. It seemed such an extraordinary, improbable thing – to be in love, to be so head-over-heels in love, at her age. She could not stop thinking about Wallace.

But the rosy border around her thoughts soon faded. Was he really a Good Thing, she wondered? Why had she confided so many of her worries and problems to him? She knew what *his* explanation would be: because she never knew what she was thinking until she heard it spoken out loud! Actually, her only reason had been to accept his commiseration . . . perhaps pick up the odd suggestion. Nothing more. The one thing she had not wanted was for him to start interfering. Even Eliot, who was actually a junior partner, had never done that.

But Eliot had never wanted to run a business, anyway; he only took that business degree to please his folks.

Did Wallace have ambitions in that line? It was hard to believe. But then who'd have believed it of Brunty? Obviously Crownfield had poured the syrup in his ear.

She thought of Crownfield plotting with Brunty, and Rosenheim and Randy Gold at loggerheads, and Wallace interviewing Sidney Gold, and Lydia hobnobbing with her friends in Leicestershire . . . all of them *doing* things, or able to do things – and herself imprisoned down here, having to hide like a common felon.

She halted and stamped a foot in frustration. This walk was a rotten idea. She was obviously going to fret her nerves to shreds. Yet if she went back to the lonely Poacher, how would it be any better?

And then she remembered she had brought "Jane Eyre" with her. She could curl up in front of the fire and reread it from cover to cover! Yes – nothing else could possibly transport her out of this misery.

She turned about, but almost immediately it struck her that she ought at least to see Chartwell. The rest of her plan she could cheerfully abandon, but she ought at least to see Chartwell.

She turned about again. What had the man said – look for a fingerpost saying Puddledock.

The only person in sight was a long way off – a man, sitting at the roadside, waiting for a rural bus, perhaps. Just beyond him was something white that might be a fingerpost. As she drew nearer she realized it was not beyond him but beside him – and it was not a fingerpost but an easel. She was suddenly filled with envy for this artist, which so consumed her that she came within twenty paces before she realized he was none other than Winston Churchill himself, standing there, solid as a rock.

He glanced at her, raised his straw hat, said, "Good morning," and returned to his work.

"D'you mind awfully if I have a quick look?" she asked as she came up behind him.

He turned round, rather testily, and then recognized her. "Mrs Somerville!" he exclaimed in surprise and began at once to lay down his brushes and water-colour palette. "But I thought you were coming down tomorrow."

"Please don't disturb yourself, Mr Churchill, or you'll make me wish I'd turned about the minute I recognized you." She gripped his wrist and gave it a token shake. "Oh, but that's beautiful! I know your work in oils, of course, but I haven't seen so many water colours by you. Is that Chartwell? I think I recognize it."

"That is Chartwell," he confirmed, his eyes darting back and forth between the scene and his painting of it.

"And that's the famous wall. It's even more impressive than the photos made it seem."

He accepted the compliment with a cheerful nod. "Have you broken down?" he asked, retrieving a brush and dabbing a deeper blue into his rendering of the lake.

"Not at all. I came out for a walk. Wallace Baker had early business in town. Well, I'll disturb you no further, especially in view of . . ."

But he cut her short. "Come, come, Mrs Somerville, I could not pray for a more welcome 'disturbance.' Spread your cape and sit beside me awhile and tell me what you think of our destiny in the skies."

For that, Julia needed no second invitation. As soon as she sat down, he offered, "Would you perhaps care to sketch while I paint?"

She was about to tell him she had her own book when, after a brief rummage in his satchel, he drew forth a sketching block and pencil. "But," he said as he offered them to her, "no indiarubber, I fear. The moving fingers, having writ, must move on."

She thanked him and began working away. There was silence while she sketched in the main areas of the scene – the skyline, the water, the woodland fringes, and the faint outline of the house. Only then did she venture to speak. "As to our destiny in the air, I think your speech to the House in March was the last word on the subject."

"Indeed, I trust it was not!"

"At least in the sense that you have set the agenda. Any future discussion must address itself to the points you raised. Baldwin and Chamberlain and people like that will always try to distract us with their crocodile tears for the taxpayer's purse . . . and the League of Nations . . . and agreements like Locarno, which all the world knows are just worthless bits of paper. Whereas you always bring us back to the real issues."

"And what are they, as you see them?"

She was pleased to discover that her facility with a pencil had not rusted away. The distant woodland was beginning to fill out in a most convincing manner. "You put it perfectly when you pointed out that the more we rely upon combined international action, the more we lay ourselves open to being led by the nose by the French or the Italians. If the fainthearts have their way, we shall be so *combined* with others that we'll end up having our foreign policy dictated for us in the Quai d'Orsay."

"I grant all that. Yet Chamberlain has a strong argument when he talks of the cost of it all, don't you think?"

"Of course it will be expensive. But if the Germans can do it, then so can we. And if they *are* doing it, then so *must* we. Even if it costs a hundred million, it is surely worth it when the alternative is the surrender of our independence?"

"Indeed," he growled. She glanced up to see him quartering the landscape with his eyes, as if every shrub or ditch concealed an army of nay-sayers. It was surely to them that he addressed his next remark: "Never were so fertile and so blessed an insurance procured so cheaply." Then, with a savage satisfaction he began to draw off the wash he had just laid over the fields. "The hardest thing of all," he went on in a more conversational tone, "is to convince people that a hostile air force will use its bombers against women and children in undefended cities. We shrink from the very suggestion and close our minds to its possibility. Yet in the heat and fury of war, even the most civilized of men will do that they would abhor in a time of peace."

He pulled back, looked critically at his painting, and gave a little grunt of approval. "Corot, you know, would simply have painted the house from this distance. That little cube of colour would have filled his entire composition. That was how he achieved those splendid, luminous landscapes in which everything seems to be on the plane of the canvas itself."

Julia stared at her sketch and replied, "If I tried that, I'd just think of all the bits I was missing out."

He chuckled. "The odd thing about Corot, though, is that those portions *aren't* missing. They may not be on the canvas, yet they are not missing. I often think the Old Masters have nothing to offer us but despair."

Greatly daring, she moved her pencil out of the loose ruck of pasture and woodland, onto the firm lines and angles of the house, where mistakes would find no hiding place. "Whatever the target," she said, reverting to his earlier point, "the fact remains that German bombers are going to be flying in at over two hundred miles an hour.

So our interceptors must be capable of three hundred. Well, even a submarine commander can probably tell you – you don't try to fly things like that off grass – not if they must do ten . . . twenty sorties a day. That's the first bullet the Air Ministry will have to bite. Give us those proper facilities and we, the aircraft industry, will provide the right planes for the job."

He digested her words in silence – to such an extent that she wondered if he'd even been listening. She said, "You don't seem surprised to hear such sentiments from me?"

He gave her that puckish smile of his. Then he grew serious once more, saying, "Like me, then, you believe it will be Germany again?"

"Nazi Germany. Funnily enough, that was on my mind while I came down the hill toward you. I was thinking to myself what a stunningly beautiful country ours is. This English jewel, and all that. And how, for almost a thousand years, no one has been able to take it from us. And then I remembered flying over Germany with Peter Rosenheim, from whom I bought Segelflug Hessen – Mickey McHugh must have mentioned him?"

He made a noise that was neither yes nor no, nor admission, nor confirmation – simply the barest invitation to proceed.

"Well, on that particular day, Rosenheim had just been harassed in a mild, pointless sort of way by a couple of Gestapo bullies. And I asked him over the intercom why he put up with it. For an answer he simply pointed at the landscape below us and said it was his fatherland, too. That's something we forget. The Nazis have taken Germany from the Germans, as well."

They continued in this way, talking and sketching for most of the day. They spoke of technical progress in the air and the peaceful hopes for air travel. He was well briefed about her, for he also asked about the SPRP. That, in turn, led to a discussion on the changing nature of poverty and the new expectations of working people. She was amazed at the fertility of his mind. He did not parade his knowledge yet she felt its weight behind every conclusion. And his voice, of course, his ready choice of the perfect word, was an absolute delight.

Until then she had shared the almost universal view among English people that Churchill was a brilliant politician whose day was done. "That man ought to accept a peerage and retire gracefully to the Lords," people would say. His self-appointed role as back-bench gadfly to the government seemed merely tiresome, like an after-dinner speaker who didn't know when to shut up and sit down. No matter that almost every word he spoke was both wise and true; no matter that the government in question was divided and inconsistent; the fellow was finished, done for.

But during those hours, which seemed so casual at the time, her estimate of him suffered the profoundest change. The nation that believed it could afford to ignore such wisdom as his, she thought, would deserve to go down in ignominy. Almost unawares, she had joined that still-small – but growing, and certainly influential – band of admirers who would not allow his greatness to pass beyond the nation's ken.

The afternoon sped by until the lowering of the sun behind them at last alerted her to the passage of time; she looked at her watch and was astonished to discover it was almost four o'clock. By then she had three sketches of Chartwell and two of its owner; he, for his part, had done three superb little landscapes – one of which, the one of the house itself, he graciously offered to her. She was so delighted she offered him all of hers in return, but he accepted only one of the sketches of himself, which he made her sign and date.

Then, expressing mutual pleasure in their anticipation of tomorrow's luncheon, they parted. From time to time as she walked back up the road toward Westerham she glanced across the fields to see him stalking among the autumn stubble – a figure in the wilderness, here as in his *other* home, the mother of parliaments; a man condemned by his very superiority to walk alone.

She remembered Wallace's opinion: a Saul on his way to Damascus. How perfect that was. At the time it had sounded like the comforting sort of Damascus which awaits most of us – one that never actually arrives. But now, suddenly, it seemed very near.

When she had passed over the brow of the hill, and Chartwell itself was out of view, it suddenly struck her that not once since she had sat down beside him had she worried about Neville's. It was not that the firm had dropped out of her consciousness; indeed, she had thought of it several times. But on each of those occasions she had brushed it aside with the realization that, in sitting there beside Churchill, talking of war, and the aircraft industry, and the international situation, and the social changes that had overtaken the classes, she was engaging in something of far greater importance, *even to Neville's!*

When she drew near the Poacher, however, all thoughts of Churchill fled. Neville's and its day-to-day problems filled her mind once more. For there on the forecourt stood a splendid old Rolls-Royce; and the gold that gleamed where others would shine silver had nothing to do with the sinking of the autumnal sun.

Sidney himself was sitting at the wheel, so absorbed in the *Sporting Life* that she had to tap on the window before he noticed her arrival. Then he was a sudden blur of activity – throwing away the paper, straightening his clothing, taking out the ignition key, and checking his hair in the mirror, all in a chubby, rolling manner – before he opened the door and gurgled, "Surprise, eh?"

"It *was,* about five minutes ago when I first spotted you," she agreed. "No prizes for guessing how you knew you'd find me here."

He winked and said with a chuckle, "No names, no cocoa."

"I don't know about cocoa, but come in and join me for tea. I'll just go up to my room and put these things away."

"You don't feel like a walk?" He looked at her clothes, at the mud on her brogues, and added, "No, I don't suppose you do."

"We'll compromise," she suggested. "If we can find a sheltered spot in the garden, where we can get the last half-hour of this sun, we'll have tea out there."

It amused her that the landlord's wife, who would certainly have refused her request at any other time, was so bowled over by the gold-plated Rolls-Royce that she agreed at once. Tea, with hot-buttered crumpets and honey and Marmite, was brought to them in a rustic summerhouse on a little knoll that was surely designed to catch the very last moments of any autumnal sun.

"I'll be mother," Julia volunteered. She poured with rapt concentration; even the smell of the brew was invigorating.

"Ta." He took his cup and sat in morose silence awhile.

"What an extraordinary run of fine weather we're having," she commented at last.

It prompted him to speak. "What d'you really think of old Crownfield?" he asked.

"As a banker? As a person . . . or what?"

"As an enemy."

She took a sip of tea before she replied. "I'd say that was putting it rather too strongly. But I'd accept *opponent.*"

"Well, that's where you're wrong," he told her.

"And why d'you say that?"

He pinched the bridge of his nose, as if to drive out a sinus pain. "There's things it'd be wrong to say, Mrs Somerville – or wrong for me to say. But if you were to, like, guess them out loud, well, that'd be different. D'you see my point?"

"Perfectly." She laughed. "If I know or suspect anything about my friend Douglas Crownfield, you want me to tell all without your risking the slightest disclosure on your part. D'you know how old I am?"

"Well, I'll tell you for nothing, he's no friend. Did he lose a heavy bet with you once or something?"

She smiled, wondering why he was concentrating so much on Crownfield and saying nothing about the real matter that must be on his mind. She decided to stir a little more. "Wallace Baker," she told him, "maintains that Crownfield found me amusing as long as the business was small. But I have become increasingly intolerable to him as it has grown larger."

"Right!" Gold exclaimed, delighted to be given a foothold at last. "That is exactly . . . I mean, not even I could have put it better. Intoler . . . what you said – intolerant! That's the very word. Would you tell me one thing, Mrs Somerville – and feel free to be as honest as you like, now – but would Neville's be in need of some kind of additional finance?"

She watched the honey melting into her crumpet. "We all like a little extra spoonful of jam on our bread, Mr Gold."

"That's not what I mean. You know what I mean."

"Perhaps . . . if you could tell me why you've waited all these years to pop this particular question?"

He looked at her askance, stammering, "What do you . . . what do you . . . oh."

"It is quite a surprising question," she added.

He took a bite of his own honeyed crumpet and chewed it thoughtfully before he tried again. "Put it this way. I've seen a fair number of faked-up balance sheets in my day. You get a sort of feeling for them – know what I mean? With me, it's a sort of itchy feeling inside my head."

"Awkward, what? Almost impossible to scratch."

"Yeah, well that's what I'm trying to do now. You see, usually the faked-up books are the ones kept on the open shelf. It's the genuine books you lock away in the safe. That's what threw me, see?" He stared directly at her, for the first time since they had sat down. "You do know what I'm talking about?"

"Go on – it might come to me."

"What – the courage to admit it?"

"Just go on!"

"See, if the fake ones are kept in the safe . . . I mean, where's the point? *Unless* it's to trick some stupid little novice who stumbles across them and takes them for the real thing."

"Stumbles?" she repeated, as if the word were giving her difficulties. "*Inside* a safe? That sounds like work for pygmies."

He raised a finger and smiled. "Now there you may very well have a point, Mrs Somerville. But suppose . . . I mean, why would anyone want to do that except to make someone else fall flat on his face?" He grinned and fixed her with his eye. "Is that why you done it?"

She shook her head. "I'm not obliged to say yes or no. You'll just have to assume I did. I will tell you that I'm not in the least bit bored by all this hypothetical talk."

"Right." He rose, crossed the lawn to the birdbath, washed the honey off his hands in its algal water, and then flailed them around to dry them. He removed the final dampness with his kerchief. "Poor old Crownfield," he said. "He's so desperate for those forgeries to be true. I can just see him packing his better judgement off on a nice long holiday."

She frowned in bewilderment. "Crownfield is not the *novice* you mentioned just now, is he? If he is, we've been talking at cross purposes."

"No, but the novice had no more sense than to go running to him."

"I see. Is that what happened?"

His cup was hardly touched. She poured herself a second before she went on, "Let's drop all this badinage. We know why I left that document there to be photographed – and we know what your son was really trying to do."

Gold slumped in his chair – so dejected, so defeated almost, she could not avoid a certain pity. "He's a strange lad," she told him. "I don't think there's real wickedness in him – despite appearances. All he really wants is a respectable place in the sun. And he was looking for a short cut to it."

"Yeah, well I . . ." His voice tailed off at the sight of her upraised finger.

She went on: "I don't think *he* considered the Savoy to be quite in that category. More of a prison, really. Five stars in the Dunlop Guide, but a prison nonetheless. It made him so desperate that . . ."

He interrupted. "Place in the sun? You mean a share in my business."

"He would think of it as *his* share. And to gain it he was prepared to go to lengths that were almost criminal. Where he gets it from I can't imagine."

Sidney Gold shot her a rueful smile. "You think I'm to blame for it, anyway."

"Not at all. I'll tell you what I think. Just as I've found life sweeter when Sidney Gold stopped being against me and came round to my side, so I think you might find the same is true with you and Randy."

His lips curled in a sneer. "I don't like being pushed."

"Then pull at your end. He'll fall flat on his face at your feet."

Gold laughed. "Can't beat you," he grumbled. "So" – he became all brisk and businesslike again – "no trouble at Neville's? Come Tuesday, you're not going to knuckle under to Crownfield?"

"I didn't say that," she replied cautiously. "Does the thought upset you?"

He stared at her long and hard, as if he simply could not size her up.

"It's turning chill," she said, rising to go back indoors.

He grinned. "I've got a sight that'll warm the cockles of your heart." He jerked his head toward the inn. "Come and look."

Through the bars he led her, into the passage, and out to the forecourt. He went directly to the boot of his car and unlocked it. But before raising the lid he turned to her and, pointing to a spot on the gravel, very close to the car, said, "Put your feet there. This is something you'll never see again."

She did as she was told.

His lips were alive with merriment, his eyes danced, as he slowly turned the handle and slowly-slowly raised the lid. At first nothing was visible. The twilight on this side of the inn was too far advanced. But when it was open about a foot, the interior lamp came on automatically – a sudden and dramatic spotlight. Then he raised the lid as fast as his muscles could manage.

Her first thought was that a game of Bulls and Bears had spilled open there. Then she saw that the banknotes were real. The entire boot was filled with them. She turned to ask him what on earth it all meant and found him enraptured, mesmerized at the sight of so much wealth.

"What's it for?" she asked.

"Insurance," he told her, pointing to himself. "I'm looking after number one again. As per usual."

CHAPTER SIXTY-TWO

"Now just calm down," Wallace said. "Get your breath back and tell me coolly and clearly. Are you saying he was offering you twenty thousand pounds? Just like that?"

She dabbed the laughter from her eyes and nodded. "That's what it amounted to."

"I had no idea that was his intention, you know. When I left him I supposed he was on his way to sort out Randolph. I went on to set Max and Imogen's minds at rest – just in case they heard anything on Monday."

"Ah, that's how he got here first."

"This twenty thousand – does he want equity?"

"He did at first." She grinned.

"So what did you beat him down to?"

"*We*, Wallace. This is your triumph, too."

He looked at her in surprise. "My, my!"

"I remembered how, long ago, when George was alive and Somerville's was under threat, we staved the bank off for weeks by my promising to assign my own small inheritance to the firm. So I talked our Sidney into depositing his cash with Crownfield and letting him know we're negotiating an equity deal. The deposit is just to show good faith."

Wallace laughed joyously. "Poor old Crownfield – he'll be absolutely furious."

"I hope he'll also be sensible, so that Sidney Gold can have his money back by this time next week. If Gold did buy equity in Neville's, Crownfield can kiss goodbye forever to any hope of forcing me to go public. So I pray he'll back down on his present assault and just hope to fight another day." She slipped her arms around him and began to kiss his neck and face. "But you were brilliant, darling. And Lydia. And Rosenheim. I'd have been sunk without you."

He pulled back as far as her embrace allowed. "A bit of a new tune?"

"I've done a lot of thinking today – and talking as a matter of fact. You'll never guess who . . ."

"Hang on. Just one more thing before we leave Sidney Gold. Why these theatricals? Why didn't he just pull out his chequebook? Why this incredible display of cash?"

She laughed. "That's just the way the man is. I wouldn't hold that against him any more. Thank God this time I wasn't so stupid and conceited as to tell him it was vulgar. I suppose I have learned something in the past seven years." Her stomach gurgled. "Oops!" she said. "Have they lost the beater for that dinner gong?"

He checked his watch. "Give them five minutes' grace. This is England, after all. So – you were about to tell me . . ."

"Oh, it's been a pretty ordinary sort of day here, don't you know. Had a long, long bath, and what the New Yorkers call brunch, and then went for a walk . . . and did a bit of sketching, and . . ."

"Oh, let me see?"

"You wouldn't be interested."

"I assure you I would."

She eyed him uncertainly. "Promise not to laugh?"

"Promise." He nodded brightly, in case she disbelieved him.

She passed the sketches to him, which she had torn out of Churchill's sketchbook. And at that moment the landlord told her she was wanted on the phone.

When she returned he was looking at Churchill's own water colour.

"That was Peter Rosenheim," she informed him. "It seems that Sidney's had a little talk with his son."

"Oh?"

"Yes. Rosenheim says Randy Gold is pulling out of the arrangement, leaving himself and Morgan to deal directly with Neville's. Our cash-in-advance arrangement is no longer conditional."

"Home and dry!" He laid the paintings down and stretched his arms toward her.

The gong sounded for dinner.

Much later that evening, when they were in their pyjamas and dressing gowns, she lay in his embrace before the dying fire.

"Penny for them?" he asked.

"I was just thinking. All my life . . . well, I suppose most people are like that, so it's not unique."

"What isn't?"

"Except that for each one of us it is the only experience we can go by."

"Yes, but what?"

"I mean, it *feels* unique."

"What, for heaven's sake?"

"That's what I'm trying to tell you, if you'd just stop interrupting. I've always had this feeling that I get only half of anything. Of everything. Like . . . I want something very much, all right? And so I work and work and work for it. And then when it comes, it seems like only half of it. I always feel something's missing."

"And you don't any more?"

She shook her head. "It just struck me today – talking with Churchill – I found out where it's been hiding all along. It's not *in* the thing, it's all round and about. I've always been looking for the missing bits *inside* whatever it is. But it's outside. It's the rest of the world."

She made an awkward gesture and half-turned to watch him suspiciously, out of the corner of her eye – afraid he might mock her semi-coherence.

But he was serious now, and looking at her with a sort of contained excitement, afraid to break a moment he considered fragile. "Go on," he murmured.

She settled back into his embrace. "I suddenly realized that what's been missing with Neville's . . . I mean, it wasn't inside, where I've always looked for it. It's everything around the company – all the things Churchill talked about with me. The whole wide world. Why couldn't I see it before?"

"It's called maturing," he whispered. "What about love?"

"Well, it's the same thing there."

"Tell me."

"All I knew was the half of it that was in here – in my heart. I never realized what was missing until I found the outside of it. And all that was waiting to be discovered out there. With you, my darling."

His lips grazed her neck, her ear, her cheek, shivering her voice, melting her insides. She eased herself away and went on, "Yesterday evening, when we went for that walk – you said you'd ask me a question."

"Oh, did I?" he replied – much too offhandedly.

"You actually did ask it."

"I have an awful memory for things like that, my love. Oh, I know! Yes! I asked could I go and see Sidney Gold."

She dug her elbow, quite hard, into his ribs. "Ooooopff!" He laughed. "Okay – I've just remembered the other question."

She waited for him to prove it.

"Will you?" he asked.

She said nothing. She froze.

"Will you marry me?"

She was silent a long time. Then she murmured his name.

"Mmmm?"

"You're not going to write all this down, are you?" she asked.

"All what?"

"You . . . me . . . everything?"

"In the *Vogue* piece, you mean?"

"Anywhere."

After a long pause he replied, "One should never say never."

After an even longer pause he asked, "Why – would it bother you?"

"I'd only permit it on one condition."

"Which is?"

"The closing words. You'd have to use the ones I dictate."

"Whatever you say."

"Well, I say your closing words will be these: *Reader – she married me!*"

He roared with laughter.

And then he laughed with delight.

And then, in quieter vein, he delighted in the thought that he was about to spend the rest of his life with this astonishing, beautiful, marvellous, wonderful, surprising, adorable – and infuriating – woman.

Here goes, then, he thought: *Reader – she married me!*

THE END